FLY BY NIGHT

FLY BY NIGHT

TARA O'CONNOR

COLORS BY
TRIONA TREE FARRELL

RH
GRAPHIC

NEW YORK

Cover art, text, and interior illustrations copyright © 2021 by Tara O'Connor

All rights reserved. Published in the United States by RH Graphic, an imprint of Random House Children's Books, a division of Penguin Random House LLC, New York.

RH Graphic with the book design is a trademark of Penguin Random House LLC.

Visit us on the web! RHKidsGraphic.com • @RHKidsGraphic

Educators and librarians, for a variety of teaching tools, visit us at RHTeachersLibrarians.com

Library of Congress Cataloging-in-Publication Data is available upon request.
ISBN 978-1-9848-5260-1 (pbk.) — ISBN 978-0-593-12530-4 (trade)
ISBN 978-1-9848-9238-6 (ebook)

Designed by Patrick Crotty
Colors by Triona Tree Farrell

MANUFACTURED IN CHINA
10 9 8 7 6 5 4 3 2 1
First Edition

A comic on every bookshelf.

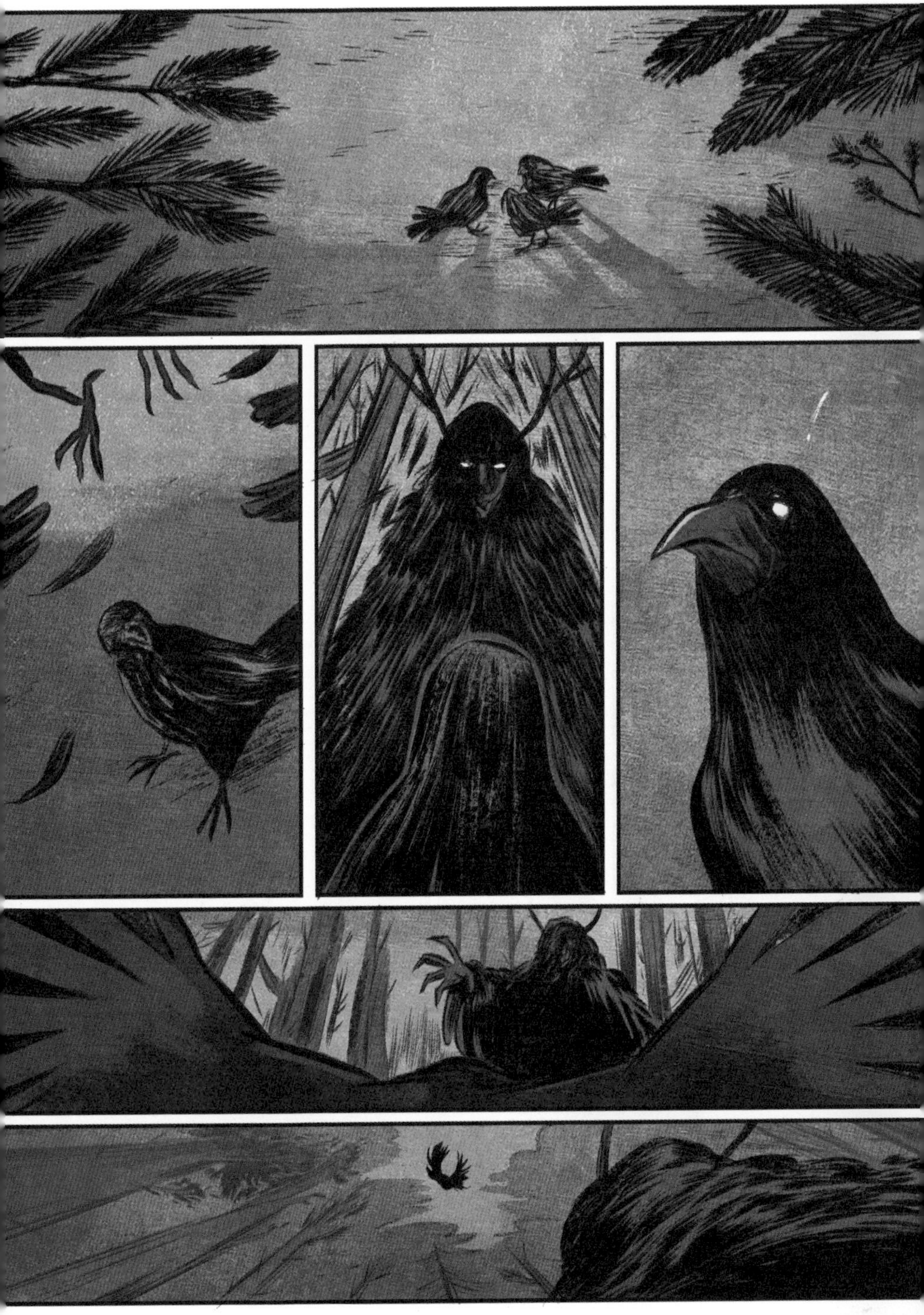

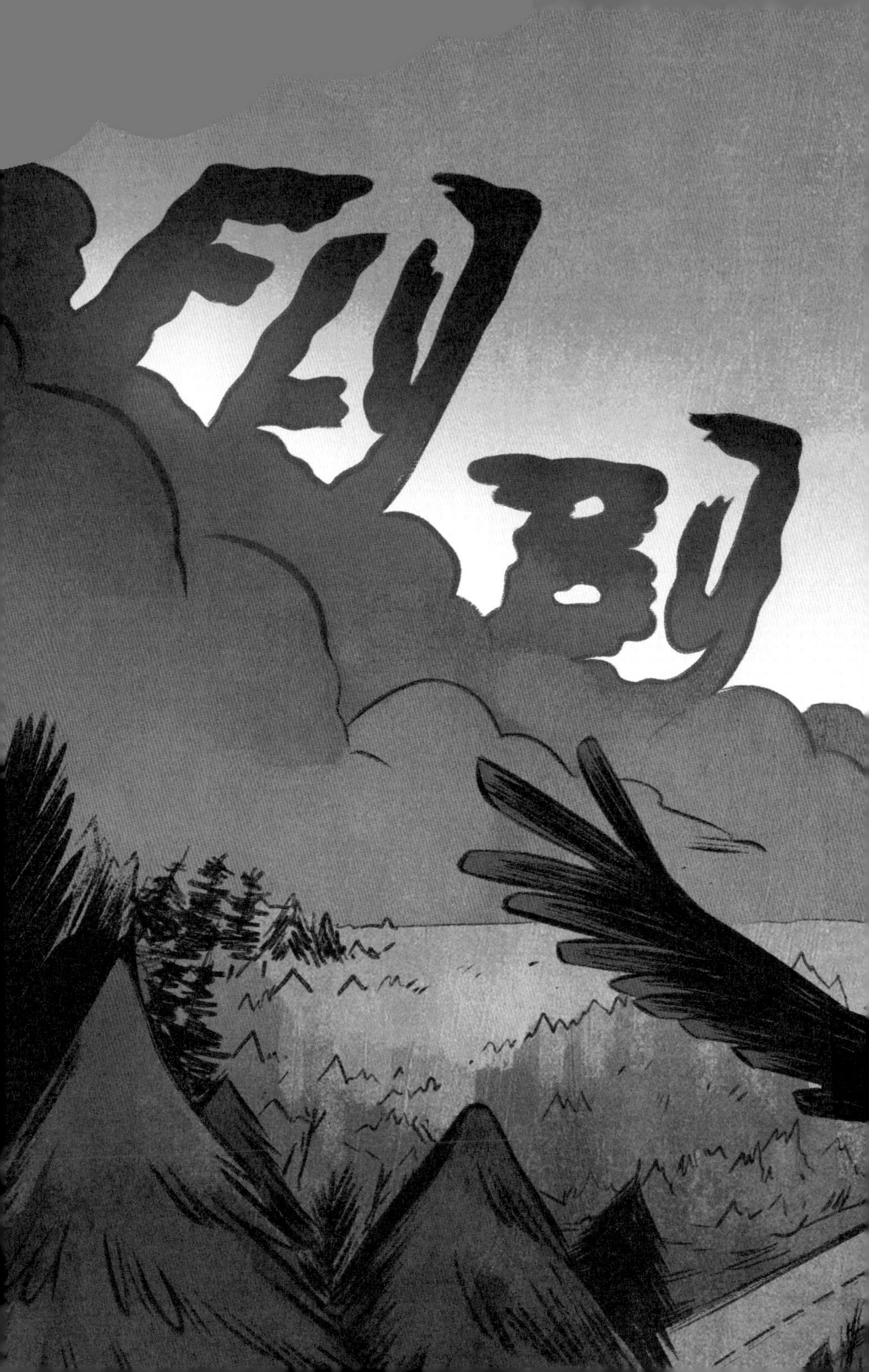
FLY BOY

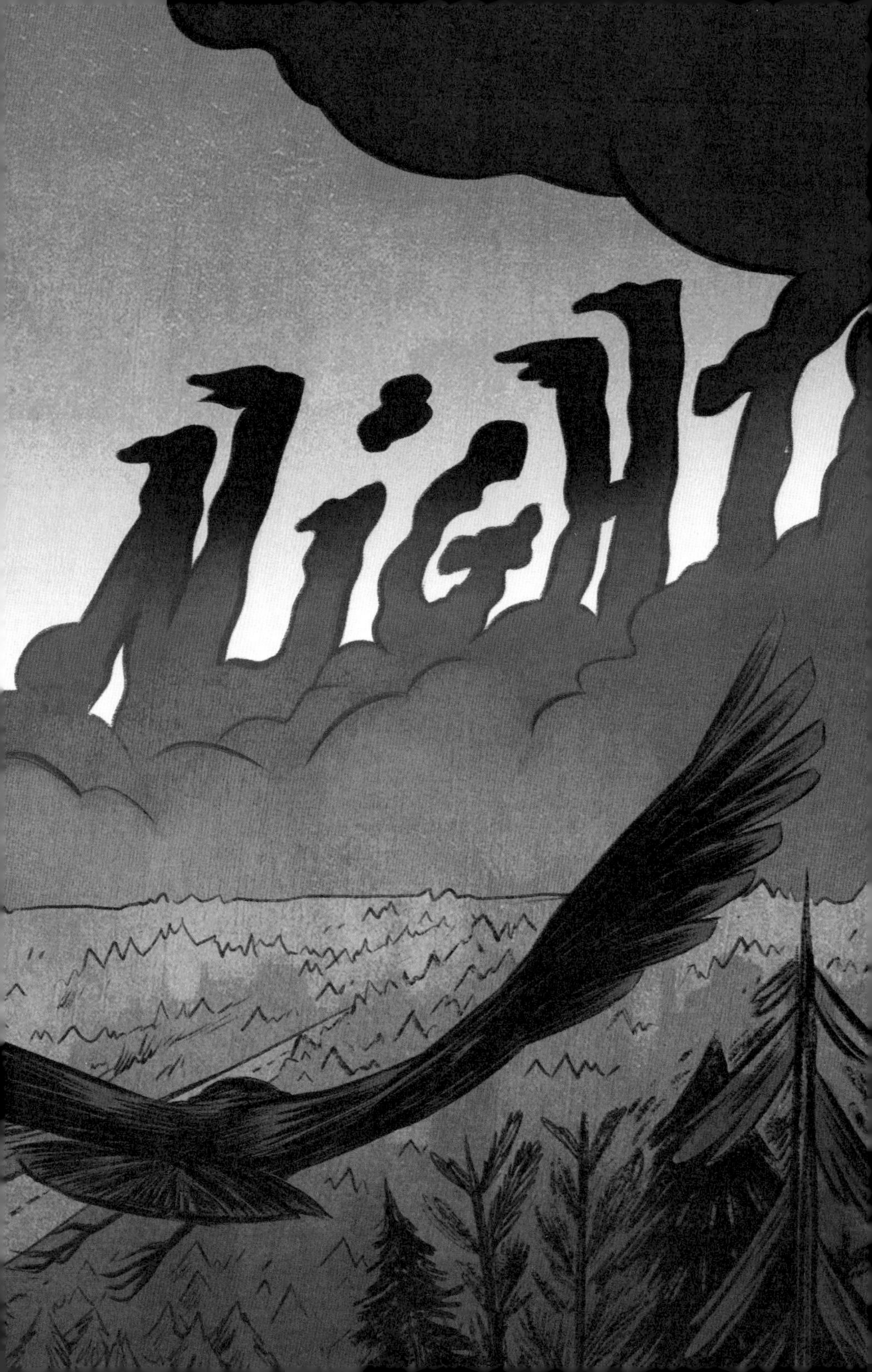
Light

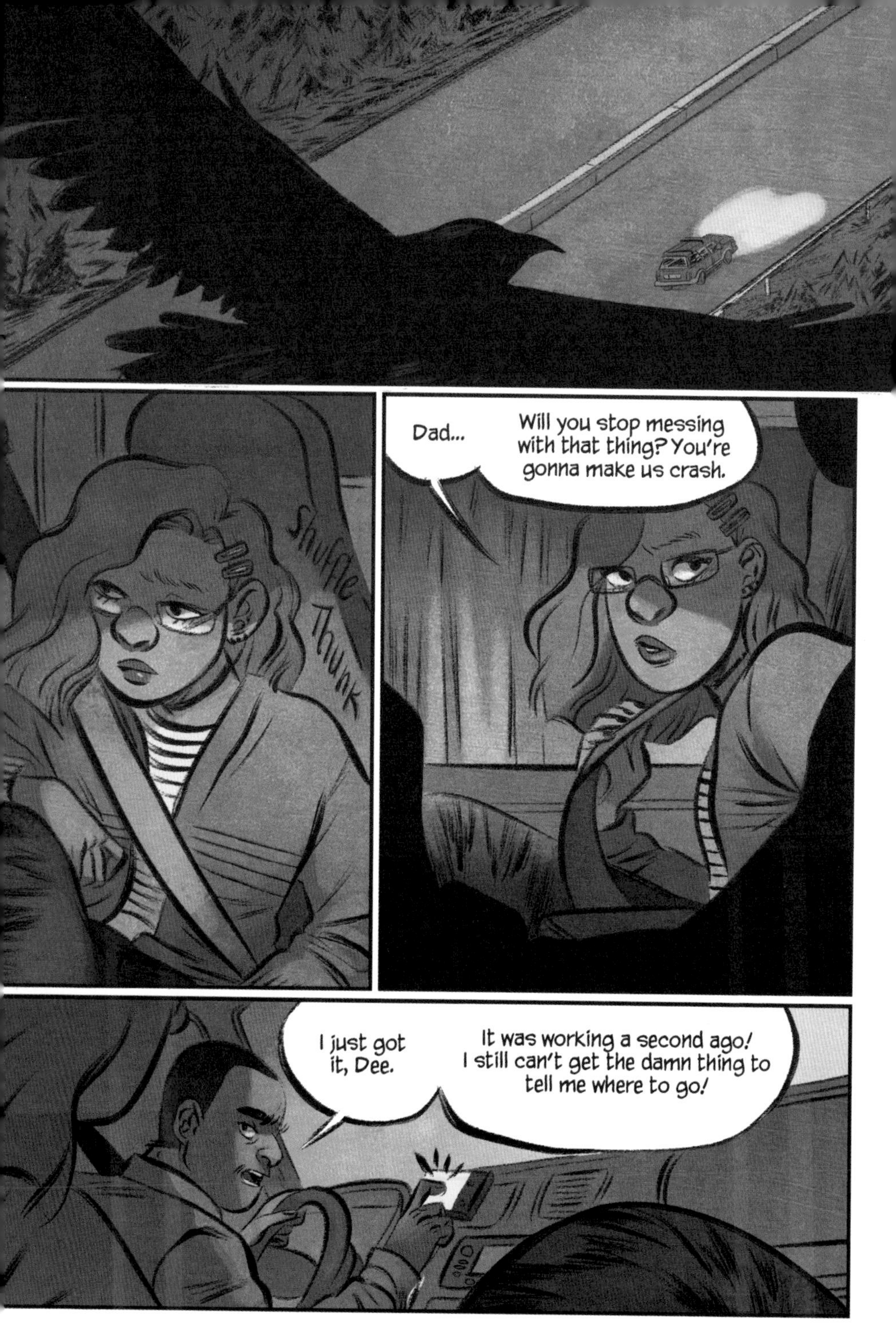
Shuffle
Thunk
Dad...
Will you stop messing with that thing? You're gonna make us crash.
I just got it, Dee.
It was working a second ago! I still can't get the damn thing to tell me where to go!

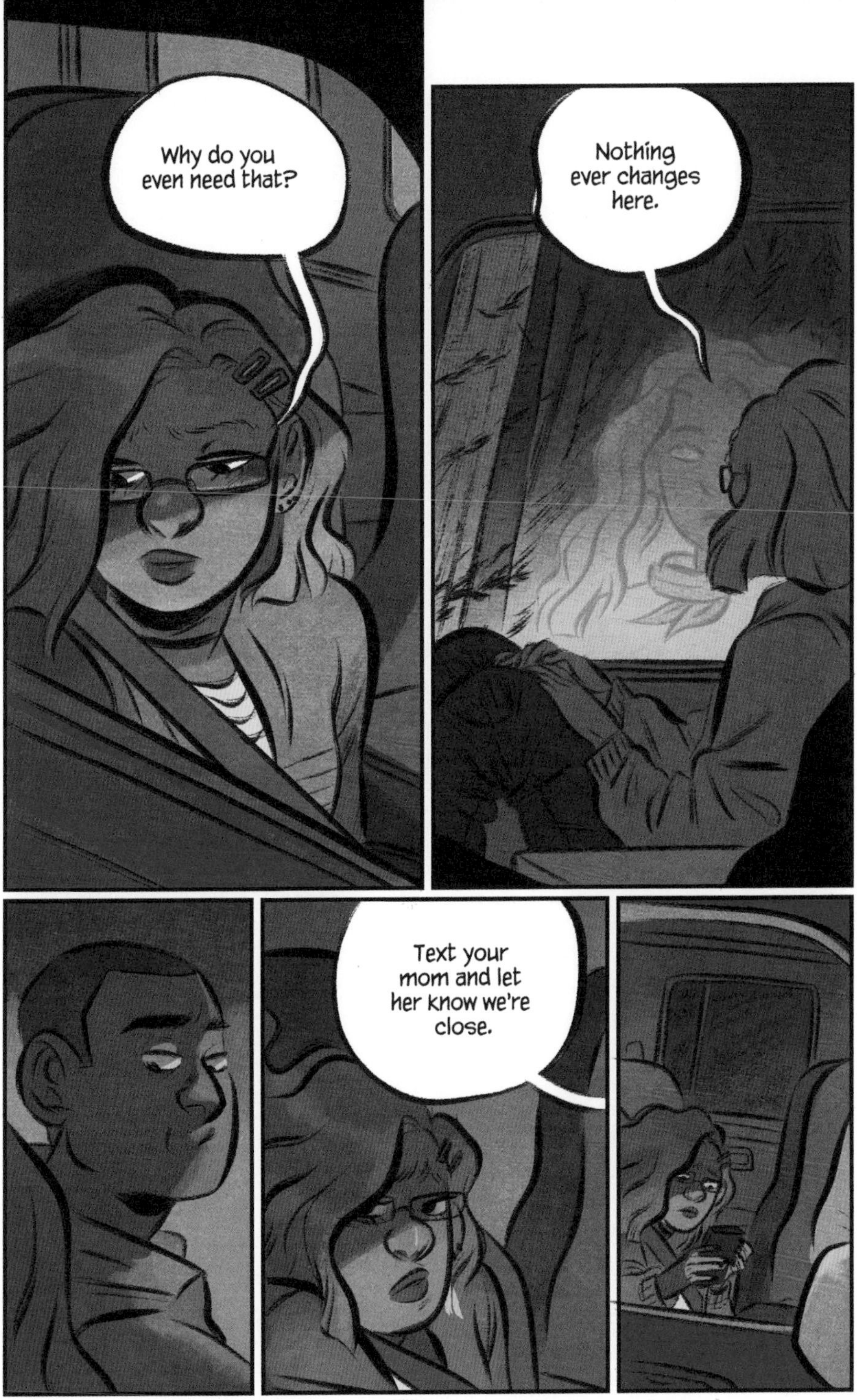

Why do you even need that?
Nothing ever changes here.
Text your mom and let her know we're close.

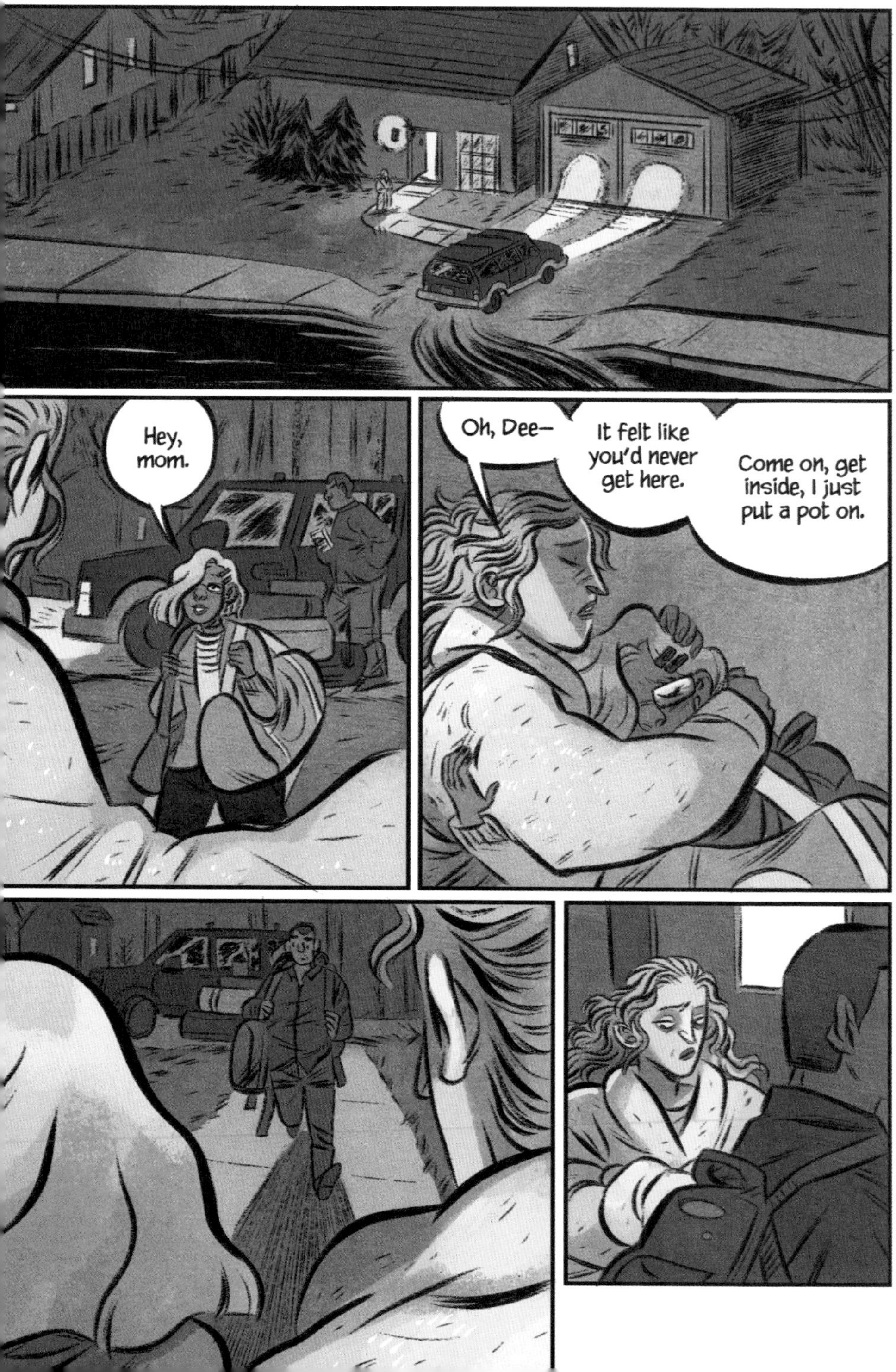

Hey, mom.
Oh, Dee—
It felt like you'd never get here.
Come on, get inside, I just put a pot on.

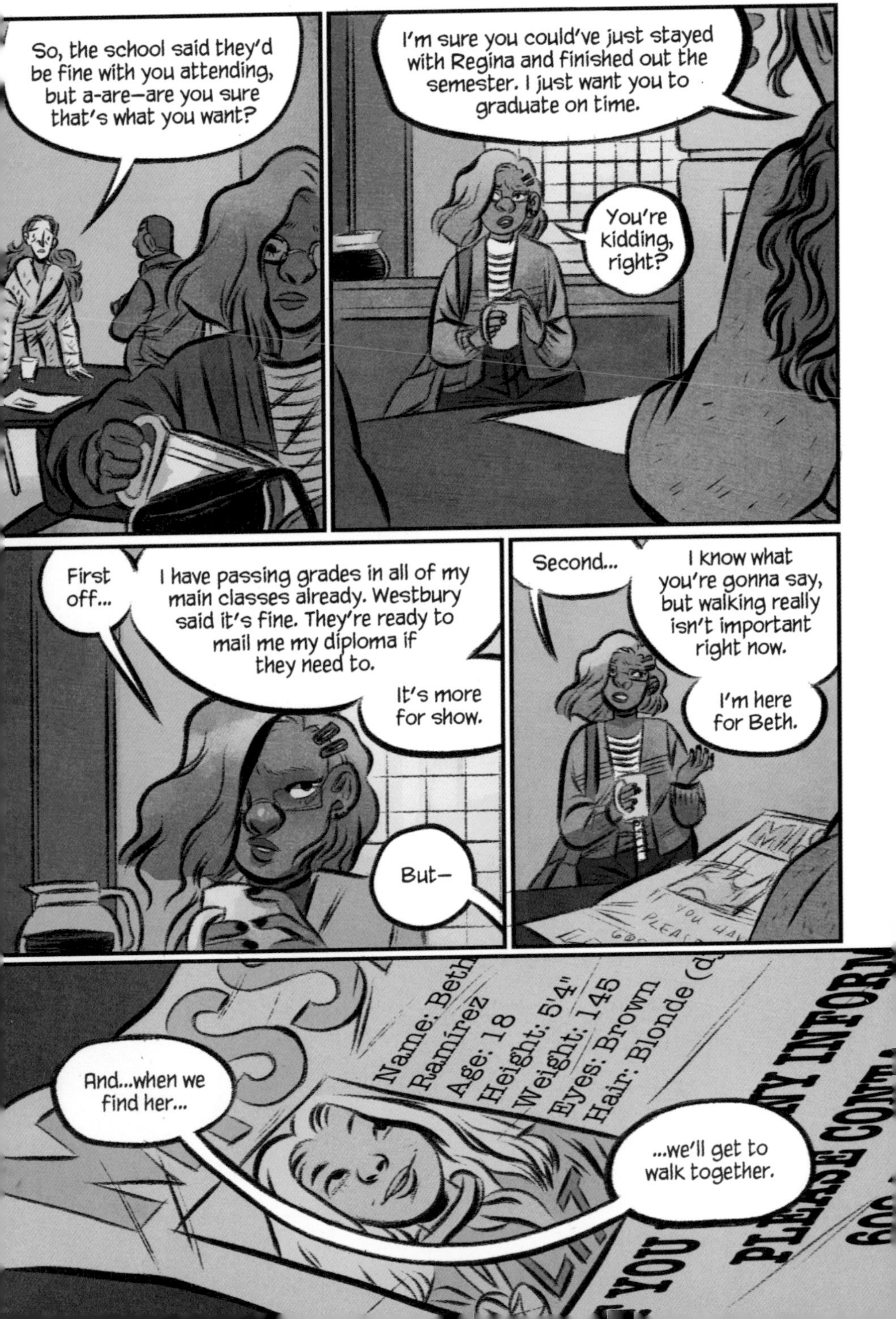
So, the school said they'd be fine with you attending, but a-are—are you sure that's what you want?
I'm sure you could've just stayed with Regina and finished out the semester. I just want you to graduate on time.
You're kidding, right?
First off...
I have passing grades in all of my main classes already. Westbury said it's fine. They're ready to mail me my diploma if they need to.
It's more for show.
But—
Second...
I know what you're gonna say, but walking really isn't important right now.
I'm here for Beth.
Name: Beth Ramirez
Age: 18
Height: 5'4"
Weight: 145
Eyes: Brown
And...when we find her...
...we'll get to walk together.

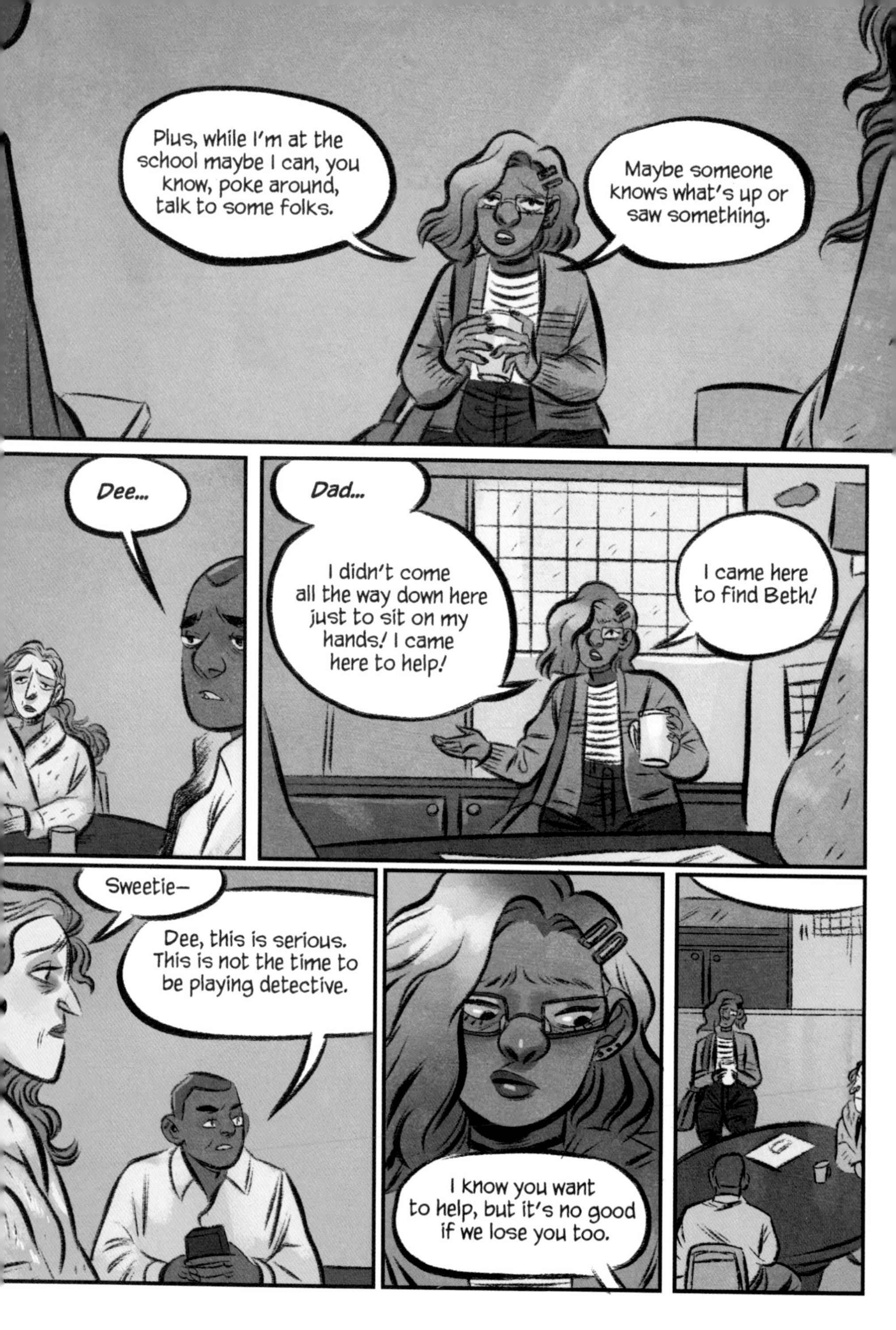
Plus, while I'm at the school maybe I can, you know, poke around, talk to some folks.
Maybe someone knows what's up or saw something.
Dee...
Dad...
I didn't come all the way down here just to sit on my hands! I came here to help!
I came here to find Beth!
Sweetie—
Dee, this is serious. This is not the time to be playing detective.
I know you want to help, but it's no good if we lose you too.

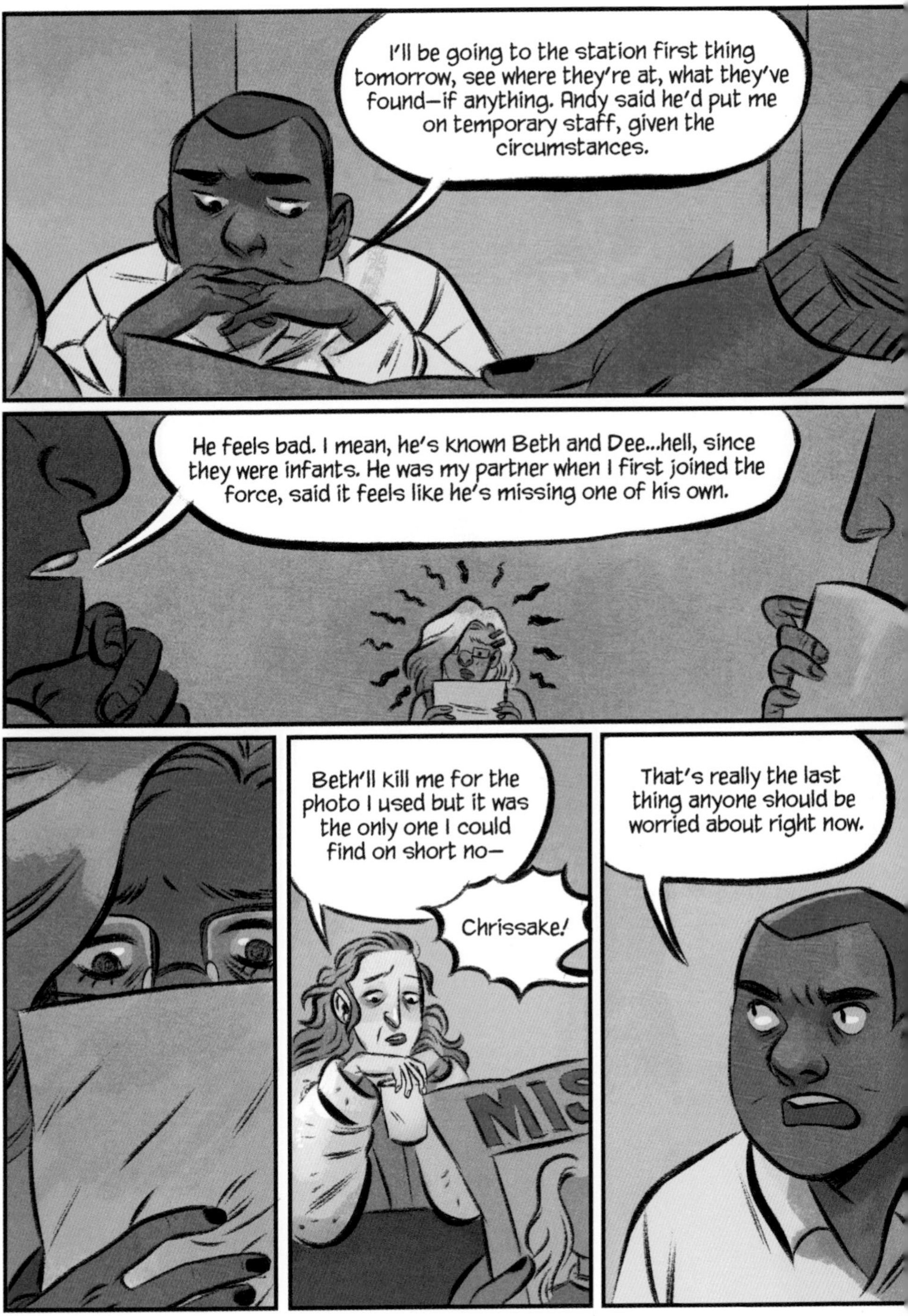
I'll be going to the station first thing tomorrow, see where they're at, what they've found—if anything. Andy said he'd put me on temporary staff, given the circumstances.
He feels bad. I mean, he's known Beth and Dee...hell, since they were infants. He was my partner when I first joined the force, said it feels like he's missing one of his own.
Beth'll kill me for the photo I used but it was the only one I could find on short no—
Chrissake!
That's really the last thing anyone should be worried about right now.
MIS

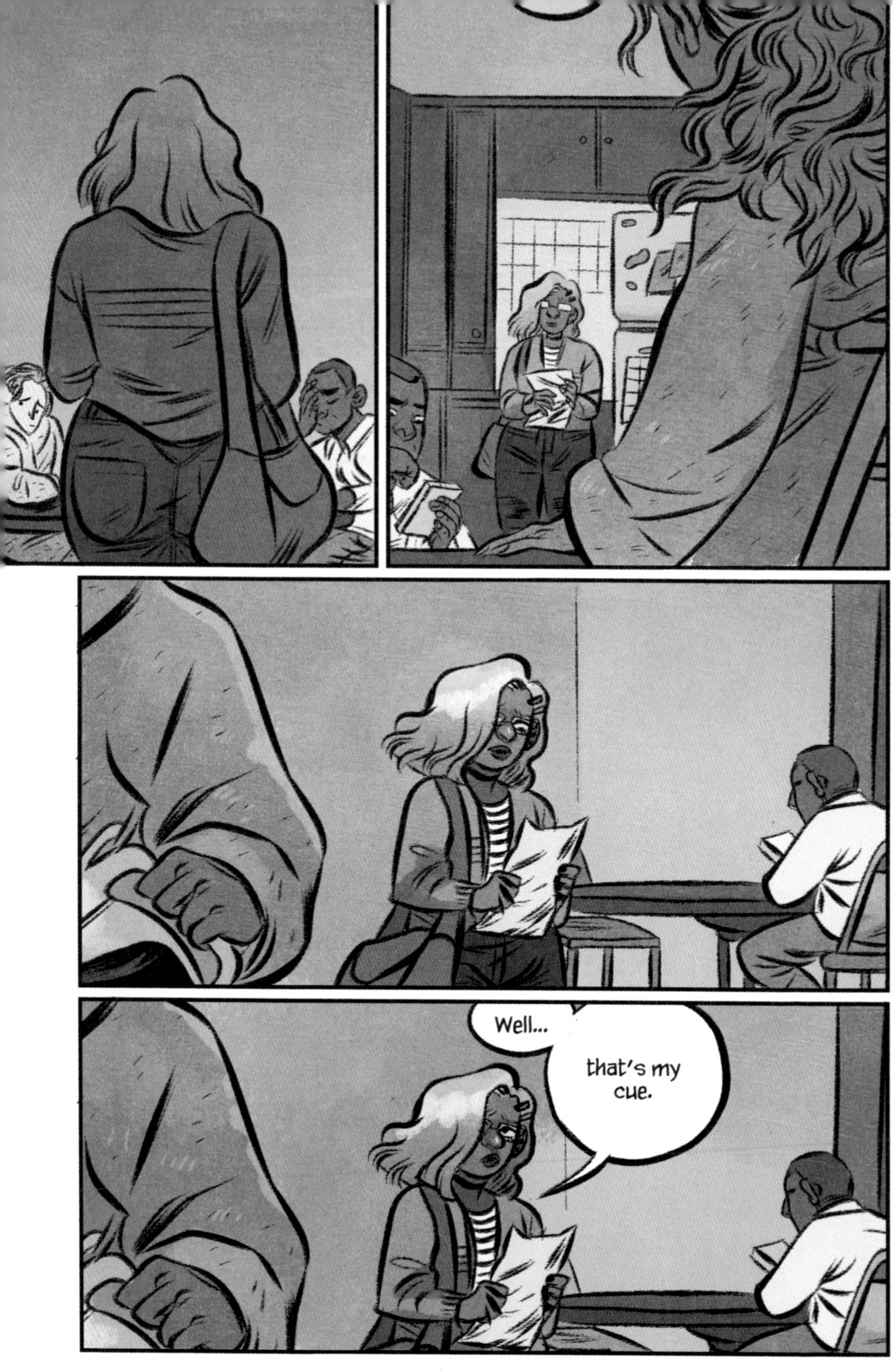
Well...
that's my cue.

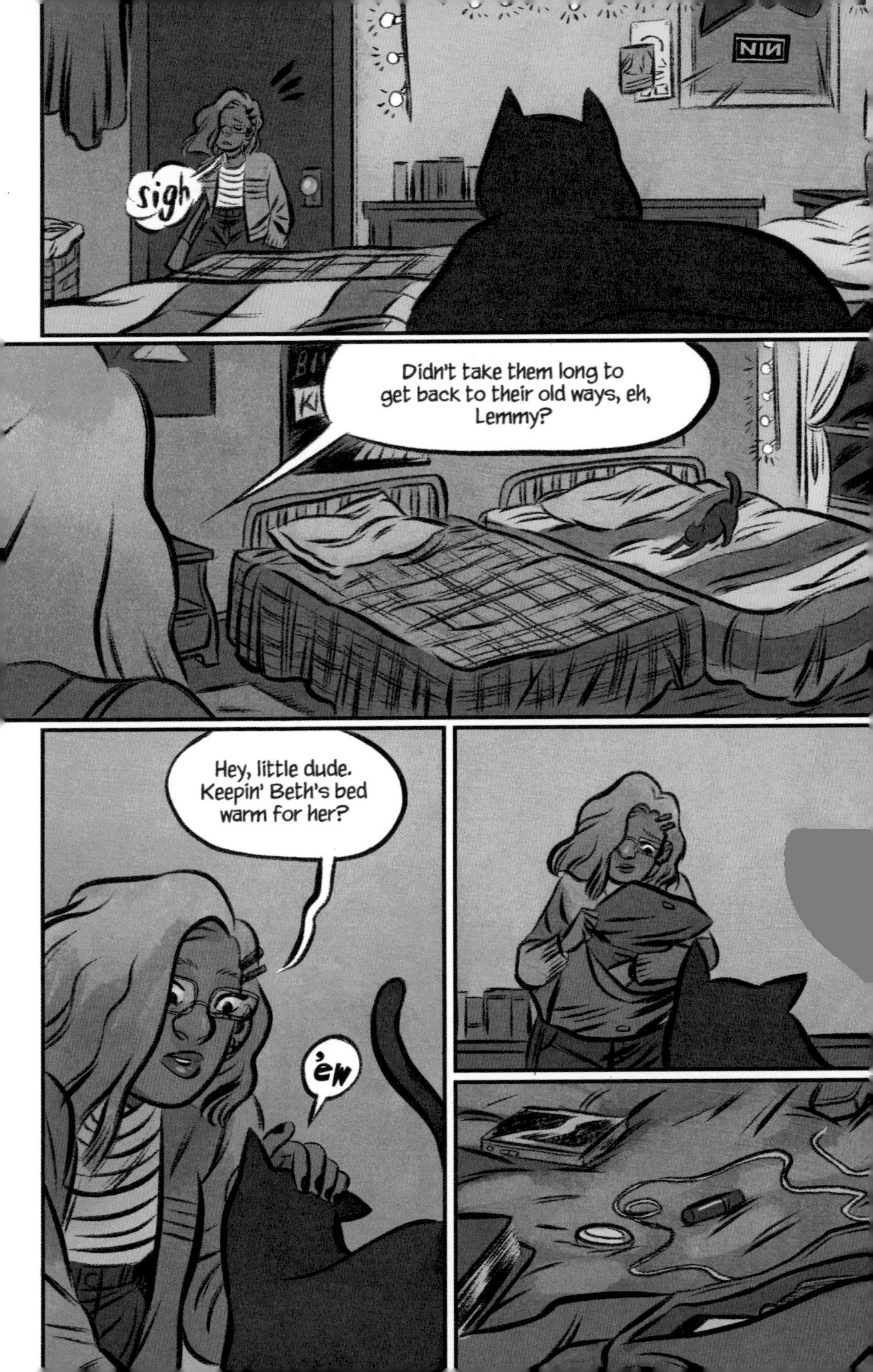
NIN
sigh
Didn't take them long to get back to their old ways, eh, Lemmy?
Hey, little dude. Keepin' Beth's bed warm for her?
'ew

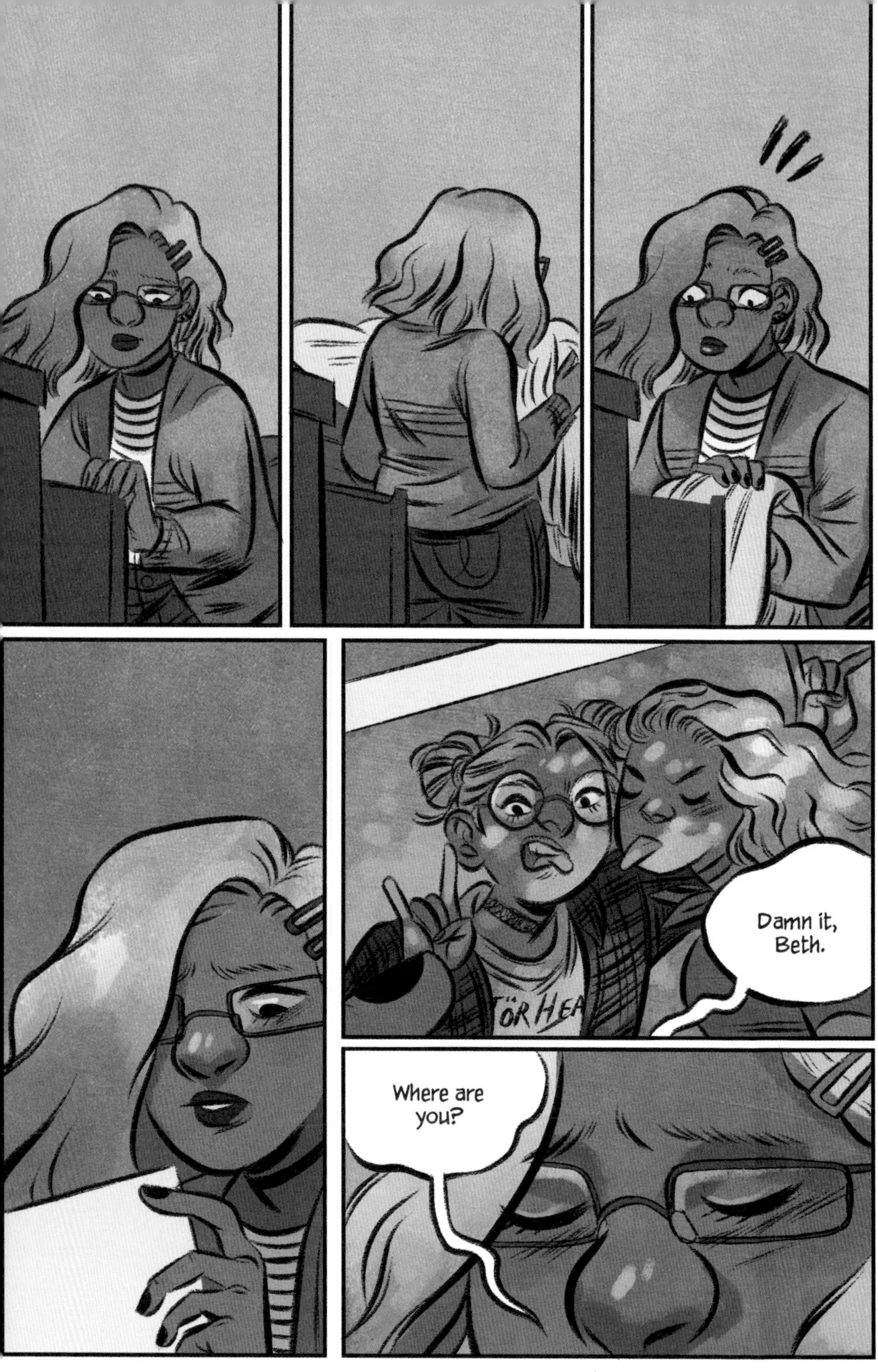
Damn it, Beth.
ÖR HEA
Where are you?

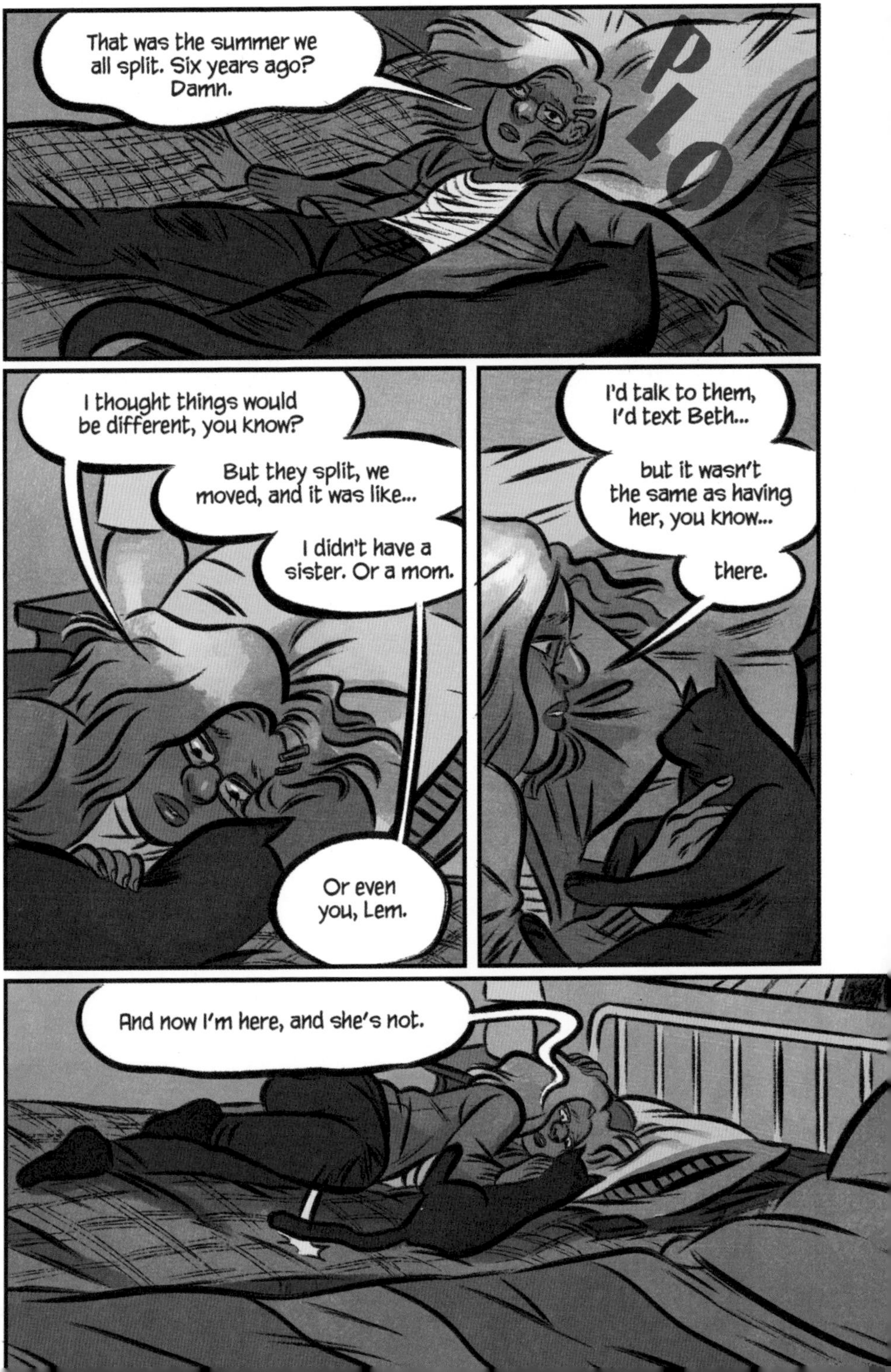
That was the summer we all split. Six years ago? Damn.
PLO
I thought things would be different, you know?
But they split, we moved, and it was like...
I didn't have a sister. Or a mom.
Or even you, Lem.
I'd talk to them, I'd text Beth...
but it wasn't the same as having her, you know...
there.
And now I'm here, and she's not.

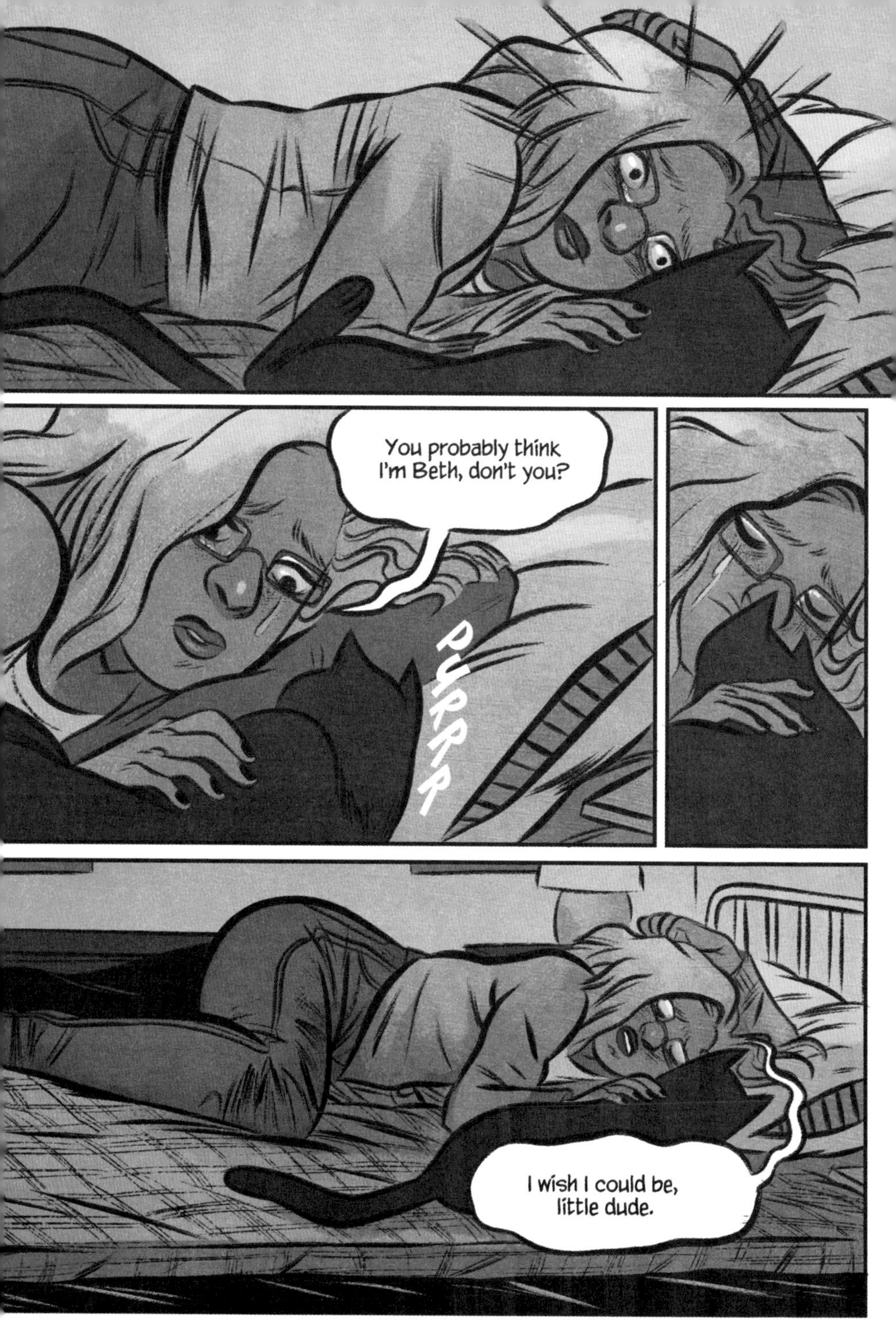

You probably think I'm Beth, don't you?
PURRR
I wish I could be, little dude.

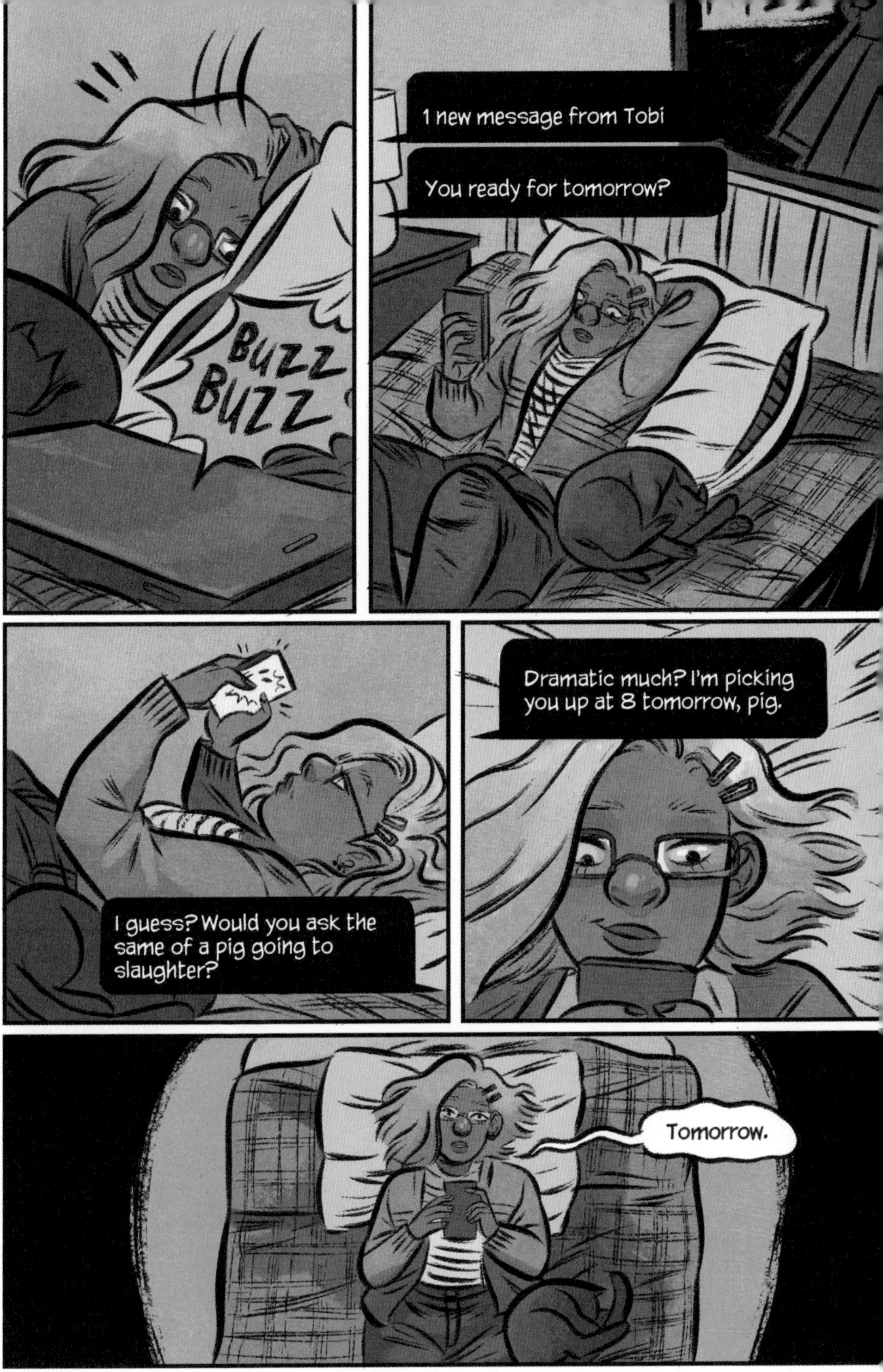
BUZZ
BUZZ
1 new message from Tobi
You ready for tomorrow?
I guess? Would you ask the same of a pig going to slaughter?
Dramatic much? I'm picking you up at 8 tomorrow, pig.
Tomorrow.

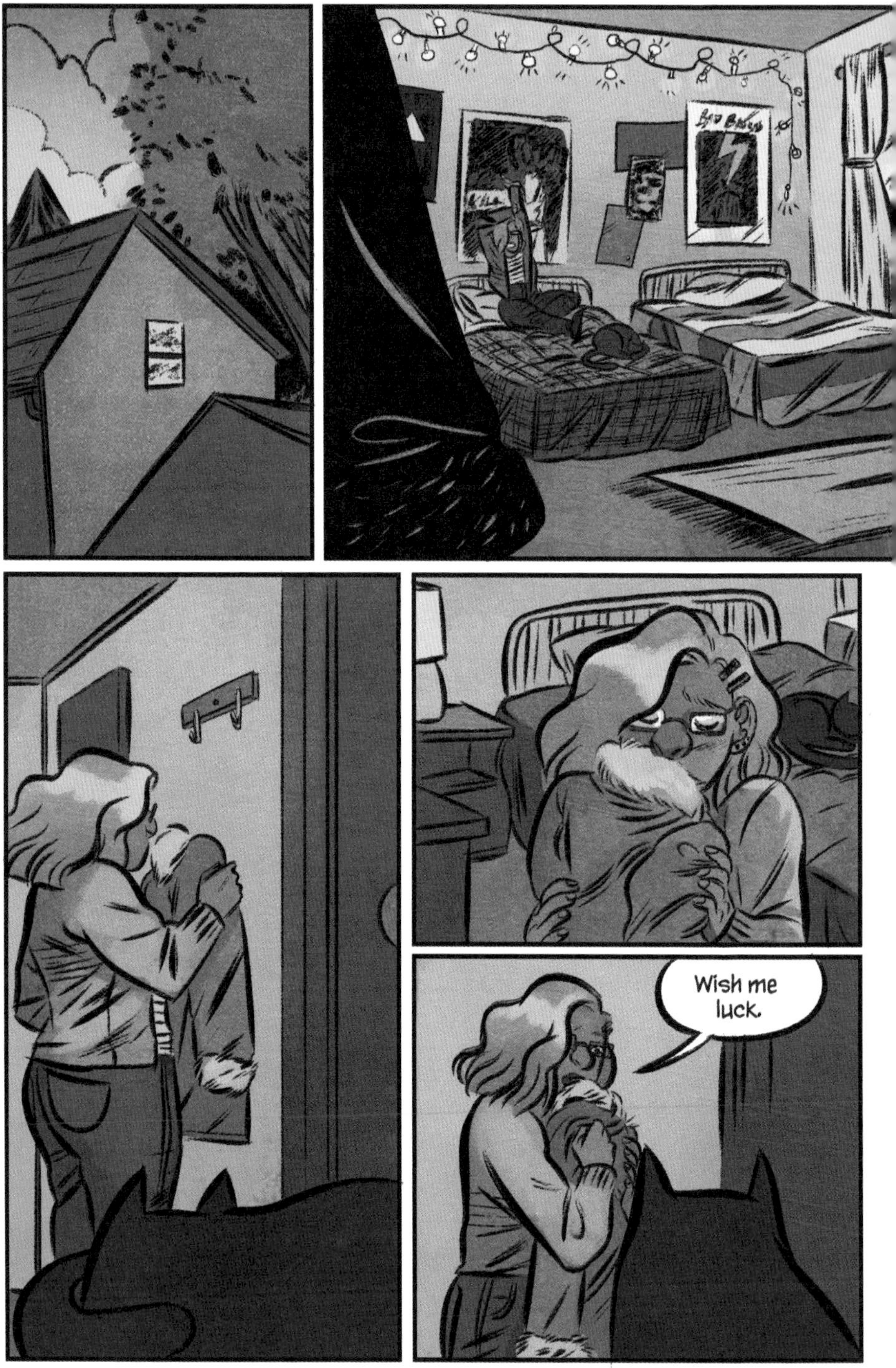
Wish me luck.

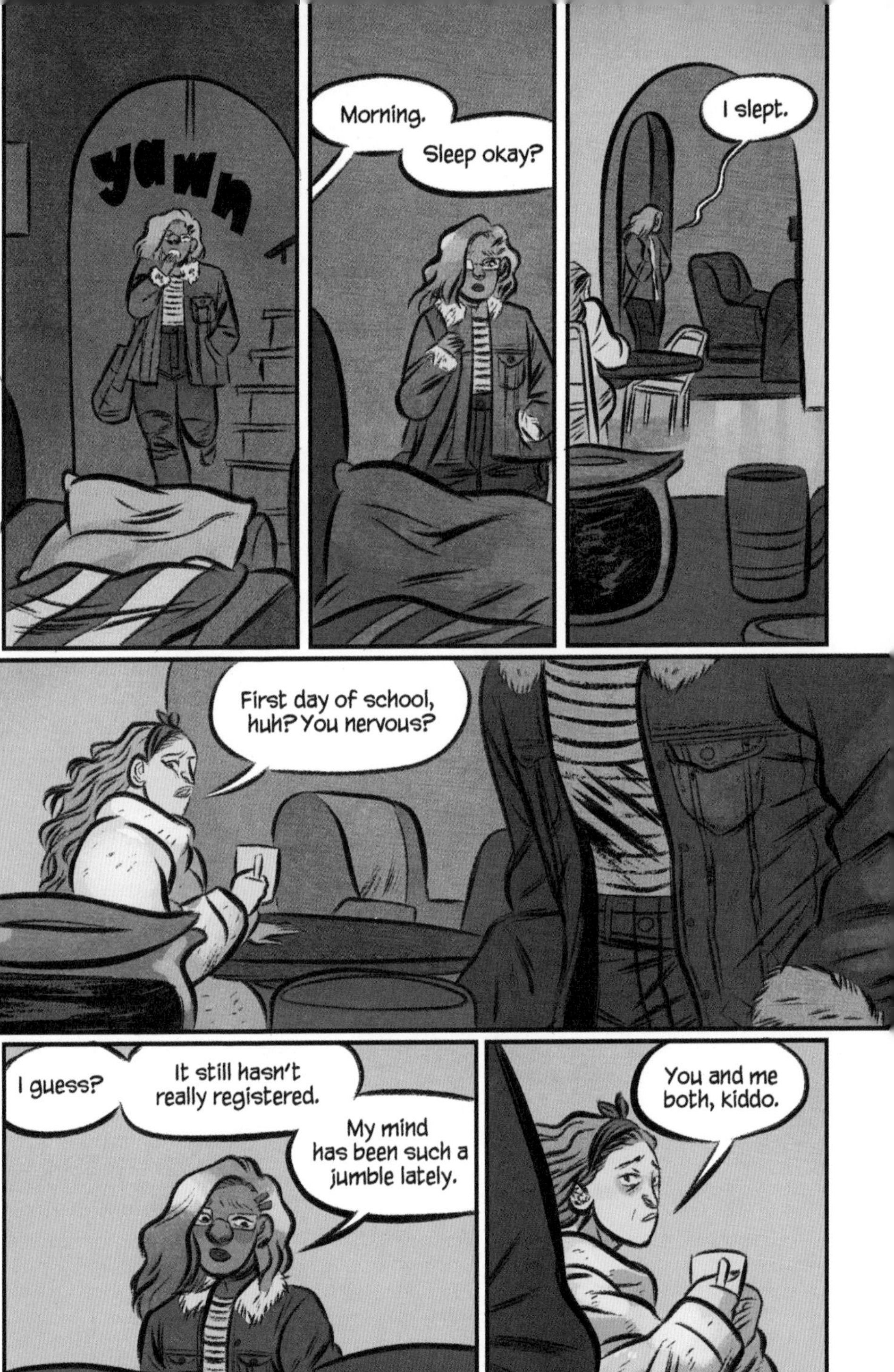
yawn
Morning.
Sleep okay?
I slept.
First day of school, huh? You nervous?
I guess?
It still hasn't really registered.
My mind has been such a jumble lately.
You and me both, kiddo.

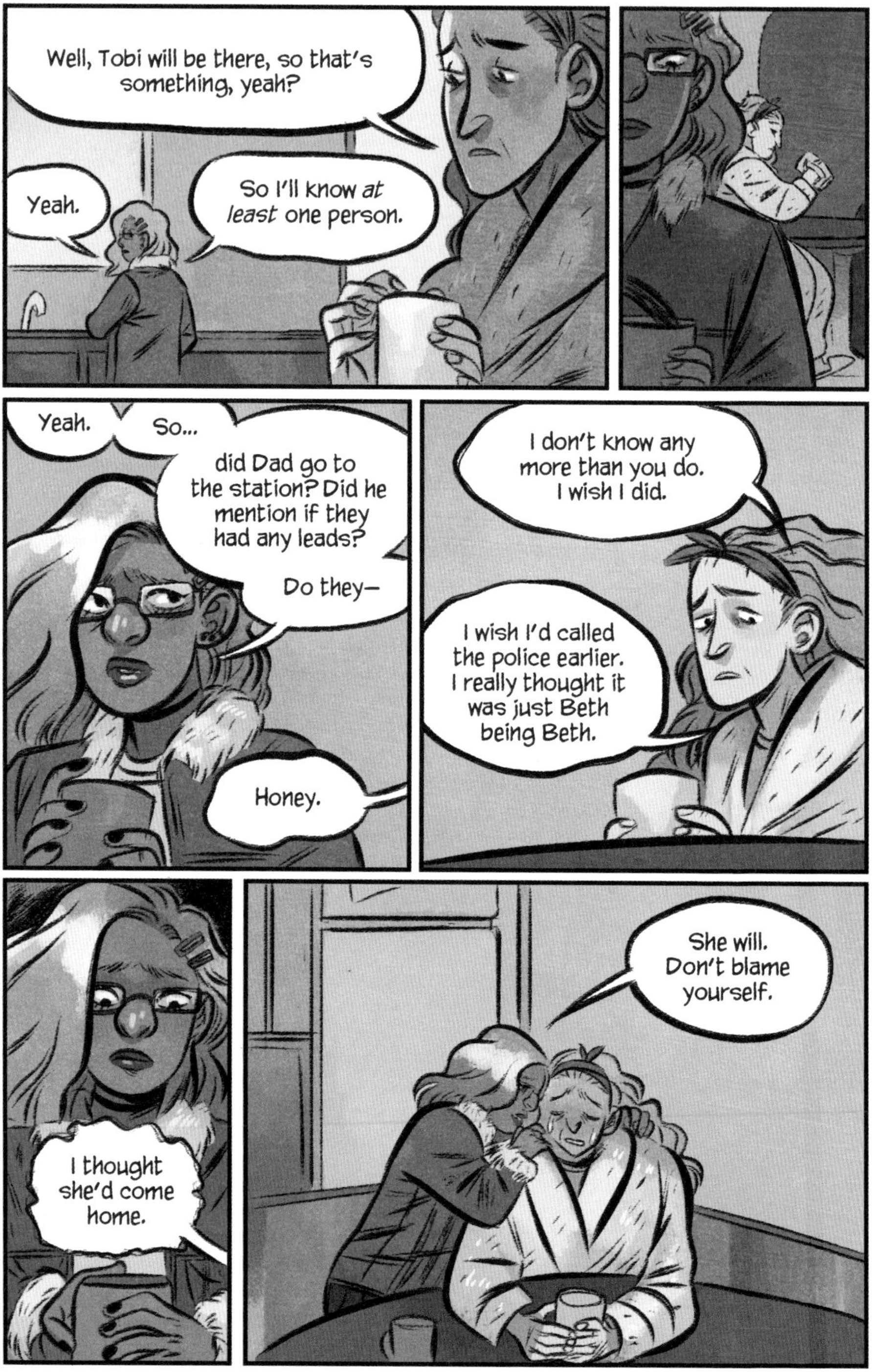
Well, Tobi will be there, so that's something, yeah?
Yeah.
So I'll know *at least* one person.
Yeah.
So...
did Dad go to the station? Did he mention if they had any leads?
Do they—
Honey.
I don't know any more than you do. I wish I did.
I wish I'd called the police earlier. I really thought it was just Beth being Beth.
I thought she'd come home.
She will. Don't blame yourself.

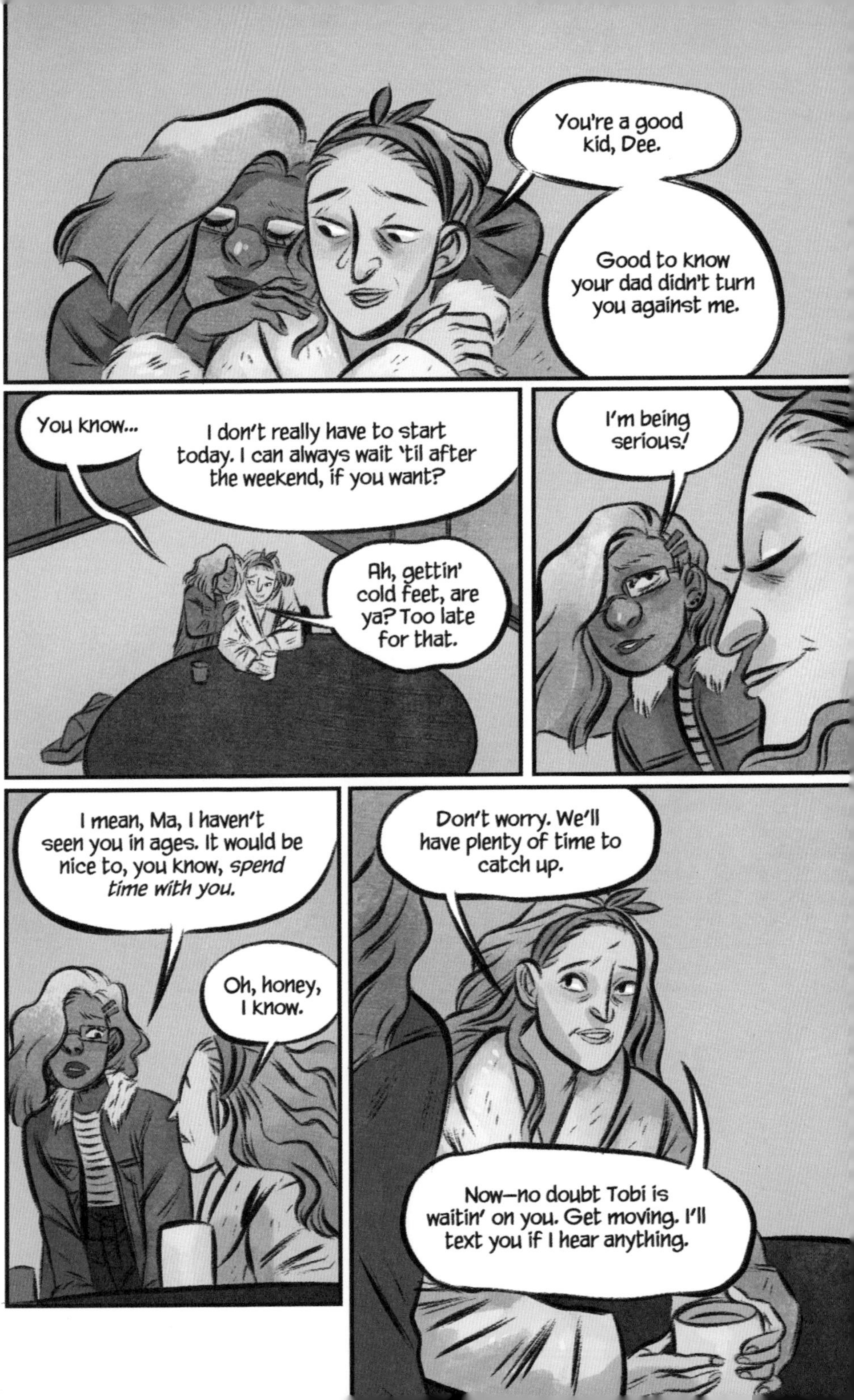

You're a good kid, Dee.
Good to know your dad didn't turn you against me.
You know...
I don't really have to start today. I can always wait 'til after the weekend, if you want?
Ah, gettin' cold feet, are ya? Too late for that.
I'm being serious!
I mean, Ma, I haven't seen you in ages. It would be nice to, you know, *spend time with you.*
Oh, honey, I know.
Don't worry. We'll have plenty of time to catch up.
Now—no doubt Tobi is waitin' on you. Get moving. I'll text you if I hear anything.

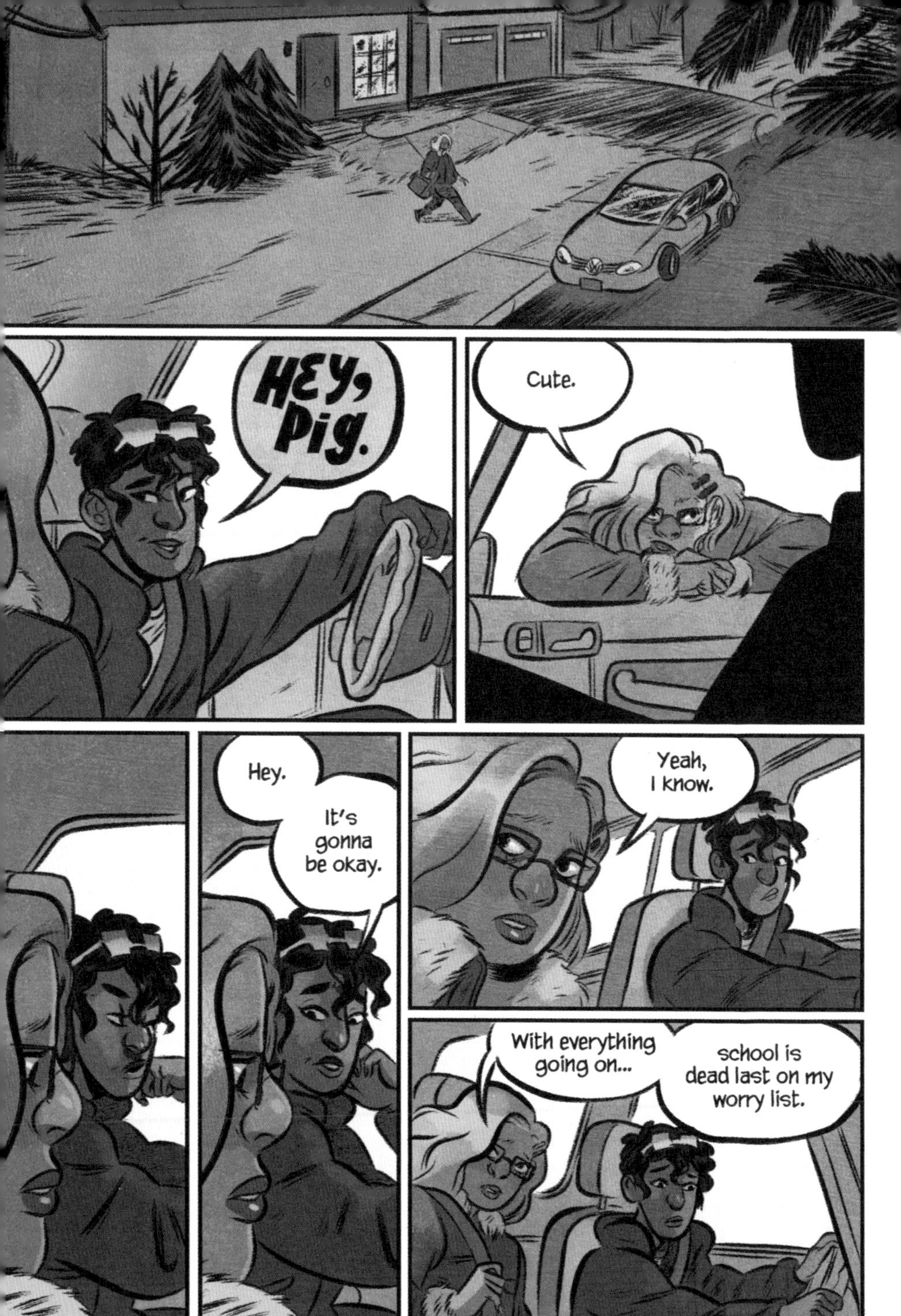
HEY, PIG.
Cute.
Hey.
It's gonna be okay.
Yeah, I know.
With everything going on...
school is dead last on my worry list.

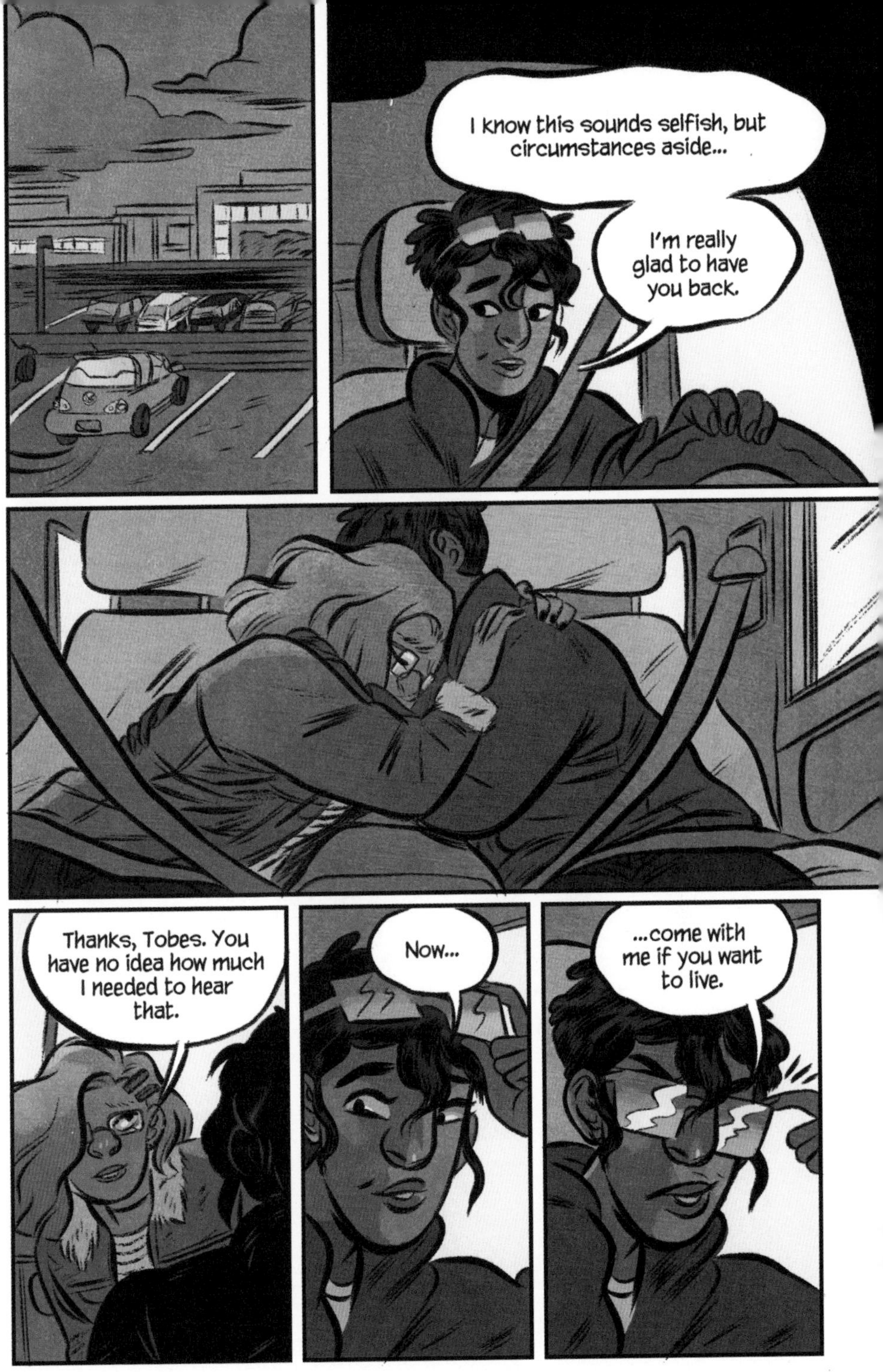
I know this sounds selfish, but circumstances aside...
I'm really glad to have you back.
Thanks, Tobes. You have no idea how much I needed to hear that.
Now...
...come with me if you want to live.

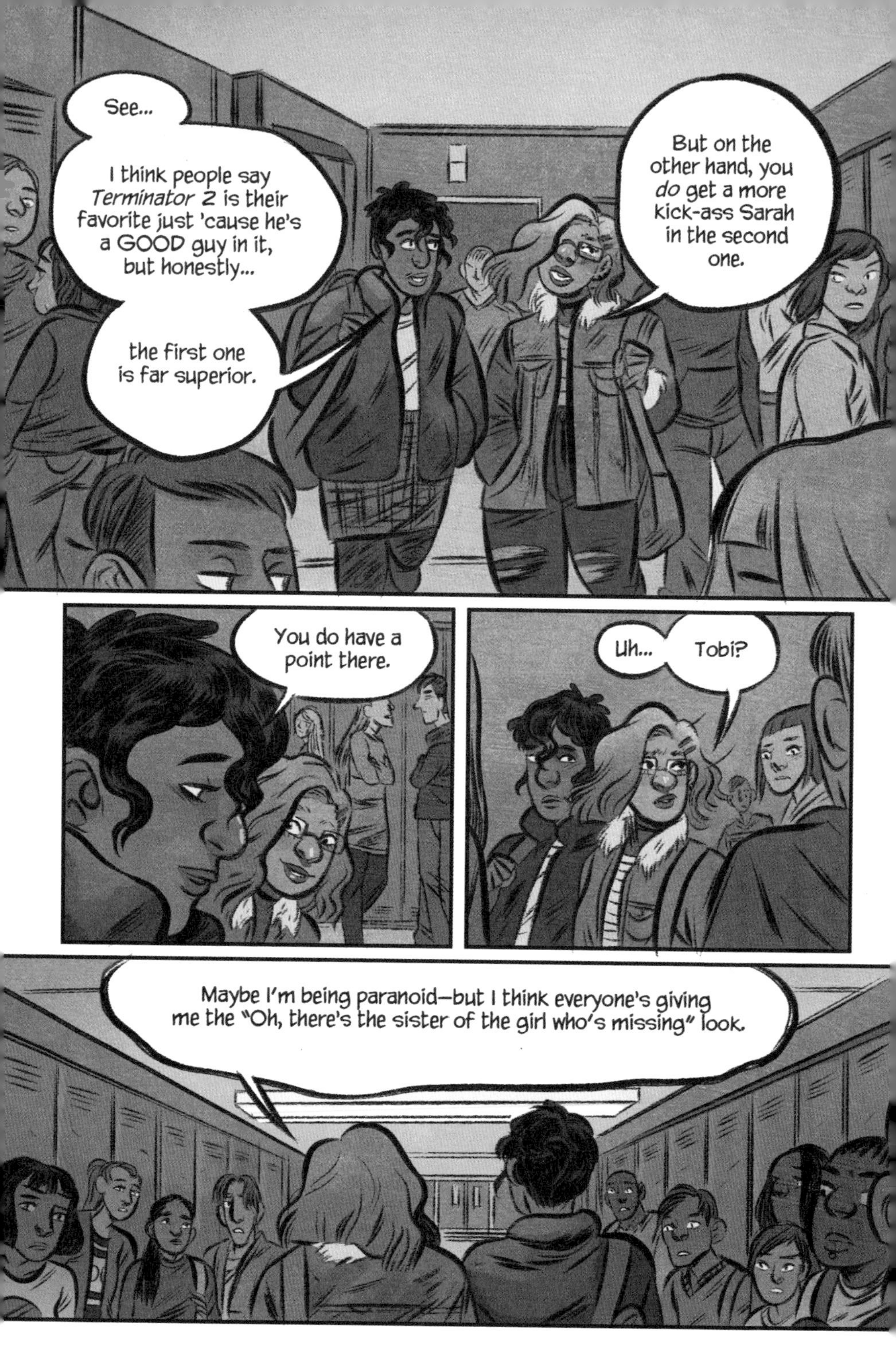
See...
I think people say *Terminator 2* is their favorite just 'cause he's a GOOD guy in it, but honestly...
the first one is far superior.
But on the other hand, you *do* get a more kick-ass Sarah in the second one.
You do have a point there.
Uh...
Tobi?
Maybe I'm being paranoid—but I think everyone's giving me the "Oh, there's the sister of the girl who's missing" look.

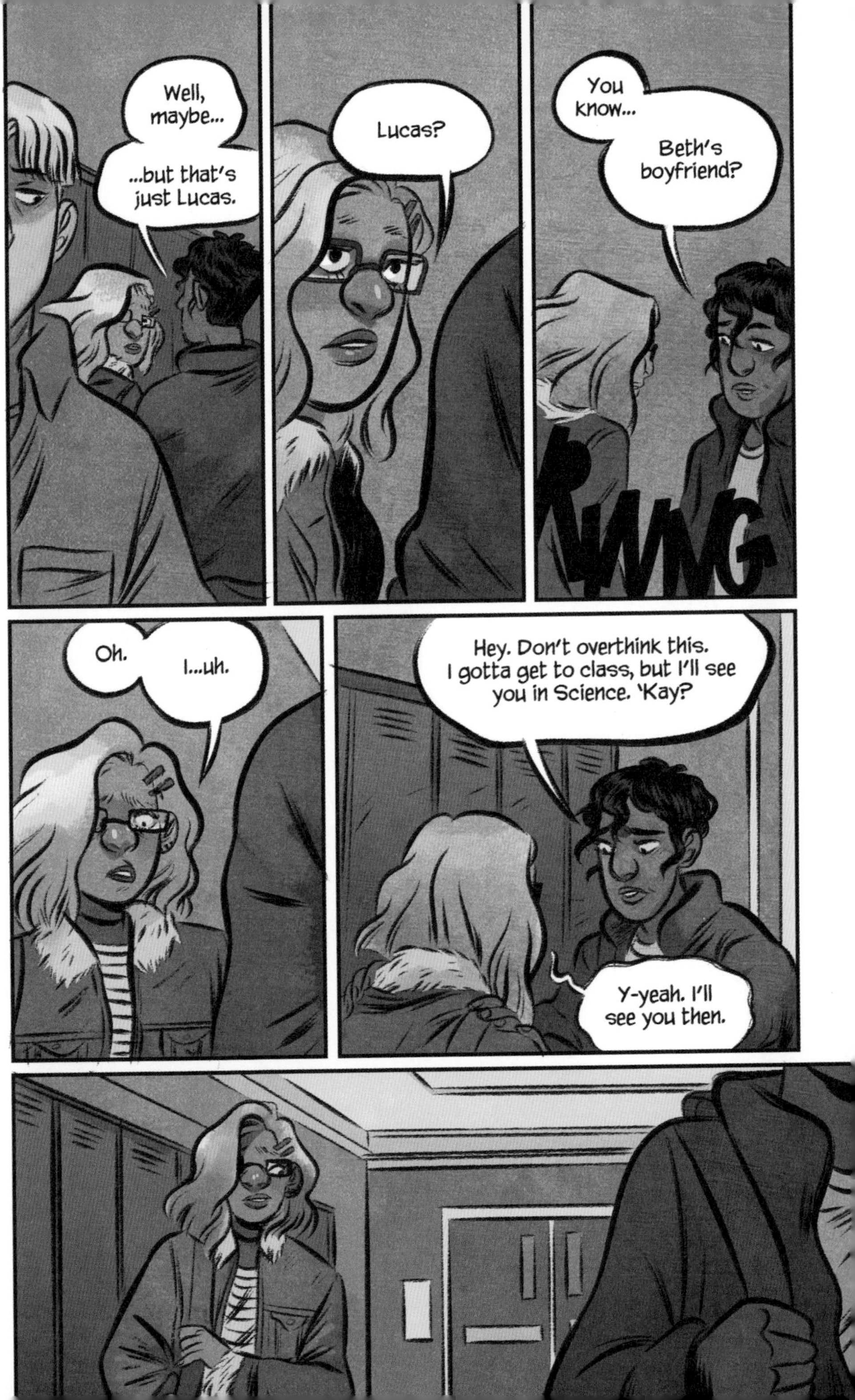
Well, maybe...
...but that's just Lucas.
Lucas?
You know...
Beth's boyfriend?
RWWNG
Oh.
I...uh.
Hey. Don't overthink this. I gotta get to class, but I'll see you in Science. 'Kay?
Y-yeah. I'll see you then.

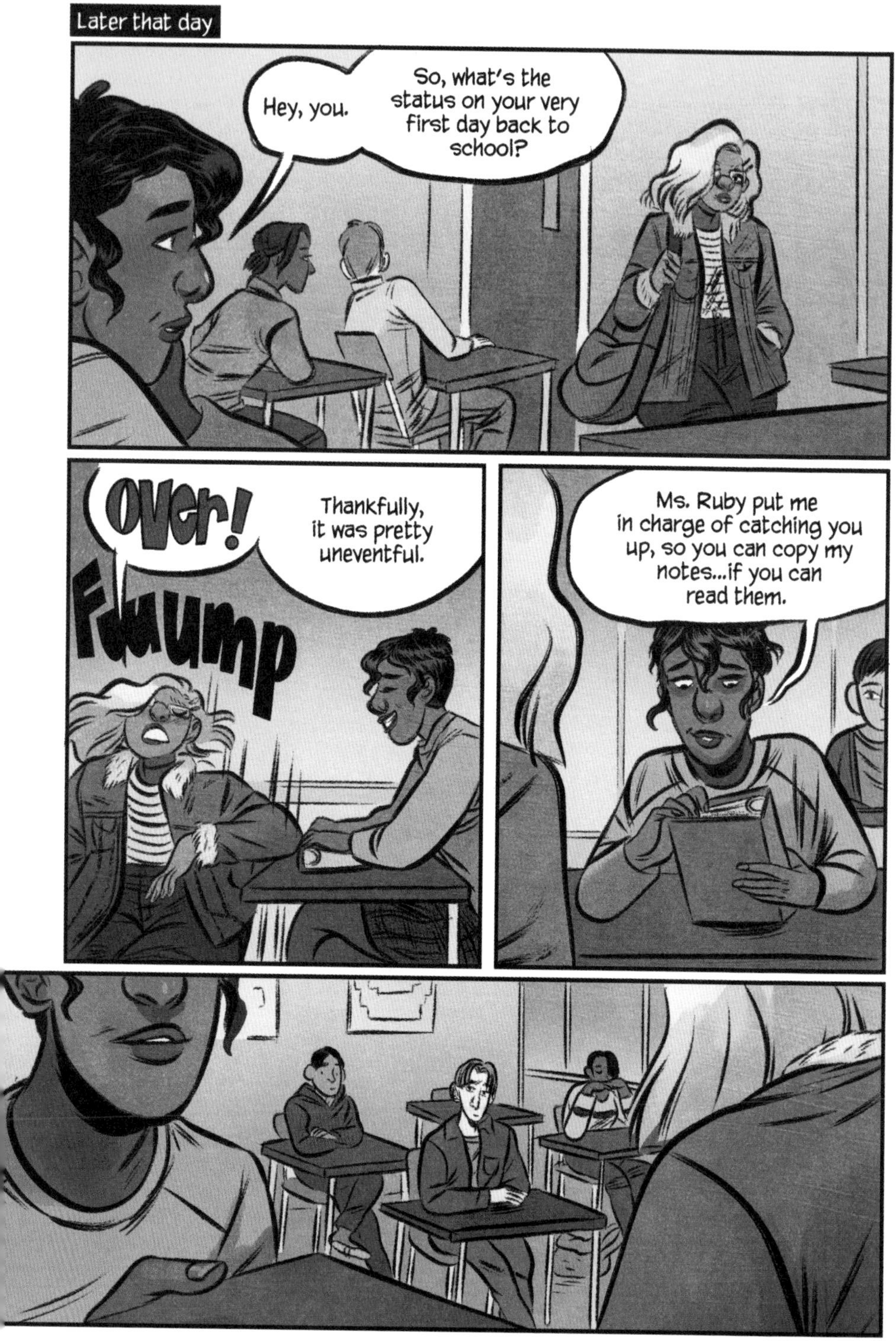
Later that day
Hey, you.
So, what's the status on your very first day back to school?
Over!
Fuuump
Thankfully, it was pretty uneventful.
Ms. Ruby put me in charge of catching you up, so you can copy my notes...if you can read them.

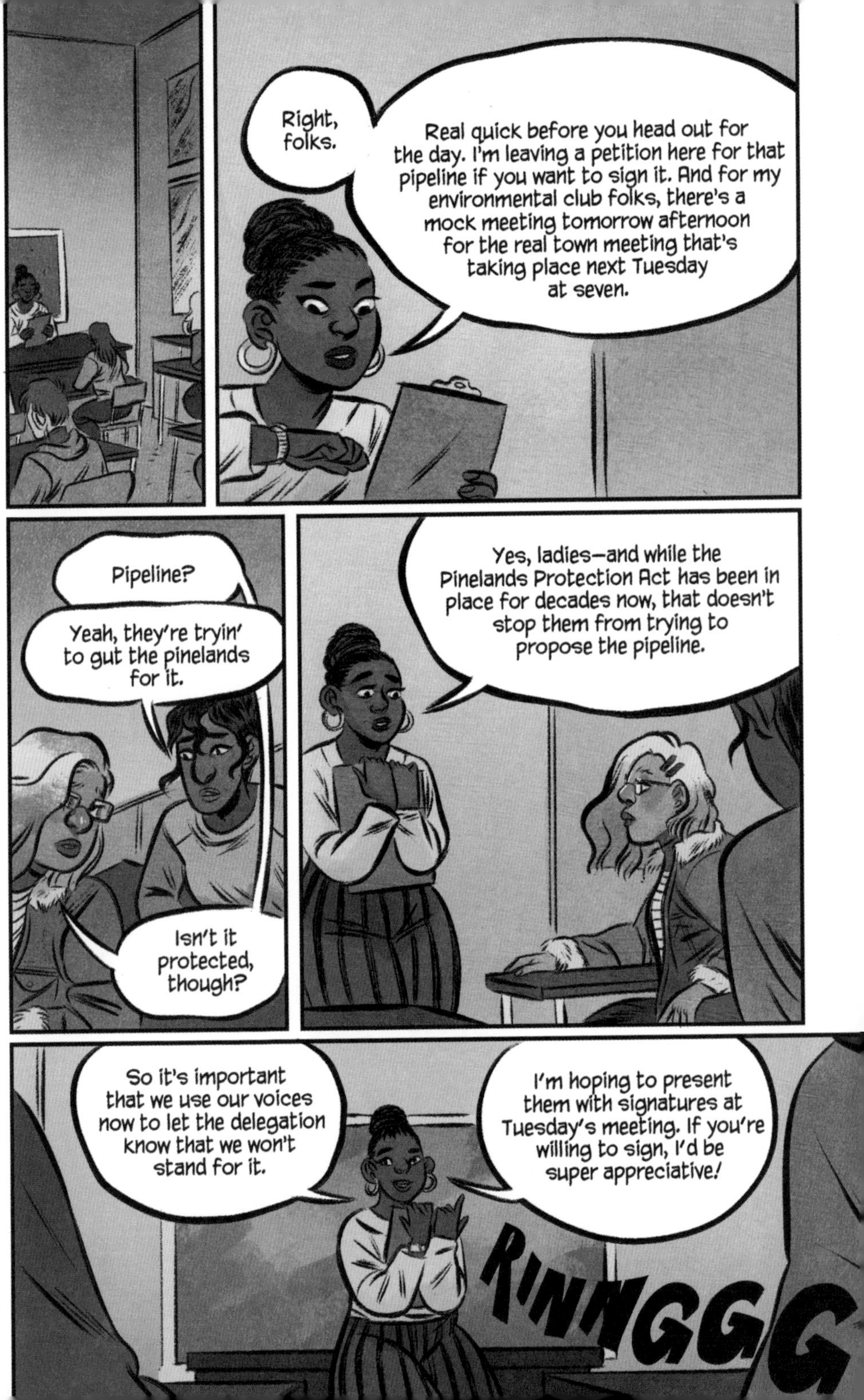
Right, folks.
Real quick before you head out for the day. I'm leaving a petition here for that pipeline if you want to sign it. And for my environmental club folks, there's a mock meeting tomorrow afternoon for the real town meeting that's taking place next Tuesday at seven.
Pipeline?
Yeah, they're tryin' to gut the pinelands for it.
Isn't it protected, though?
Yes, ladies—and while the Pinelands Protection Act has been in place for decades now, that doesn't stop them from trying to propose the pipeline.
So it's important that we use our voices now to let the delegation know that we won't stand for it.
I'm hoping to present them with signatures at Tuesday's meeting. If you're willing to sign, I'd be super appreciative!
RINNGGG

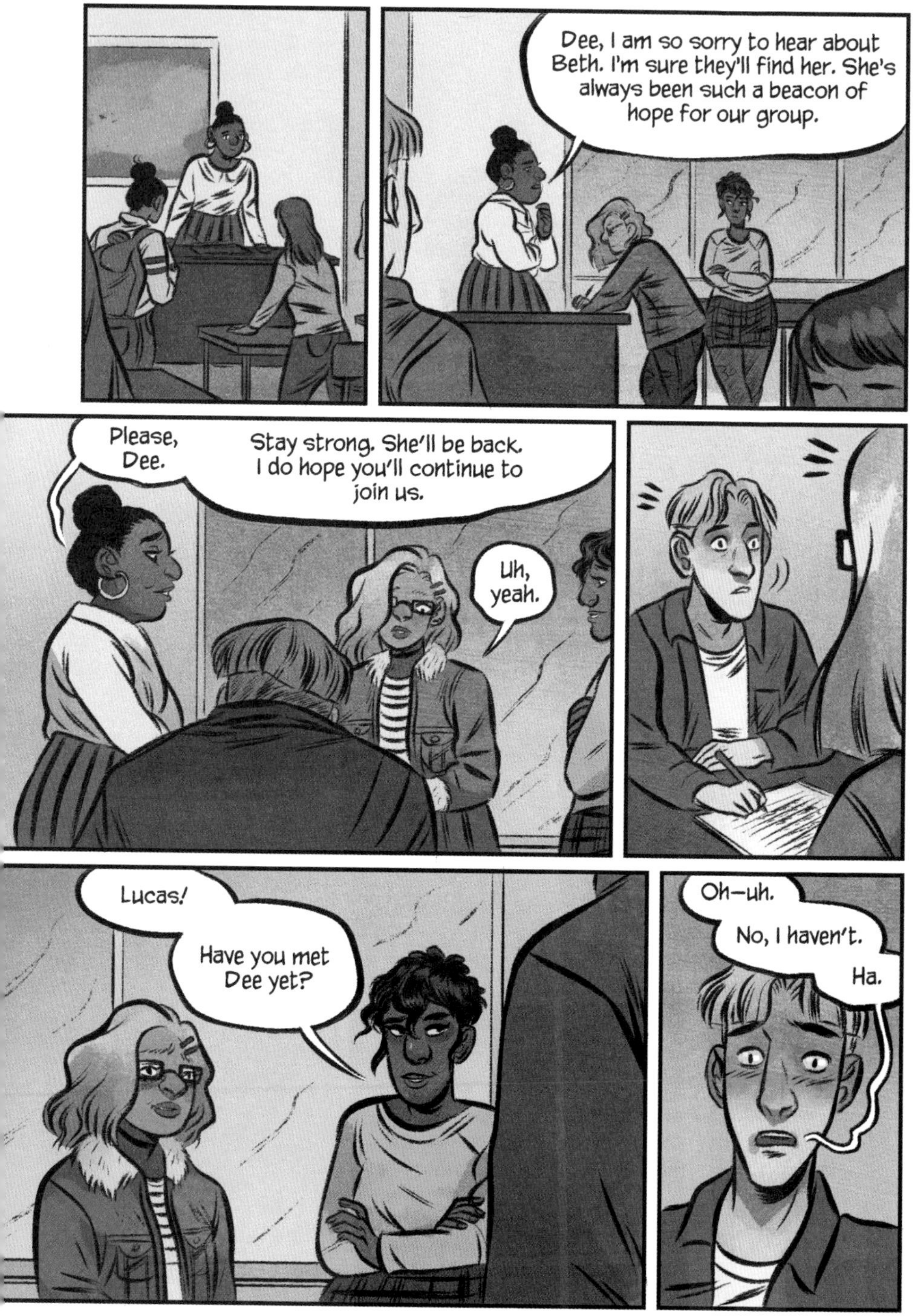
Dee, I am so sorry to hear about Beth. I'm sure they'll find her. She's always been such a beacon of hope for our group.
Please, Dee.
Stay strong. She'll be back. I do hope you'll continue to join us.
Uh, yeah.
Lucas!
Have you met Dee yet?
Oh—uh.
No, I haven't.
Ha.

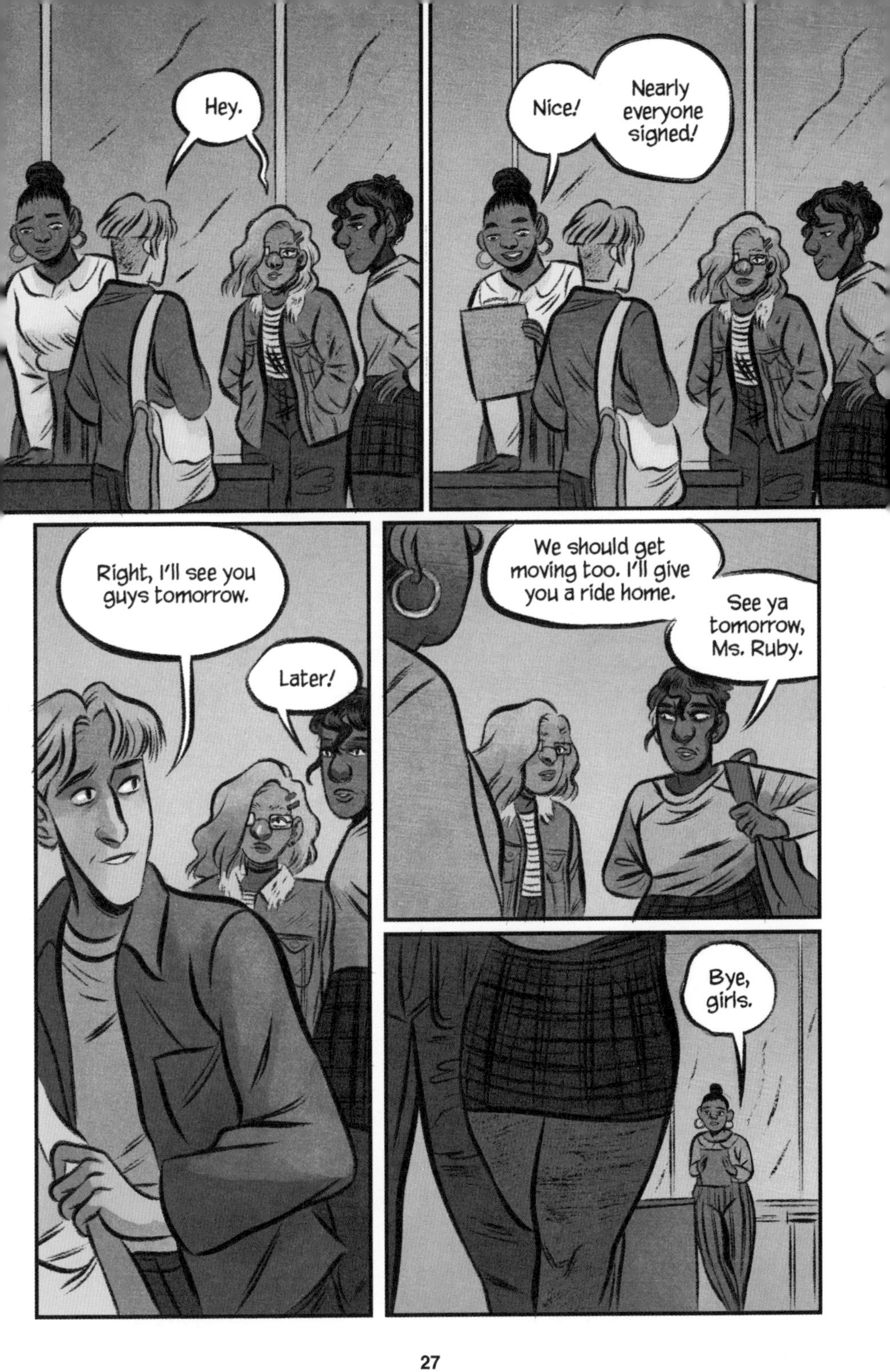

Hey.
Nice!
Nearly everyone signed!
Right, I'll see you guys tomorrow.
Later!
We should get moving too. I'll give you a ride home.
See ya tomorrow, Ms. Ruby.
Bye, girls.

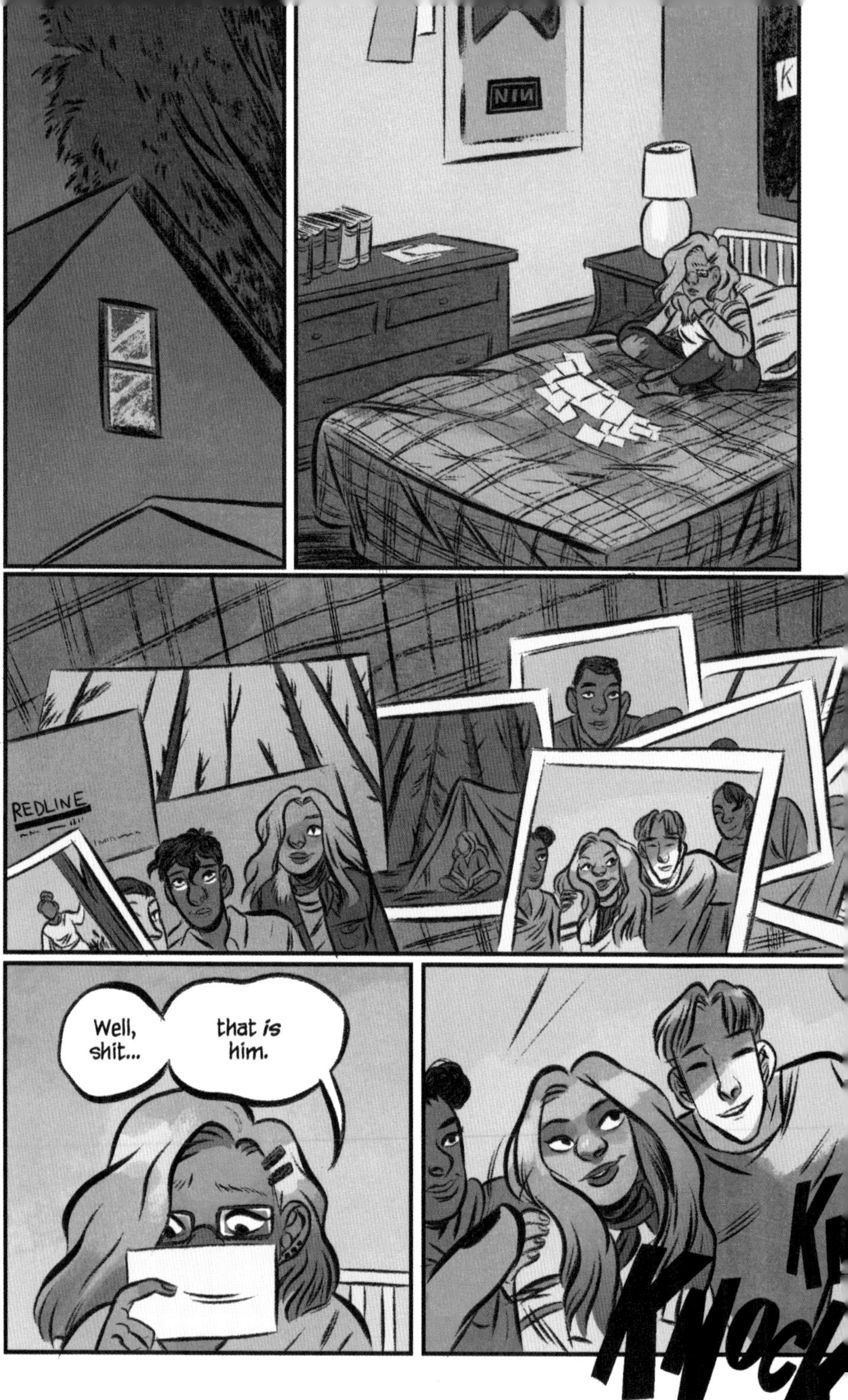
NIN
K
REDLINE
Well, shit...
that *is* him.

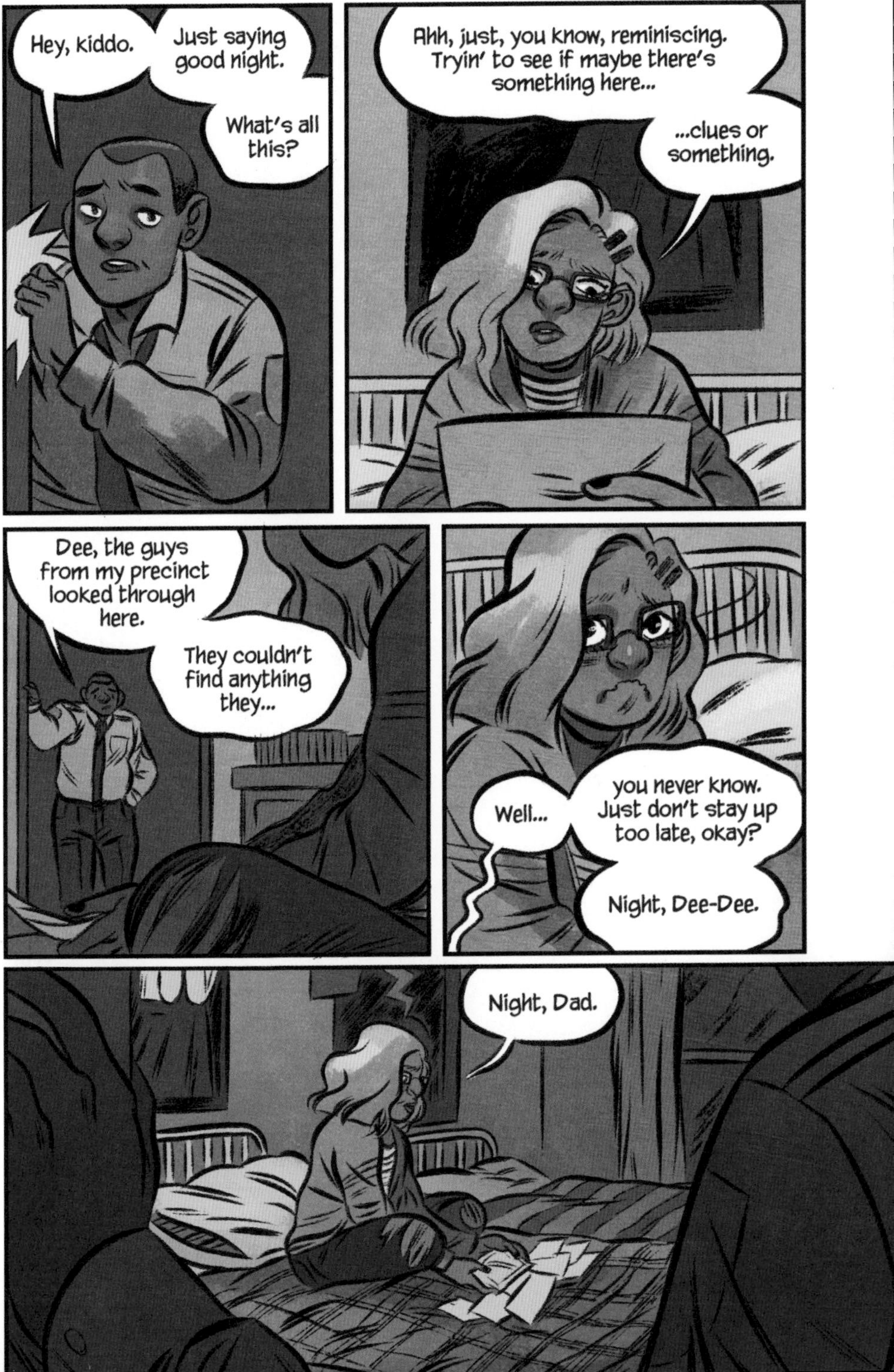
Hey, kiddo.
Just saying good night.
What's all this?
Ahh, just, you know, reminiscing. Tryin' to see if maybe there's something here...
...clues or something.
Dee, the guys from my precinct looked through here.
They couldn't find anything they...
Well...
you never know. Just don't stay up too late, okay?
Night, Dee-Dee.
Night, Dad.

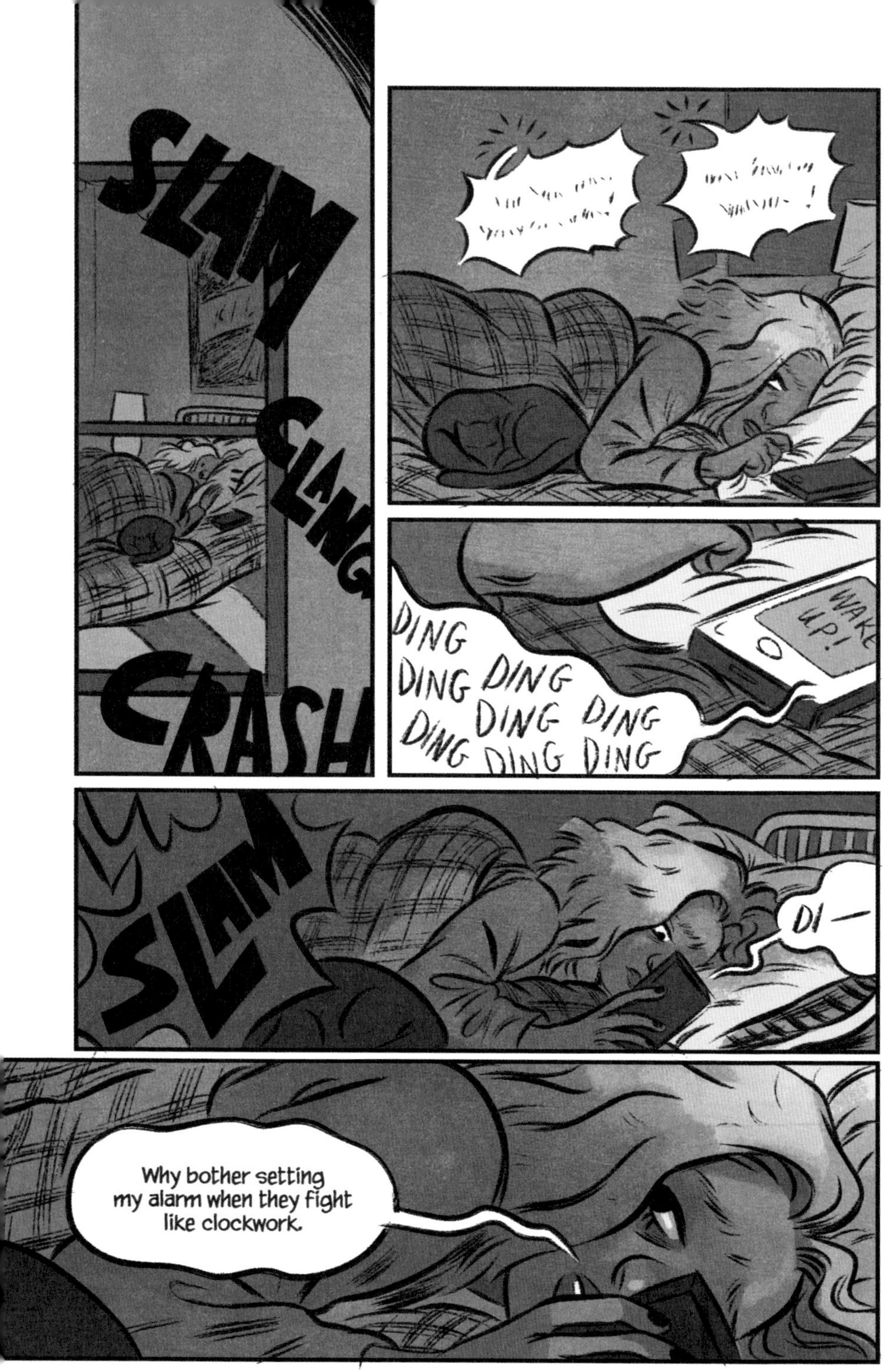
SLAM
CLANG
CRASH
DING DING DING DING DING DING DING DING
WAKE UP!
SLAM
DI—
Why bother setting my alarm when they fight like clockwork.

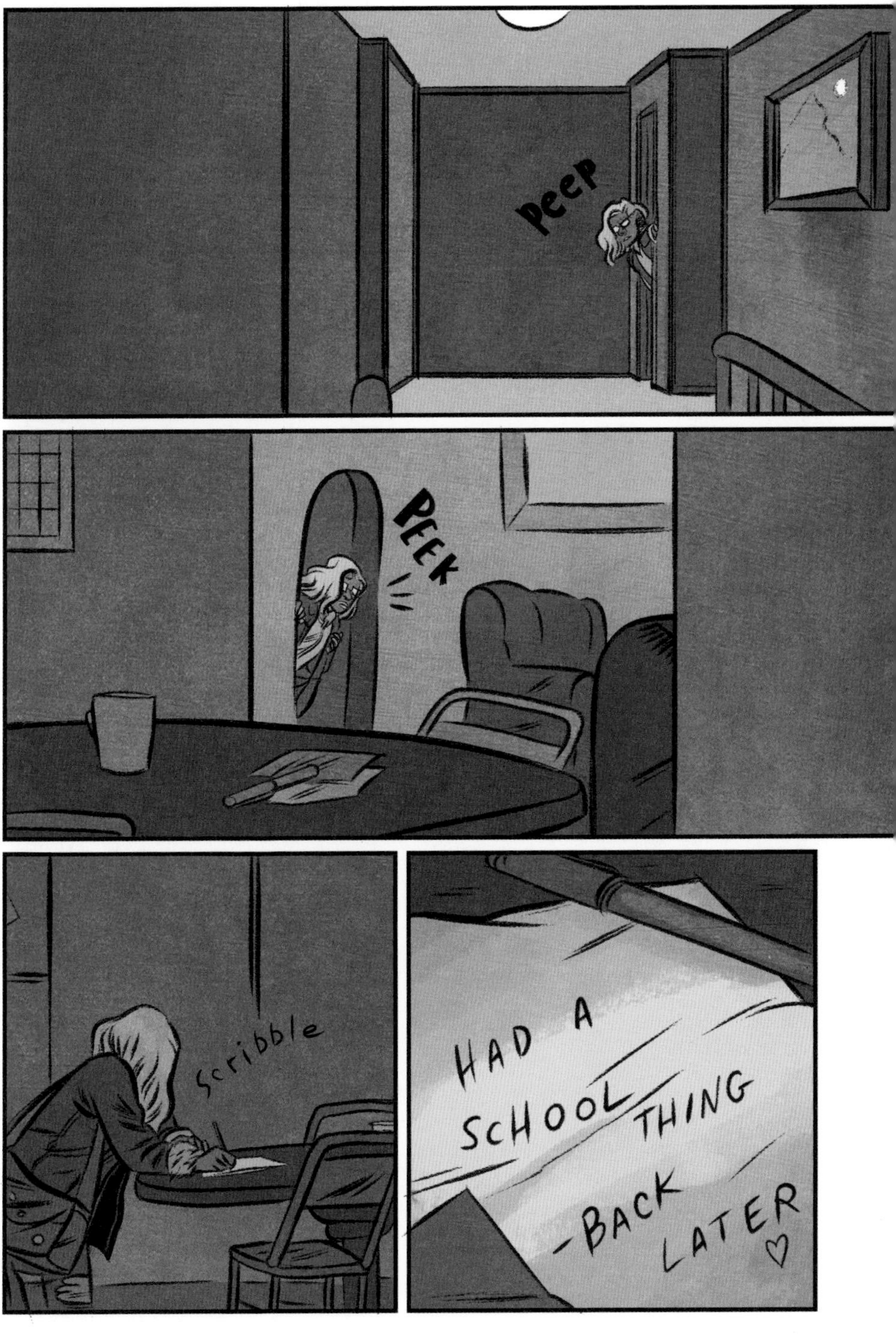
PEEP
PEEK
scribble
HAD A SCHOOL THING
-BACK LATER ♡

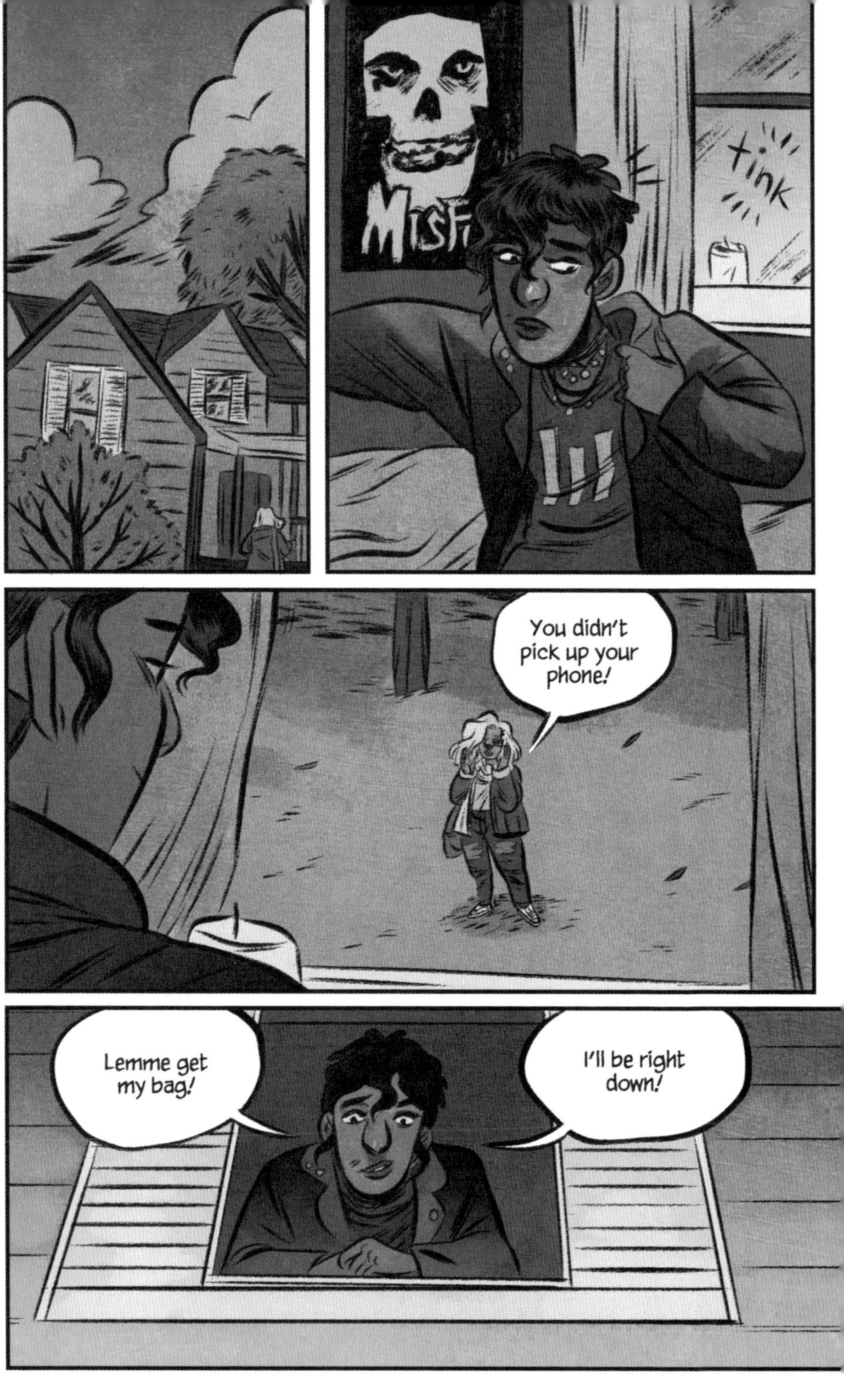
MISFI
tink
You didn't pick up your phone!
Lemme get my bag!
I'll be right down!

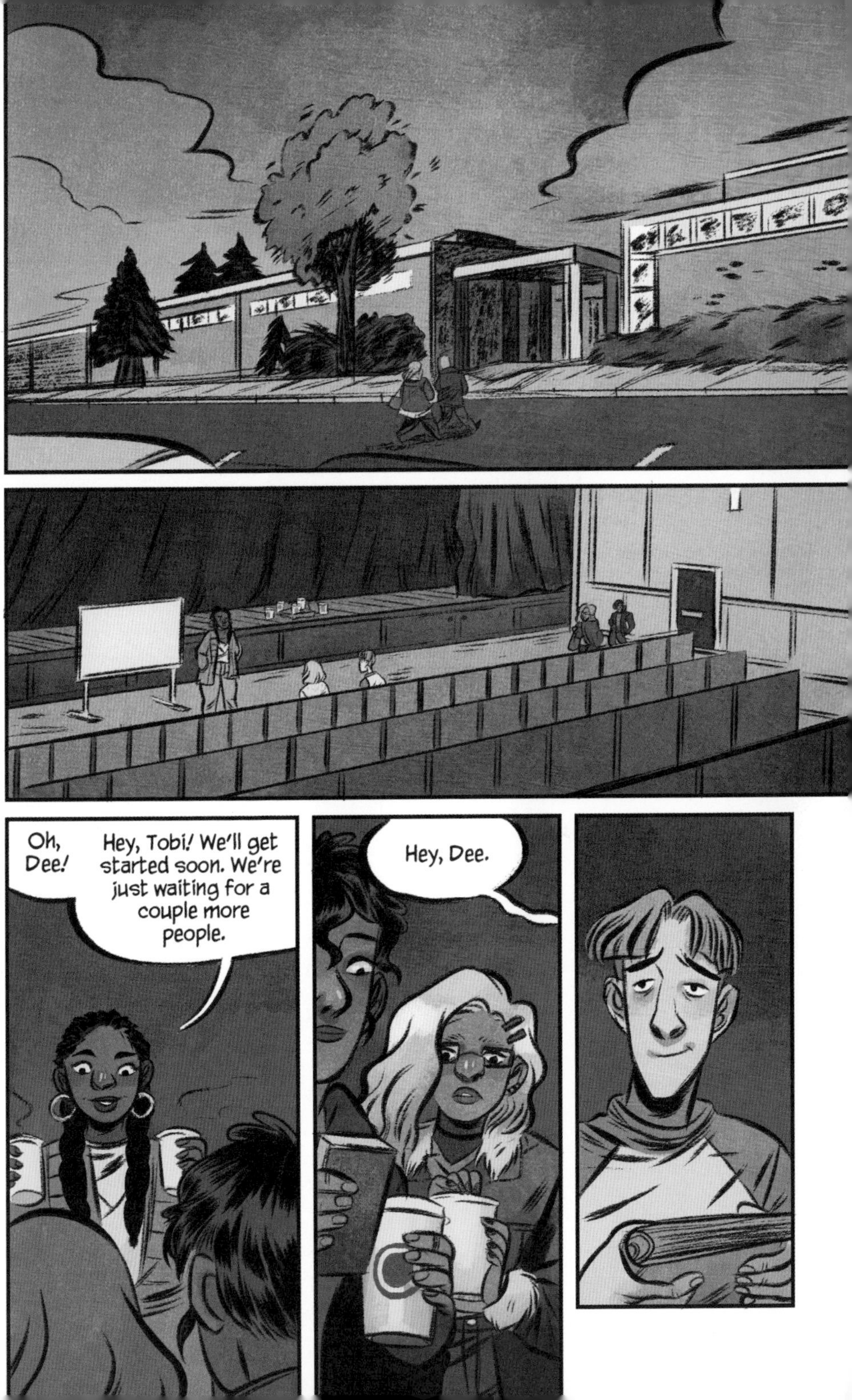
Oh, Dee!
Hey, Tobi! We'll get started soon. We're just waiting for a couple more people.
Hey, Dee.

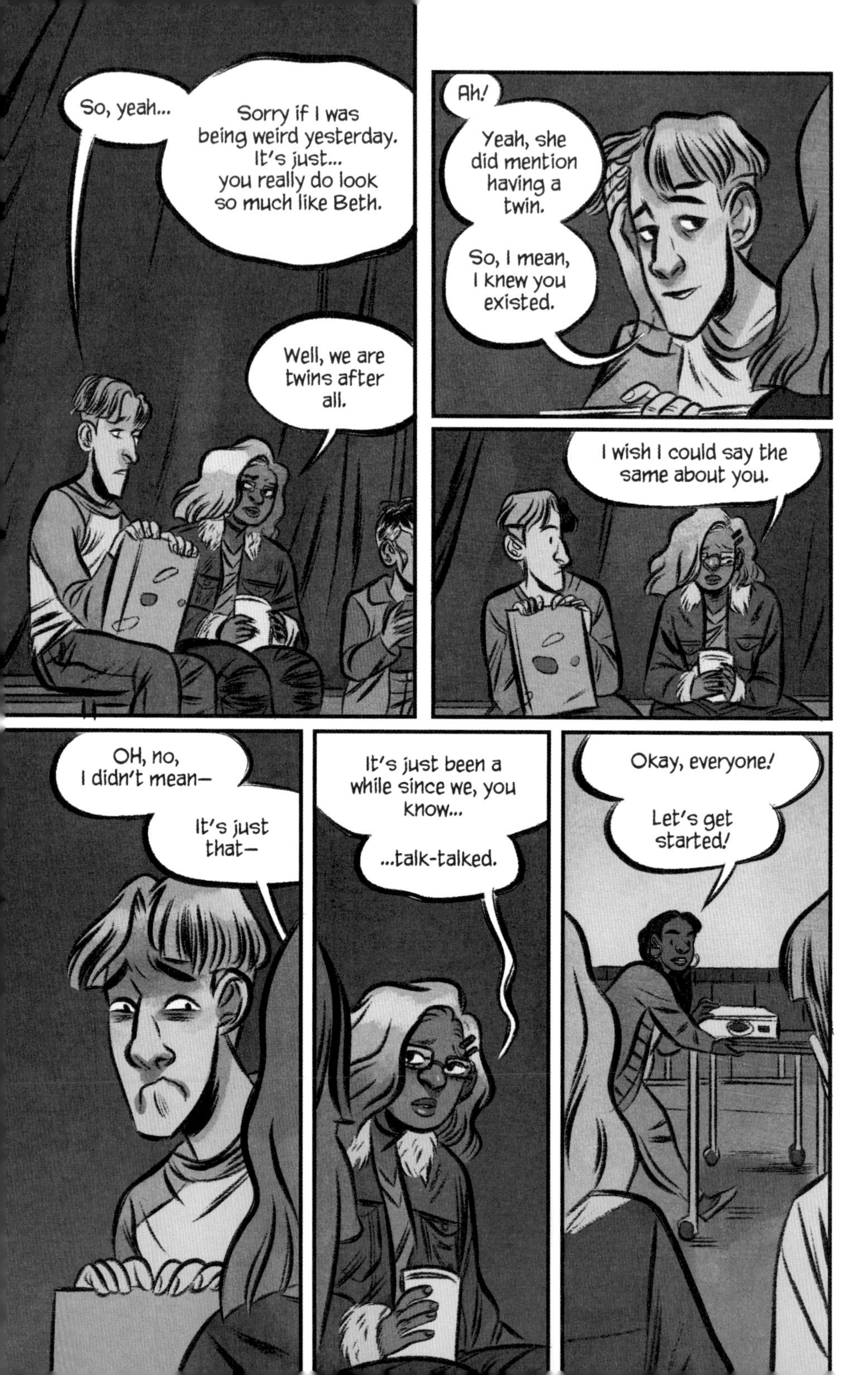
So, yeah...
Sorry if I was being weird yesterday. It's just... you really do look so much like Beth.
Well, we are twins after all.
Ah!
Yeah, she did mention having a twin.
So, I mean, I knew you existed.
I wish I could say the same about you.
OH, no, I didn't mean—
It's just that—
It's just been a while since we, you know...
...talk-talked.
Okay, everyone!
Let's get started!

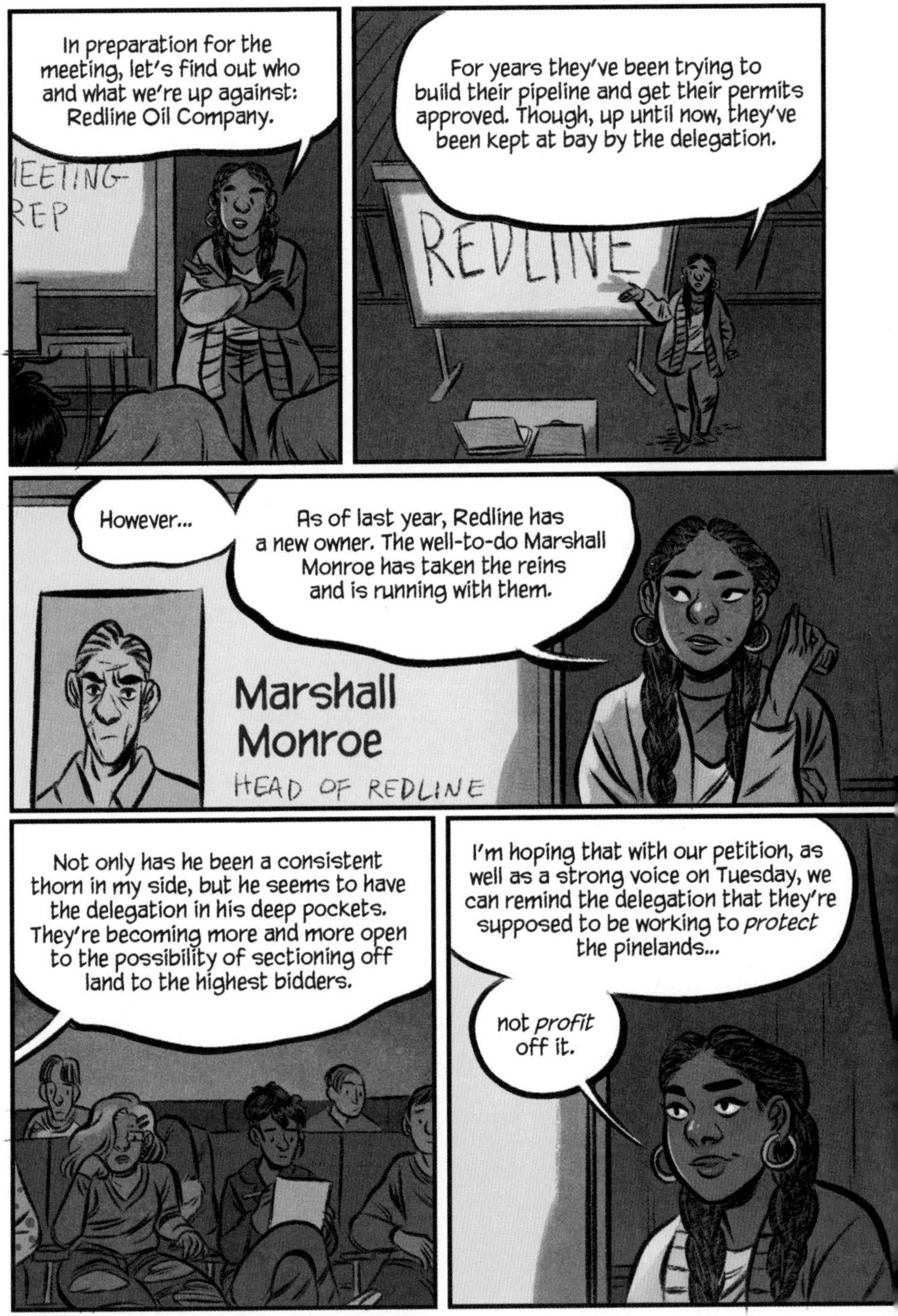
In preparation for the meeting, let's find out who and what we're up against: Redline Oil Company.
MEETING PREP
For years they've been trying to build their pipeline and get their permits approved. Though, up until now, they've been kept at bay by the delegation.
REDLINE
However...
As of last year, Redline has a new owner. The well-to-do Marshall Monroe has taken the reins and is running with them.
Marshall Monroe
HEAD OF REDLINE
Not only has he been a consistent thorn in my side, but he seems to have the delegation in his deep pockets. They're becoming more and more open to the possibility of sectioning off land to the highest bidders.
I'm hoping that with our petition, as well as a strong voice on Tuesday, we can remind the delegation that they're supposed to be working to *protect* the pinelands...
not *profit* off it.

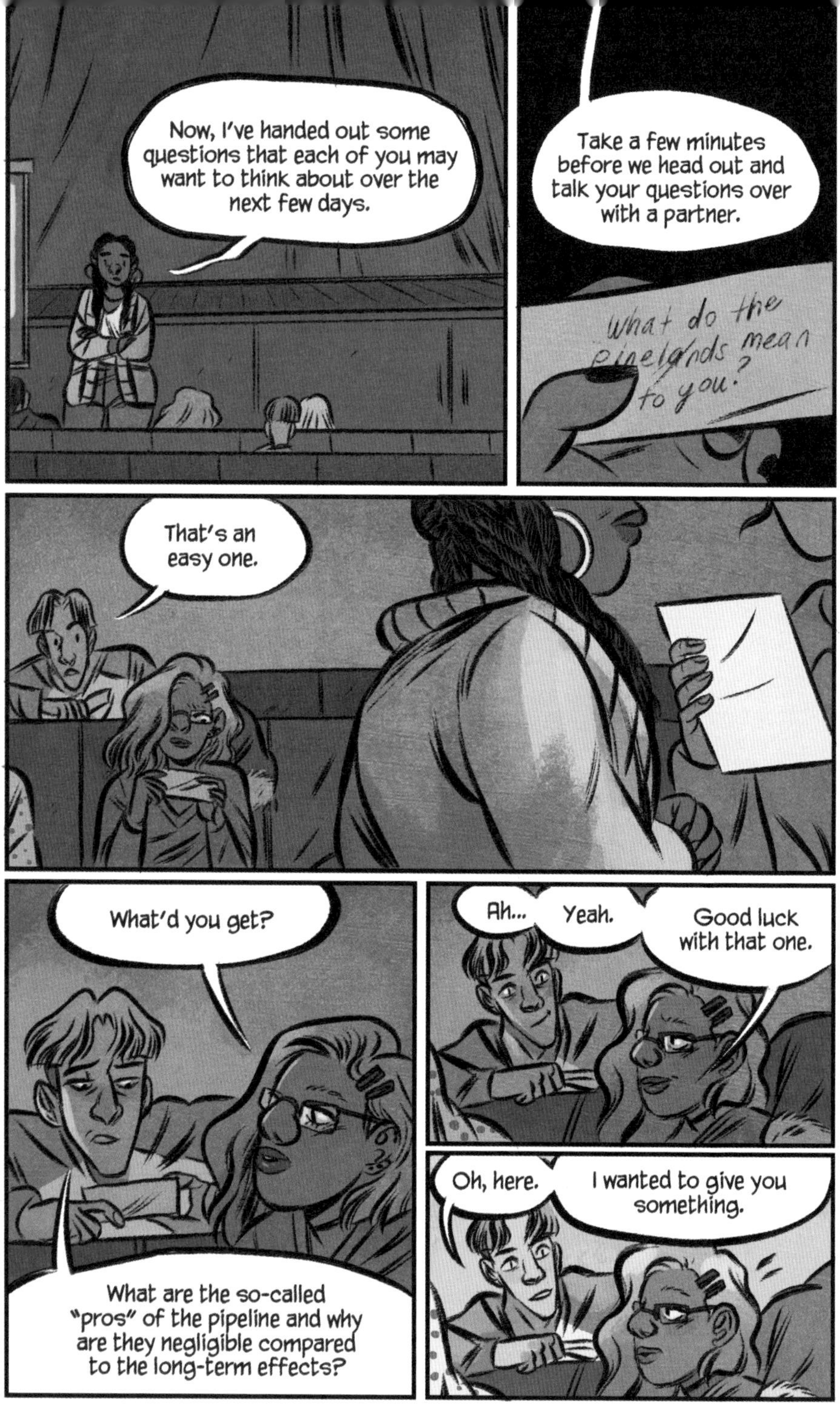
Now, I've handed out some questions that each of you may want to think about over the next few days.
Take a few minutes before we head out and talk your questions over with a partner.
what do the pinelands mean to you?
That's an easy one.
What'd you get?
What are the so-called "pros" of the pipeline and why are they negligible compared to the long-term effects?
Ah...
Yeah.
Good luck with that one.
Oh, here.
I wanted to give you something.

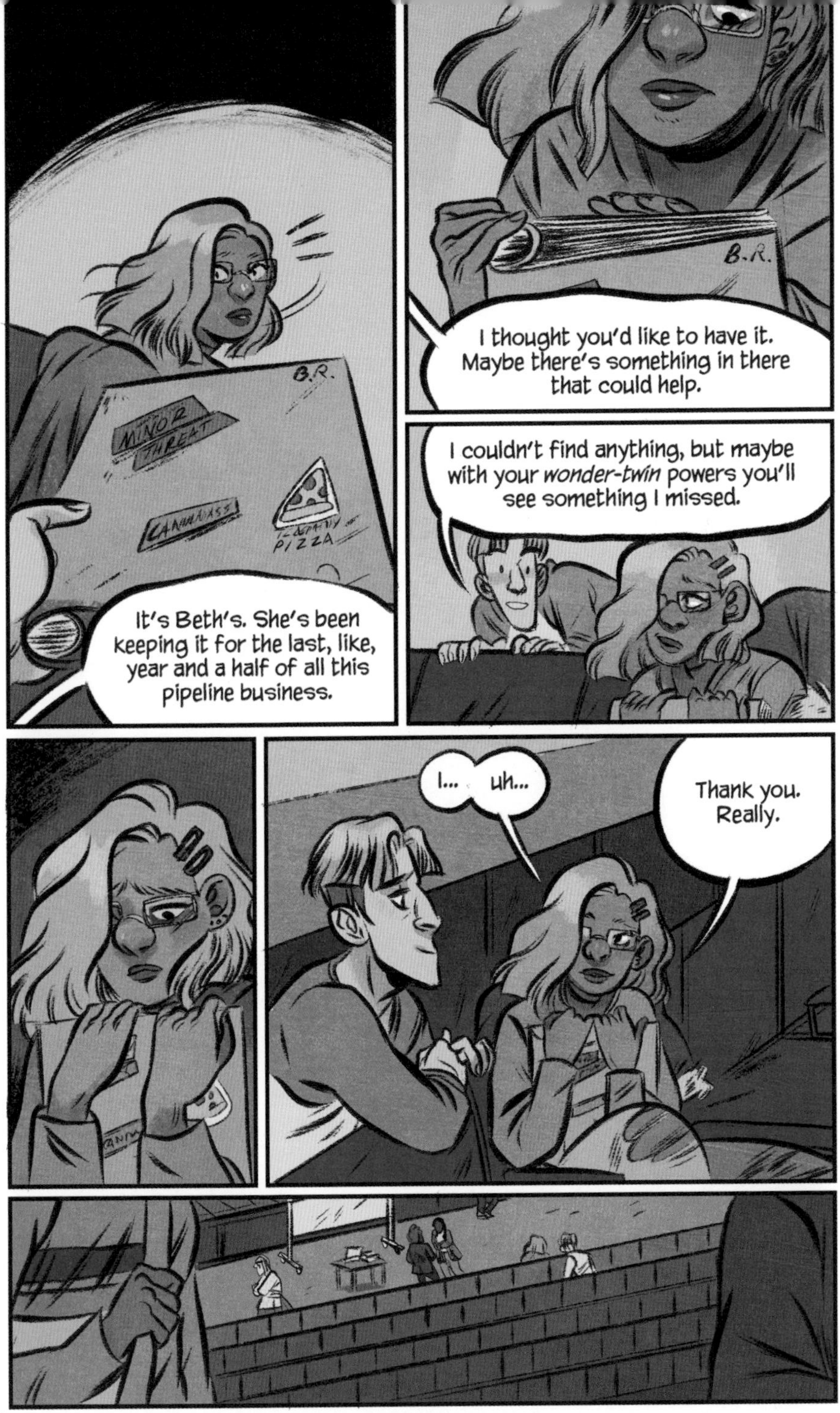
B.R.
MINOR THREAT
PIZZA
It's Beth's. She's been keeping it for the last, like, year and a half of all this pipeline business.
B.R.
I thought you'd like to have it. Maybe there's something in there that could help.
I couldn't find anything, but maybe with your *wonder-twin* powers you'll see something I missed.
I... uh...
Thank you. Really.

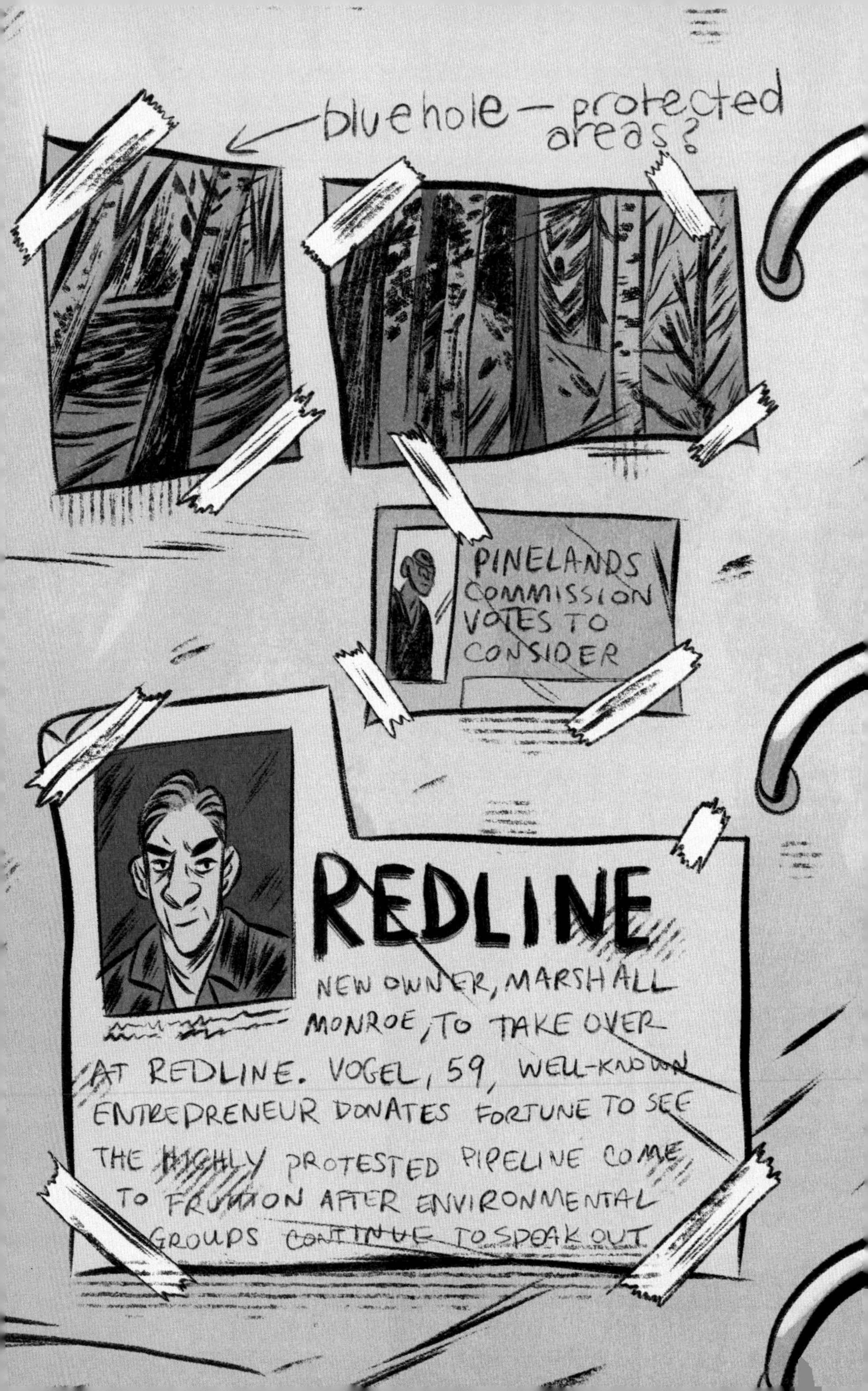
bluehole — protected areas?
PINELANDS COMMISSION VOTES TO CONSIDER
REDLINE
NEW OWNER, MARSHALL MONROE, TO TAKE OVER AT REDLINE. VOGEL, 59, WELL-KNOWN ENTREPRENEUR DONATES FORTUNE TO SEE THE HIGHLY PROTESTED PIPELINE COME TO FRUITION AFTER ENVIRONMENTAL GROUPS CONTINUE TO SPEAK OUT

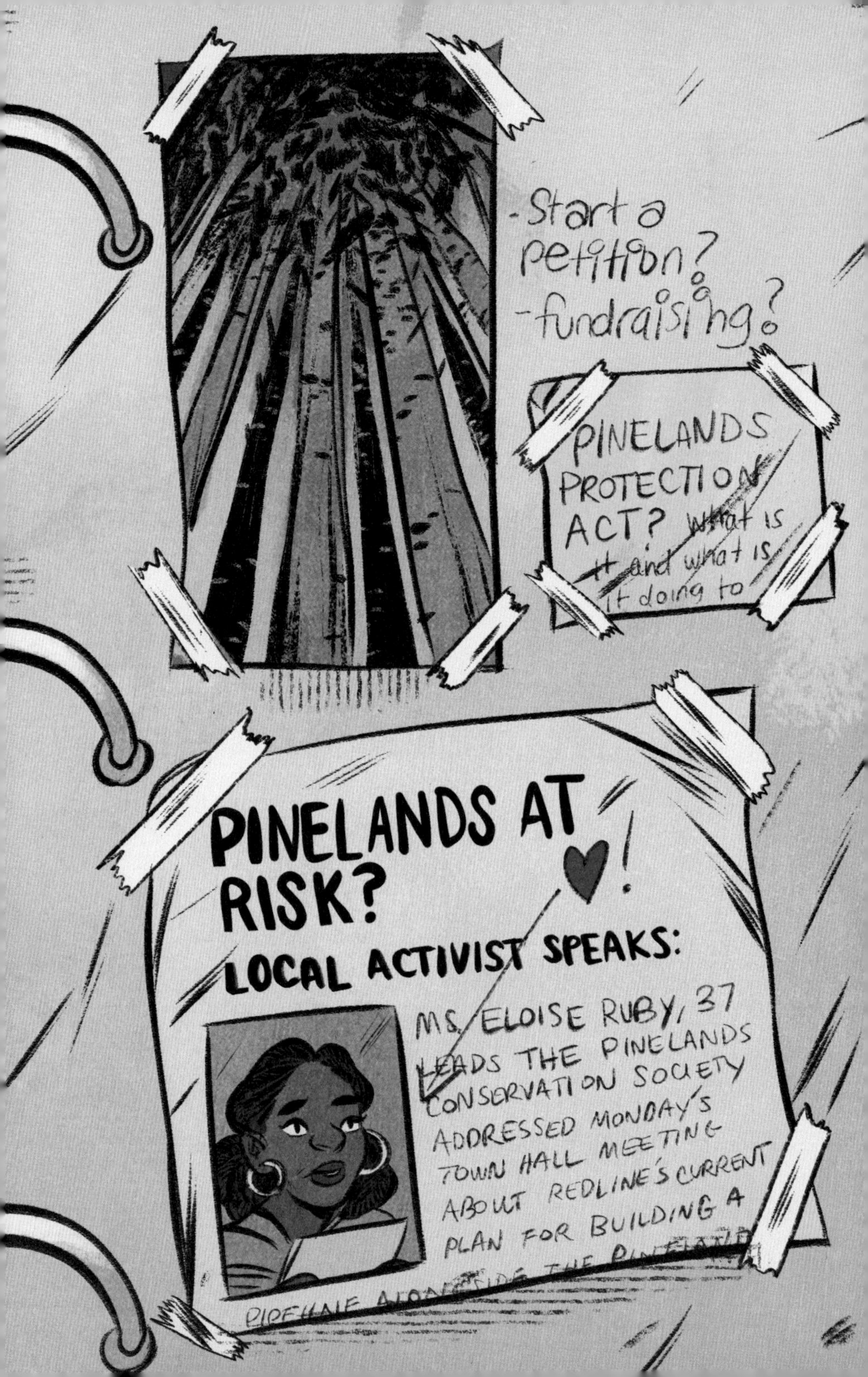
-Start a petition?
-fundraising?
PINELANDS PROTECTION ACT? What is it and what is it doing to
PINELANDS AT RISK?
LOCAL ACTIVIST SPEAKS:
MS. ELOISE RUBY, 37 LEADS THE PINELANDS CONSERVATION SOCIETY ADDRESSED MONDAY'S TOWN HALL MEETING ABOUT REDLINE'S CURRENT PLAN FOR BUILDING A

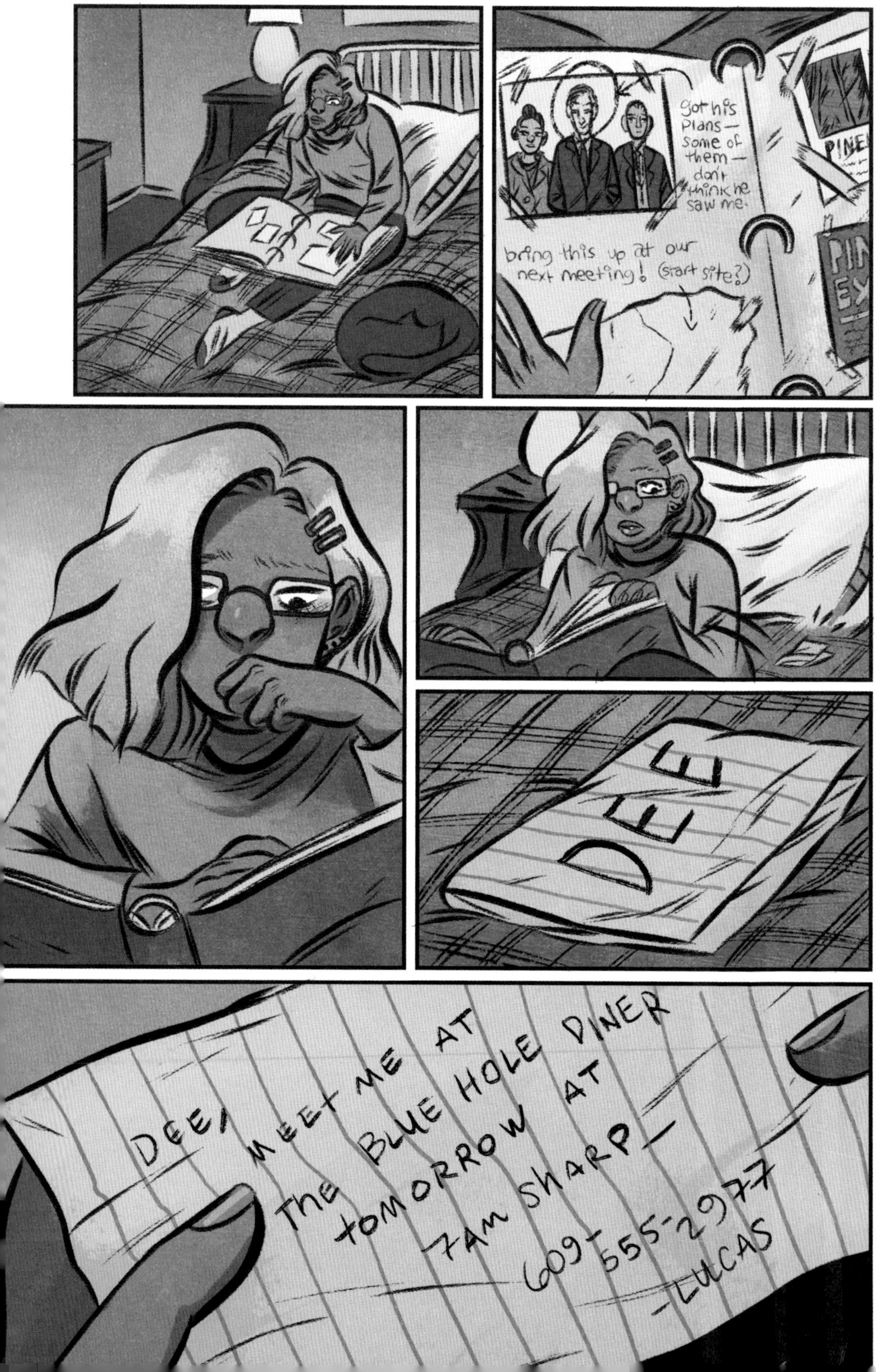
got his plans — some of them — don't think he saw me.
bring this up at our next meeting! (start site?)
DEE
DEE, MEET ME AT THE BLUE HOLE DINER TOMORROW AT 7AM SHARP — 609-555-2977 — LUCAS

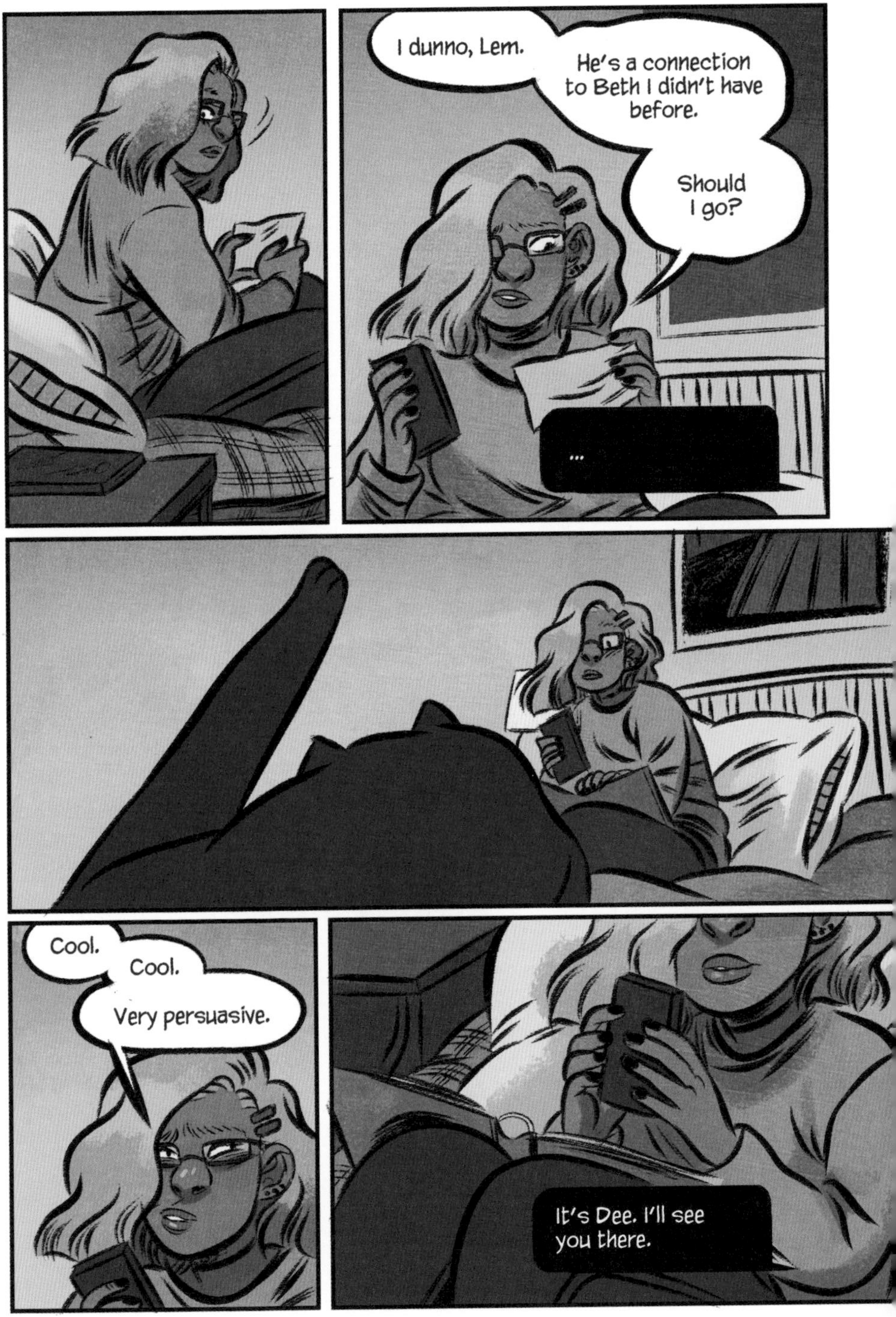
I dunno, Lem.
He's a connection to Beth I didn't have before.
Should I go?
...
Cool.
Cool.
Very persuasive.
It's Dee. I'll see you there.

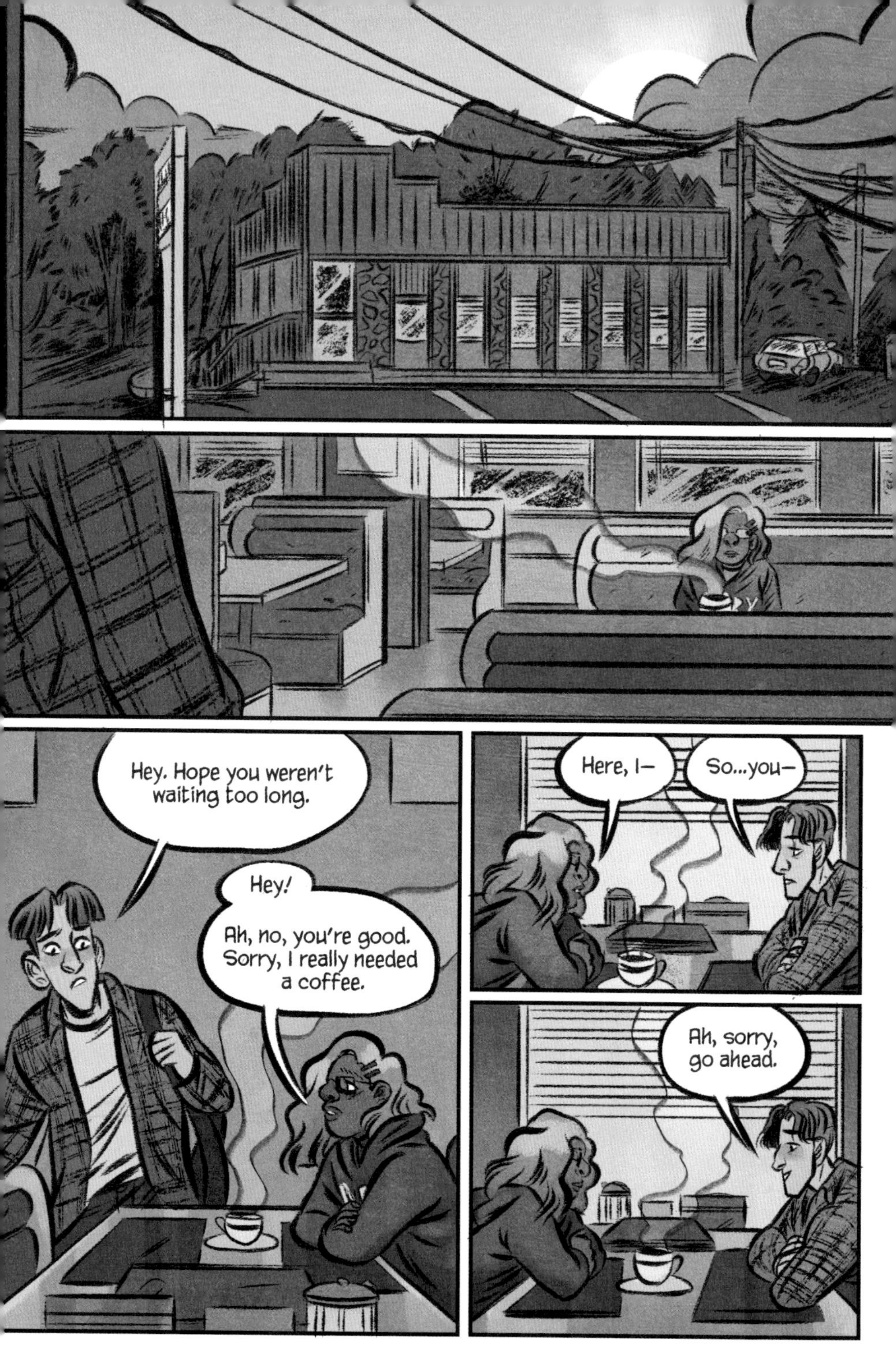

Hey. Hope you weren't waiting too long.
Hey!
Ah, no, you're good. Sorry, I really needed a coffee.
Here, I—
So...you—
Ah, sorry, go ahead.

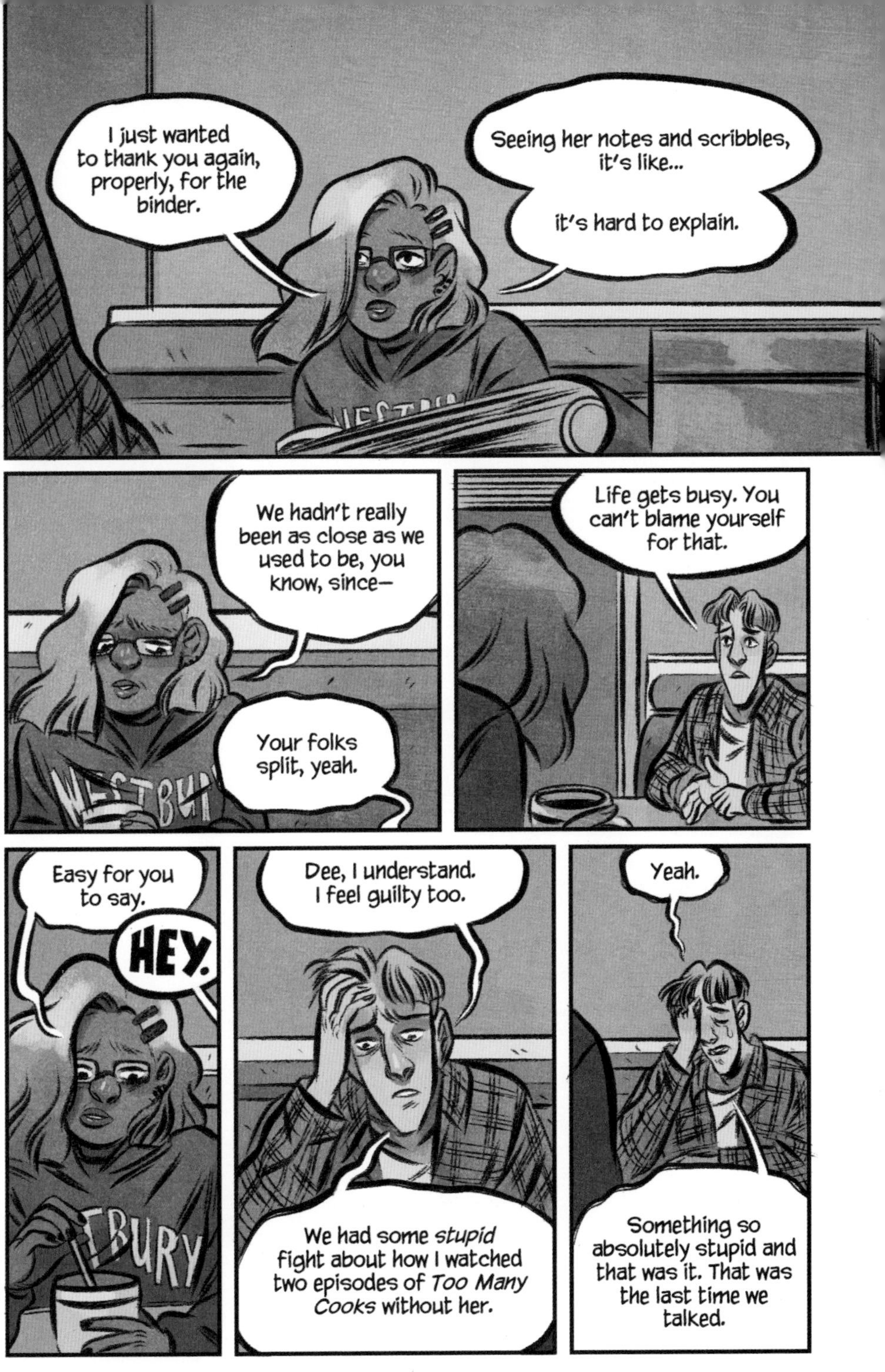
I just wanted to thank you again, properly, for the binder.
Seeing her notes and scribbles, it's like...
it's hard to explain.
We hadn't really been as close as we used to be, you know, since—
Your folks split, yeah.
Life gets busy. You can't blame yourself for that.
Easy for you to say.
HEY.
Dee, I understand. I feel guilty too.
We had some *stupid* fight about how I watched two episodes of *Too Many Cooks* without her.
Yeah.
Something so absolutely stupid and that was it. That was the last time we talked.

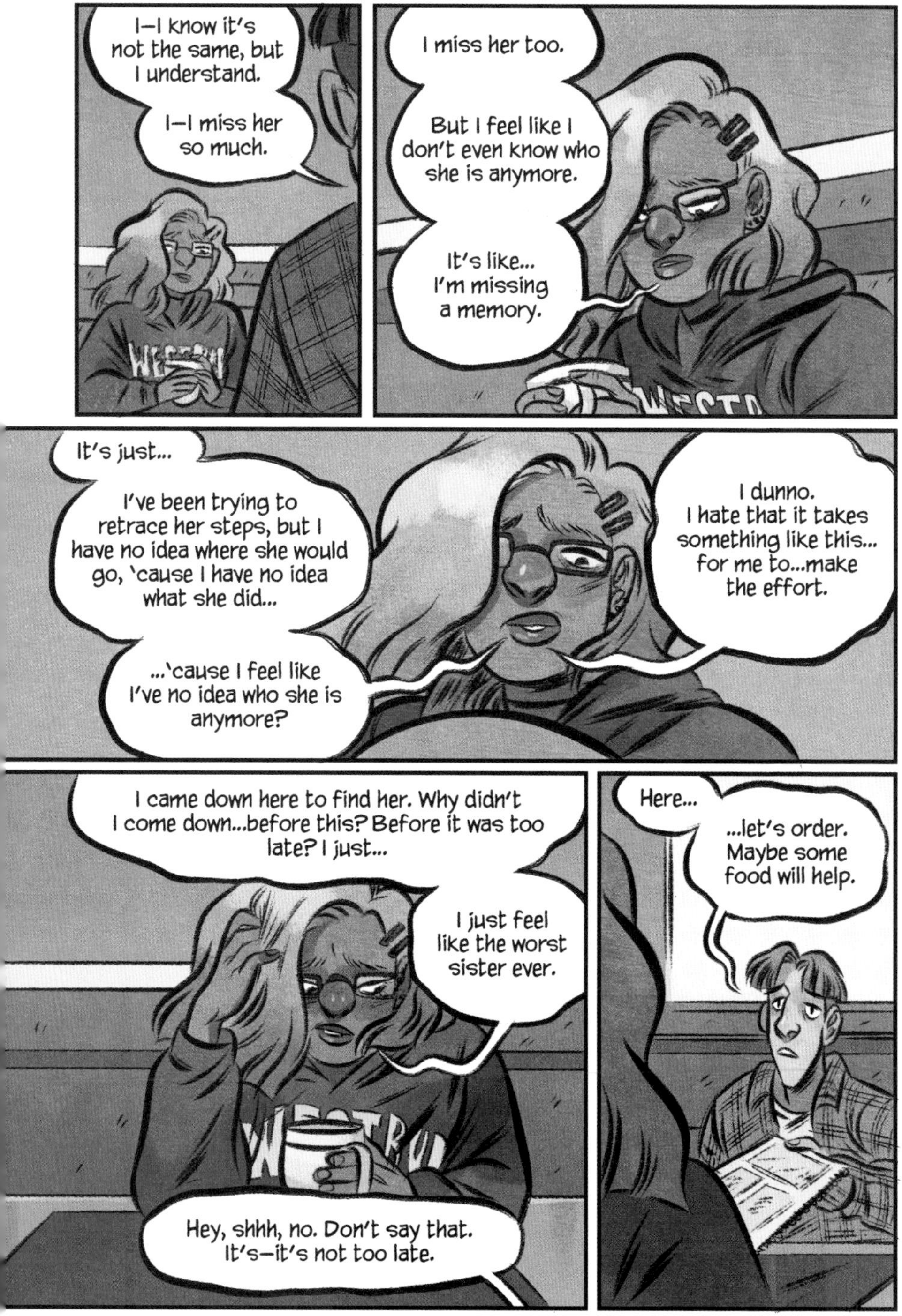
I—I know it's not the same, but I understand.
I—I miss her so much.
I miss her too.
But I feel like I don't even know who she is anymore.
It's like... I'm missing a memory.
It's just...
I've been trying to retrace her steps, but I have no idea where she would go, 'cause I have no idea what she did...
...'cause I feel like I've no idea who she is anymore?
I dunno. I hate that it takes something like this... for me to...make the effort.
I came down here to find her. Why didn't I come down...before this? Before it was too late? I just...
I just feel like the worst sister ever.
Hey, shhh, no. Don't say that. It's—it's not too late.
Here...
...let's order. Maybe some food will help.

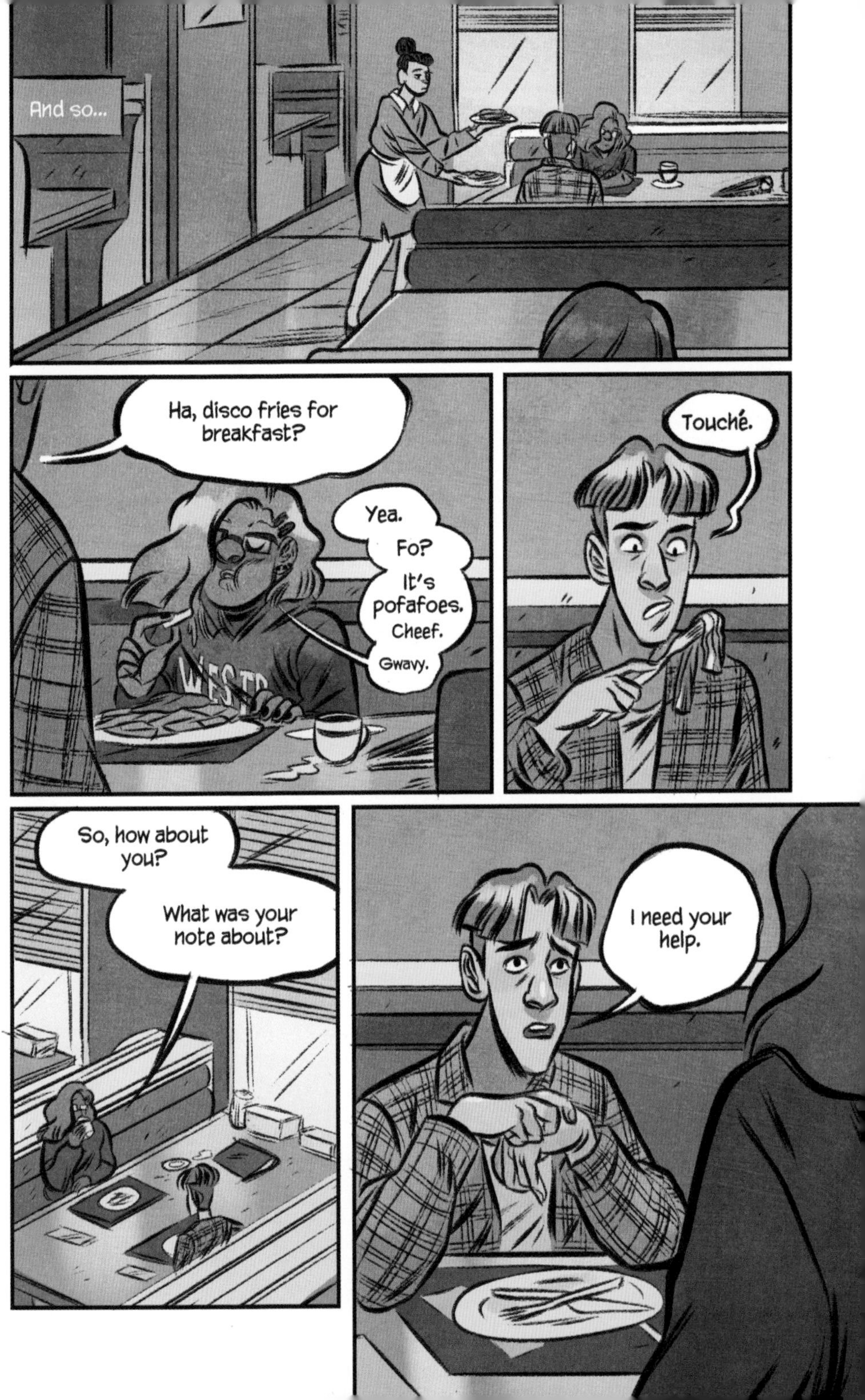
And so...
Ha, disco fries for breakfast?
Yea.
Fo?
It's pofafoes.
Cheef.
Gwavy.
Touché.
So, how about you?
What was your note about?
I need your help.

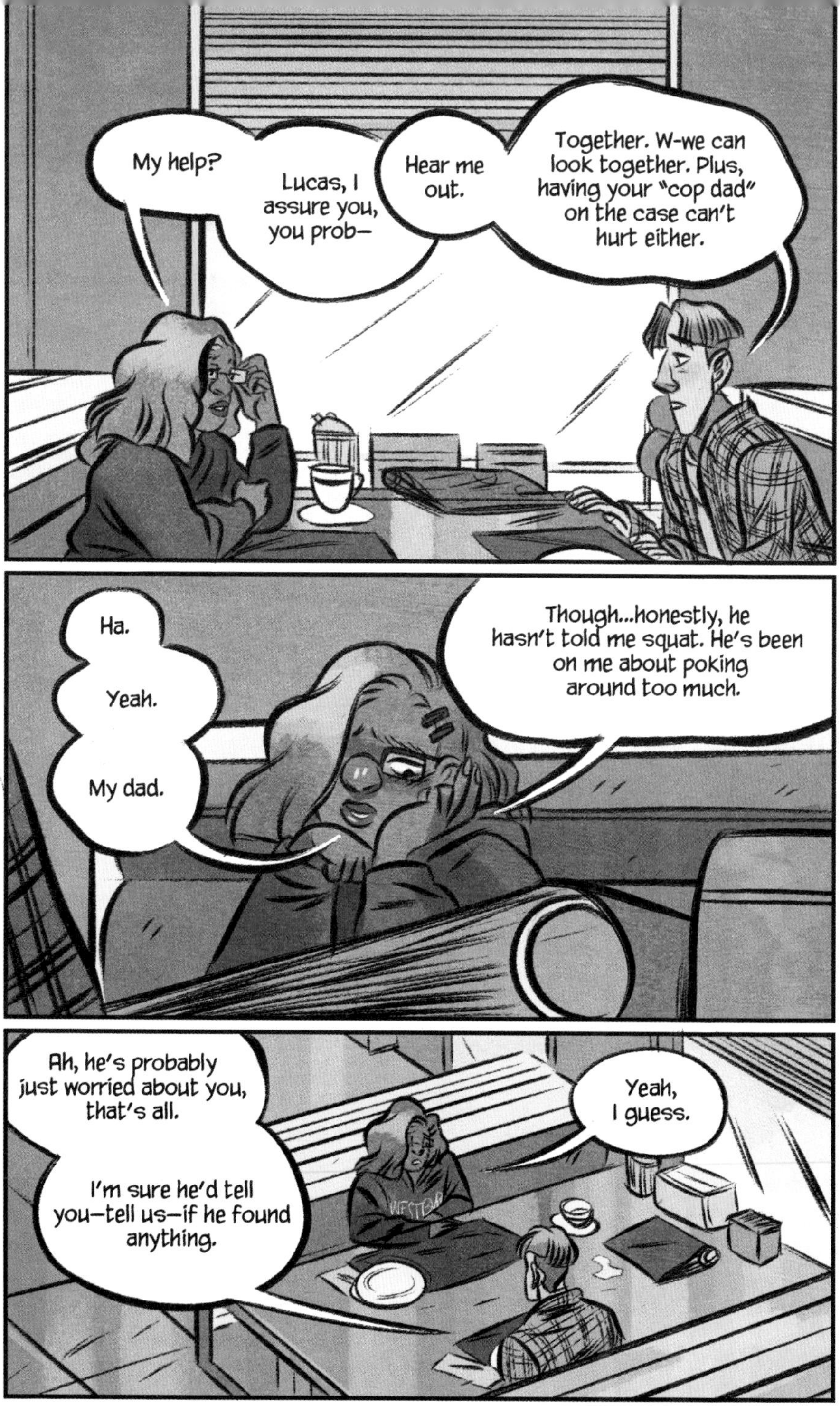
My help?
Lucas, I assure you, you prob—
Hear me out.
Together. W-we can look together. Plus, having your "cop dad" on the case can't hurt either.
Ha.
Yeah.
My dad.
Though...honestly, he hasn't told me squat. He's been on me about poking around too much.
Ah, he's probably just worried about you, that's all.
I'm sure he'd tell you—tell us—if he found anything.
Yeah, I guess.

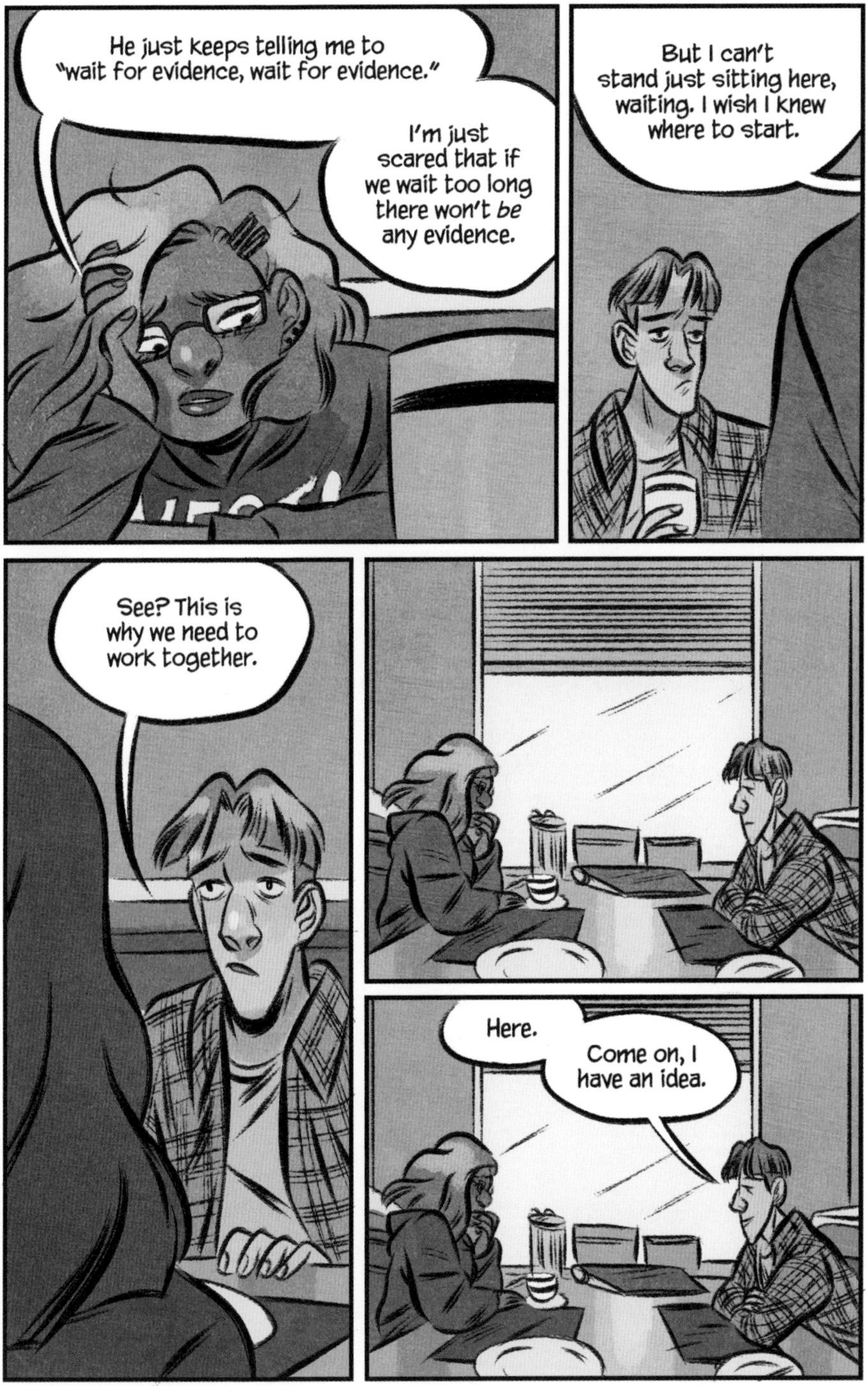
He just keeps telling me to "wait for evidence, wait for evidence."
I'm just scared that if we wait too long there won't *be* any evidence.
But I can't stand just sitting here, waiting. I wish I knew where to start.
See? This is why we need to work together.
Here.
Come on, I have an idea.

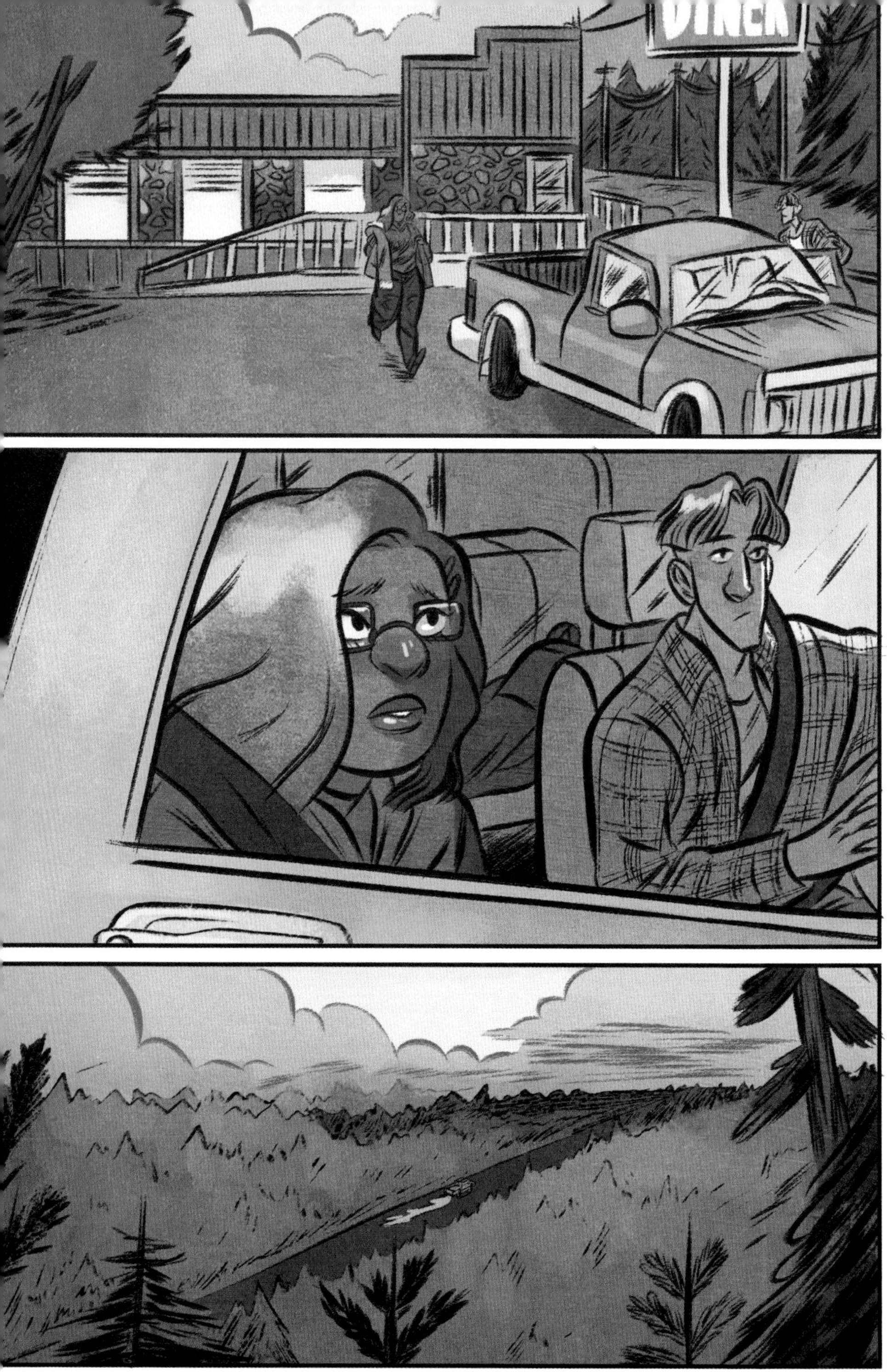

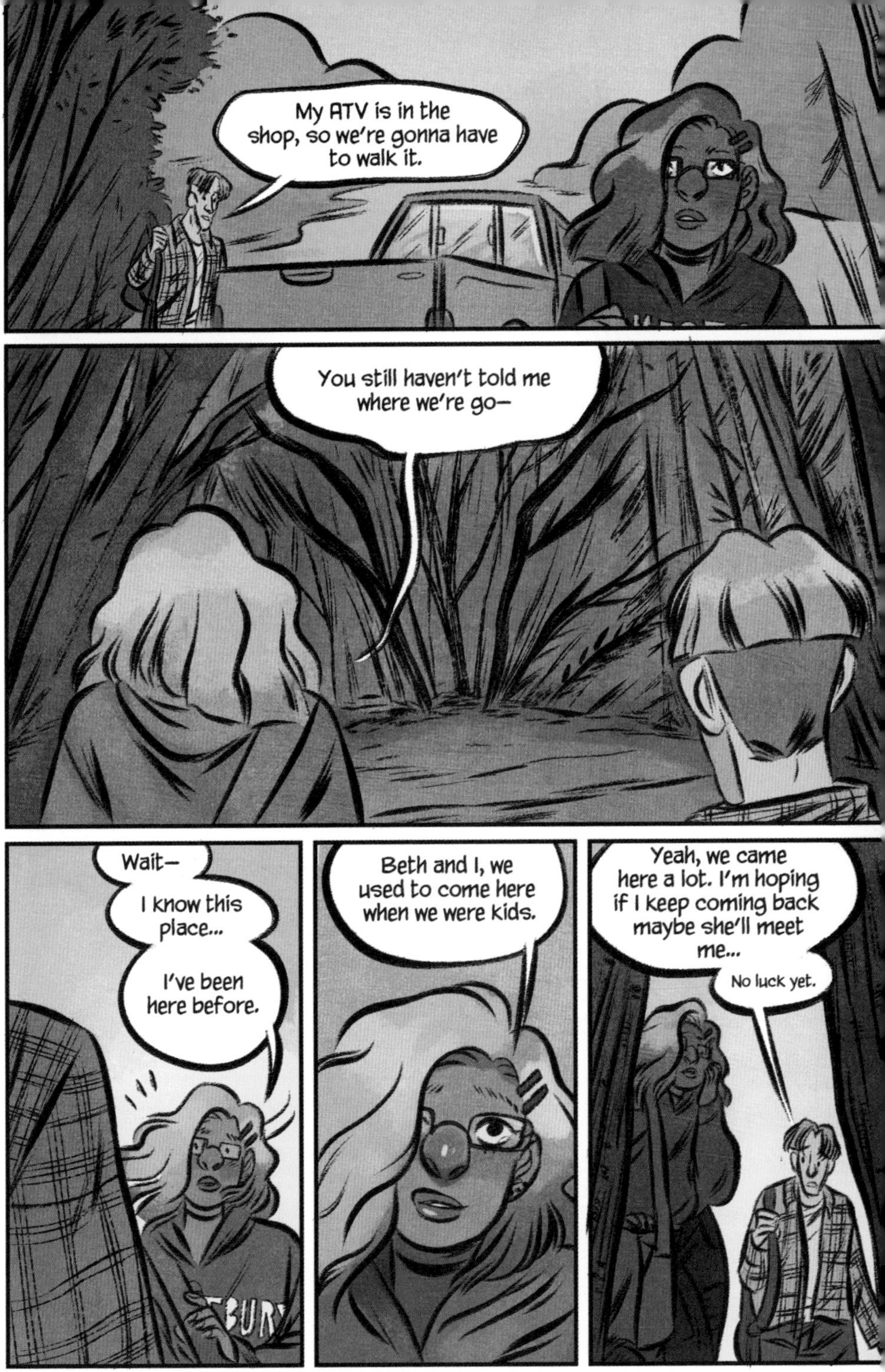
My ATV is in the shop, so we're gonna have to walk it.
You still haven't told me where we're go—
Wait—
I know this place...
I've been here before.
Beth and I, we used to come here when we were kids.
Yeah, we came here a lot. I'm hoping if I keep coming back maybe she'll meet me...
No luck yet.

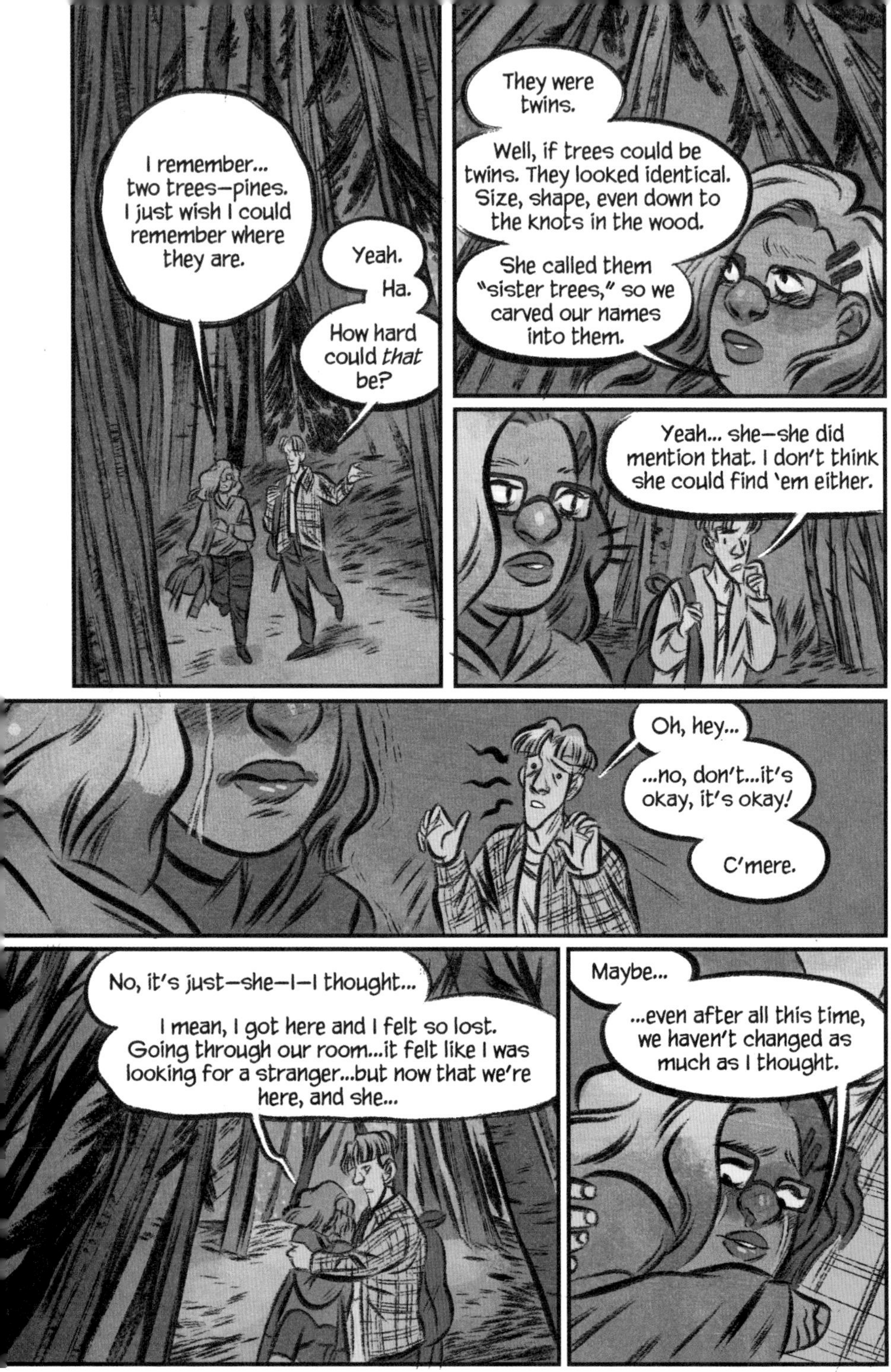
I remember... two trees—pines. I just wish I could remember where they are.
Yeah.
Ha.
How hard could *that* be?
They were twins.
Well, if trees could be twins. They looked identical. Size, shape, even down to the knots in the wood.
She called them "sister trees," so we carved our names into them.
Yeah... she—she did mention that. I don't think she could find 'em either.
Oh, hey...
...no, don't...it's okay, it's okay!
C'mere.
No, it's just—she—I—I thought...
I mean, I got here and I felt so lost. Going through our room...it felt like I was looking for a stranger...but now that we're here, and she...
Maybe...
...even after all this time, we haven't changed as much as I thought.

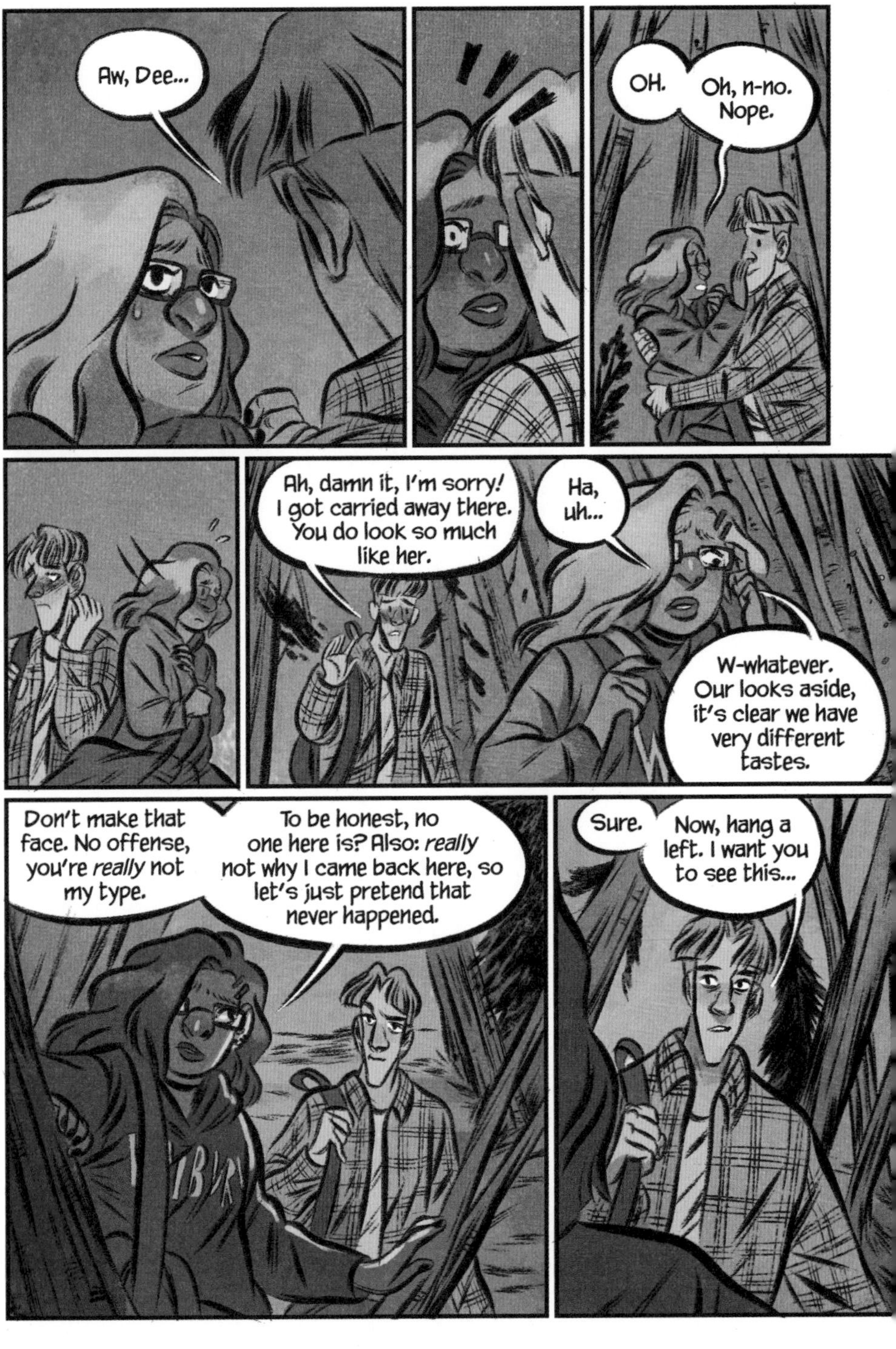
Aw, Dee...
OH.
Oh, n-no. Nope.
Ah, damn it, I'm sorry! I got carried away there. You do look so much like her.
Ha, uh...
W-whatever. Our looks aside, it's clear we have very different tastes.
Don't make that face. No offense, you're *really* not my type.
To be honest, no one here is? Also: *really* not why I came back here, so let's just pretend that never happened.
Sure.
Now, hang a left. I want you to see this...

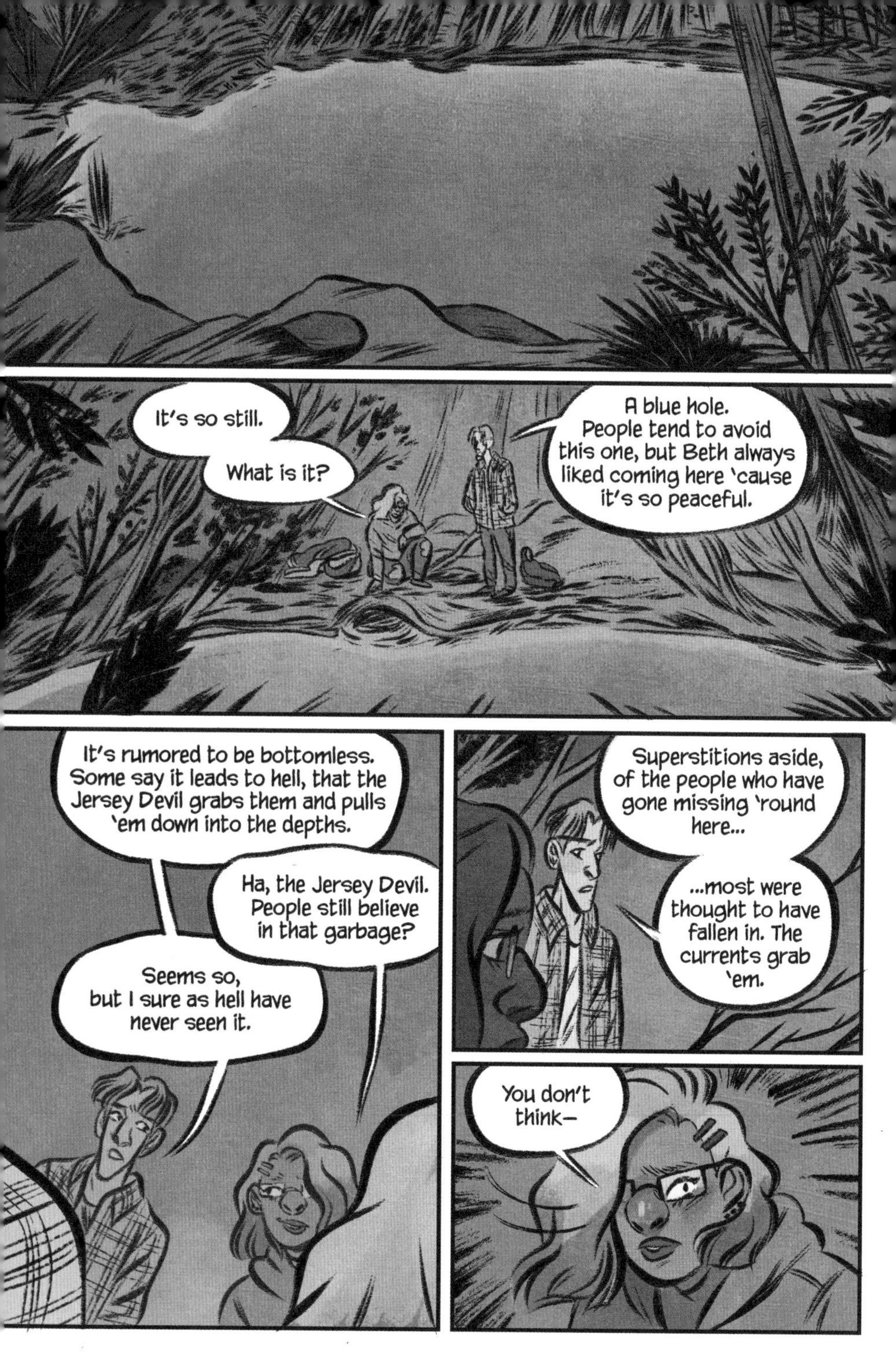
It's so still.
What is it?
A blue hole. People tend to avoid this one, but Beth always liked coming here 'cause it's so peaceful.
It's rumored to be bottomless. Some say it leads to hell, that the Jersey Devil grabs them and pulls 'em down into the depths.
Ha, the Jersey Devil. People still believe in that garbage?
Seems so, but I sure as hell have never seen it.
Superstitions aside, of the people who have gone missing 'round here...
...most were thought to have fallen in. The currents grab 'em.
You don't think—

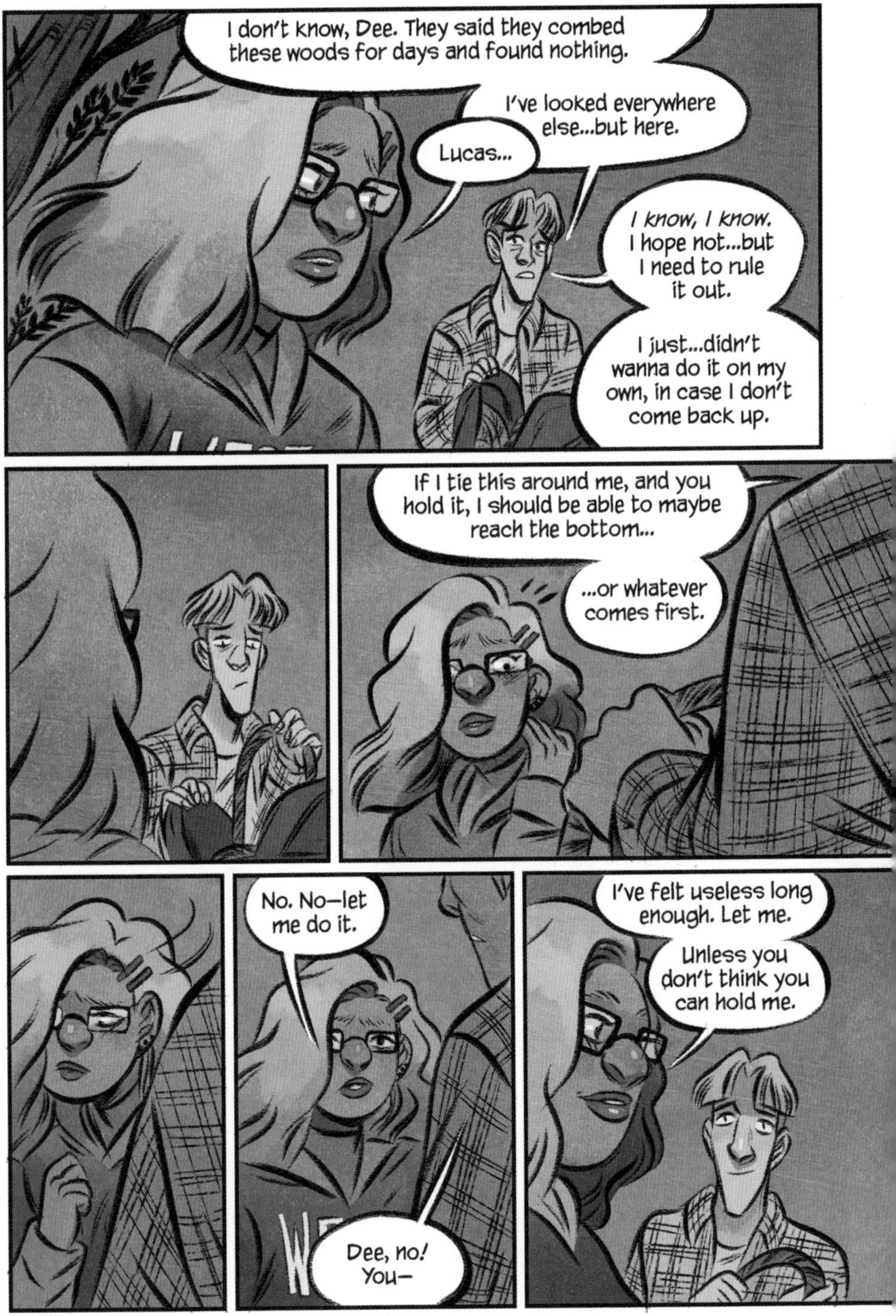
I don't know, Dee. They said they combed these woods for days and found nothing.
I've looked everywhere else...but here.
Lucas...
I know, I know. I hope not...but I need to rule it out.
I just...didn't wanna do it on my own, in case I don't come back up.
If I tie this around me, and you hold it, I should be able to maybe reach the bottom...
...or whatever comes first.
No. No—let me do it.
Dee, no! You—
I've felt useless long enough. Let me.
Unless you don't think you can hold me.

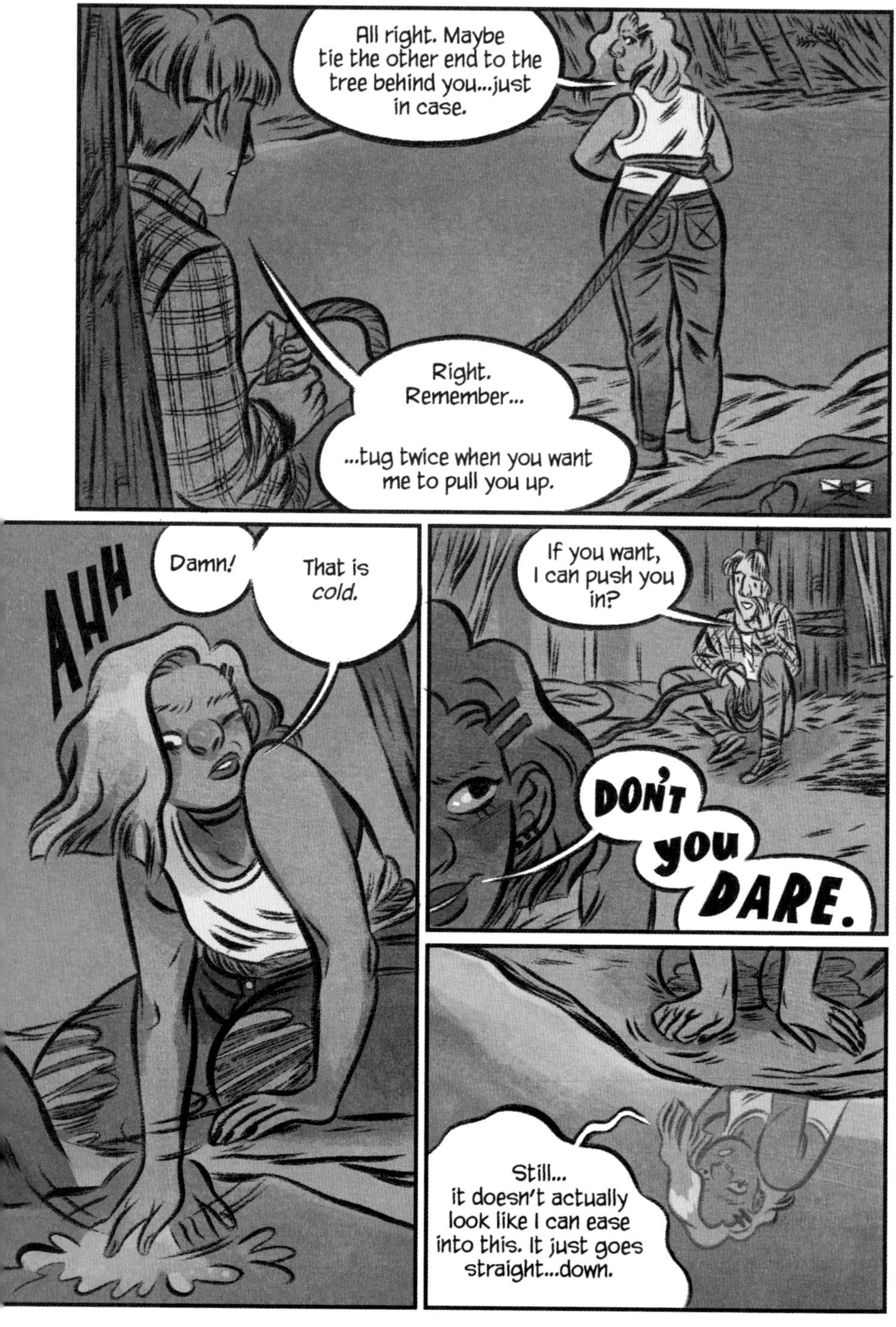
All right. Maybe tie the other end to the tree behind you...just in case.
Right. Remember...
...tug twice when you want me to pull you up.
AHH
Damn!
That is *cold.*
If you want, I can push you in?
DON'T you DARE.
Still... it doesn't actually look like I can ease into this. It just goes straight...down.

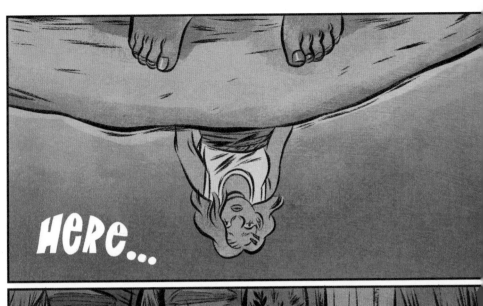

HERE...

GOES...

NOTHING!

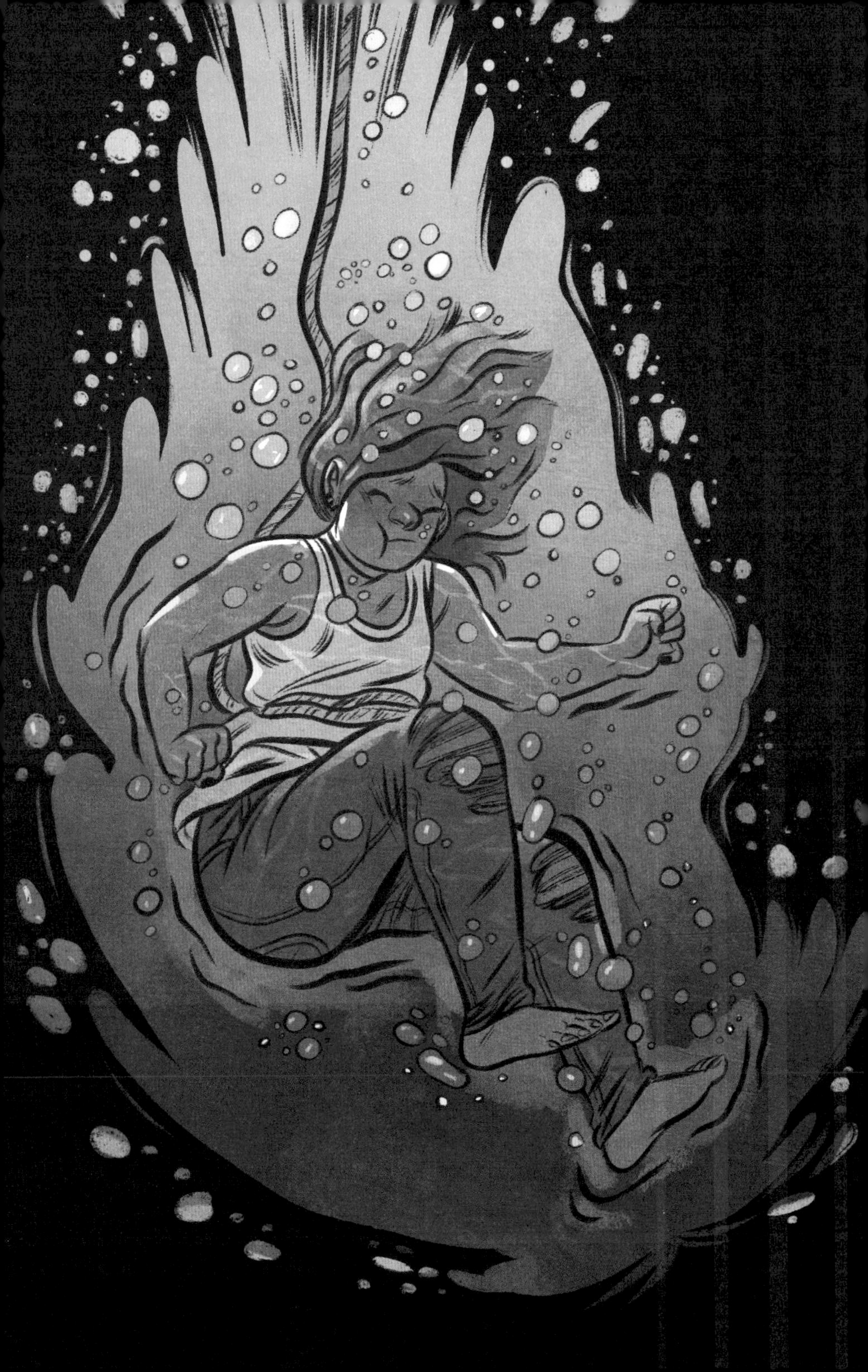

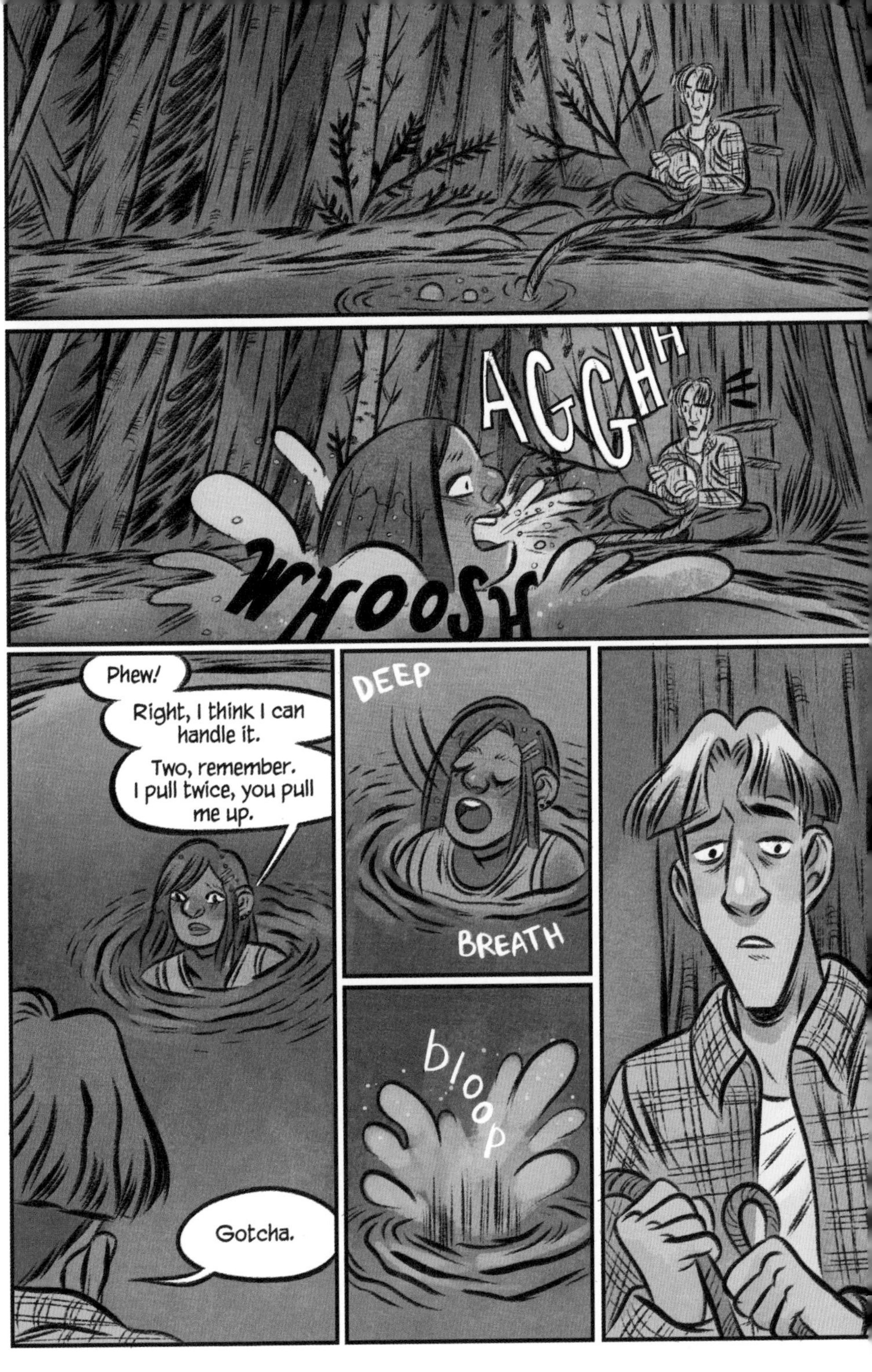
AGGHH
WHOOSH
Phew!
Right, I think I can handle it.
Two, remember. I pull twice, you pull me up.
Gotcha.
DEEP
BREATH
bloop

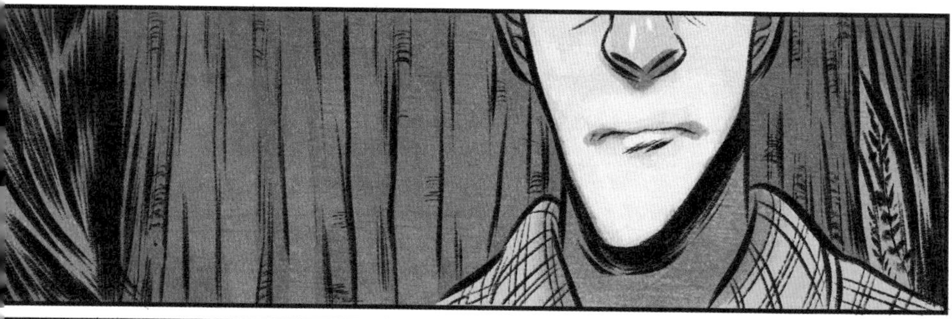

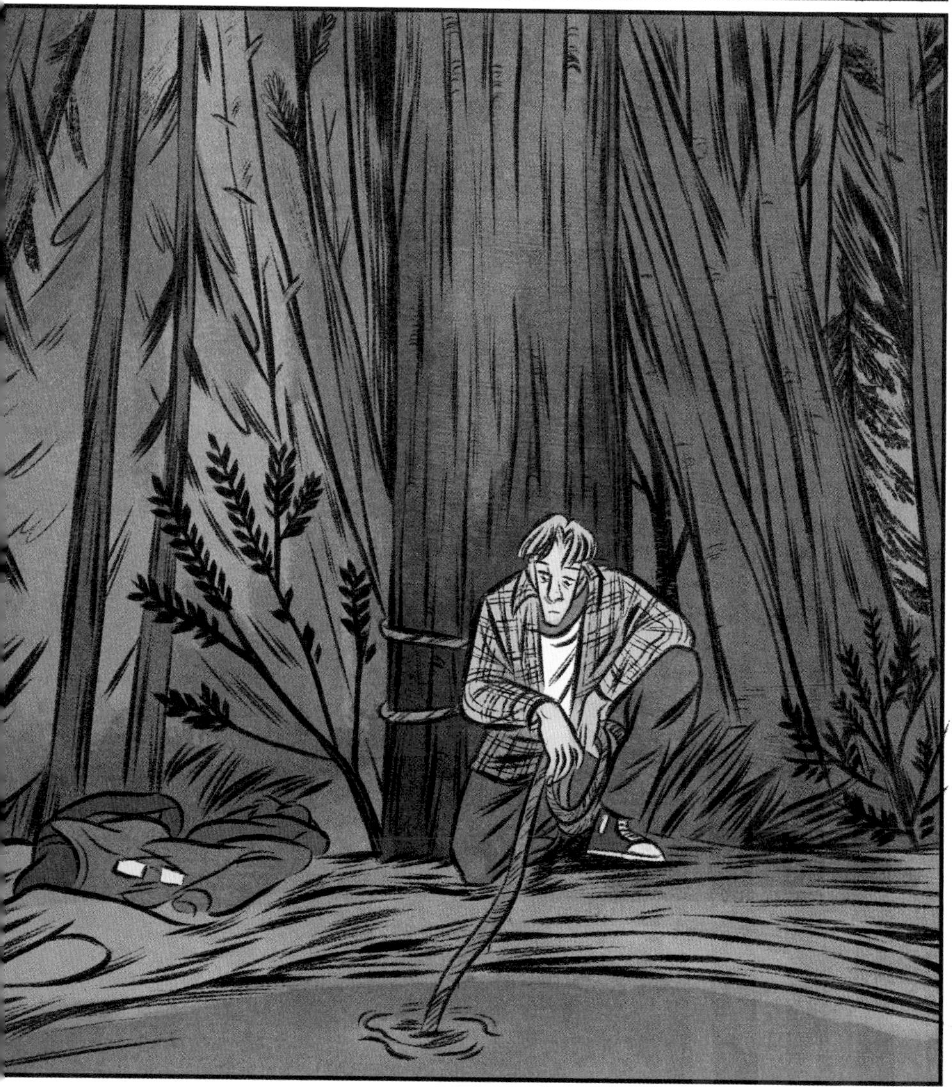

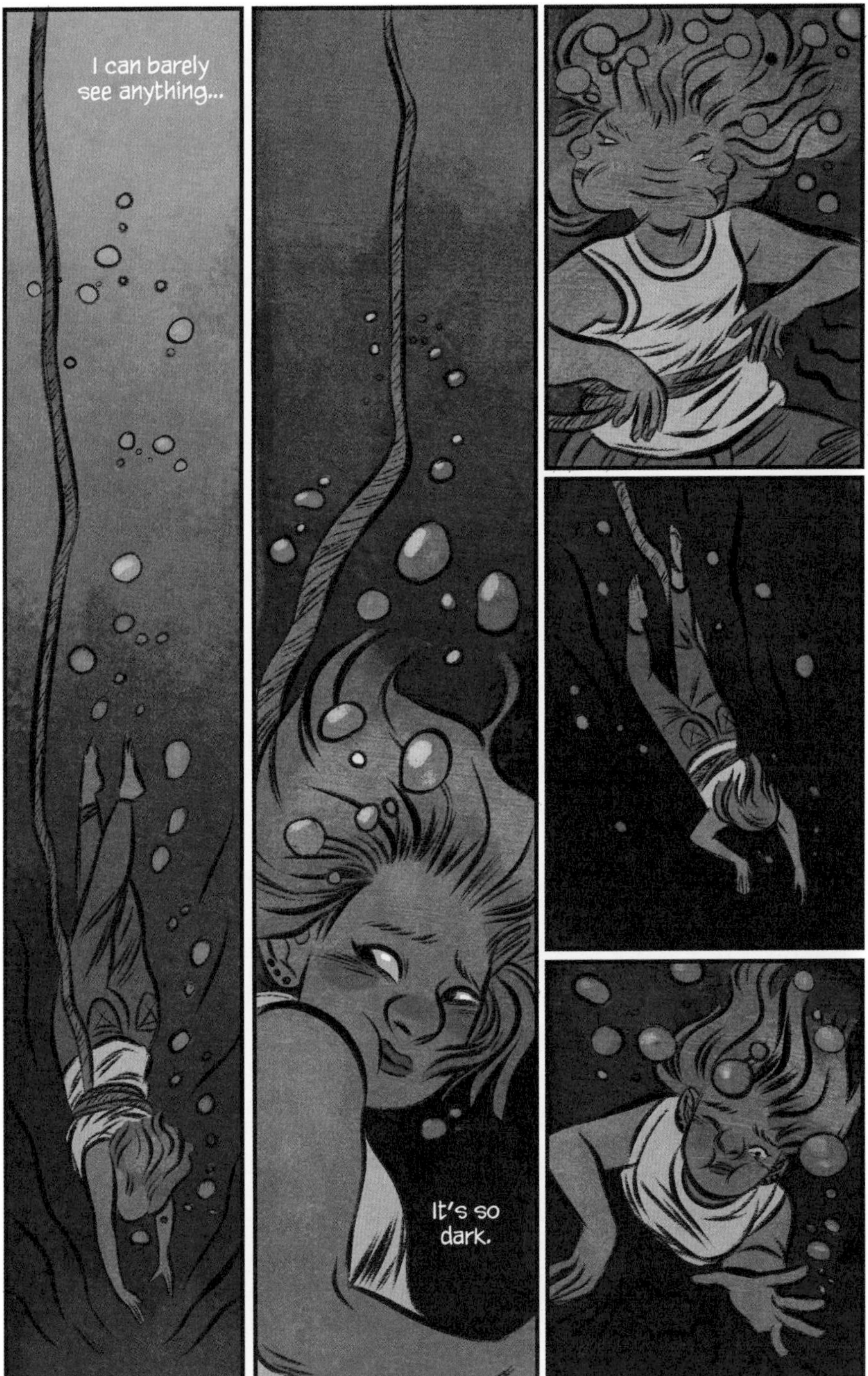
I can barely see anything...
It's so dark.

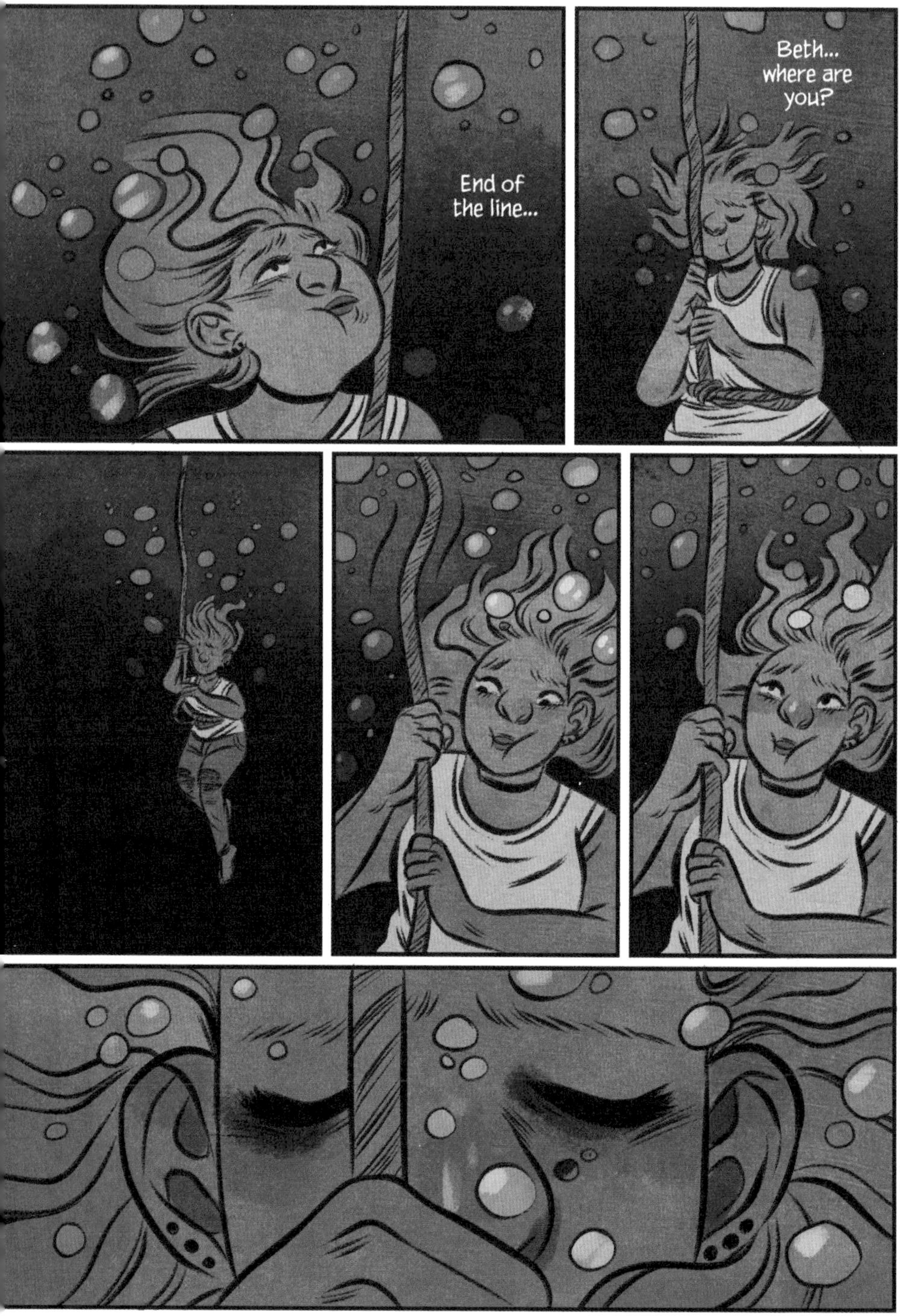
End of the line...
Beth... where are you?

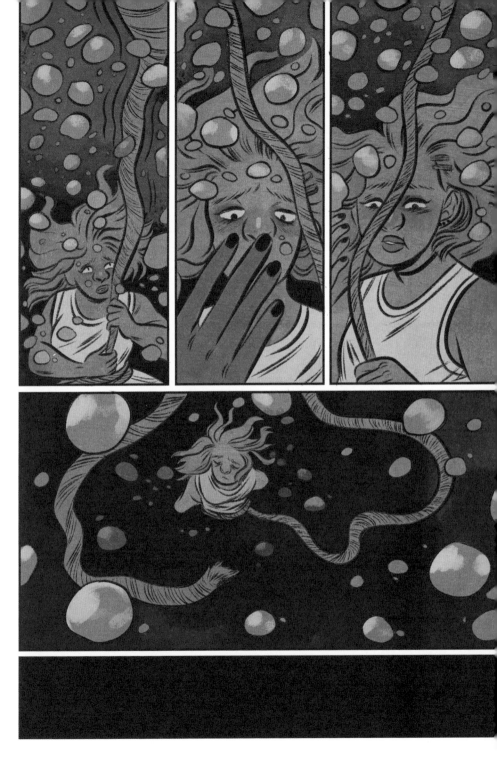

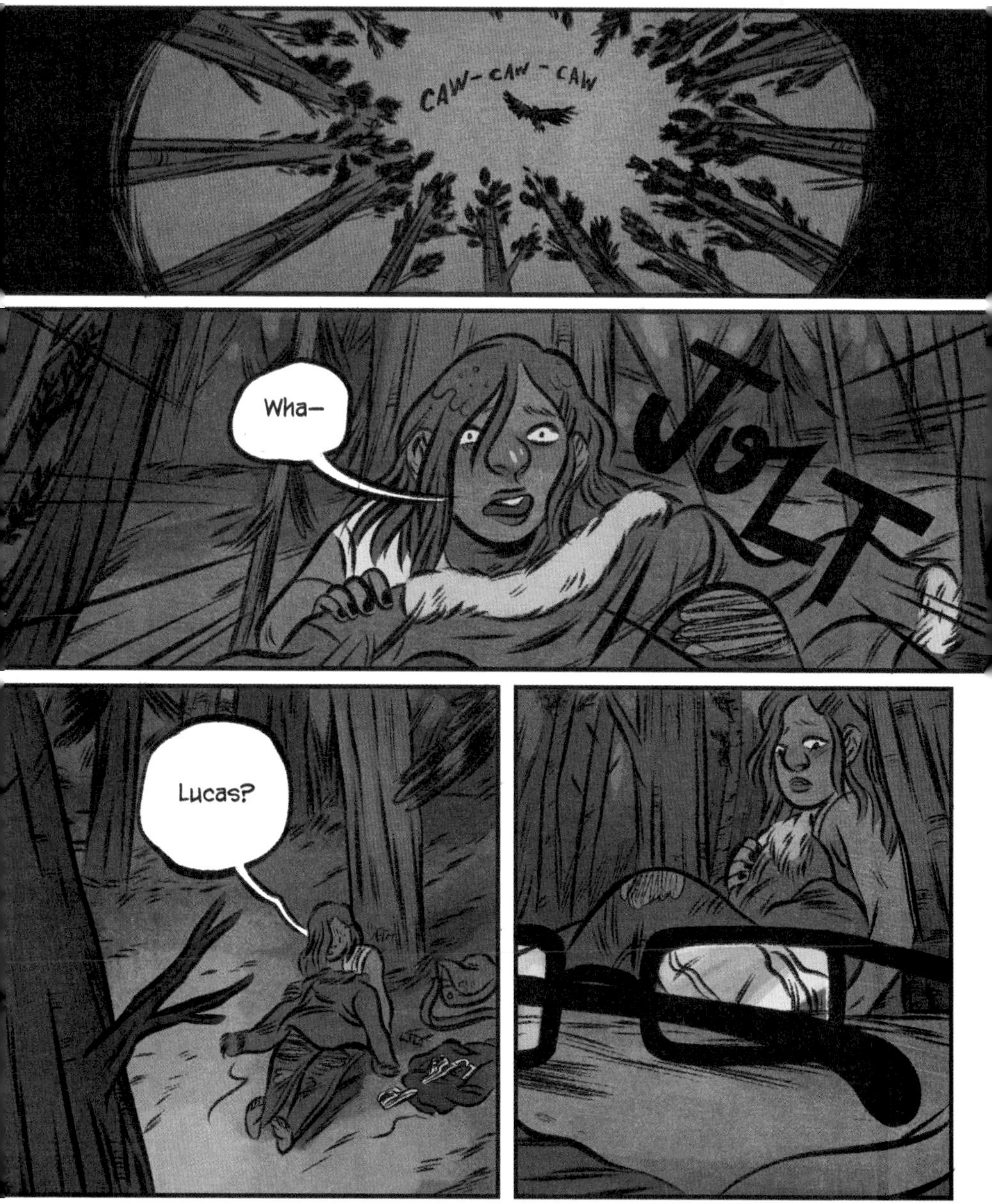
CAW-CAW-CAW
Wha–
JOLT
Lucas?

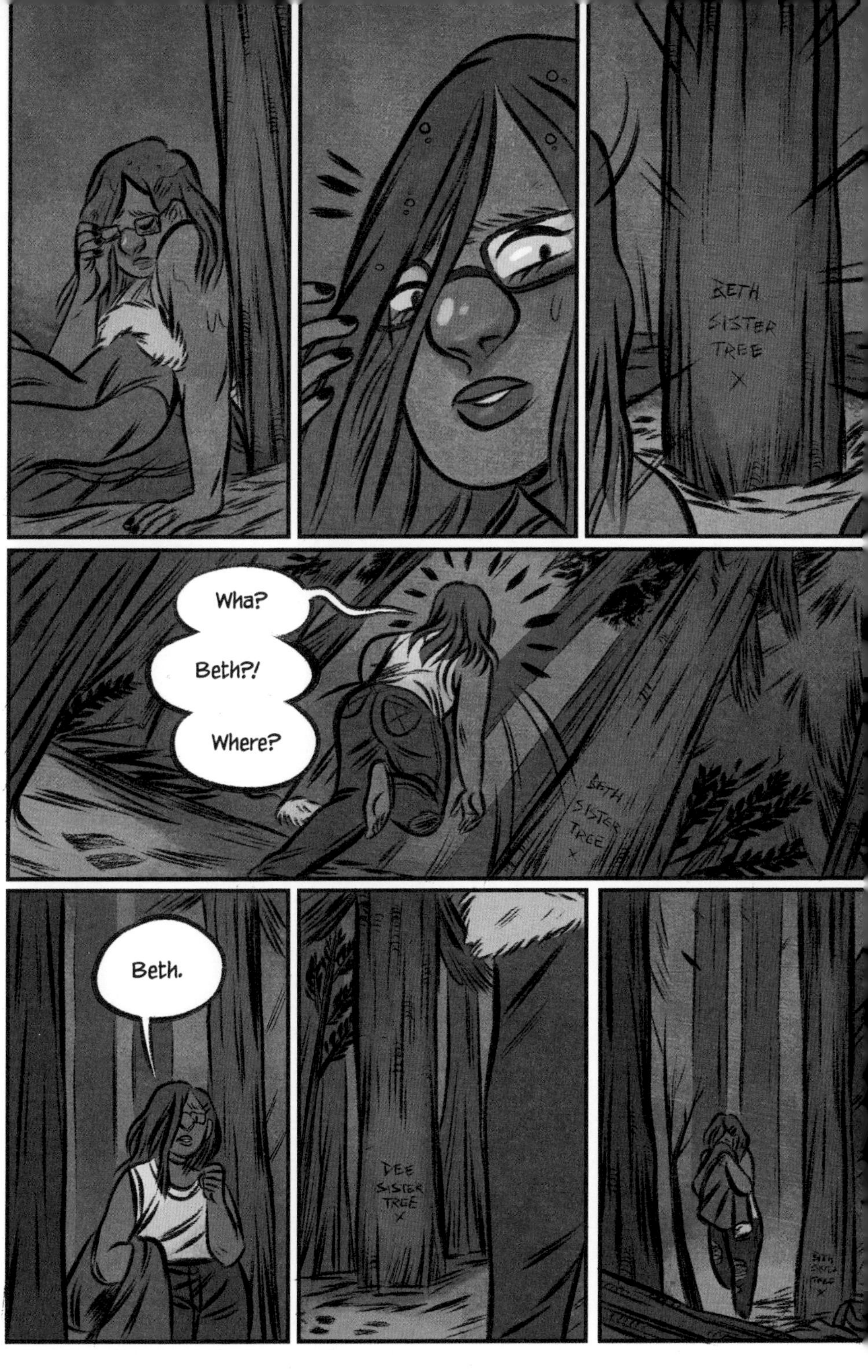
BETH
SISTER
TREE
Wha?
Beth?!
Where?
BETH
SISTER
TREE
Beth.
DEE
SISTER
TREE

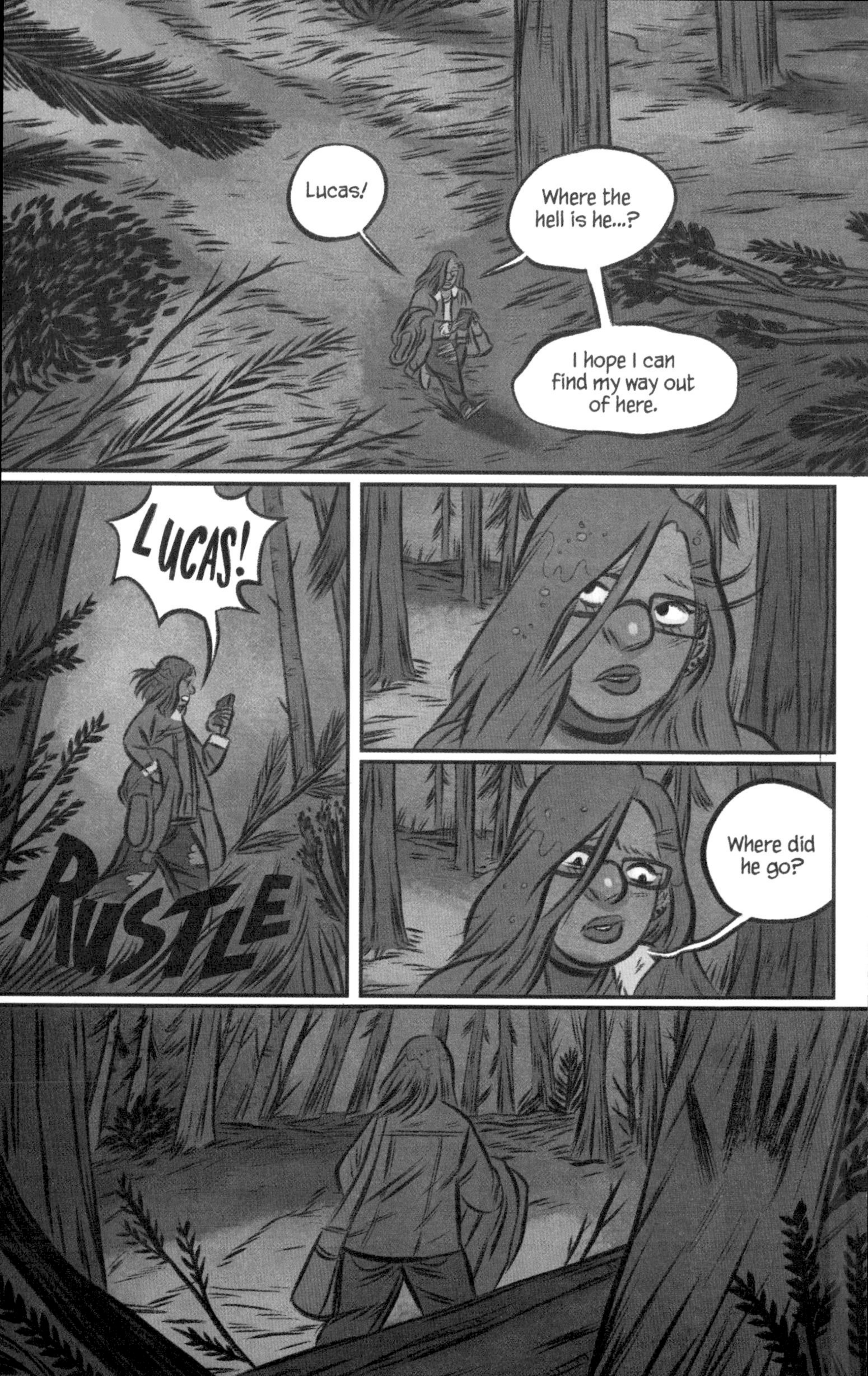

Lucas!
Where the hell is he...?
I hope I can find my way out of here.
LUCAS!
RUSTLE
Where did he go?

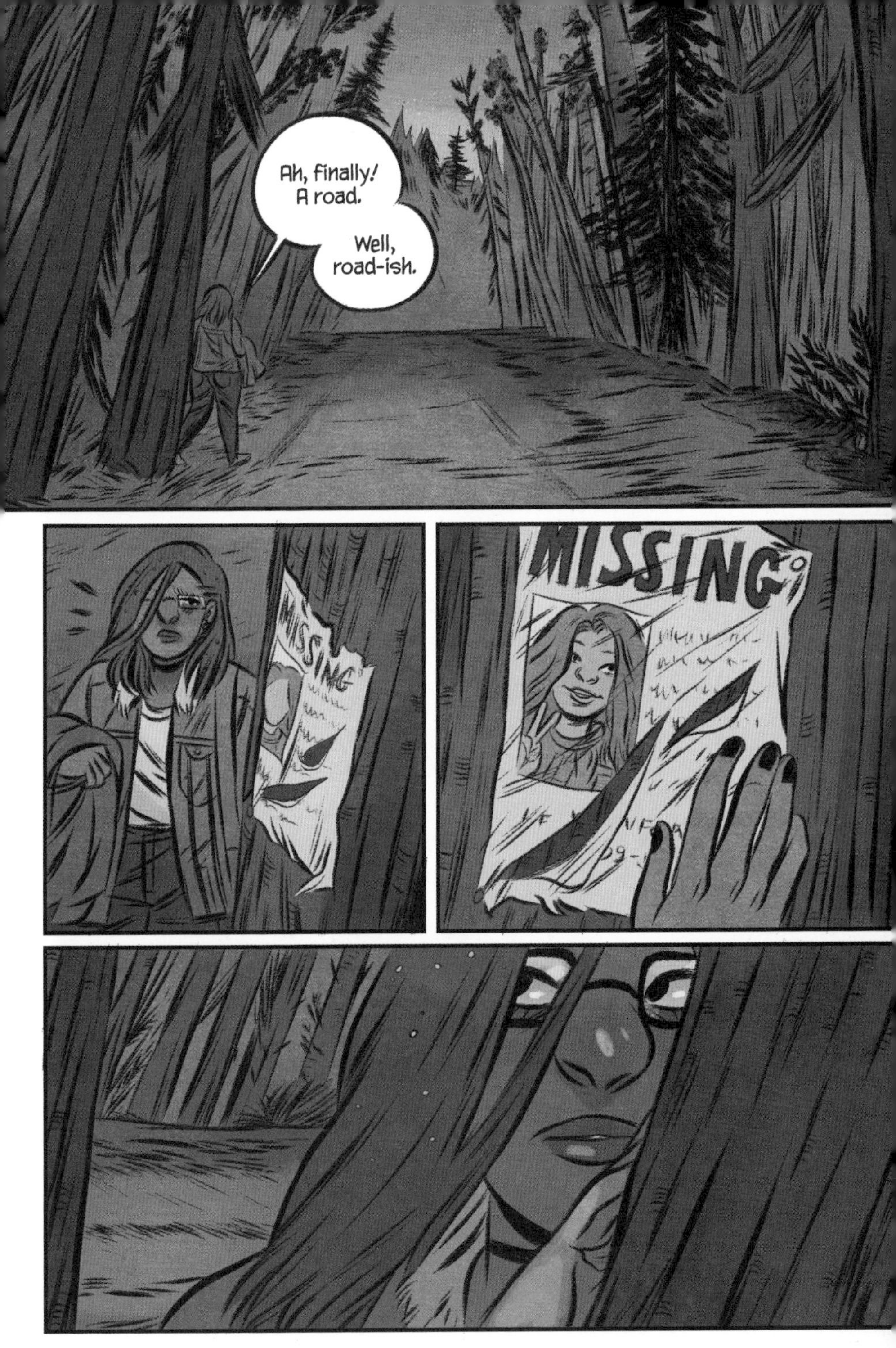
Ah, finally! A road.
Well, road-ish.
MISSING
MISSING

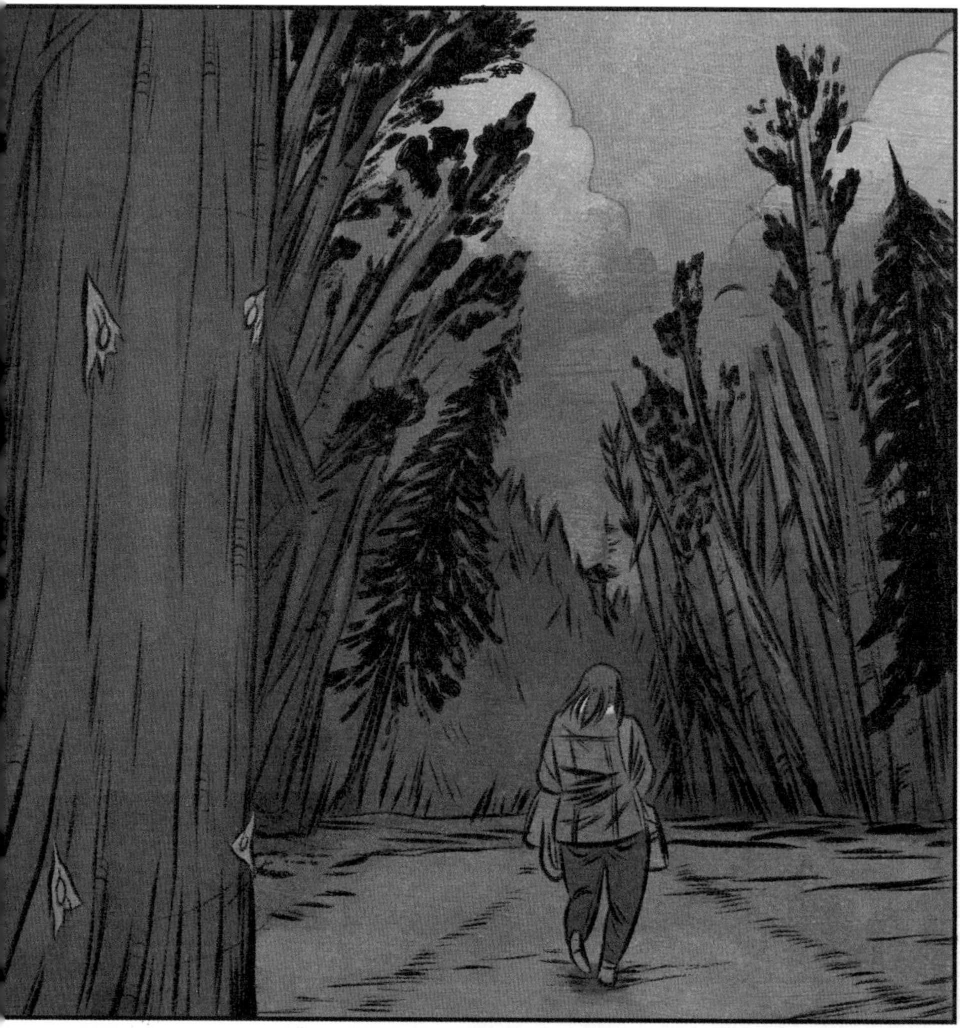

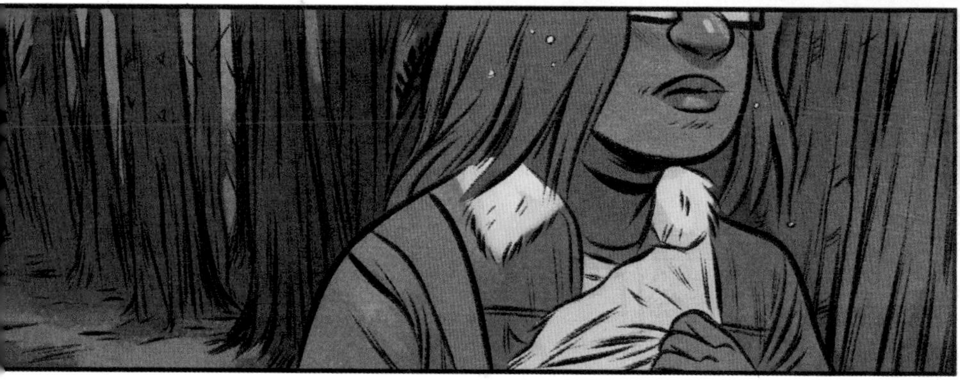

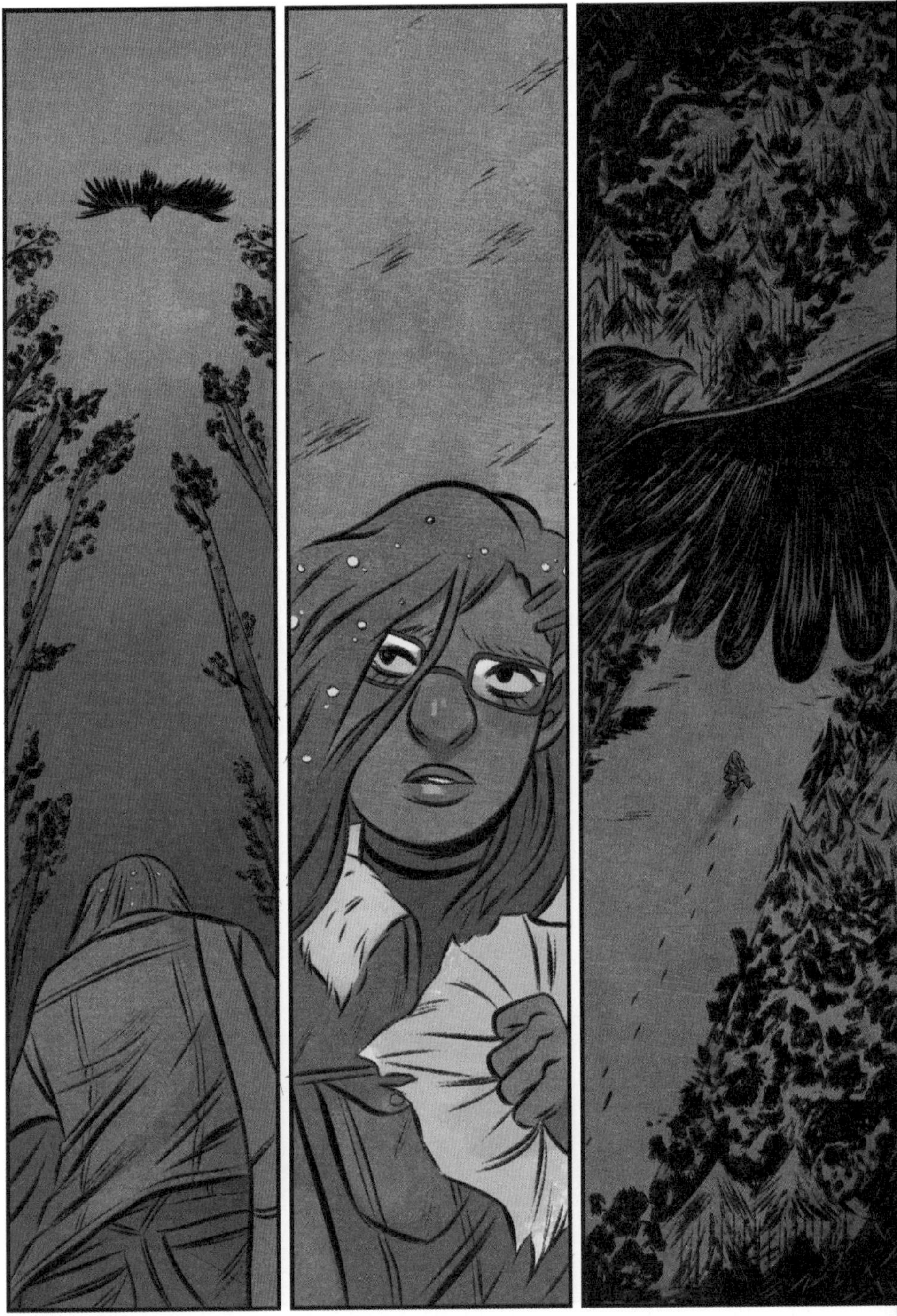

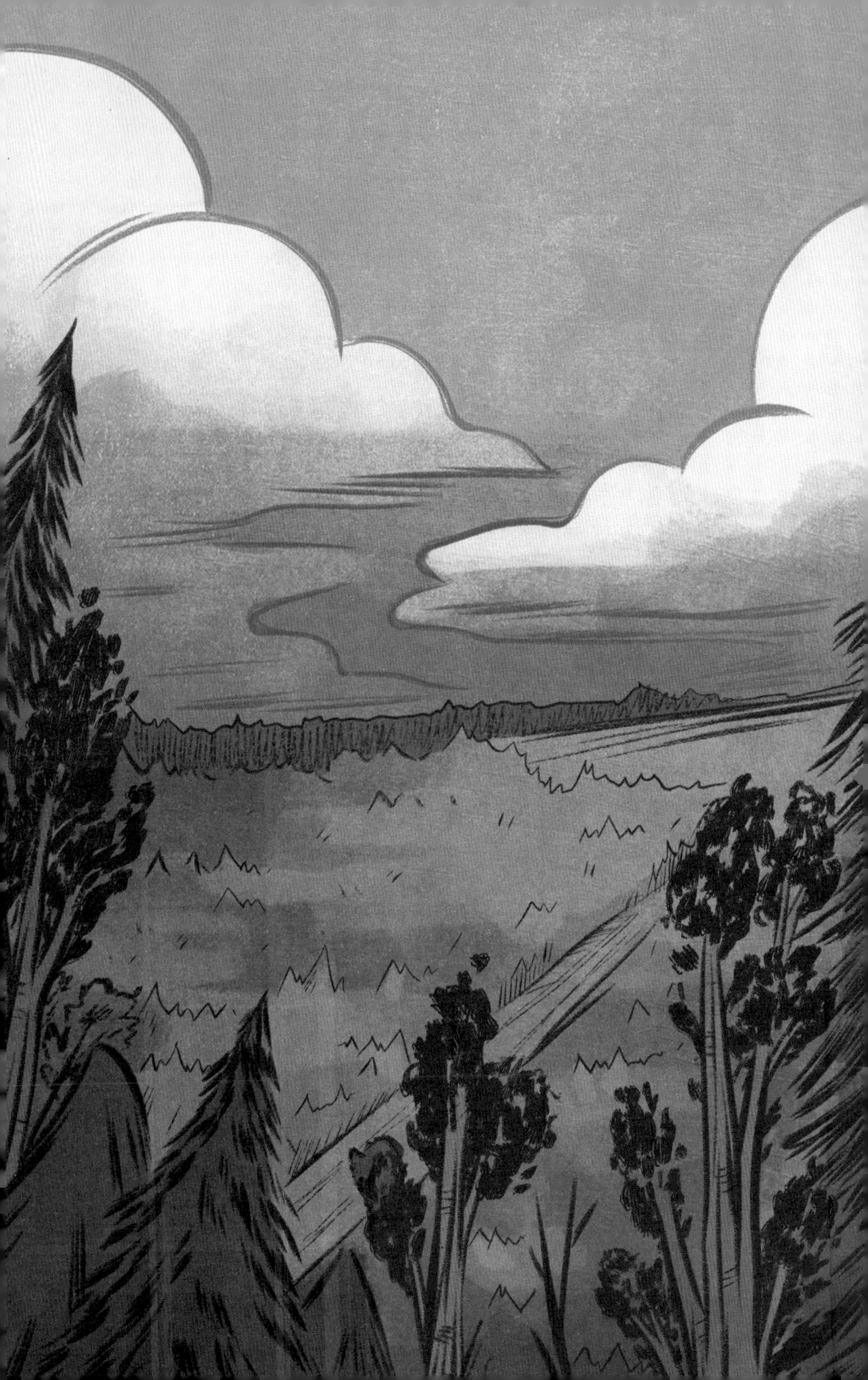

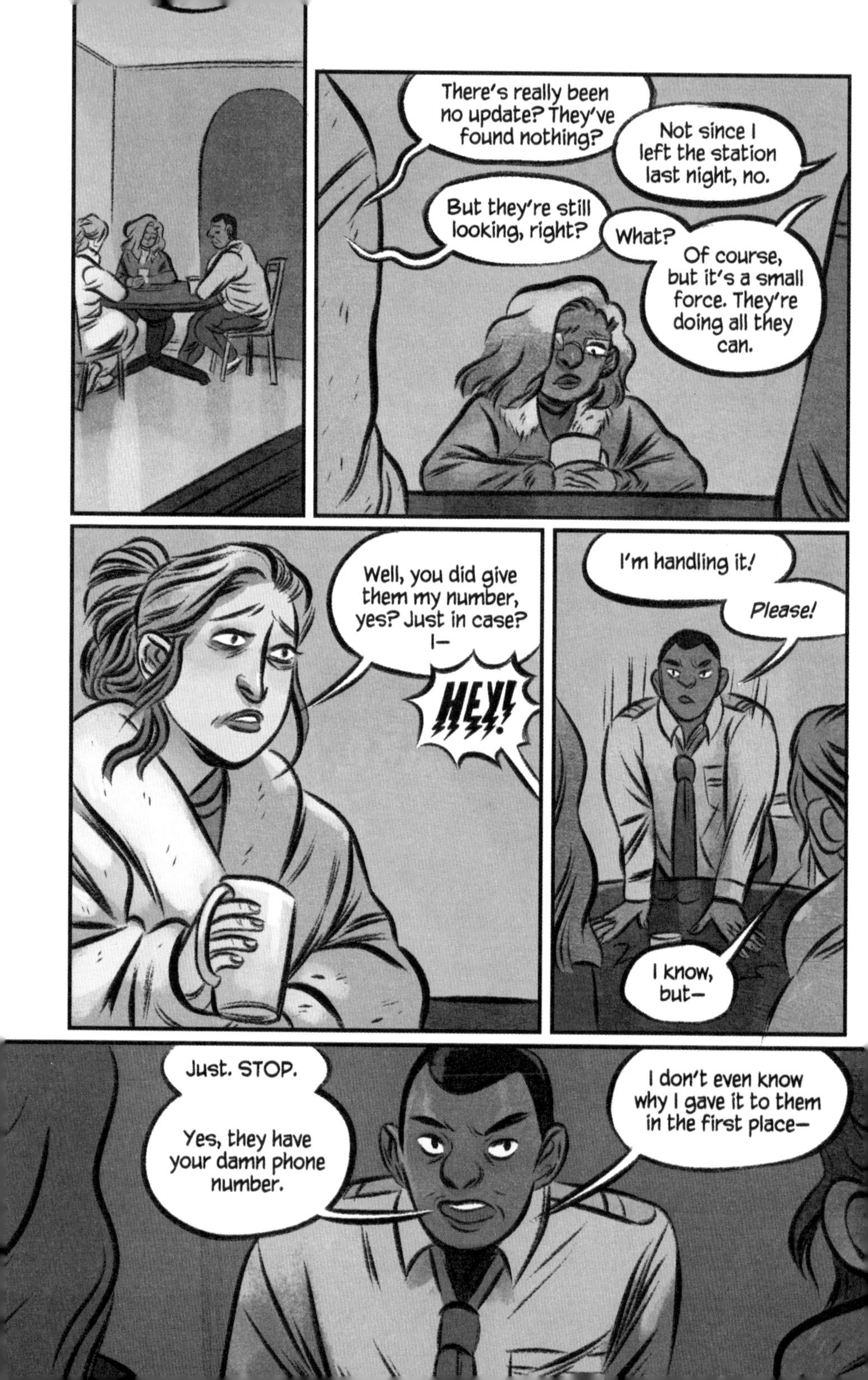
There's really been no update? They've found nothing?
Not since I left the station last night, no.
But they're still looking, right?
What?
Of course, but it's a small force. They're doing all they can.
Well, you did give them my number, yes? Just in case? I—
HEY!
I'm handling it!
Please!
I know, but—
Just. STOP.
Yes, they have your damn phone number.
I don't even know why I gave it to them in the first place—

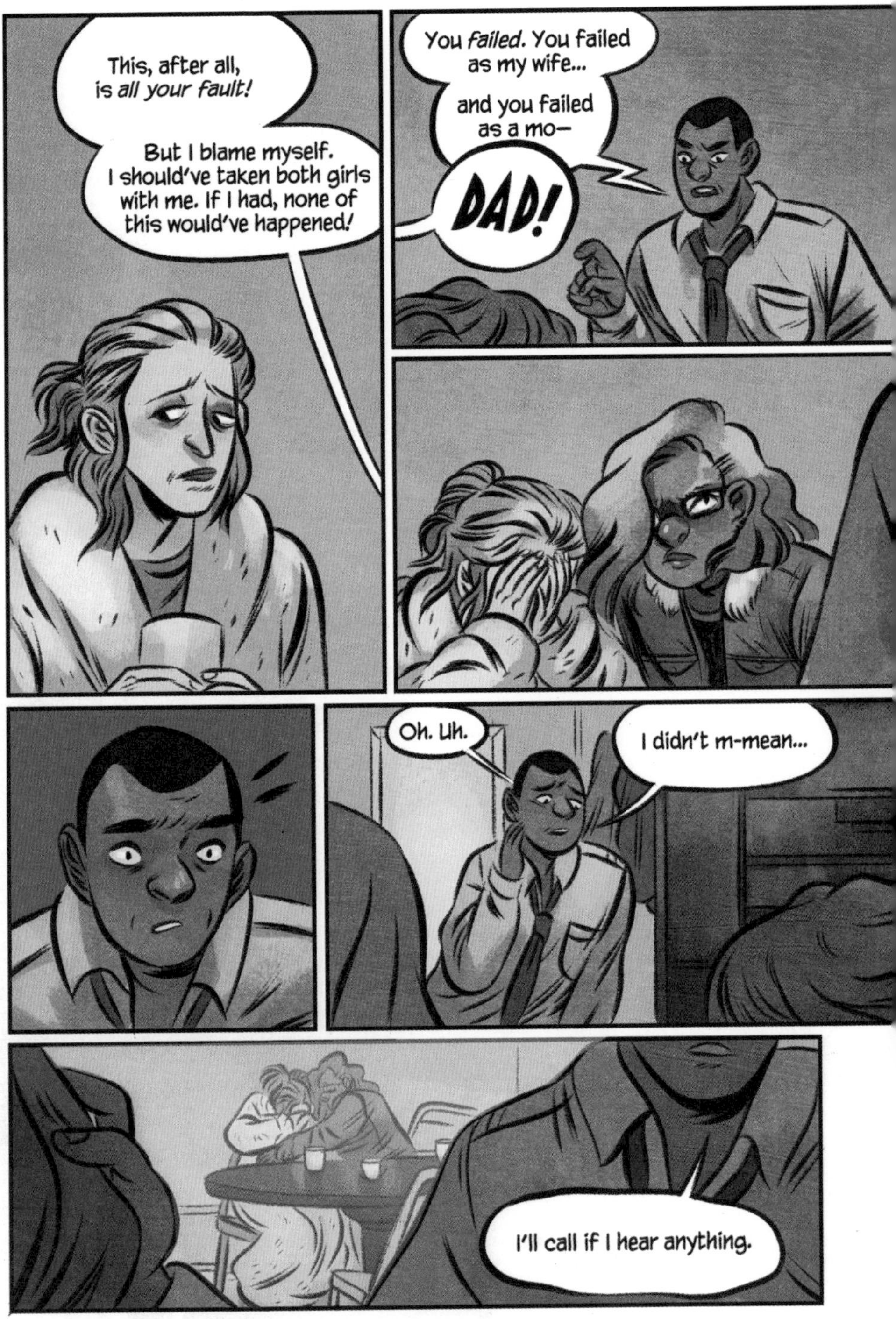
This, after all, is *all your fault!*
But I blame myself. I should've taken both girls with me. If I had, none of this would've happened!
You *failed.* You failed as my wife...
and you failed as a mo–
DAD!
Oh. Uh.
I didn't m-mean...
I'll call if I hear anything.

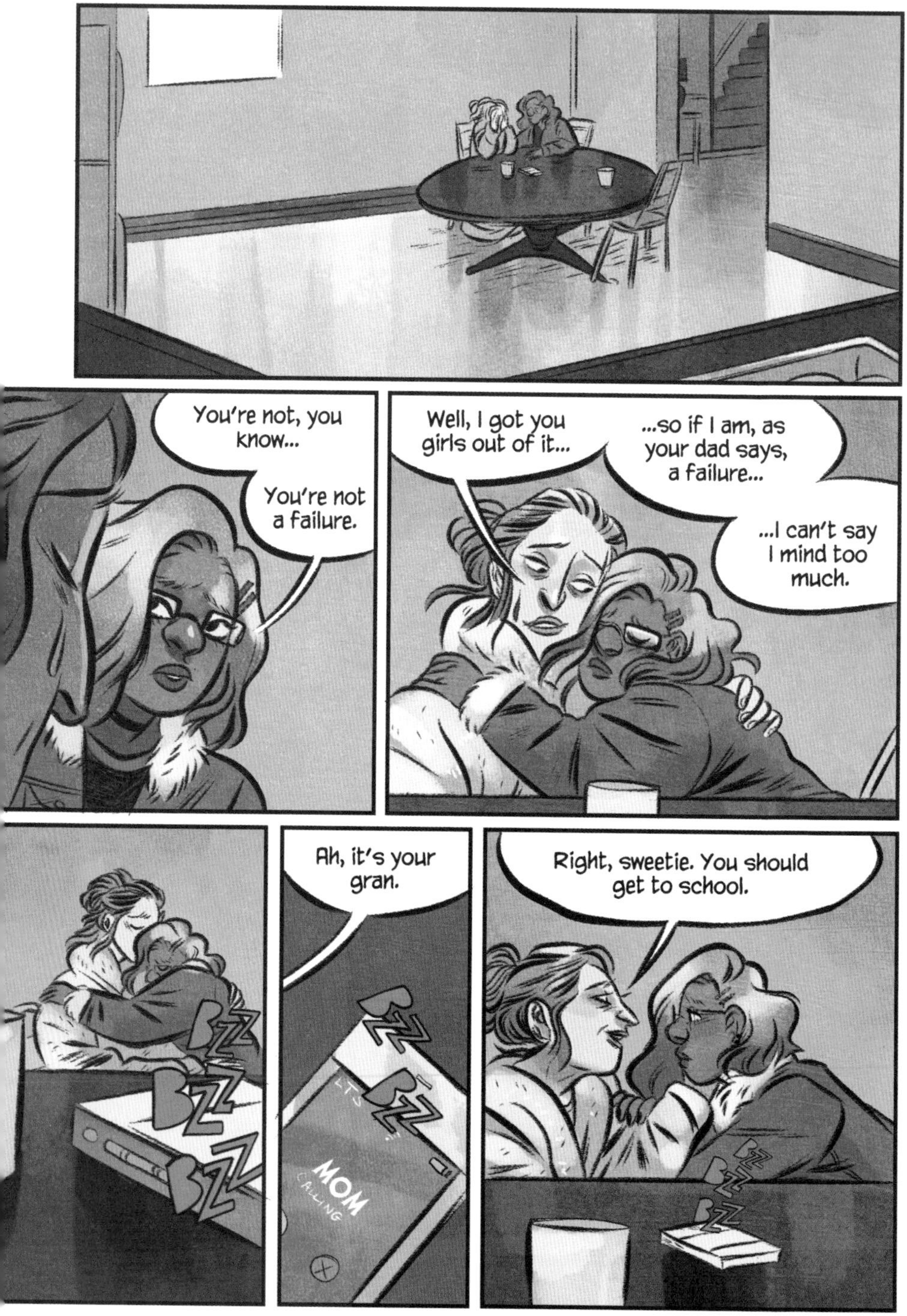
You're not, you know...
You're not a failure.
Well, I got you girls out of it...
...so if I am, as your dad says, a failure...
...I can't say I mind too much.
BZZ
BZZ
BZZ
Ah, it's your gran.
BZZ
BZZ
MOM
CALLING
Right, sweetie. You should get to school.
BZZ
BZZ
BZZ

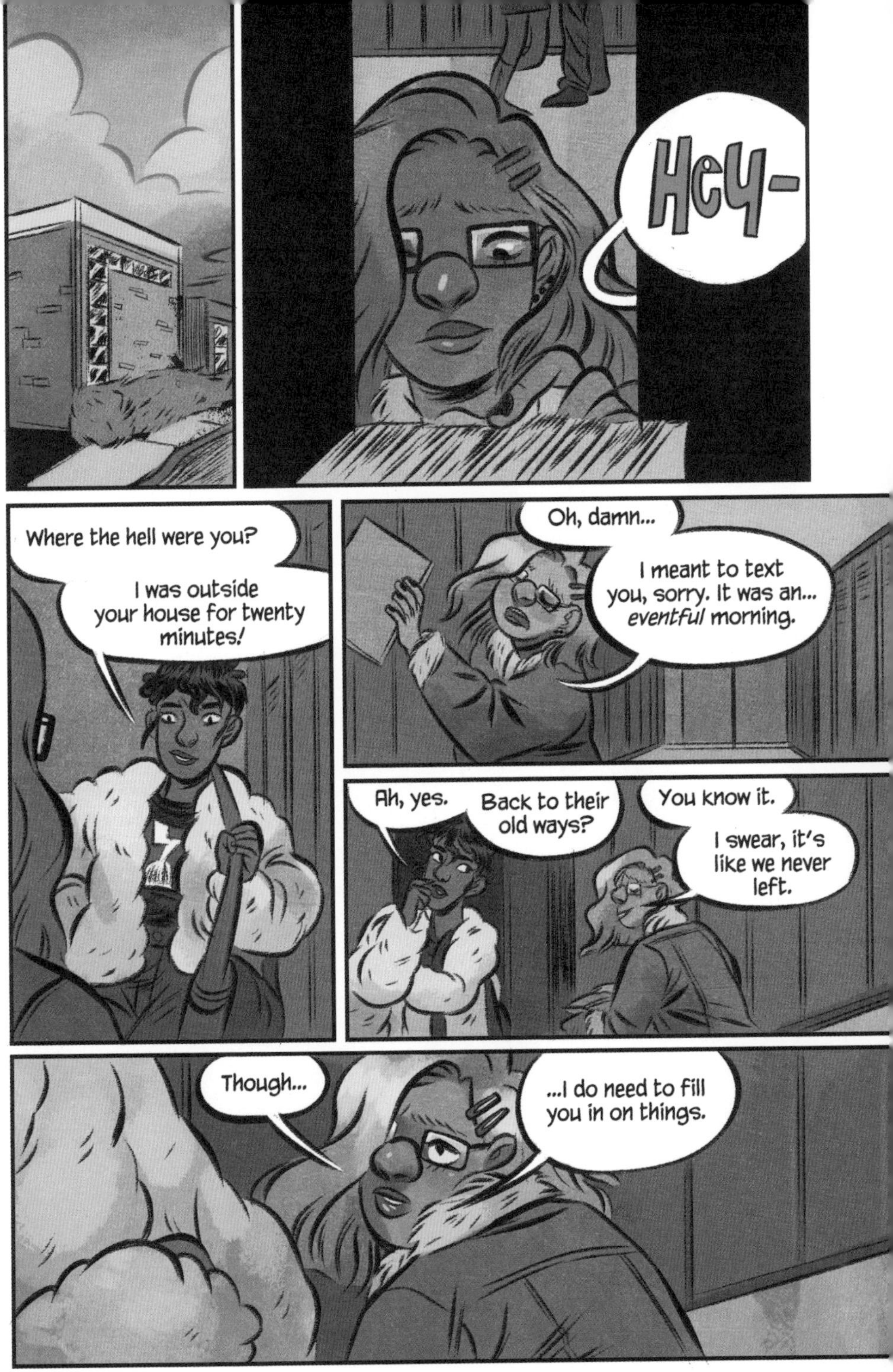

Hey-
Where the hell were you?
I was outside your house for twenty minutes!
Oh, damn...
I meant to text you, sorry. It was an... *eventful* morning.
Ah, yes.
Back to their old ways?
You know it.
I swear, it's like we never left.
Though...
...I do need to fill you in on things.

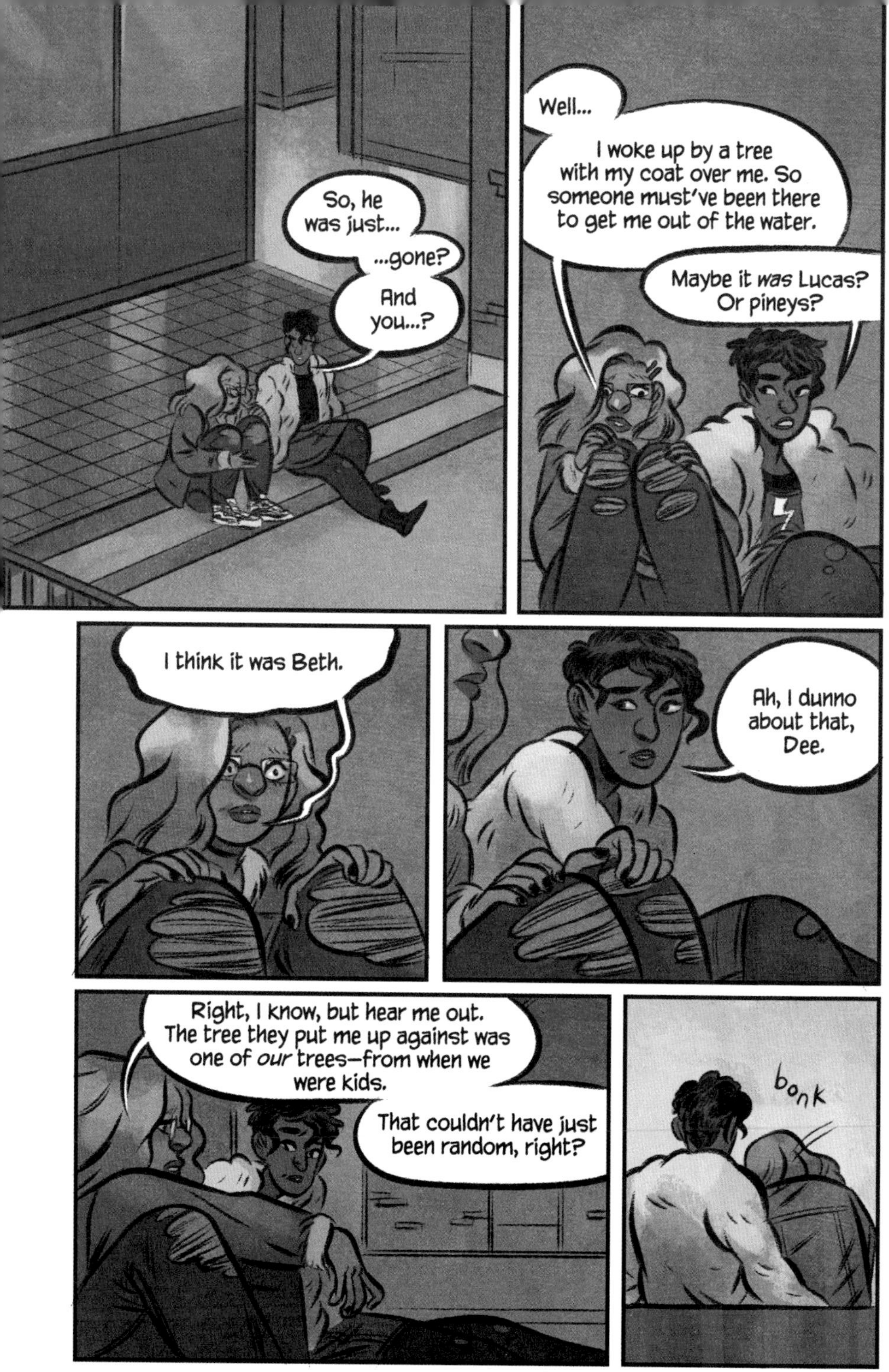
So, he was just...
...gone?
And you...?
Well...
I woke up by a tree with my coat over me. So someone must've been there to get me out of the water.
Maybe it *was* Lucas? Or pineys?
I think it was Beth.
Ah, I dunno about that, Dee.
Right, I know, but hear me out. The tree they put me up against was one of *our* trees—from when we were kids.
That couldn't have just been random, right?
bonk

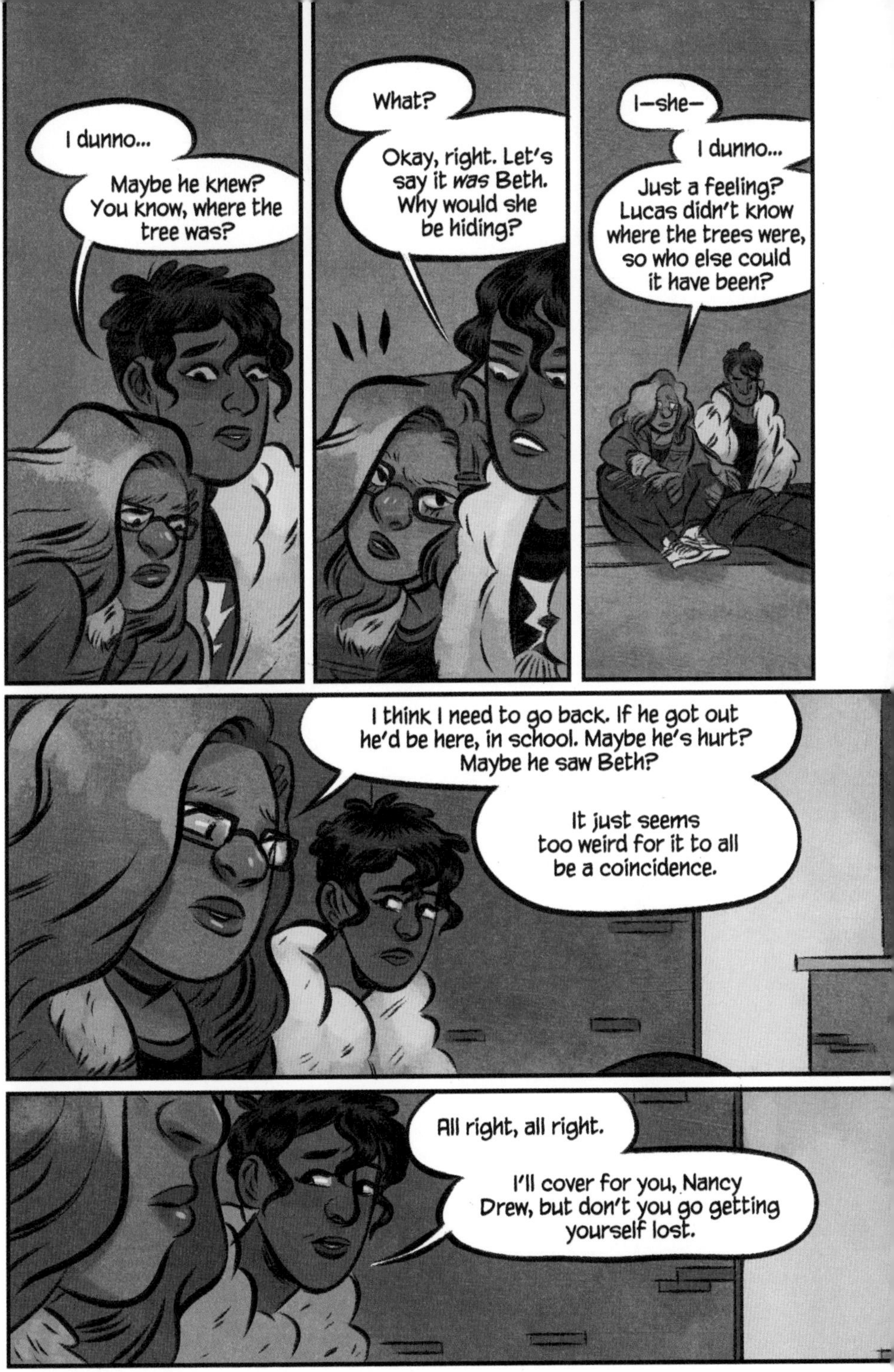
I dunno...
Maybe he knew? You know, where the tree was?
What?
Okay, right. Let's say it *was* Beth. Why would she be hiding?
I—she—
I dunno...
Just a feeling? Lucas didn't know where the trees were, so who else could it have been?
I think I need to go back. If he got out he'd be here, in school. Maybe he's hurt? Maybe he saw Beth?
It just seems too weird for it to all be a coincidence.
All right, all right.
I'll cover for you, Nancy Drew, but don't you go getting yourself lost.

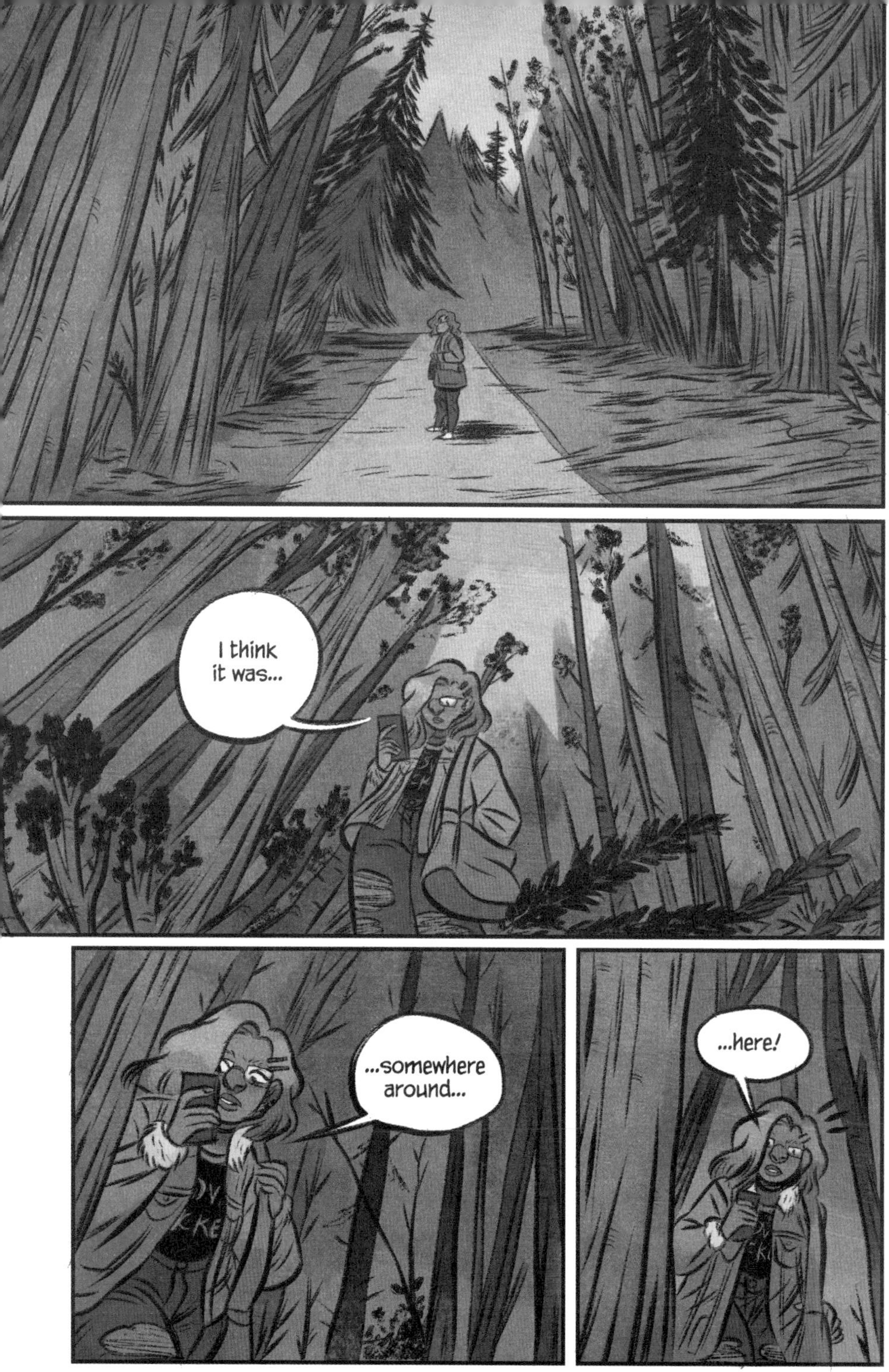
I think it was...
...somewhere around...
...here!

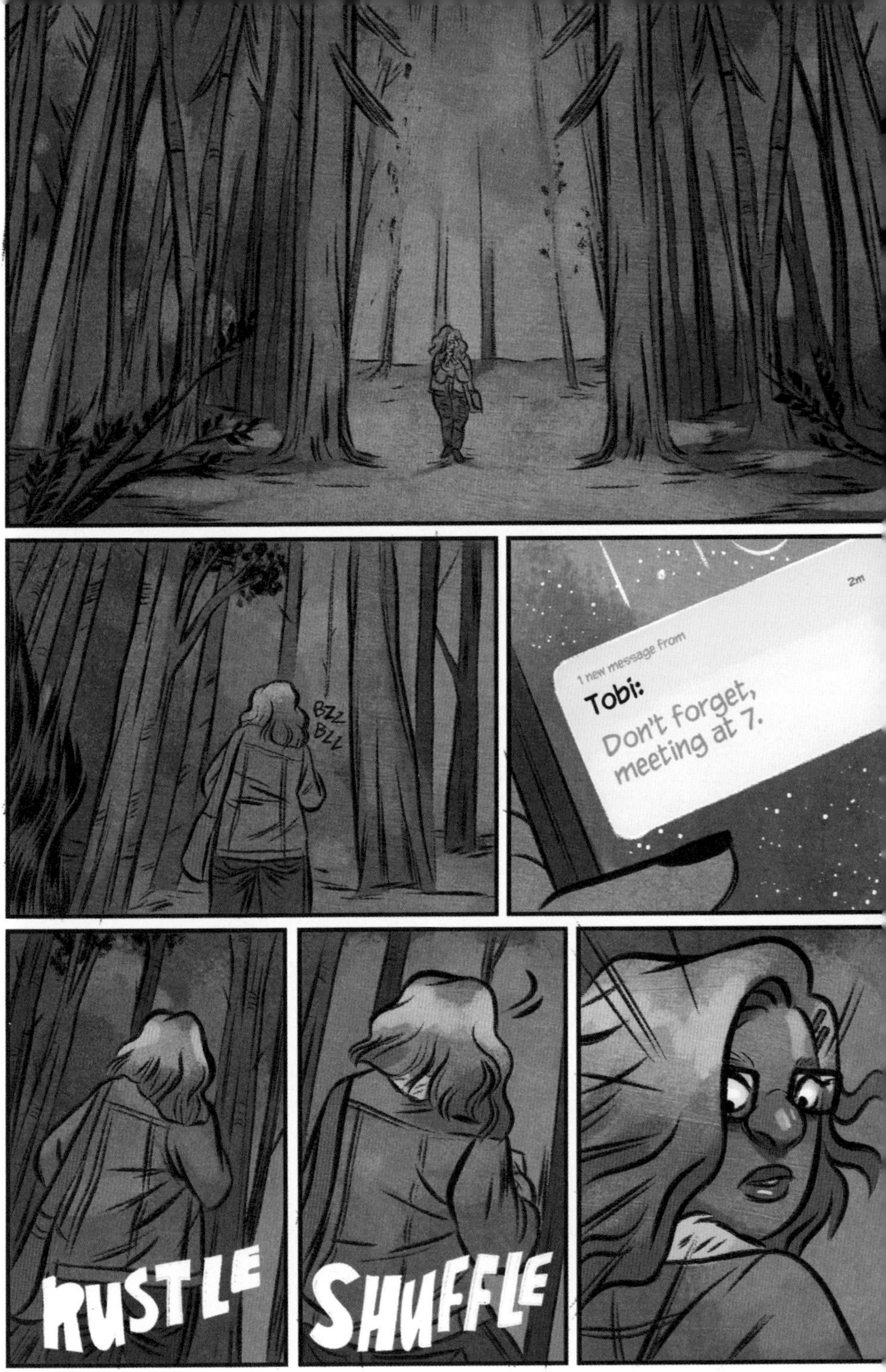

BZZ BZZ
1 new message from
Tobi:
Don't forget, meeting at 7.
2m
RUSTLE
SHUFFLE

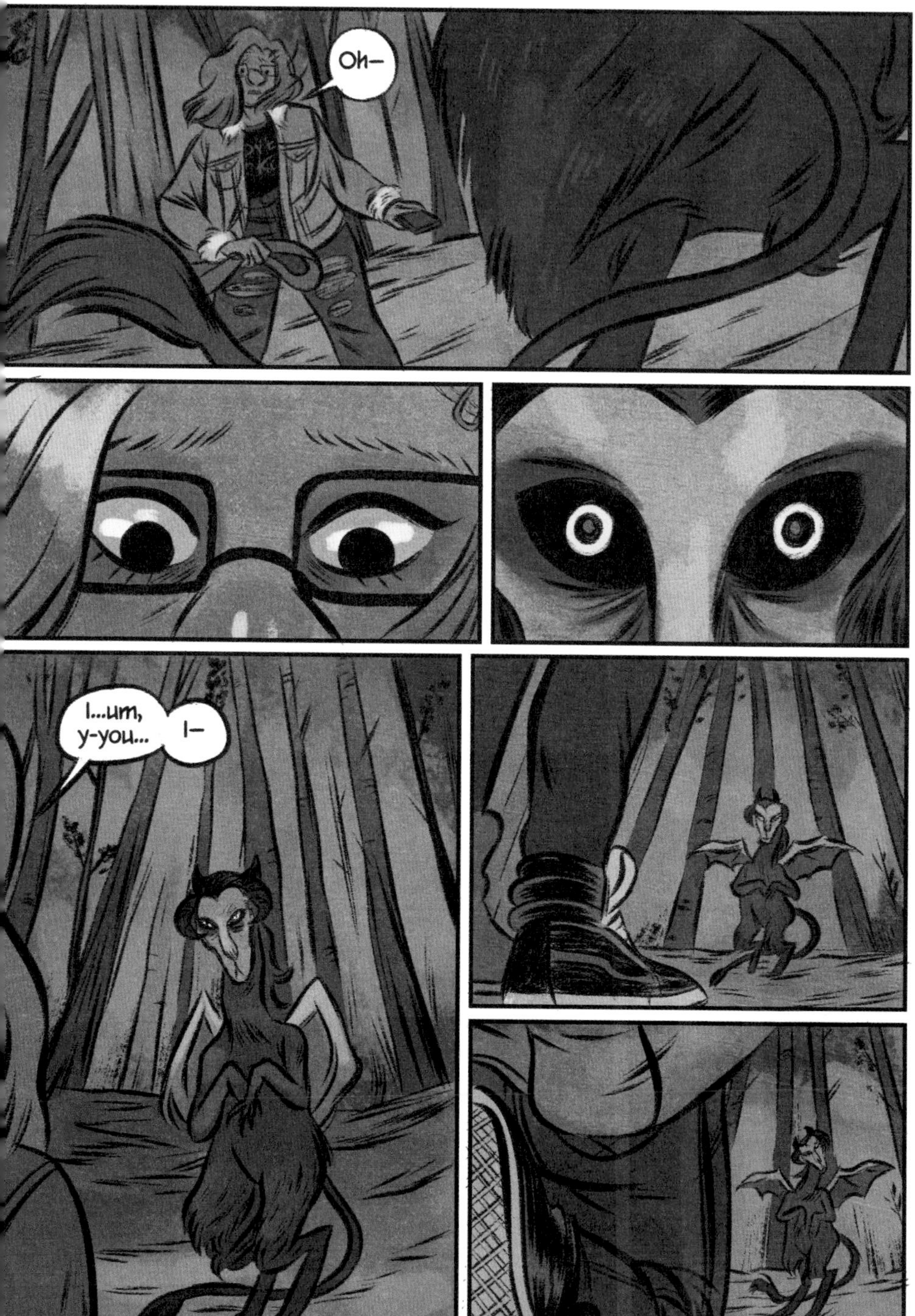
Oh–
I...um, y-you...
I–

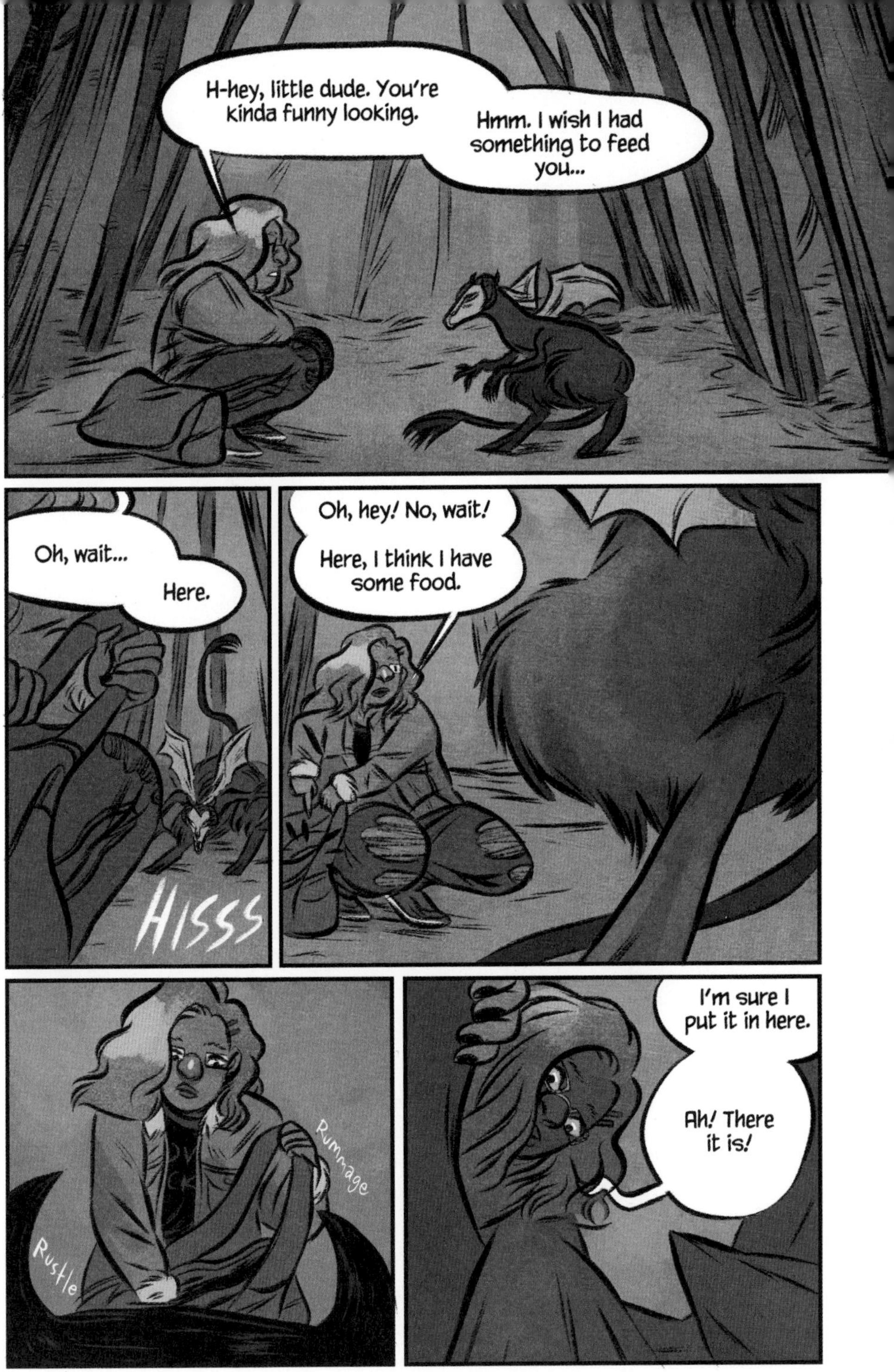
H-hey, little dude. You're kinda funny looking.
Hmm. I wish I had something to feed you...
Oh, wait...
Here.
HISSS
Oh, hey! No, wait!
Here, I think I have some food.
Rummage
Rustle
I'm sure I put it in here.
Ah! There it is!

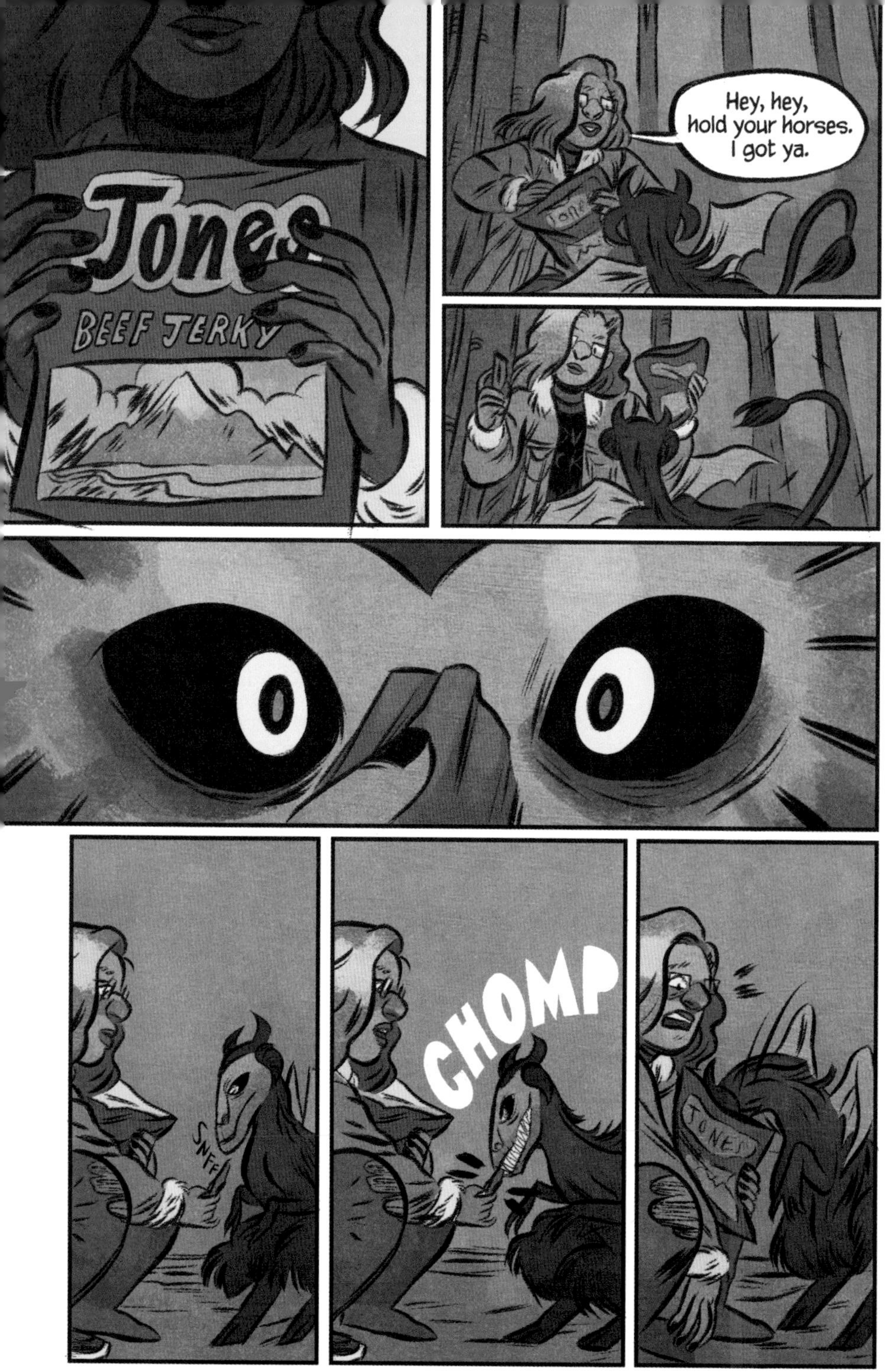
Jones
BEEF JERKY
Hey, hey, hold your horses. I got ya.
SNFF
CHOMP
JONES

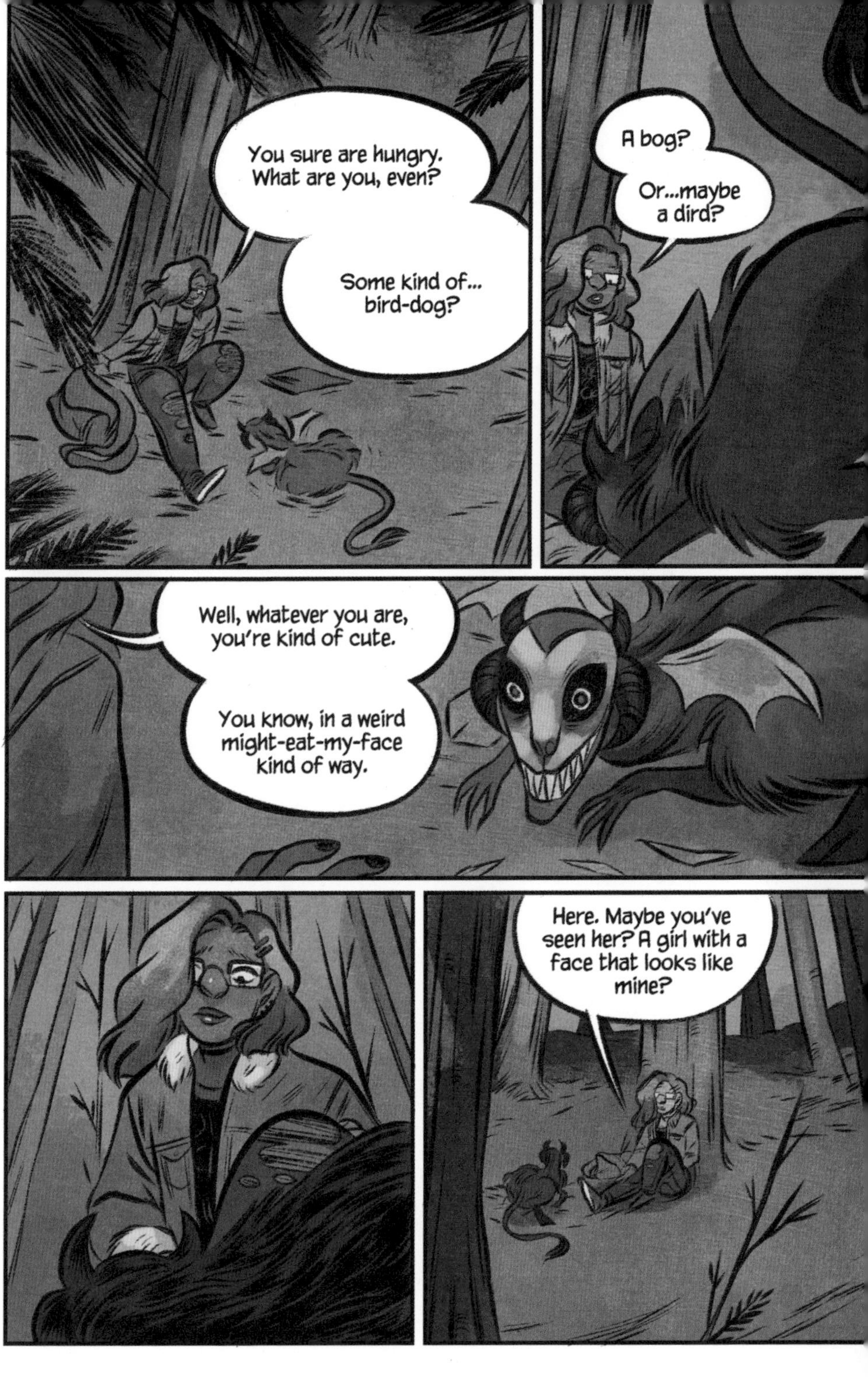
You sure are hungry. What are you, even?
Some kind of... bird-dog?
A bog?
Or...maybe a dird?
Well, whatever you are, you're kind of cute.
You know, in a weird might-eat-my-face kind of way.
Here. Maybe you've seen her? A girl with a face that looks like mine?

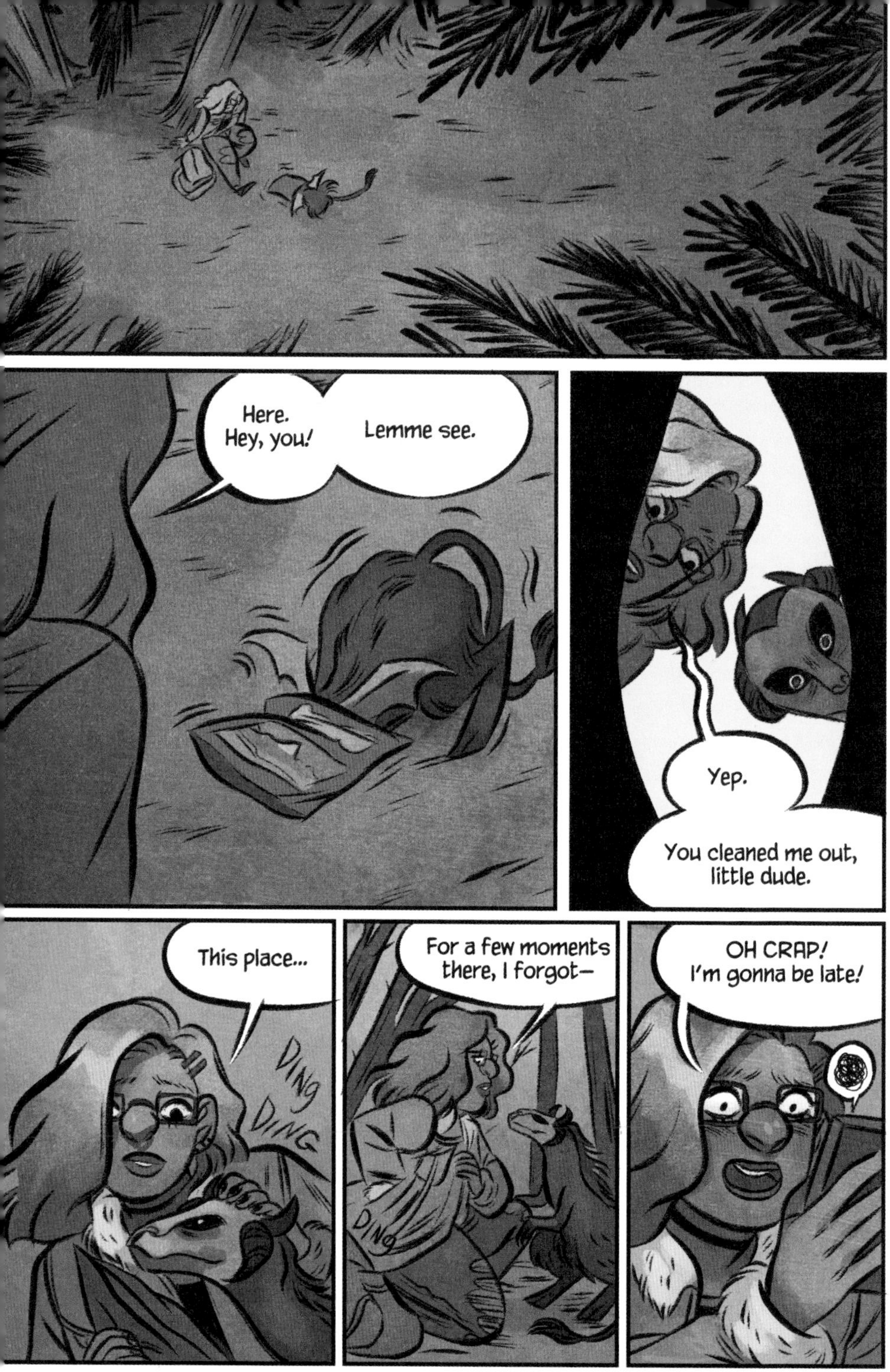
Here.
Hey, you!
Lemme see.
Yep.
You cleaned me out, little dude.
This place...
DING DING
For a few moments there, I forgot—
DING
OH CRAP!
I'm gonna be late!

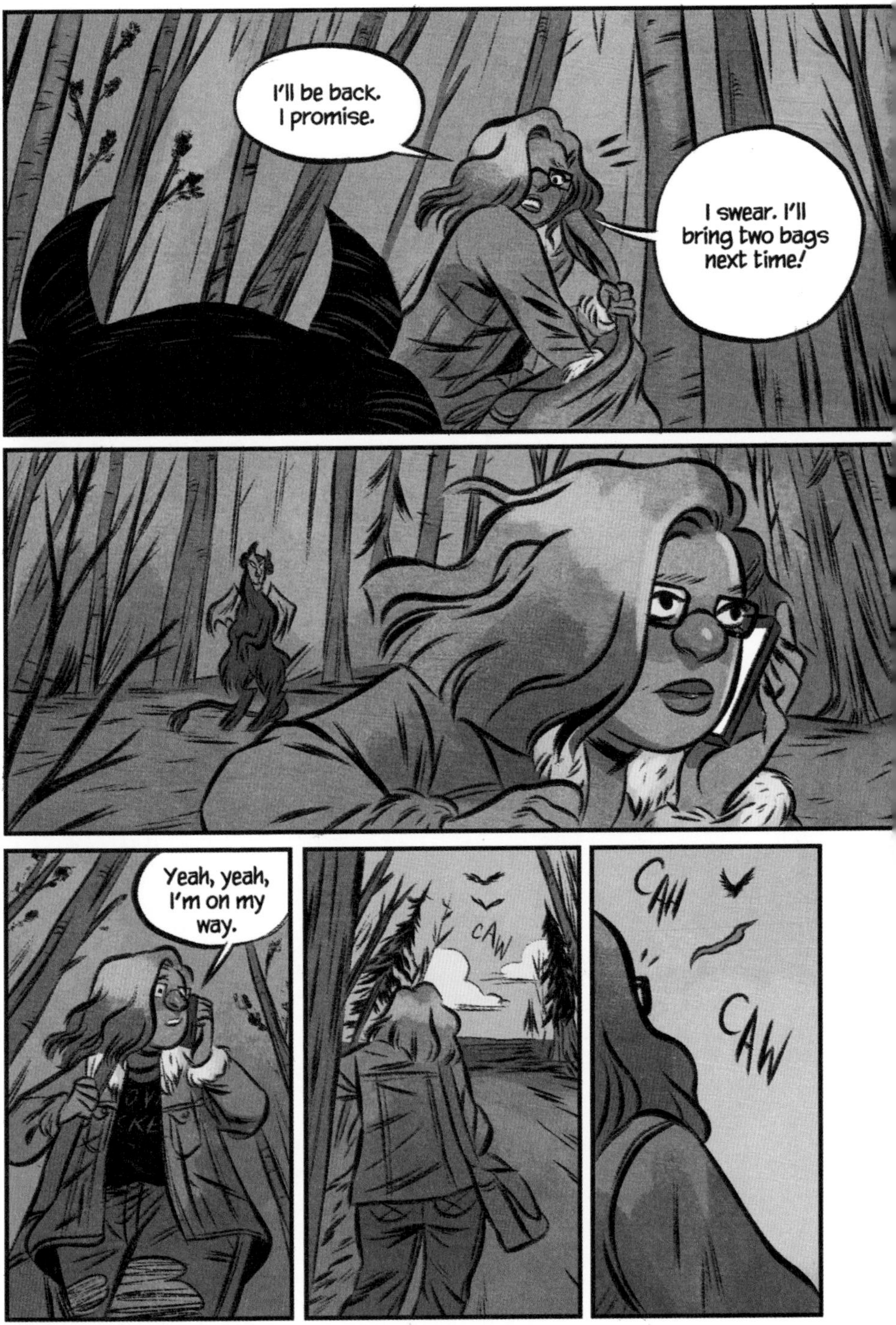
I'll be back.
I promise.
I swear. I'll bring two bags next time!
Yeah, yeah, I'm on my way.
CAW
CAW
CAW

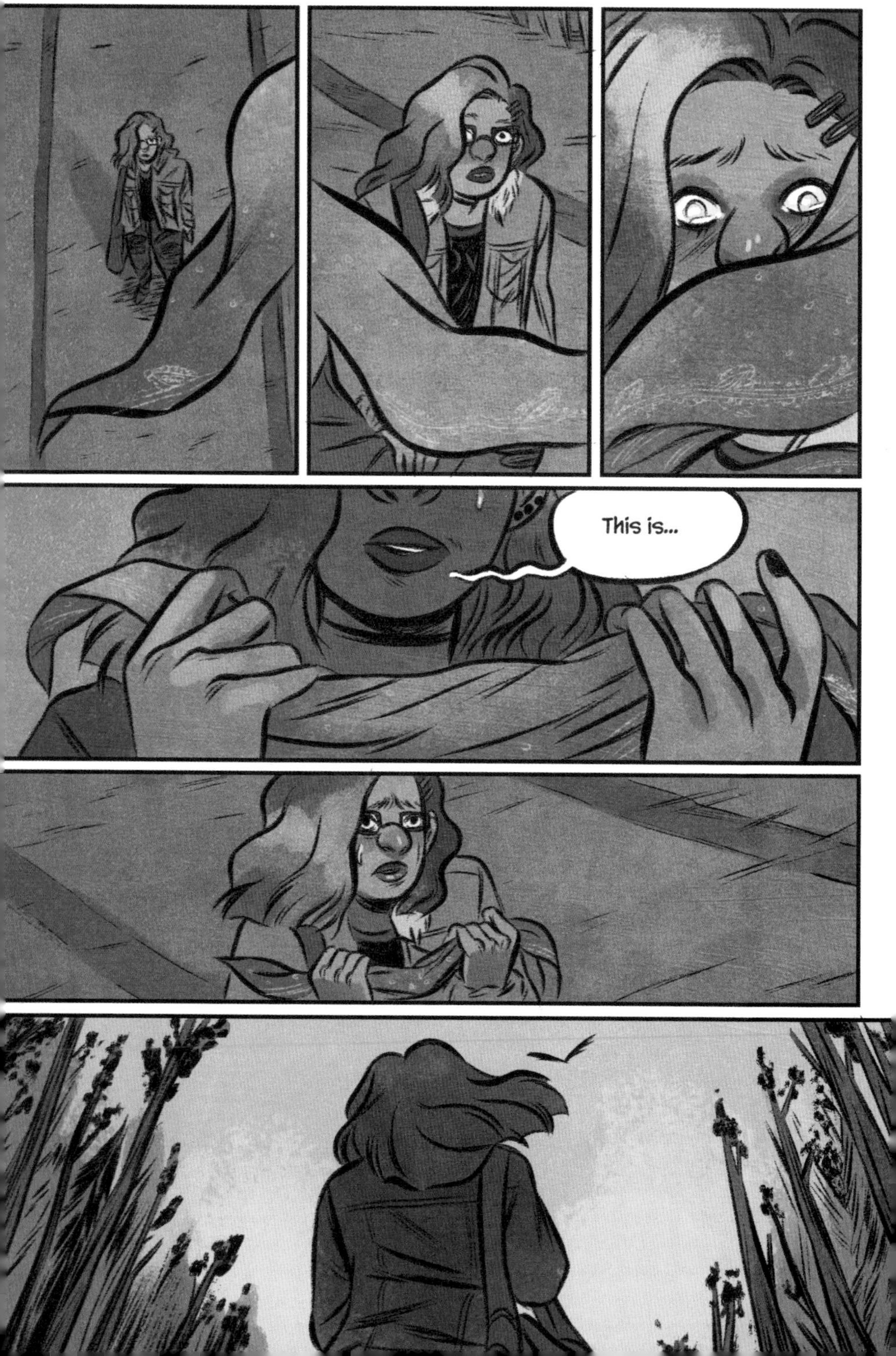
This is...

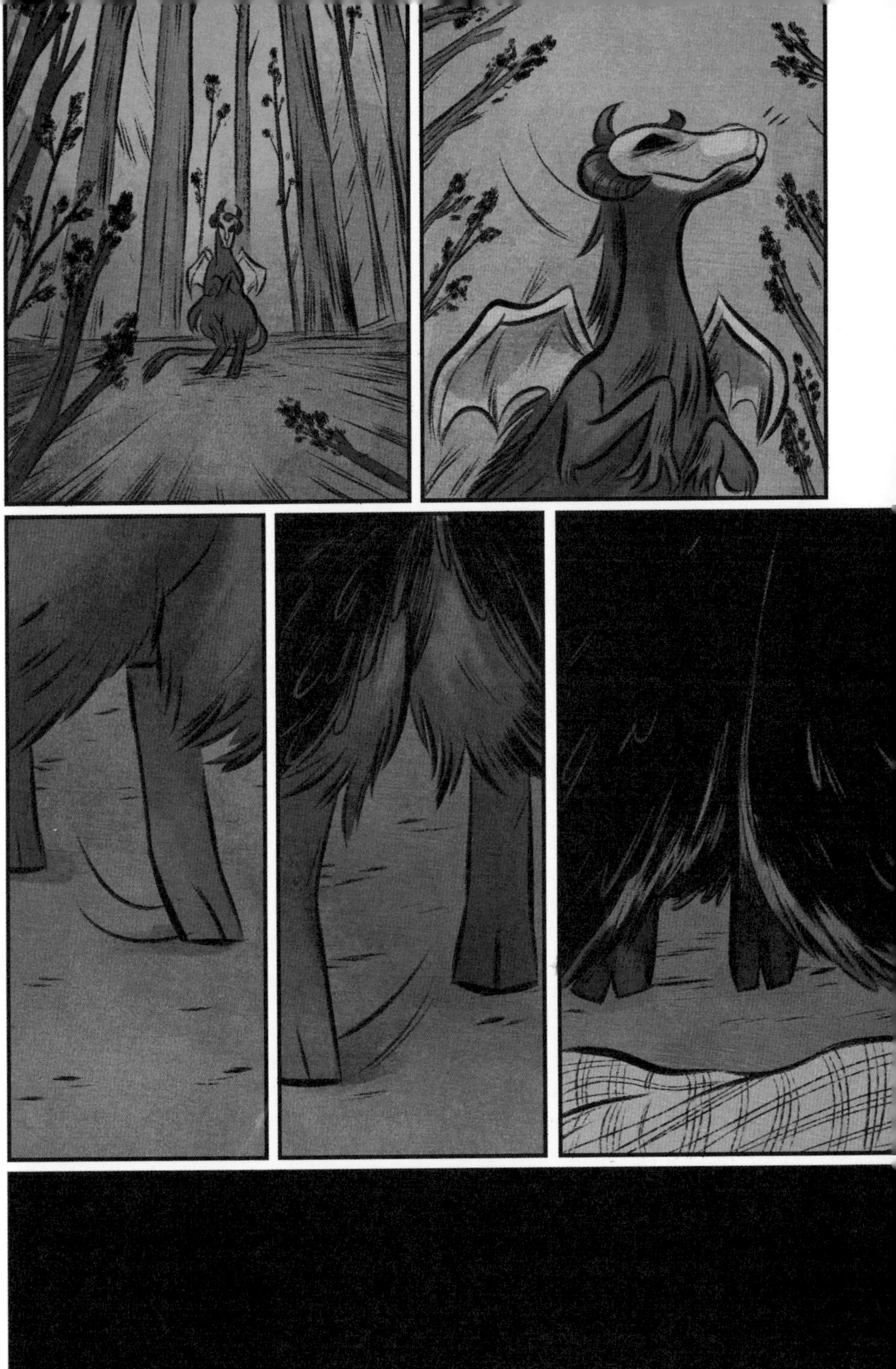

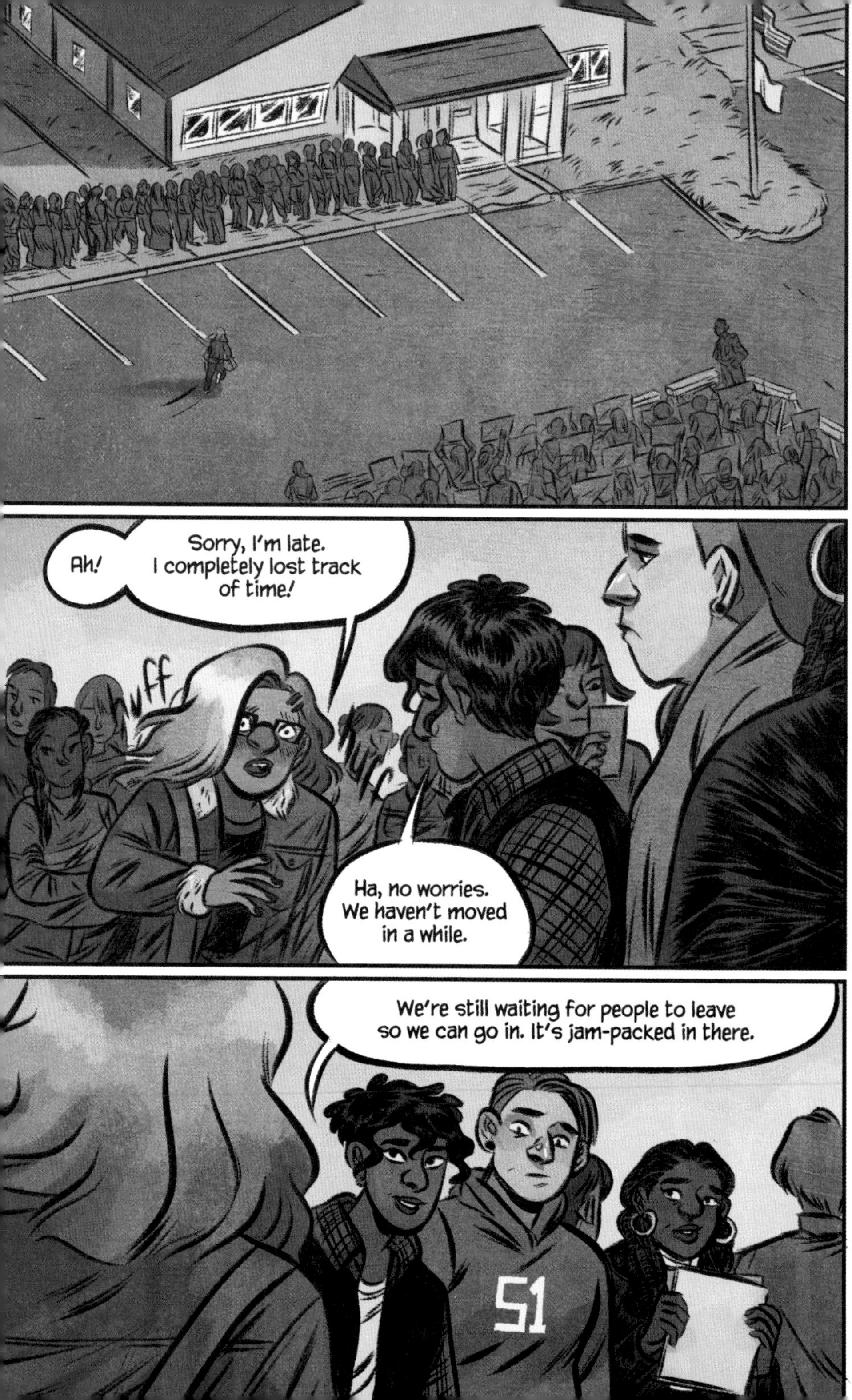

Ah!
Sorry, I'm late. I completely lost track of time!
uff
Ha, no worries. We haven't moved in a while.
We're still waiting for people to leave so we can go in. It's jam-packed in there.
51

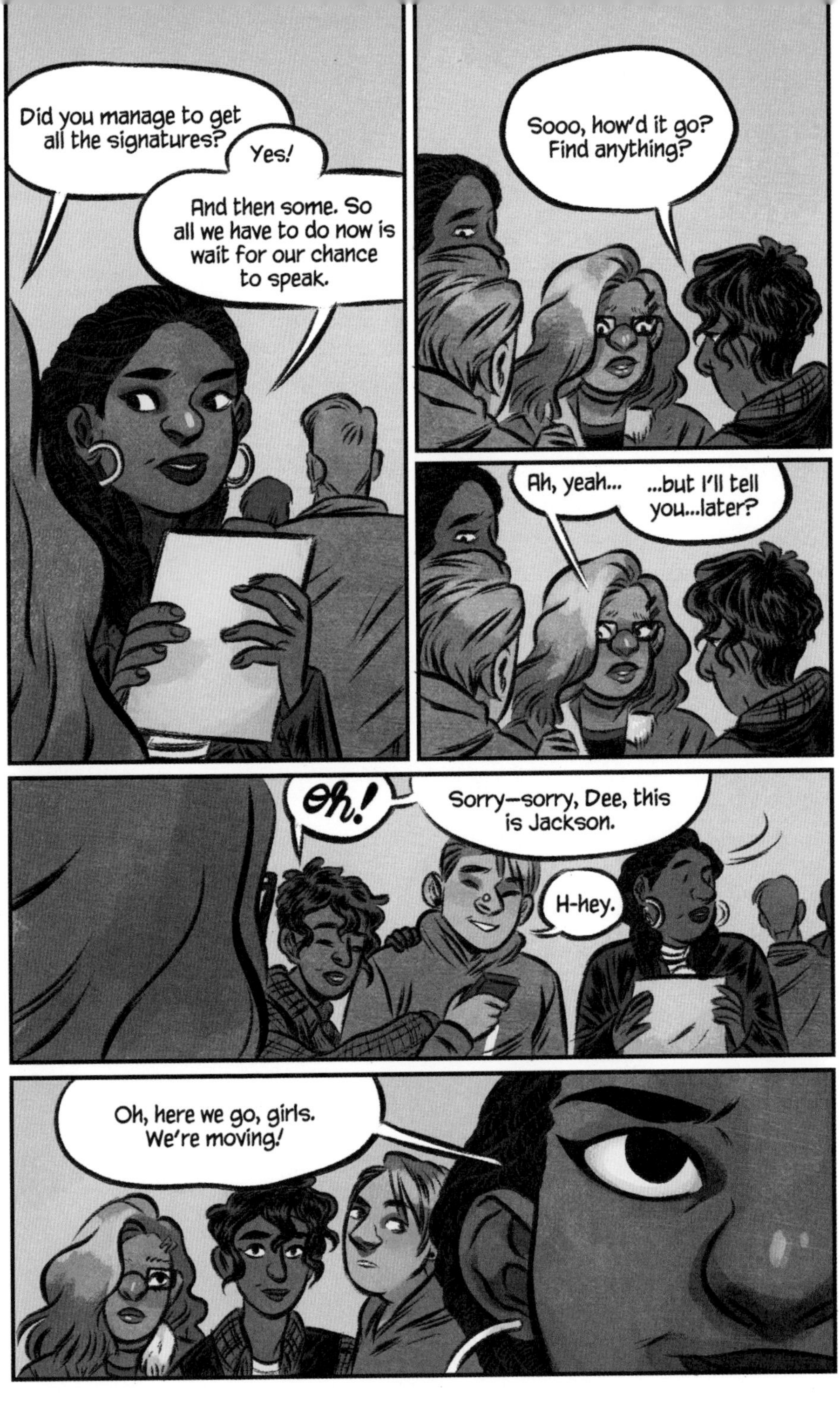
Did you manage to get all the signatures?
Yes!
And then some. So all we have to do now is wait for our chance to speak.
Sooo, how'd it go? Find anything?
Ah, yeah...
...but I'll tell you...later?
Oh!
Sorry—sorry, Dee, this is Jackson.
H-hey.
Oh, here we go, girls. We're moving!

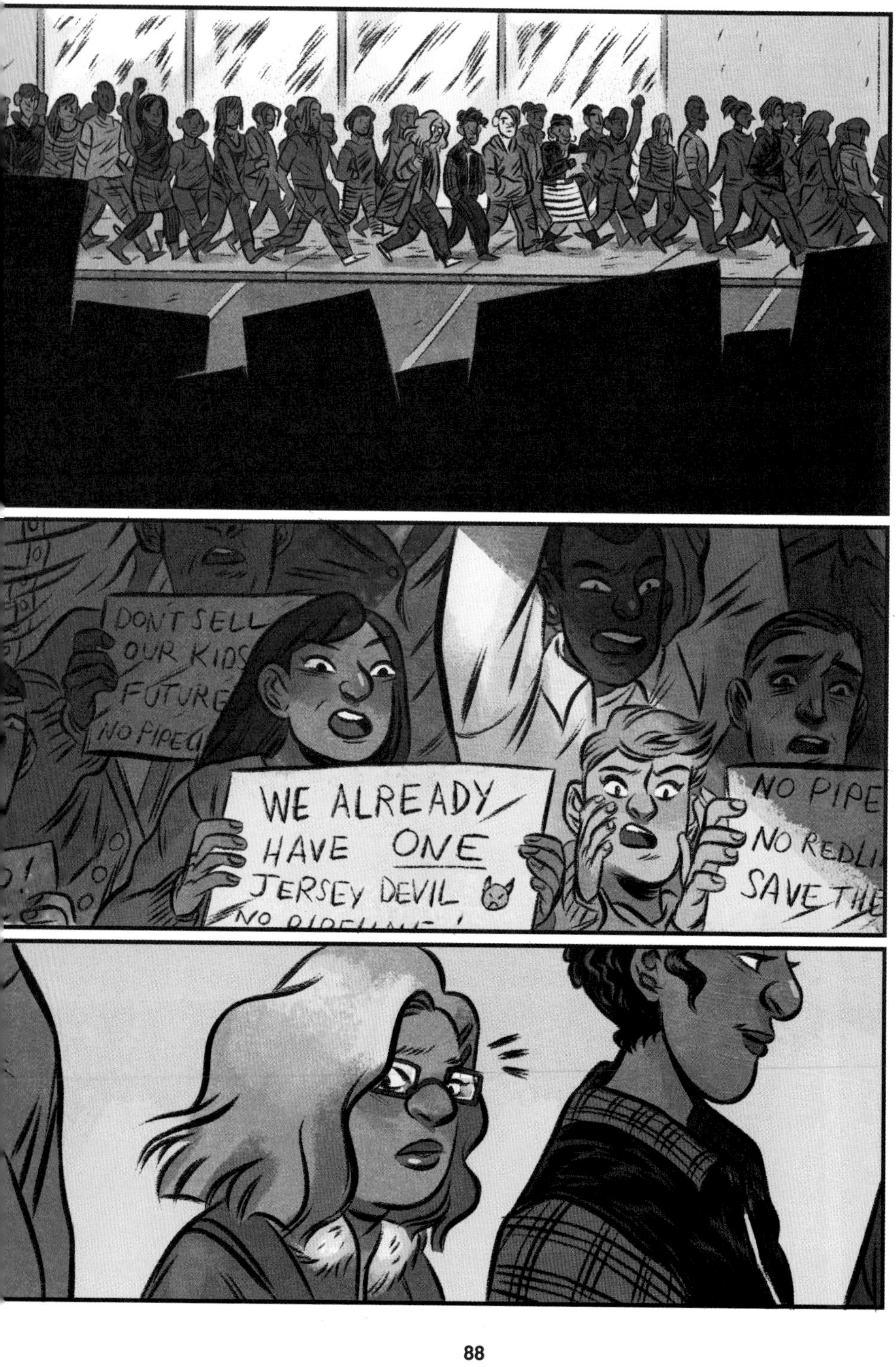
DON'T SELL
OUR KIDS
FUTURE
NO PIPEL
WE ALREADY HAVE ONE JERSEY DEVIL
NO PIPE
NO REDLI
SAVE THE

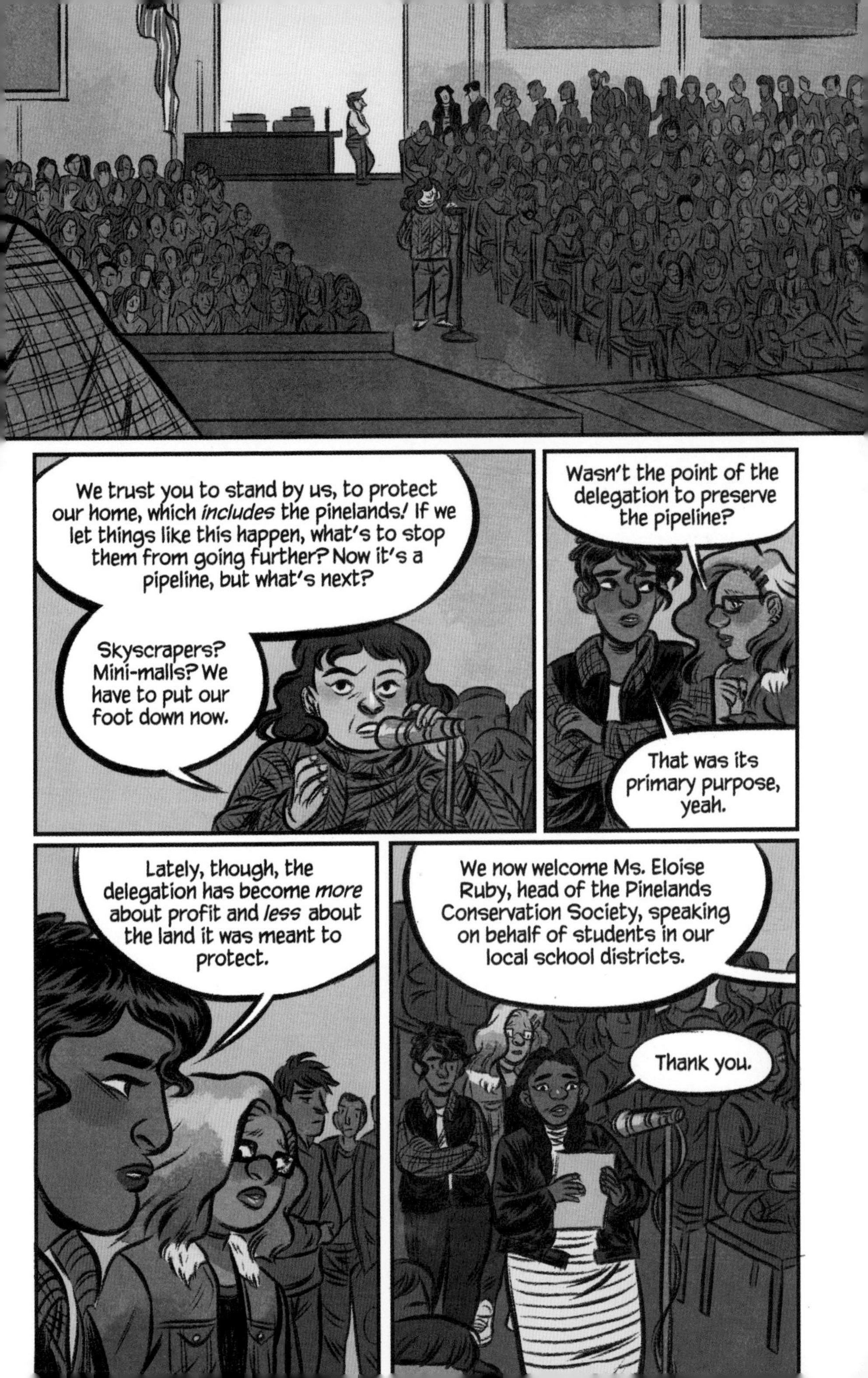
We trust you to stand by us, to protect our home, which *includes* the pinelands! If we let things like this happen, what's to stop them from going further? Now it's a pipeline, but what's next?
Skyscrapers? Mini-malls? We have to put our foot down now.
Wasn't the point of the delegation to preserve the pipeline?
That was its primary purpose, yeah.
Lately, though, the delegation has become *more* about profit and *less* about the land it was meant to protect.
We now welcome Ms. Eloise Ruby, head of the Pinelands Conservation Society, speaking on behalf of students in our local school districts.
Thank you.

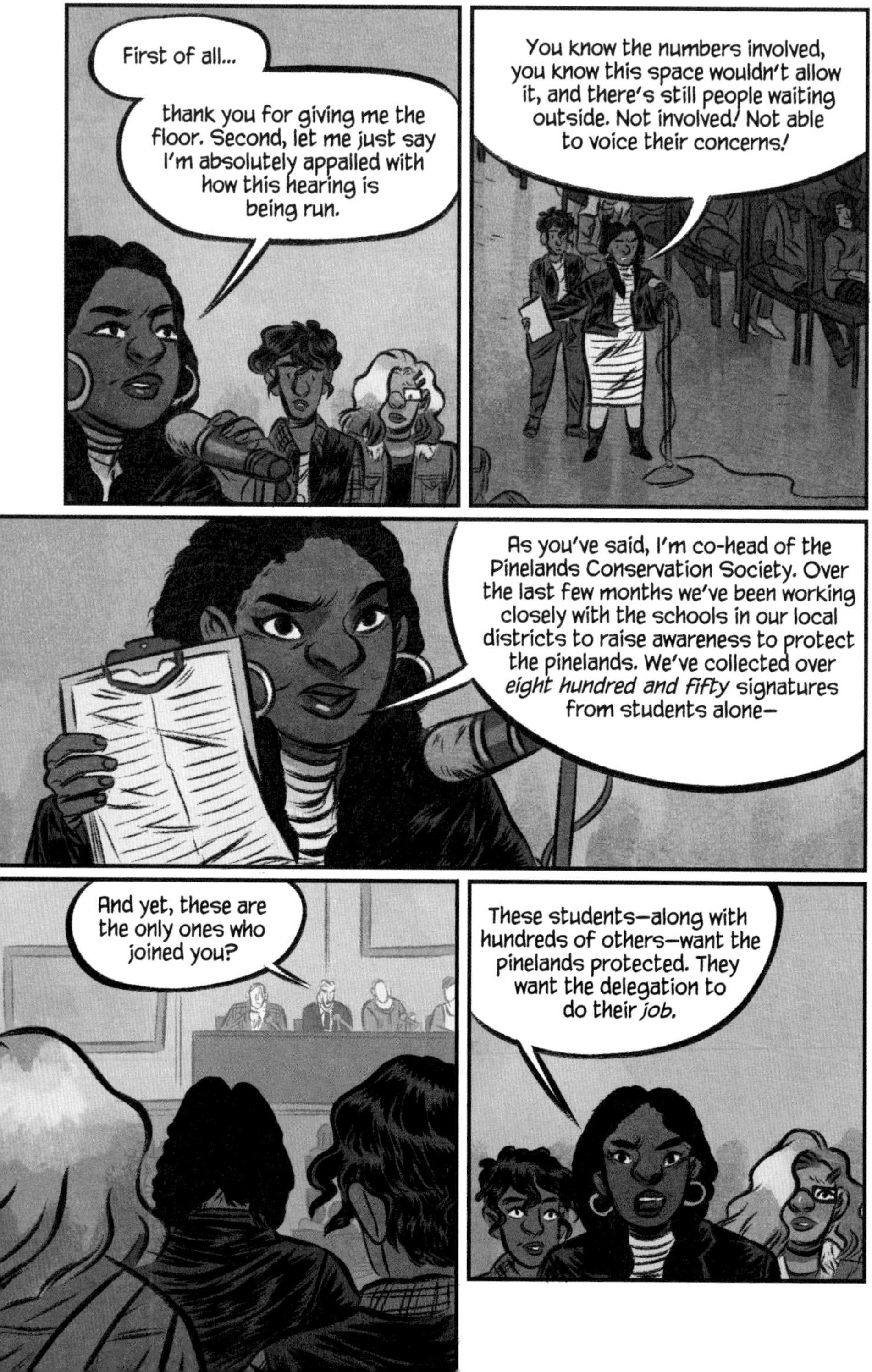
First of all...
thank you for giving me the floor. Second, let me just say I'm absolutely appalled with how this hearing is being run.
You know the numbers involved, you know this space wouldn't allow it, and there's still people waiting outside. Not involved! Not able to voice their concerns!
As you've said, I'm co-head of the Pinelands Conservation Society. Over the last few months we've been working closely with the schools in our local districts to raise awareness to protect the pinelands. We've collected over *eight hundred and fifty* signatures from students alone—
And yet, these are the only ones who joined you?
These students—along with hundreds of others—want the pinelands protected. They want the delegation to do their *job.*

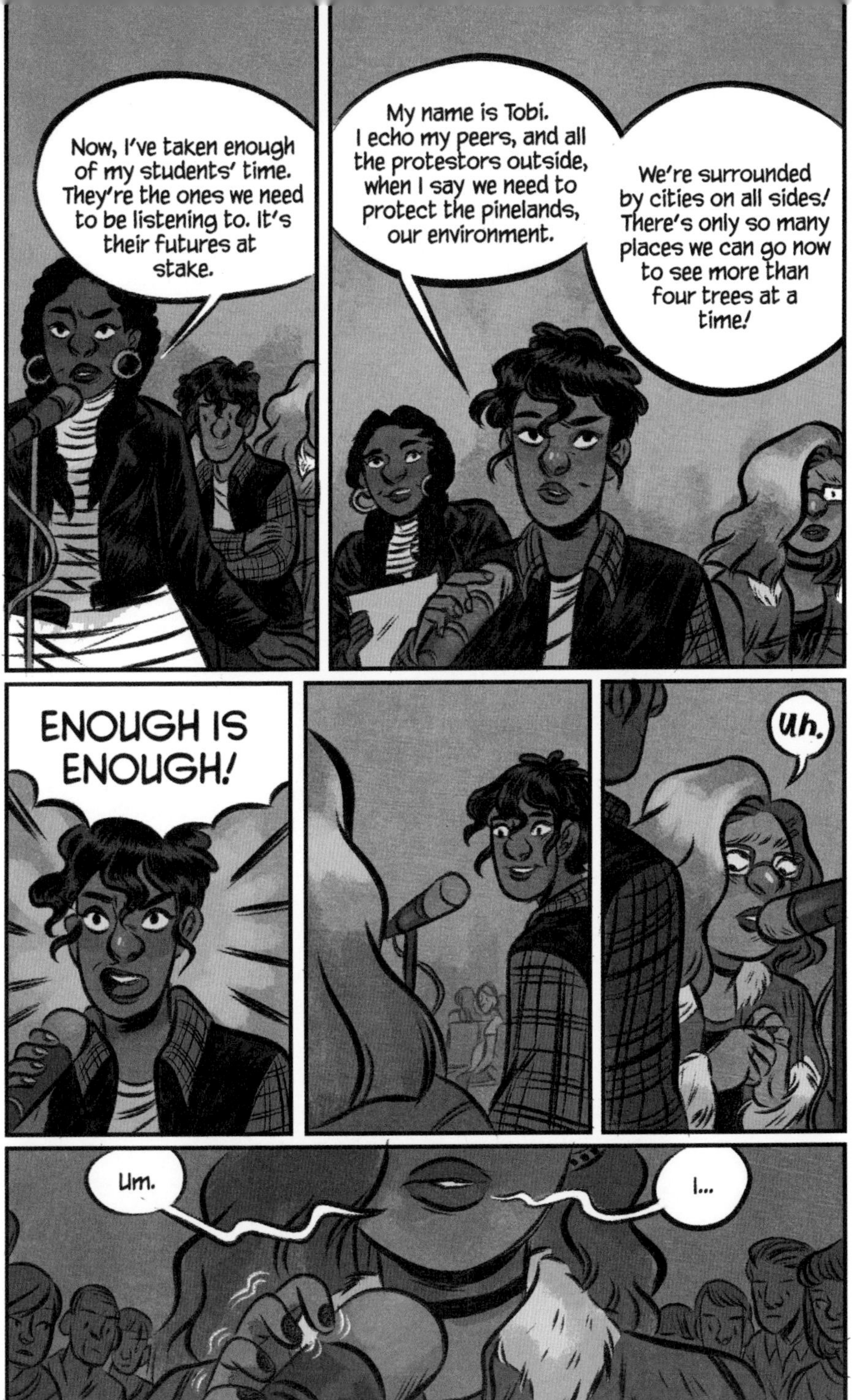
Now, I've taken enough of my students' time. They're the ones we need to be listening to. It's their futures at stake.
My name is Tobi. I echo my peers, and all the protestors outside, when I say we need to protect the pinelands, our environment.
We're surrounded by cities on all sides! There's only so many places we can go now to see more than four trees at a time!
ENOUGH IS ENOUGH!
Uh.
Um.
I...

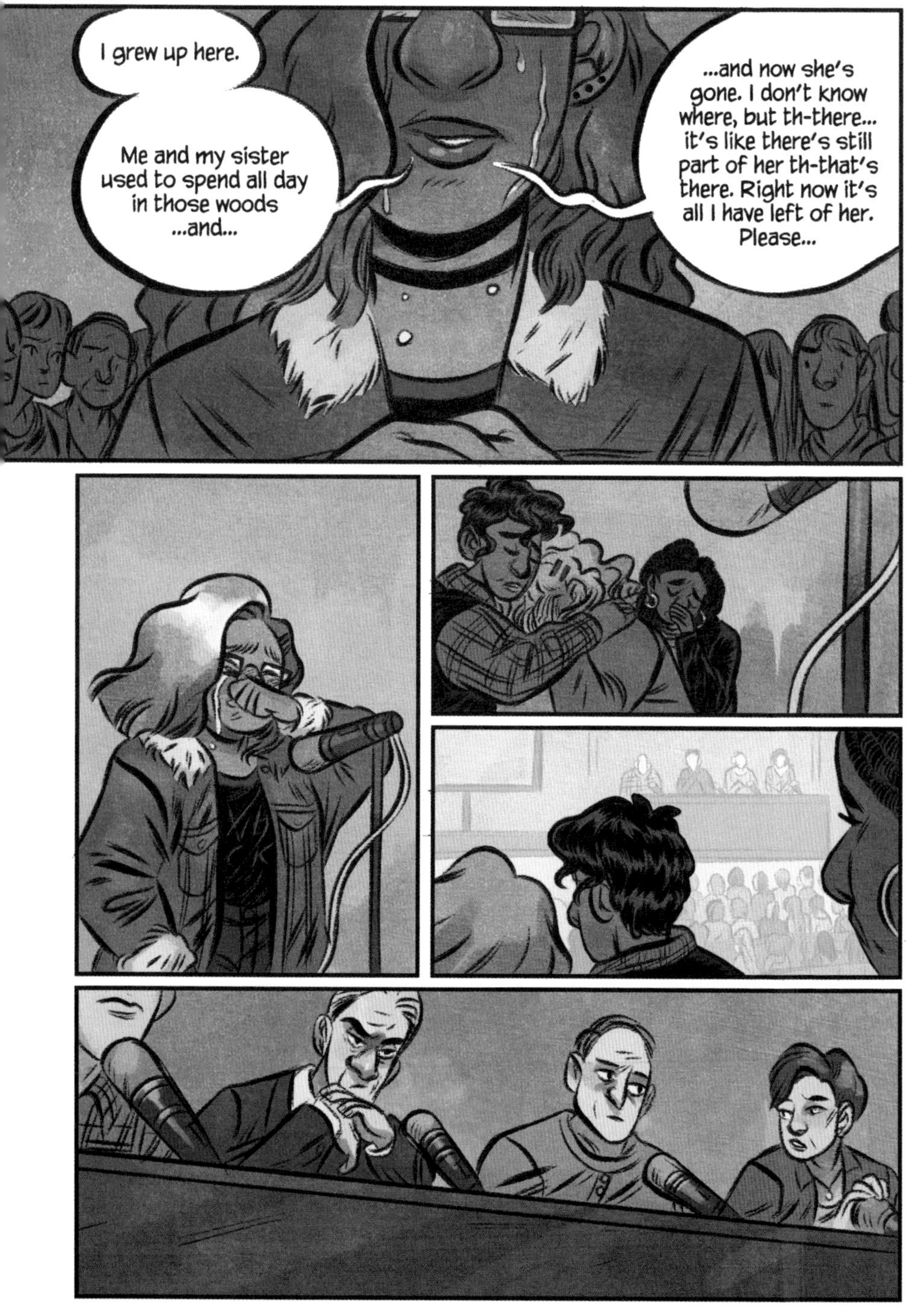
I grew up here.
Me and my sister used to spend all day in those woods ...and...
...and now she's gone. I don't know where, but th-there... it's like there's still part of her th-that's there. Right now it's all I have left of her. Please...

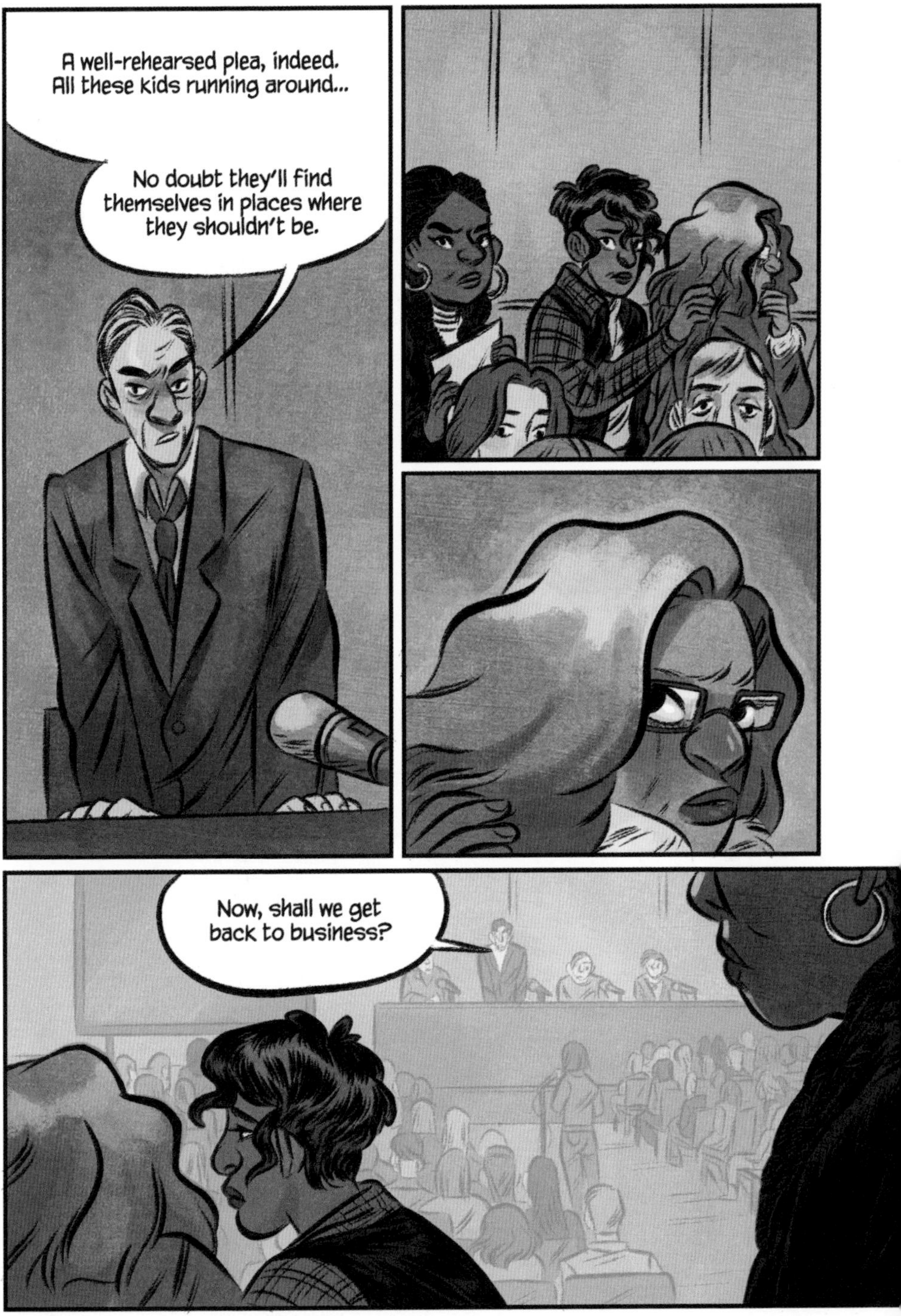
A well-rehearsed plea, indeed.
All these kids running around...
No doubt they'll find themselves in places where they shouldn't be.
Now, shall we get back to business?

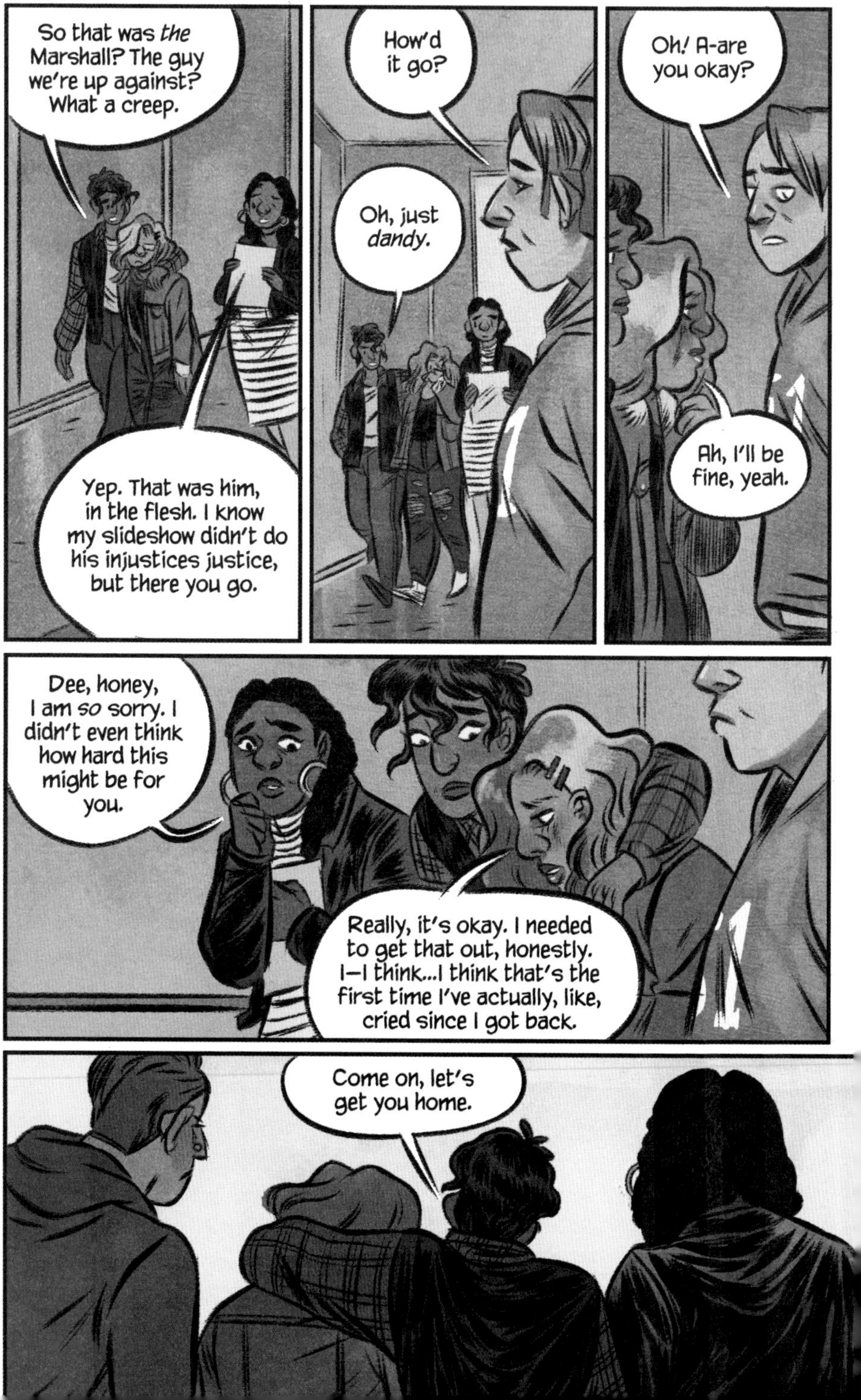
So that was *the* Marshall? The guy we're up against? What a creep.
Yep. That was him, in the flesh. I know my slideshow didn't do his injustices justice, but there you go.
How'd it go?
Oh, just *dandy*.
Oh! A-are you okay?
Ah, I'll be fine, yeah.
Dee, honey, I am *so* sorry. I didn't even think how hard this might be for you.
Really, it's okay. I needed to get that out, honestly. I—I think...I think that's the first time I've actually, like, cried since I got back.
Come on, let's get you home.

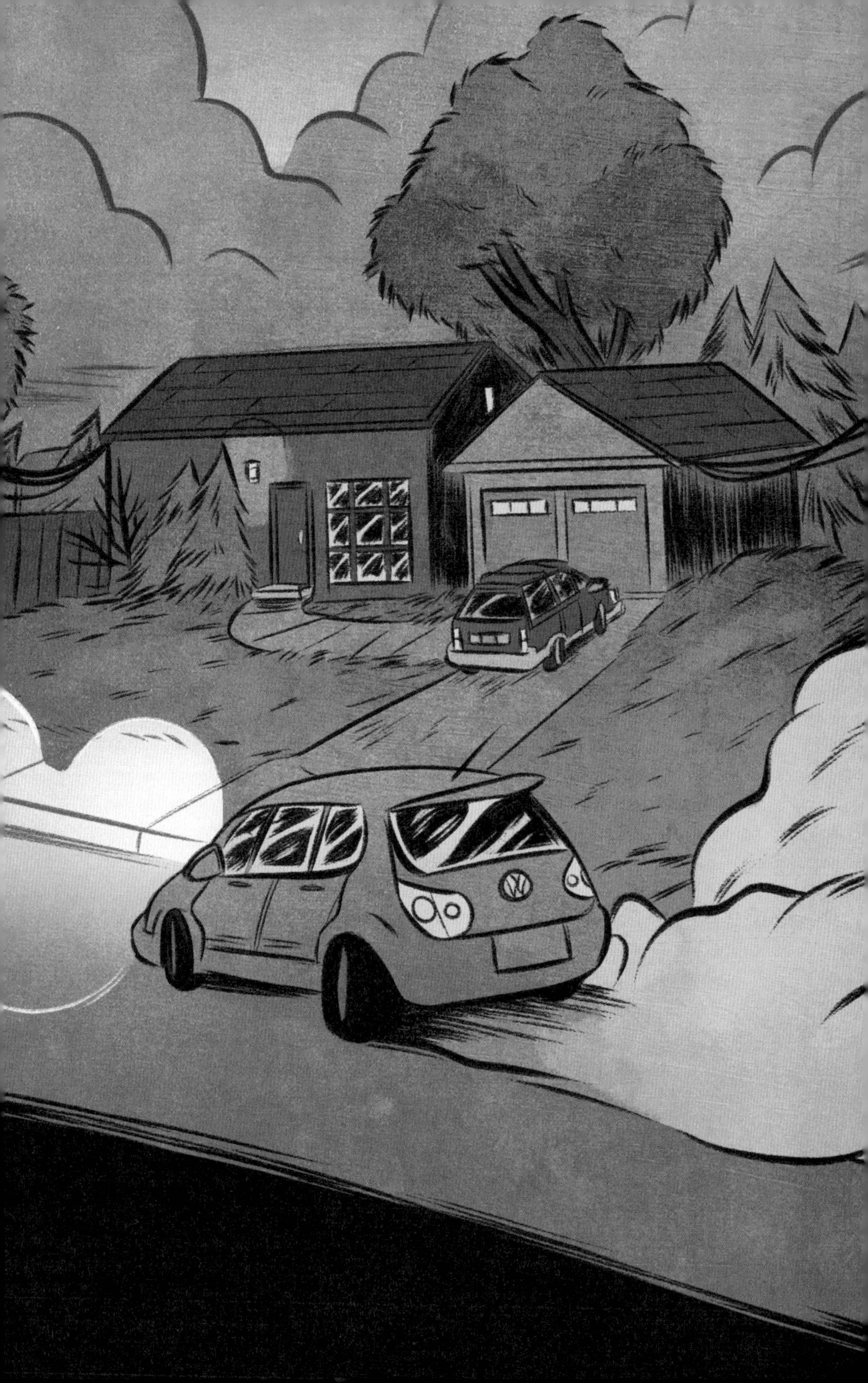

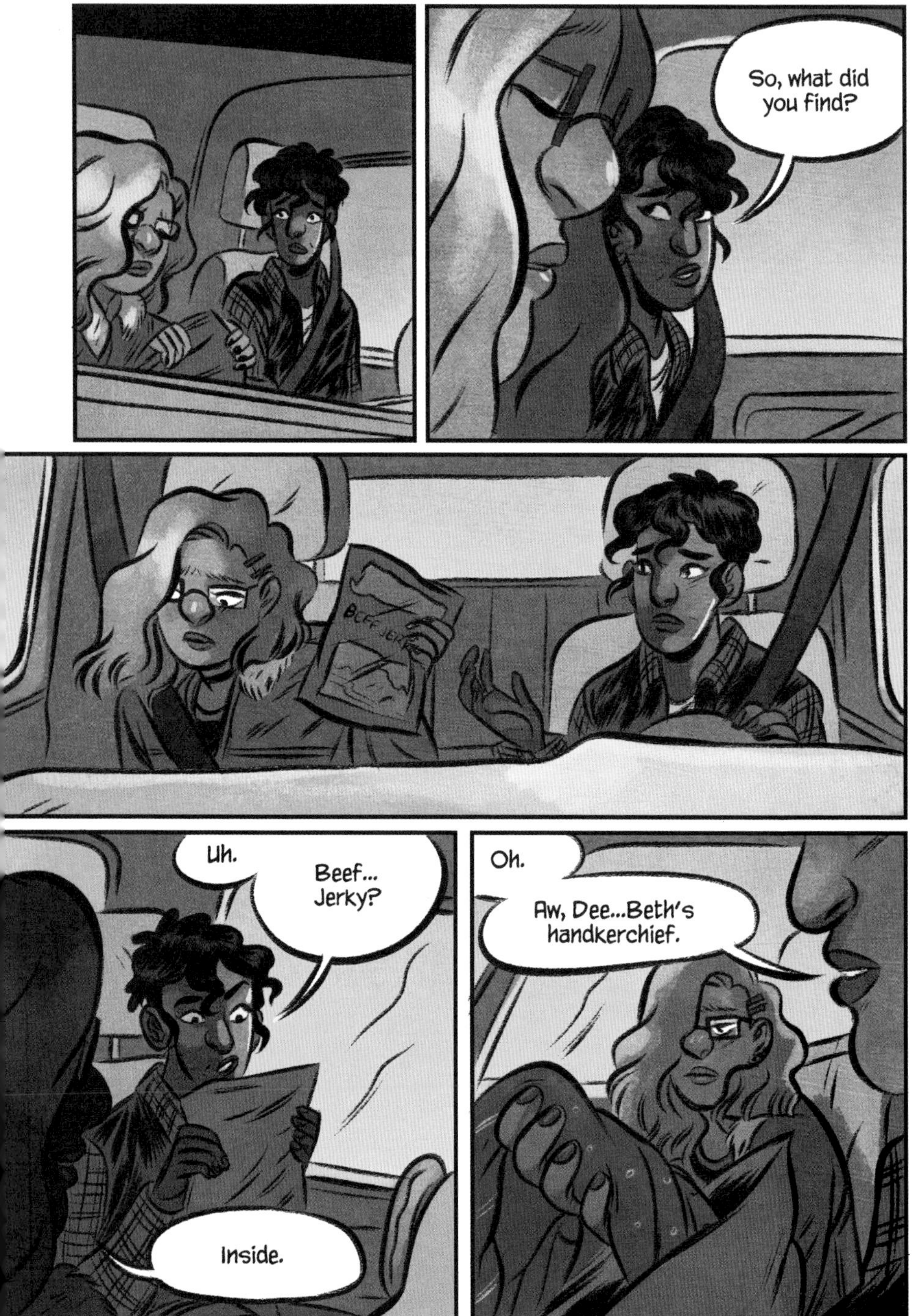
So, what did you find?
BEEF JERKY
Uh.
Beef... Jerky?
Inside.
Oh.
Aw, Dee...Beth's handkerchief.

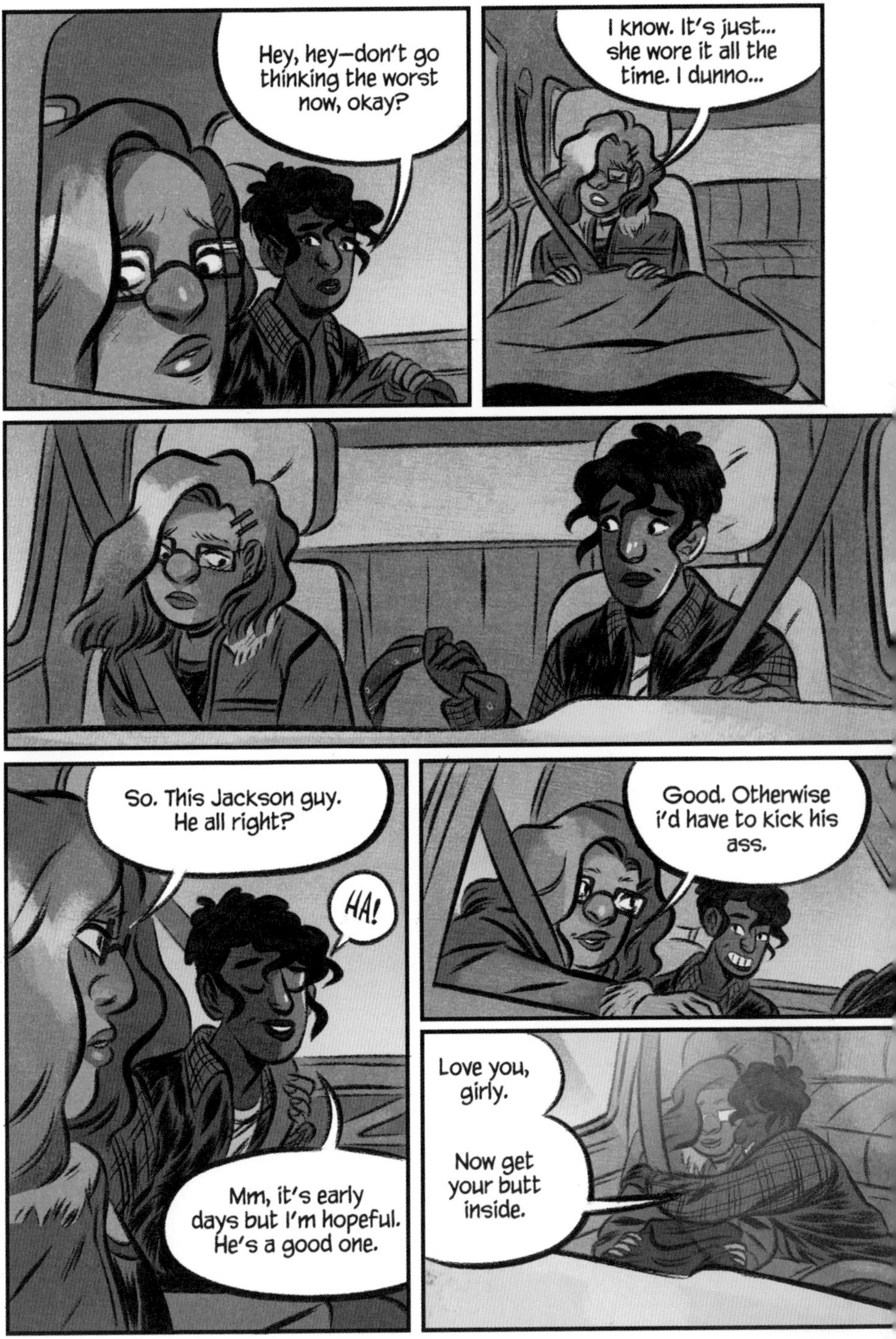
Hey, hey—don't go thinking the worst now, okay?
I know. It's just... she wore it all the time. I dunno...
So. This Jackson guy. He all right?
HA!
Mm, it's early days but I'm hopeful. He's a good one.
Good. Otherwise i'd have to kick his ass.
Love you, girly.
Now get your butt inside.

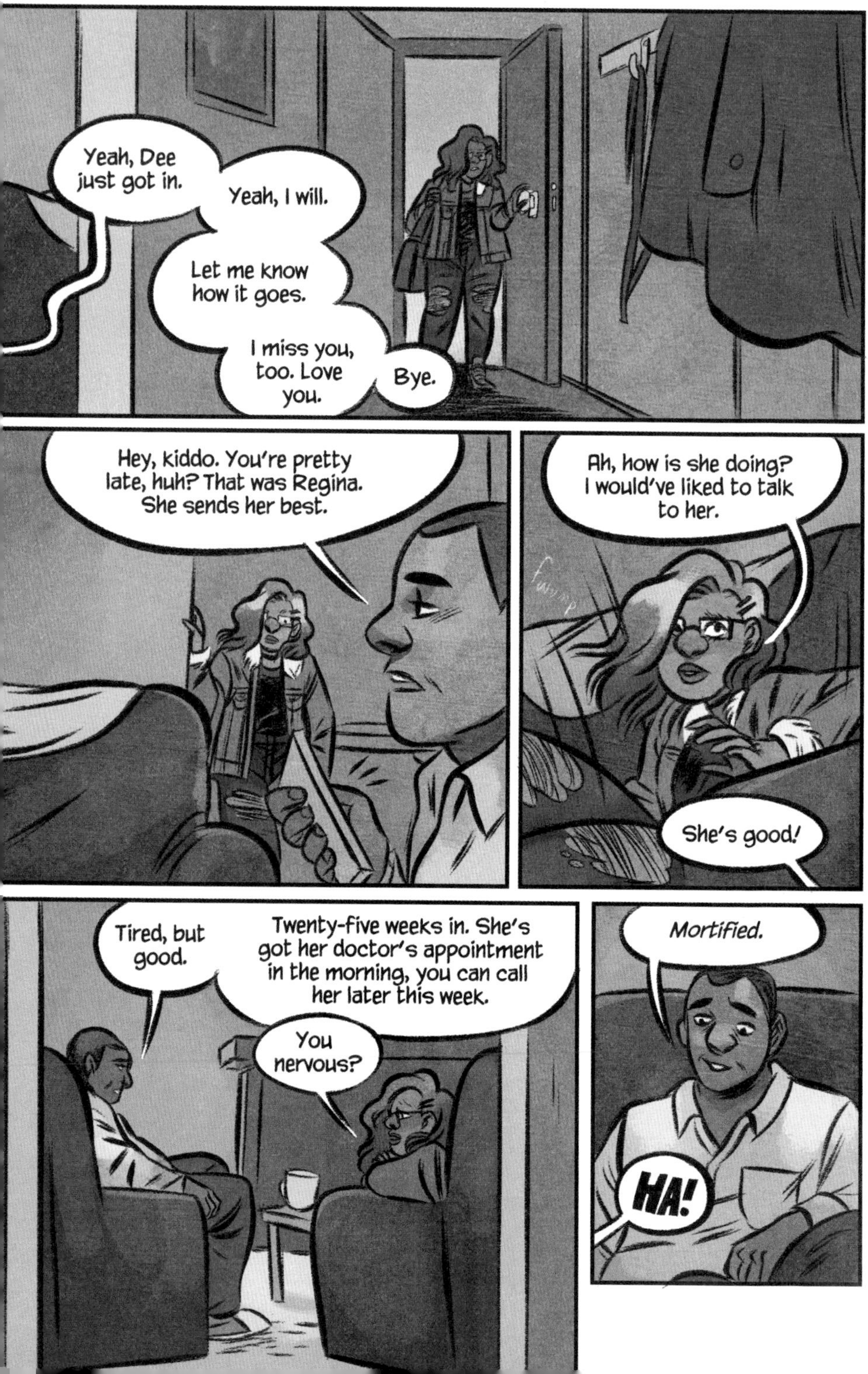

Yeah, Dee just got in.
Yeah, I will.
Let me know how it goes.
I miss you, too. Love you.
Bye.
Hey, kiddo. You're pretty late, huh? That was Regina. She sends her best.
Ah, how is she doing? I would've liked to talk to her.
She's good!
Tired, but good.
Twenty-five weeks in. She's got her doctor's appointment in the morning, you can call her later this week.
You nervous?
Mortified.
HA!

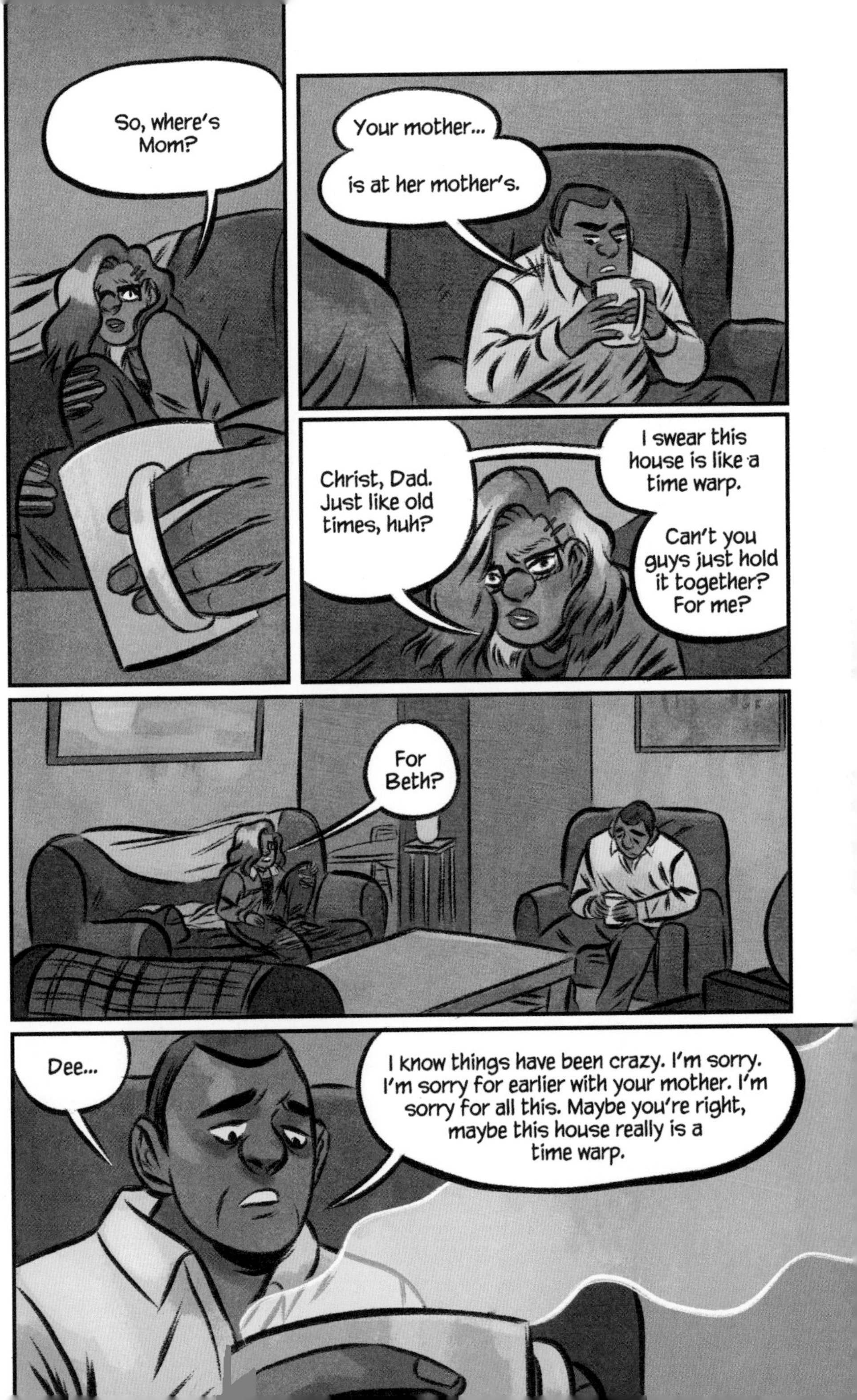
So, where's Mom?
Your mother...
is at her mother's.
I swear this house is like a time warp.
Christ, Dad. Just like old times, huh?
Can't you guys just hold it together? For me?
For Beth?
Dee...
I know things have been crazy. I'm sorry. I'm sorry for earlier with your mother. I'm sorry for all this. Maybe you're right, maybe this house really is a time warp.

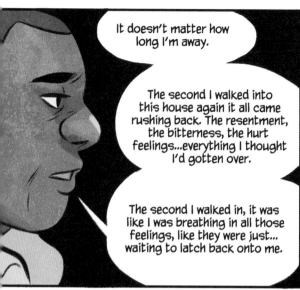

It doesn't matter how long I'm away.

The second I walked into this house again it all came rushing back. The resentment, the bitterness, the hurt feelings...everything I thought I'd gotten over.

The second I walked in, it was like I was breathing in all those feelings, like they were just... waiting to latch back onto me.

Yeah, I get that.

Like...negative energy reopening wounds.

I remember early on...when you guys first split...

I secretly hoped you would work it out. You know, get back together. Obviously, I know better now.

Aw, Dee...

No, I'm serious! You're better apart, I see that now. I mean, I've known it for years, but being back here makes it *crystal* clear.

Dad, it's okay, really.

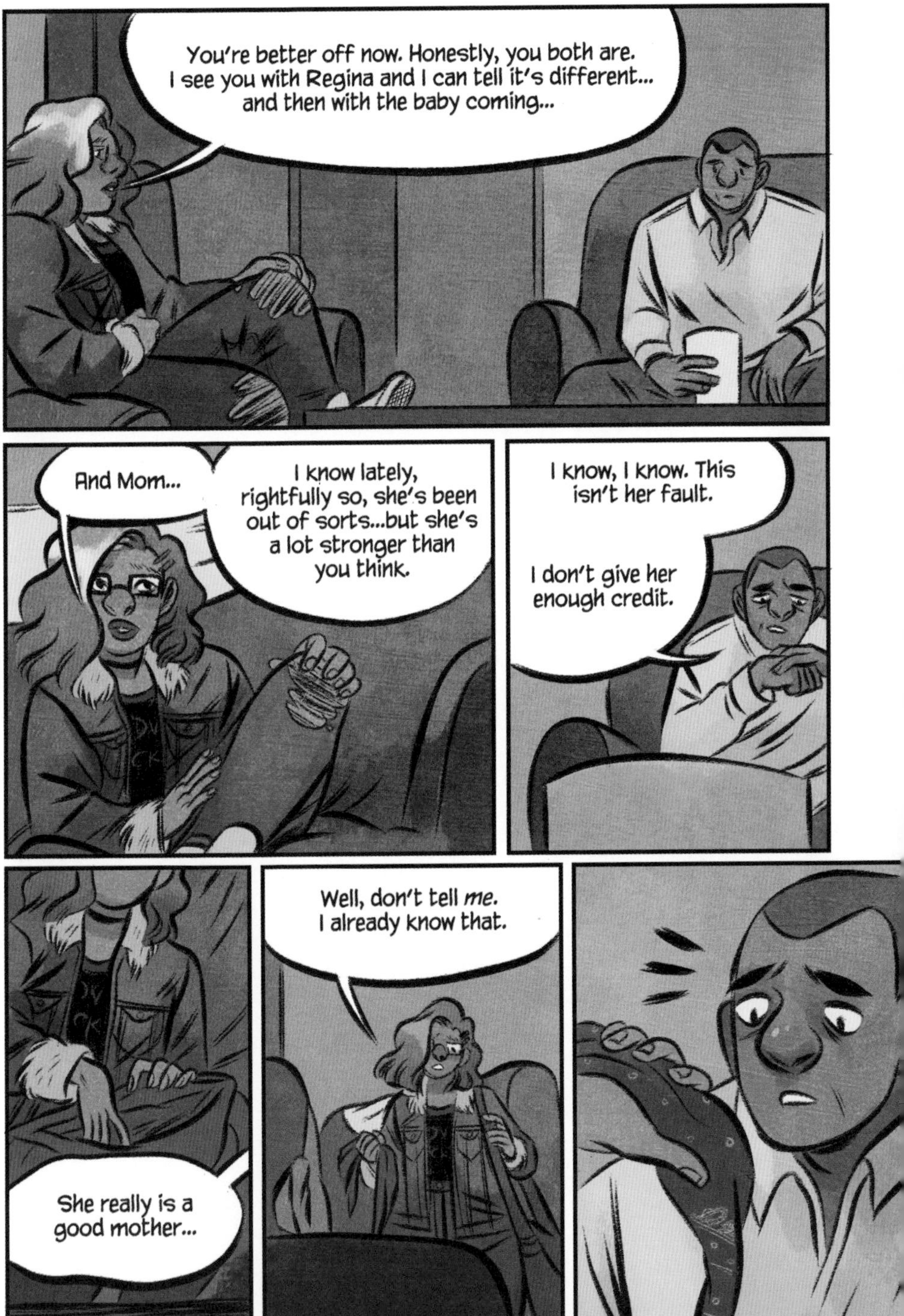
You're better off now. Honestly, you both are. I see you with Regina and I can tell it's different... and then with the baby coming...
And Mom...
I know lately, rightfully so, she's been out of sorts...but she's a lot stronger than you think.
I know, I know. This isn't her fault.
I don't give her enough credit.
She really is a good mother...
Well, don't tell *me*. I already know that.

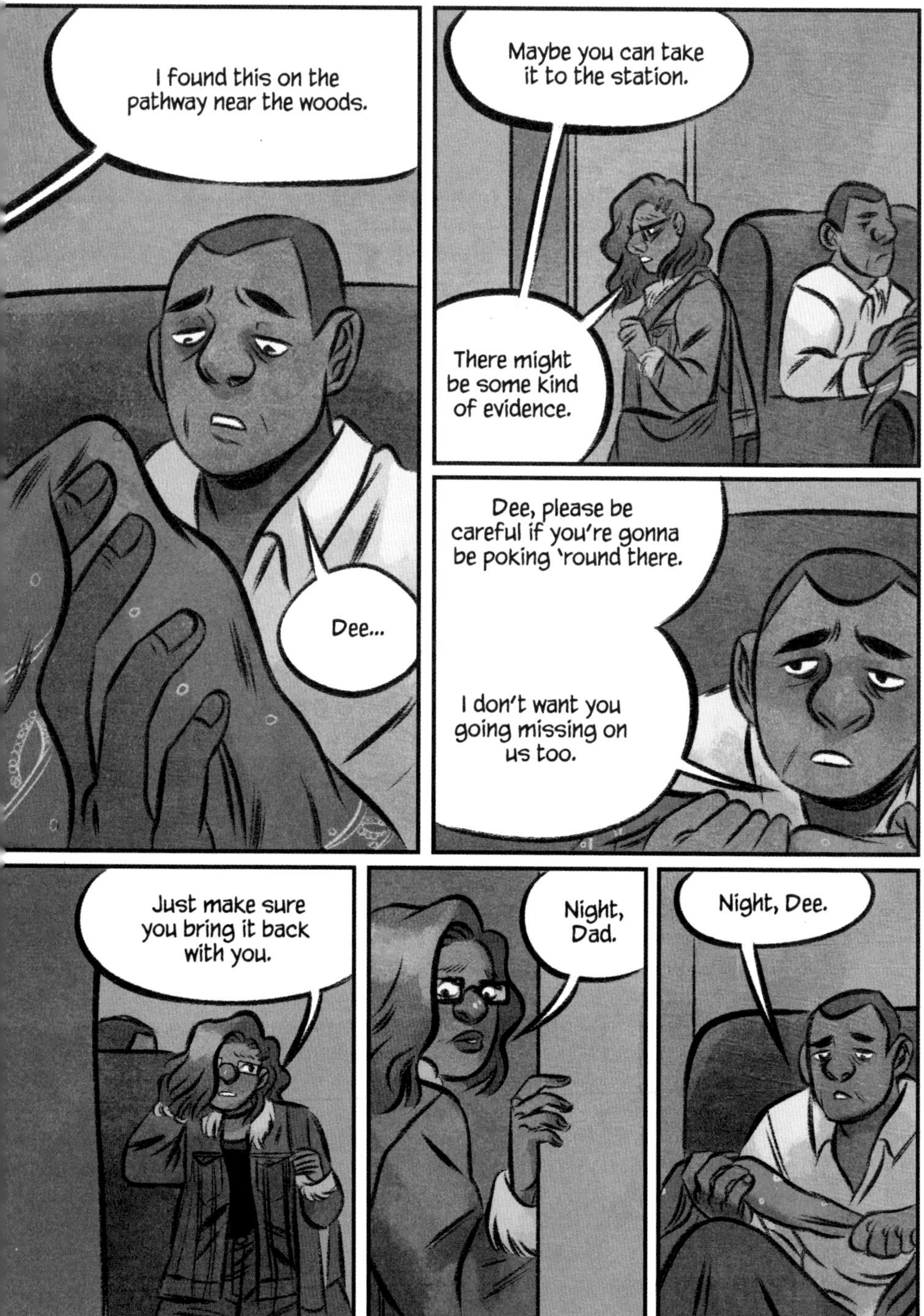
I found this on the pathway near the woods.
Dee...
Maybe you can take it to the station.
There might be some kind of evidence.
Dee, please be careful if you're gonna be poking 'round there.
I don't want you going missing on us too.
Just make sure you bring it back with you.
Night, Dad.
Night, Dee.

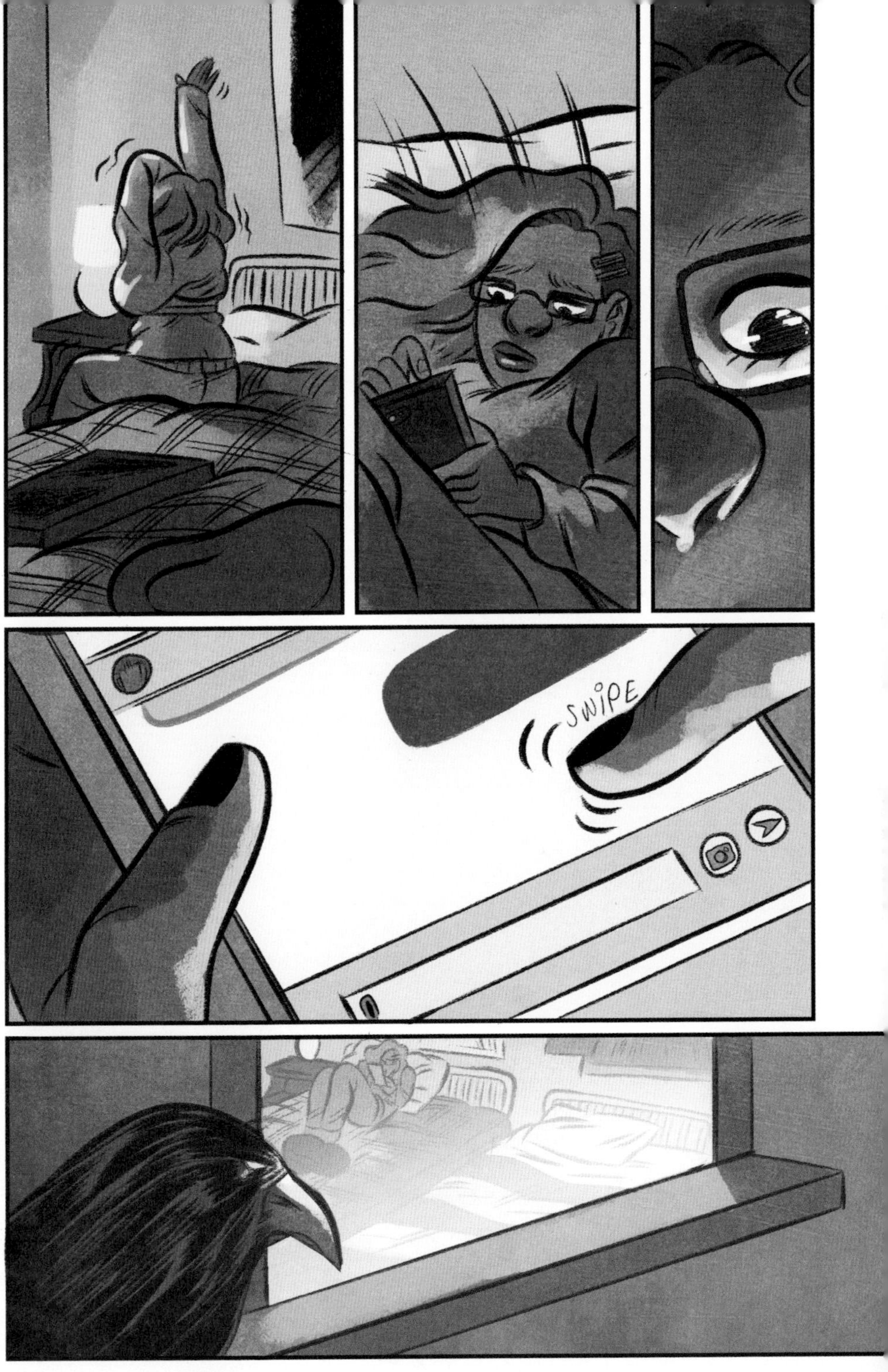
SWIPE

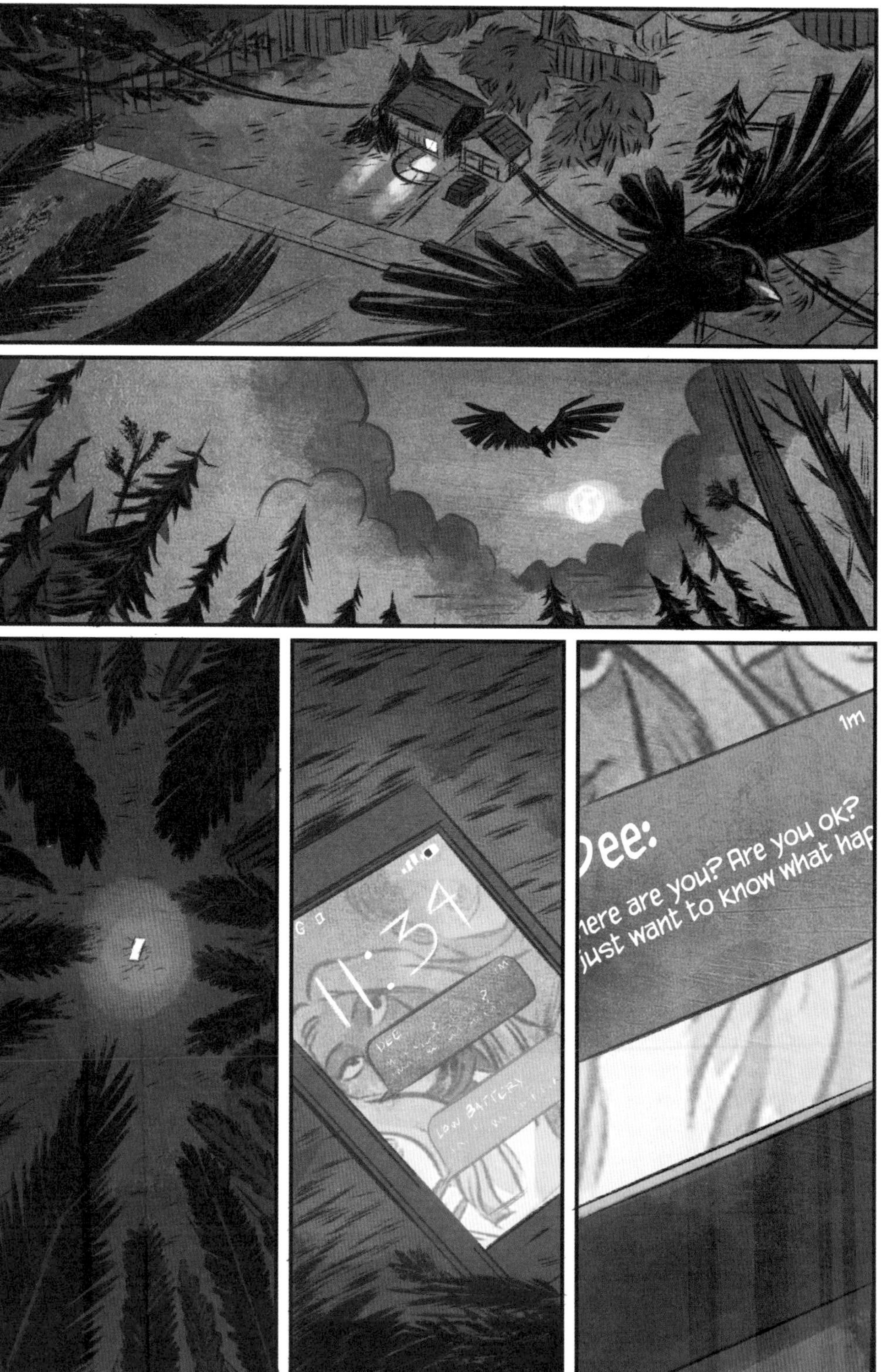
11:34
DEE
LOW BATTERY
1m
Dee:
here are you? Are you ok?
just want to know what hap

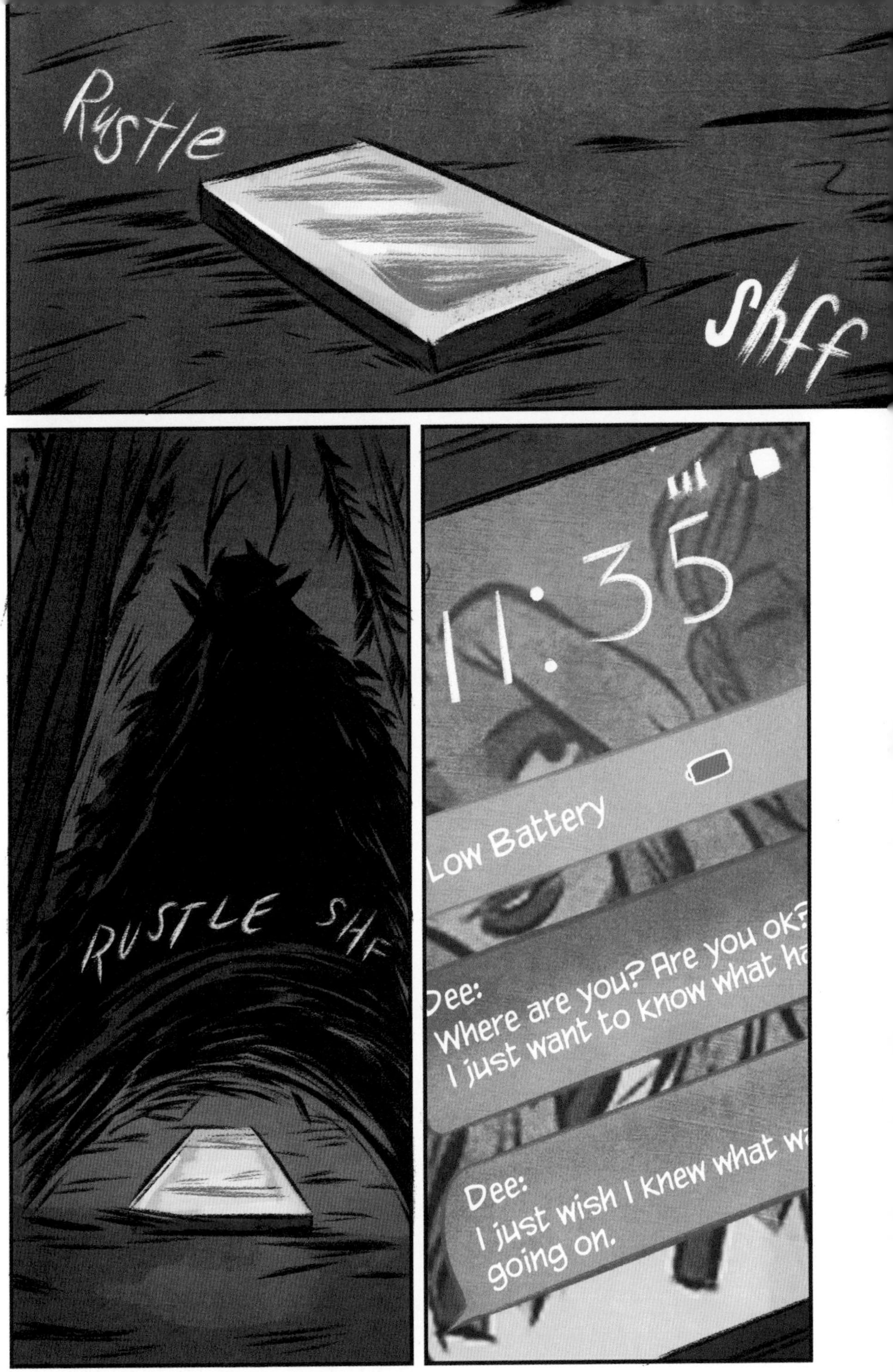
Rustle
shff
RUSTLE SHF
11:35
Low Battery
Dee:
Where are you? Are you ok?
I just want to know what ha
Dee:
I just wish I knew what wa
going on.

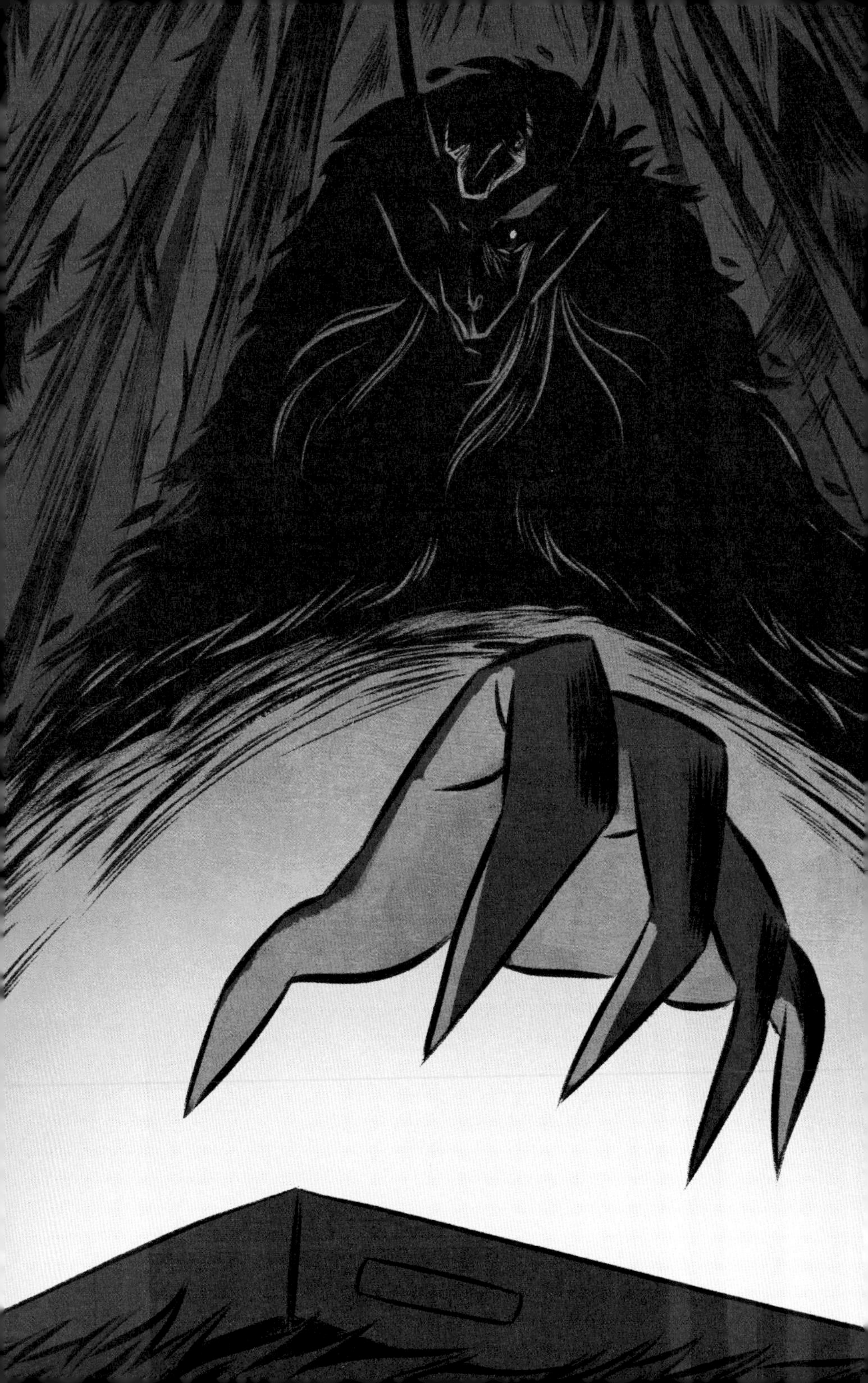

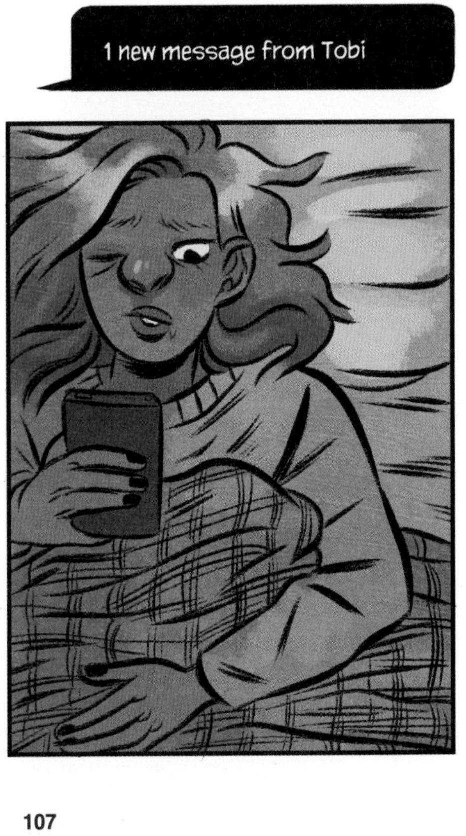
1 new message from Tobi

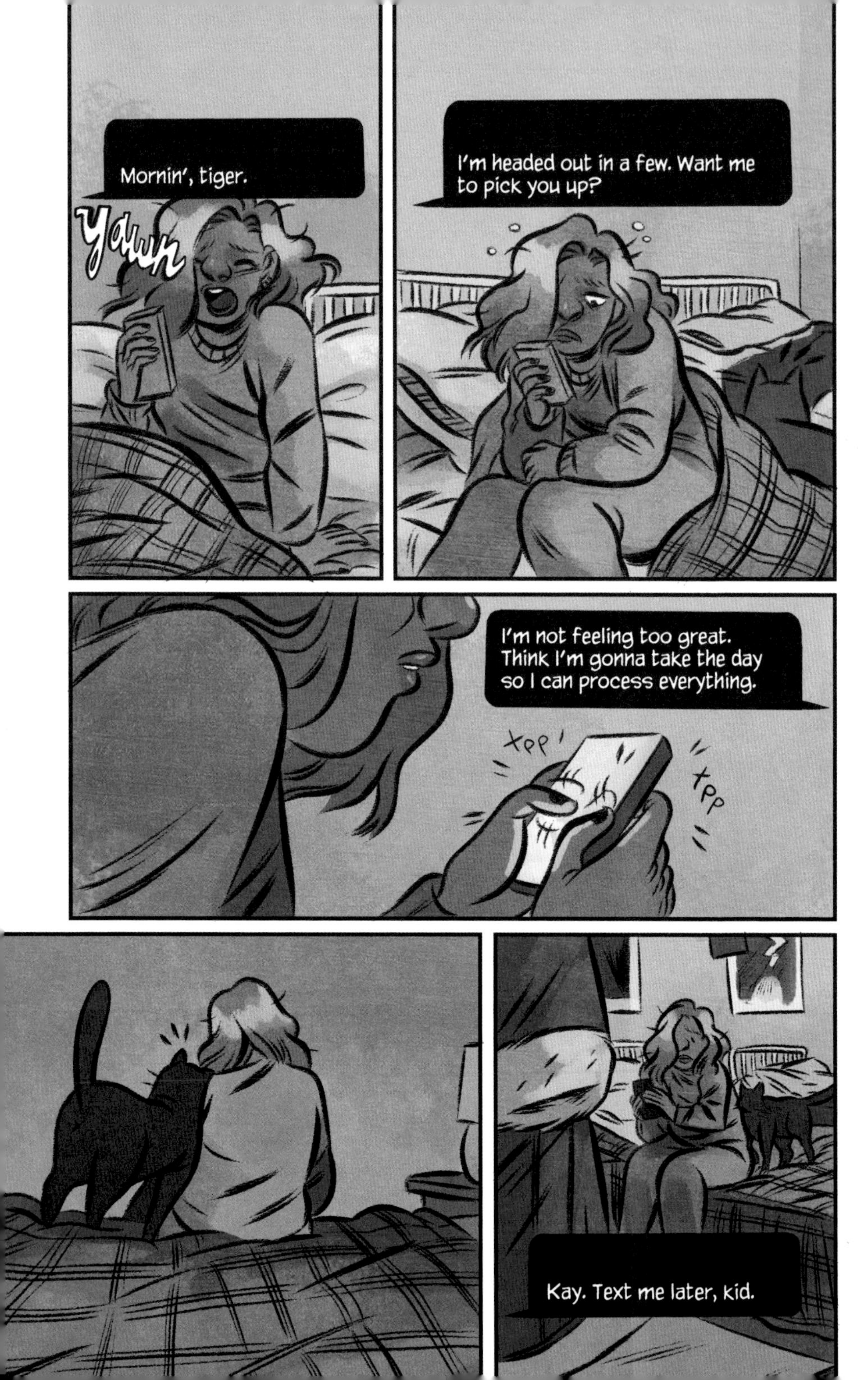
Mornin', tiger.
yawn
I'm headed out in a few. Want me to pick you up?
I'm not feeling too great. Think I'm gonna take the day so I can process everything.
tpp
tpp
Kay. Text me later, kid.

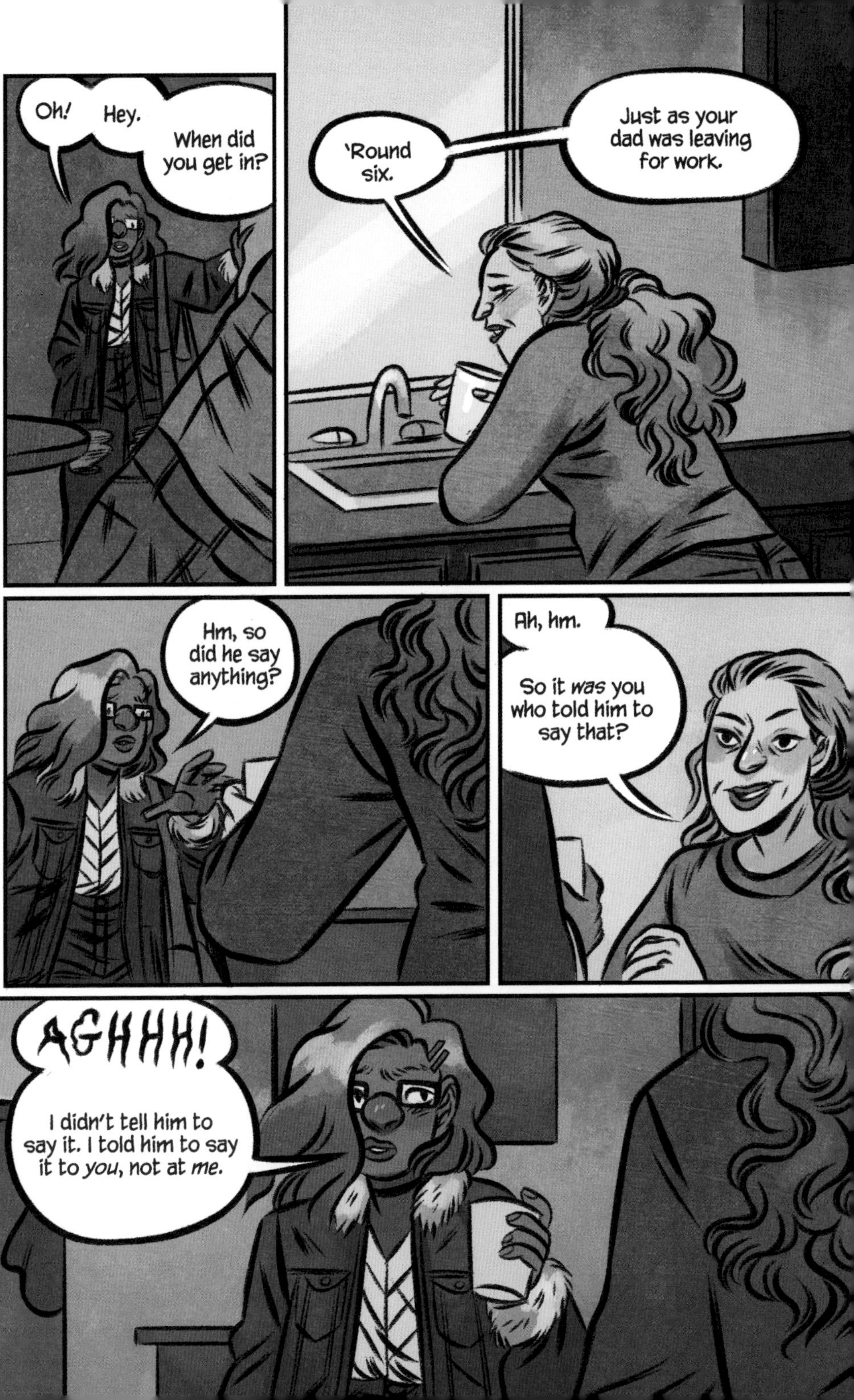
Oh!
Hey.
When did you get in?
'Round six.
Just as your dad was leaving for work.
Hm, so did he say anything?
Ah, hm.
So it *was* you who told him to say that?
AGHHH!
I didn't tell him to say it. I told him to say it to *you*, not at *me*.

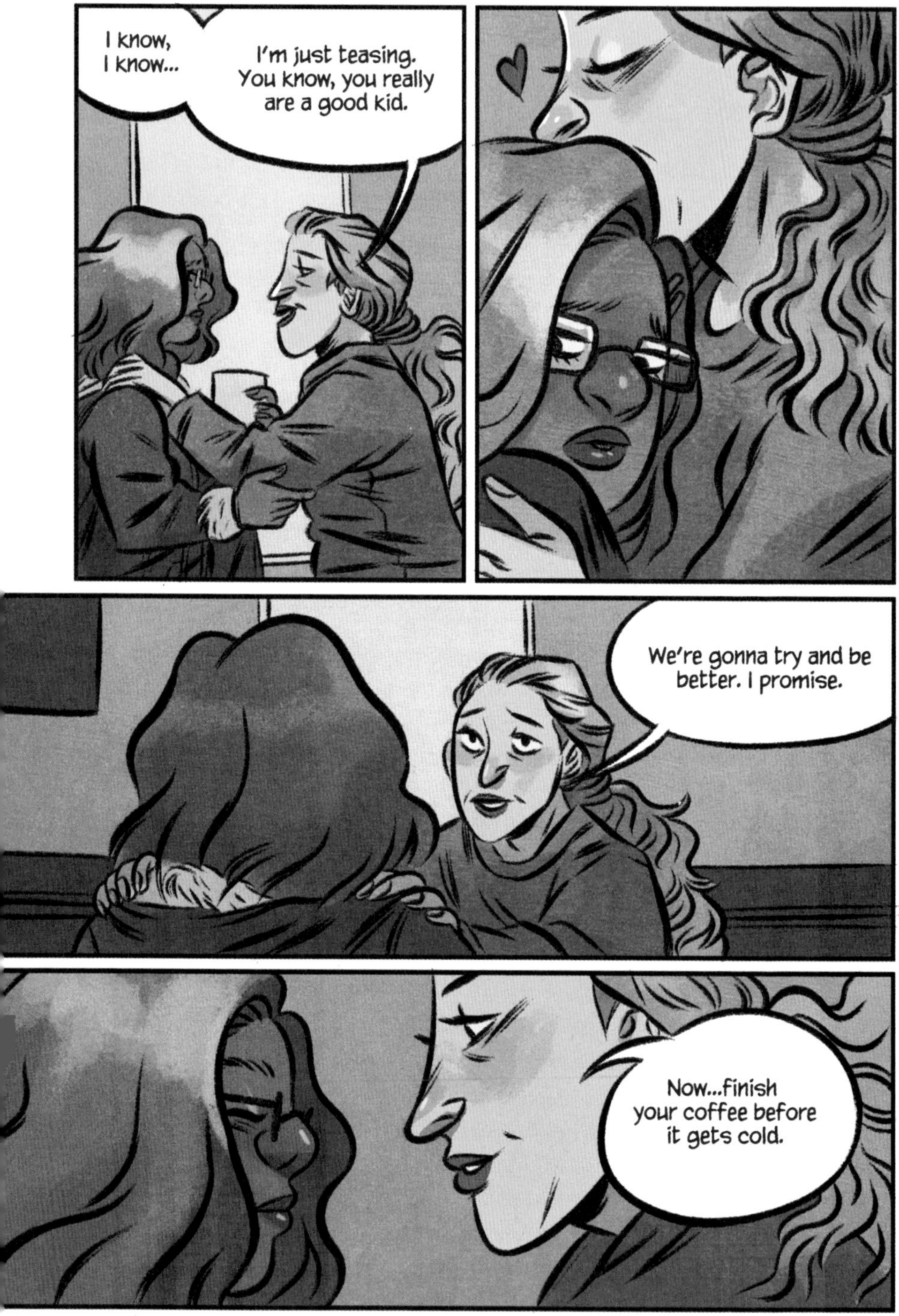
I know, I know...
I'm just teasing. You know, you really are a good kid.
We're gonna try and be better. I promise.
Now...finish your coffee before it gets cold.

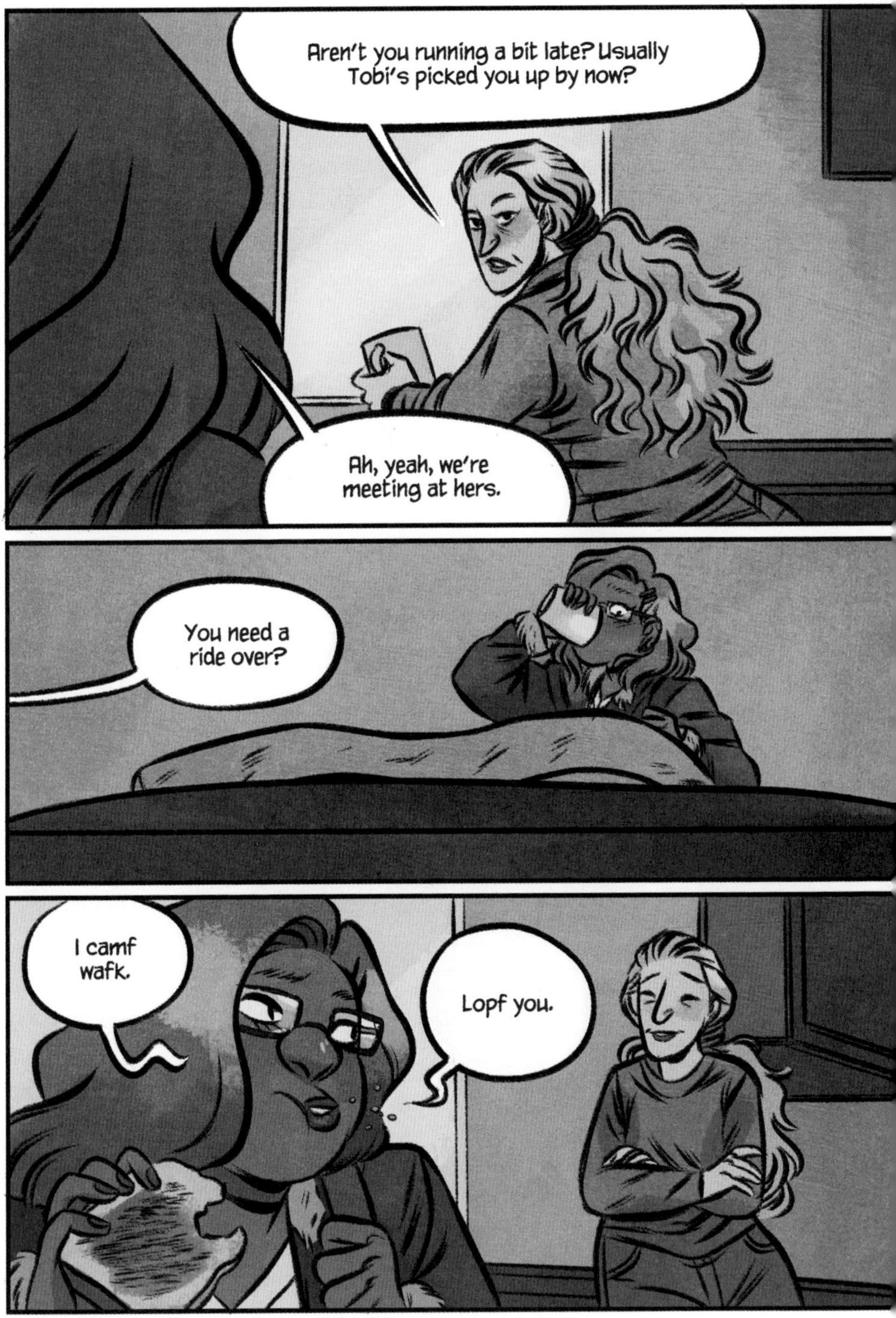
Aren't you running a bit late? Usually Tobi's picked you up by now?
Ah, yeah, we're meeting at hers.
You need a ride over?
I camf wafk.
Lopf you.

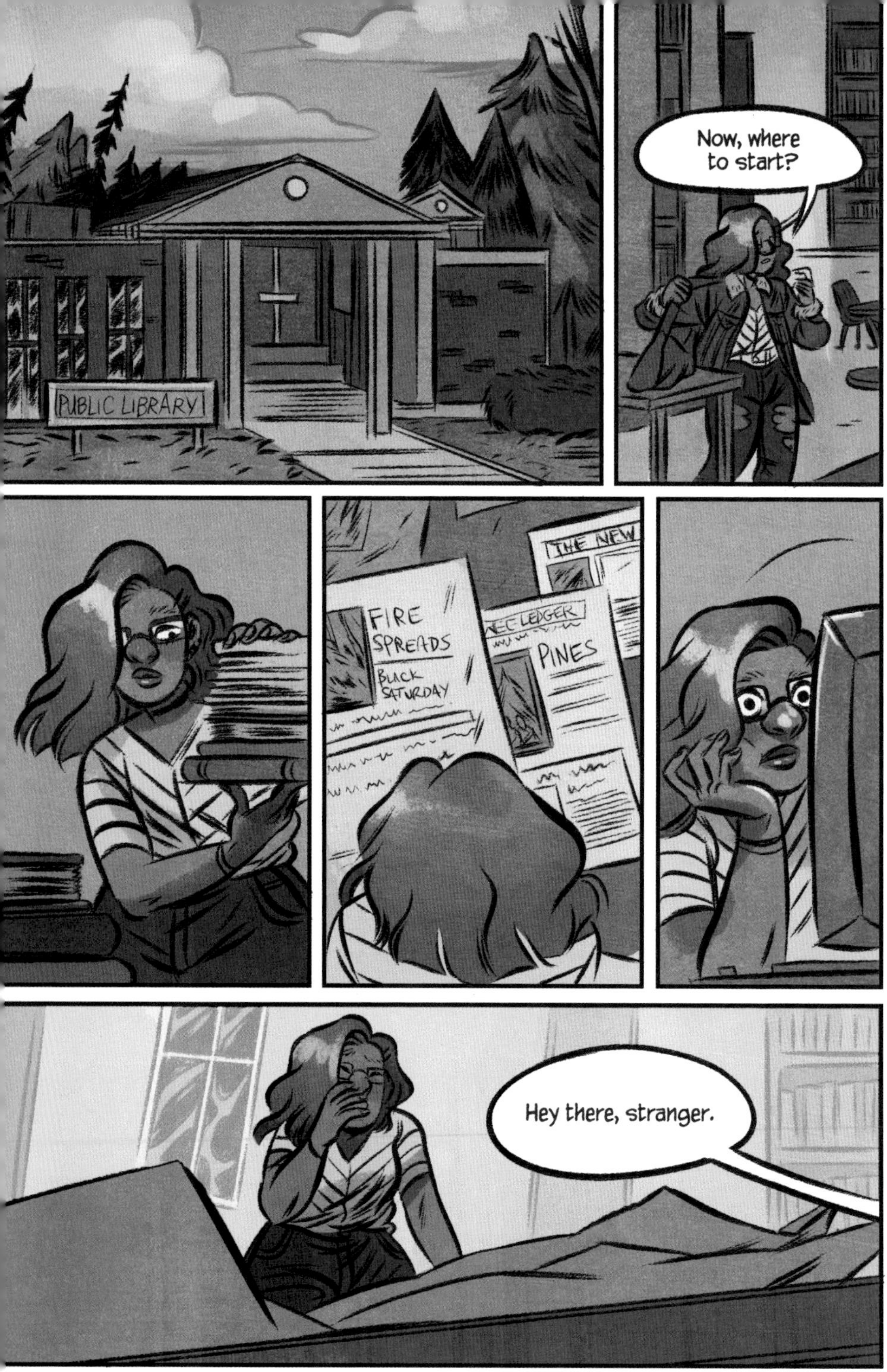
PUBLIC LIBRARY
Now, where to start?
THE NEW
FIRE SPREADS
BLACK SATURDAY
LEDGER
PINES
Hey there, stranger.

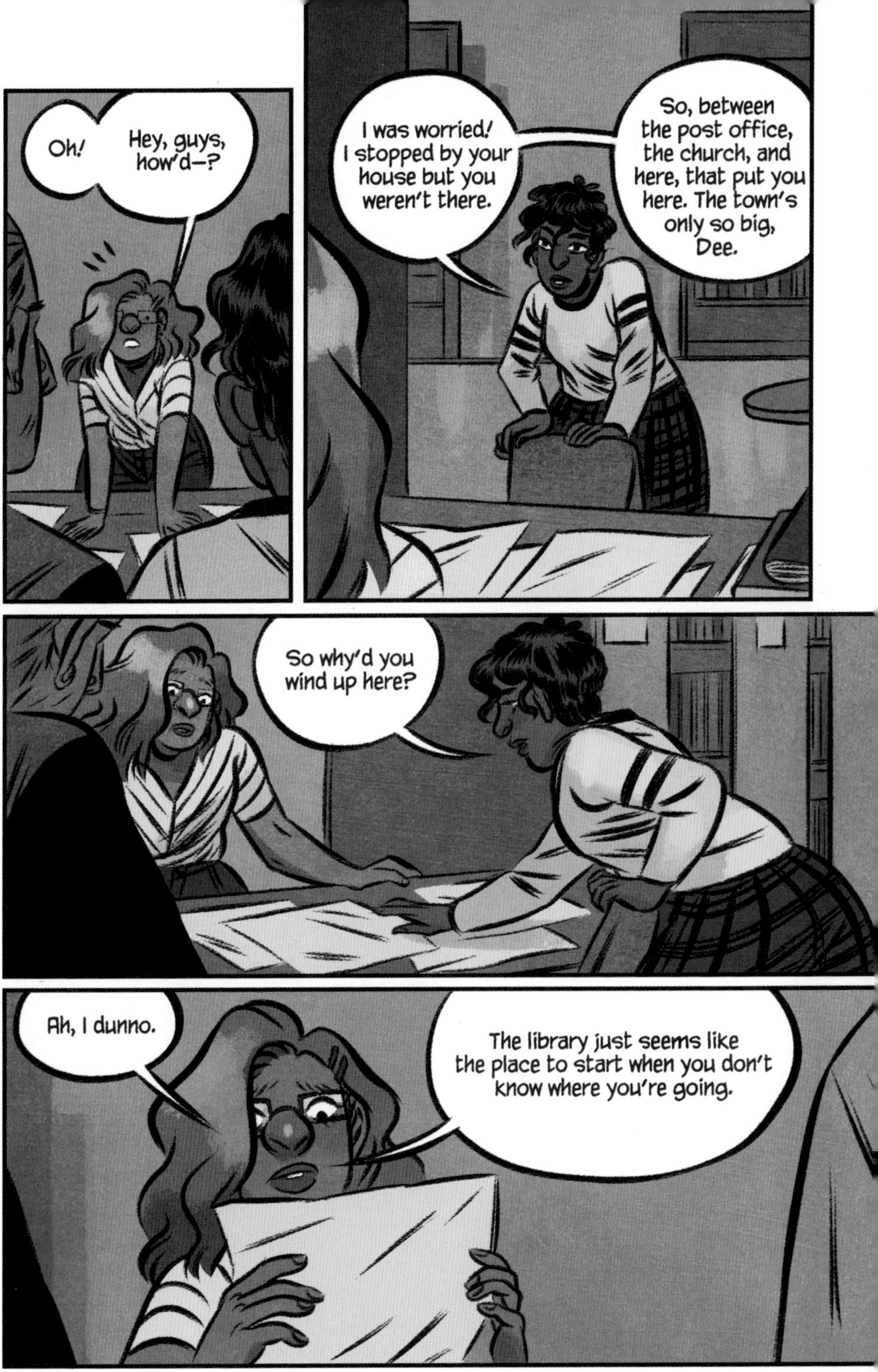
Oh!
Hey, guys, how'd—?
I was worried! I stopped by your house but you weren't there.
So, between the post office, the church, and here, that put you here. The town's only so big, Dee.
So why'd you wind up here?
Ah, I dunno.
The library just seems like the place to start when you don't know where you're going.

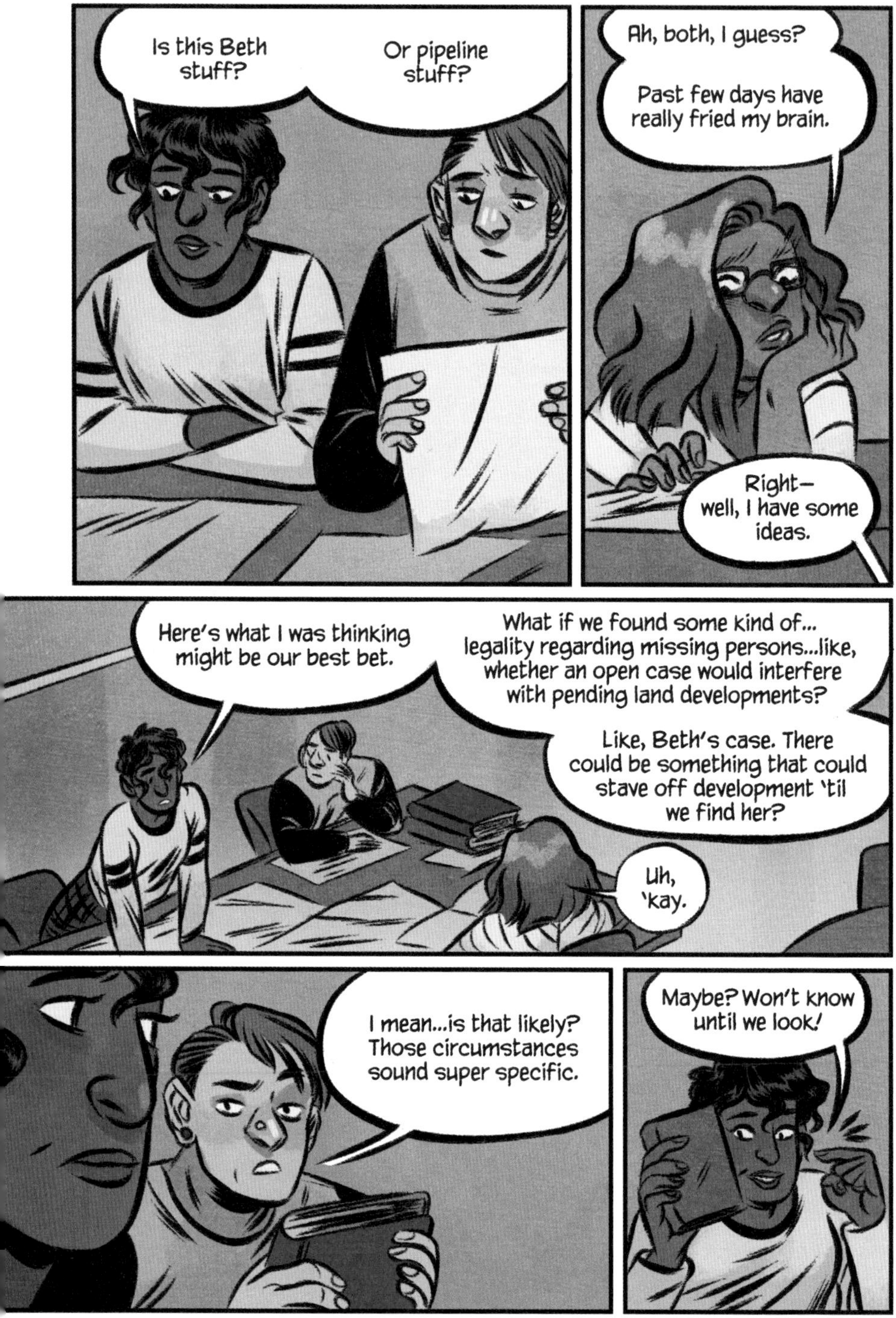

Is this Beth stuff?
Or pipeline stuff?
Ah, both, I guess?
Past few days have really fried my brain.
Right— well, I have some ideas.
Here's what I was thinking might be our best bet.
What if we found some kind of... legality regarding missing persons...like, whether an open case would interfere with pending land developments?
Like, Beth's case. There could be something that could stave off development 'til we find her?
Uh, 'kay.
I mean...is that likely? Those circumstances sound super specific.
Maybe? Won't know until we look!

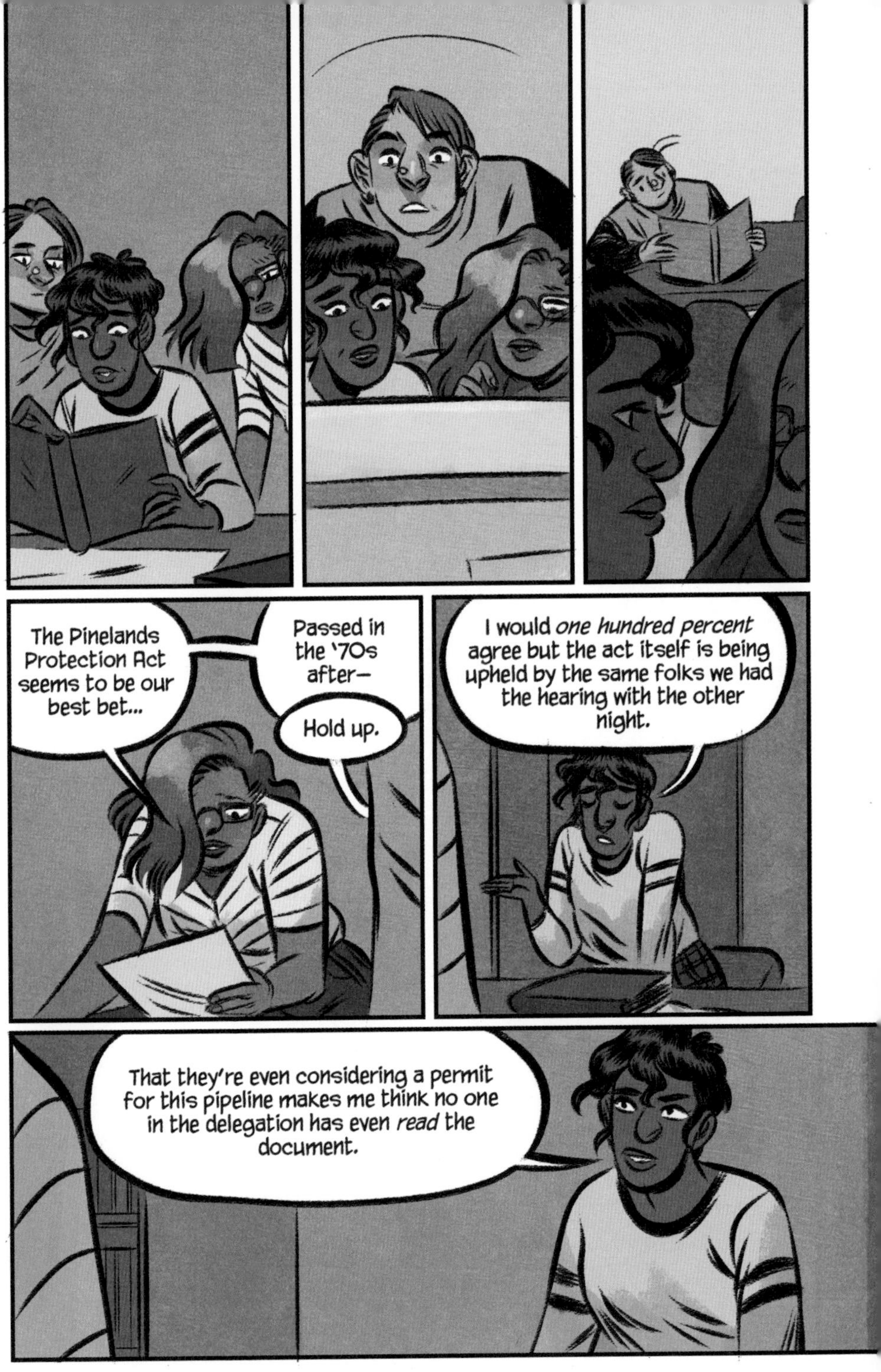

The Pinelands Protection Act seems to be our best bet...
Passed in the '70s after—
Hold up.
I would *one hundred percent* agree but the act itself is being upheld by the same folks we had the hearing with the other night.
That they're even considering a permit for this pipeline makes me think no one in the delegation has even *read* the document.

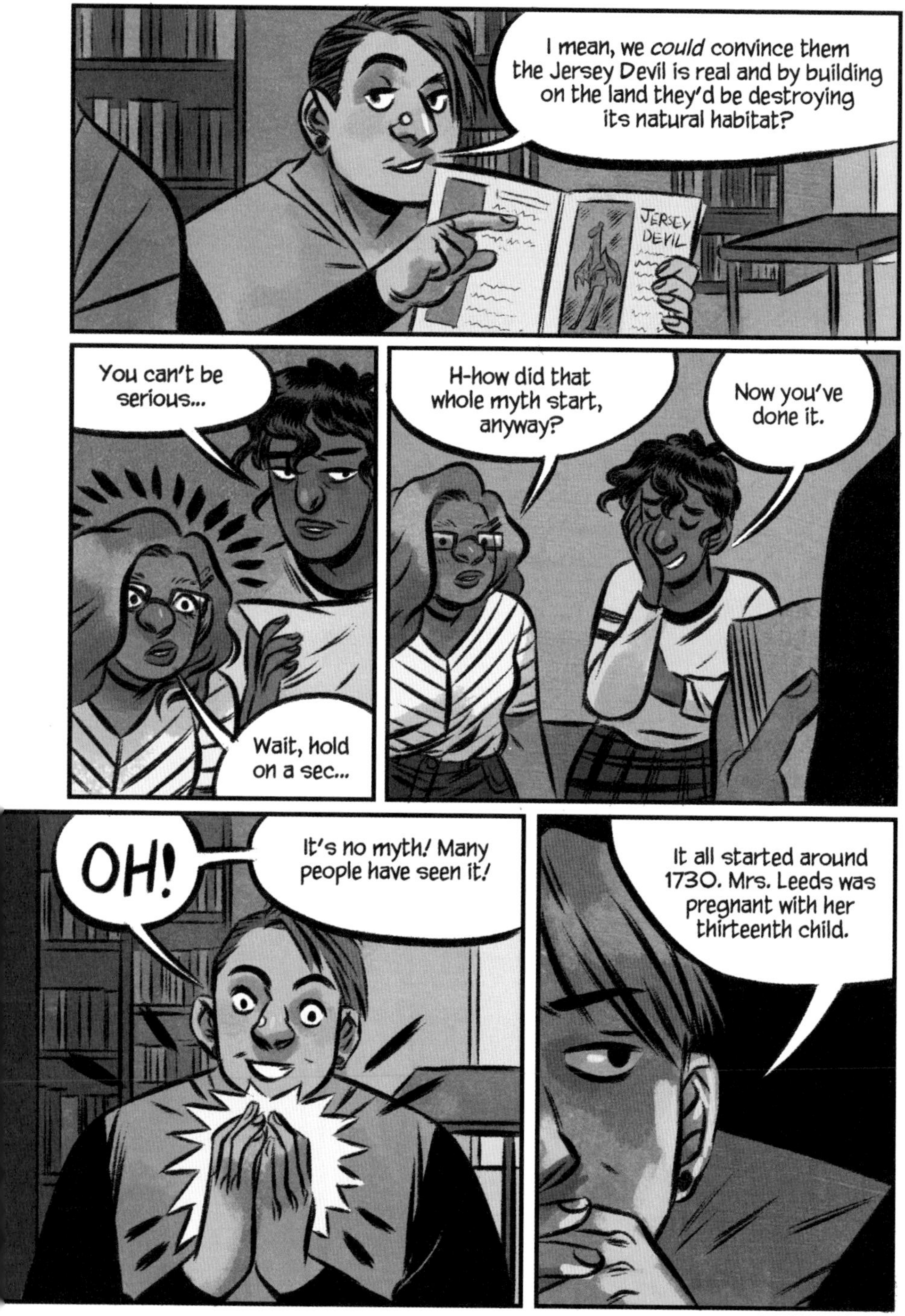
I mean, we *could* convince them the Jersey Devil is real and by building on the land they'd be destroying its natural habitat?
JERSEY DEVIL
You can't be serious...
Wait, hold on a sec...
H-how did that whole myth start, anyway?
Now you've done it.
OH!
It's no myth! Many people have seen it!
It all started around 1730. Mrs. Leeds was pregnant with her thirteenth child.

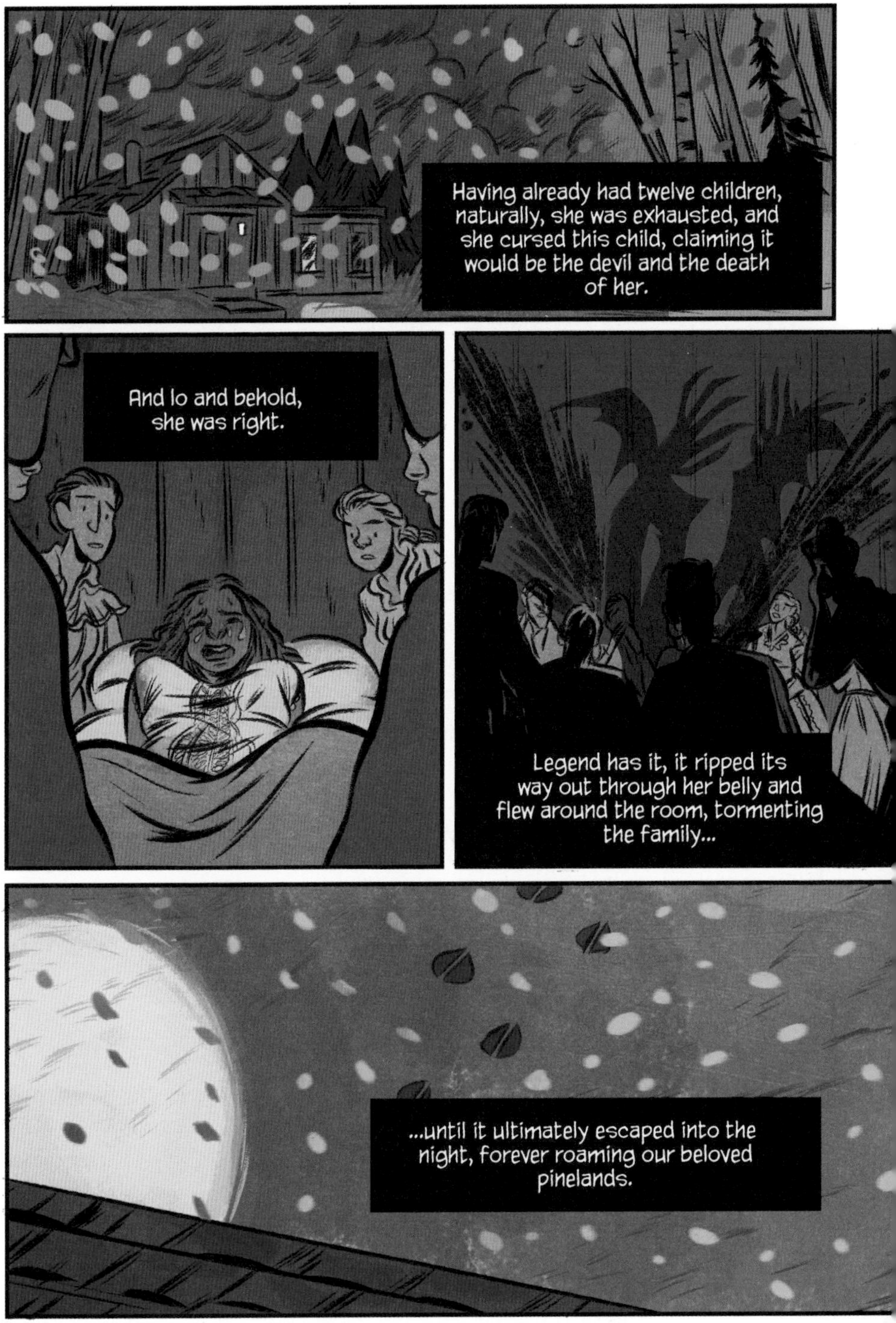
Having already had twelve children, naturally, she was exhausted, and she cursed this child, claiming it would be the devil and the death of her.
And lo and behold, she was right.
Legend has it, it ripped its way out through her belly and flew around the room, tormenting the family...
...until it ultimately escaped into the night, forever roaming our beloved pinelands.

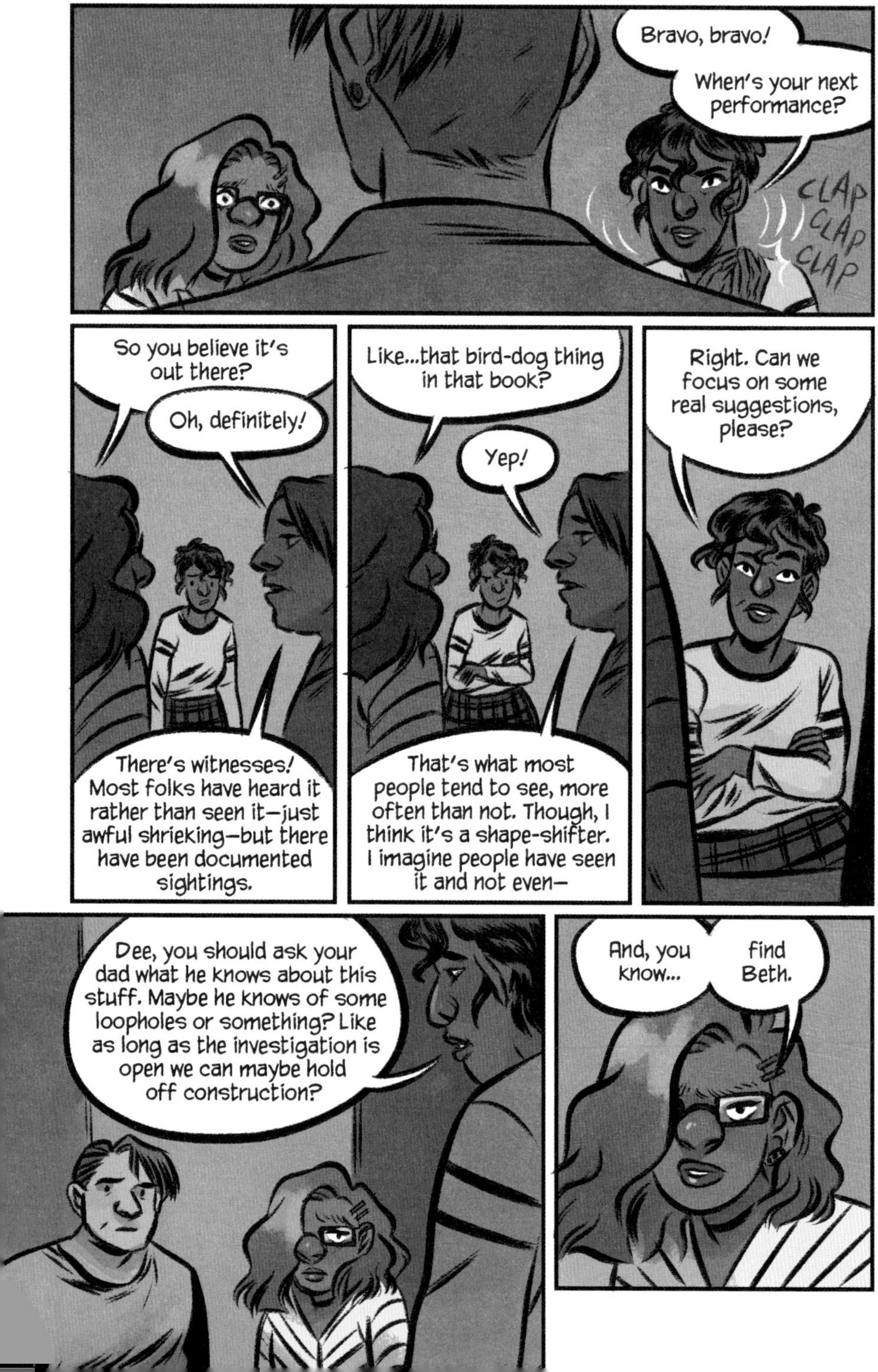
Bravo, bravo!
When's your next performance?
CLAP CLAP CLAP
So you believe it's out there?
Oh, definitely!
There's witnesses! Most folks have heard it rather than seen it—just awful shrieking—but there have been documented sightings.
Like...that bird-dog thing in that book?
Yep!
That's what most people tend to see, more often than not. Though, I think it's a shape-shifter. I imagine people have seen it and not even—
Right. Can we focus on some real suggestions, please?
Dee, you should ask your dad what he knows about this stuff. Maybe he knows of some loopholes or something? Like as long as the investigation is open we can maybe hold off construction?
And, you know...
find Beth.

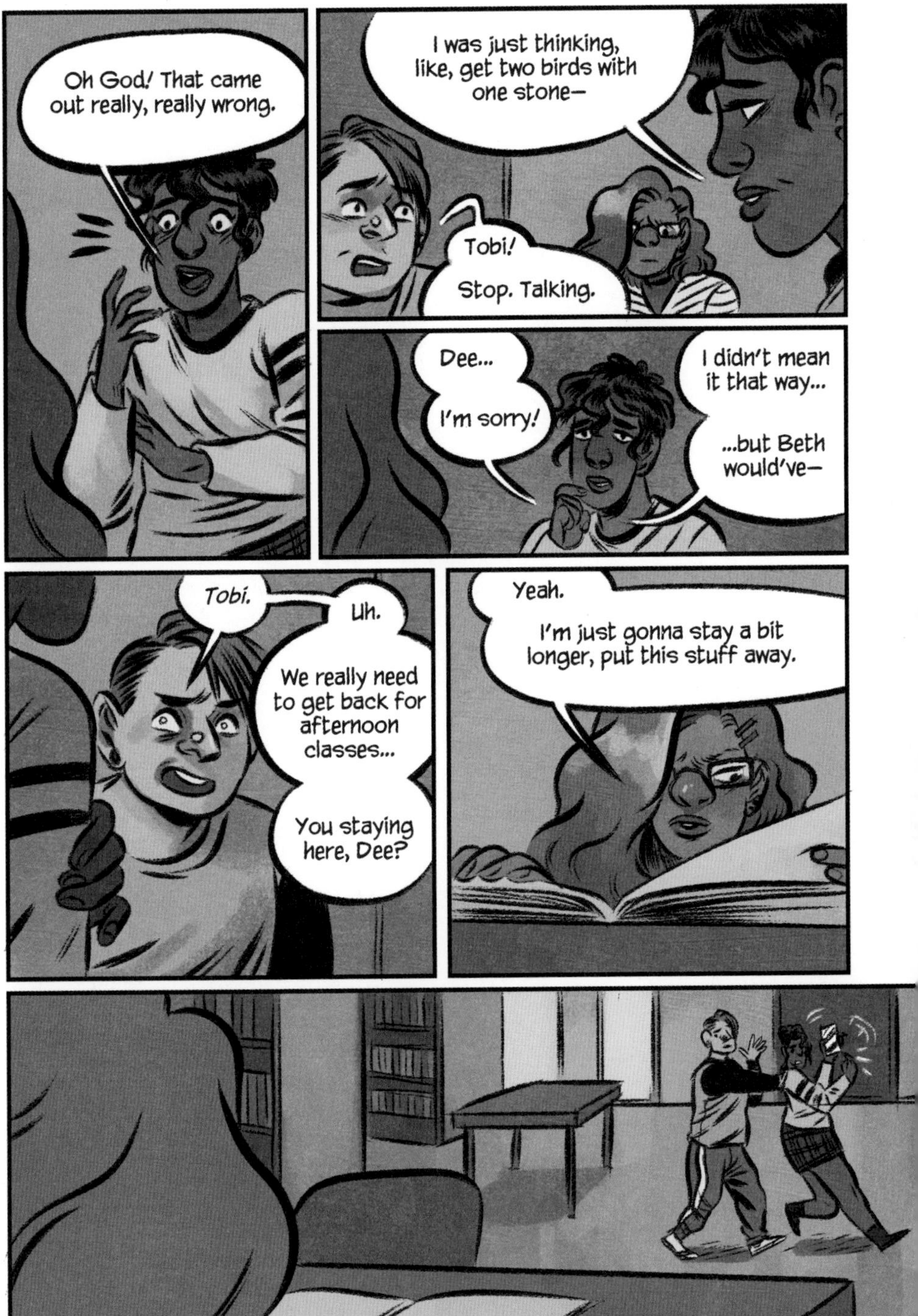
Oh God! That came out really, really wrong.
I was just thinking, like, get two birds with one stone—
Tobi!
Stop. Talking.
Dee...
I'm sorry!
I didn't mean it that way...
...but Beth would've—
Tobi.
Uh.
We really need to get back for afternoon classes...
You staying here, Dee?
Yeah.
I'm just gonna stay a bit longer, put this stuff away.

I'll call you later if I can ever manage to get my foot outta my mouth.

DEVIL

FIRE CLEAN UP

Legend has it that Mrs. Leeds gave birth to her thirteenth child. She cursed it and it was born a devil.

It escaped into the night and is said to inhabit the pinelands and terrorize locals.

Various sightings over the ... made believers of even

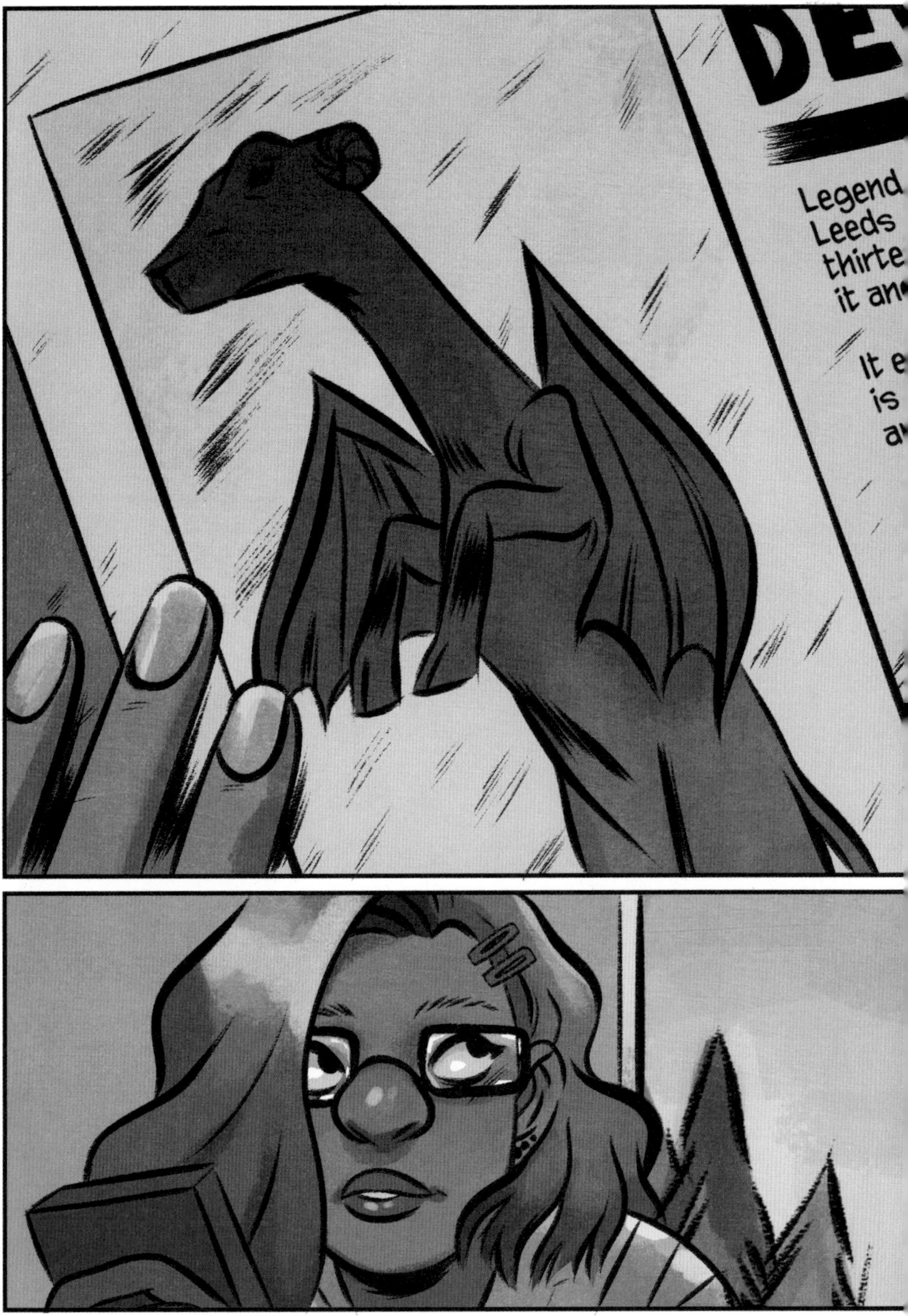
Legend
Leeds
thirte
it an
It e
is

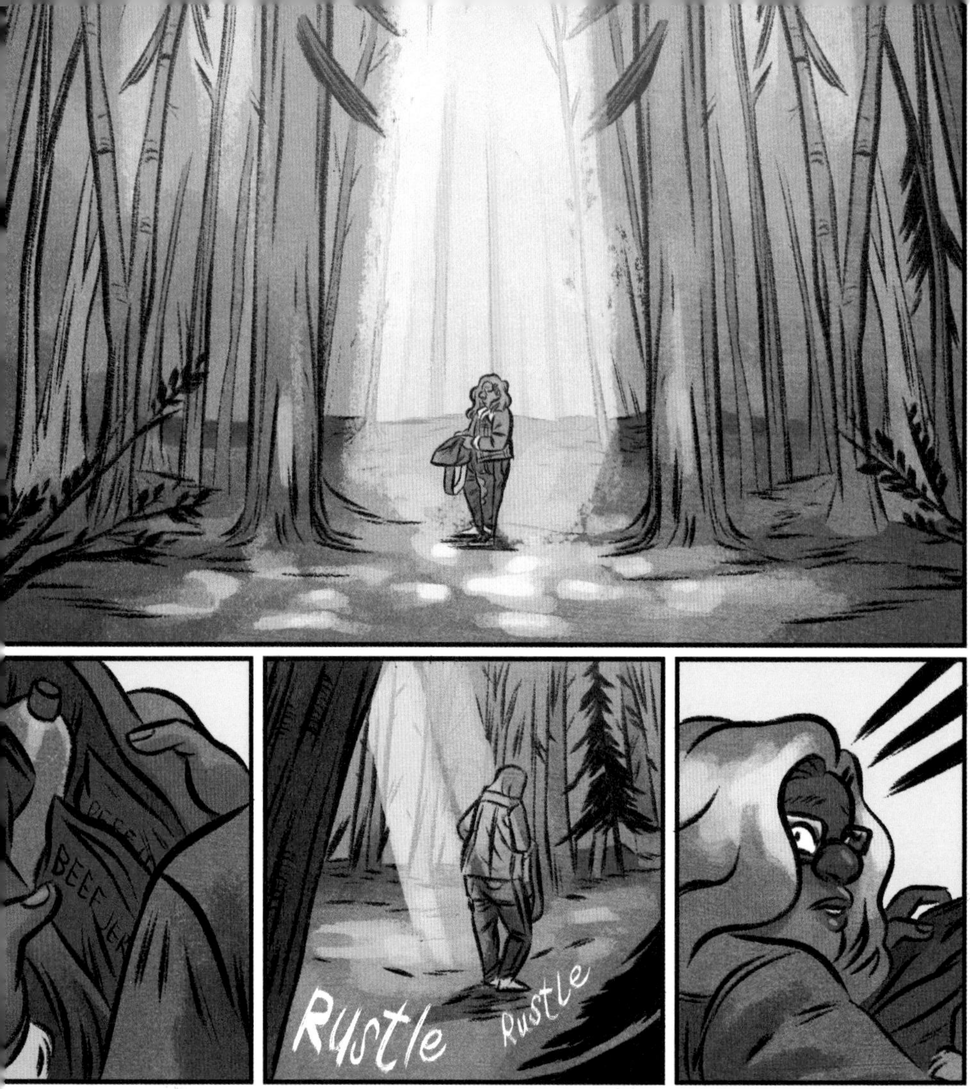
BEEF JER
Rustle
Rustle
WHOOSH

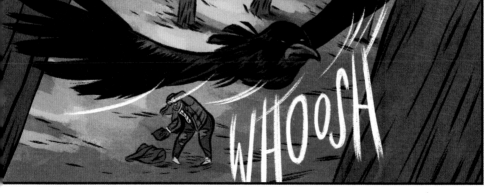

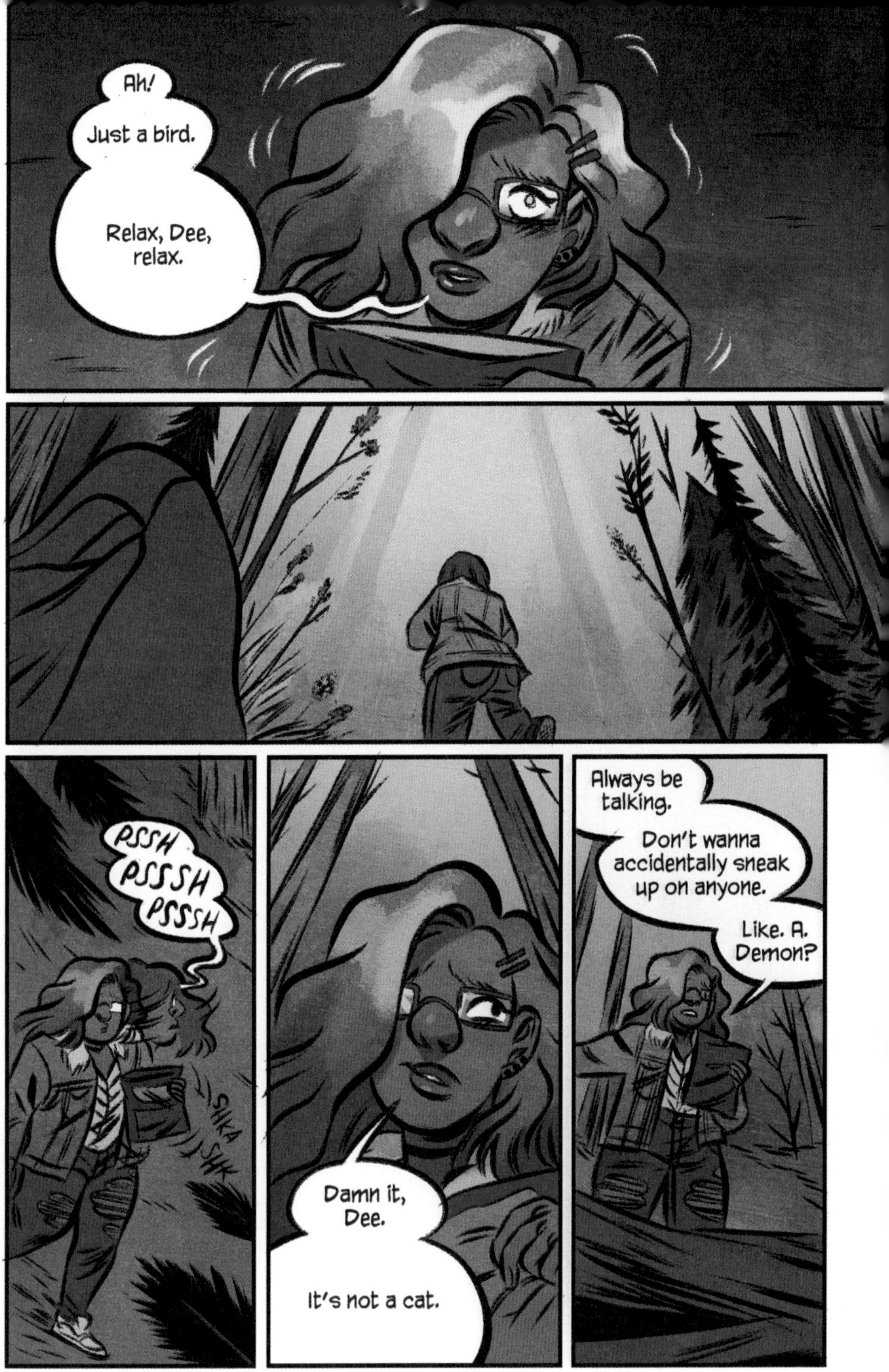
Ah!
Just a bird.
Relax, Dee, relax.
PSSH PSSSH PSSSH
SHKA SHK
Damn it, Dee.
It's not a cat.
Always be talking.
Don't wanna accidentally sneak up on anyone.
Like. A. Demon?

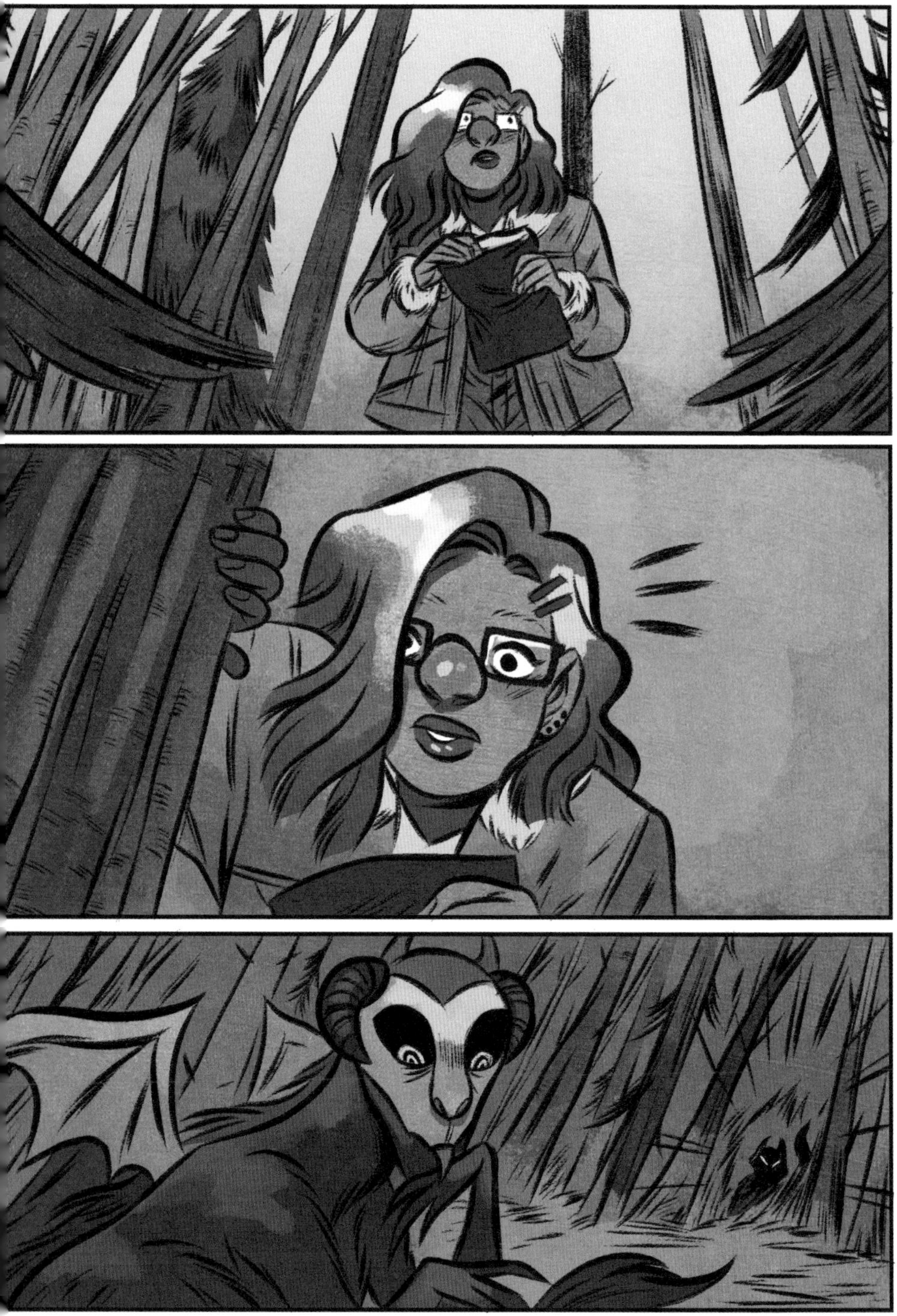

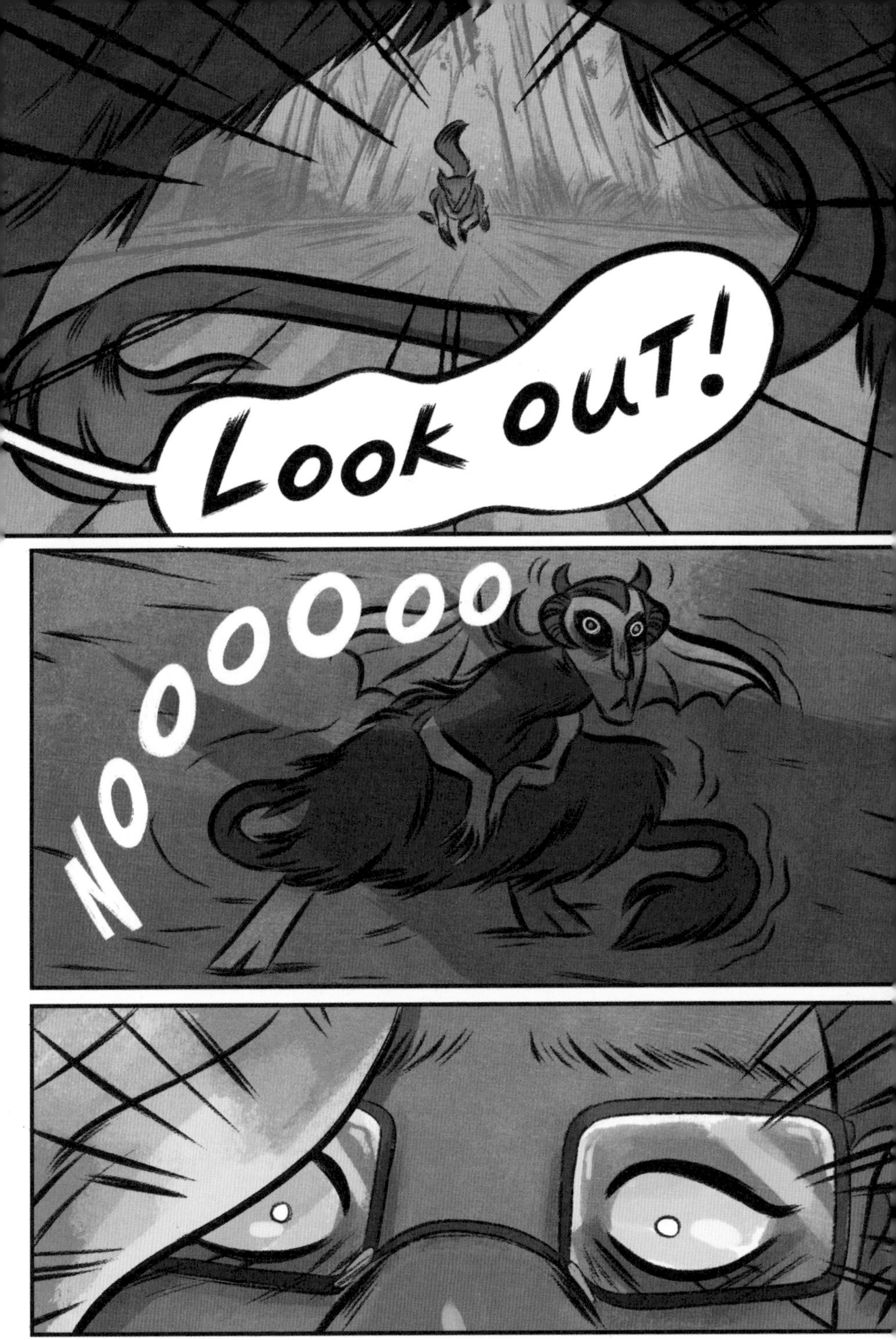
Look out!
NOOOOOO

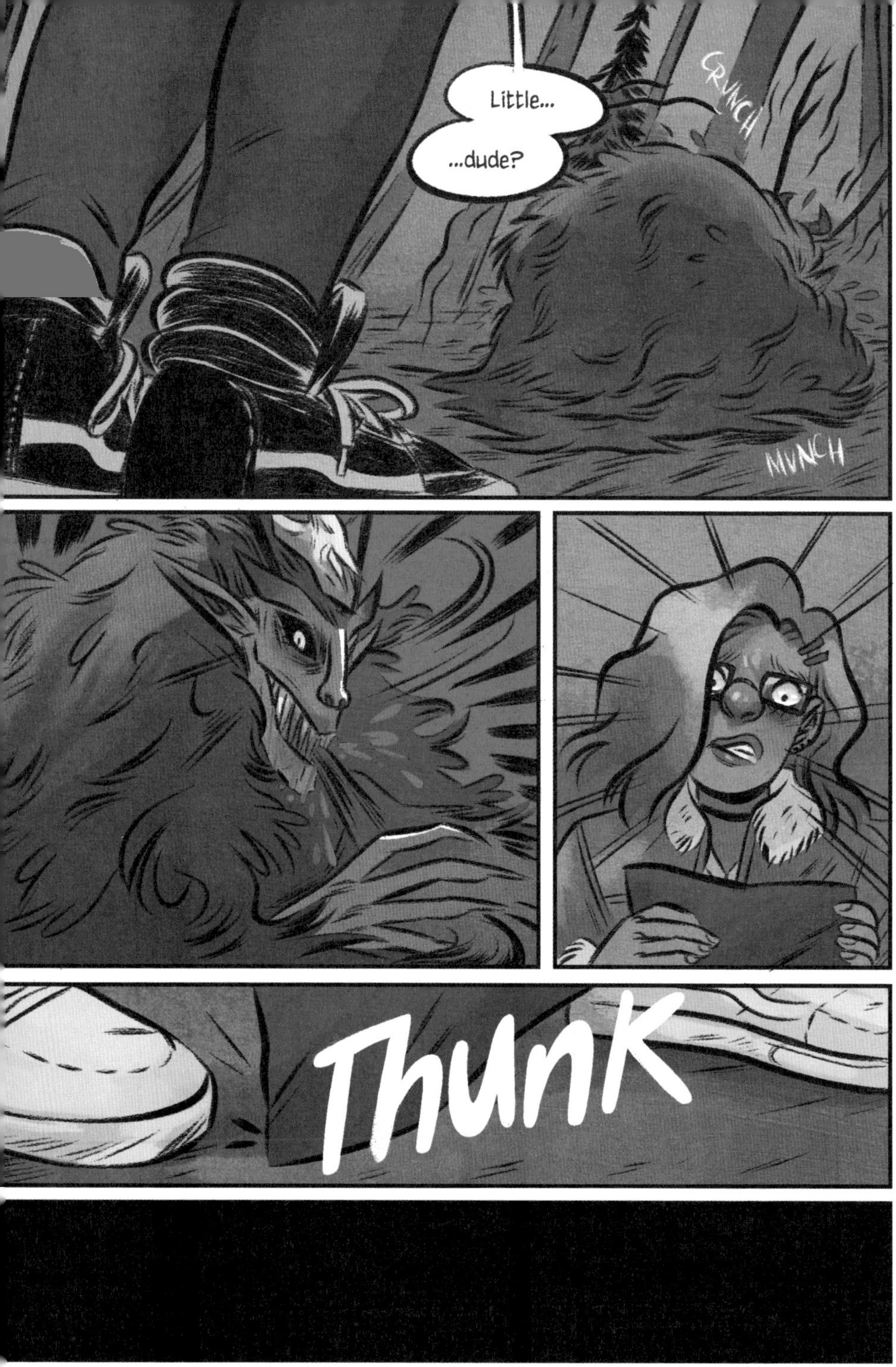
Little...
...dude?
CRUNCH
MUNCH
Thunk

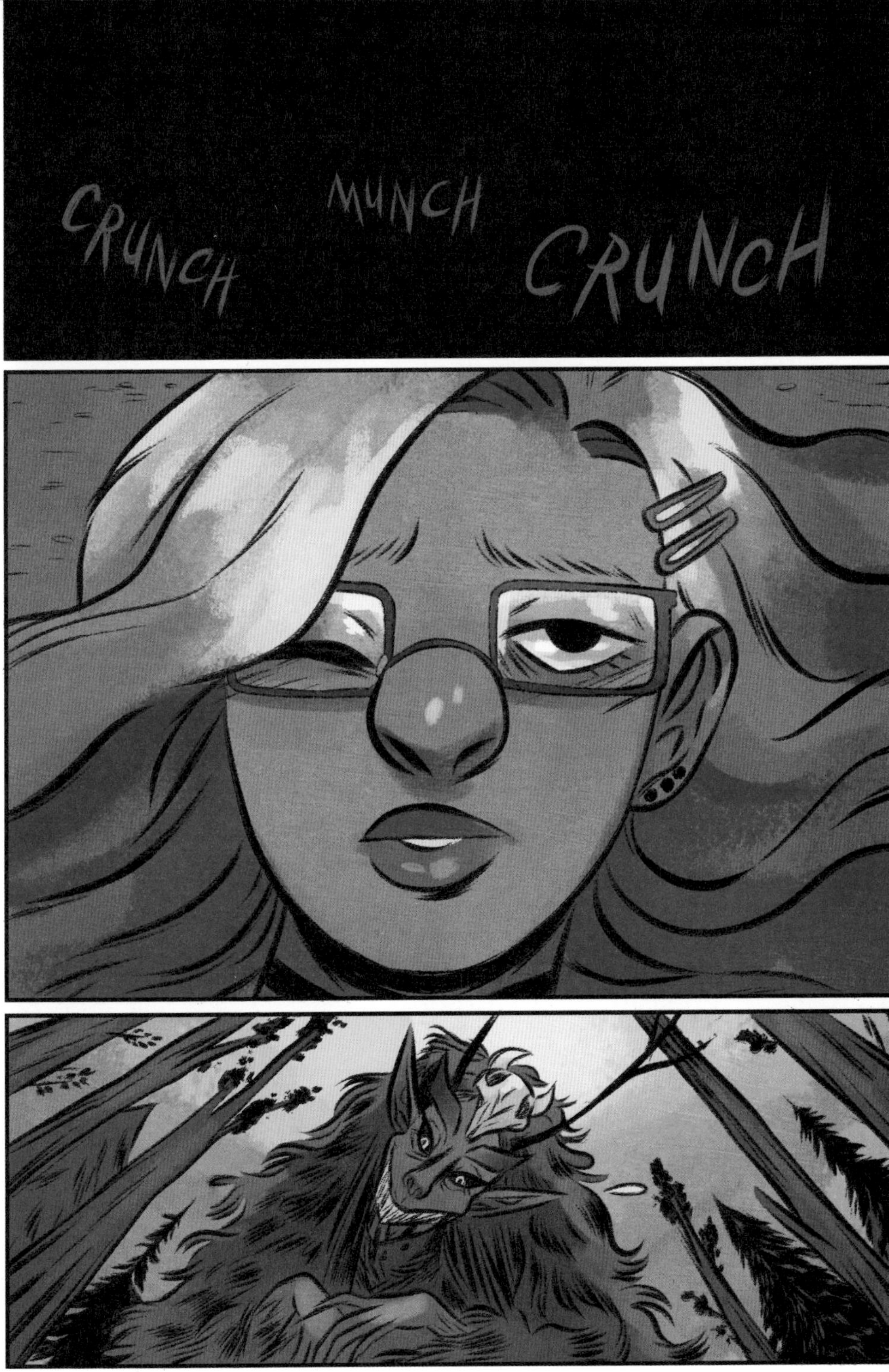
CRUNCH
MUNCH
CRUNCH

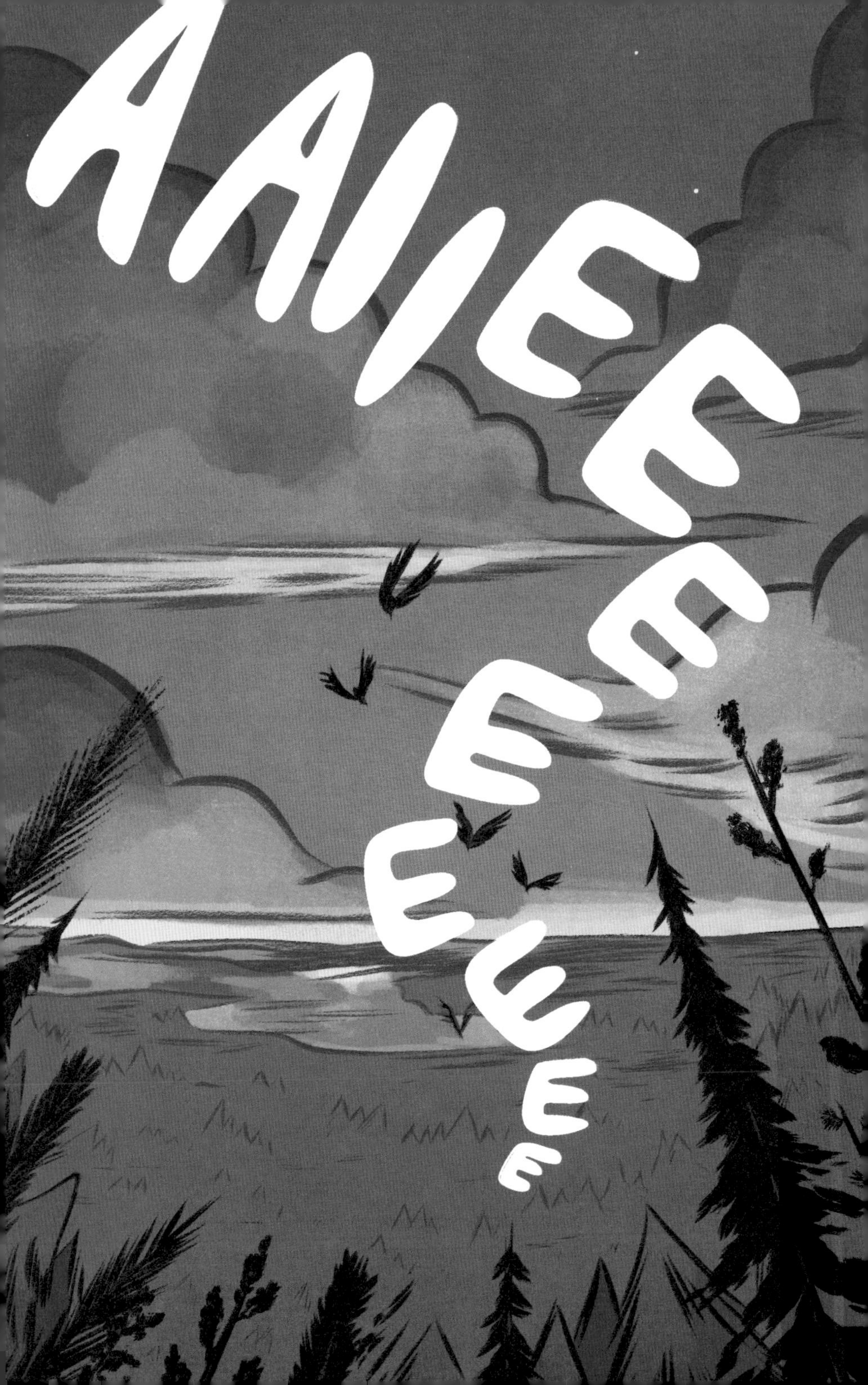
AAIIEEEEEEEE

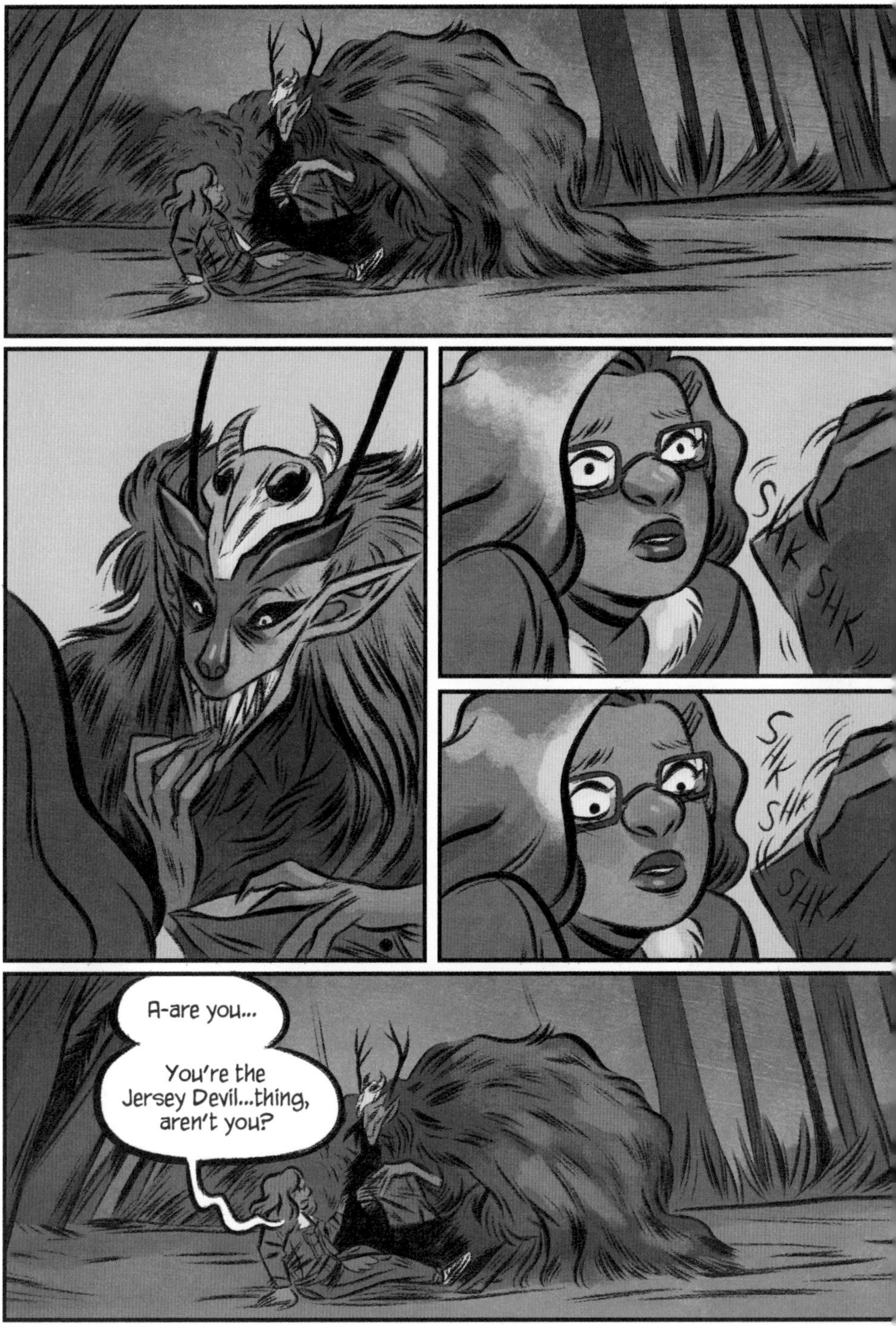
SHK SHK SHK
SHK SHK SHK
A-are you...
You're the Jersey Devil...thing, aren't you?

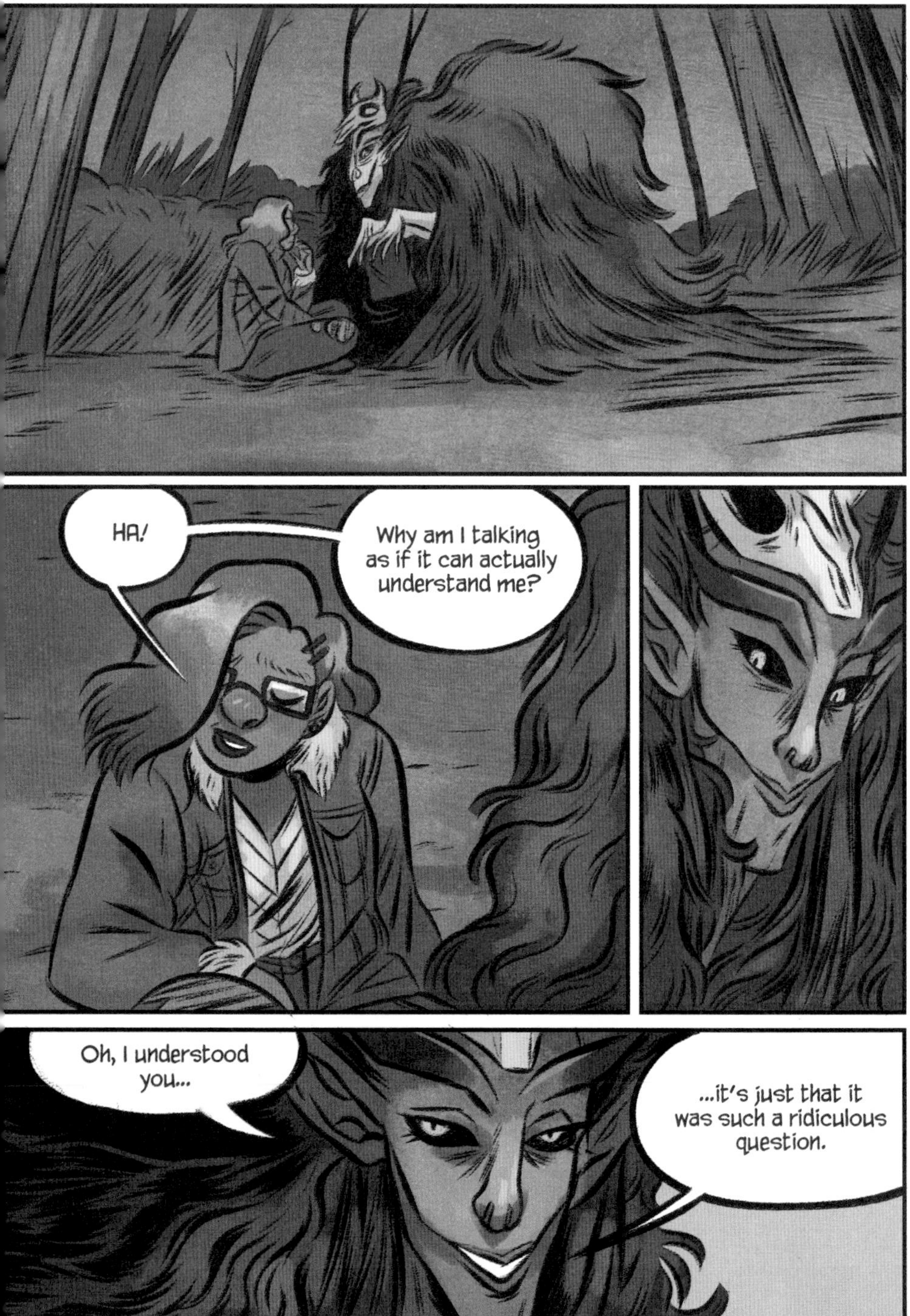
HA!
Why am I talking as if it can actually understand me?
Oh, I understood you...
...it's just that it was such a ridiculous question.

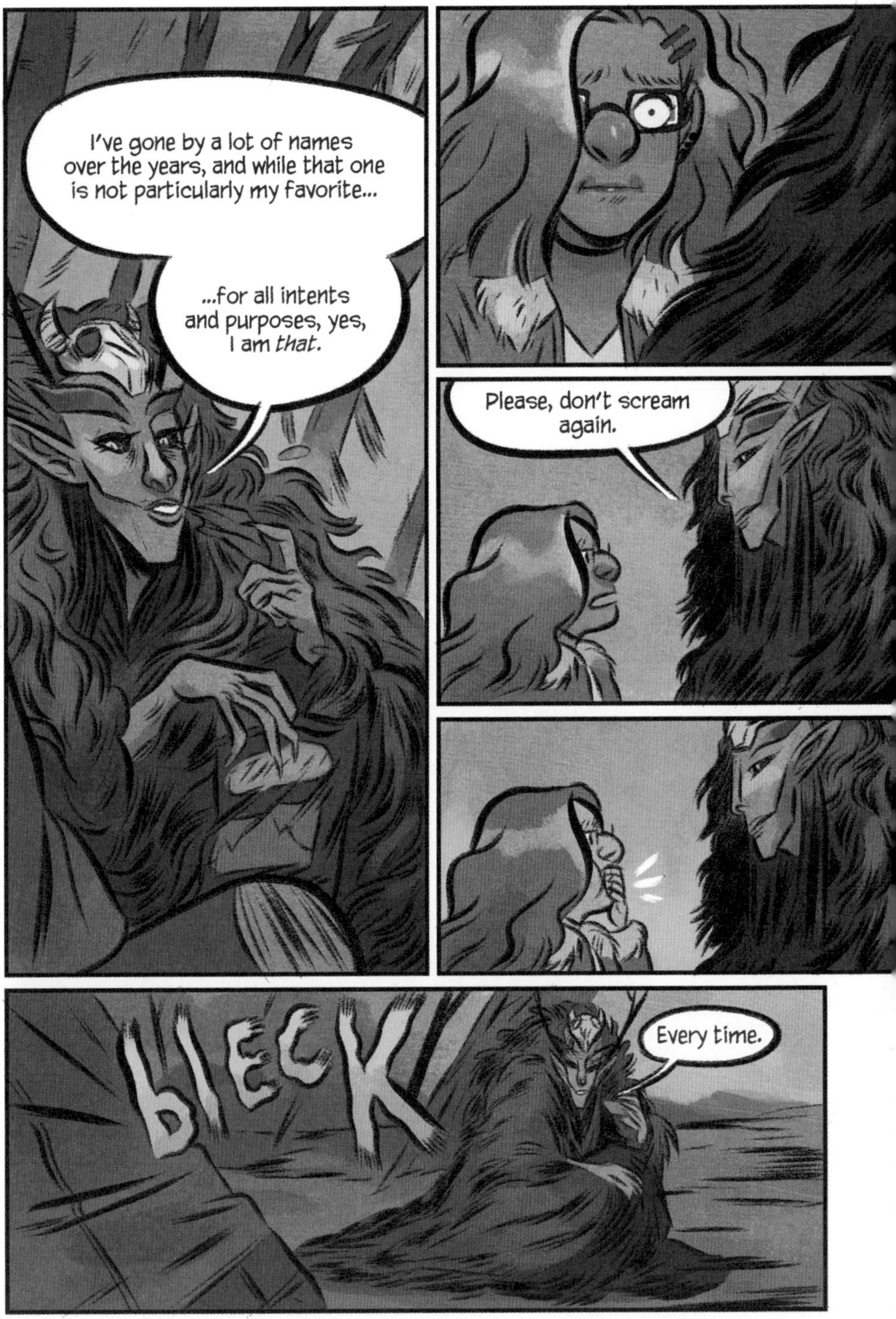
I've gone by a lot of names over the years, and while that one is not particularly my favorite...
...for all intents and purposes, yes, I am *that*.
Please, don't scream again.
BLECK
Every time.

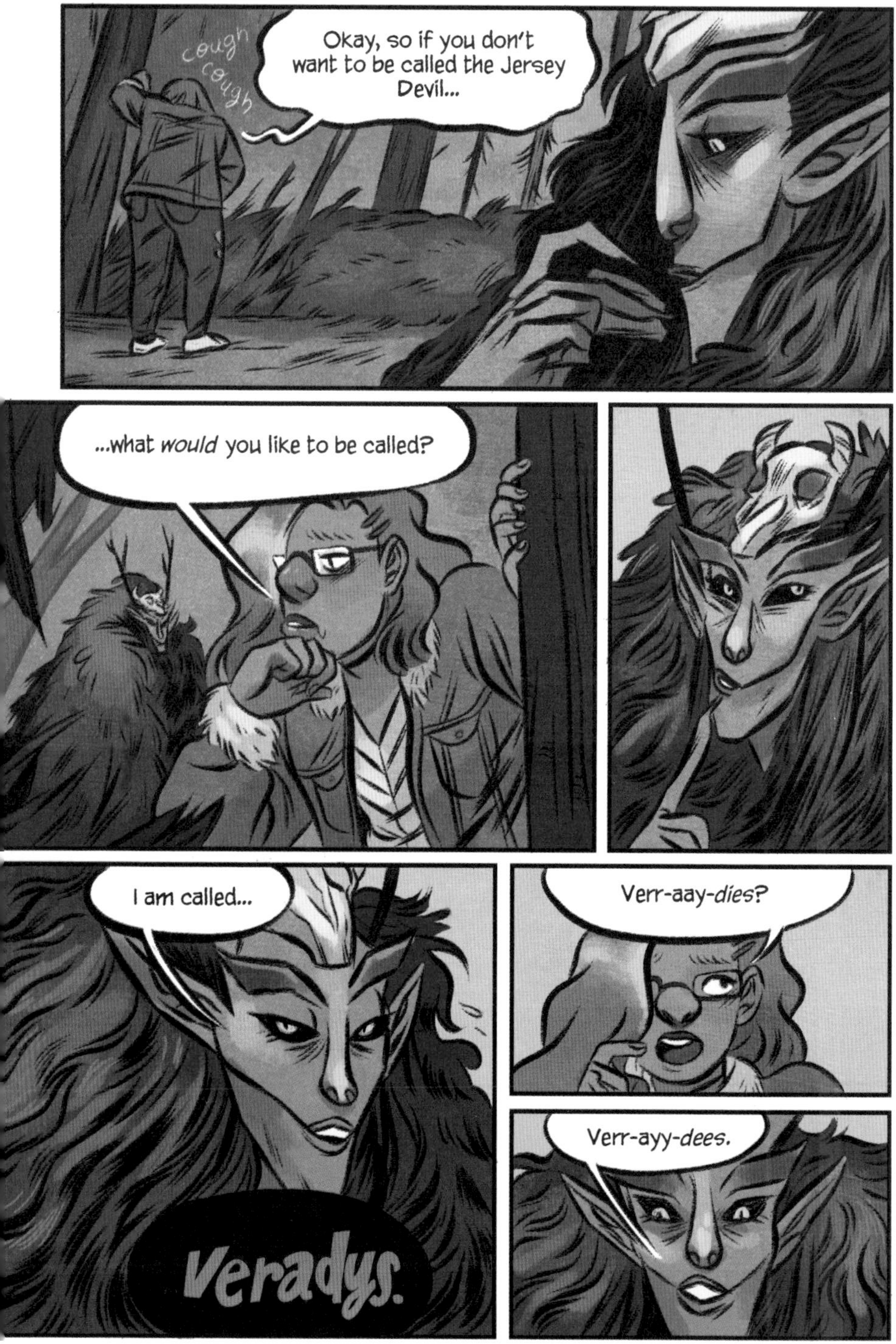
cough cough
Okay, so if you don't want to be called the Jersey Devil...
...what *would* you like to be called?
I am called...
Veradys.
Verr-aay-*dies*?
Verr-ayy-*dees*.

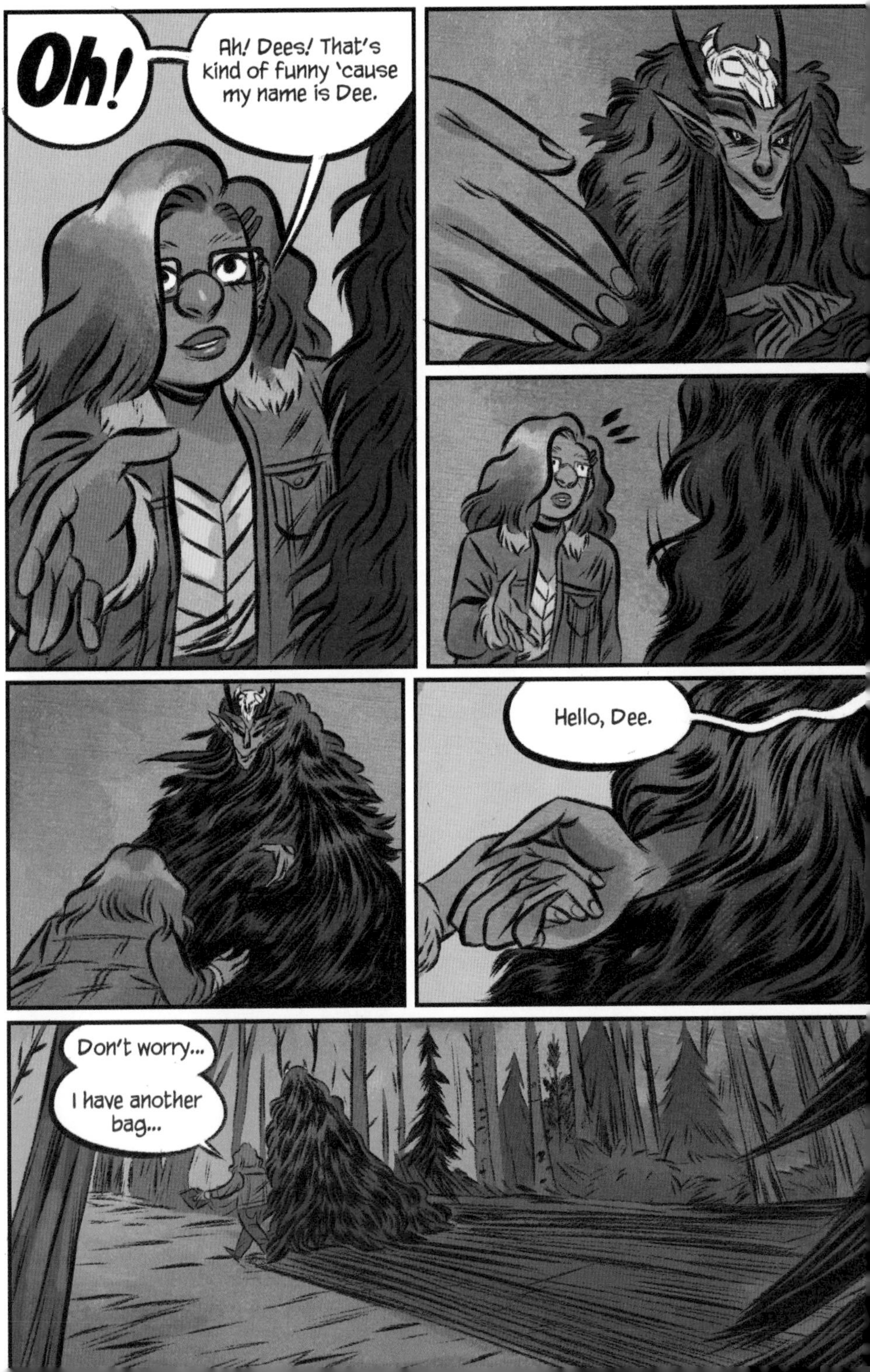
Oh!
Ah! Dees! That's kind of funny 'cause my name is Dee.
Hello, Dee.
Don't worry...
I have another bag...

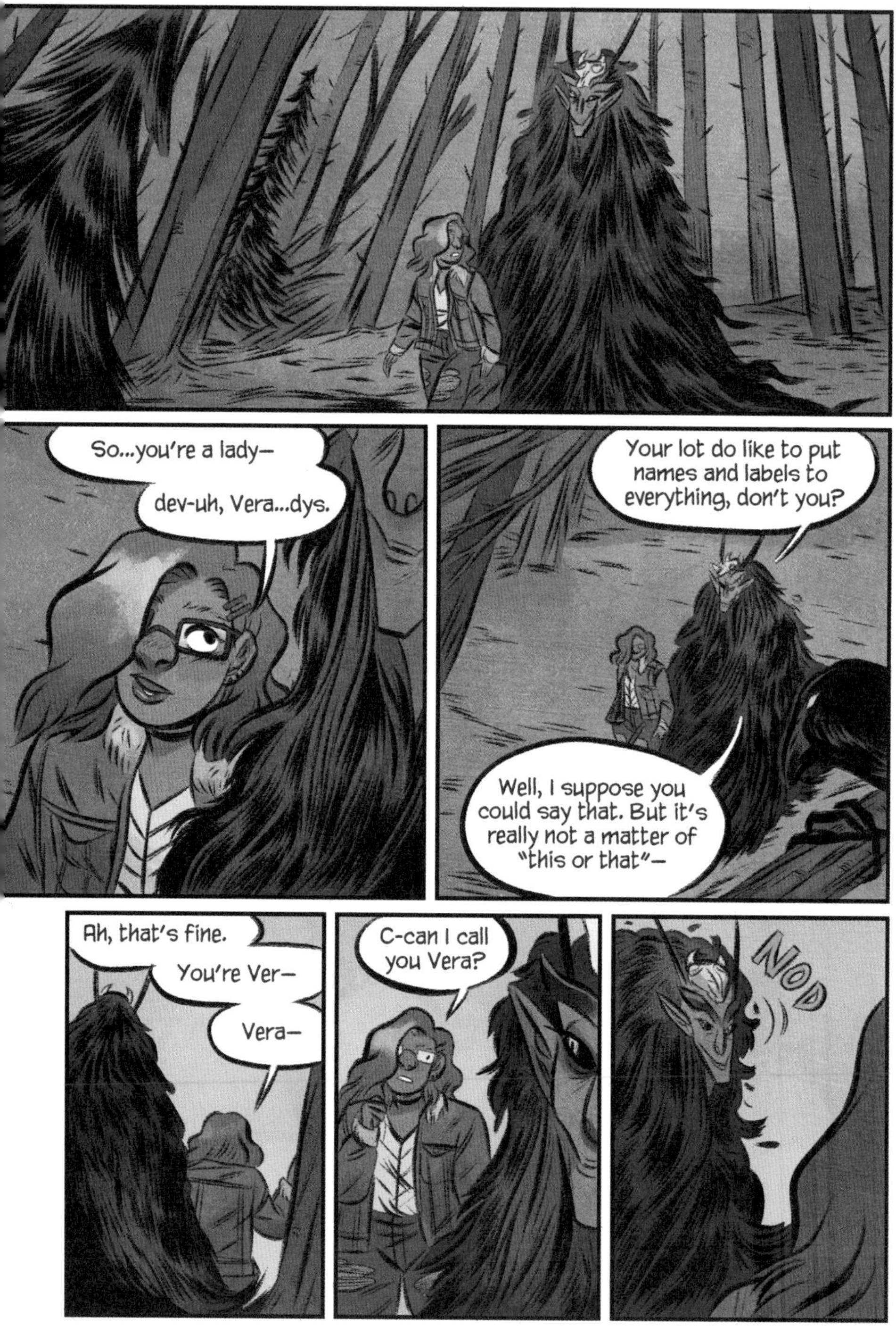
So...you're a lady—
dev-uh, Vera...dys.
Your lot do like to put names and labels to everything, don't you?
Well, I suppose you could say that. But it's really not a matter of "this or that"—
Ah, that's fine.
You're Ver—
Vera—
C-can I call you Vera?
NOD

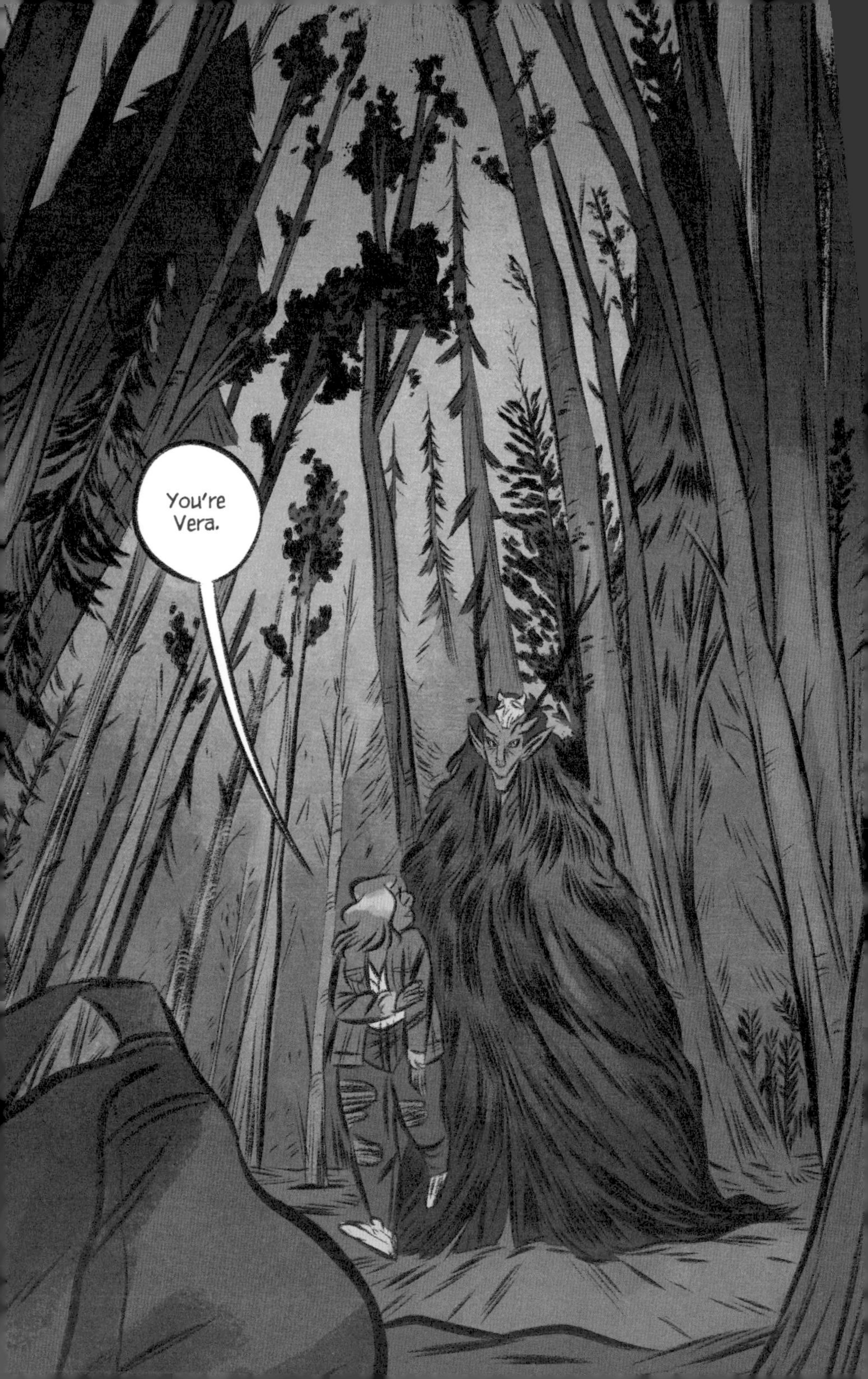
You're Vera.

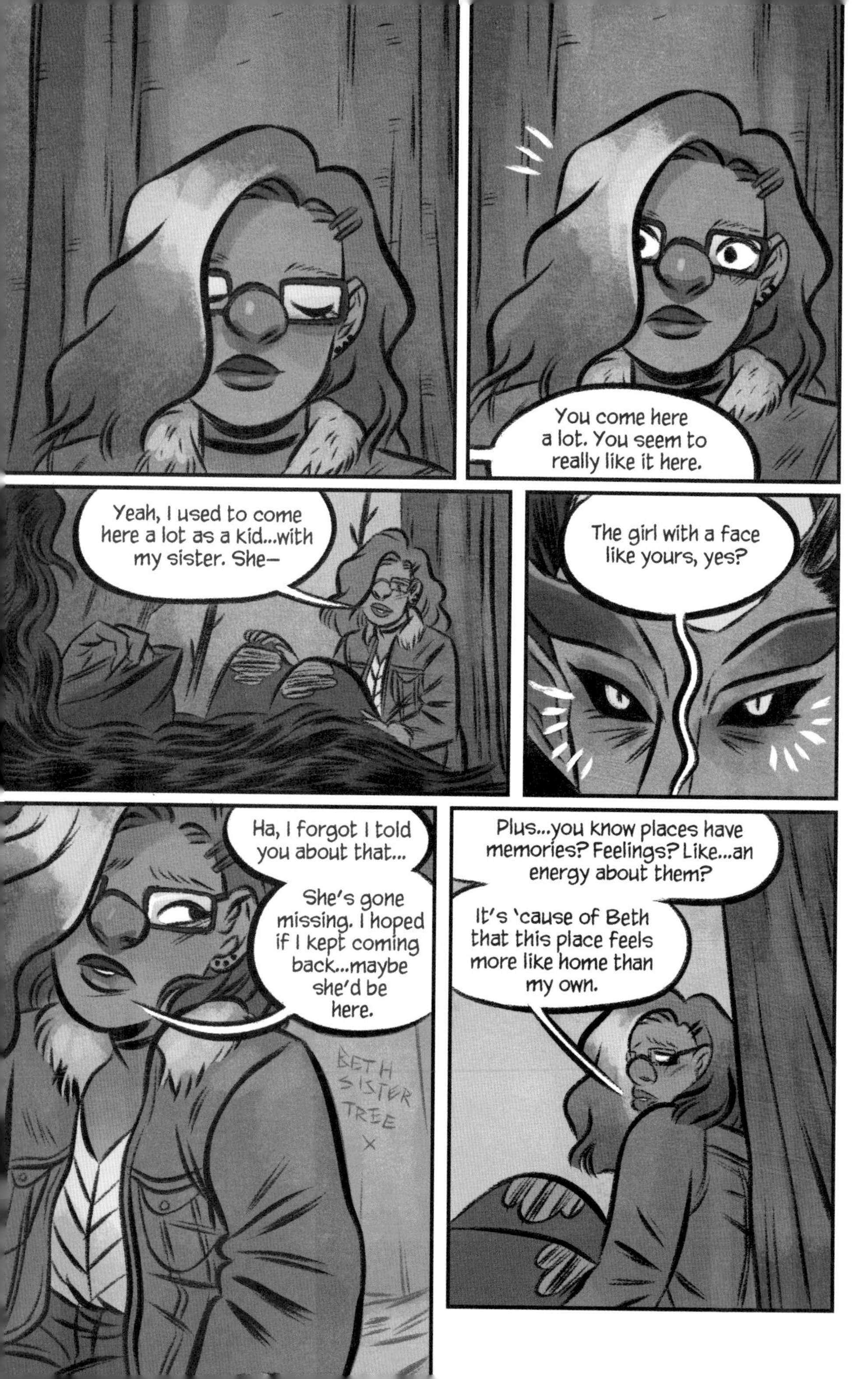
You come here a lot. You seem to really like it here.
Yeah, I used to come here a lot as a kid...with my sister. She—
The girl with a face like yours, yes?
Ha, I forgot I told you about that...
She's gone missing. I hoped if I kept coming back...maybe she'd be here.
BETH SISTER TREE
Plus...you know places have memories? Feelings? Like...an energy about them?
It's 'cause of Beth that this place feels more like home than my own.

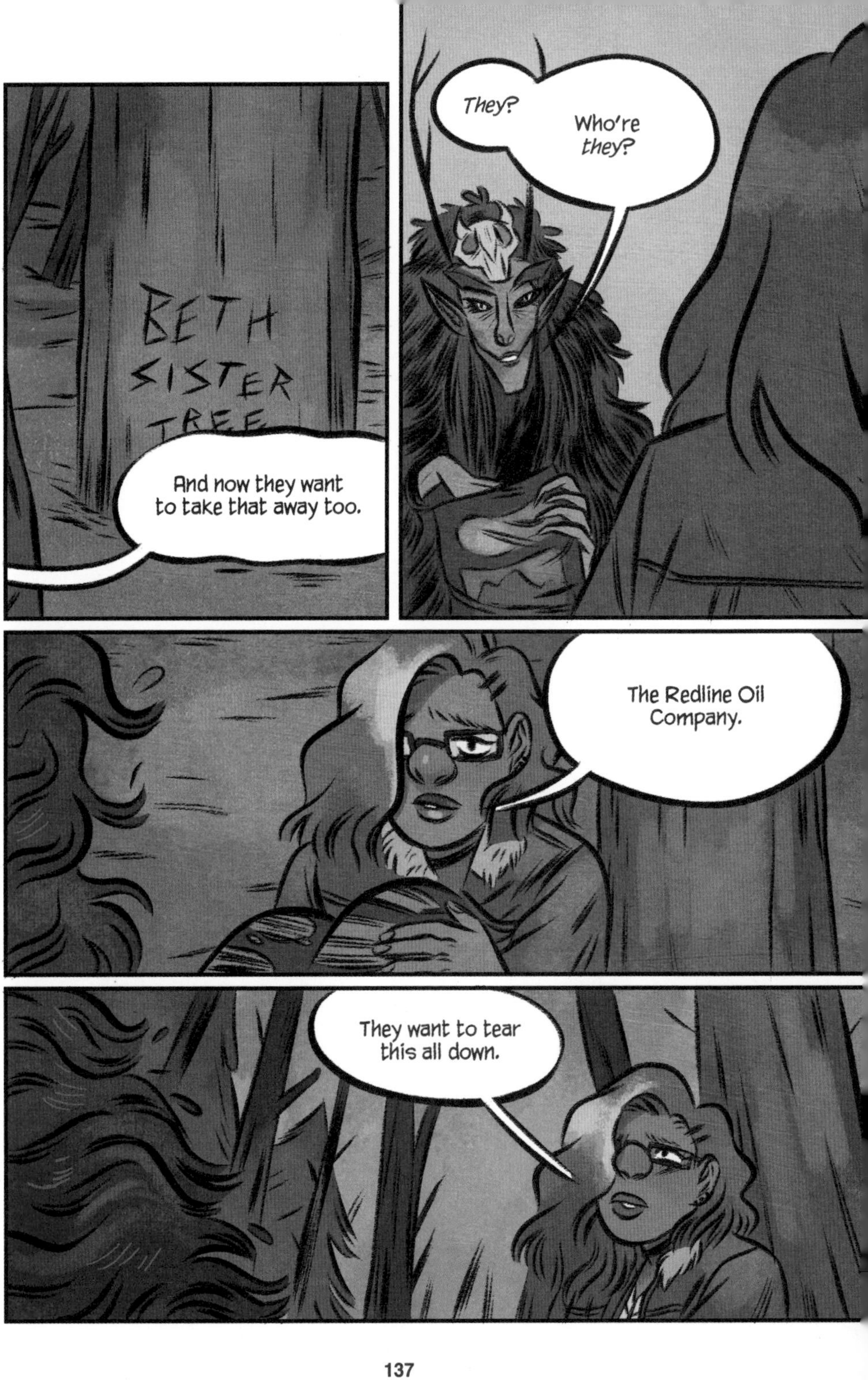
BETH SISTER TREE
And now they want to take that away too.
They?
Who're they?
The Redline Oil Company.
They want to tear this all down.

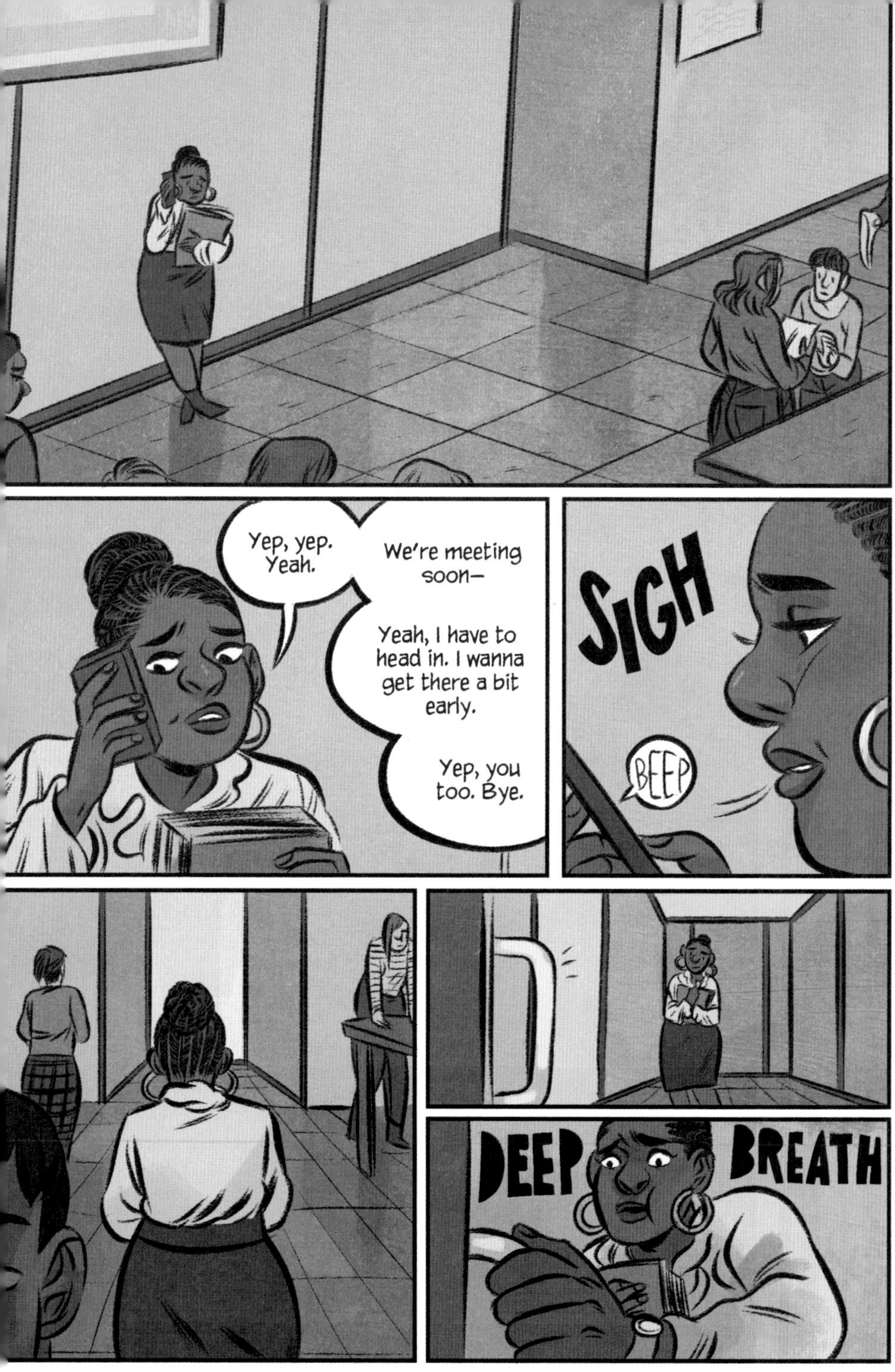
Yep, yep. Yeah.
We're meeting soon—
Yeah, I have to head in. I wanna get there a bit early.
Yep, you too. Bye.
SIGH
BEEP
DEEP BREATH

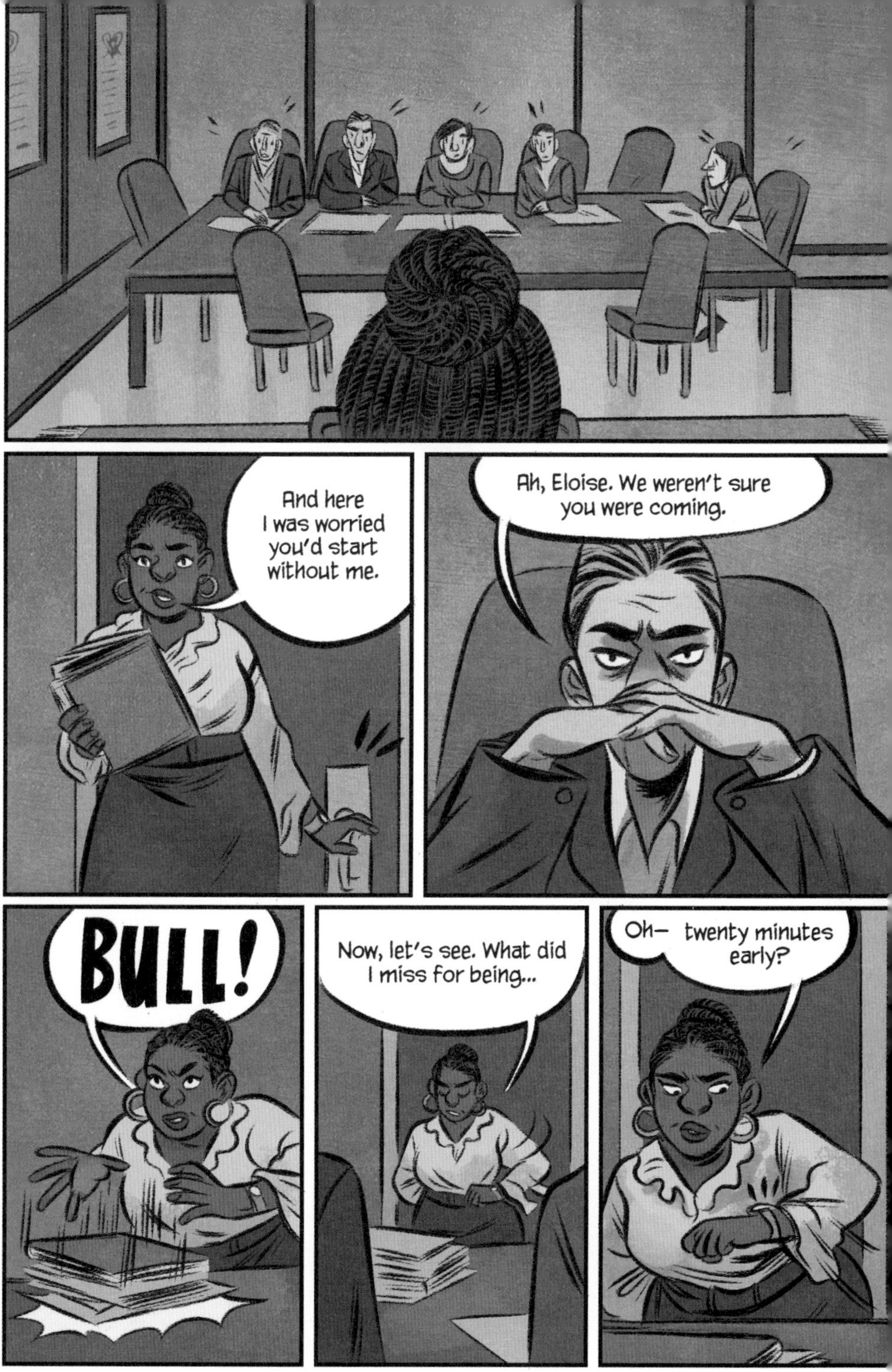
And here I was worried you'd start without me.
Ah, Eloise. We weren't sure you were coming.
BULL!
Now, let's see. What did I miss for being...
Oh— twenty minutes early?

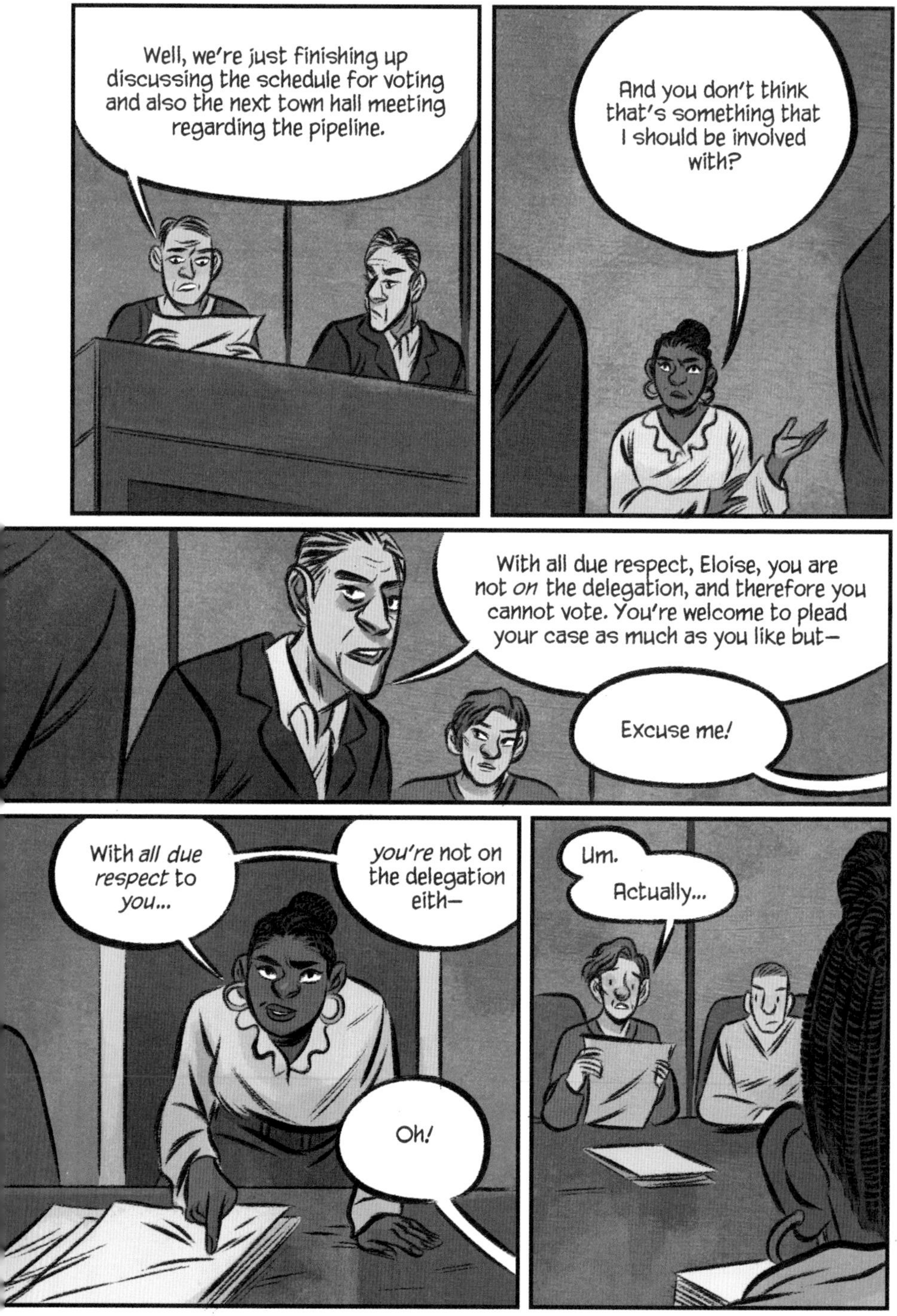
Well, we're just finishing up discussing the schedule for voting and also the next town hall meeting regarding the pipeline.
And you don't think that's something that I should be involved with?
With all due respect, Eloise, you are not *on* the delegation, and therefore you cannot vote. You're welcome to plead your case as much as you like but—
Excuse me!
With *all due respect* to *you*...
you're not on the delegation eith—
Oh!
Um.
Actually...

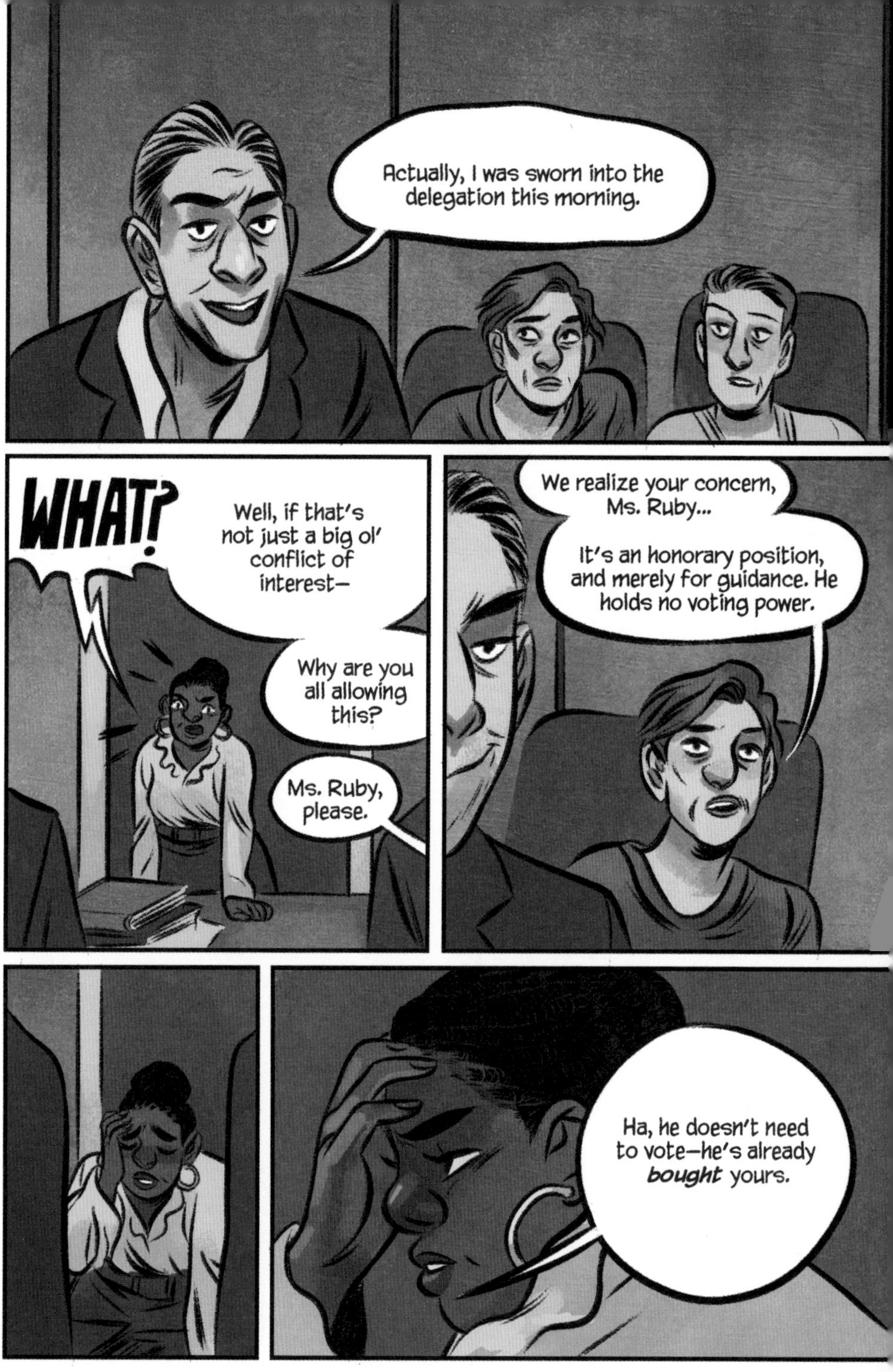
Actually, I was sworn into the delegation this morning.
WHAT?
Well, if that's not just a big ol' conflict of interest—
Why are you all allowing this?
Ms. Ruby, please.
We realize your concern, Ms. Ruby...
It's an honorary position, and merely for guidance. He holds no voting power.
Ha, he doesn't need to vote—he's already *bought* yours.

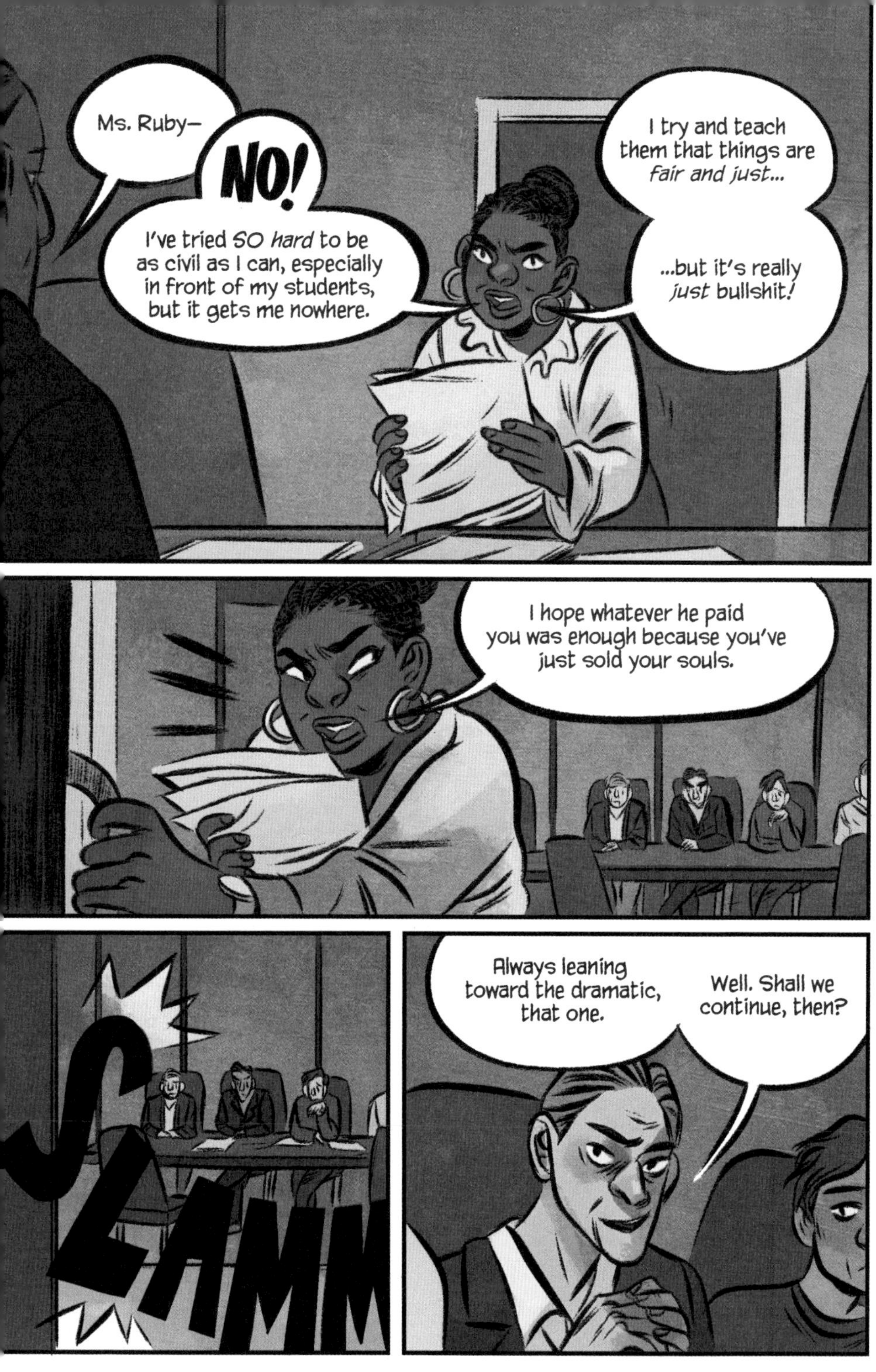
Ms. Ruby—
NO!
I've tried *SO hard* to be as civil as I can, especially in front of my students, but it gets me nowhere.
I try and teach them that things are *fair and just...*
...but it's really *just* bullshit!
I hope whatever he paid you was enough because you've just sold your souls.
SLAMM
Always leaning toward the dramatic, that one.
Well. Shall we continue, then?

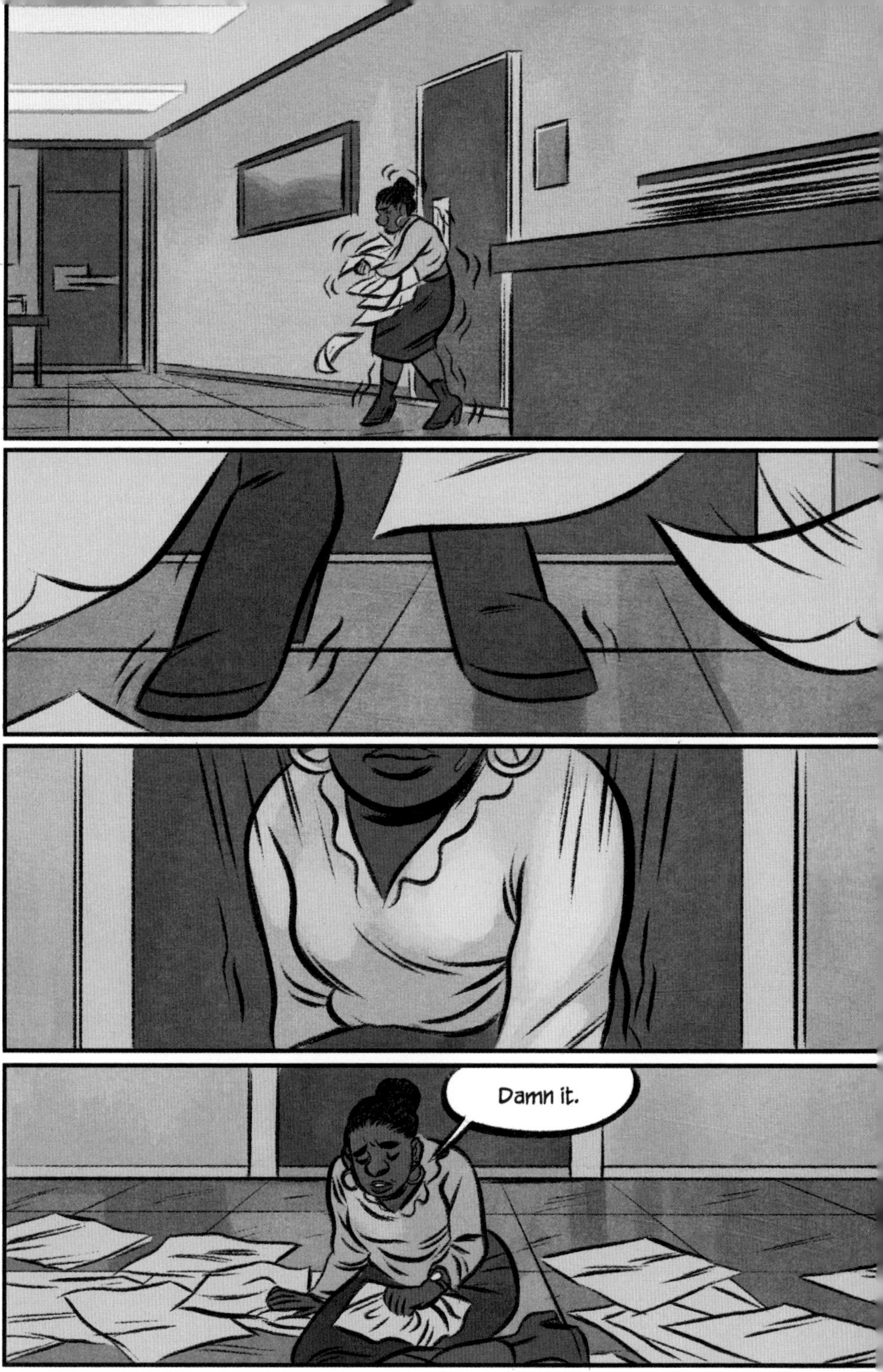
Damn it.

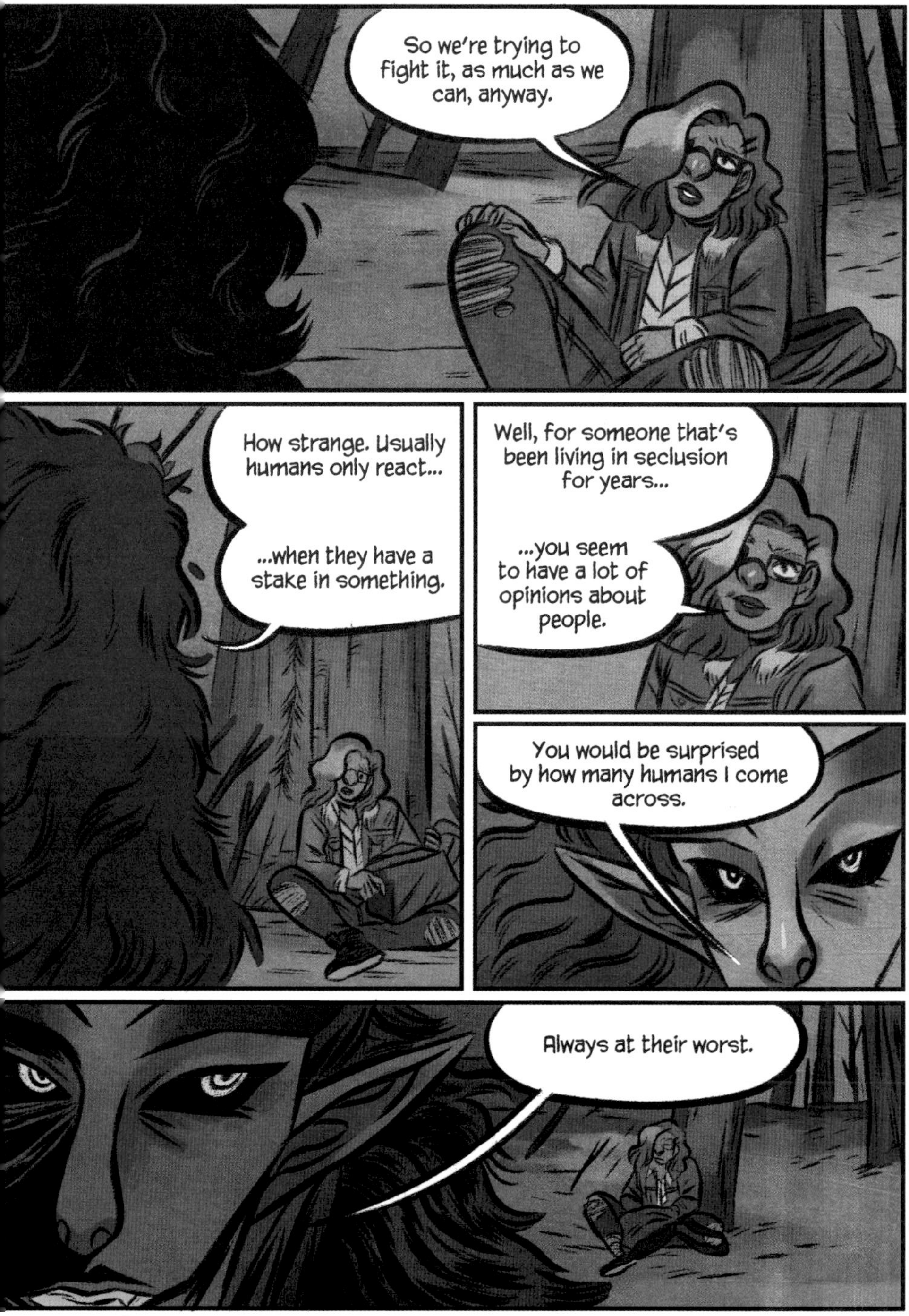

So we're trying to fight it, as much as we can, anyway.
How strange. Usually humans only react...
...when they have a stake in something.
Well, for someone that's been living in seclusion for years...
...you seem to have a lot of opinions about people.
You would be surprised by how many humans I come across.
Always at their worst.

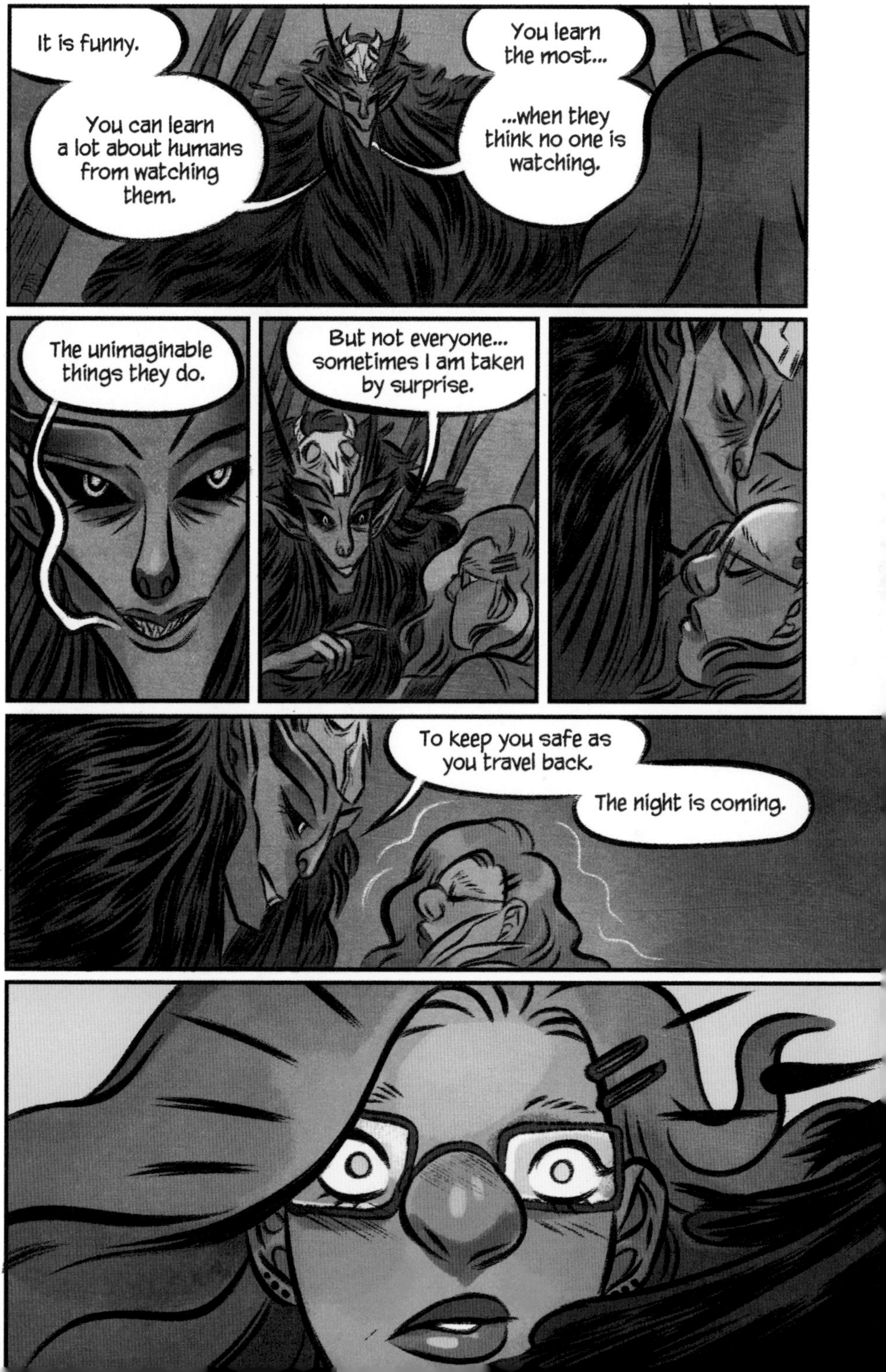
It is funny.
You can learn a lot about humans from watching them.
You learn the most...
...when they think no one is watching.
The unimaginable things they do.
But not everyone... sometimes I am taken by surprise.
To keep you safe as you travel back.
The night is coming.

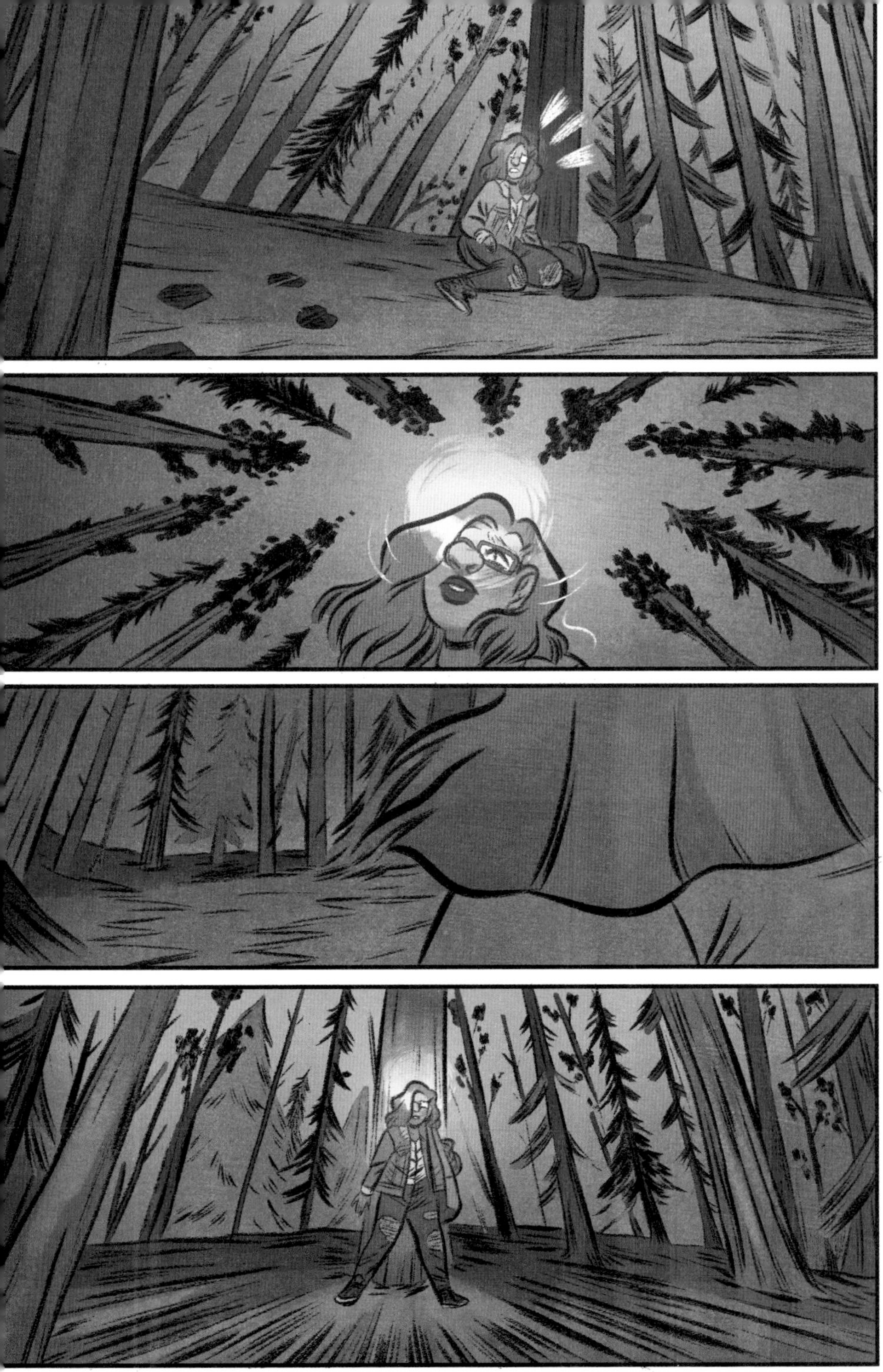

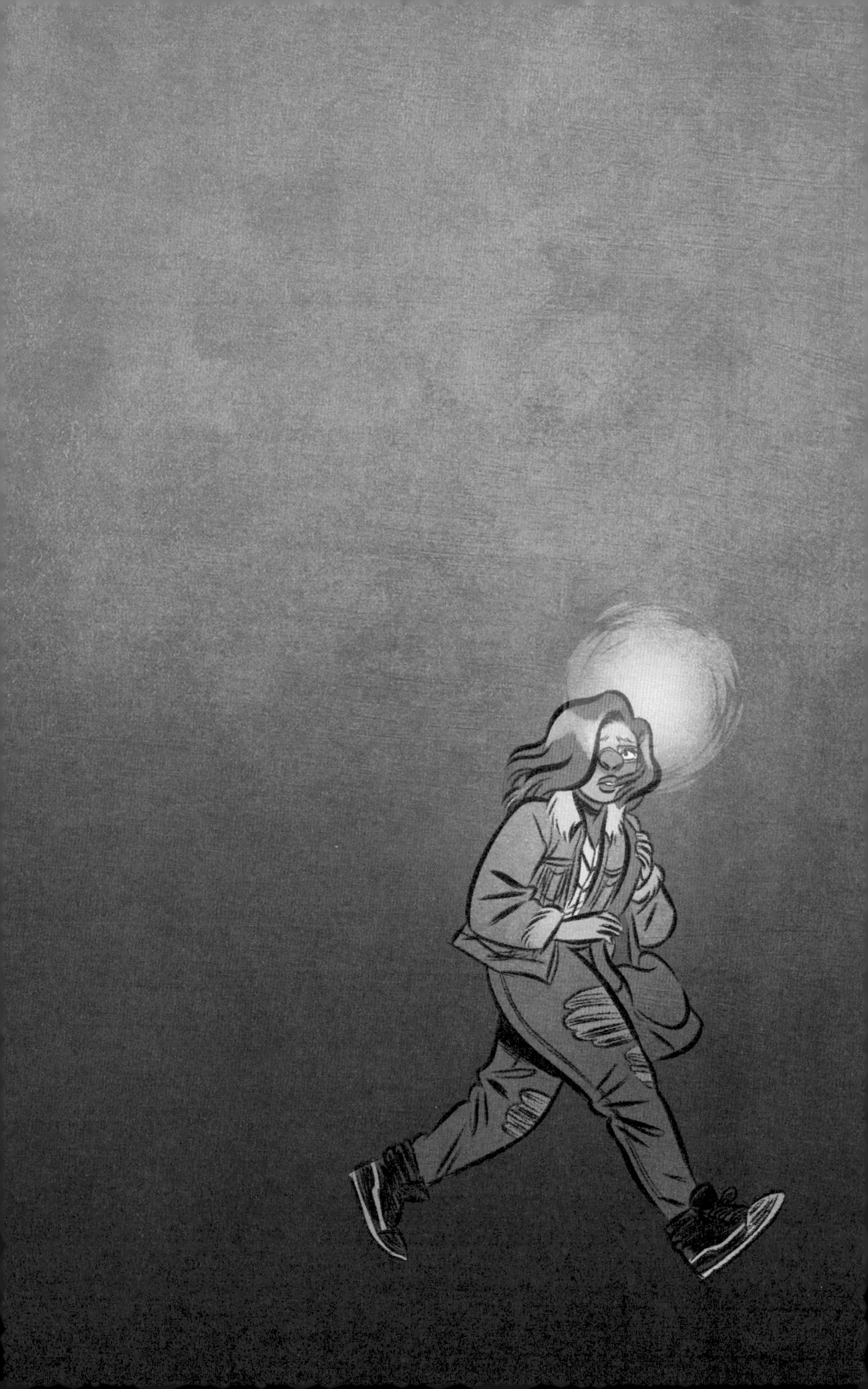

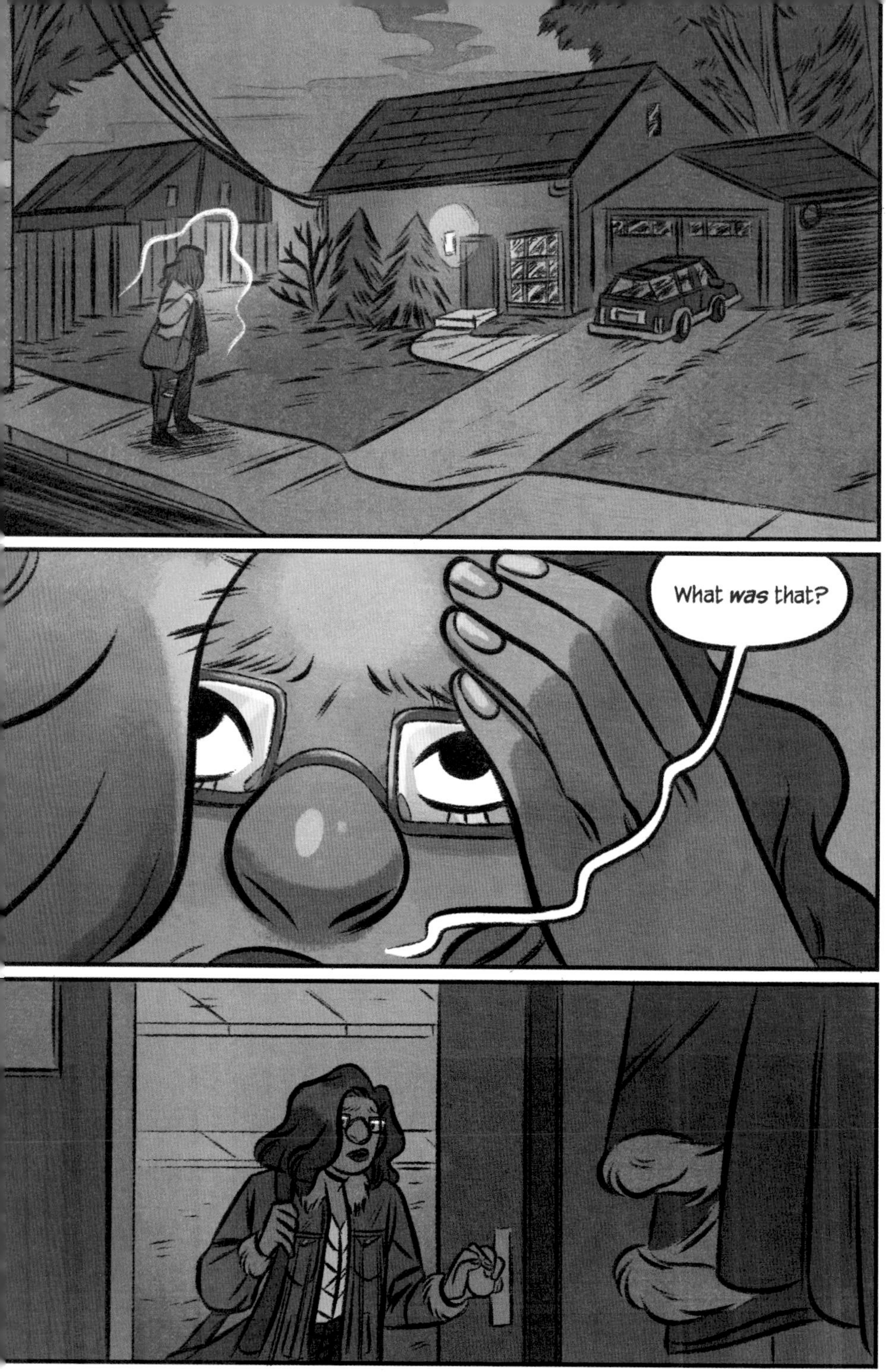
What *was* that?

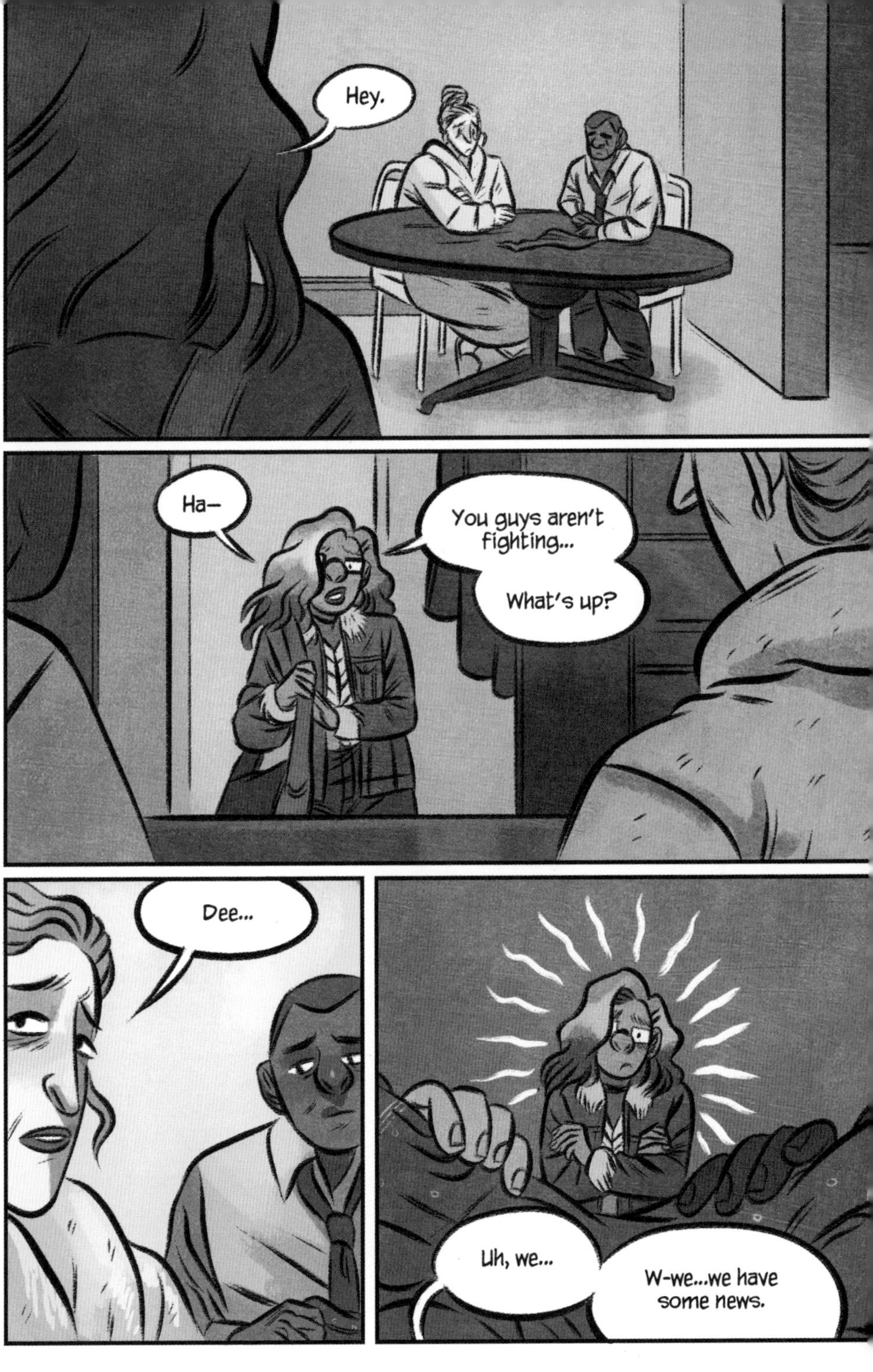
Hey.
Ha—
You guys aren't fighting...
What's up?
Dee...
Uh, we...
W-we...we have some news.

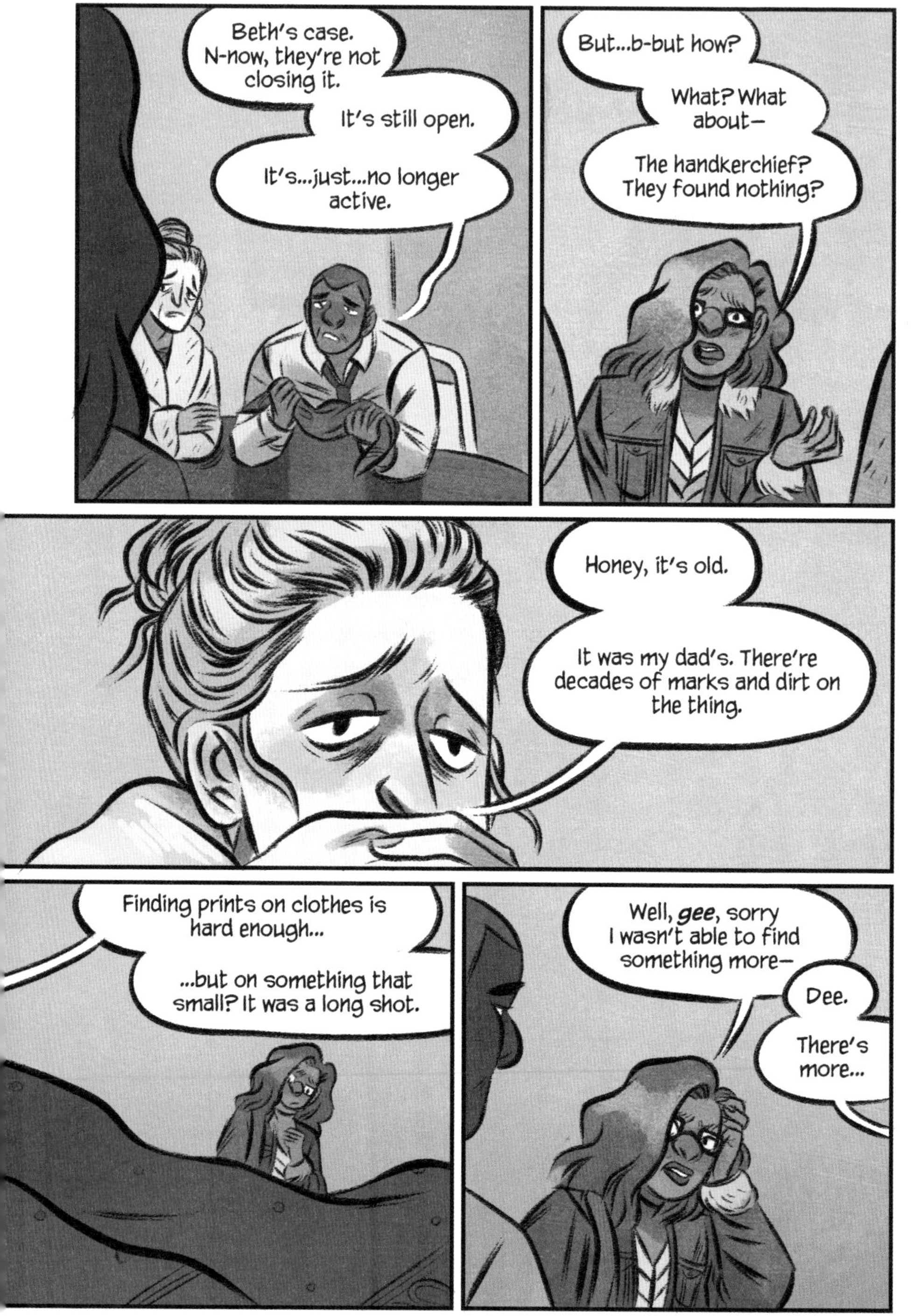
Beth's case. N-now, they're not closing it.
It's still open.
It's...just...no longer active.
But...b-but how?
What? What about—
The handkerchief? They found nothing?
Honey, it's old.
It was my dad's. There're decades of marks and dirt on the thing.
Finding prints on clothes is hard enough...
...but on something that small? It was a long shot.
Well, *gee*, sorry I wasn't able to find something more—
Dee.
There's more...

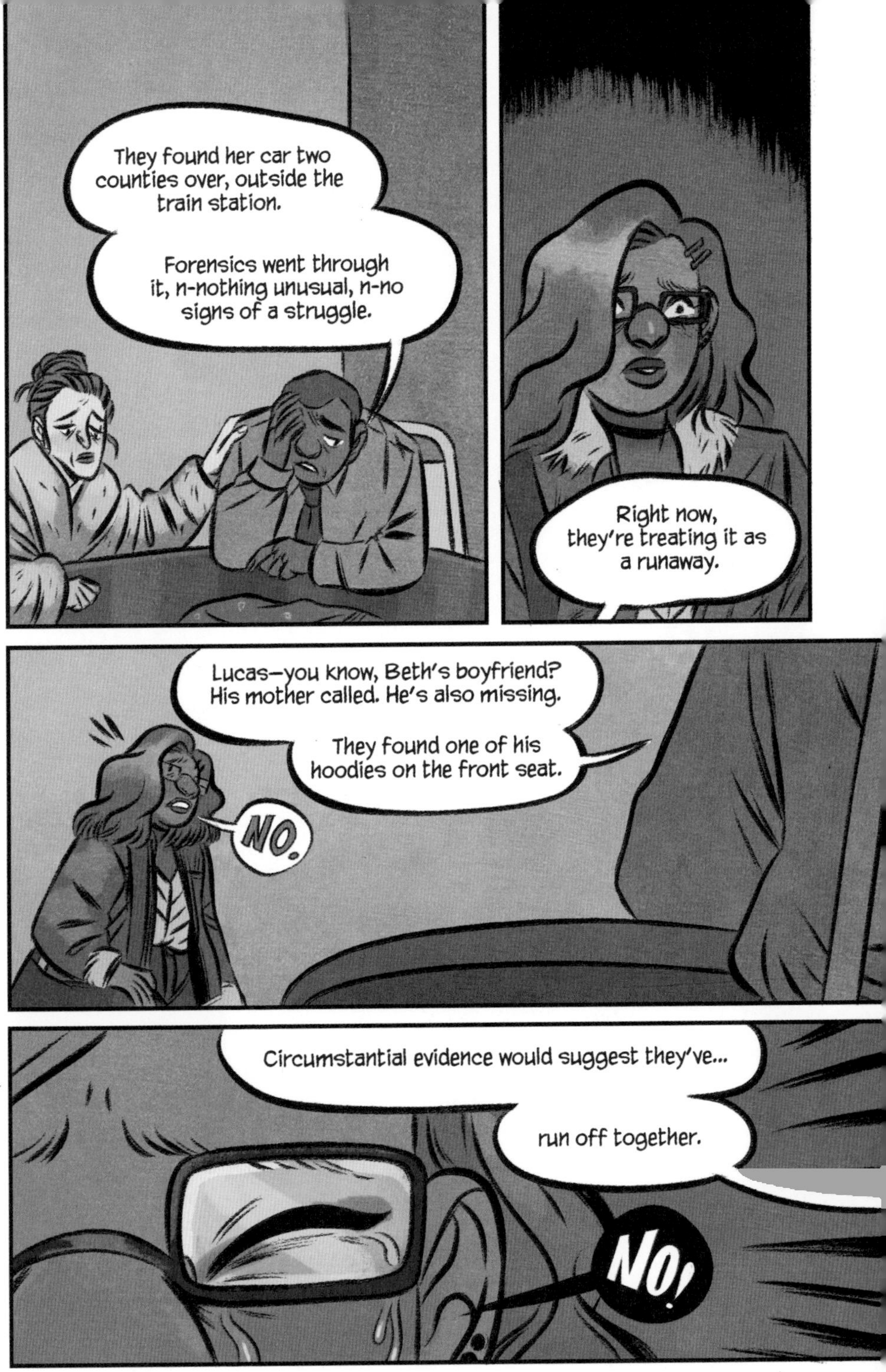
They found her car two counties over, outside the train station.
Forensics went through it, n-nothing unusual, n-no signs of a struggle.
Right now, they're treating it as a runaway.
Lucas—you know, Beth's boyfriend? His mother called. He's also missing.
They found one of his hoodies on the front seat.
NO.
Circumstantial evidence would suggest they've...
run off together.
NO!

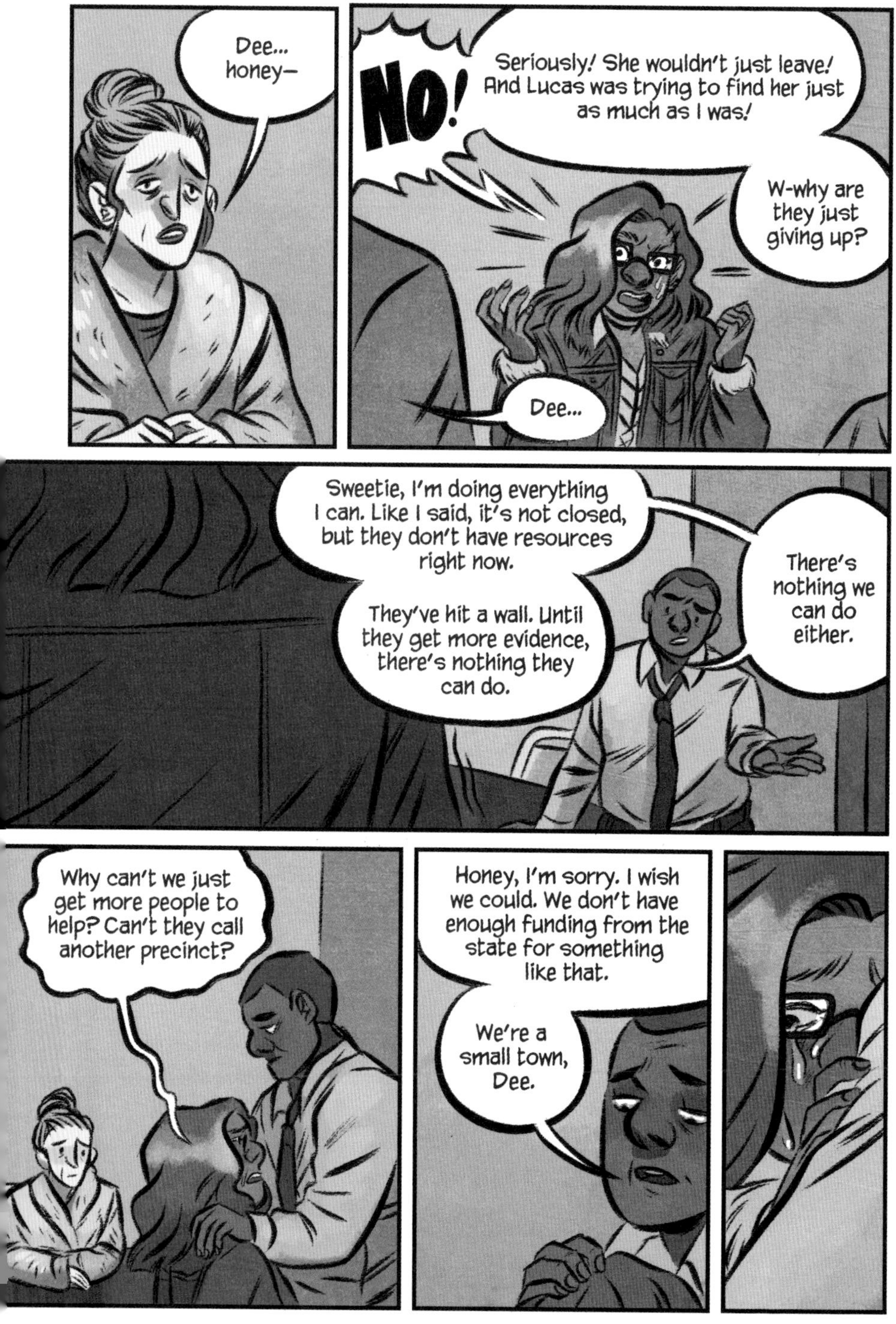
Dee... honey—
NO!
Seriously! She wouldn't just leave! And Lucas was trying to find her just as much as I was!
W-why are they just giving up?
Dee...
Sweetie, I'm doing everything I can. Like I said, it's not closed, but they don't have resources right now.
They've hit a wall. Until they get more evidence, there's nothing they can do.
There's nothing we can do either.
Why can't we just get more people to help? Can't they call another precinct?
Honey, I'm sorry. I wish we could. We don't have enough funding from the state for something like that.
We're a small town, Dee.

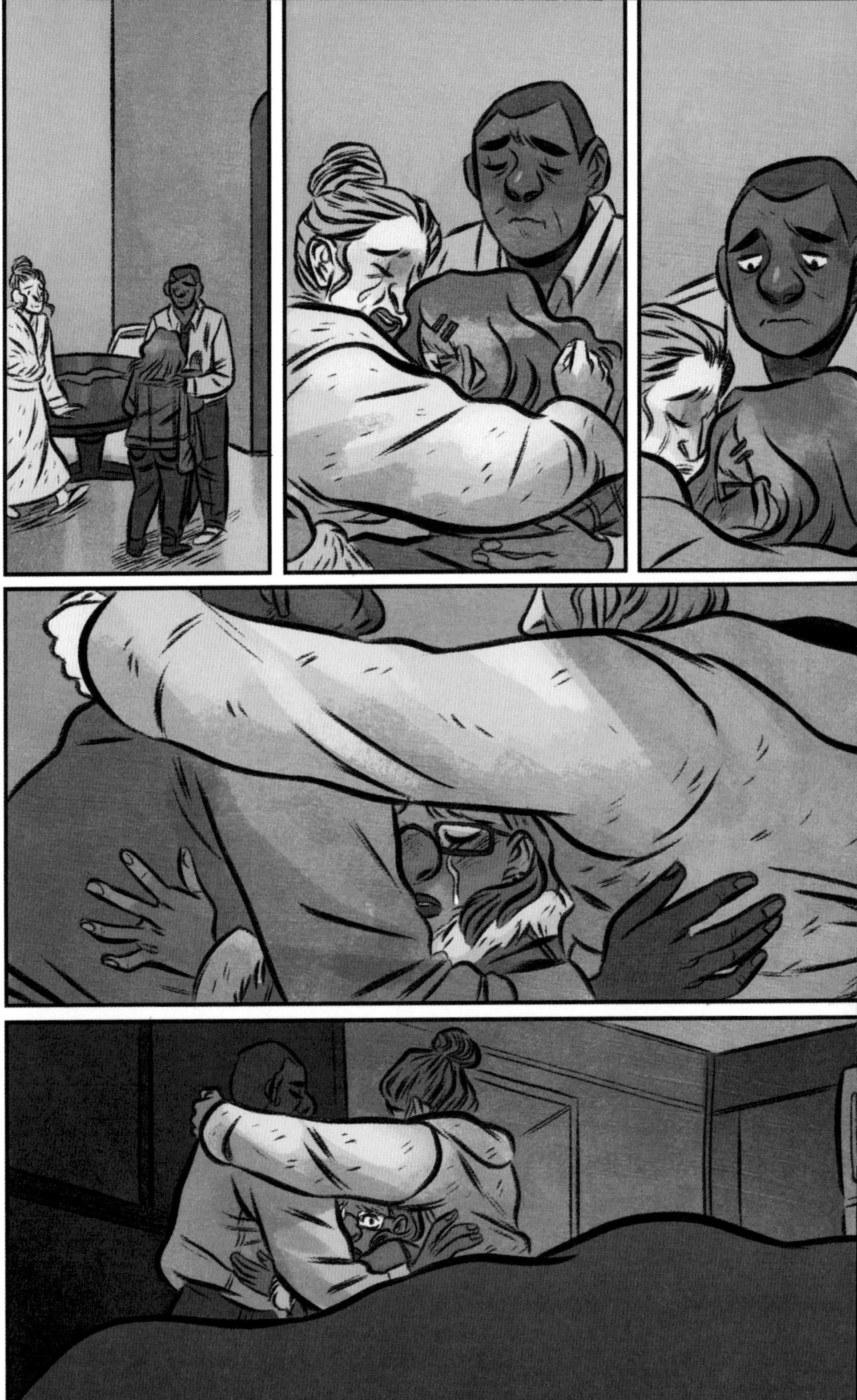

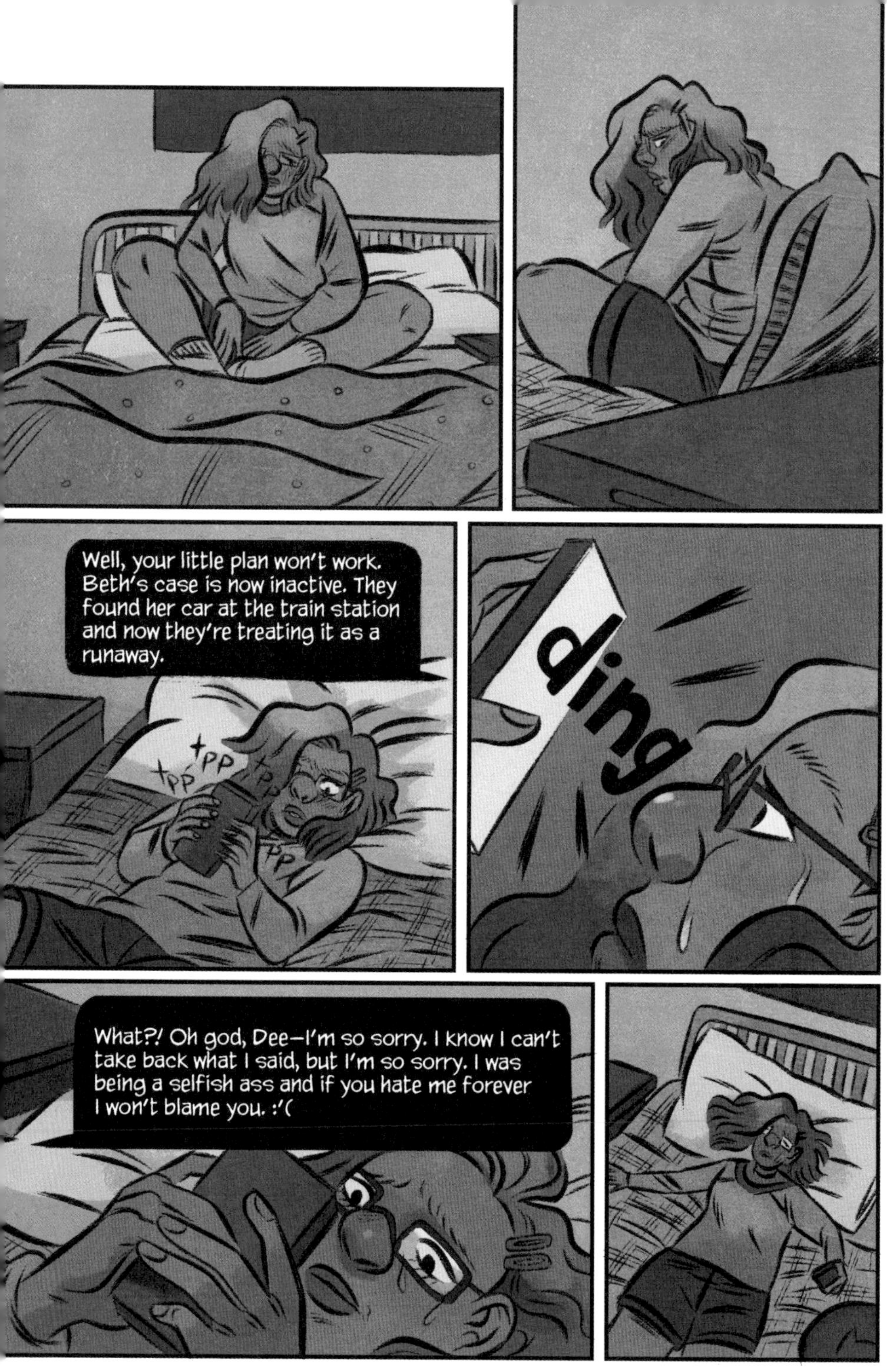
Well, your little plan won't work. Beth's case is now inactive. They found her car at the train station and now they're treating it as a runaway.
tpp
tpp
tpp
tpp
ding
What?! Oh god, Dee—I'm so sorry. I know I can't take back what I said, but I'm so sorry. I was being a selfish ass and if you hate me forever I won't blame you. :'(

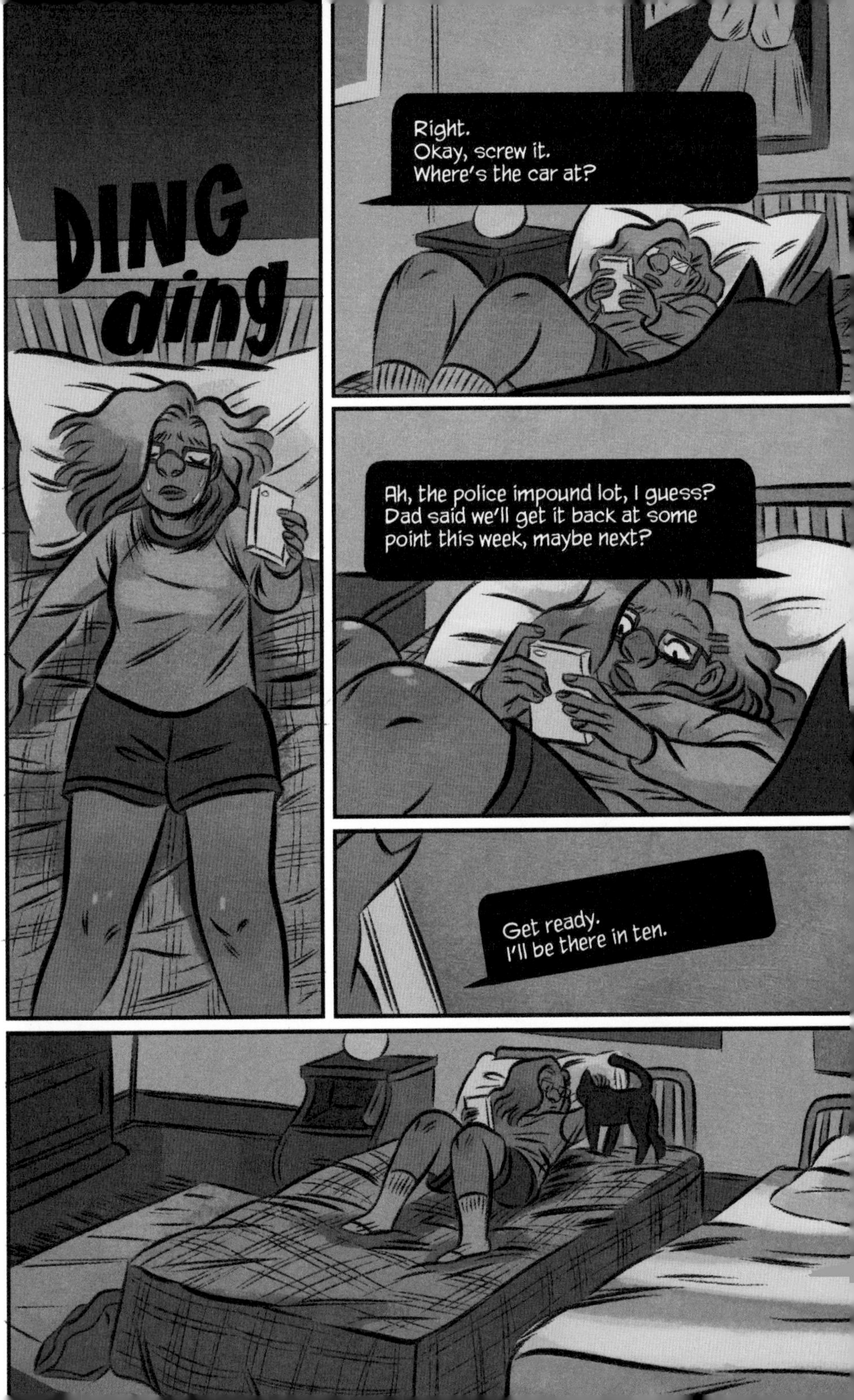
DING
ding
Right.
Okay, screw it.
Where's the car at?
Ah, the police impound lot, I guess?
Dad said we'll get it back at some
point this week, maybe next?
Get ready.
I'll be there in ten.

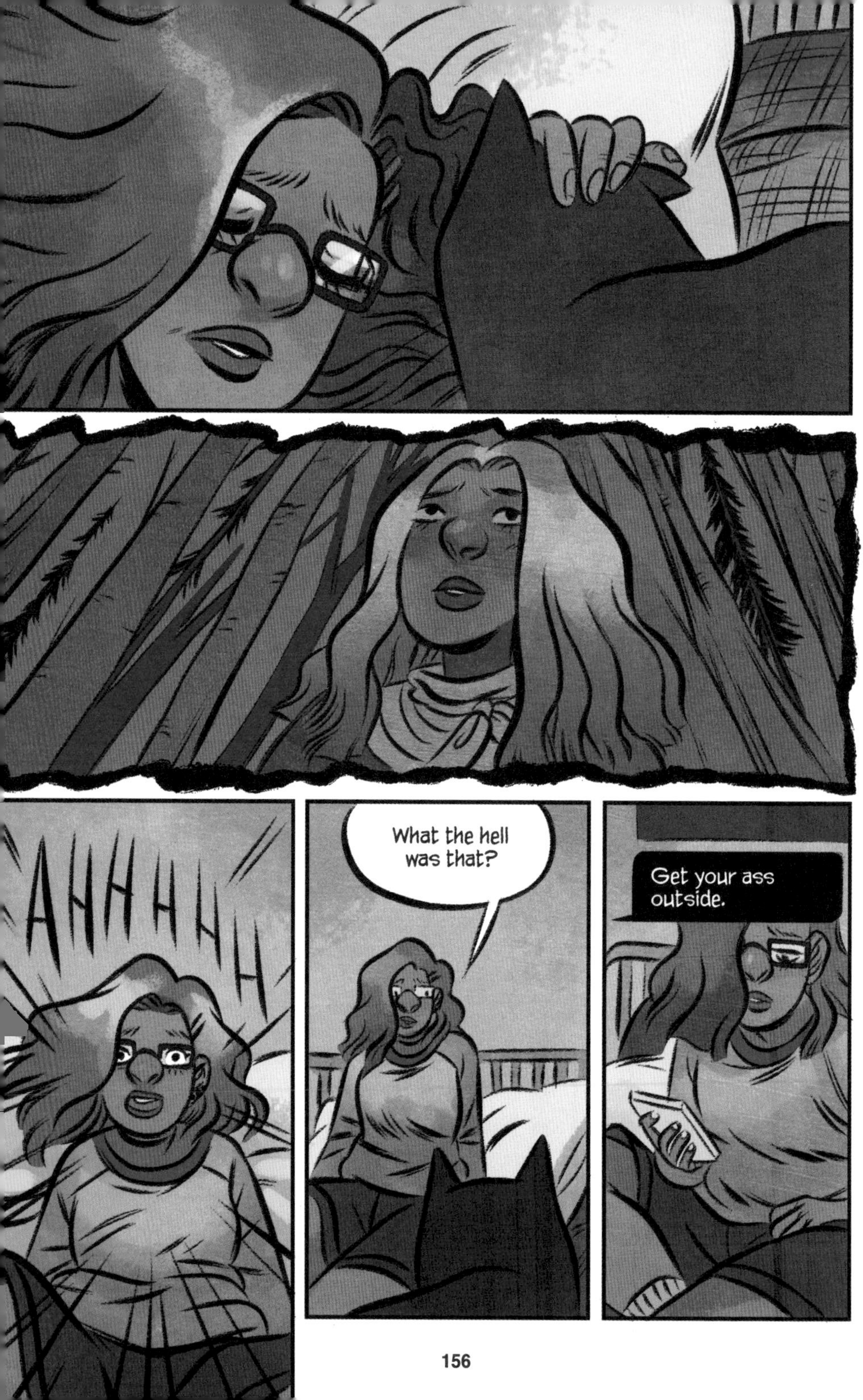
AHHHHHH
What the hell was that?
Get your ass outside.

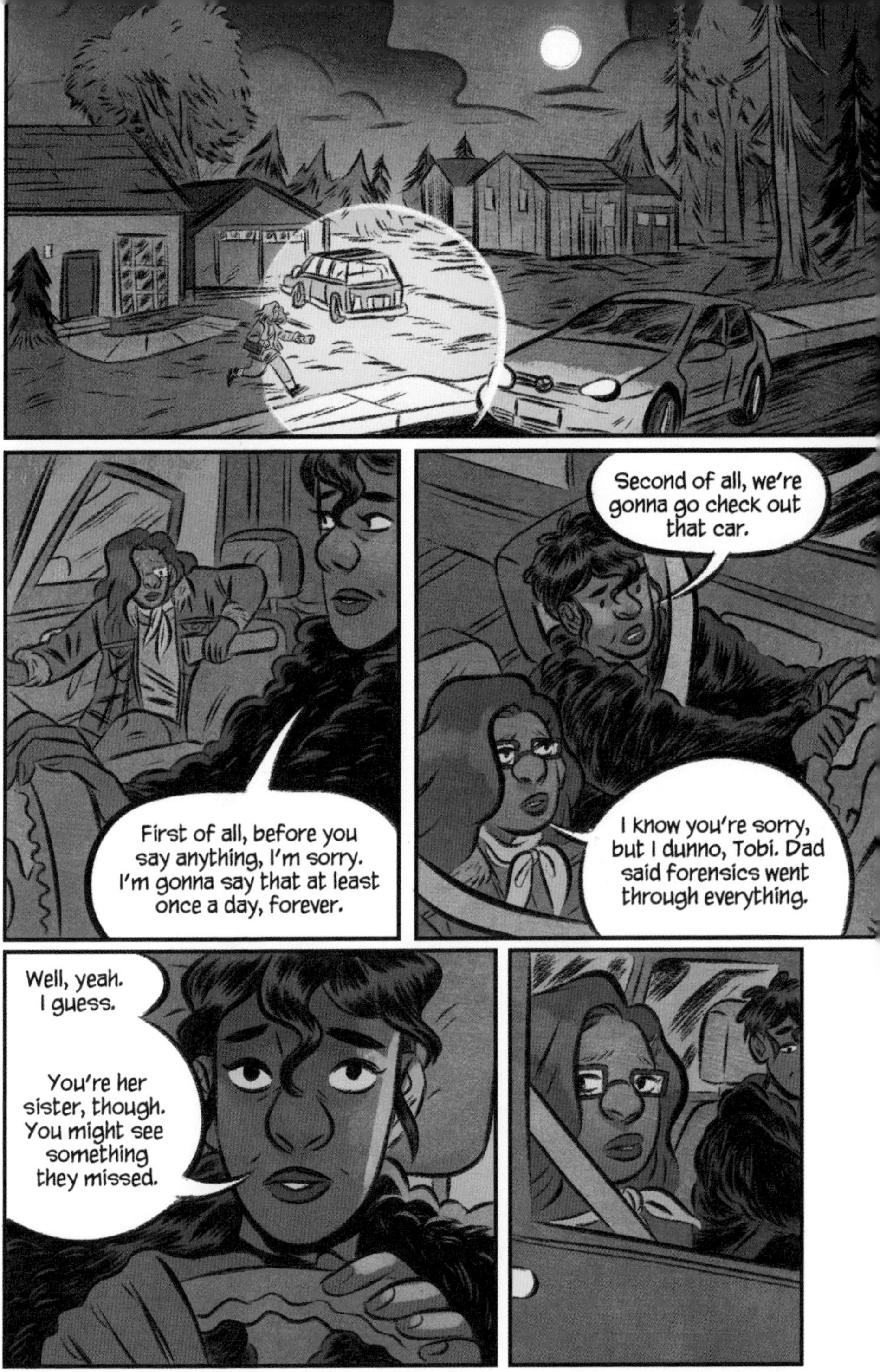
First of all, before you say anything, I'm sorry. I'm gonna say that at least once a day, forever.
Second of all, we're gonna go check out that car.
I know you're sorry, but I dunno, Tobi. Dad said forensics went through everything.
Well, yeah. I guess.
You're her sister, though. You might see something they missed.

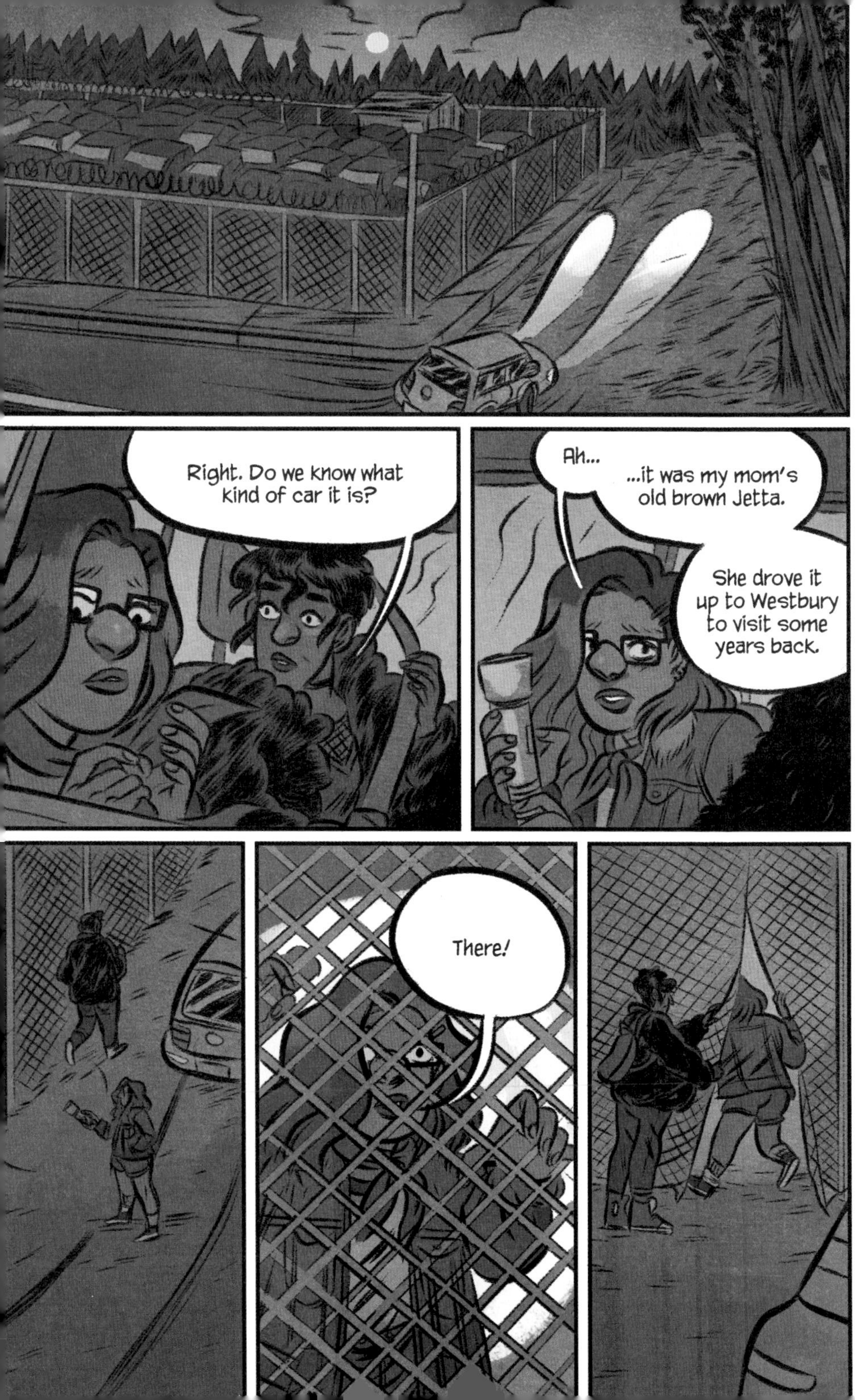
Right. Do we know what kind of car it is?
Ah...
...it was my mom's old brown Jetta.
She drove it up to Westbury to visit some years back.
There!

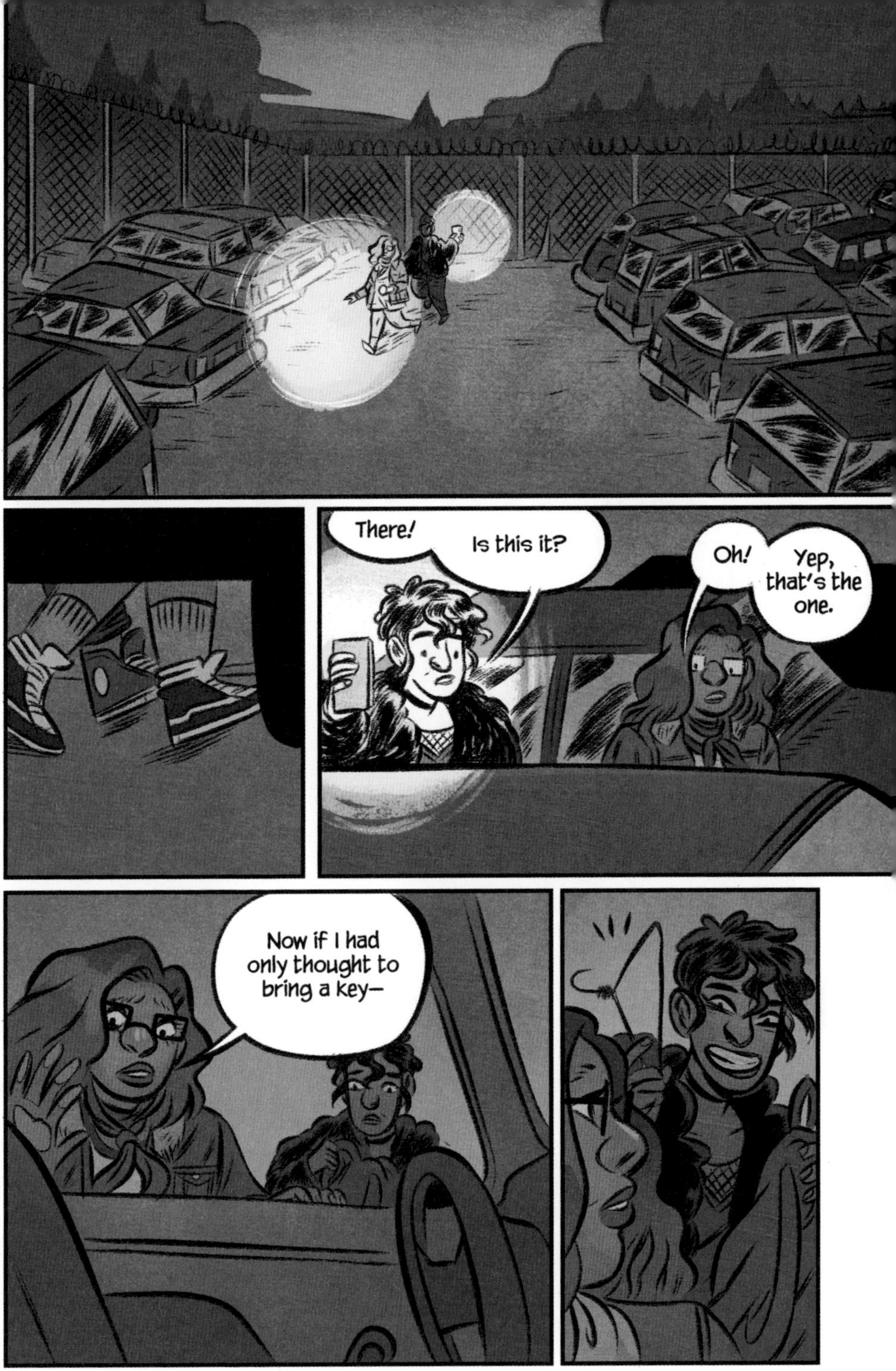
There!
Is this it?
Oh!
Yep, that's the one.
Now if I had only thought to bring a key—

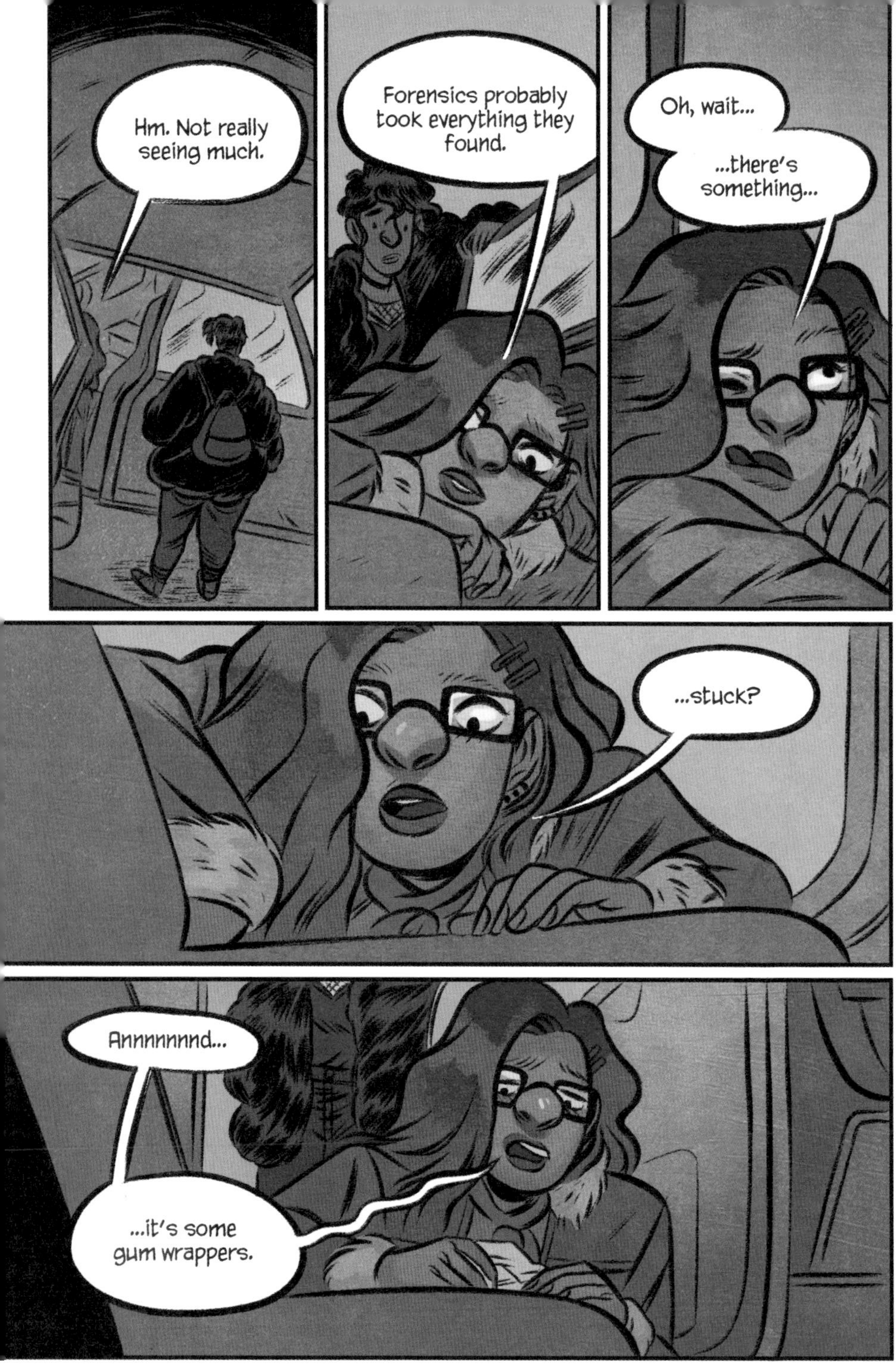
Hm. Not really seeing much.
Forensics probably took everything they found.
Oh, wait...
...there's something...
...stuck?
Annnnnnnd...
...it's some gum wrappers.

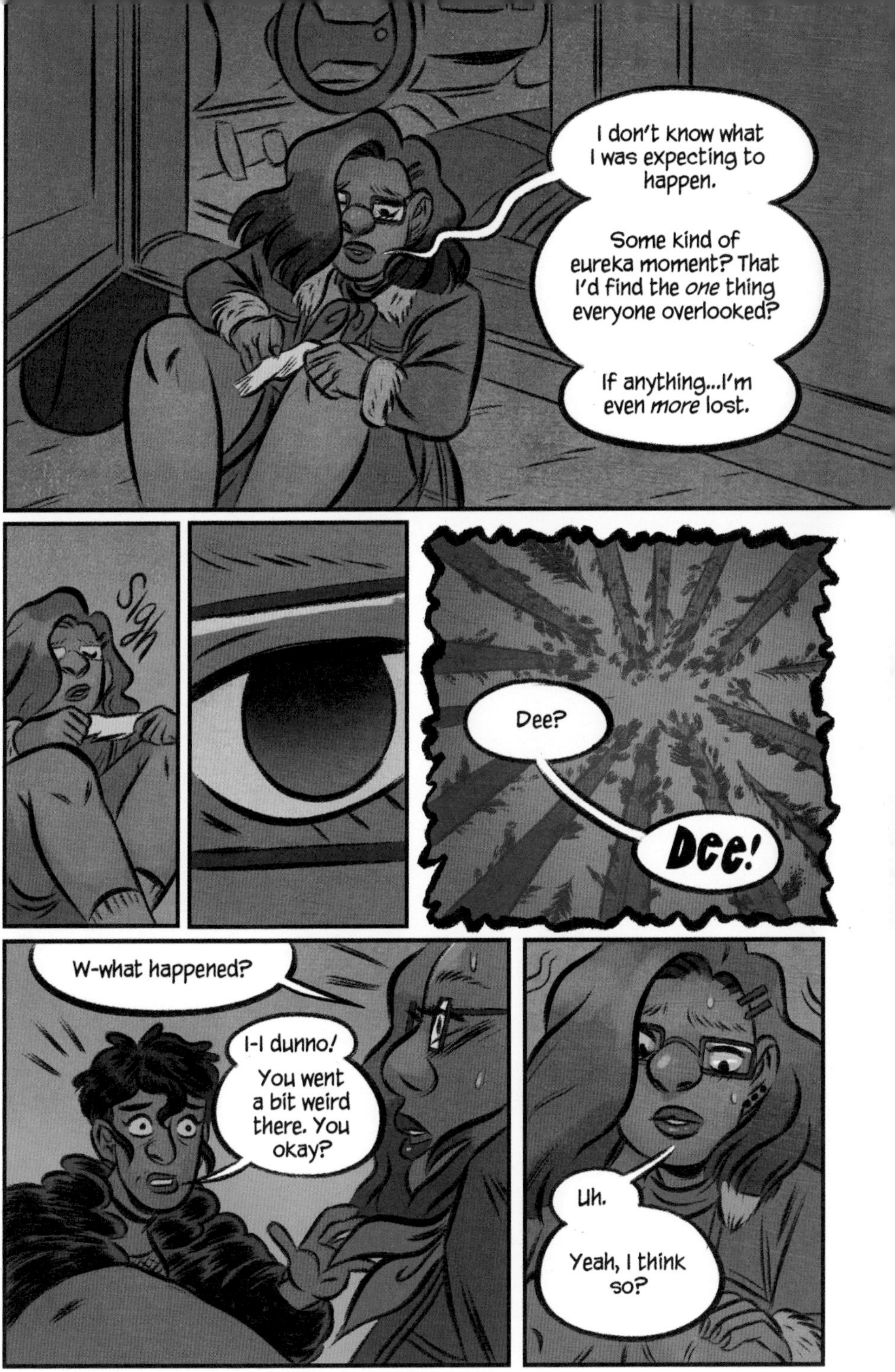
I don't know what I was expecting to happen.
Some kind of eureka moment? That I'd find the *one* thing everyone overlooked?
If anything...I'm even *more* lost.
Sigh
Dee?
Dee!
W-what happened?
I-I dunno!
You went a bit weird there. You okay?
Uh.
Yeah, I think so?

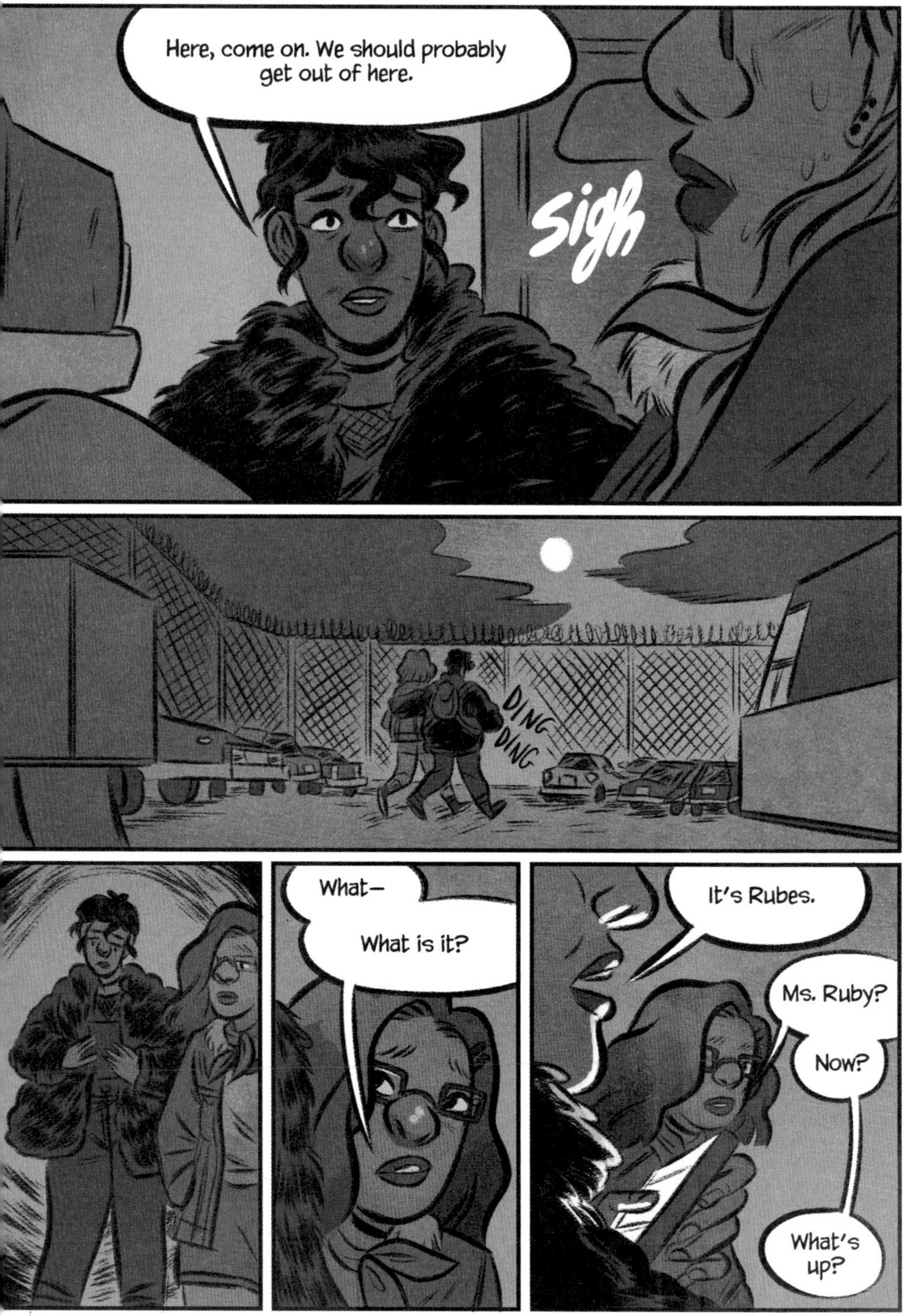
Here, come on. We should probably get out of here.
Sigh
DING DING
What—
What is it?
It's Rubes.
Ms. Ruby?
Now?
What's up?

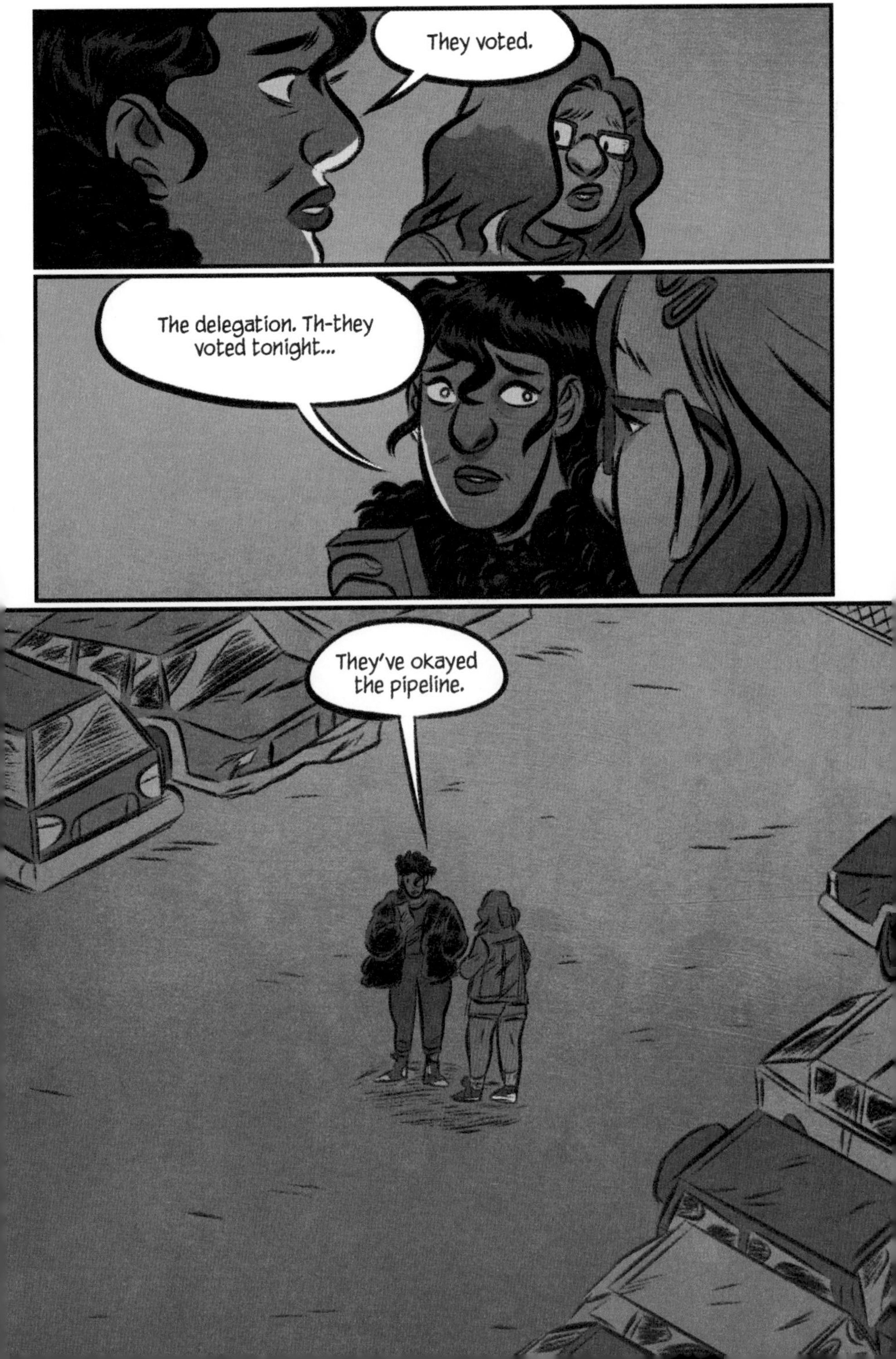
They voted.
The delegation. Th-they voted tonight...
They've okayed the pipeline.

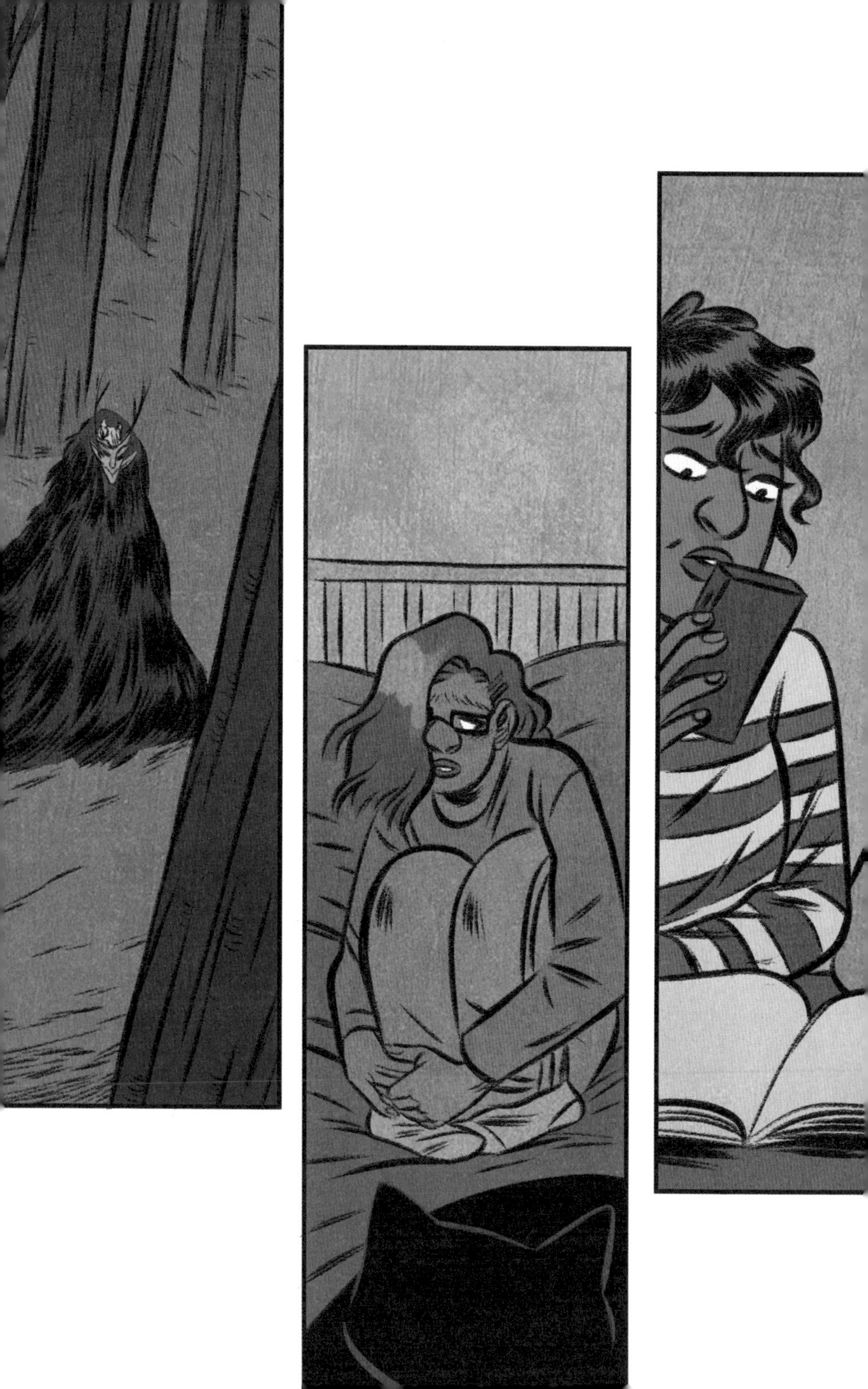

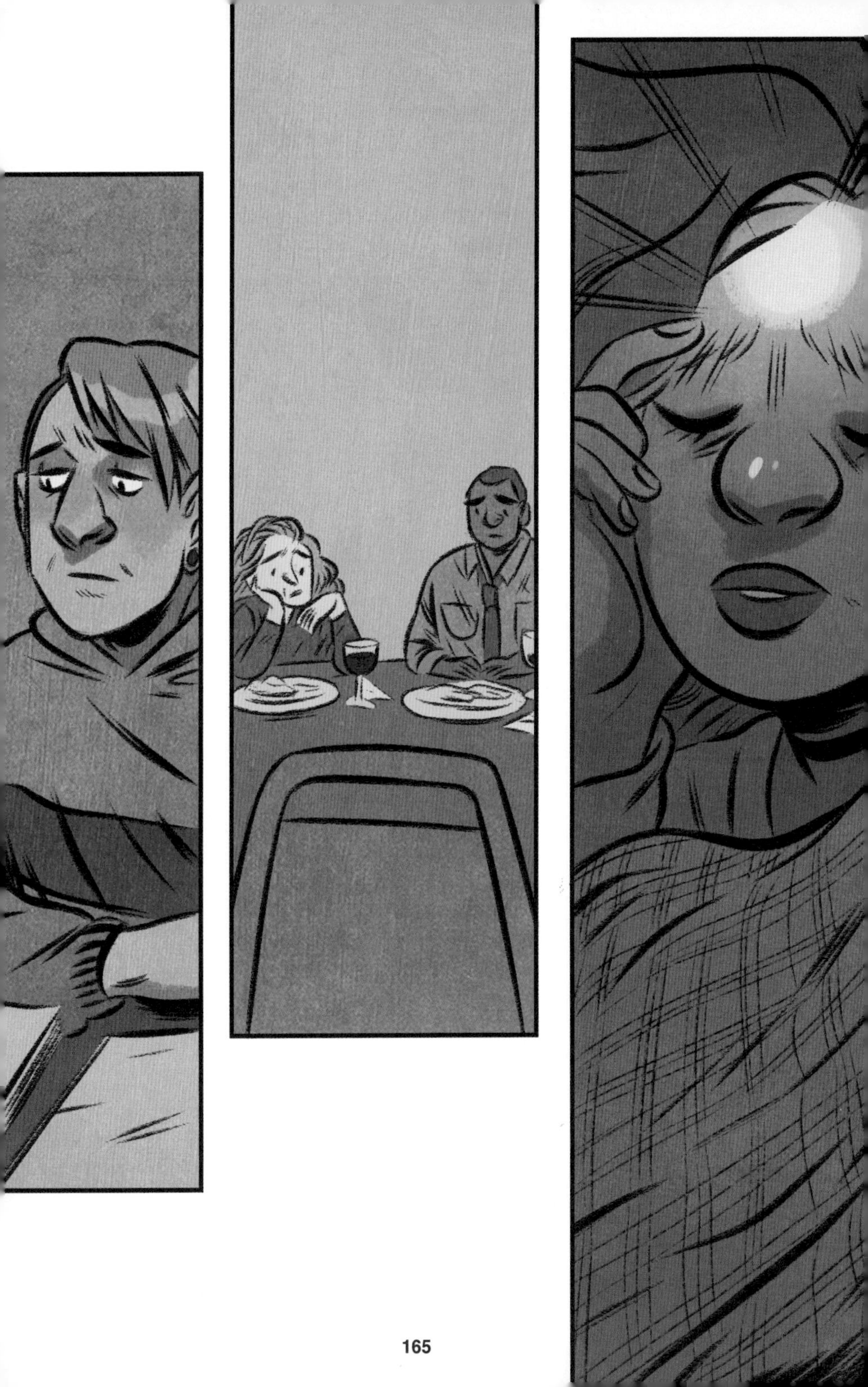

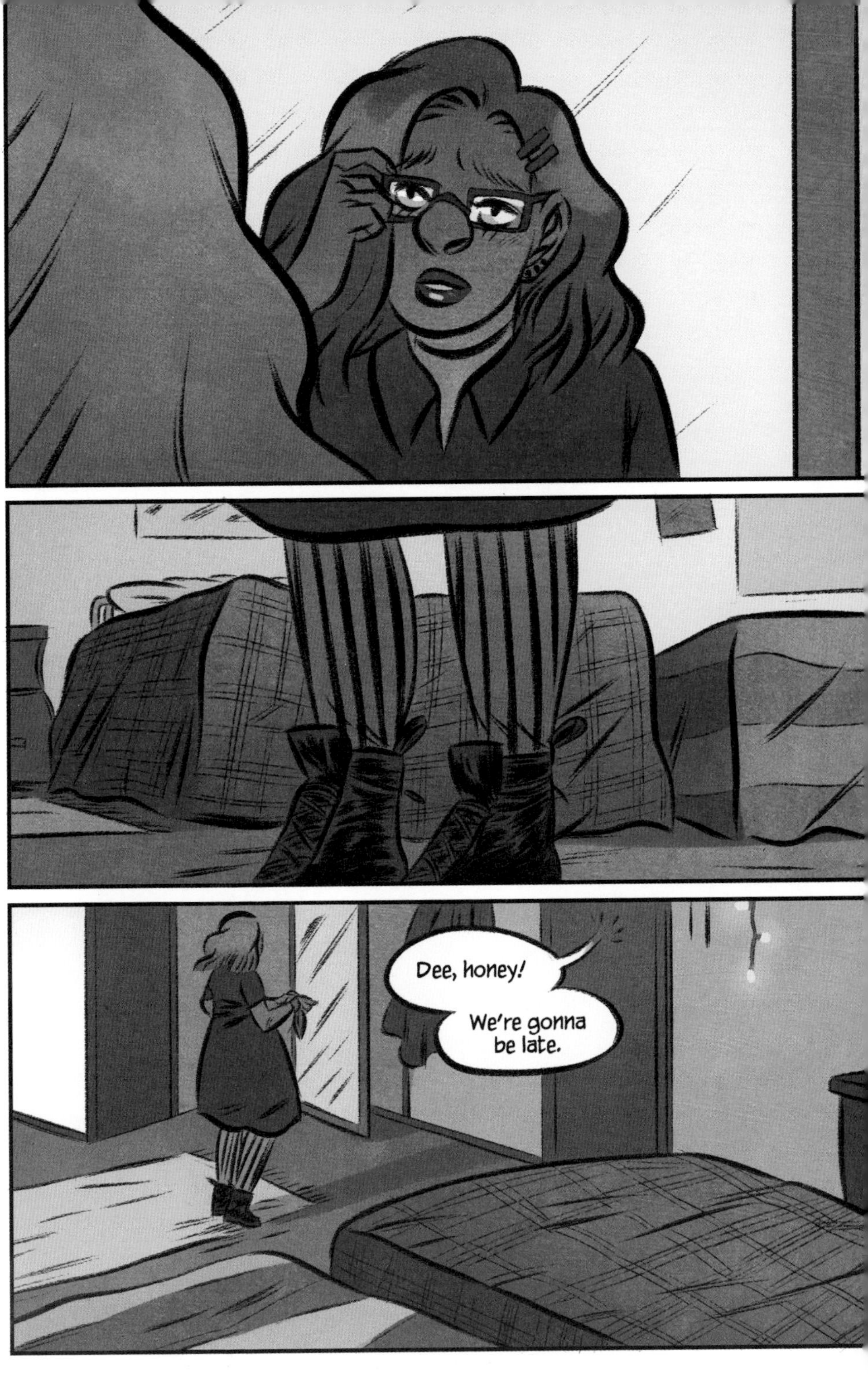
Dee, honey!
We're gonna be late.

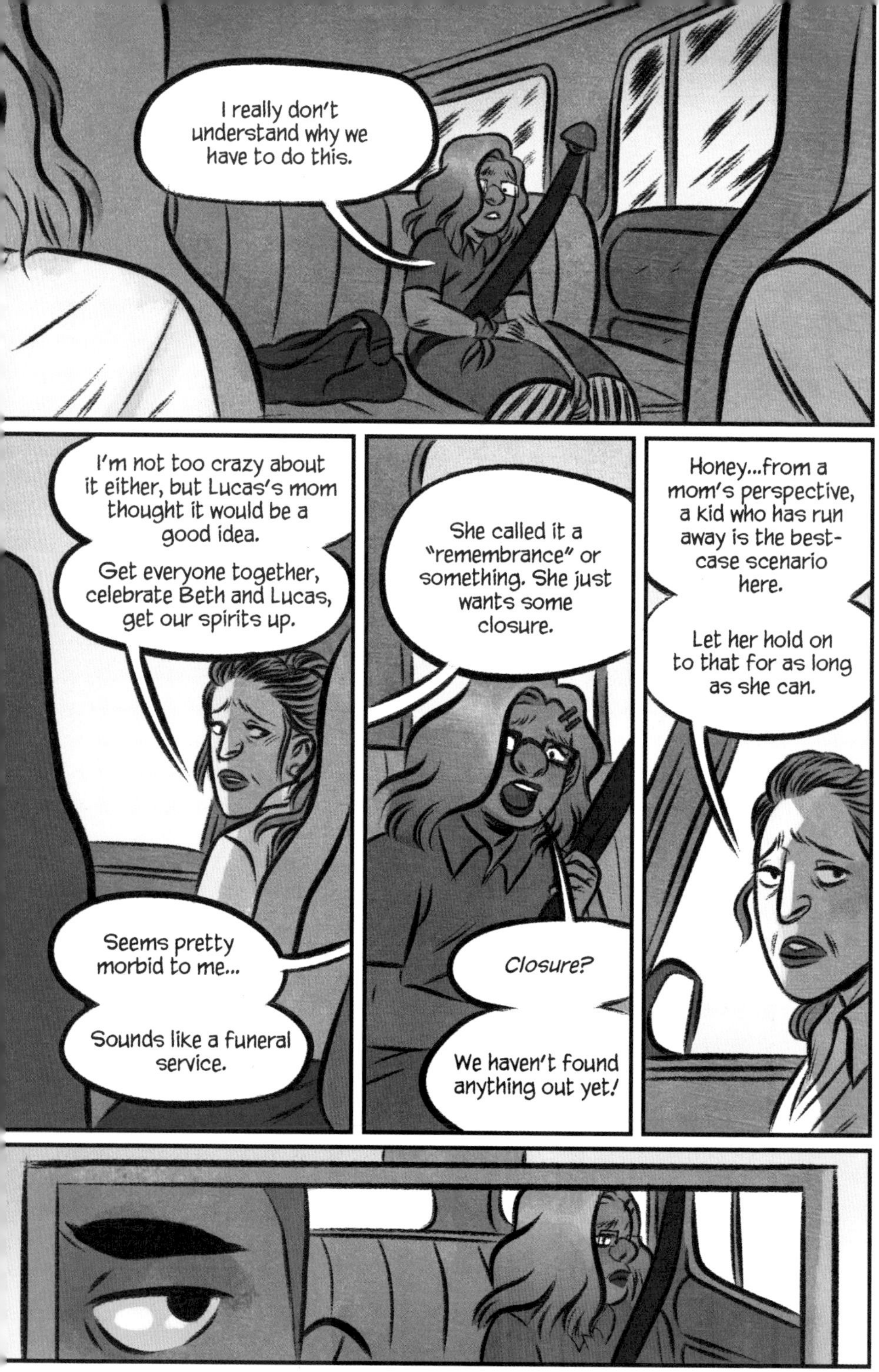
I really don't understand why we have to do this.
I'm not too crazy about it either, but Lucas's mom thought it would be a good idea.
Get everyone together, celebrate Beth and Lucas, get our spirits up.
Seems pretty morbid to me...
Sounds like a funeral service.
She called it a "remembrance" or something. She just wants some closure.
Closure?
We haven't found anything out yet!
Honey...from a mom's perspective, a kid who has run away is the best-case scenario here.
Let her hold on to that for as long as she can.

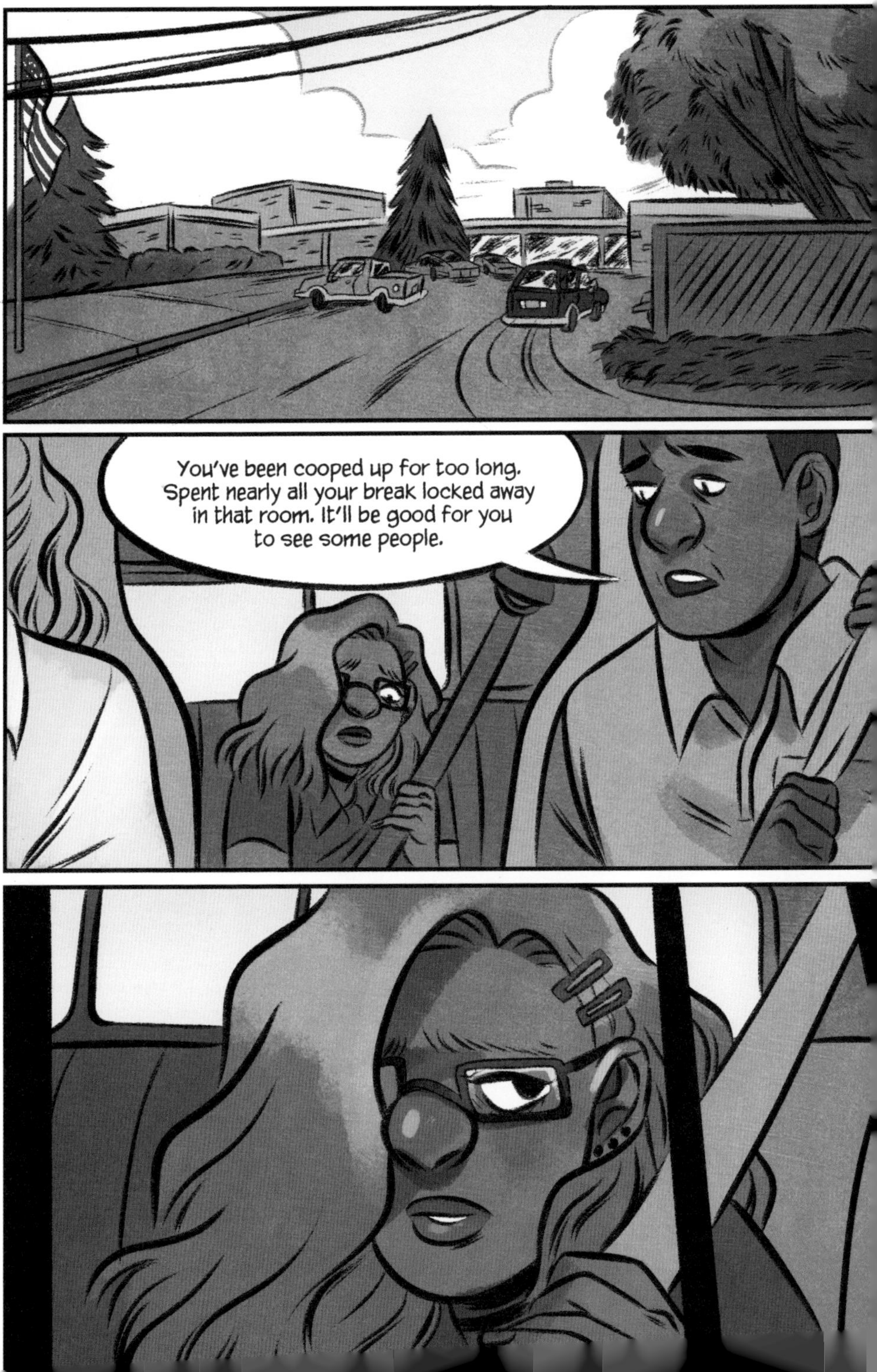
You've been cooped up for too long. Spent nearly all your break locked away in that room. It'll be good for you to see some people.

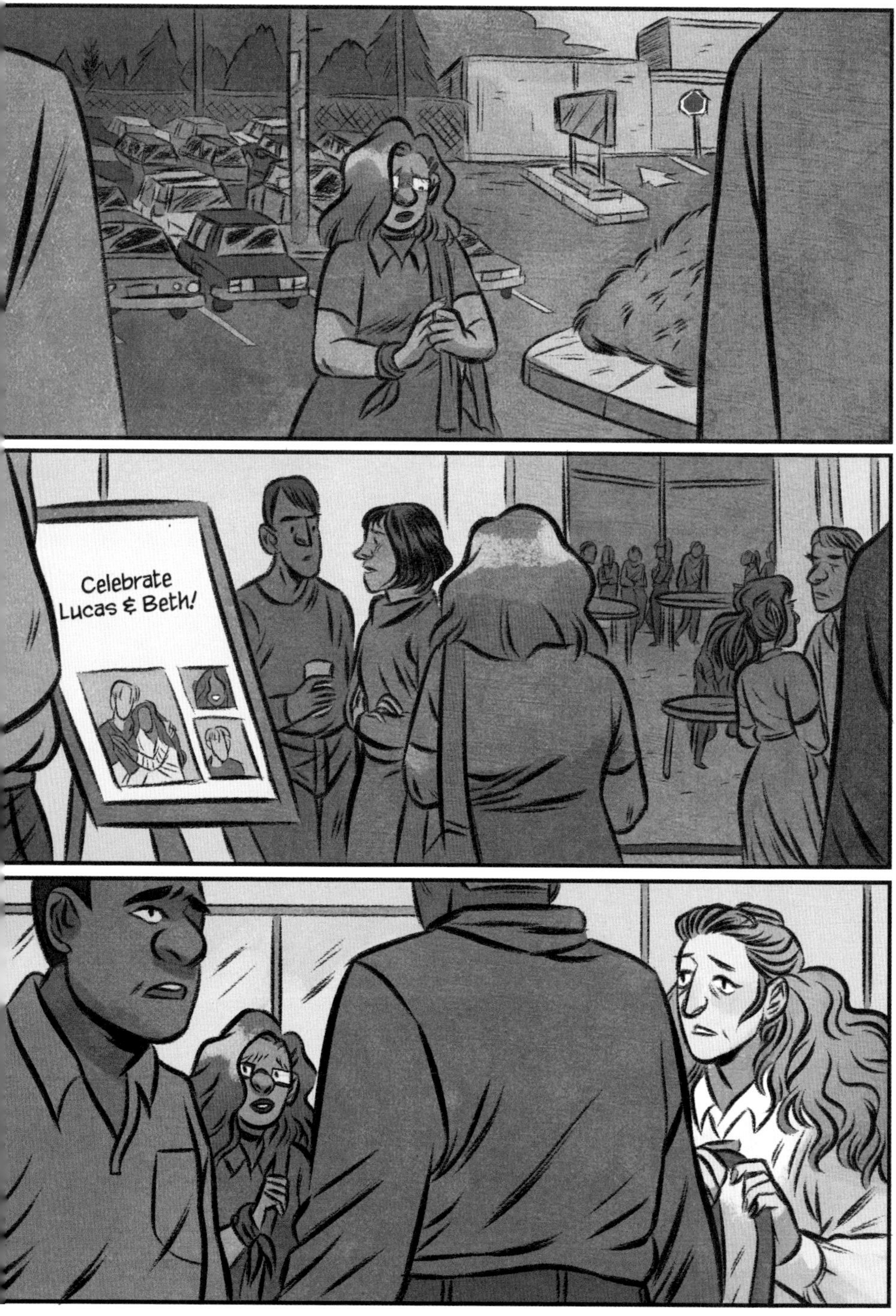
Celebrate
Lucas & Beth!

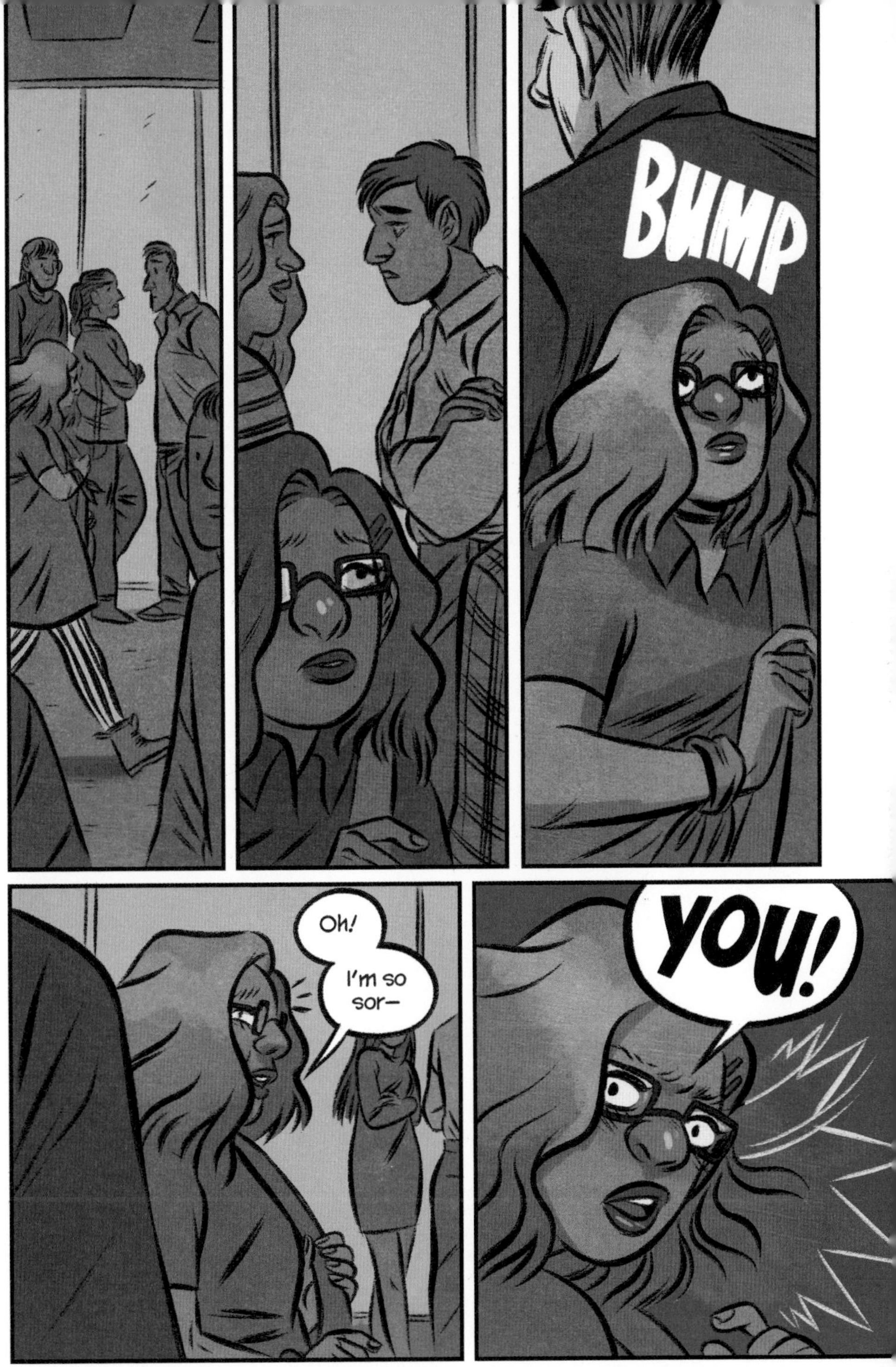
BUMP
Oh!
I'm so sor–
YOU!

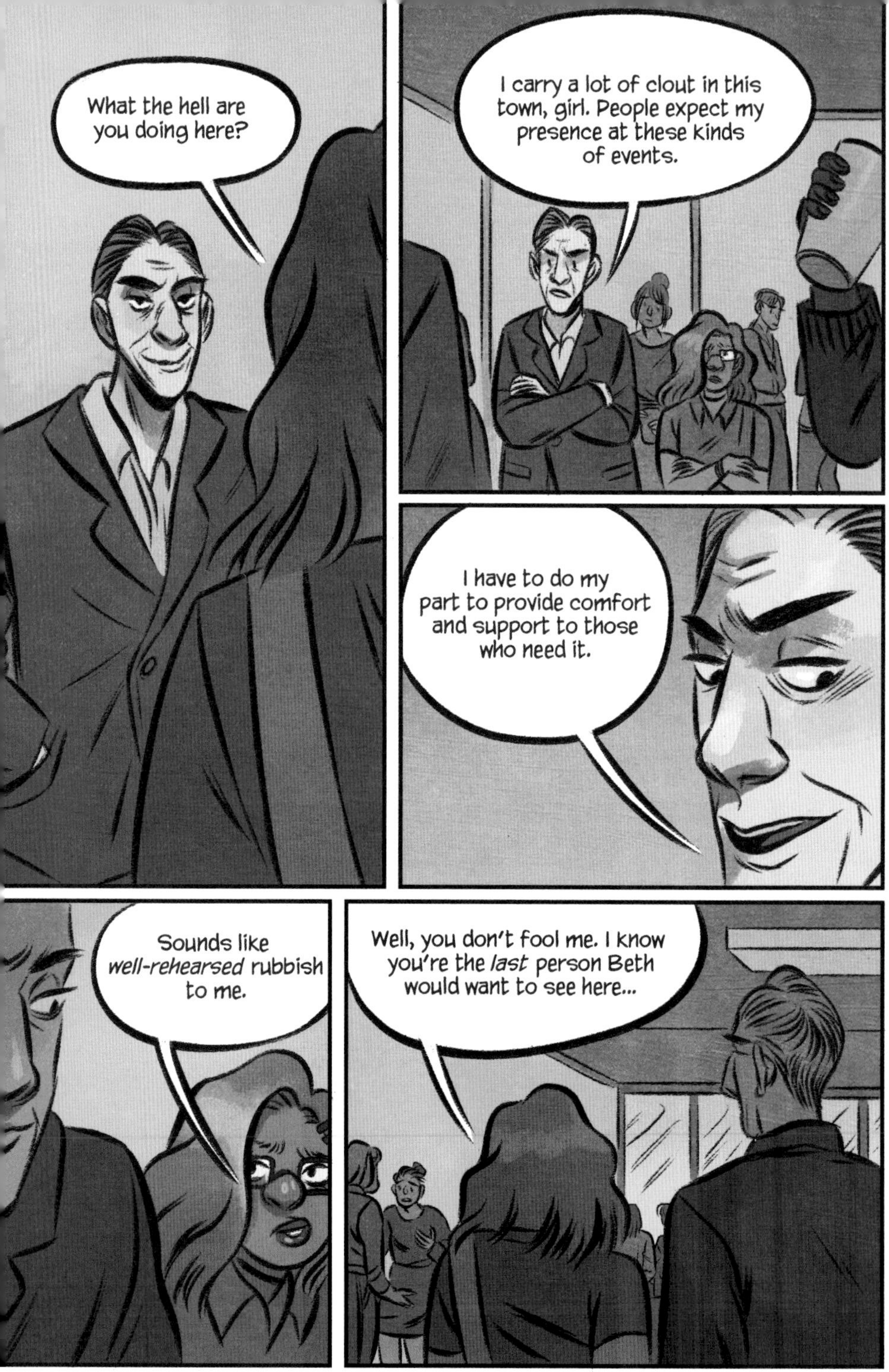
What the hell are you doing here?
I carry a lot of clout in this town, girl. People expect my presence at these kinds of events.
I have to do my part to provide comfort and support to those who need it.
Sounds like *well-rehearsed* rubbish to me.
Well, you don't fool me. I know you're the *last* person Beth would want to see here...

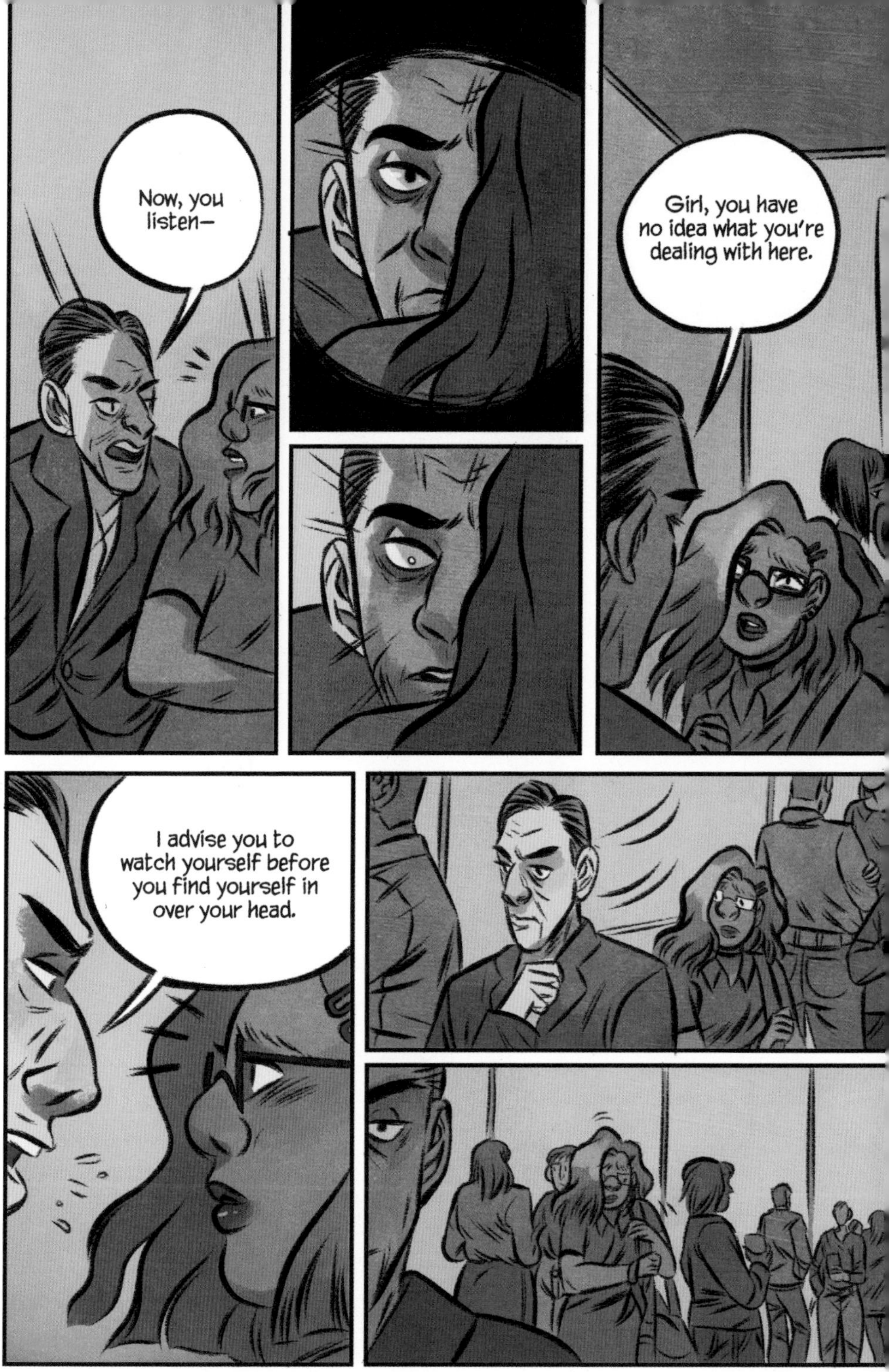
Now, you listen—
Girl, you have no idea what you're dealing with here.
I advise you to watch yourself before you find yourself in over your head.

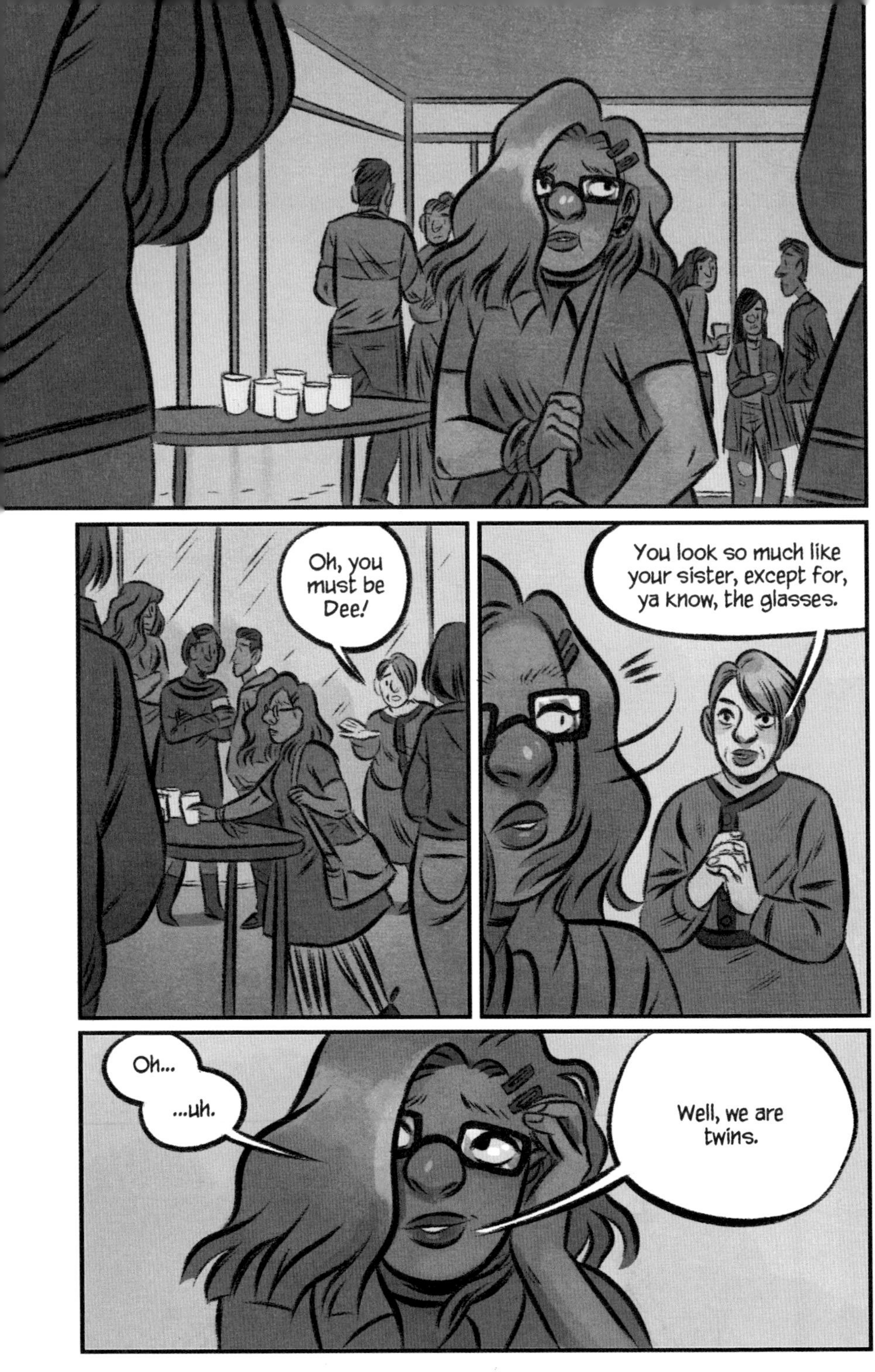
Oh, you must be Dee!
You look so much like your sister, except for, ya know, the glasses.
Oh...
...uh.
Well, we are twins.

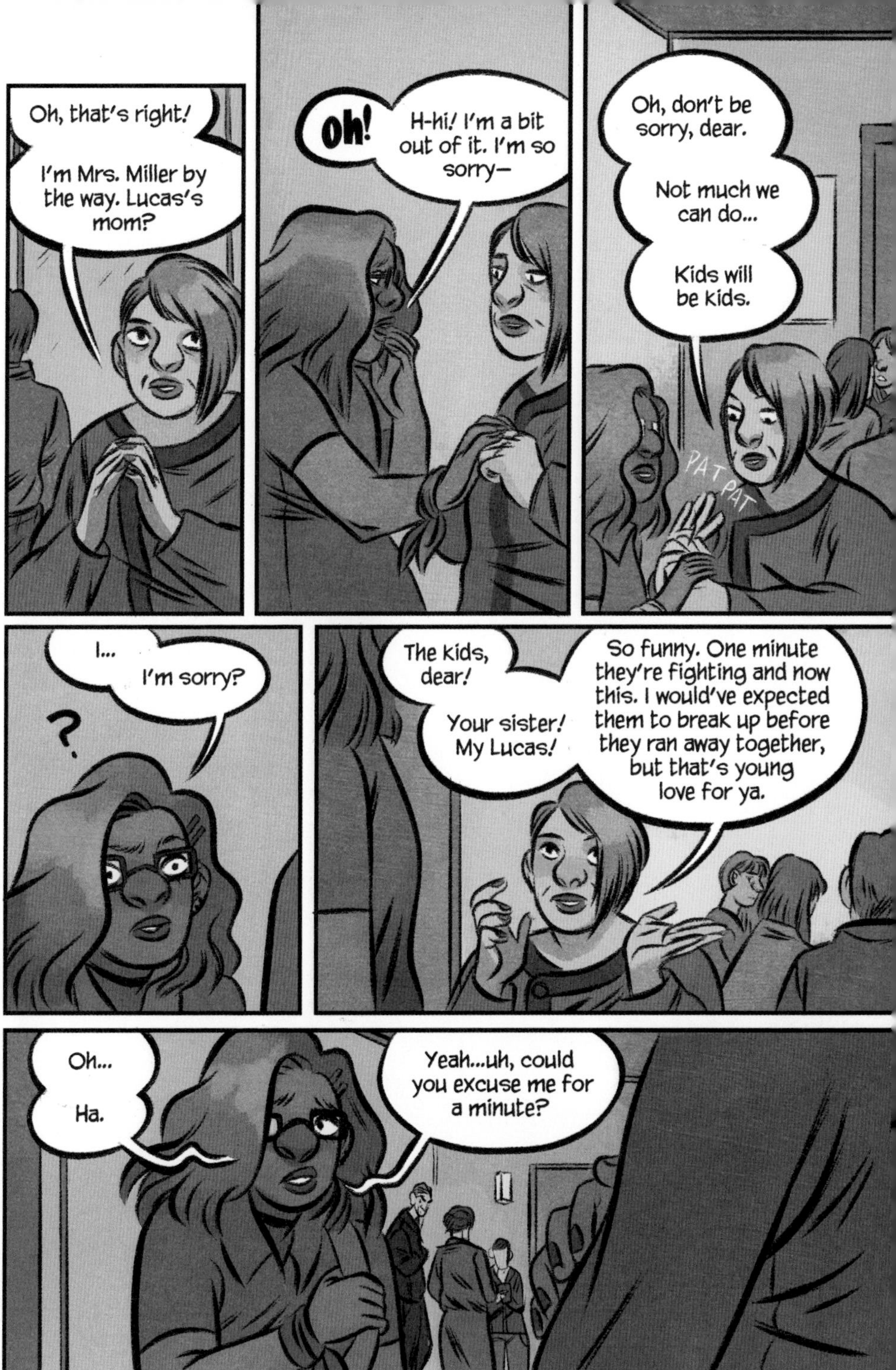
Oh, that's right!
I'm Mrs. Miller by the way. Lucas's mom?
Oh!
H-hi! I'm a bit out of it. I'm so sorry—
Oh, don't be sorry, dear.
Not much we can do...
Kids will be kids.
PAT PAT
I...
I'm sorry?
?
The kids, dear!
Your sister! My Lucas!
So funny. One minute they're fighting and now this. I would've expected them to break up before they ran away together, but that's young love for ya.
Oh...
Ha.
Yeah...uh, could you excuse me for a minute?

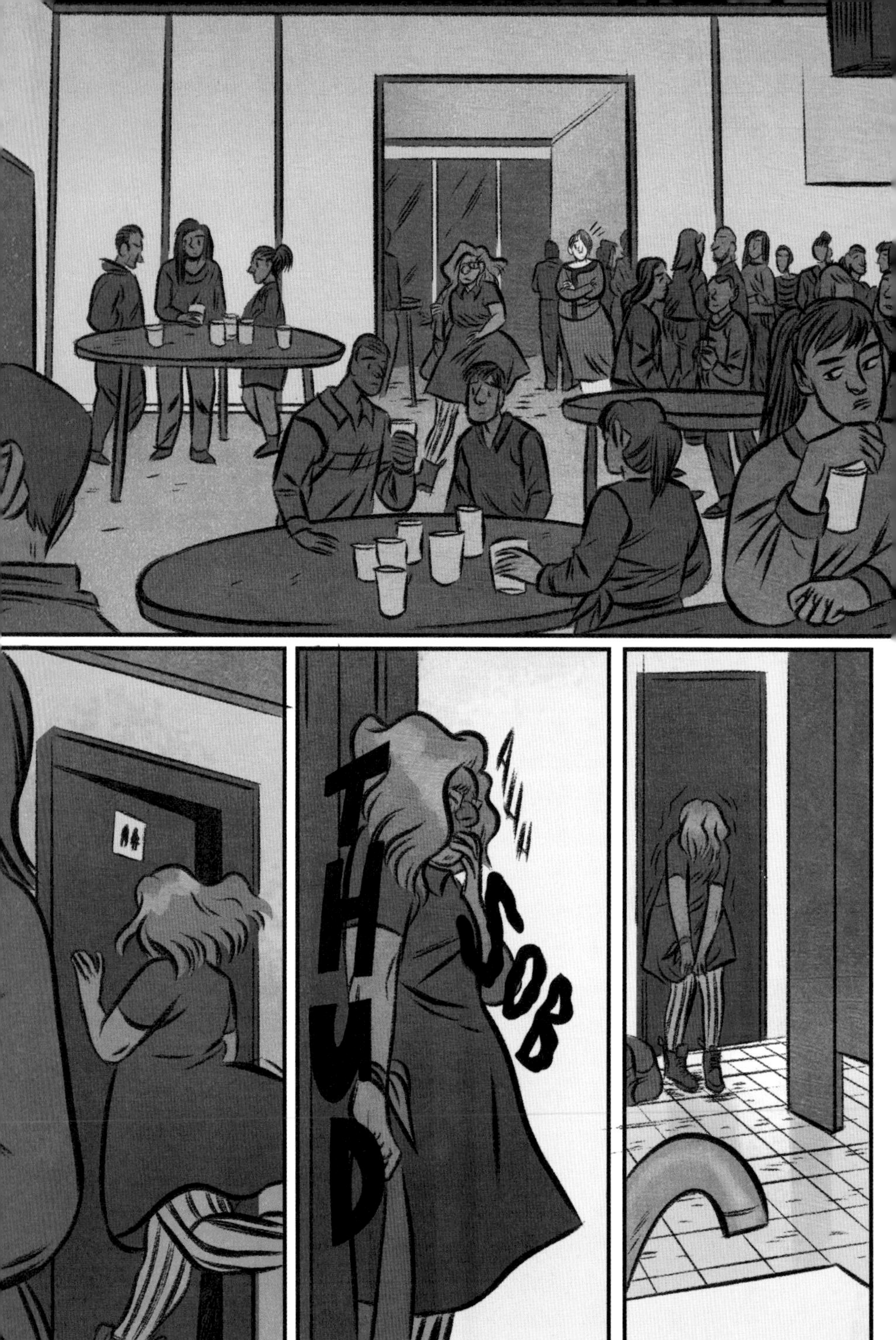
THUD
SOB

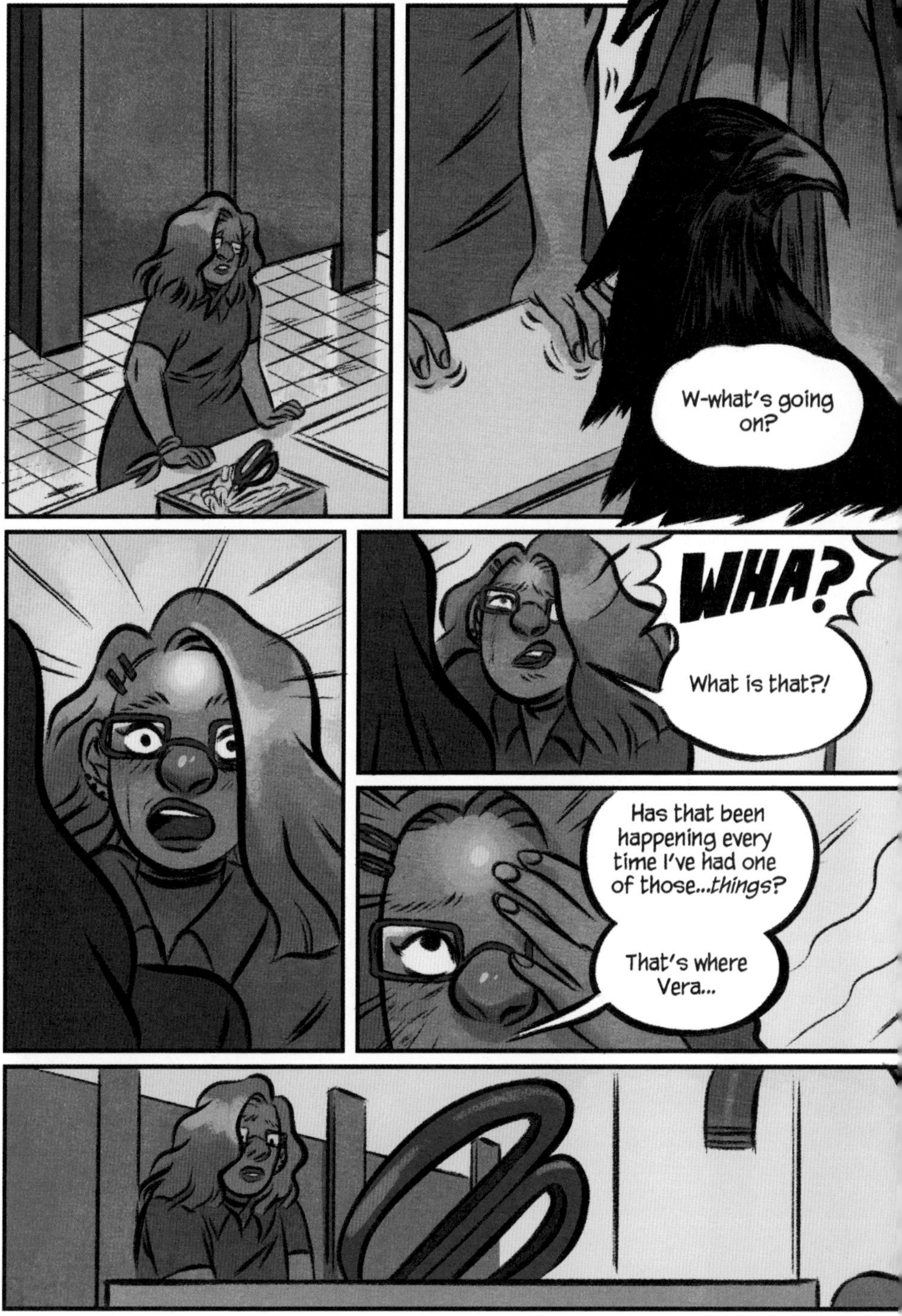
W-what's going on?
WHA?
What is that?!
Has that been happening every time I've had one of those...*things*?
That's where Vera...

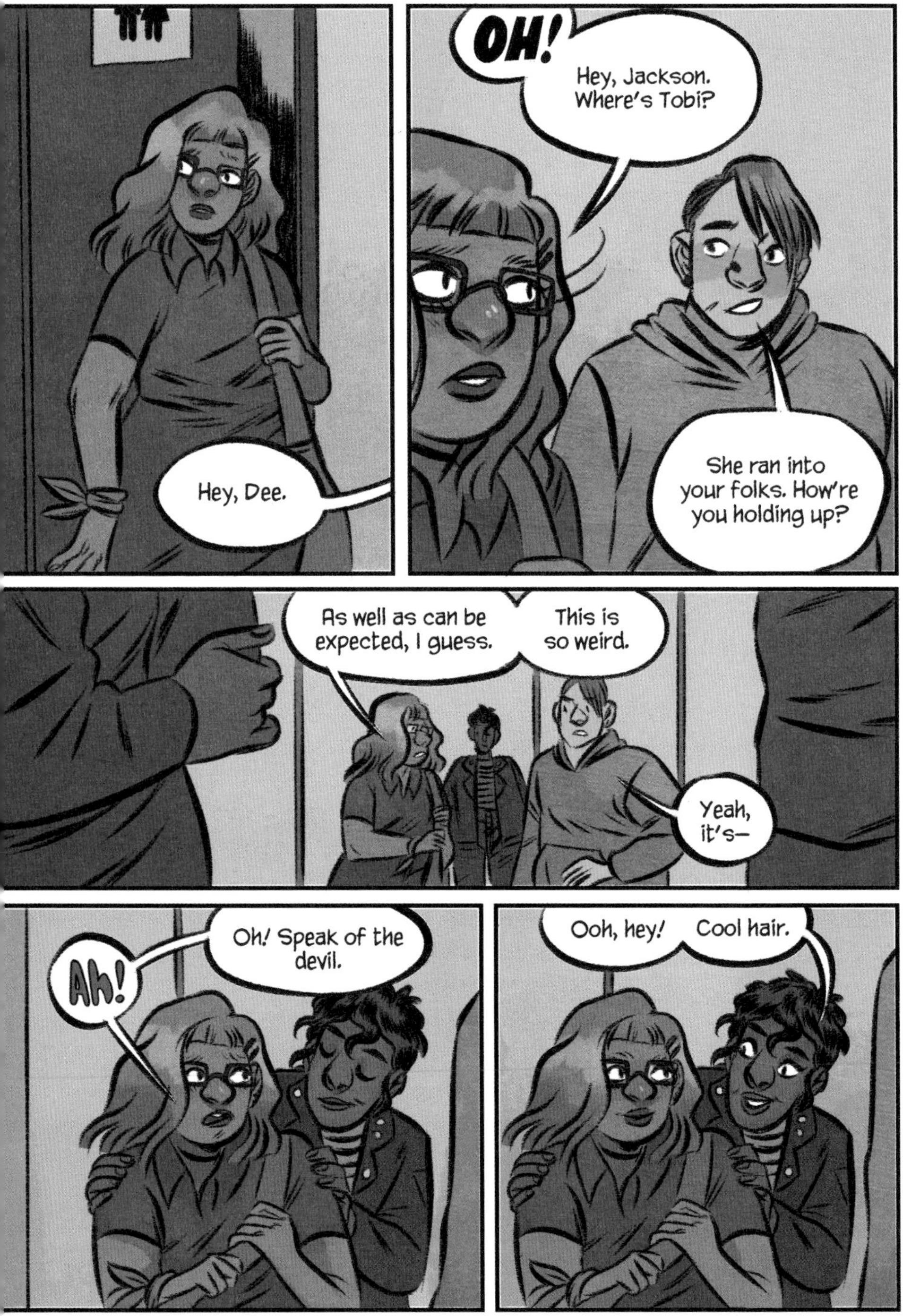
Hey, Dee.
OH!
Hey, Jackson. Where's Tobi?
She ran into your folks. How're you holding up?
As well as can be expected, I guess.
This is so weird.
Yeah, it's—
Ah!
Oh! Speak of the devil.
Ooh, hey!
Cool hair.

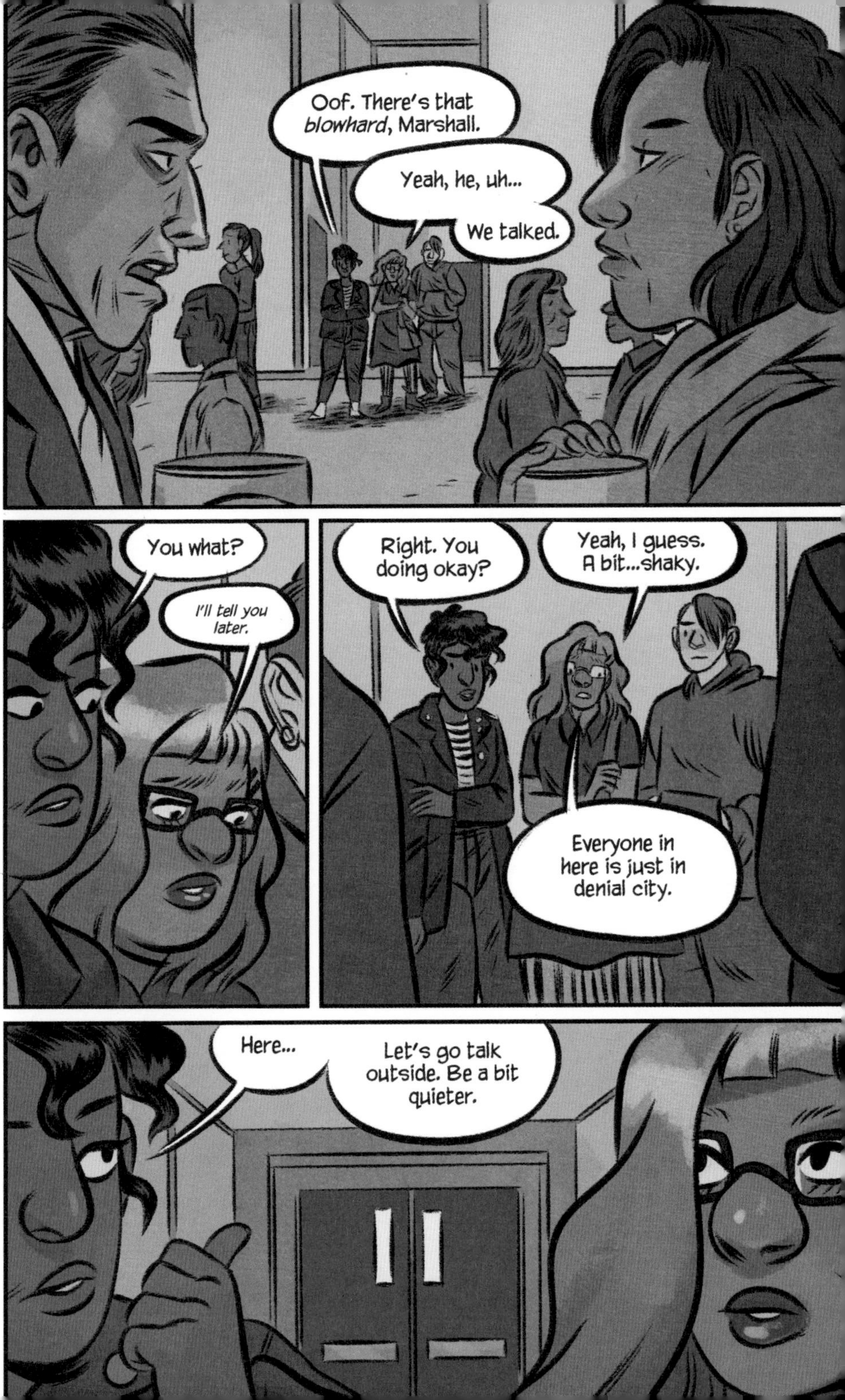

Oof. There's that *blowhard*, Marshall.
Yeah, he, uh...
We talked.
You what?
I'll tell you later.
Right. You doing okay?
Yeah, I guess. A bit...shaky.
Everyone in here is just in denial city.
Here...
Let's go talk outside. Be a bit quieter.

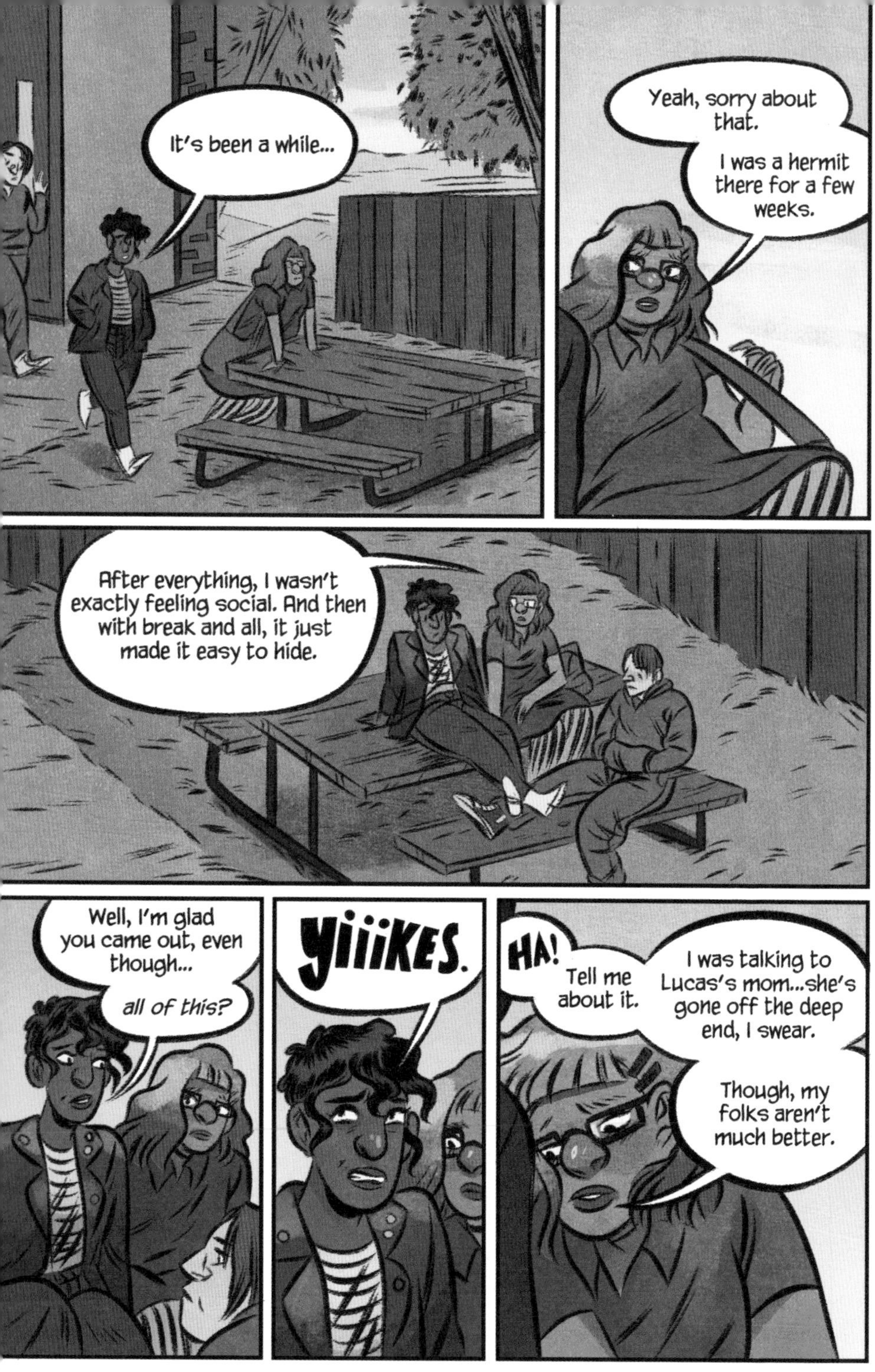
It's been a while...
Yeah, sorry about that.
I was a hermit there for a few weeks.
After everything, I wasn't exactly feeling social. And then with break and all, it just made it easy to hide.
Well, I'm glad you came out, even though...
all of this?
yiiiKES.
HA!
Tell me about it.
I was talking to Lucas's mom...she's gone off the deep end, I swear.
Though, my folks aren't much better.

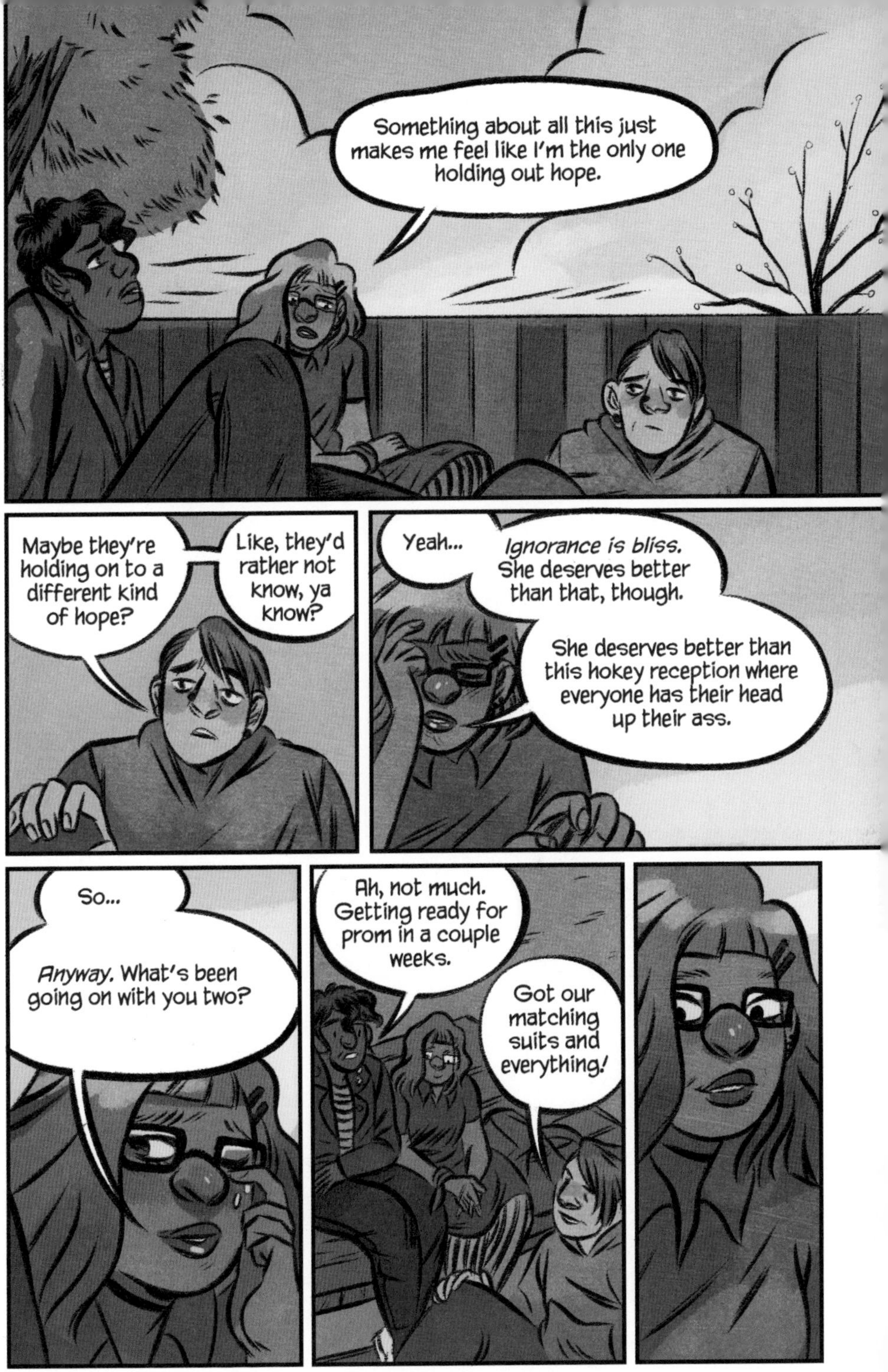
Something about all this just makes me feel like I'm the only one holding out hope.
Maybe they're holding on to a different kind of hope?
Like, they'd rather not know, ya know?
Yeah...
Ignorance is bliss. She deserves better than that, though.
She deserves better than this hokey reception where everyone has their head up their ass.
So...
Anyway. What's been going on with you two?
Ah, not much. Getting ready for prom in a couple weeks.
Got our matching suits and everything!

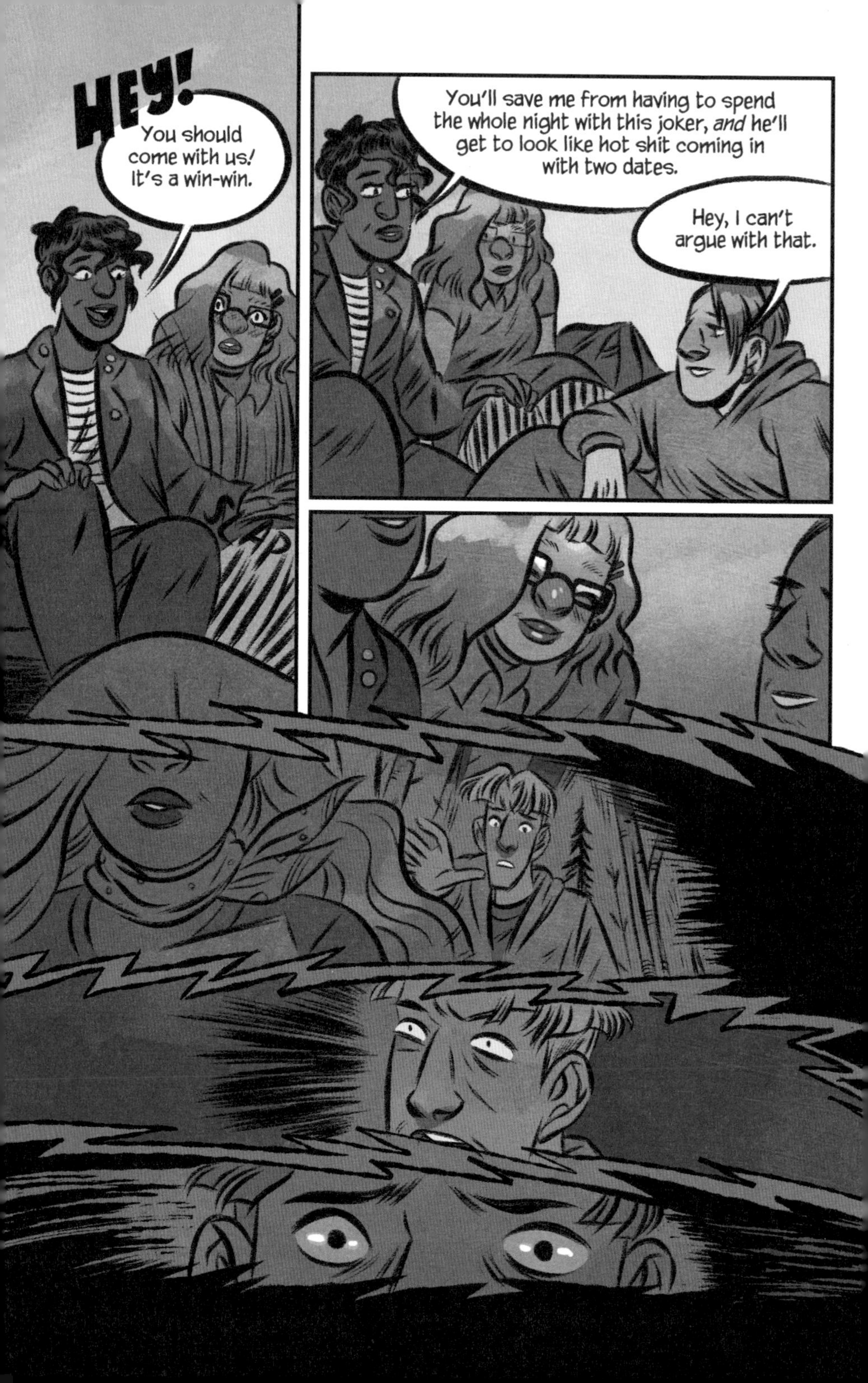
HEY!
You should come with us! It's a win-win.
You'll save me from having to spend the whole night with this joker, *and* he'll get to look like hot shit coming in with two dates.
Hey, I can't argue with that.

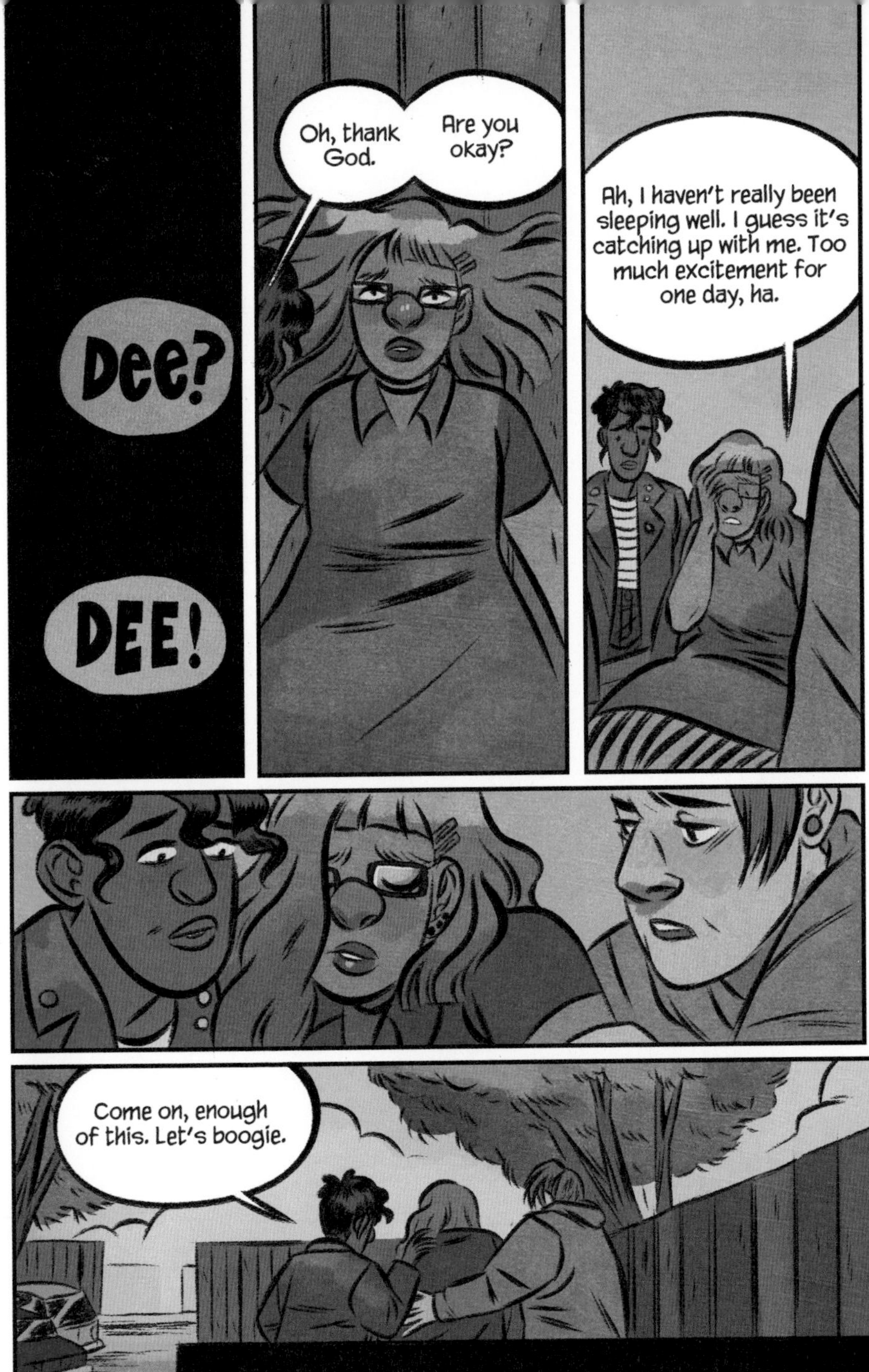
Dee?
DEE!
Oh, thank God.
Are you okay?
Ah, I haven't really been sleeping well. I guess it's catching up with me. Too much excitement for one day, ha.
Come on, enough of this. Let's boogie.

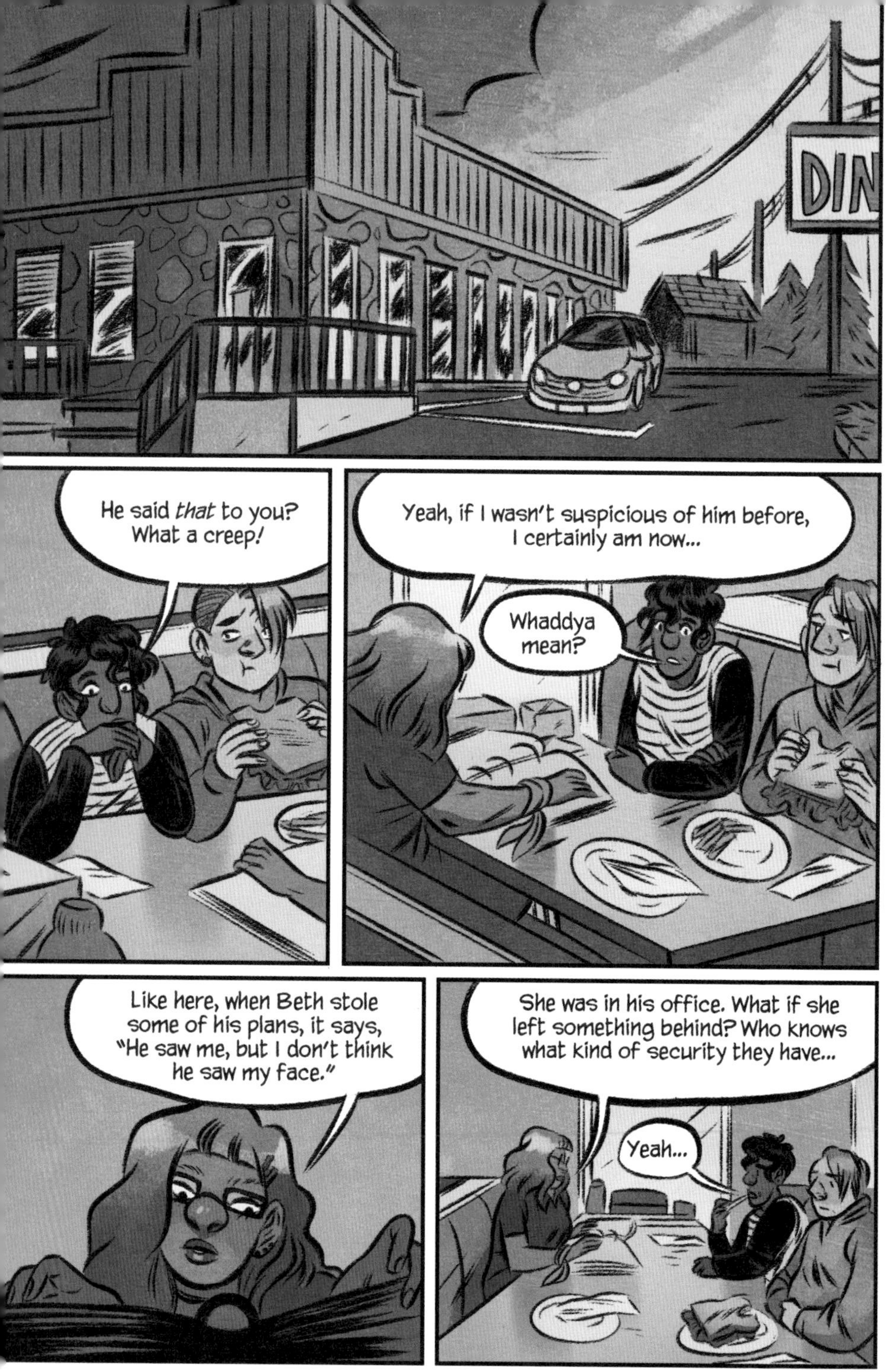
DIN
He said *that* to you? What a creep!
Yeah, if I wasn't suspicious of him before, I certainly am now...
Whaddya mean?
Like here, when Beth stole some of his plans, it says, "He saw me, but I don't think he saw my face."
She was in his office. What if she left something behind? Who knows what kind of security they have...
Yeah...

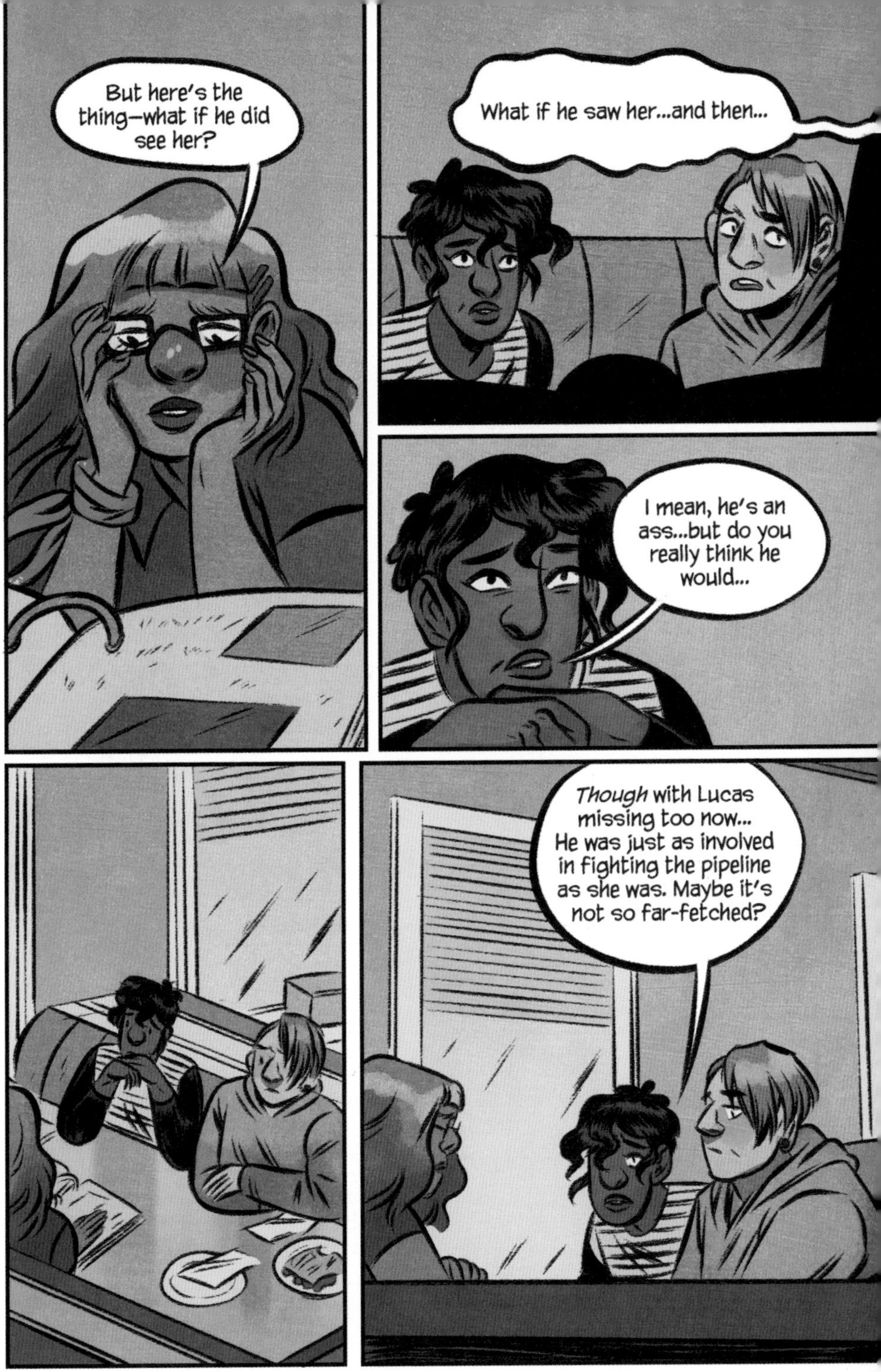

But here's the thing—what if he did see her?
What if he saw her...and then...
I mean, he's an ass...but do you really think he would...
Though with Lucas missing too now... He was just as involved in fighting the pipeline as she was. Maybe it's not so far-fetched?

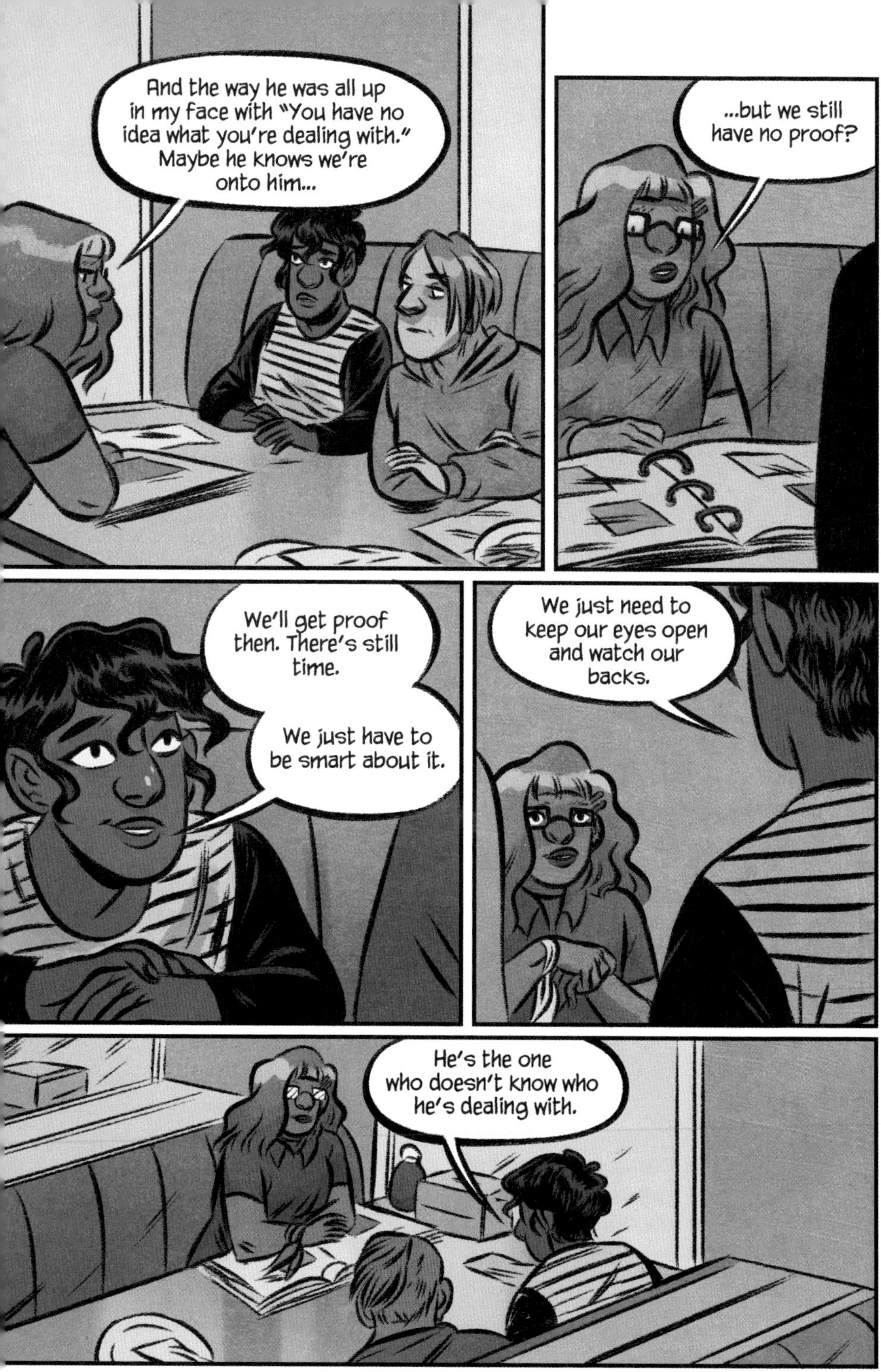
And the way he was all up in my face with "You have no idea what you're dealing with." Maybe he knows we're onto him...
...but we still have no proof?
We'll get proof then. There's still time.
We just have to be smart about it.
We just need to keep our eyes open and watch our backs.
He's the one who doesn't know who he's dealing with.

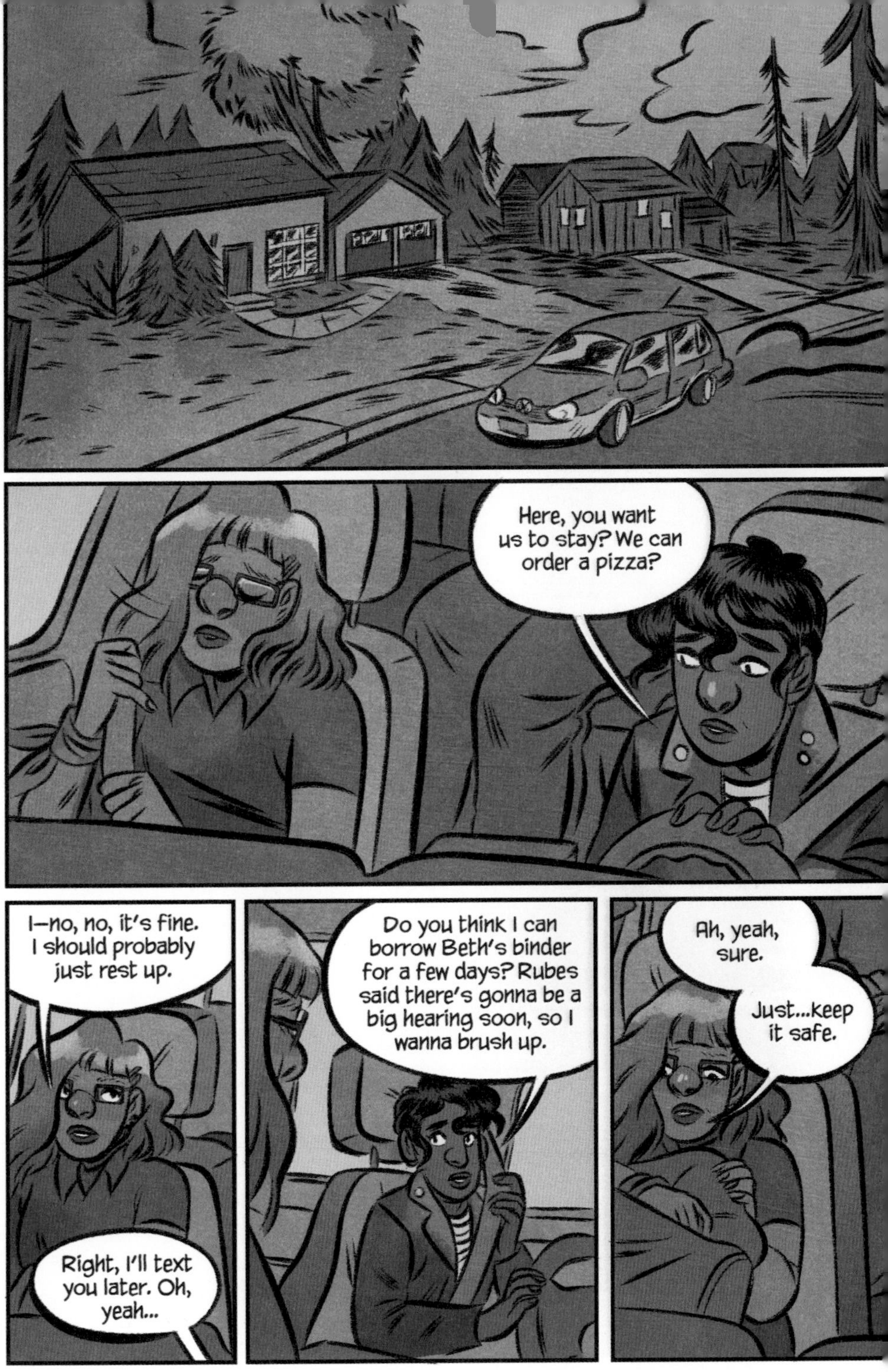
Here, you want us to stay? We can order a pizza?
I—no, no, it's fine. I should probably just rest up.
Right, I'll text you later. Oh, yeah...
Do you think I can borrow Beth's binder for a few days? Rubes said there's gonna be a big hearing soon, so I wanna brush up.
Ah, yeah, sure.
Just...keep it safe.

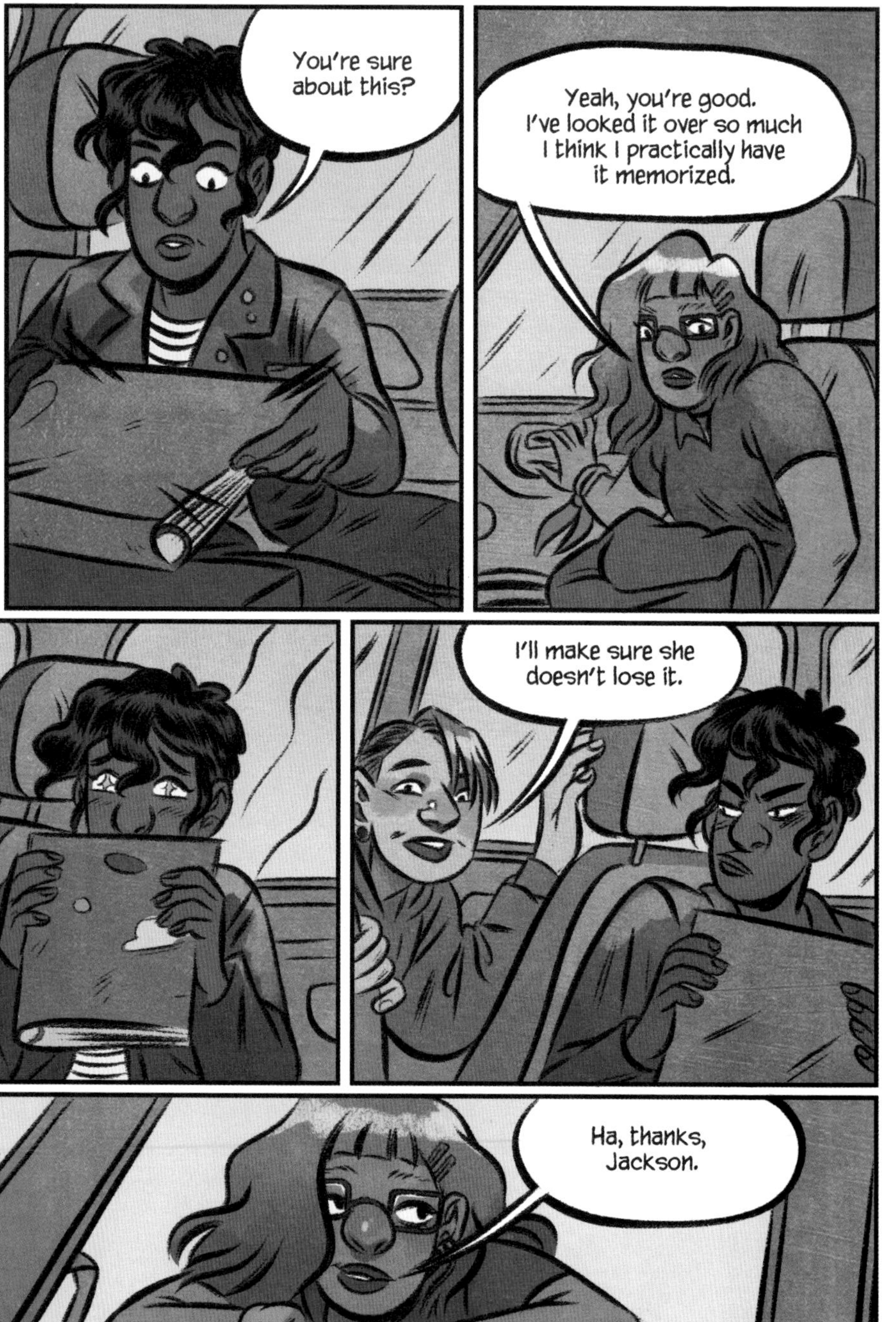
You're sure about this?
Yeah, you're good. I've looked it over so much I think I practically have it memorized.
I'll make sure she doesn't lose it.
Ha, thanks, Jackson.

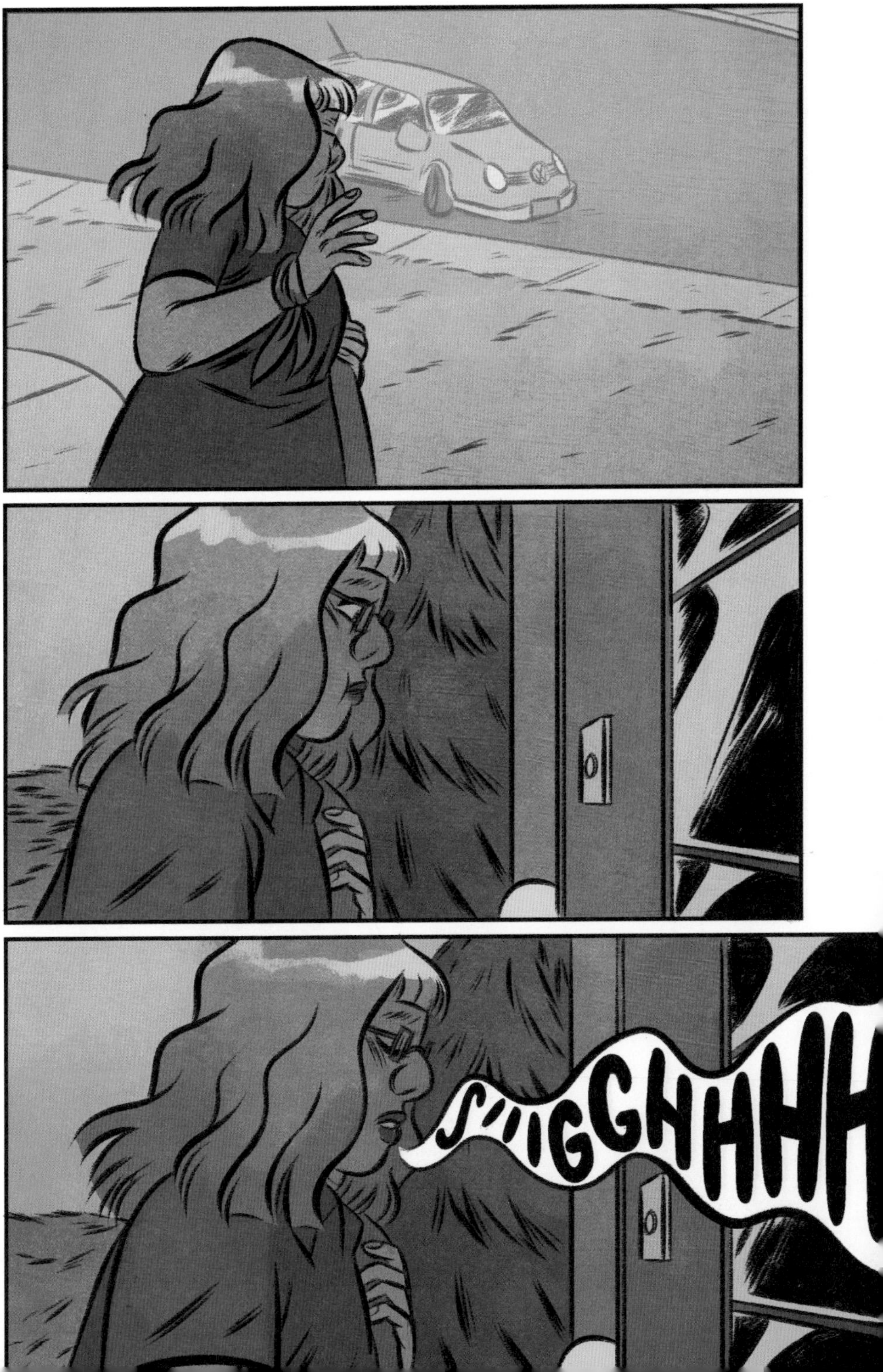
SIIIGGHHHHH

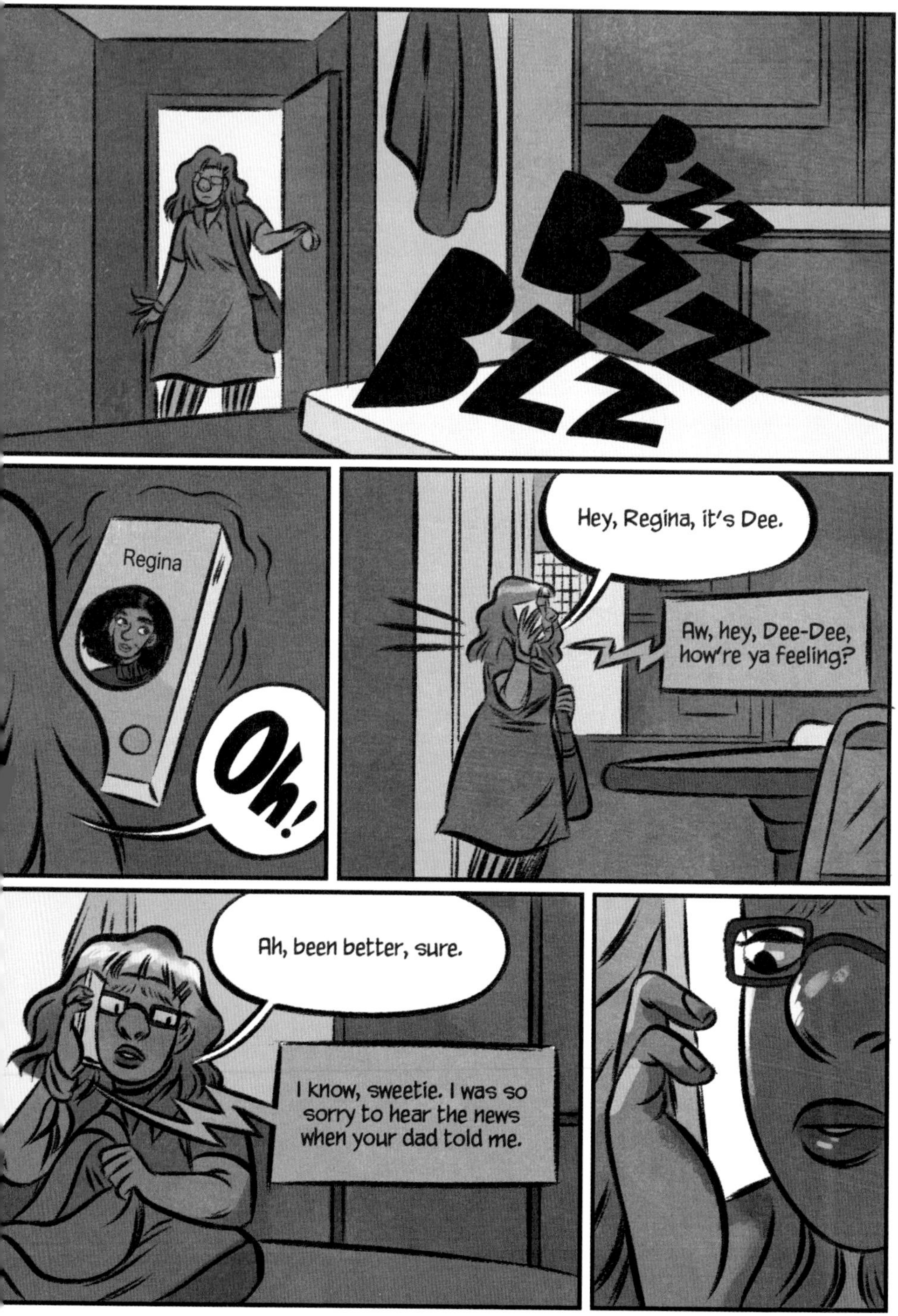
BZZ BZZ BZZ
Regina
Oh!
Hey, Regina, it's Dee.
Aw, hey, Dee-Dee, how're ya feeling?
Ah, been better, sure.
I know, sweetie. I was so sorry to hear the news when your dad told me.

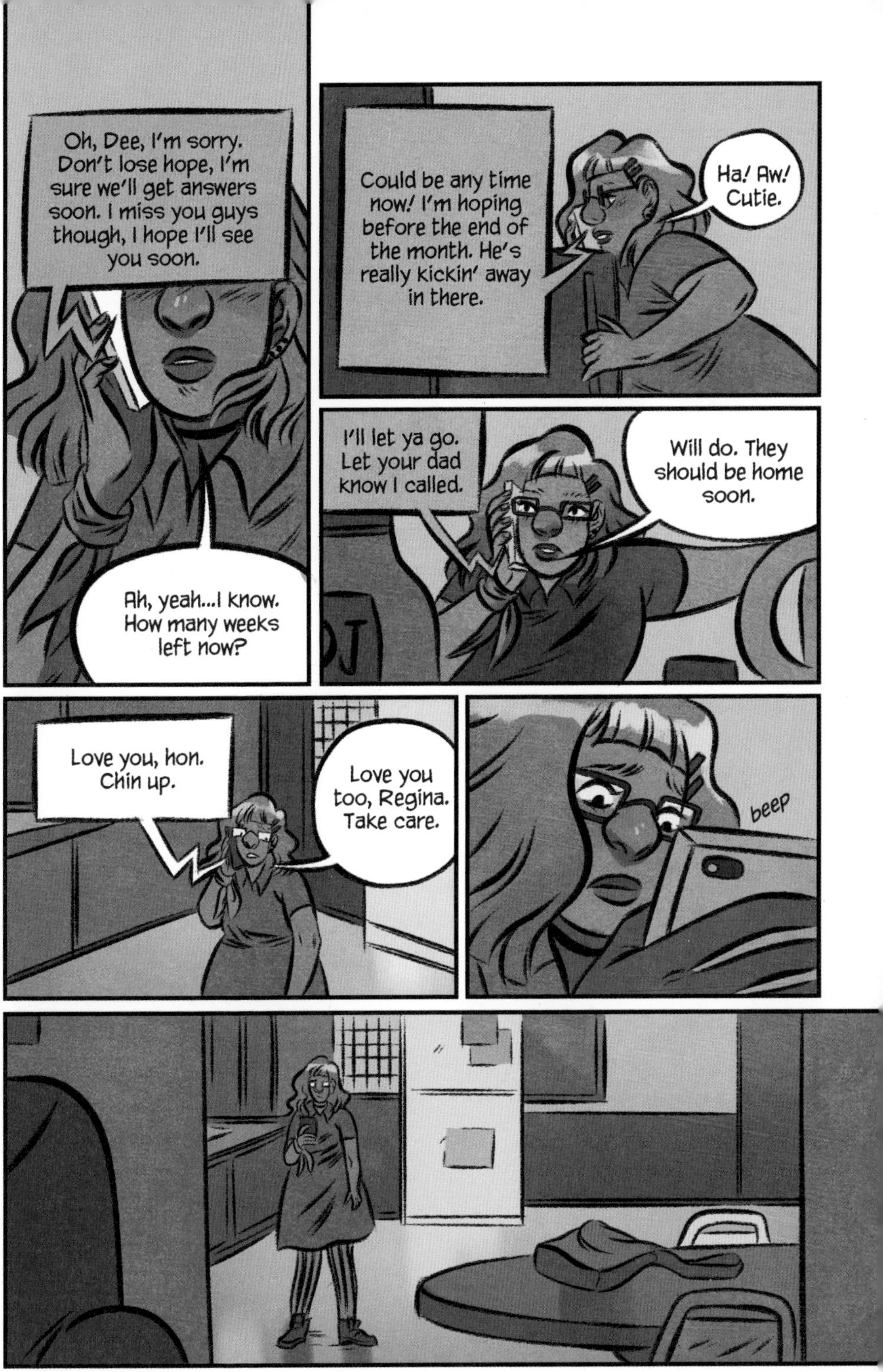
Oh, Dee, I'm sorry. Don't lose hope, I'm sure we'll get answers soon. I miss you guys though, I hope I'll see you soon.
Ah, yeah...I know. How many weeks left now?
Could be any time now! I'm hoping before the end of the month. He's really kickin' away in there.
Ha! Aw! Cutie.
I'll let ya go. Let your dad know I called.
Will do. They should be home soon.
Love you, hon. Chin up.
Love you too, Regina. Take care.
beep

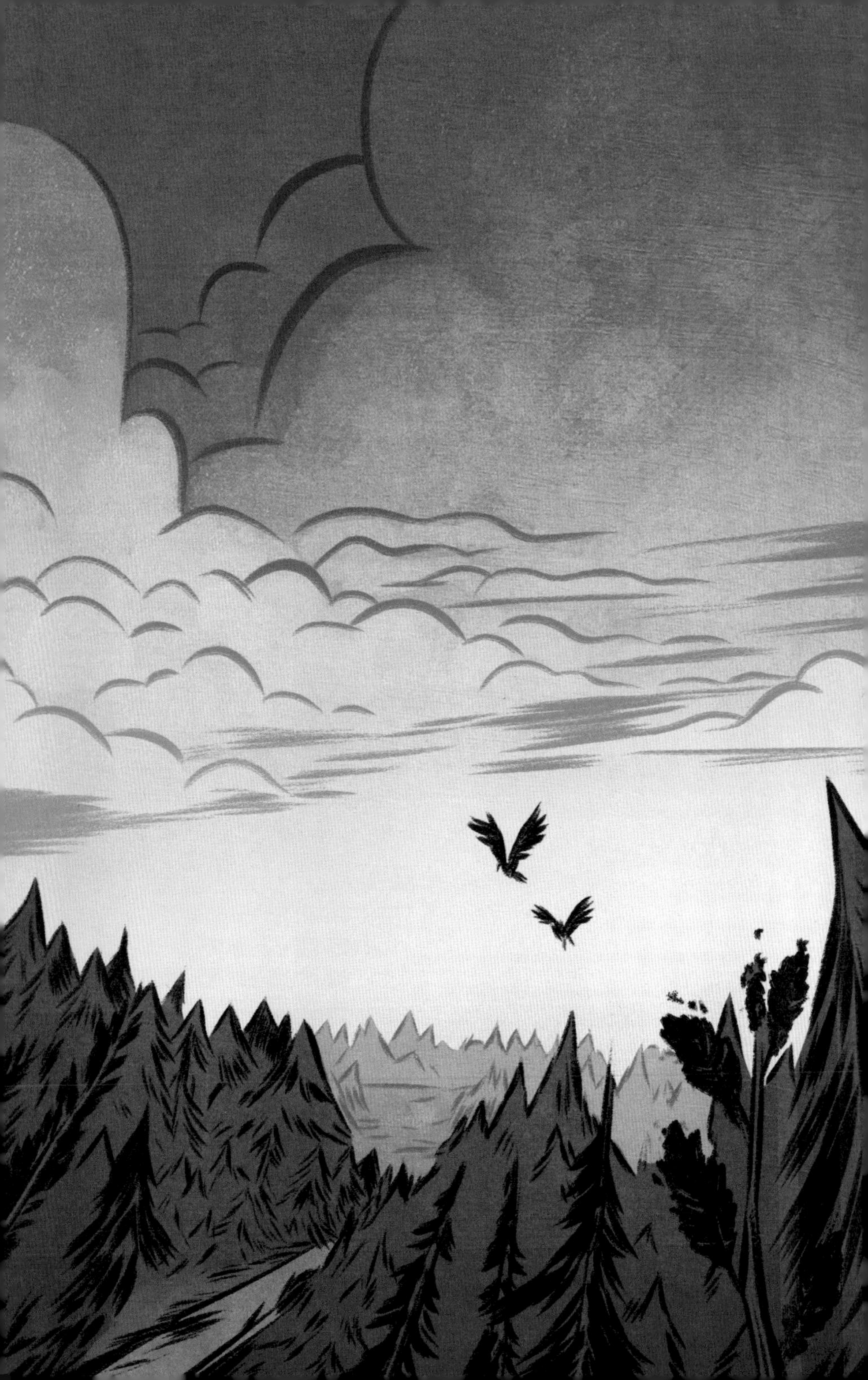

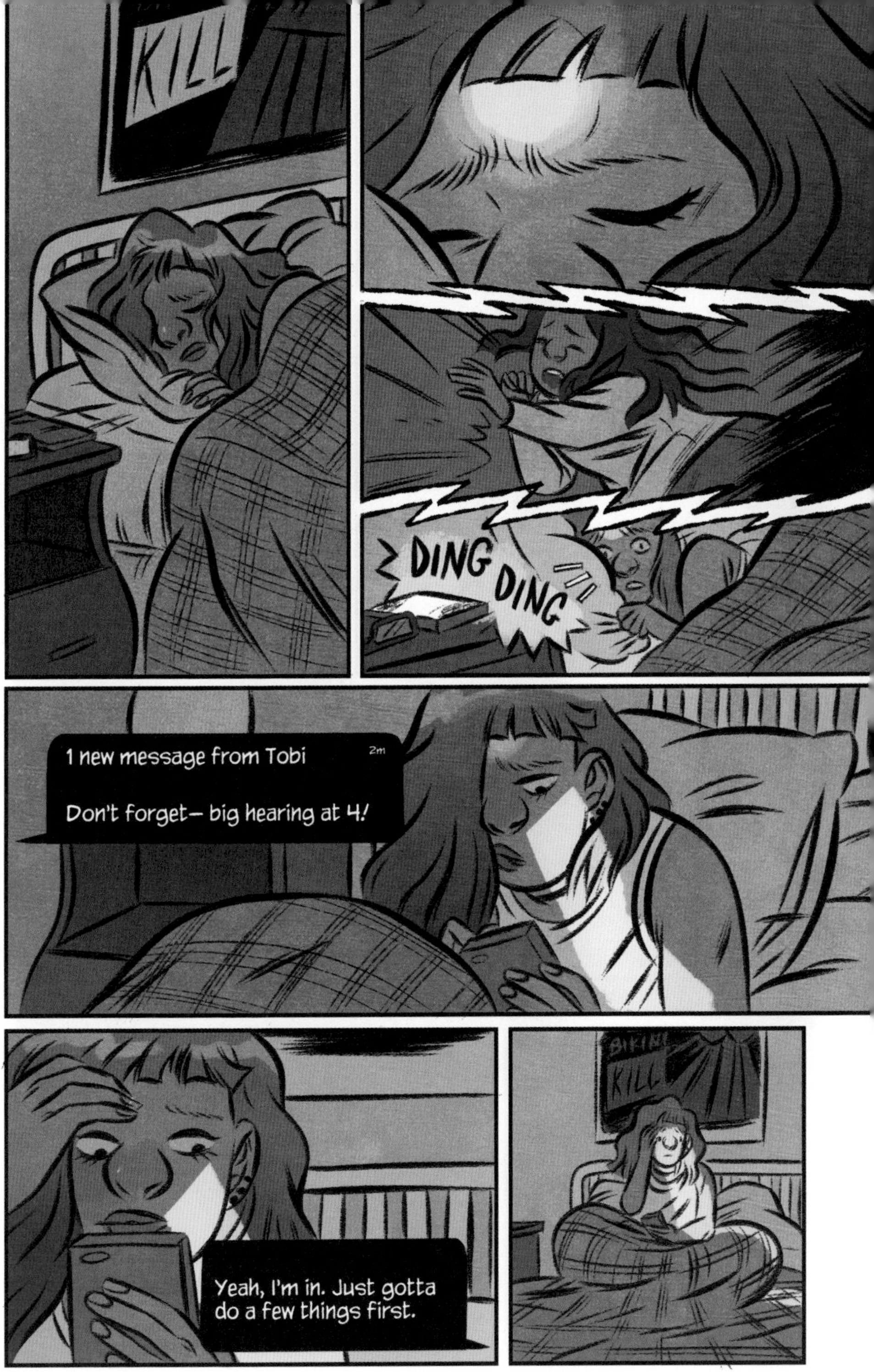
KILL
DING DING
1 new message from Tobi
2m
Don't forget— big hearing at 4!
Yeah, I'm in. Just gotta do a few things first.

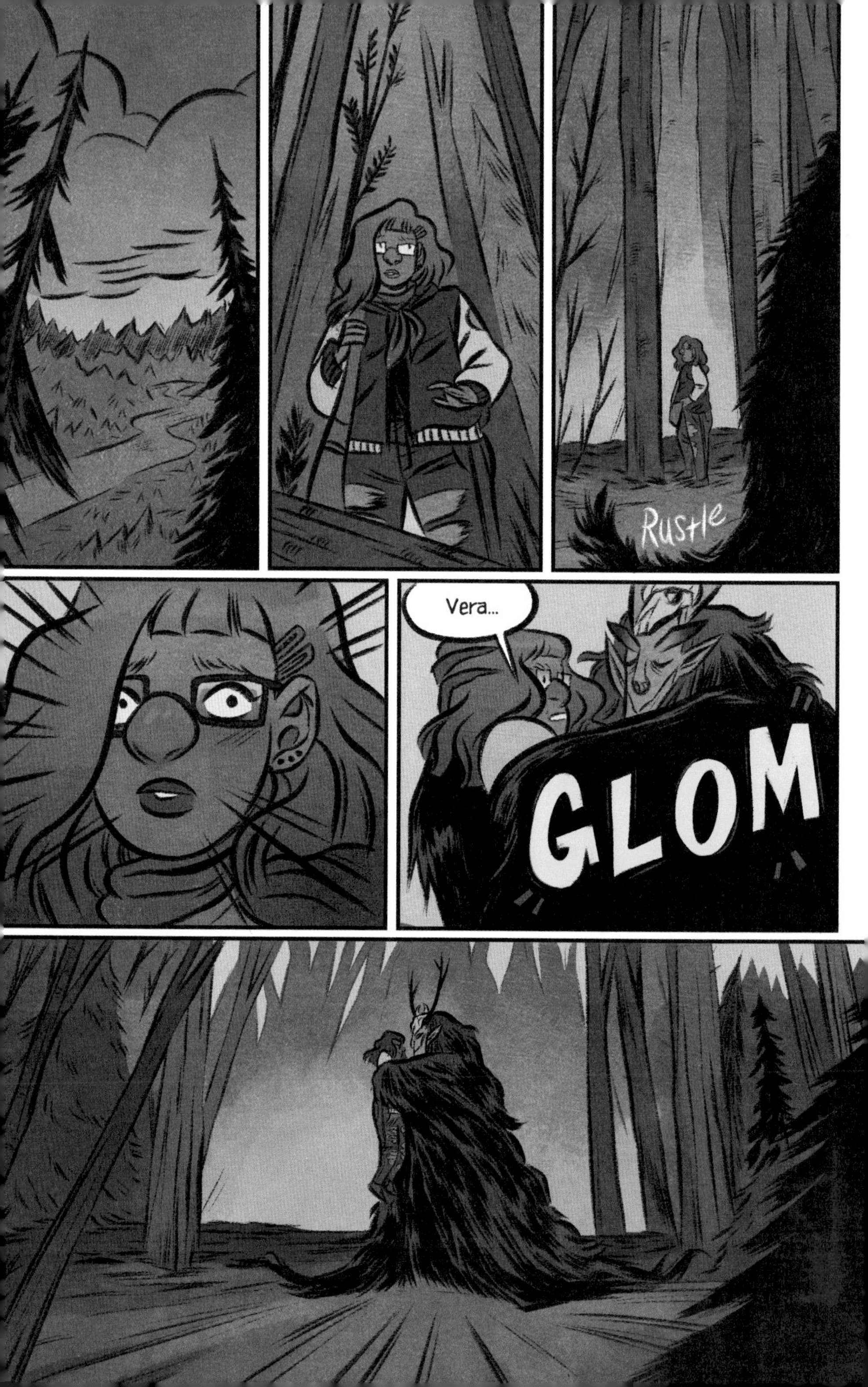
Rustle
Vera...
GLOM

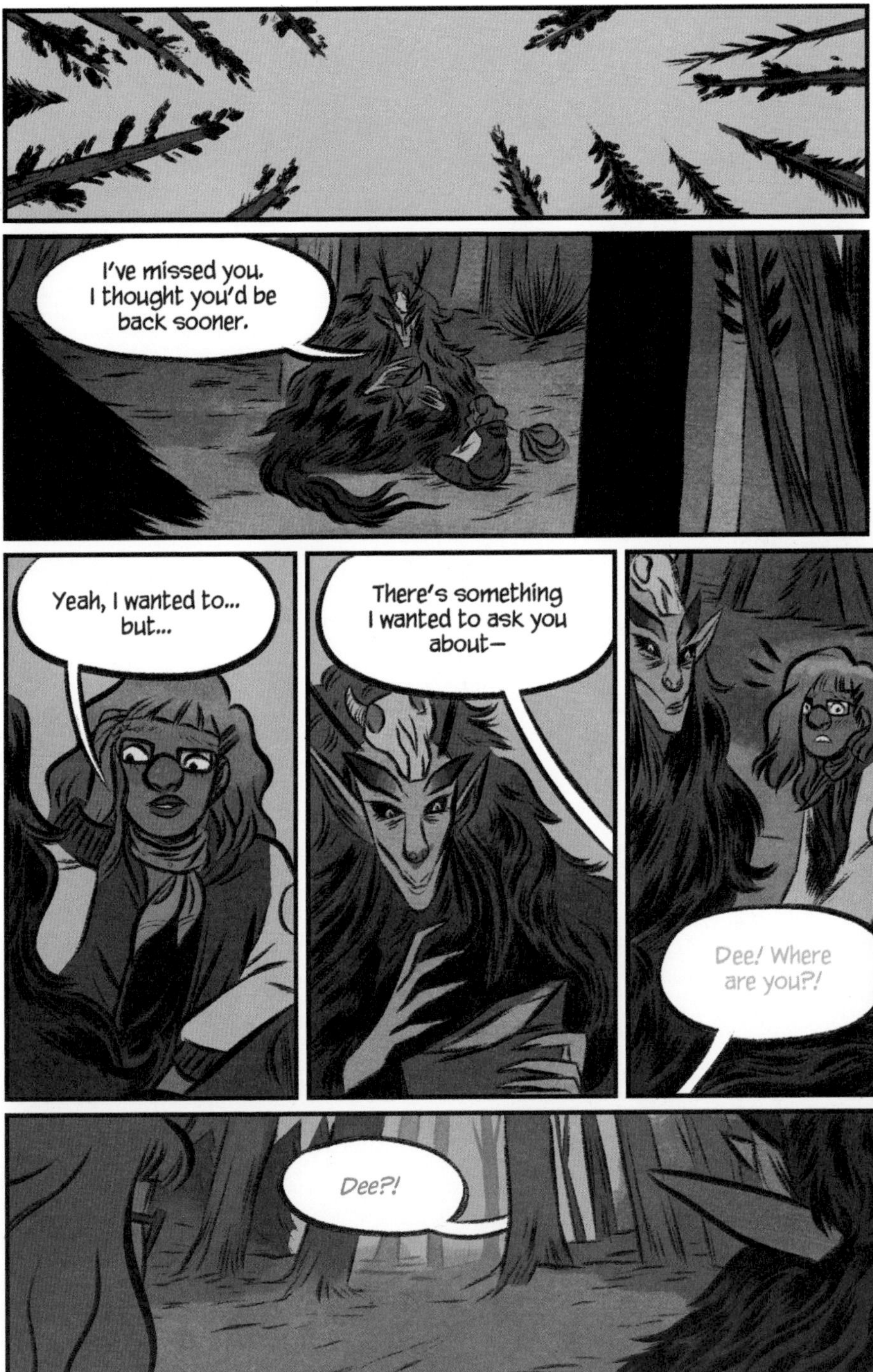
I've missed you. I thought you'd be back sooner.
Yeah, I wanted to... but...
There's something I wanted to ask you about—
Dee! Where are you?!
Dee?!

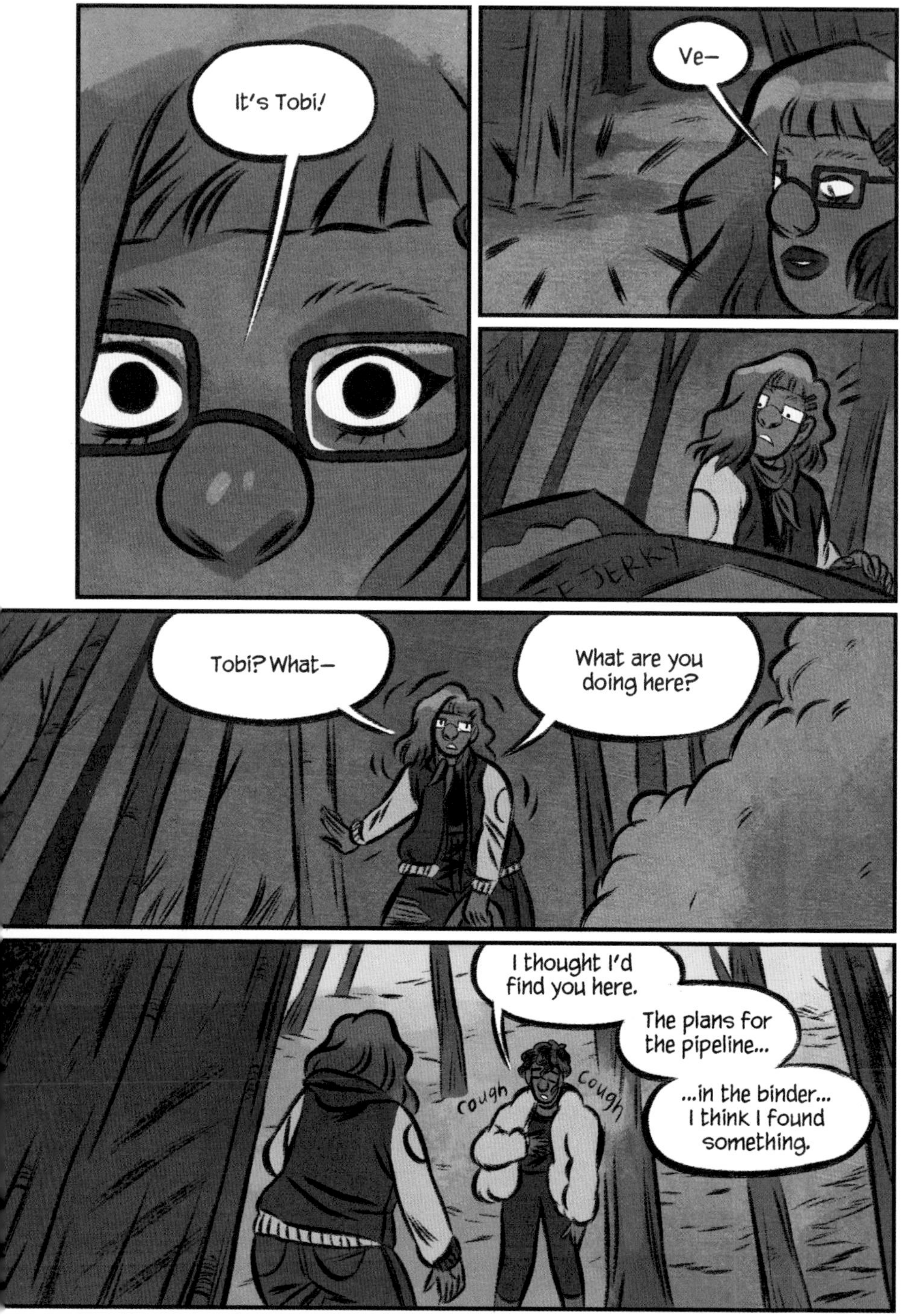
It's Tobi!
Ve–
JERKY
Tobi? What–
What are you doing here?
I thought I'd find you here.
cough
cough
The plans for the pipeline...
...in the binder... I think I found something.

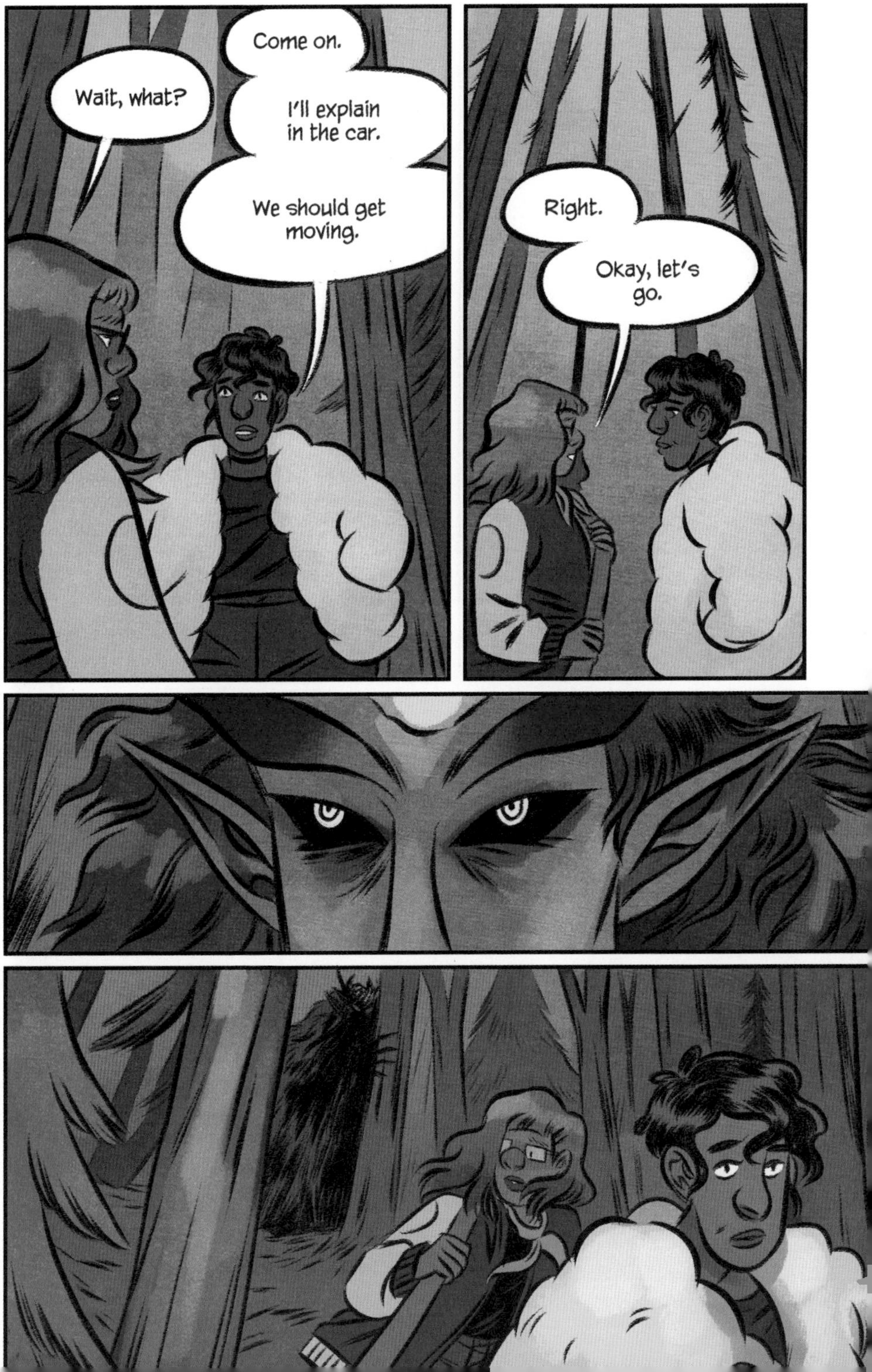
Wait, what?
Come on.
I'll explain in the car.
We should get moving.
Right.
Okay, let's go.

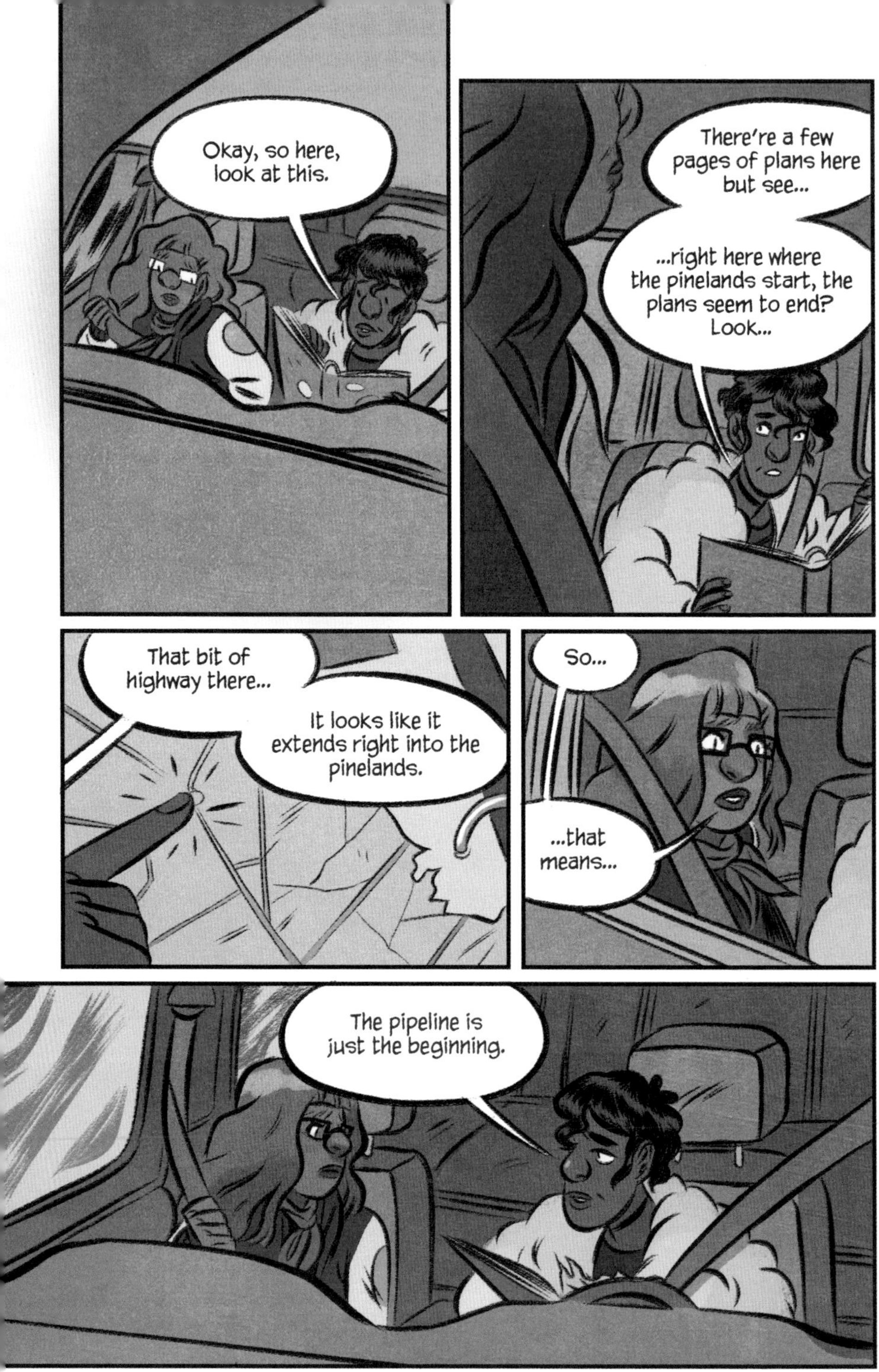
Okay, so here, look at this.
There're a few pages of plans here but see...
...right here where the pinelands start, the plans seem to end? Look...
That bit of highway there...
It looks like it extends right into the pinelands.
So...
...that means...
The pipeline is just the beginning.

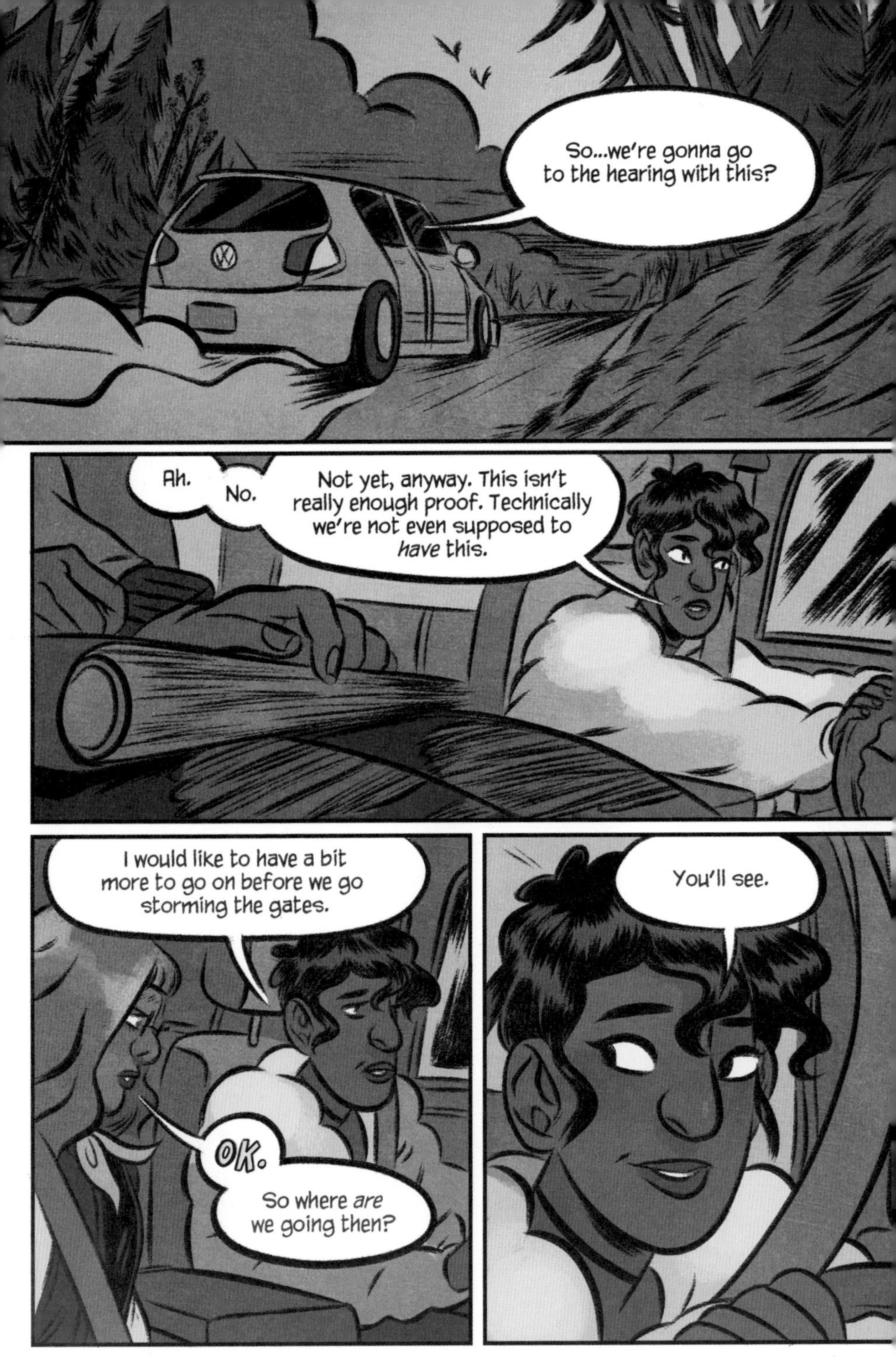
So...we're gonna go to the hearing with this?
Ah.
No.
Not yet, anyway. This isn't really enough proof. Technically we're not even supposed to *have* this.
I would like to have a bit more to go on before we go storming the gates.
OK.
So where *are* we going then?
You'll see.

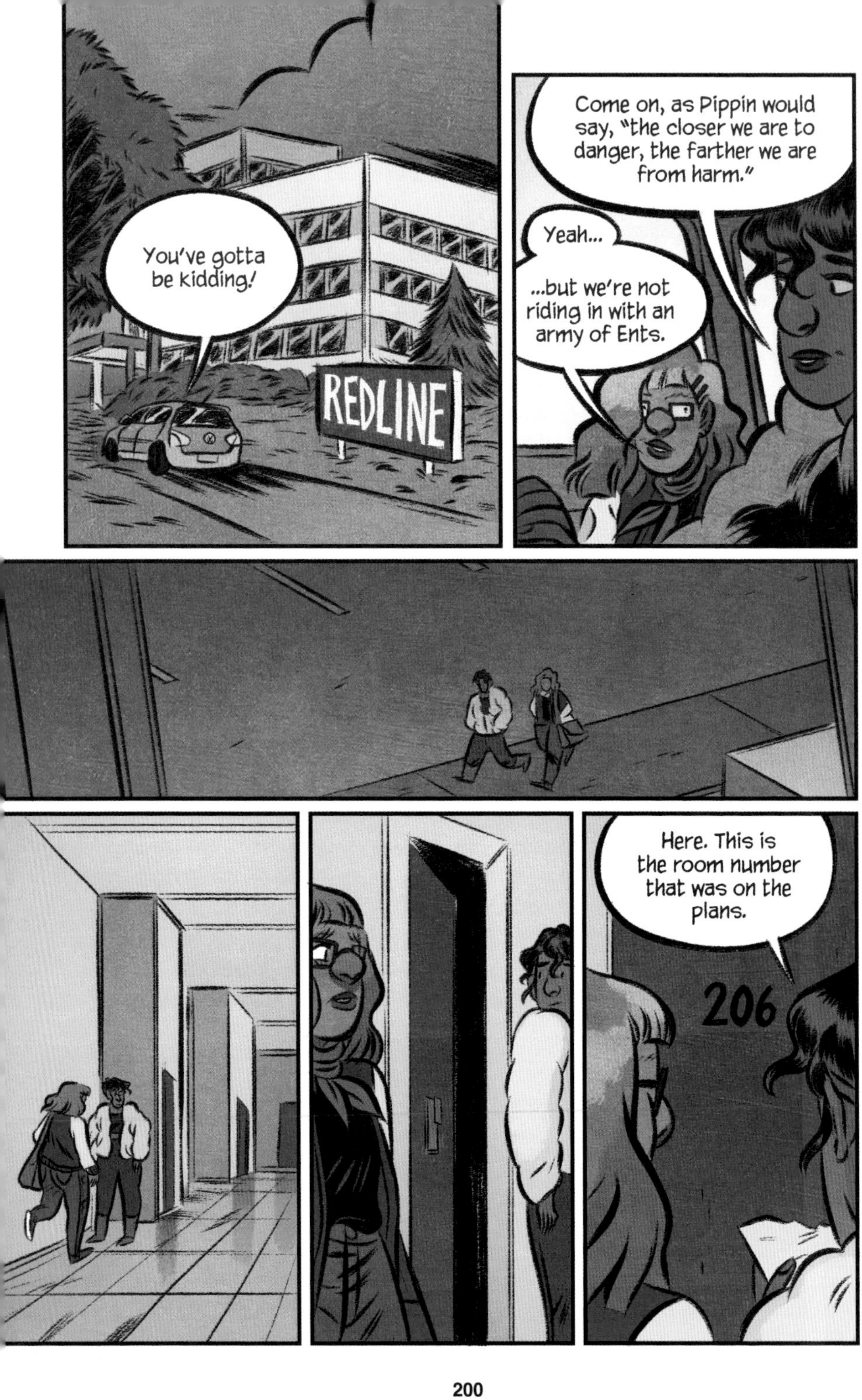
REDLINE
You've gotta be kidding!
Come on, as Pippin would say, "the closer we are to danger, the farther we are from harm."
Yeah...
...but we're not riding in with an army of Ents.
Here. This is the room number that was on the plans.
206

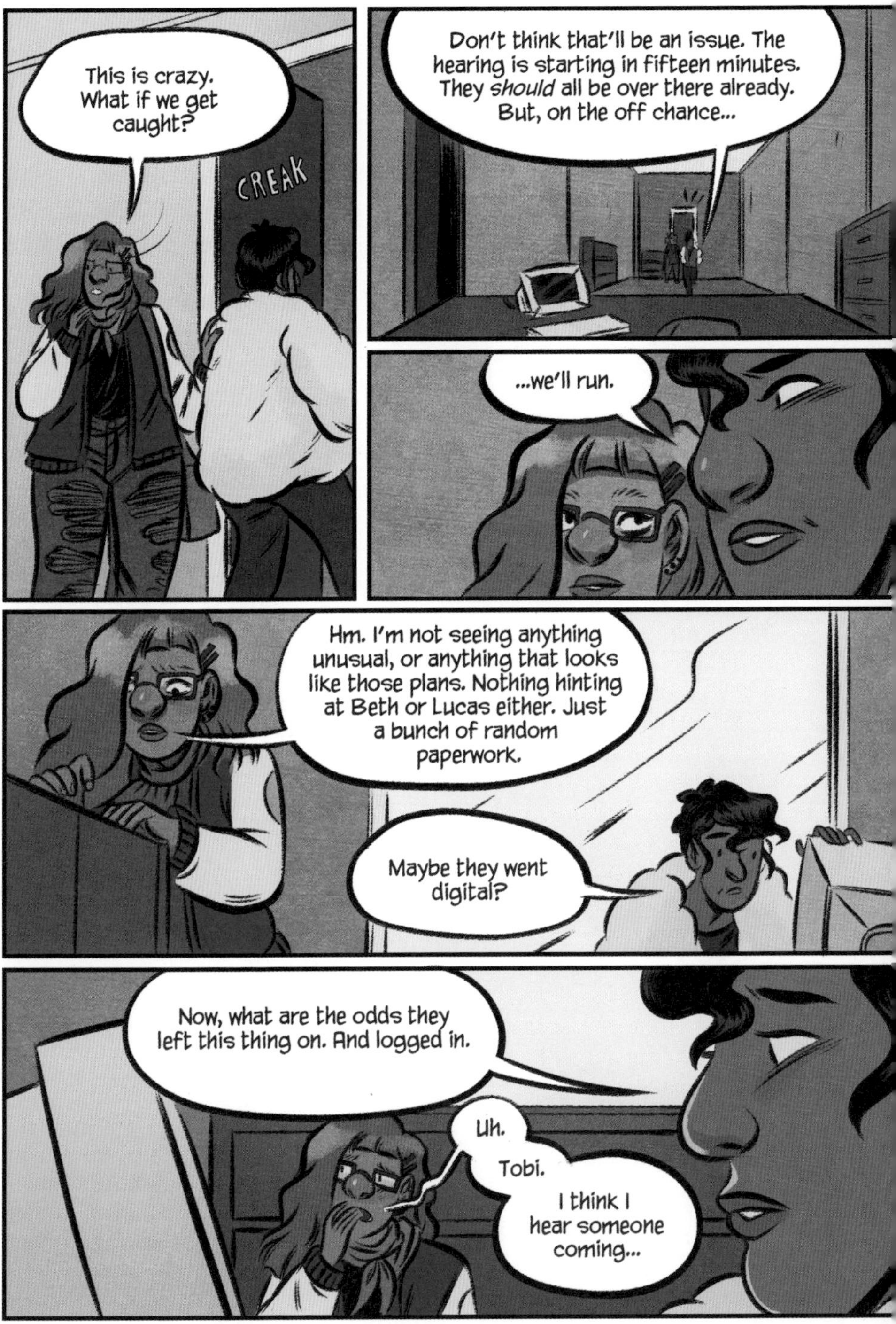
This is crazy. What if we get caught?
CREAK
Don't think that'll be an issue. The hearing is starting in fifteen minutes. They *should* all be over there already. But, on the off chance...
...we'll run.
Hm. I'm not seeing anything unusual, or anything that looks like those plans. Nothing hinting at Beth or Lucas either. Just a bunch of random paperwork.
Maybe they went digital?
Now, what are the odds they left this thing on. And logged in.
Uh.
Tobi.
I think I hear someone coming...

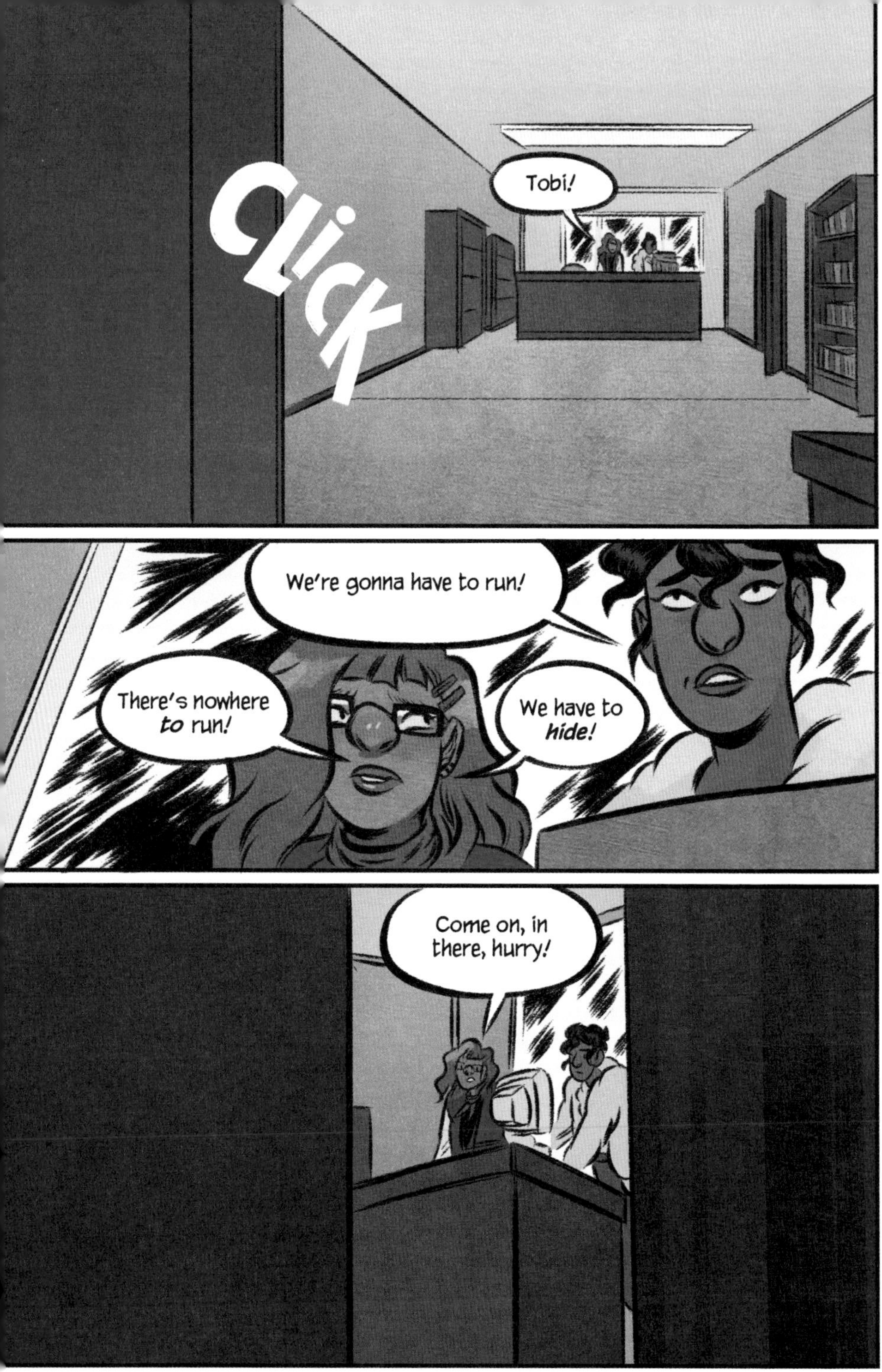
Tobi!
CLICK
We're gonna have to run!
There's nowhere *to* run!
We have to *hide*!
Come on, in there, hurry!

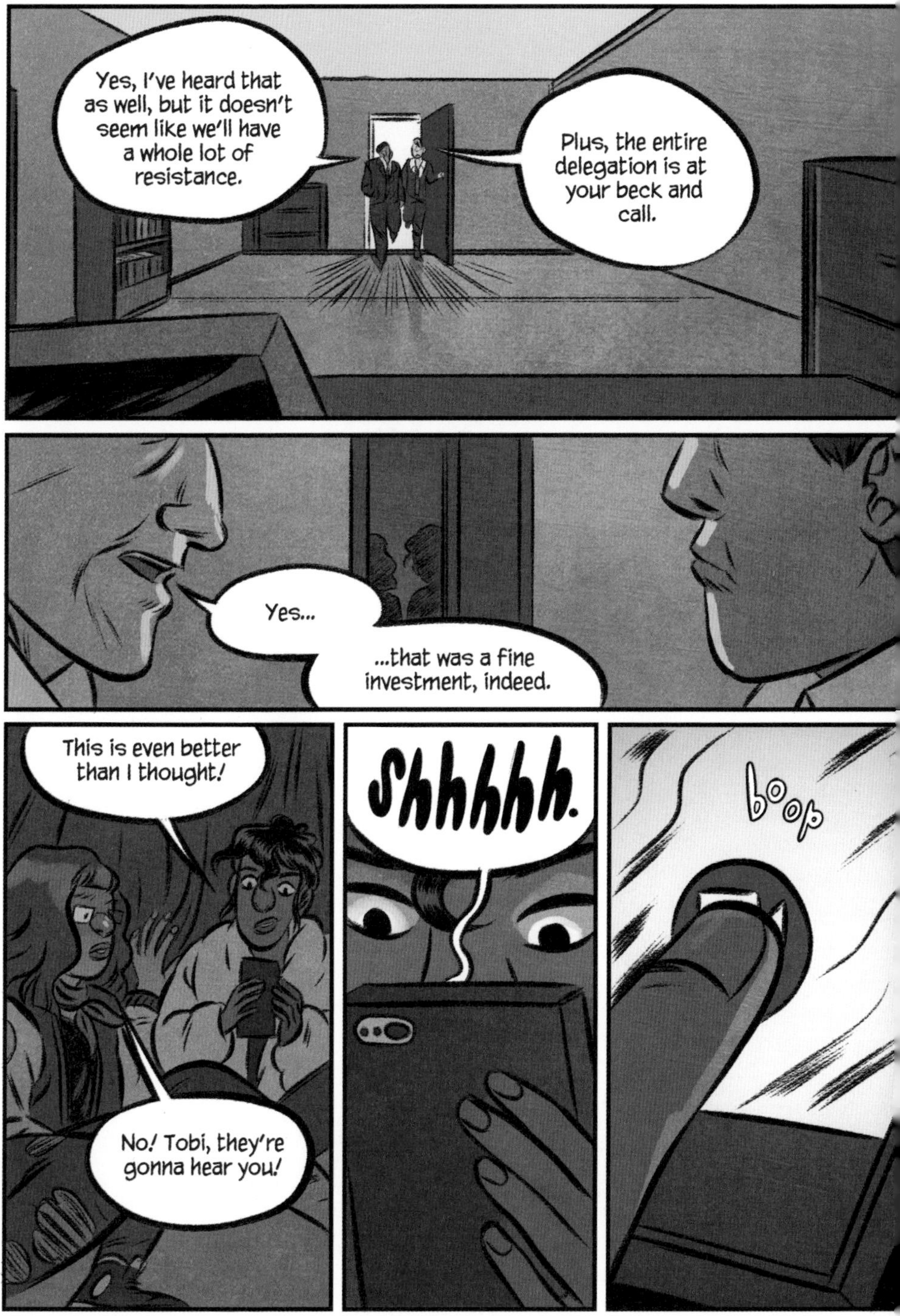
Yes, I've heard that as well, but it doesn't seem like we'll have a whole lot of resistance.
Plus, the entire delegation is at your beck and call.
Yes...
...that was a fine investment, indeed.
This is even better than I thought!
No! Tobi, they're gonna hear you!
Shhhhh.
boop

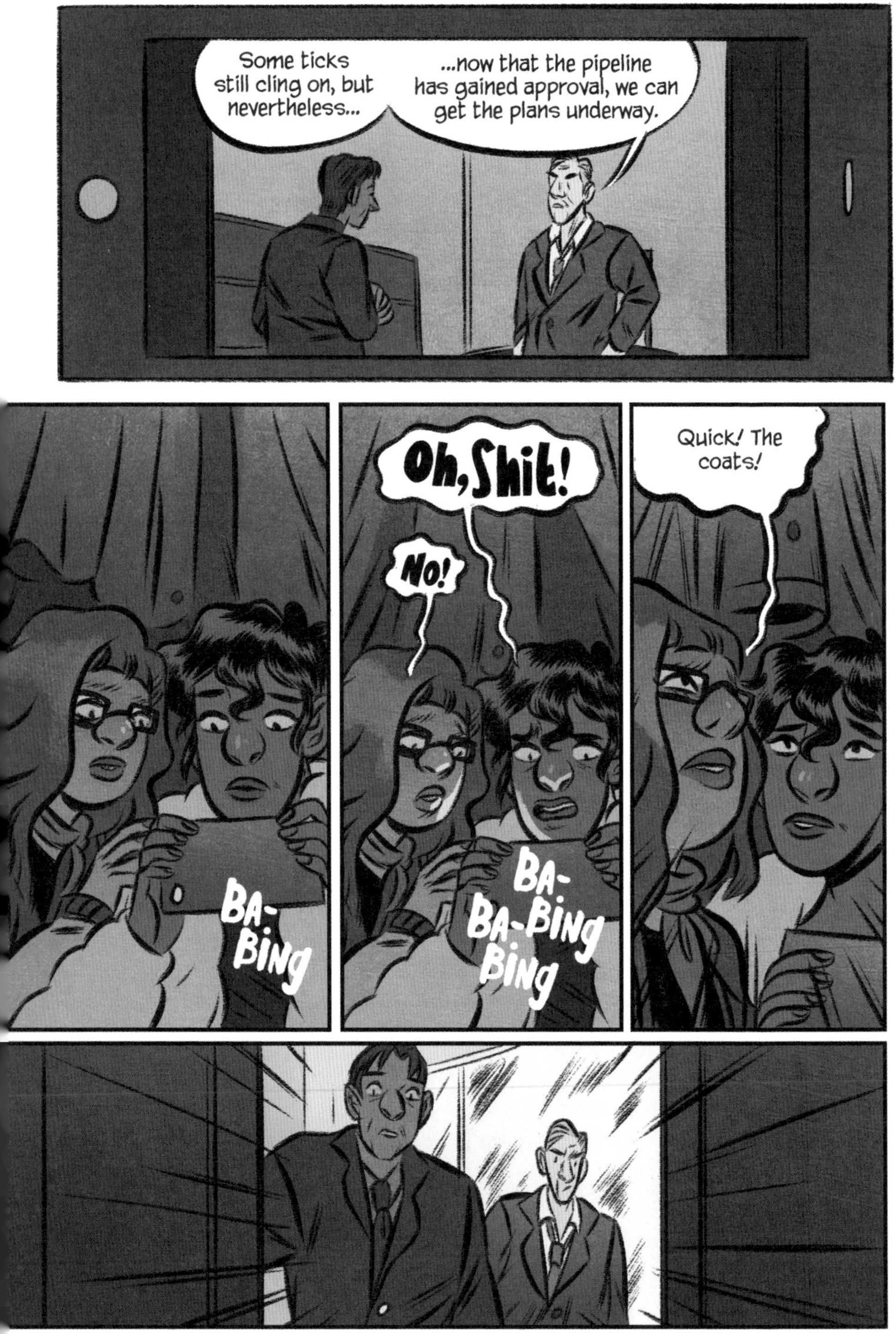

Some ticks still cling on, but nevertheless...
...now that the pipeline has gained approval, we can get the plans underway.
BA-BING
Oh, Shit!
NO!
BA-BA-BING BING
Quick! The coats!

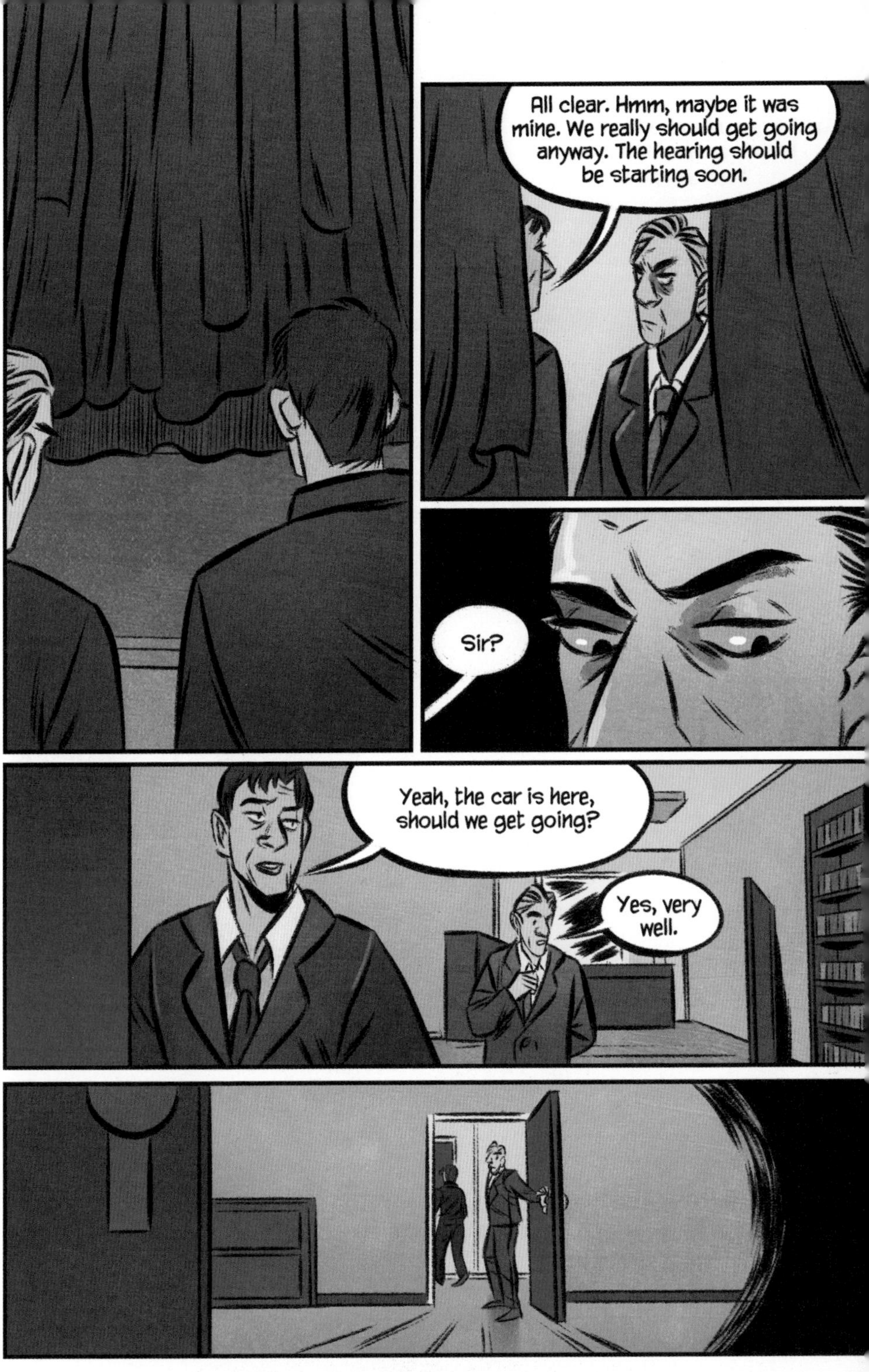
All clear. Hmm, maybe it was mine. We really should get going anyway. The hearing should be starting soon.
Sir?
Yeah, the car is here, should we get going?
Yes, very well.

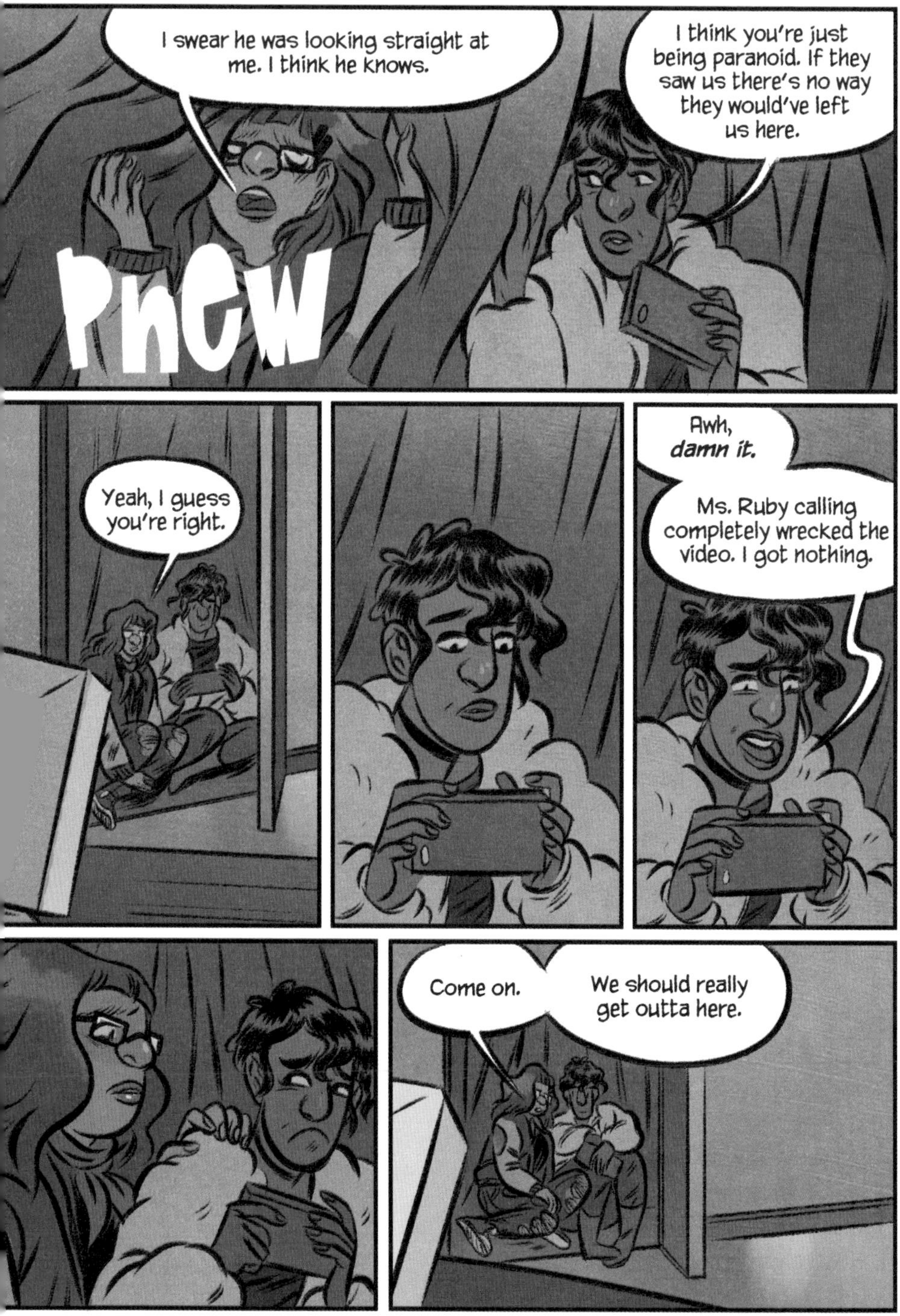
I swear he was looking straight at me. I think he knows.
I think you're just being paranoid. If they saw us there's no way they would've left us here.
PHEW
Yeah, I guess you're right.
Awh, *damn it.*
Ms. Ruby calling completely wrecked the video. I got nothing.
Come on.
We should really get outta here.

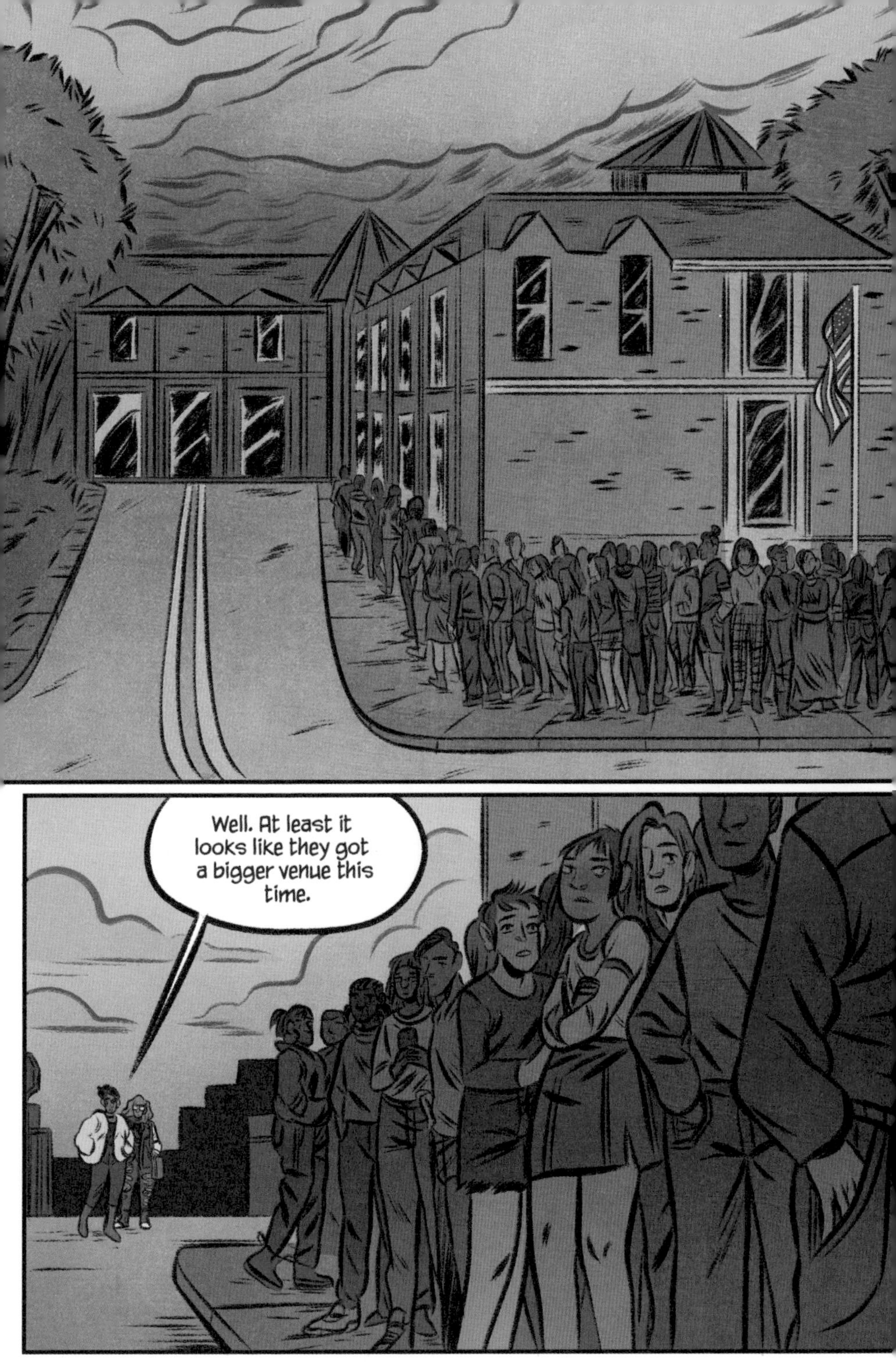
Well. At least it looks like they got a bigger venue this time.

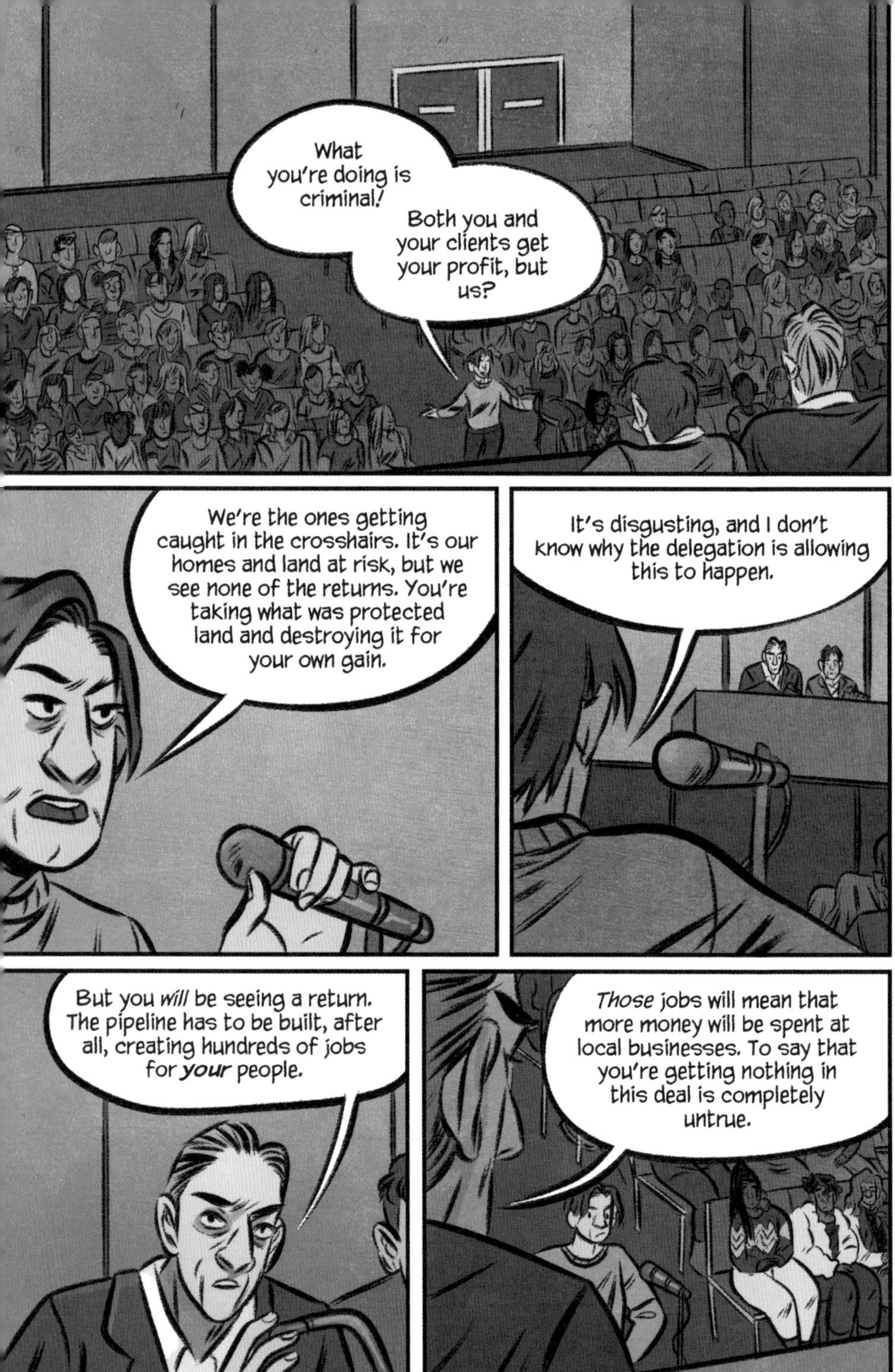
What you're doing is criminal!
Both you and your clients get your profit, but us?
We're the ones getting caught in the crosshairs. It's our homes and land at risk, but we see none of the returns. You're taking what was protected land and destroying it for your own gain.
It's disgusting, and I don't know why the delegation is allowing this to happen.
But you *will* be seeing a return. The pipeline has to be built, after all, creating hundreds of jobs for ***your*** people.
Those jobs will mean that more money will be spent at local businesses. To say that you're getting nothing in this deal is completely untrue.

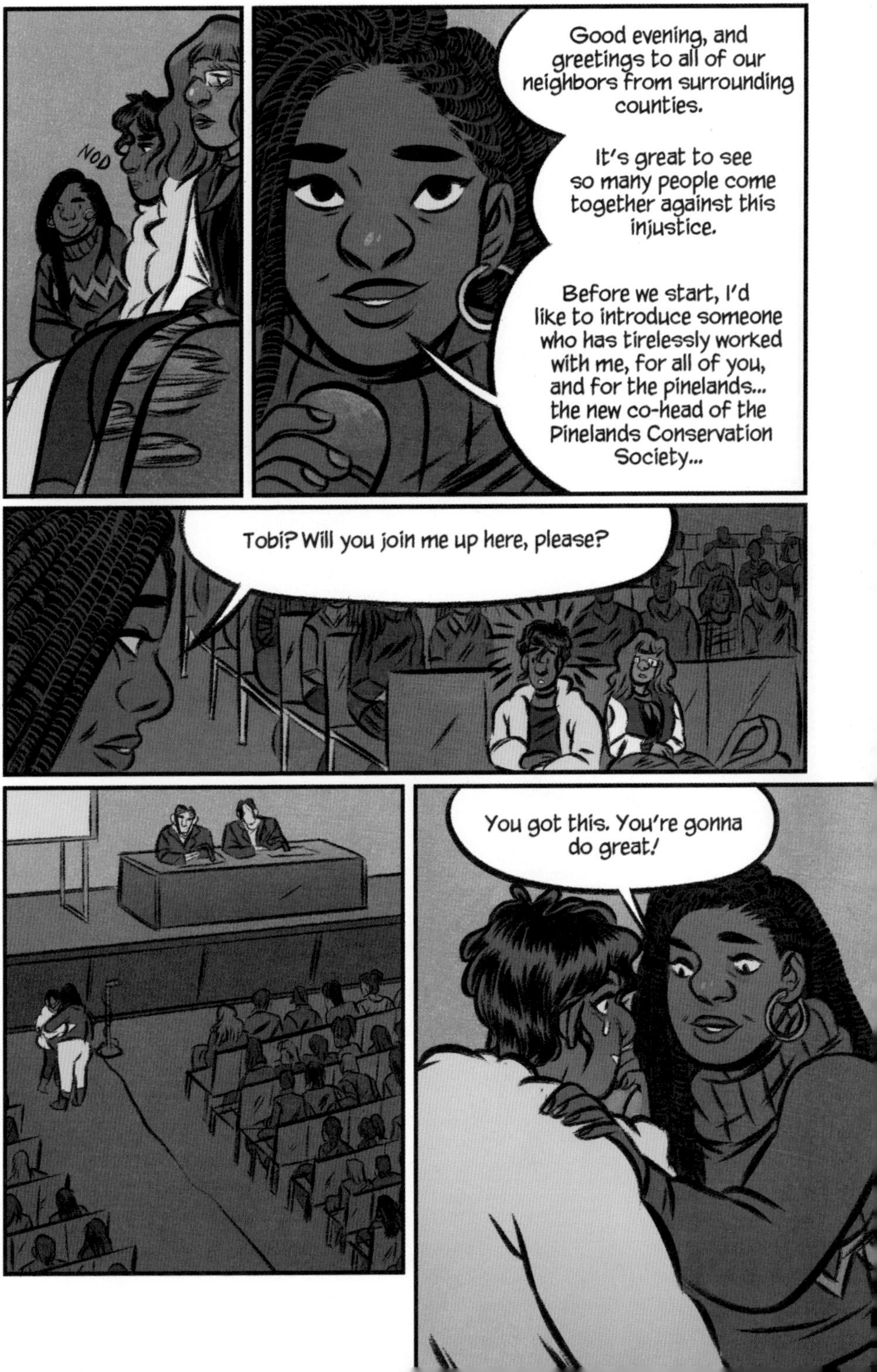
NOD
Good evening, and greetings to all of our neighbors from surrounding counties.
It's great to see so many people come together against this injustice.
Before we start, I'd like to introduce someone who has tirelessly worked with me, for all of you, and for the pinelands... the new co-head of the Pinelands Conservation Society...
Tobi? Will you join me up here, please?
You got this. You're gonna do great!

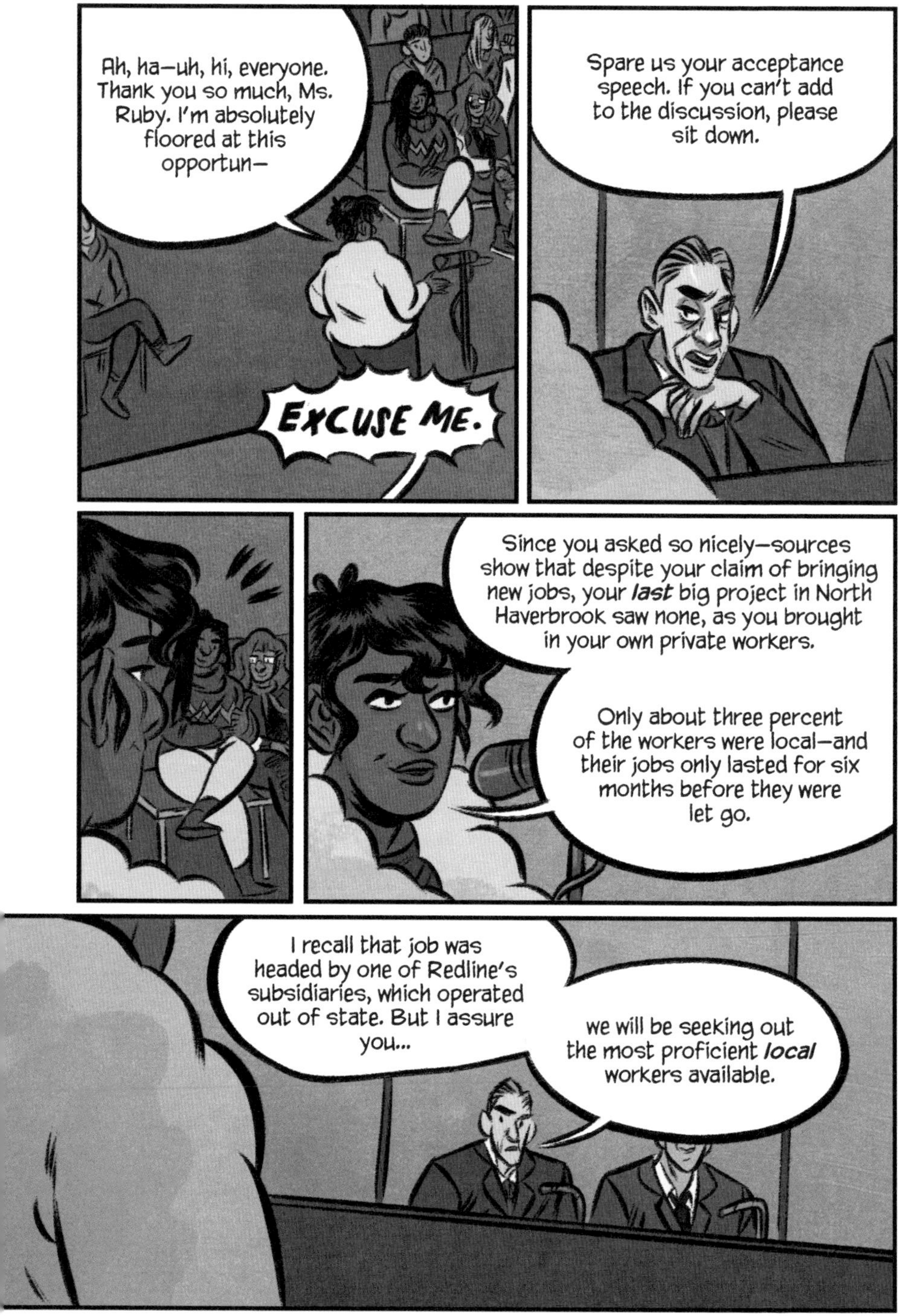
Ah, ha—uh, hi, everyone. Thank you so much, Ms. Ruby. I'm absolutely floored at this opportun—
EXCUSE ME.
Spare us your acceptance speech. If you can't add to the discussion, please sit down.
Since you asked so nicely—sources show that despite your claim of bringing new jobs, your *last* big project in North Haverbrook saw none, as you brought in your own private workers.
Only about three percent of the workers were local—and their jobs only lasted for six months before they were let go.
I recall that job was headed by one of Redline's subsidiaries, which operated out of state. But I assure you...
we will be seeking out the most proficient *local* workers available.

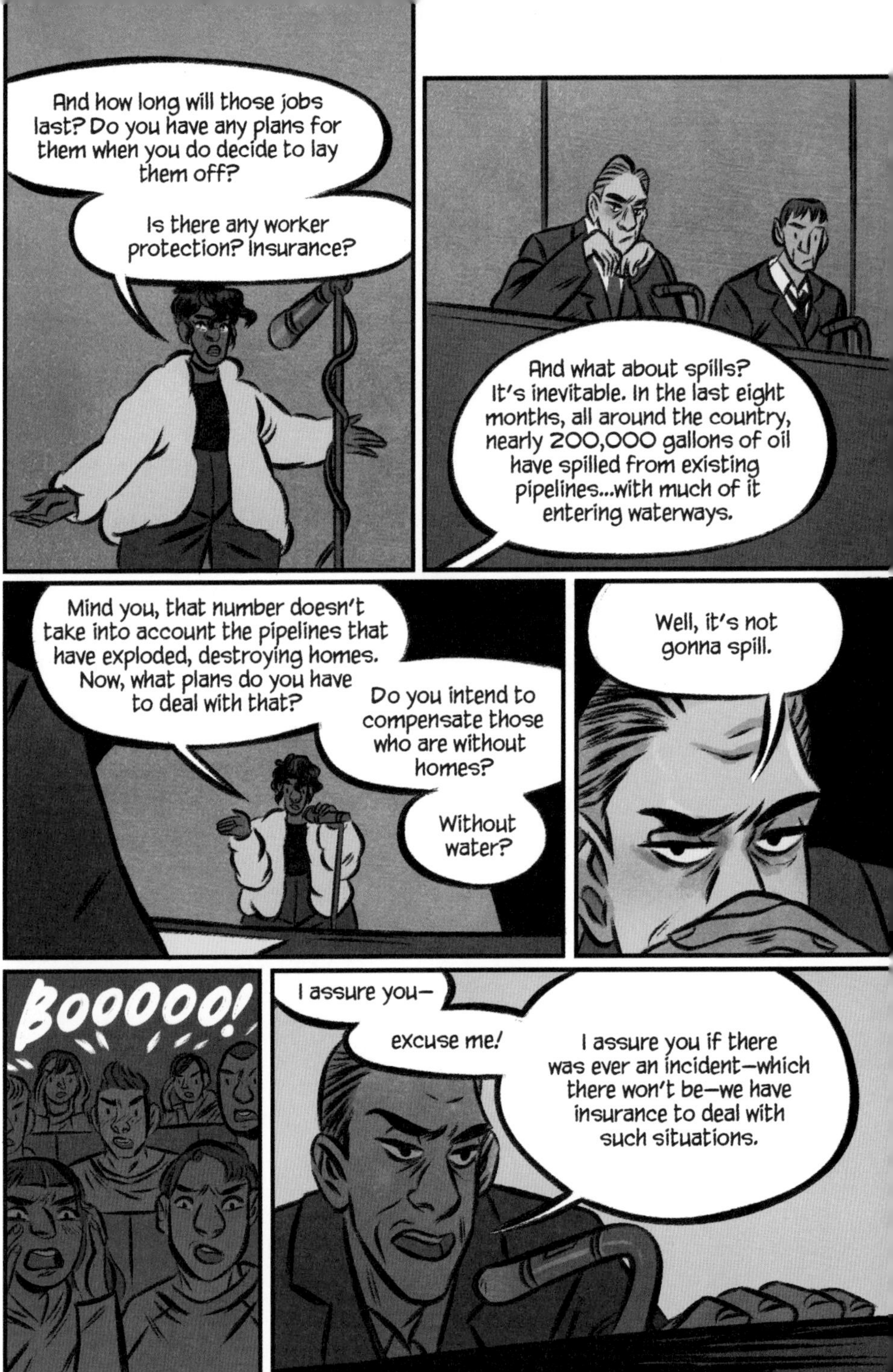
And how long will those jobs last? Do you have any plans for them when you do decide to lay them off?
Is there any worker protection? Insurance?
And what about spills? It's inevitable. In the last eight months, all around the country, nearly 200,000 gallons of oil have spilled from existing pipelines...with much of it entering waterways.
Mind you, that number doesn't take into account the pipelines that have exploded, destroying homes. Now, what plans do you have to deal with that?
Do you intend to compensate those who are without homes?
Without water?
Well, it's not gonna spill.
BOOOOO!
I assure you—
excuse me!
I assure you if there was ever an incident—which there won't be—we have insurance to deal with such situations.

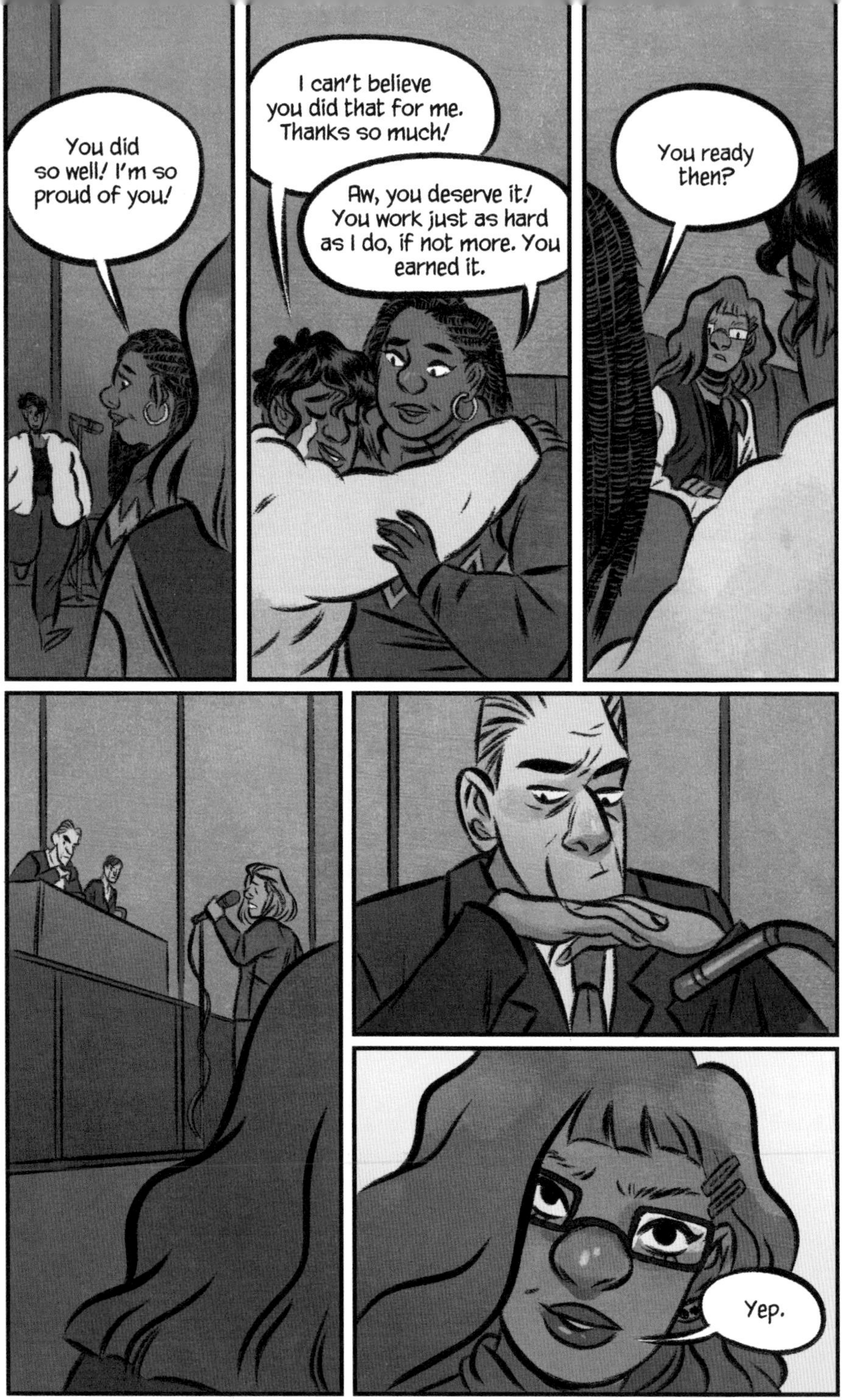
You did so well! I'm so proud of you!
I can't believe you did that for me. Thanks so much!
Aw, you deserve it! You work just as hard as I do, if not more. You earned it.
You ready then?
Yep.

Not long ago was the anniversary of one of the biggest fires in the history of the pinelands...in 1963, numerous fires broke out and destroyed hundreds of thousands of acres.

Surely you're aware of the history of the pinelands, sir.

I've heard about that, yes.

And your *point*?

Well, if you knew *anything* about the pinelands, you'd be aware of the numerous fires that break out every single year. So my *point* is...

...why would anyone be dumb enough to put such extremely flammable material in and around a million-acre fire hazard? That's just asking for a disaster to happen.

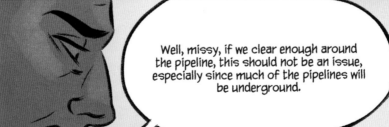

Well, missy, if we clear enough around the pipeline, this should not be an issue, especially since much of the pipelines will be underground.

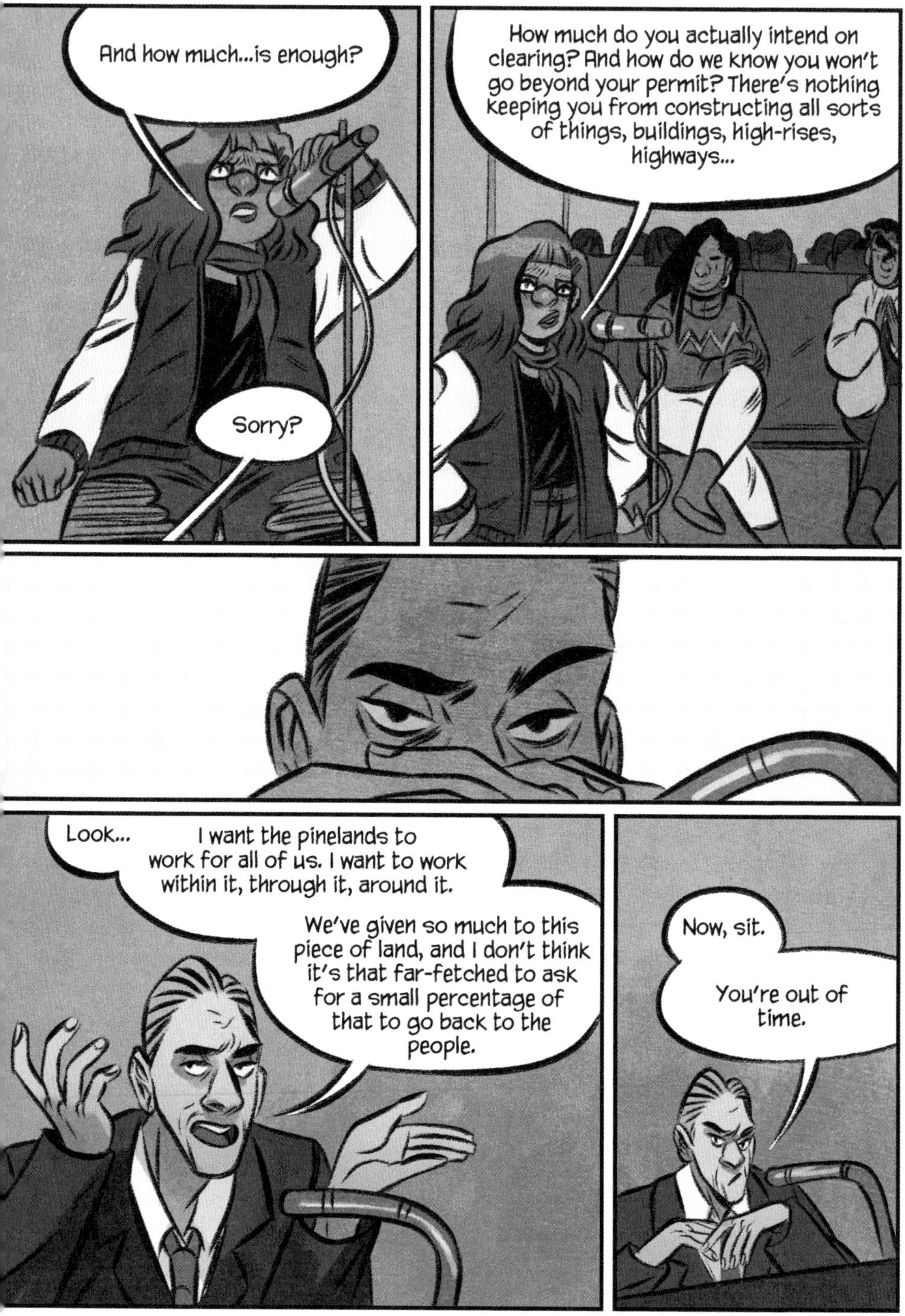
And how much...is enough?
Sorry?
How much do you actually intend on clearing? And how do we know you won't go beyond your permit? There's nothing keeping you from constructing all sorts of things, buildings, high-rises, highways...
Look...
I want the pinelands to work for all of us. I want to work within it, through it, around it.
We've given so much to this piece of land, and I don't think it's that far-fetched to ask for a small percentage of that to go back to the people.
Now, sit.
You're out of time.

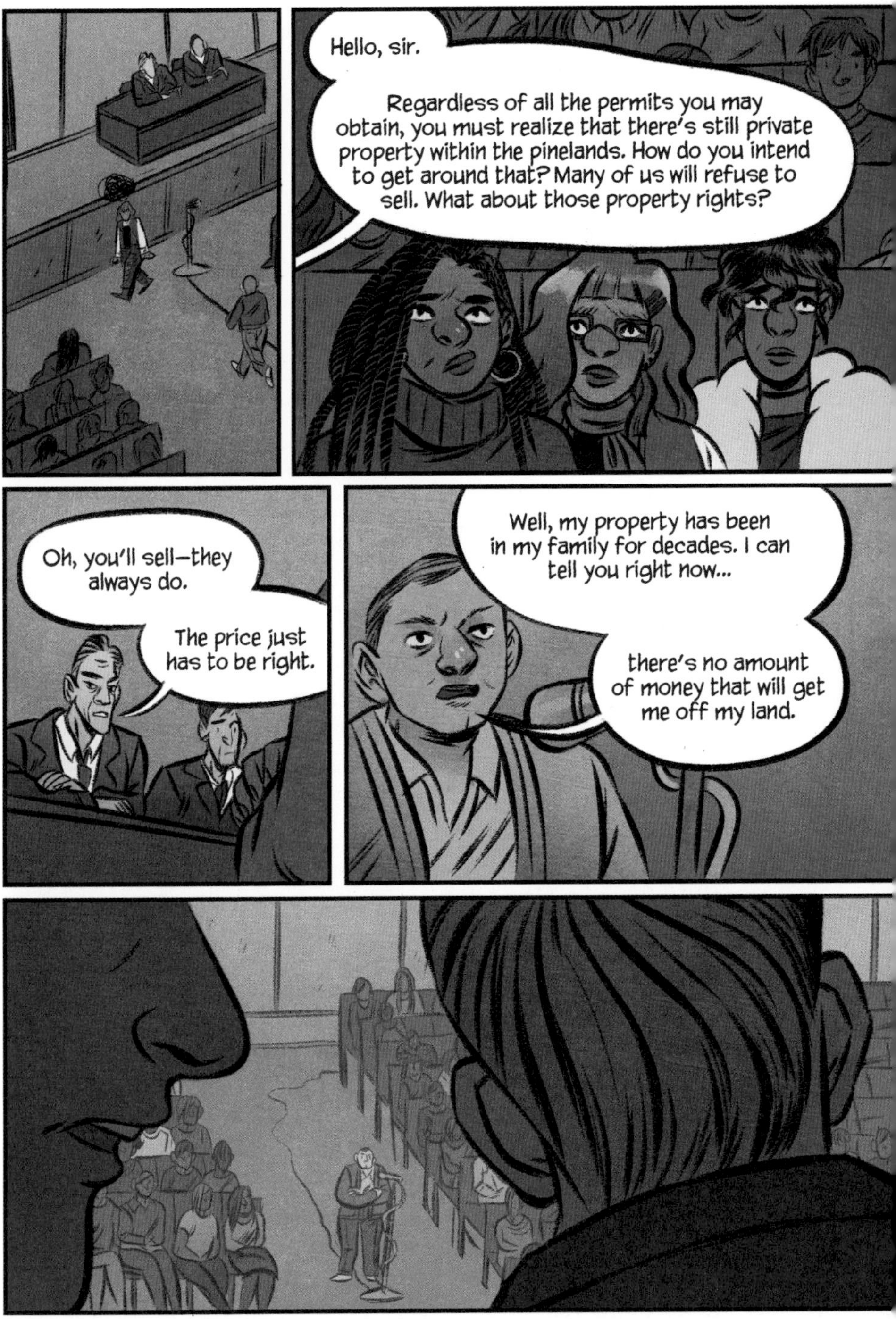
Hello, sir.
Regardless of all the permits you may obtain, you must realize that there's still private property within the pinelands. How do you intend to get around that? Many of us will refuse to sell. What about those property rights?
Oh, you'll sell—they always do.
The price just has to be right.
Well, my property has been in my family for decades. I can tell you right now...
there's no amount of money that will get me off my land.

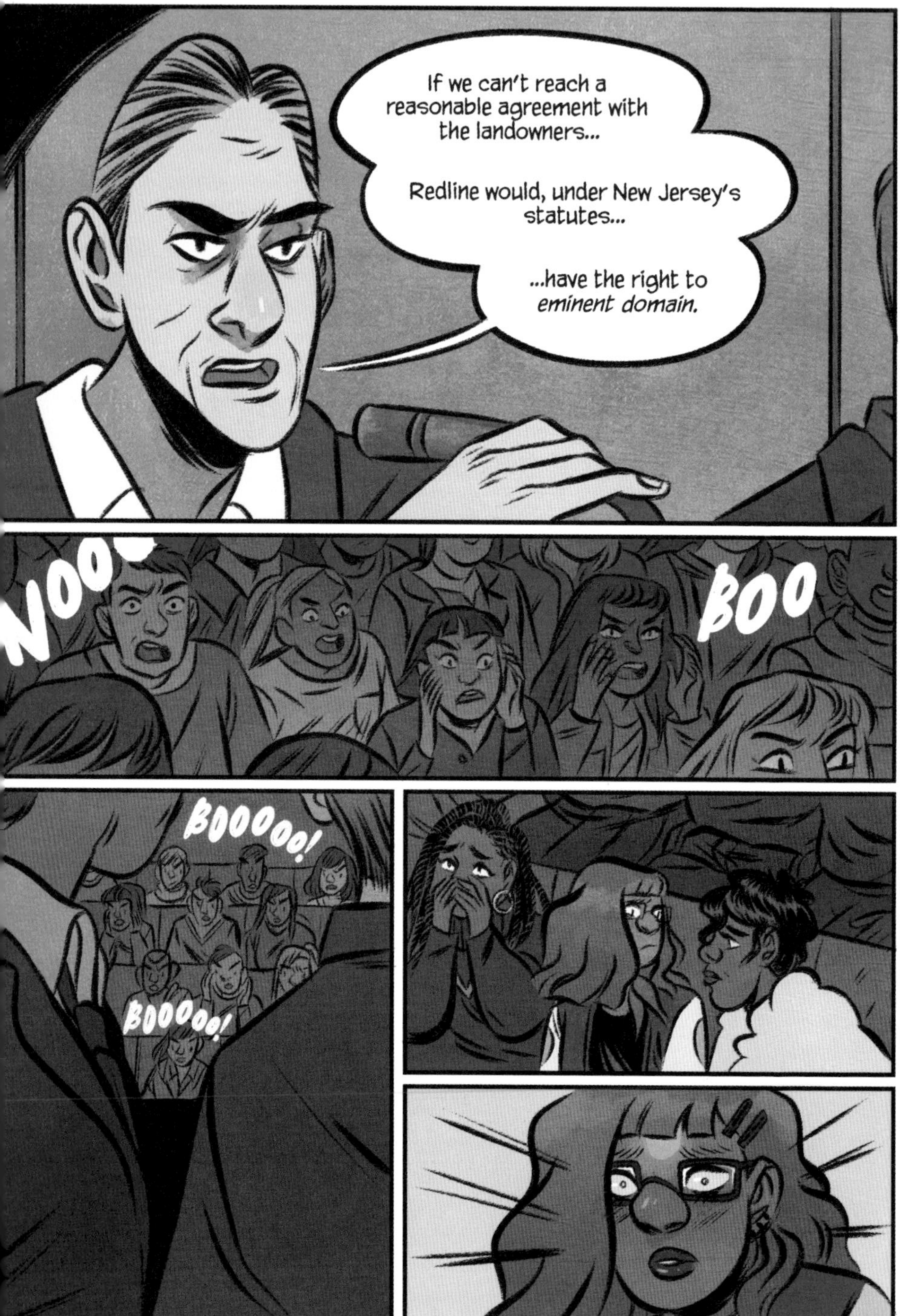
If we can't reach a reasonable agreement with the landowners...
Redline would, under New Jersey's statutes...
...have the right to *eminent domain.*
NOO
BOO
BOOOOO!
BOOOOO!

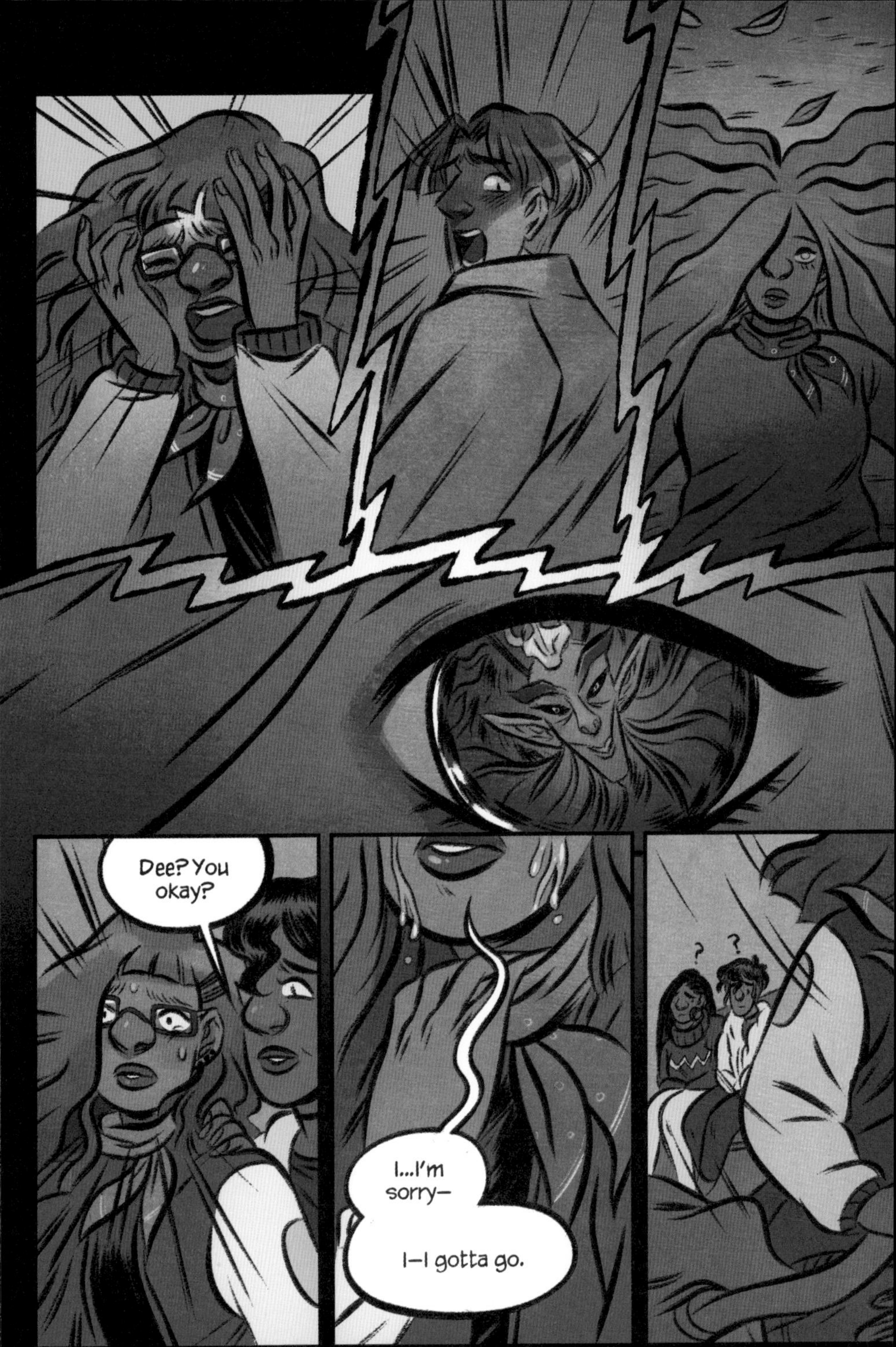
Dee? You okay?
I...I'm sorry—
I—I gotta go.
?
?

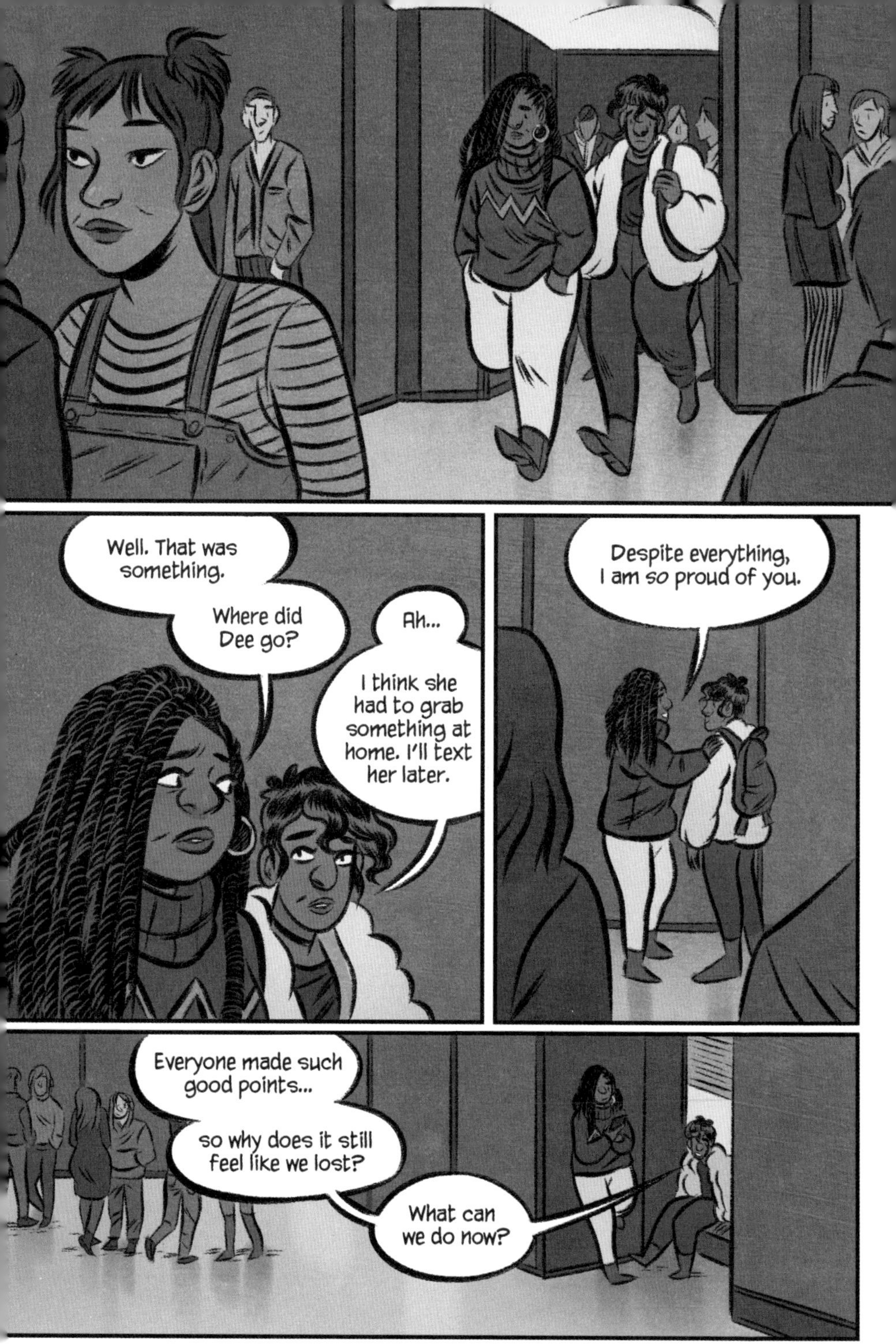
Well. That was something.
Where did Dee go?
Ah...
I think she had to grab something at home. I'll text her later.
Despite everything, I am *so* proud of you.
Everyone made such good points...
so why does it still feel like we lost?
What can we do now?

Do we stand a chance against eminent domain?

Without a court order? Not likely.

Yeah. Hmm.

We've had the hearings, signed petitions, asked all the right questions and still there's always another wall... what else can we do?

NO PIPELINE

SAY NO REDLINE SAVE OUR PROTE

MONRO YOU M GO

Perhaps it's time to join the ranks.

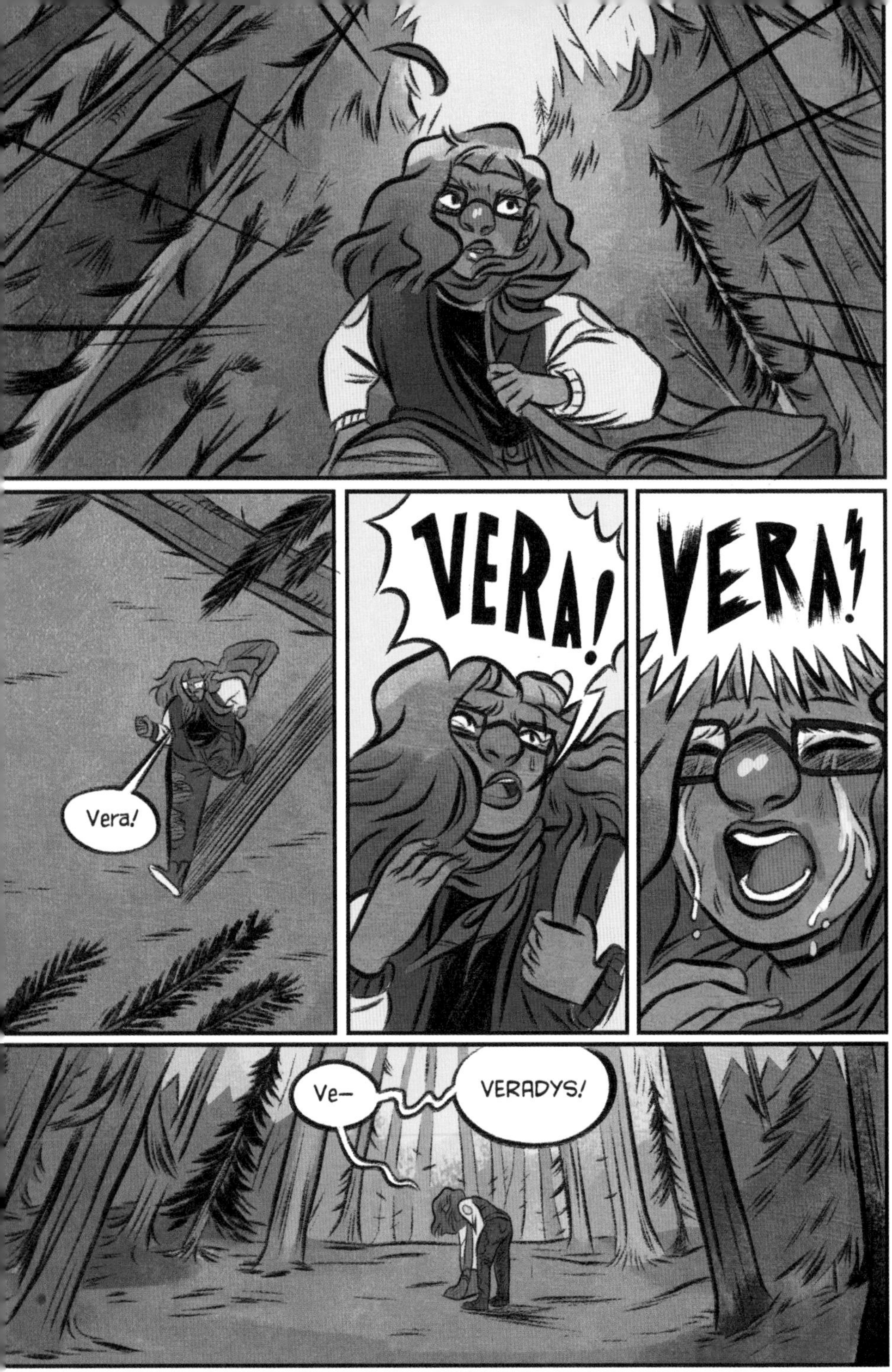
Vera!
VERA!
VERA!
Ve–
VERADYS!

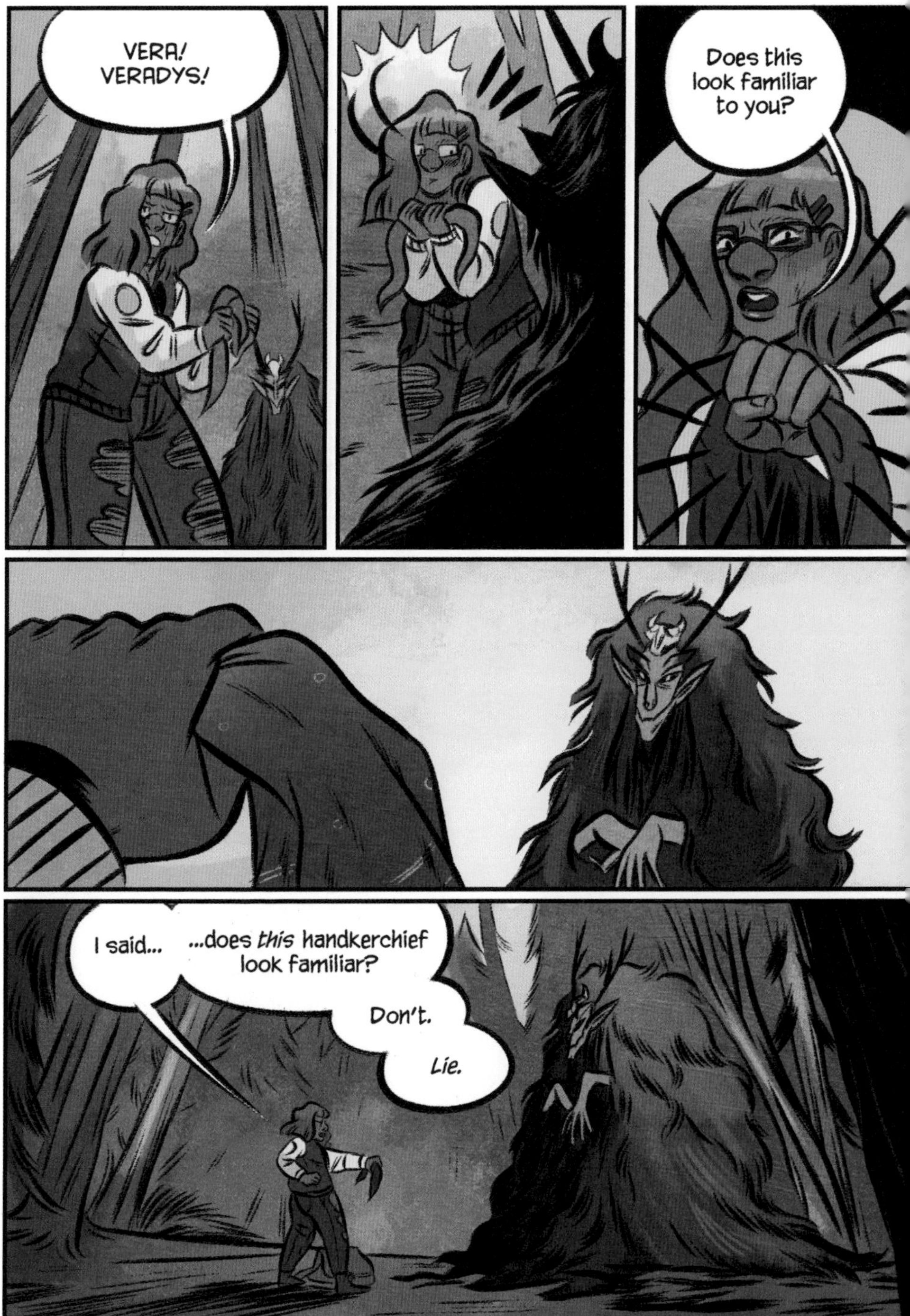
VERA! VERADYS!
Does this look familiar to you?
I said... ...does *this* handkerchief look familiar?
Don't.
Lie.

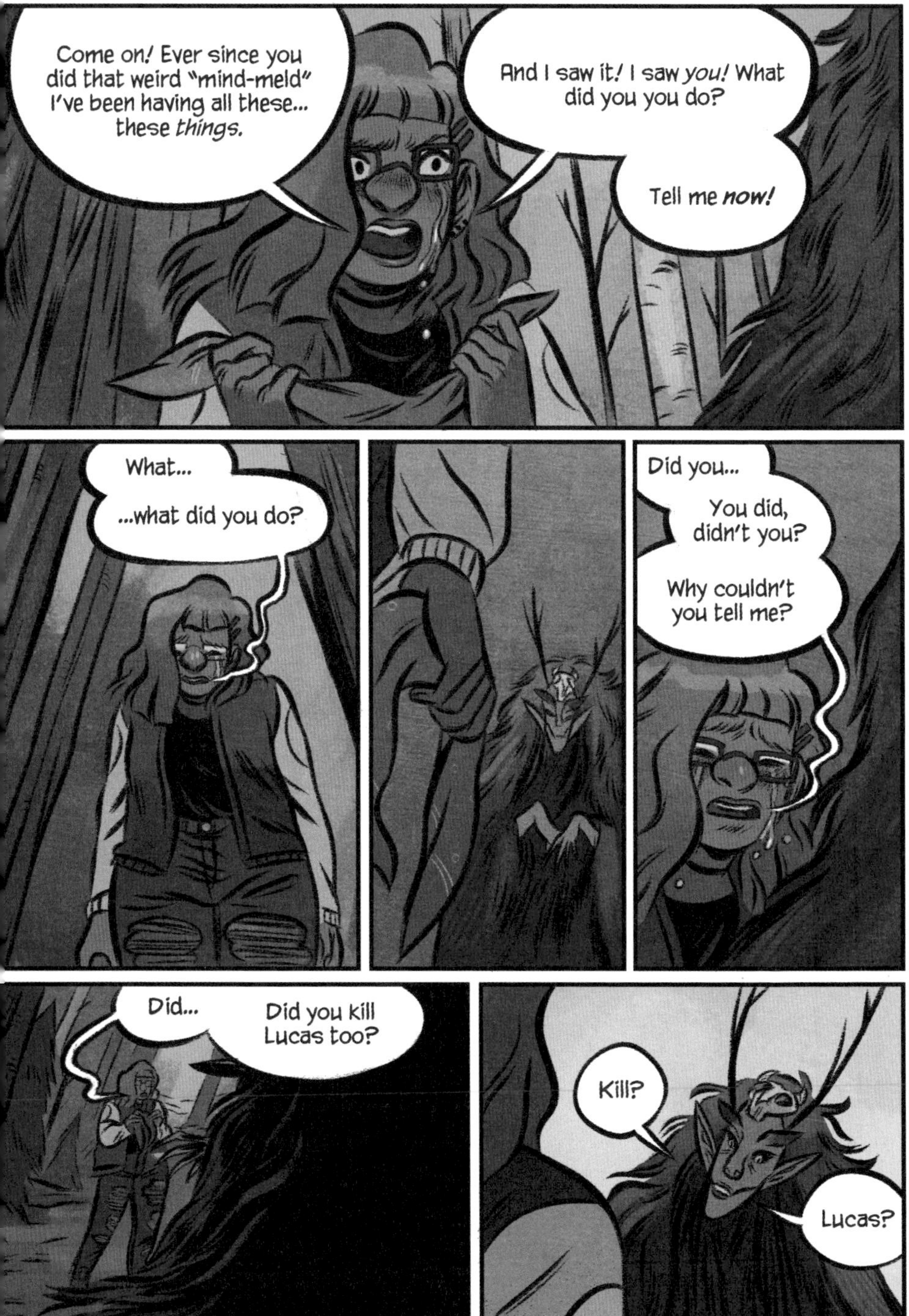

Come on! Ever since you did that weird "mind-meld" I've been having all these... these *things.*
And I saw it! I saw *you!* What did you you do?
Tell me ***now!***
What...
...what did you do?
Did you...
You did, didn't you?
Why couldn't you tell me?
Did...
Did you kill Lucas too?
Kill?
Lucas?

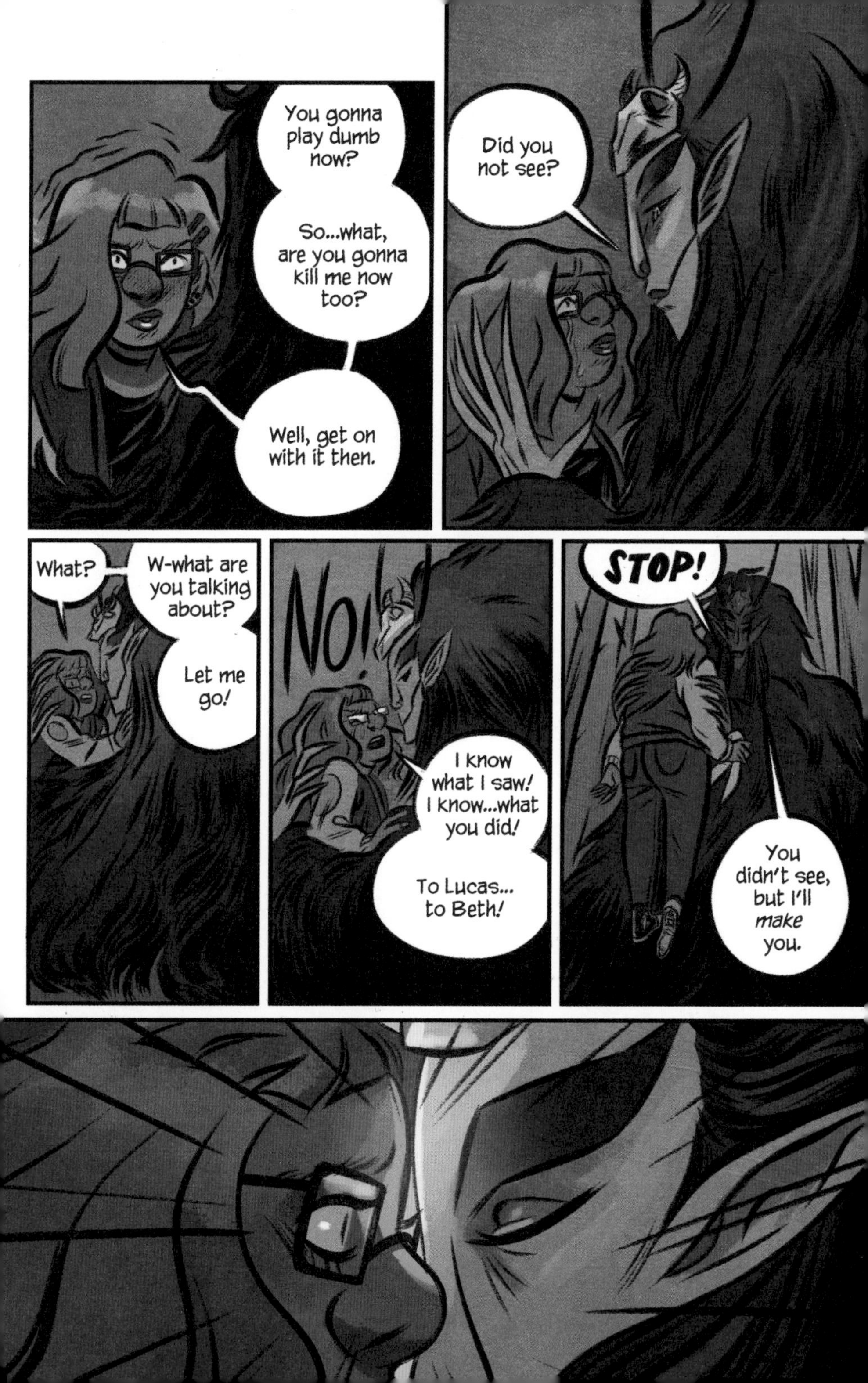

You gonna play dumb now?
So...what, are you gonna kill me now too?
Well, get on with it then.
Did you not see?
What?
W-what are you talking about?
Let me go!
NO!
I know what I saw! I know...what you did!
To Lucas... to Beth!
STOP!
You didn't see, but I'll *make* you.

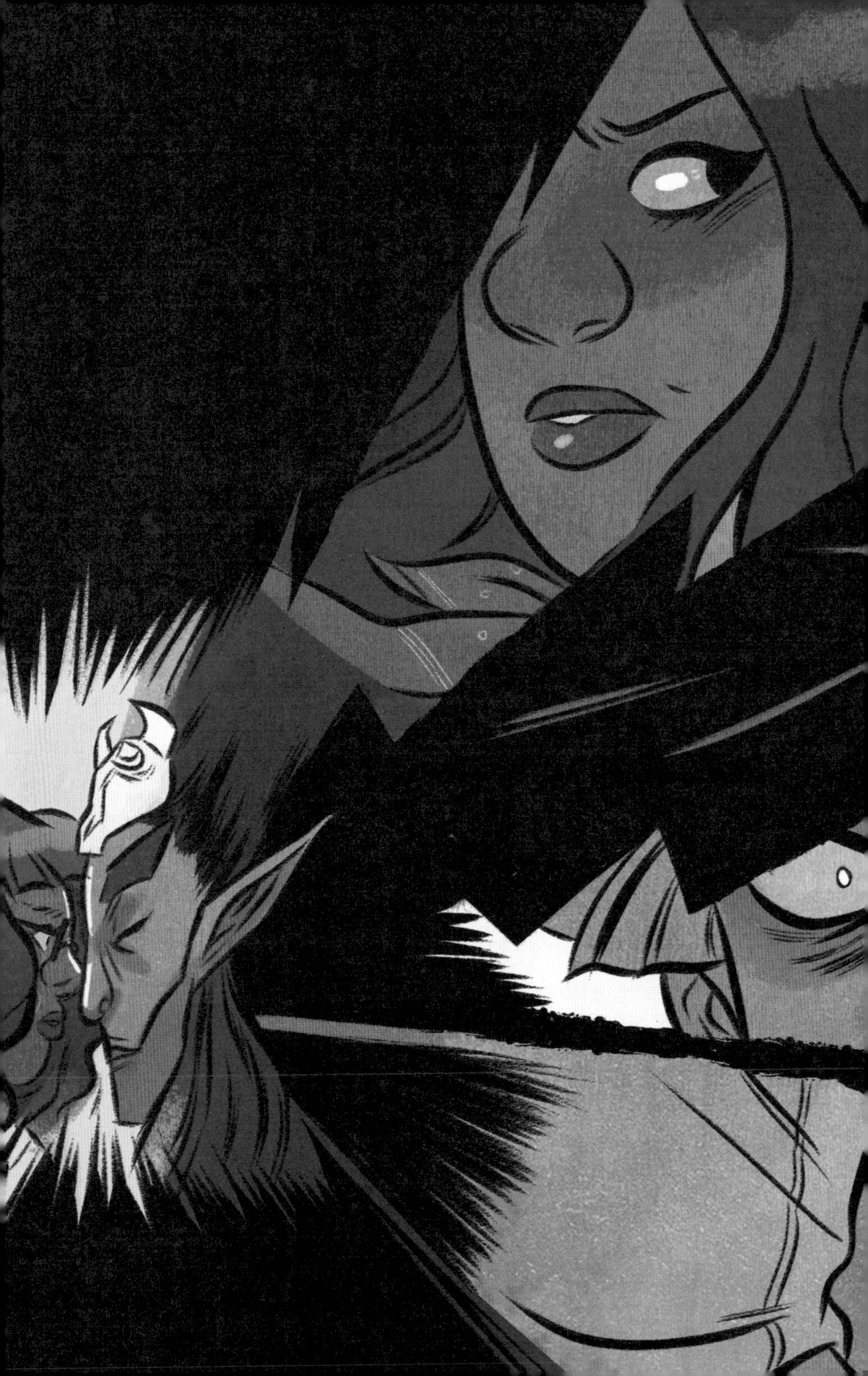

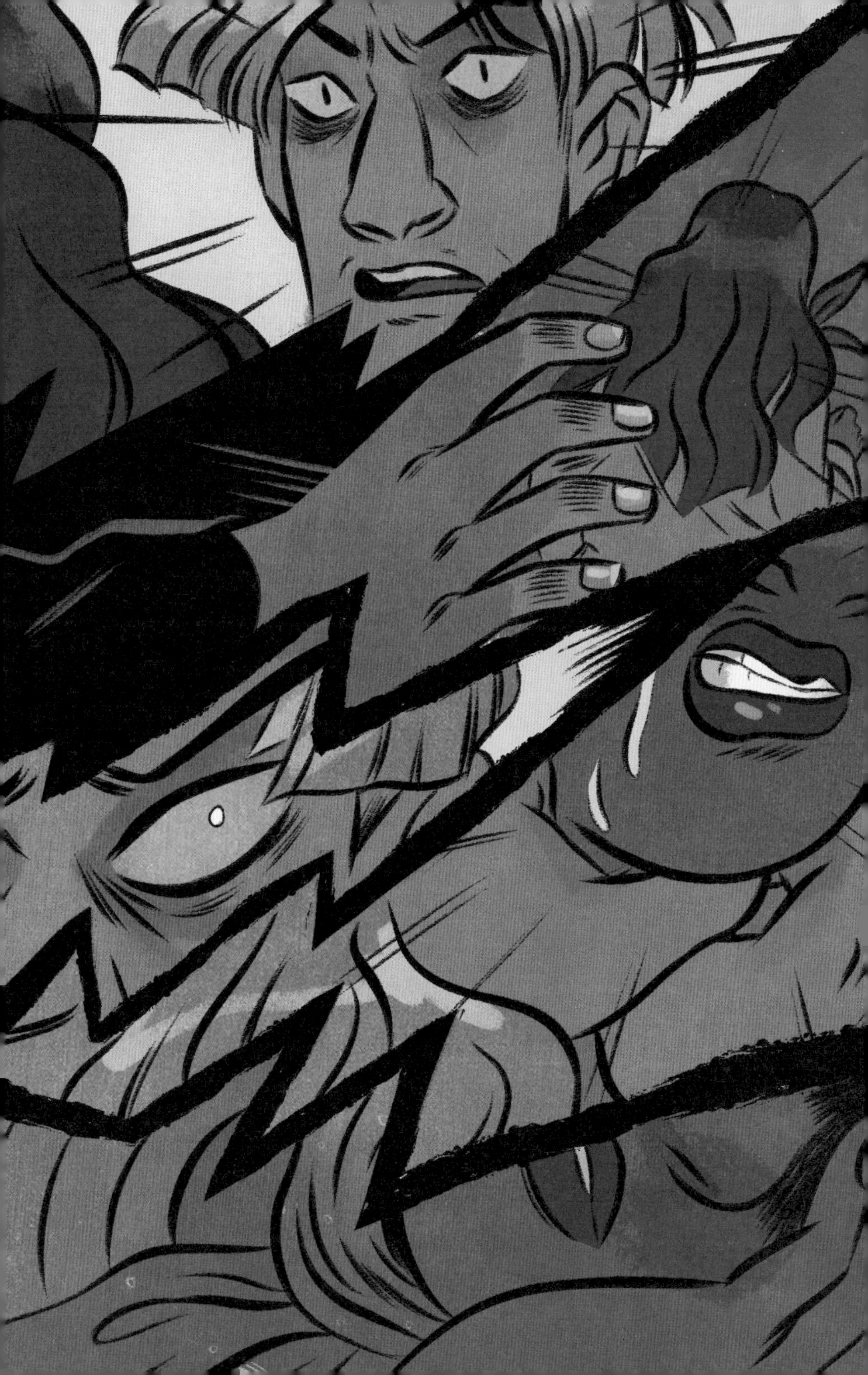

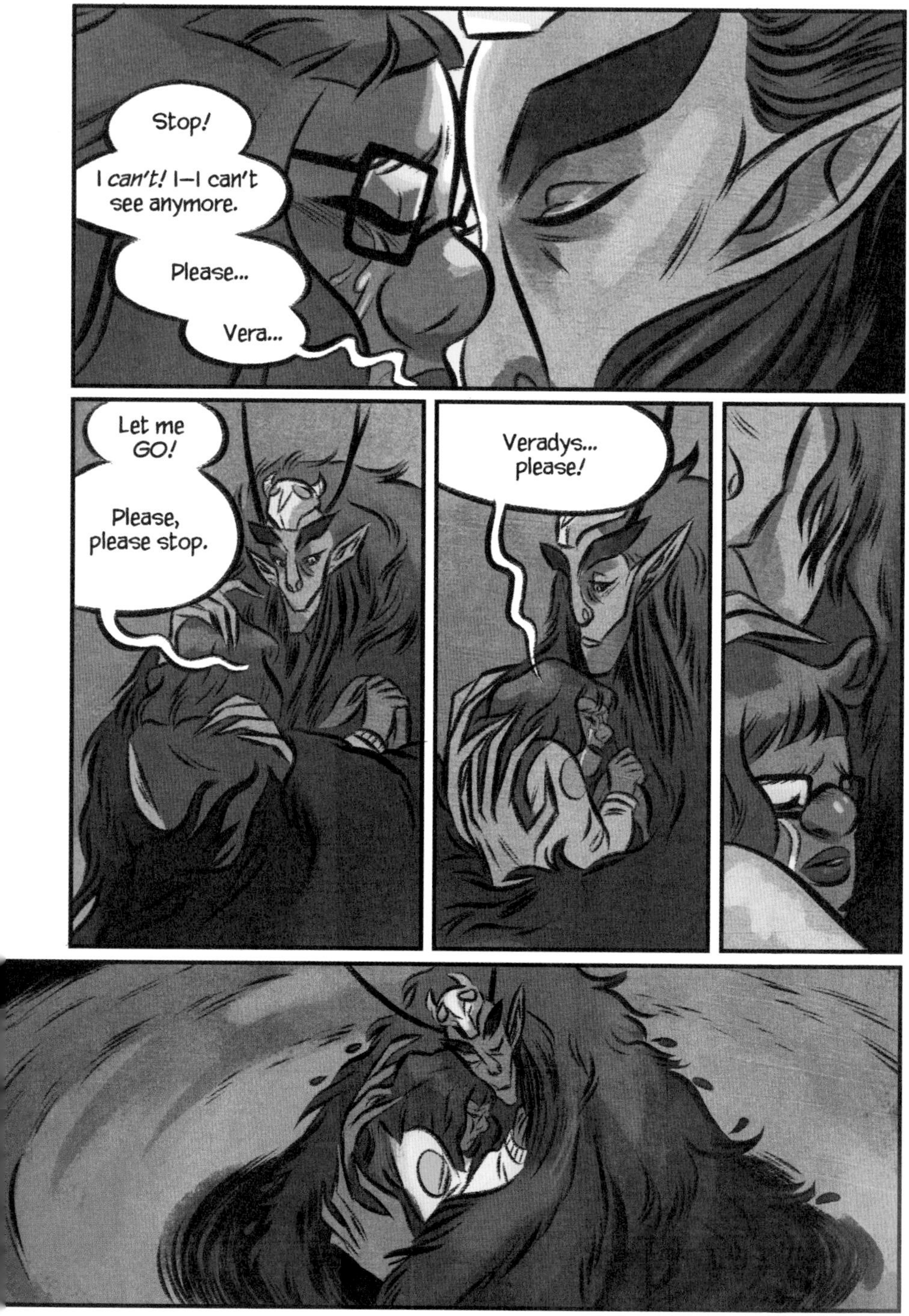
Stop!
I *can't!* I—I can't see anymore.
Please...
Vera...
Let me *GO!*
Please, please stop.
Veradys... please!

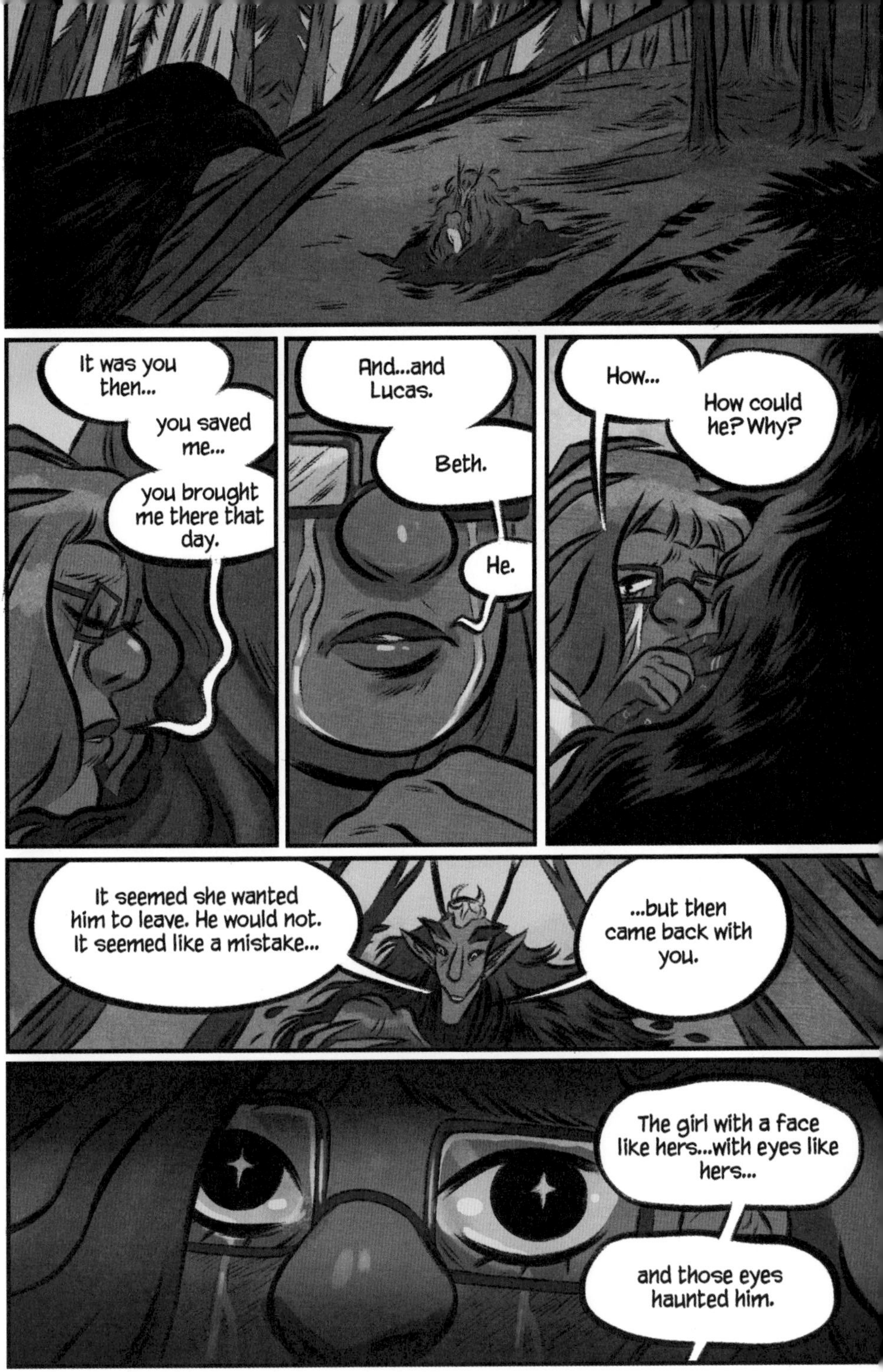
It was you then...
you saved me...
you brought me there that day.
And...and Lucas.
Beth.
He.
How...
How could he? Why?
It seemed she wanted him to leave. He would not. It seemed like a mistake...
...but then came back with you.
The girl with a face like hers...with eyes like hers...
and those eyes haunted him.

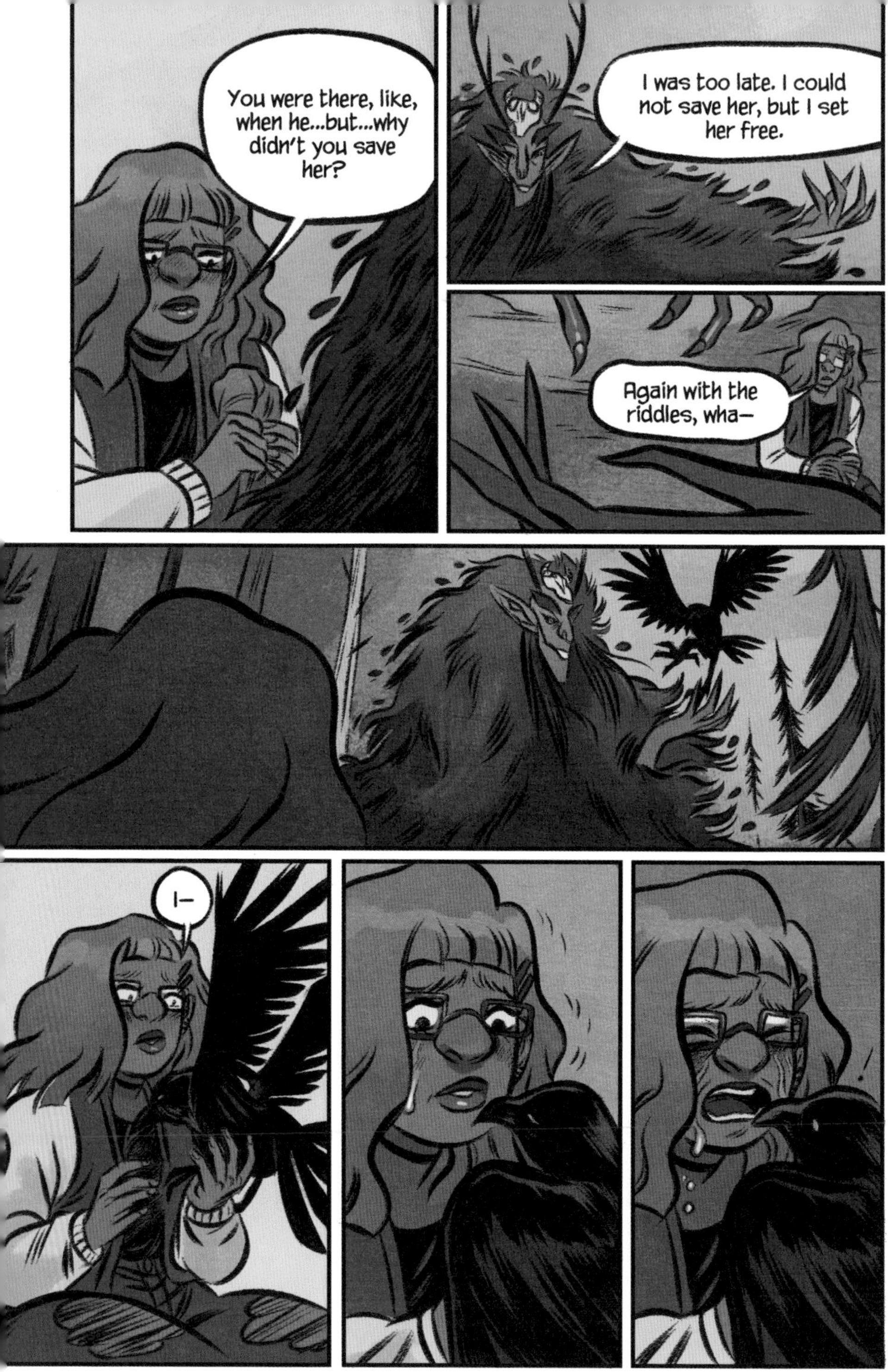
You were there, like, when he...but...why didn't you save her?
I was too late. I could not save her, but I set her free.
Again with the riddles, wha—
I—

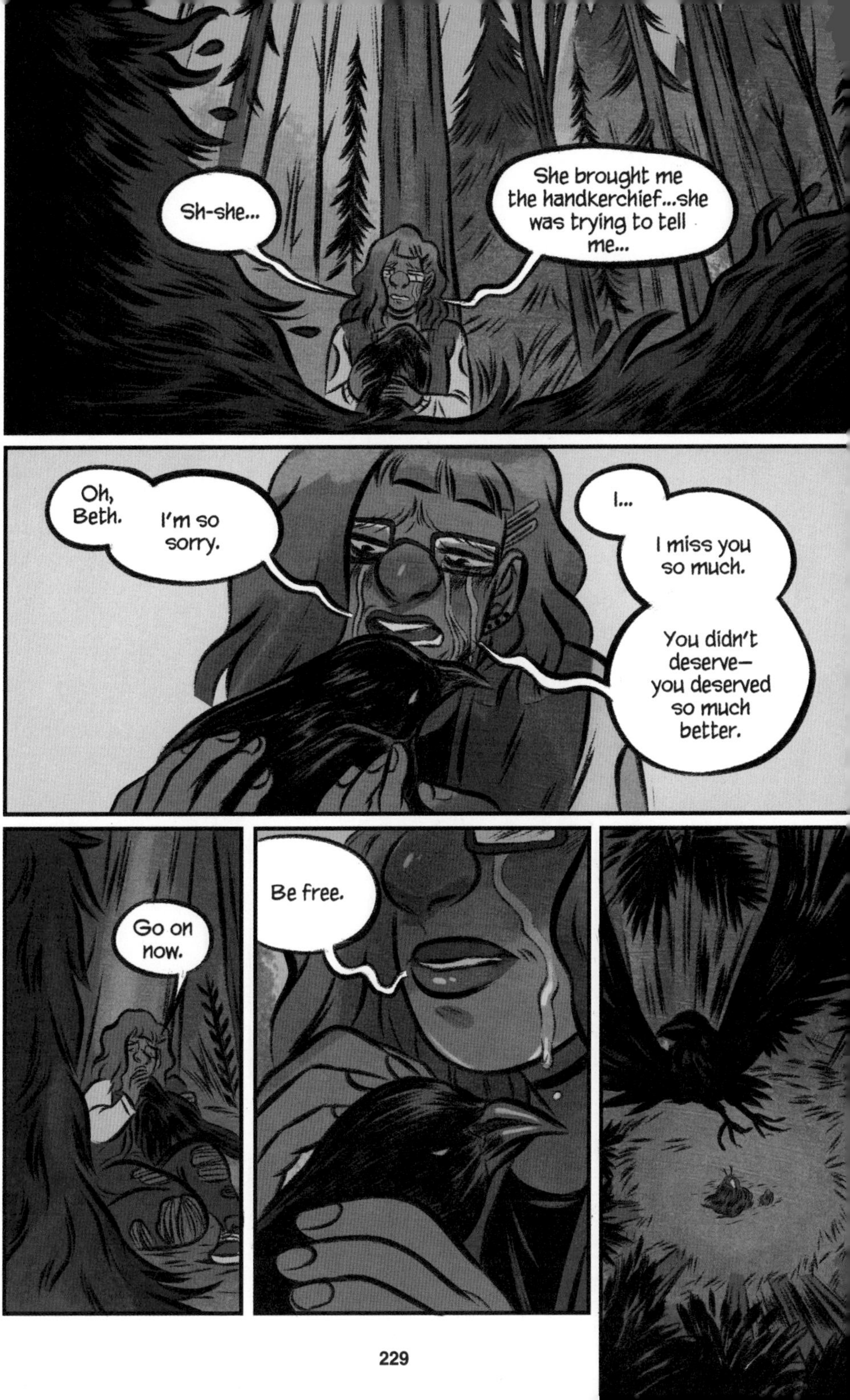
Sh-she...
She brought me the handkerchief...she was trying to tell me...
Oh, Beth.
I'm so sorry.
I...
I miss you so much.
You didn't deserve— you deserved so much better.
Go on now.
Be free.

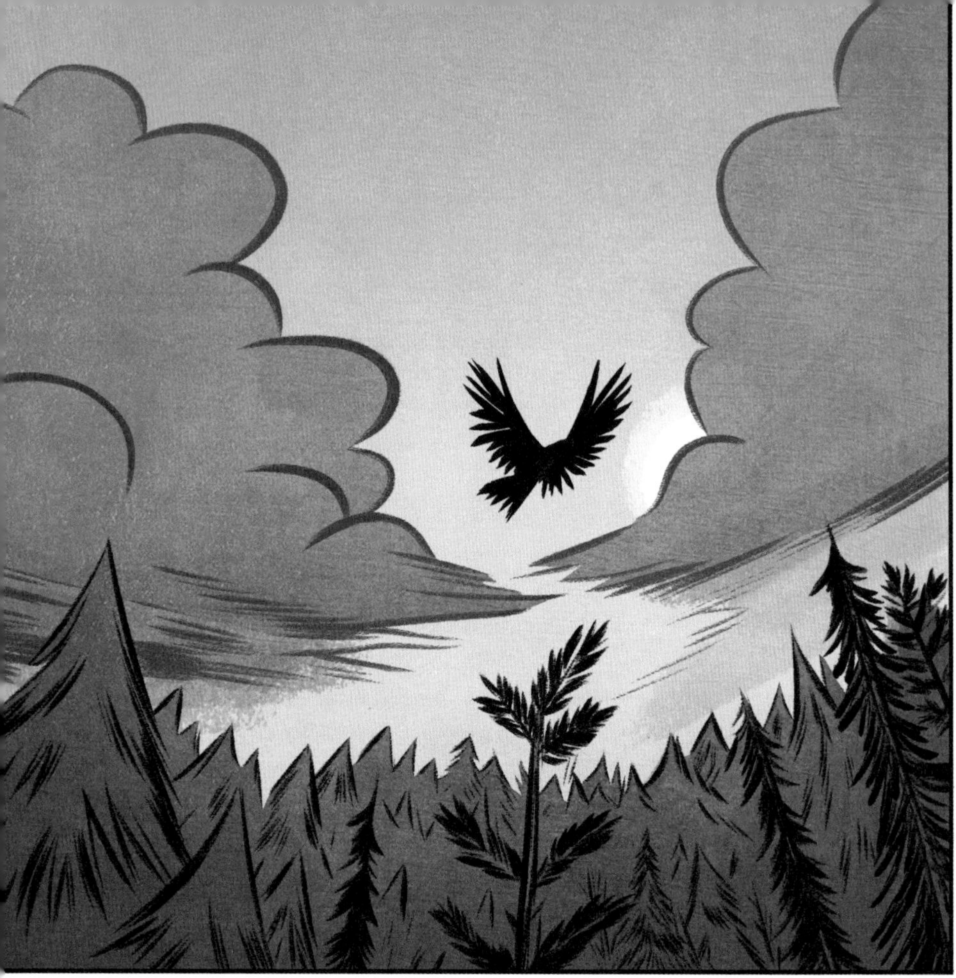

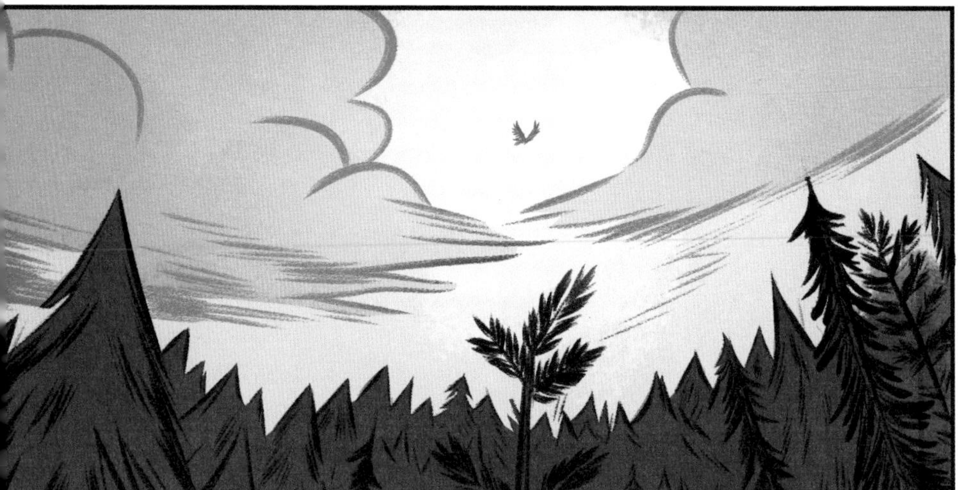

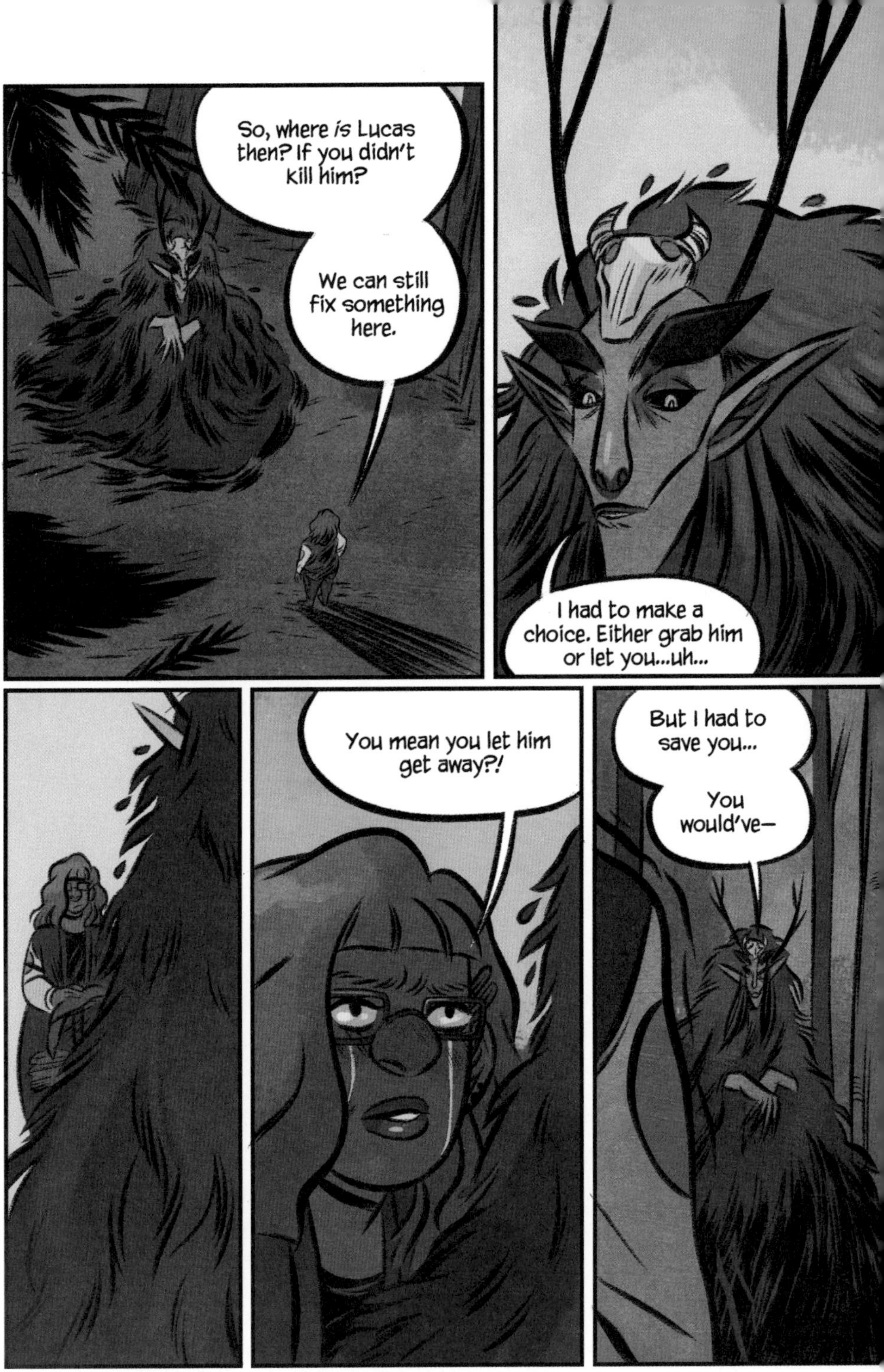
So, where *is* Lucas then? If you didn't kill him?
We can still fix something here.
I had to make a choice. Either grab him or let you...uh...
You mean you let him get away?!
But I had to save you...
You would've—

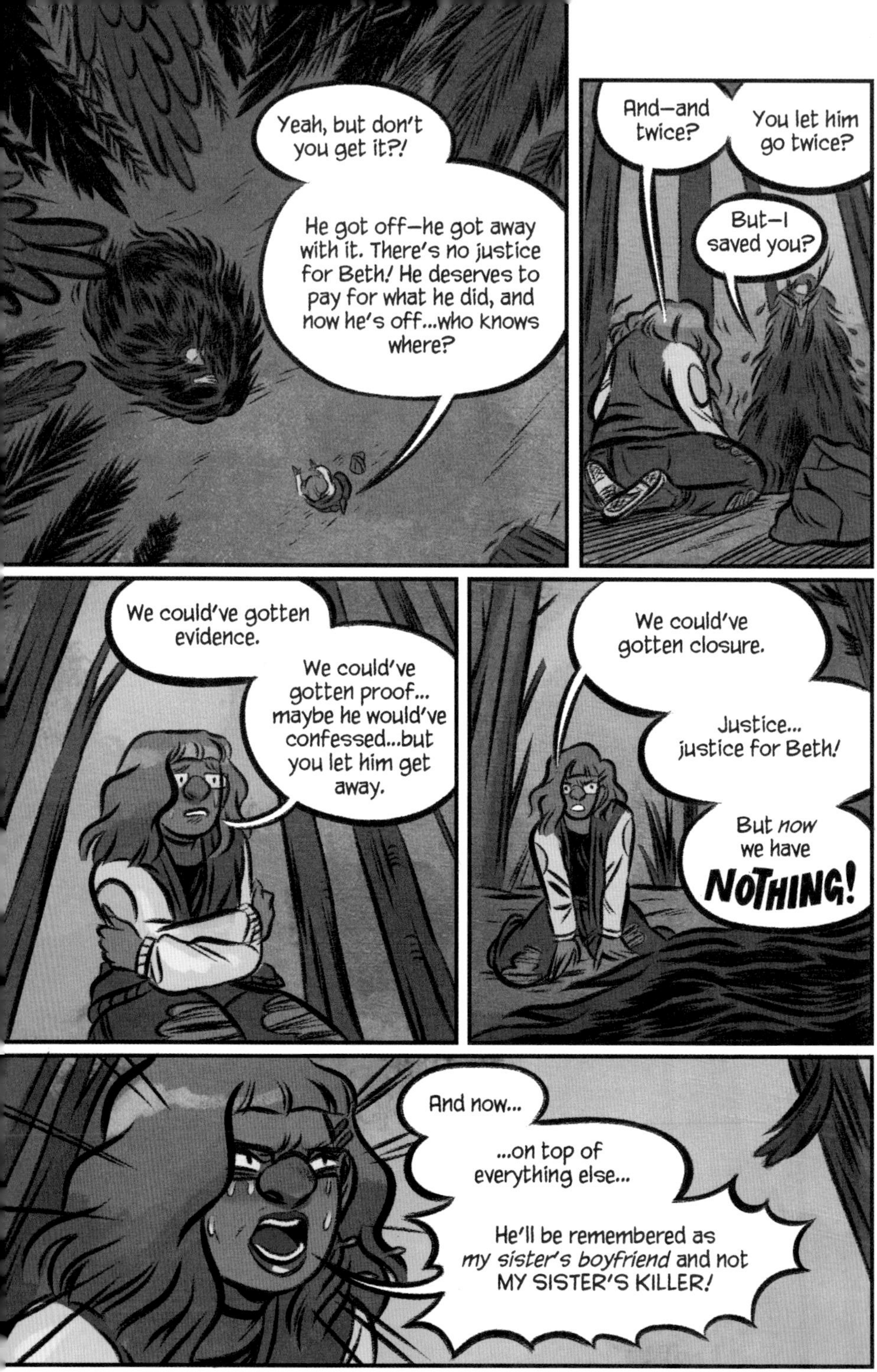
Yeah, but don't you get it?!
He got off—he got away with it. There's no justice for Beth! He deserves to pay for what he did, and now he's off...who knows where?
And—and twice?
You let him go twice?
But—I saved you?
We could've gotten evidence.
We could've gotten proof... maybe he would've confessed...but you let him get away.
We could've gotten closure.
Justice... justice for Beth!
But *now* we have NOTHING!
And now...
...on top of everything else...
He'll be remembered as *my sister's boyfriend* and not MY SISTER'S KILLER!

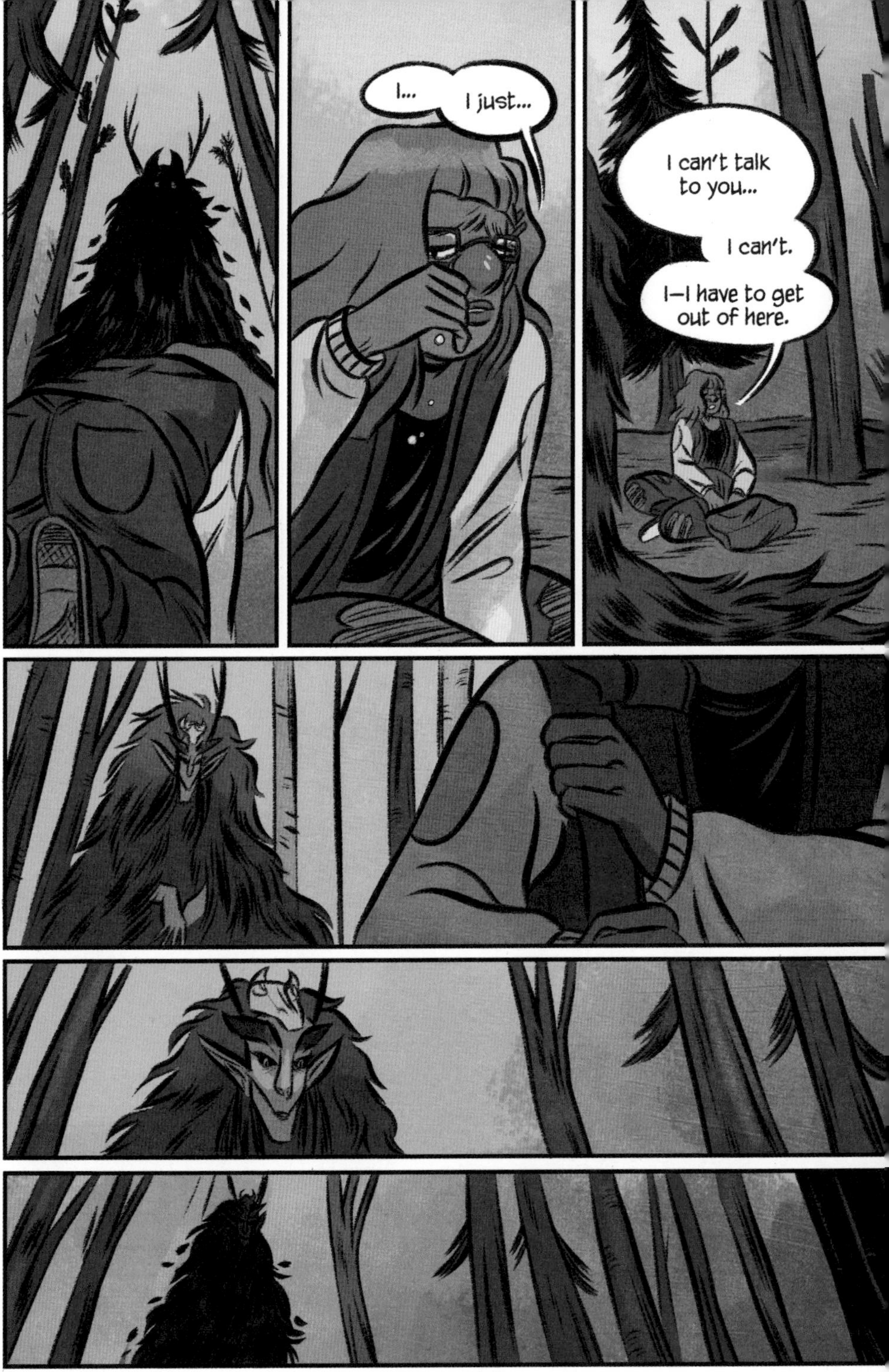
I...
I just...
I can't talk to you...
I can't.
I—I have to get out of here.

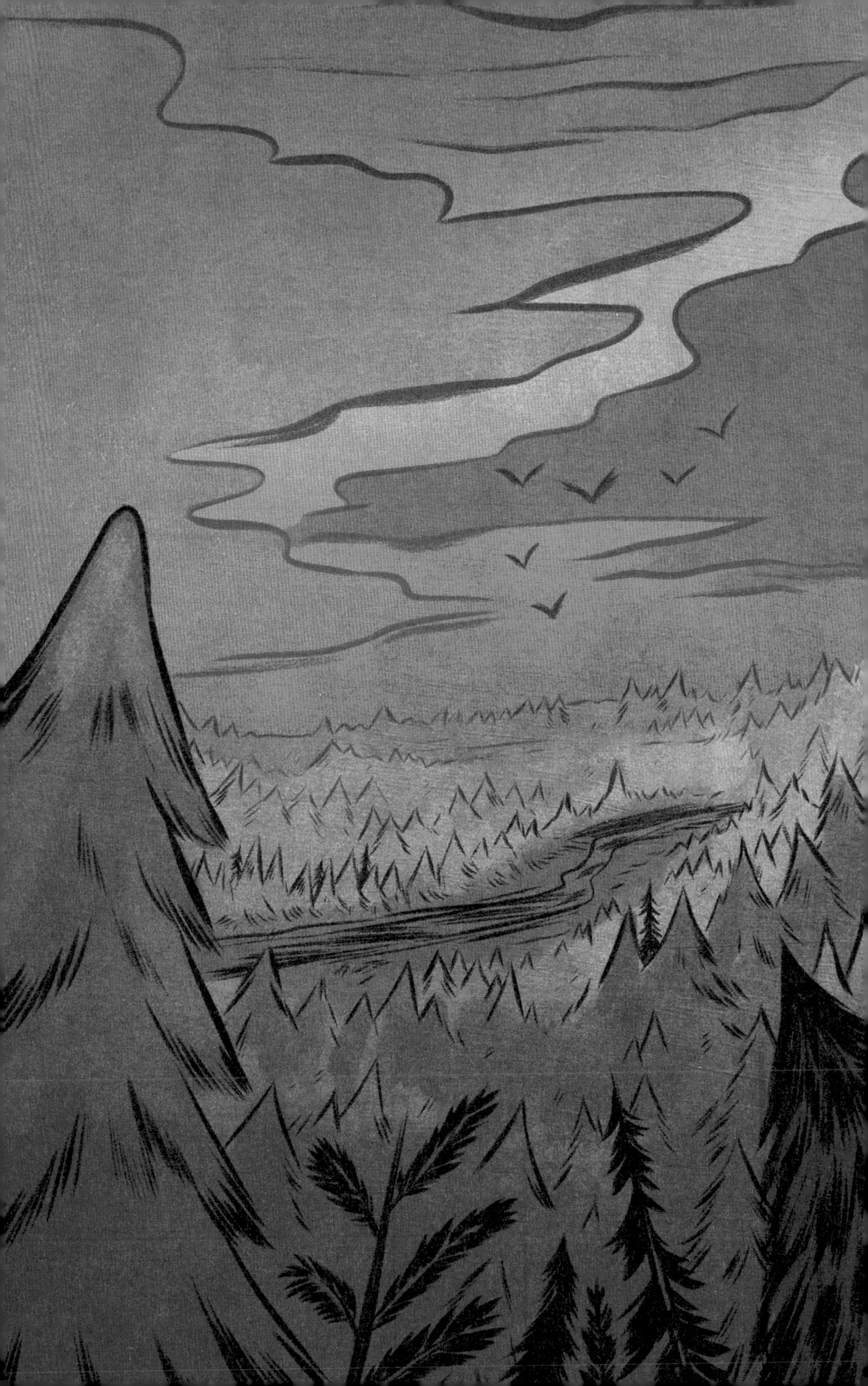

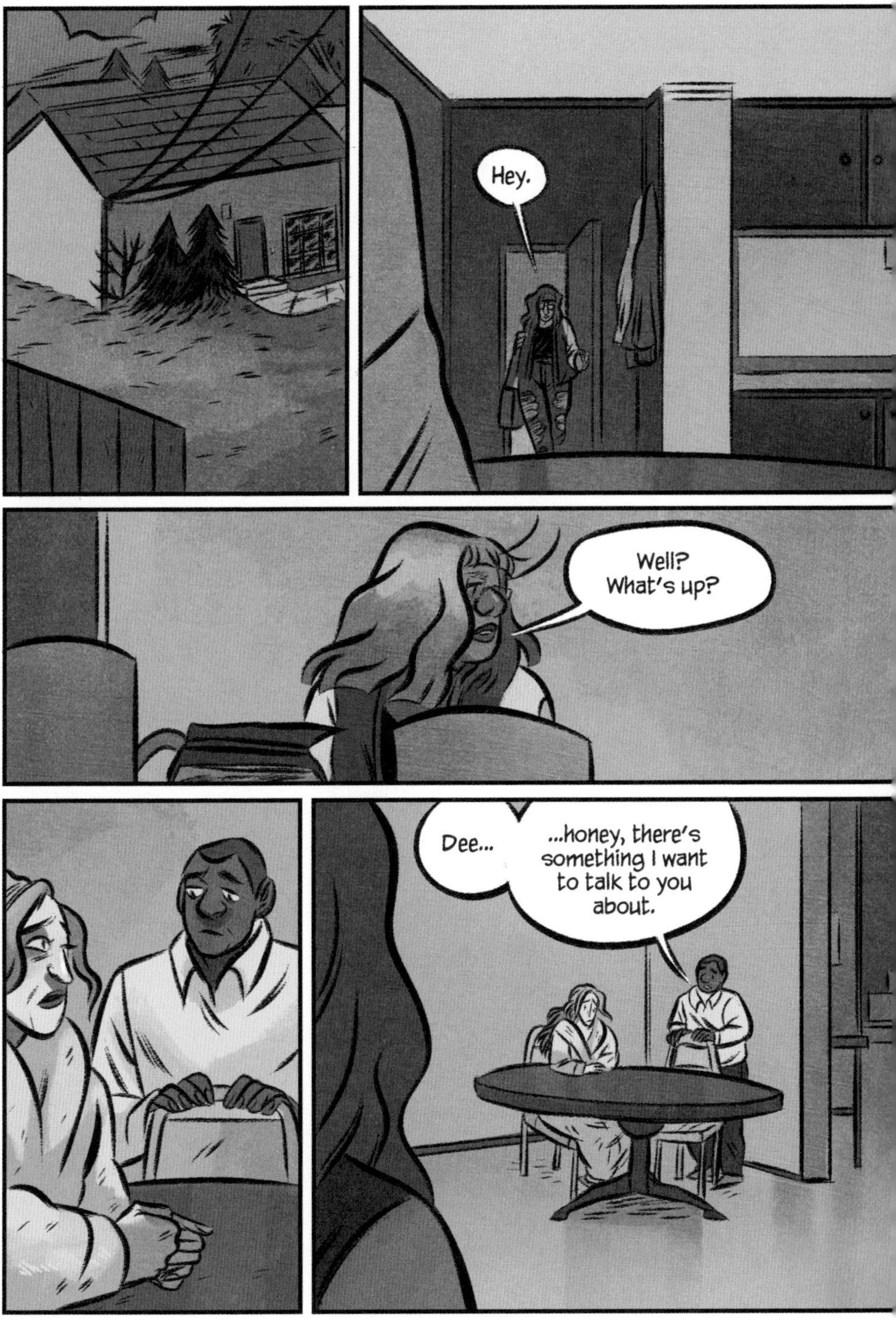
Hey.
Well? What's up?
Dee...
...honey, there's something I want to talk to you about.

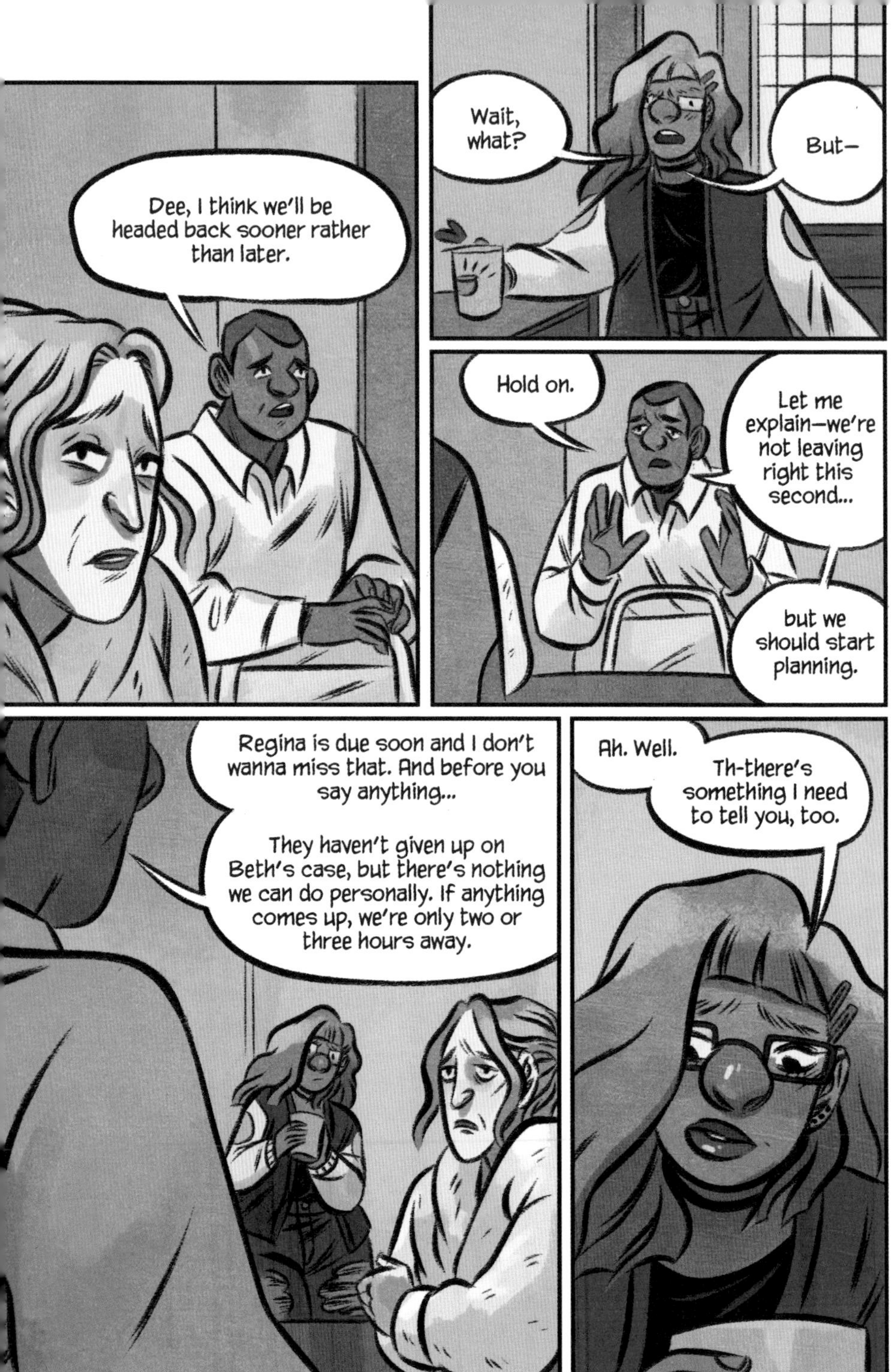
Dee, I think we'll be headed back sooner rather than later.
Wait, what?
But–
Hold on.
Let me explain—we're not leaving right this second...
but we should start planning.
Regina is due soon and I don't wanna miss that. And before you say anything...
They haven't given up on Beth's case, but there's nothing we can do personally. If anything comes up, we're only two or three hours away.
Ah. Well.
Th-there's something I need to tell you, too.

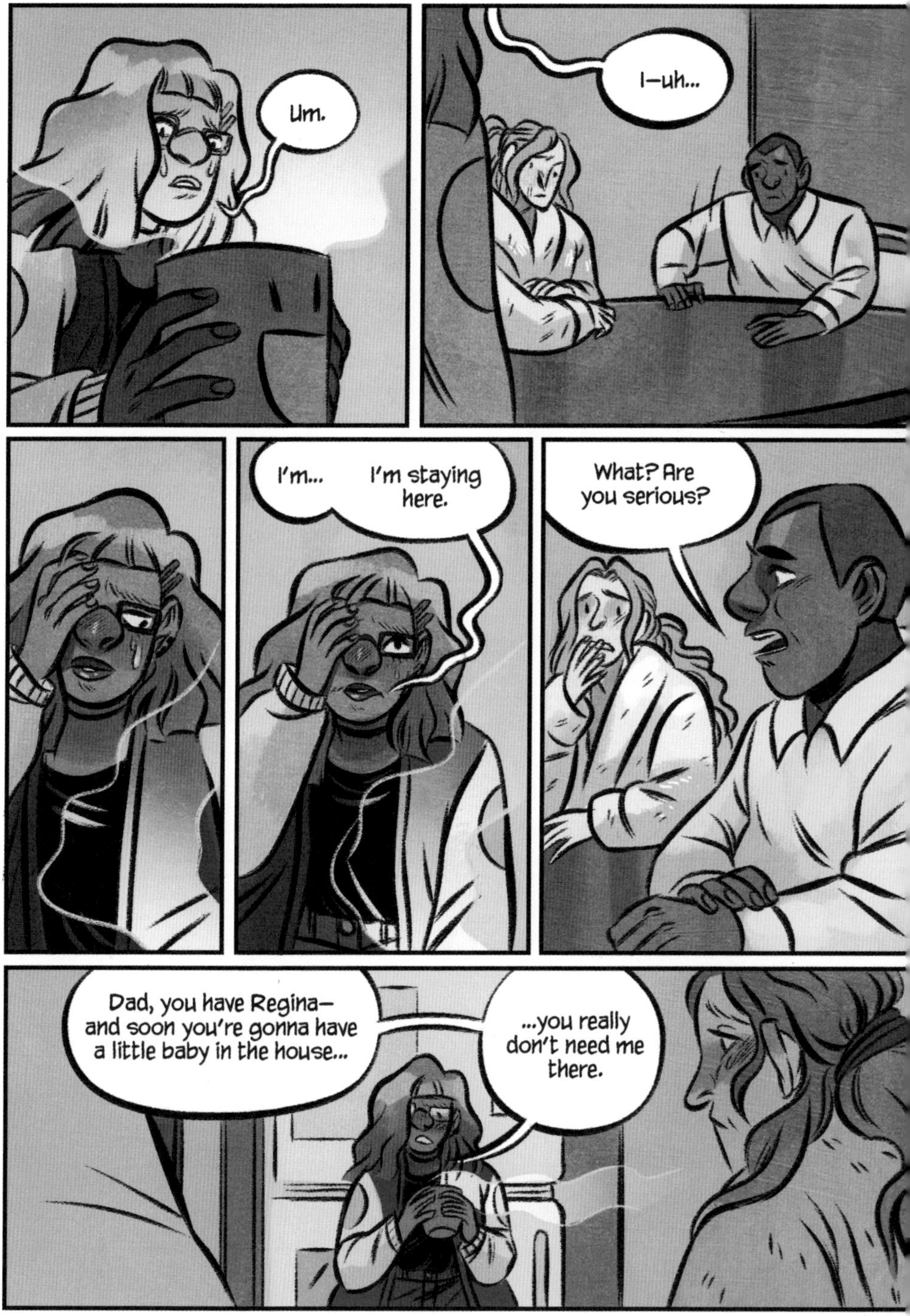
Um.
I—uh...
I'm...
I'm staying here.
What? Are you serious?
Dad, you have Regina—and soon you're gonna have a little baby in the house...
...you really don't need me there.

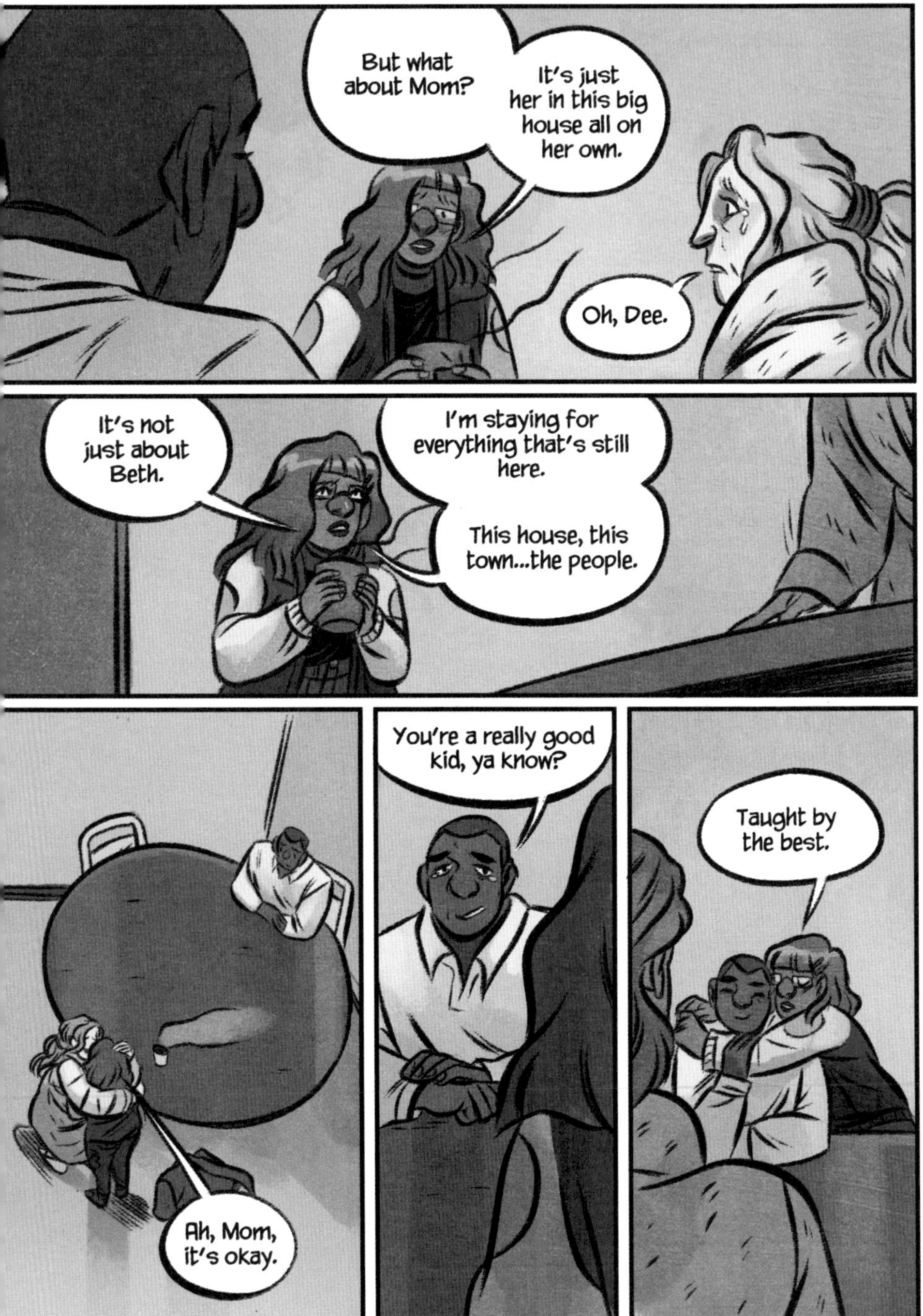
But what about Mom?
It's just her in this big house all on her own.
Oh, Dee.
It's not just about Beth.
I'm staying for everything that's still here.
This house, this town...the people.
Ah, Mom, it's okay.
You're a really good kid, ya know?
Taught by the best.

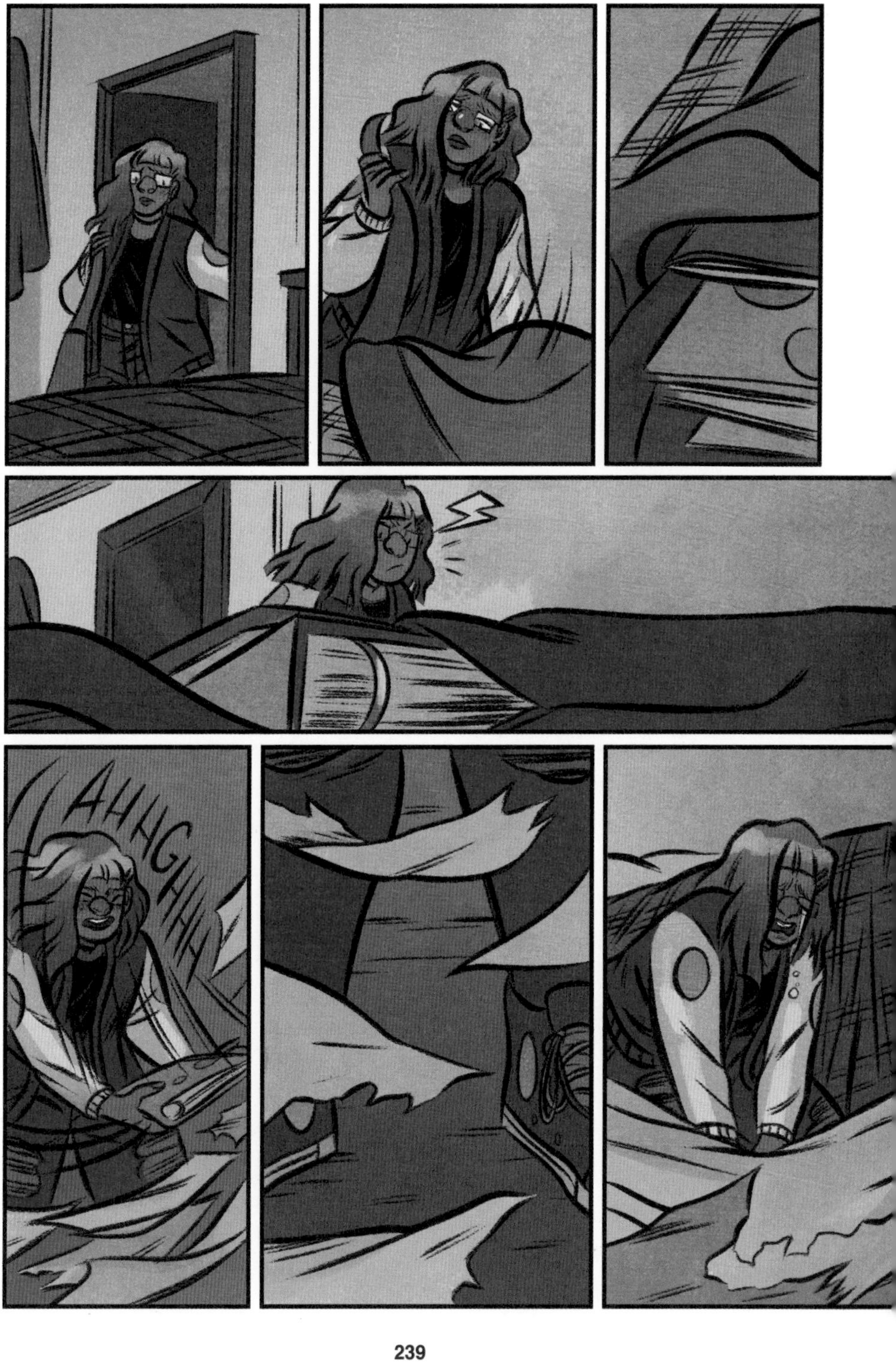
AHHGHHH

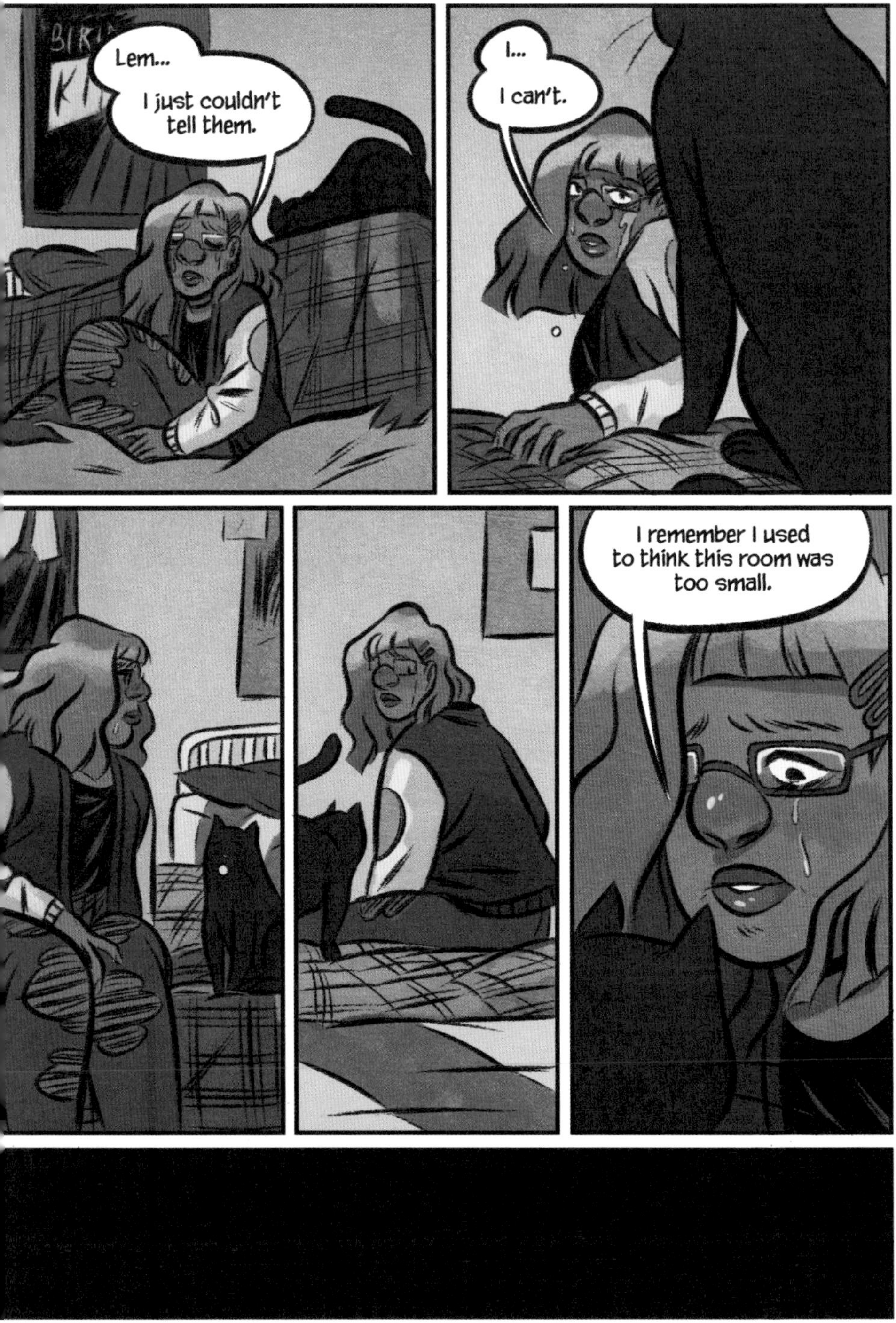
Lem...
I just couldn't tell them.
I...
I can't.
I remember I used to think this room was too small.

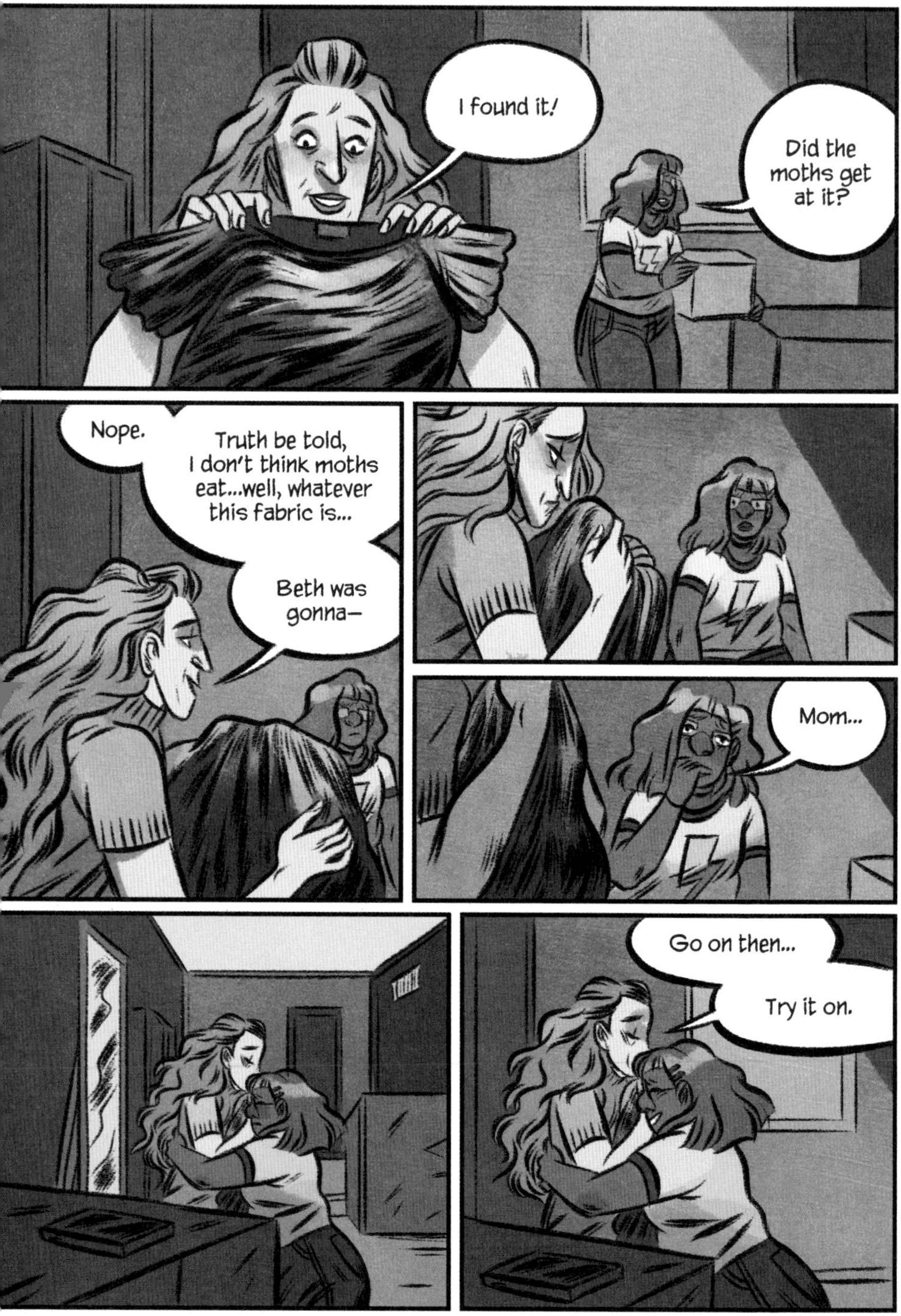
I found it!
Did the moths get at it?
Nope.
Truth be told, I don't think moths eat...well, whatever this fabric is...
Beth was gonna—
Mom...
Go on then...
Try it on.

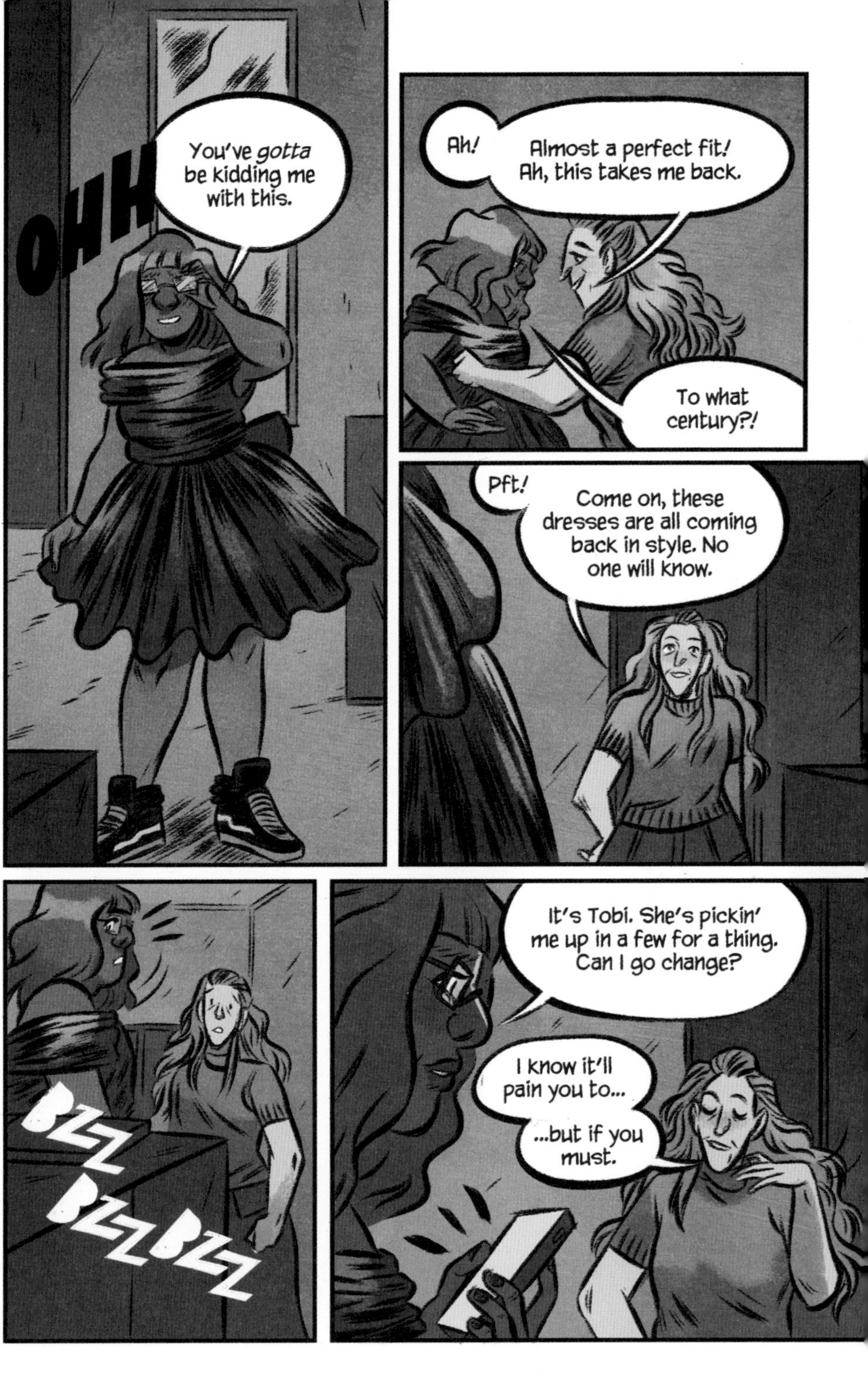
OHH
You've *gotta* be kidding me with this.
Ah!
Almost a perfect fit! Ah, this takes me back.
To what century?!
Pft!
Come on, these dresses are all coming back in style. No one will know.
BZZ BZZ BZZ
It's Tobi. She's pickin' me up in a few for a thing. Can I go change?
I know it'll pain you to...
...but if you must.

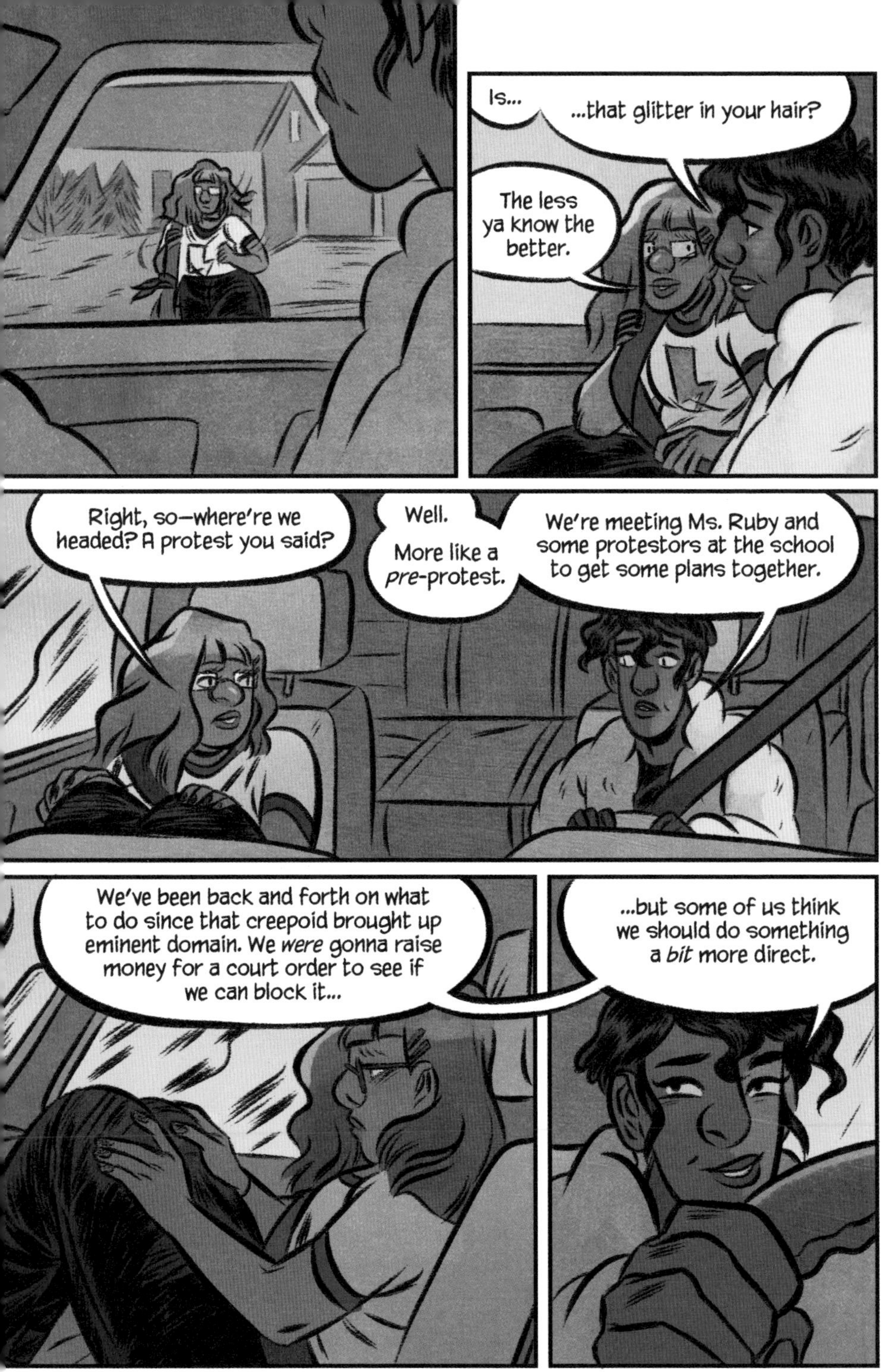

Is...
...that glitter in your hair?
The less ya know the better.
Right, so—where're we headed? A protest you said?
Well.
More like a *pre*-protest.
We're meeting Ms. Ruby and some protestors at the school to get some plans together.
We've been back and forth on what to do since that creepoid brought up eminent domain. We *were* gonna raise money for a court order to see if we can block it...
...but some of us think we should do something a *bit* more direct.

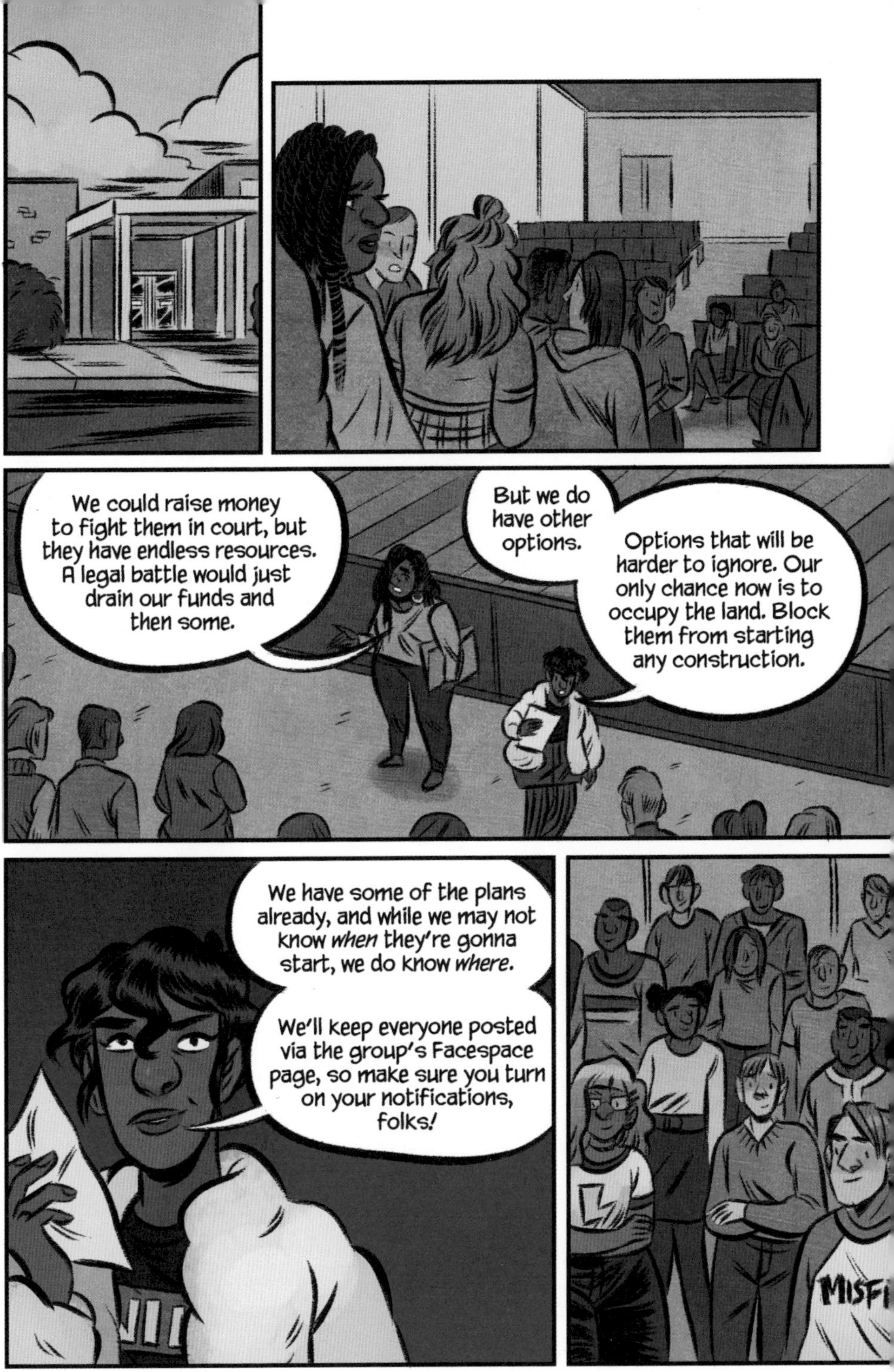
We could raise money to fight them in court, but they have endless resources. A legal battle would just drain our funds and then some.
But we do have other options.
Options that will be harder to ignore. Our only chance now is to occupy the land. Block them from starting any construction.
We have some of the plans already, and while we may not know *when* they're gonna start, we do know *where*.
We'll keep everyone posted via the group's Facespace page, so make sure you turn on your notifications, folks!
MISFI

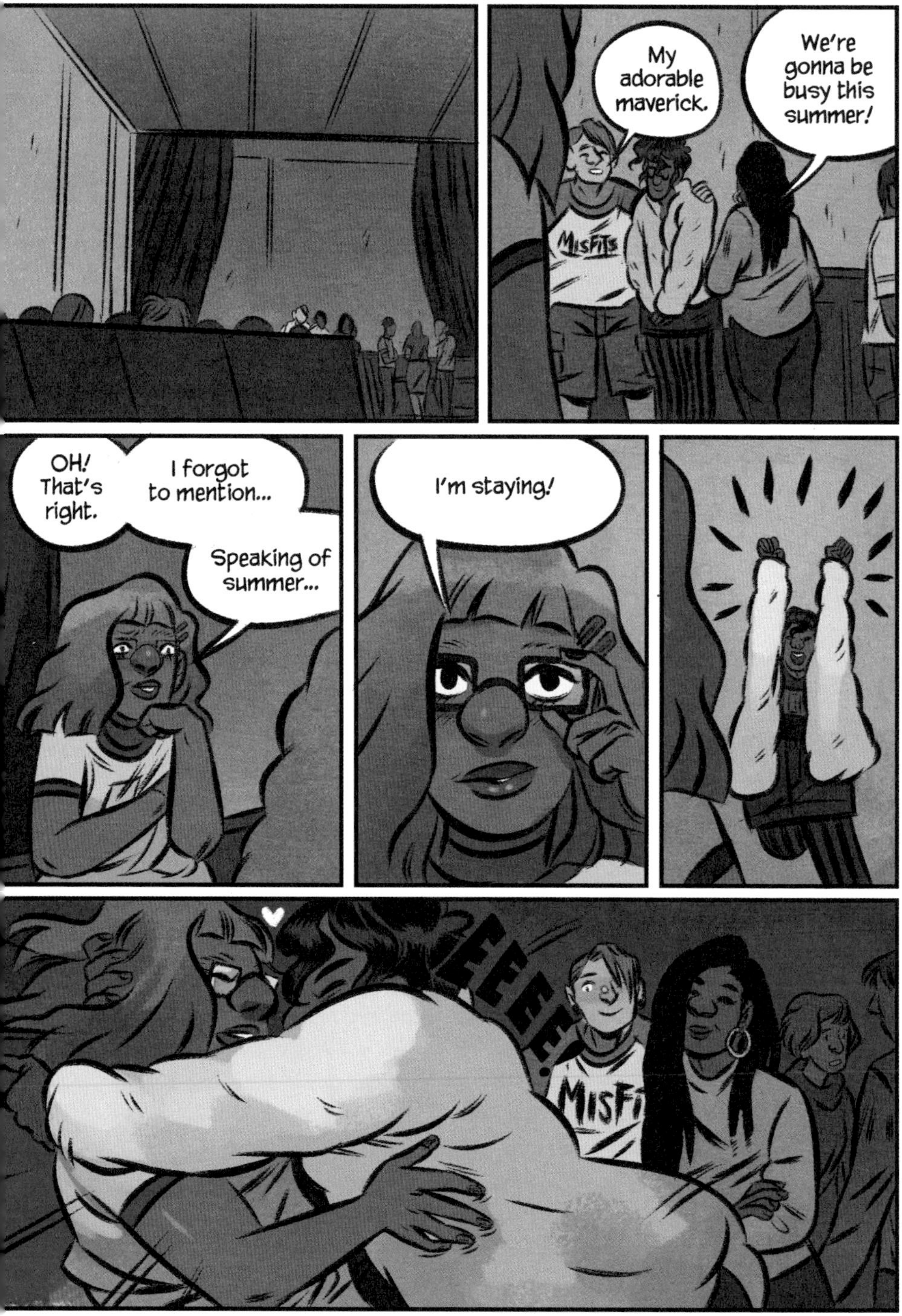
My adorable maverick.
We're gonna be busy this summer!
OH! That's right.
I forgot to mention...
Speaking of summer...
I'm staying!
EEEE!
MISFITS

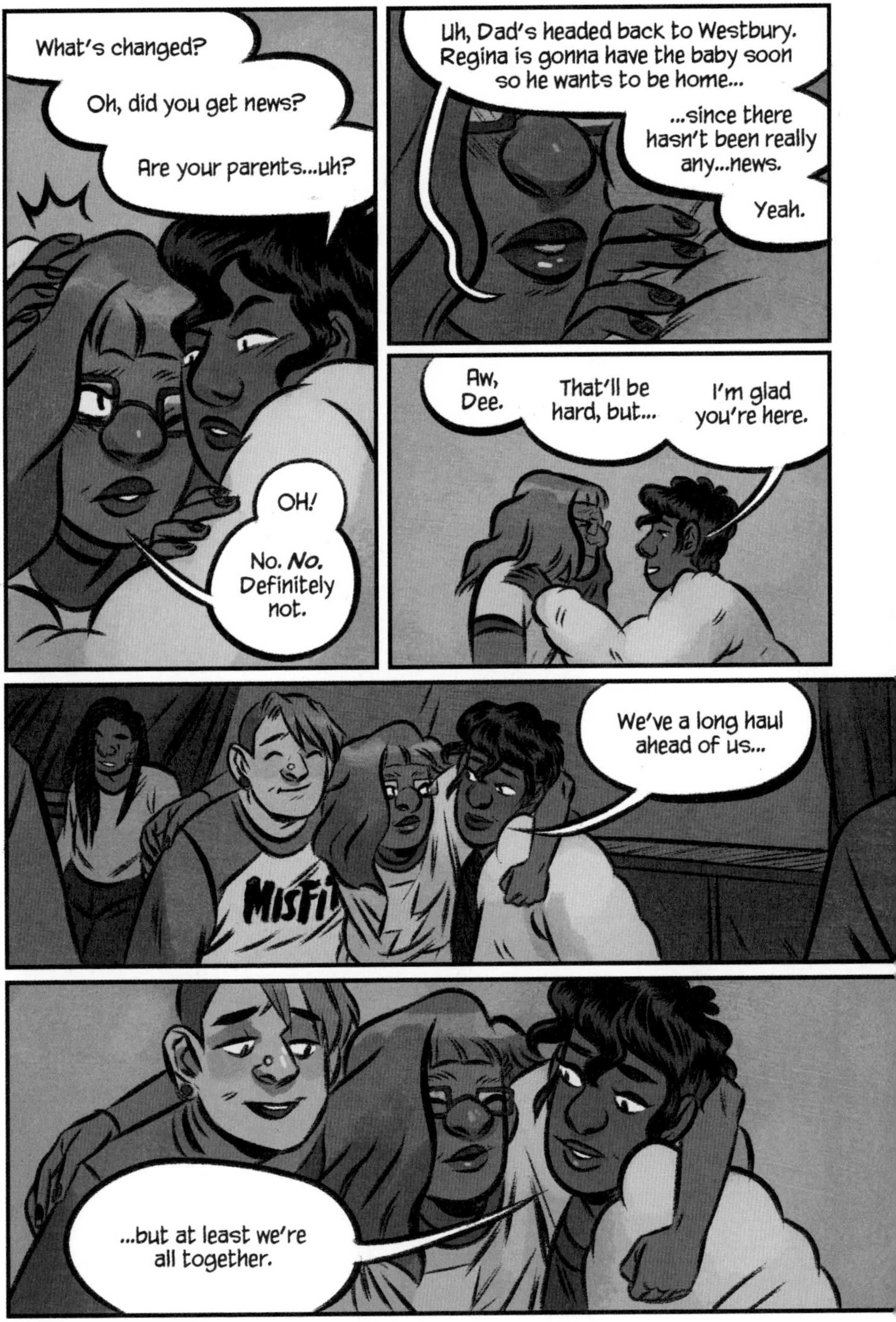
What's changed?
Oh, did you get news?
Are your parents...uh?
OH!
No. *No.* Definitely not.
Uh, Dad's headed back to Westbury. Regina is gonna have the baby soon so he wants to be home...
...since there hasn't been really any...news.
Yeah.
Aw, Dee.
That'll be hard, but...
I'm glad you're here.
MISFIT
We've a long haul ahead of us...
...but at least we're all together.

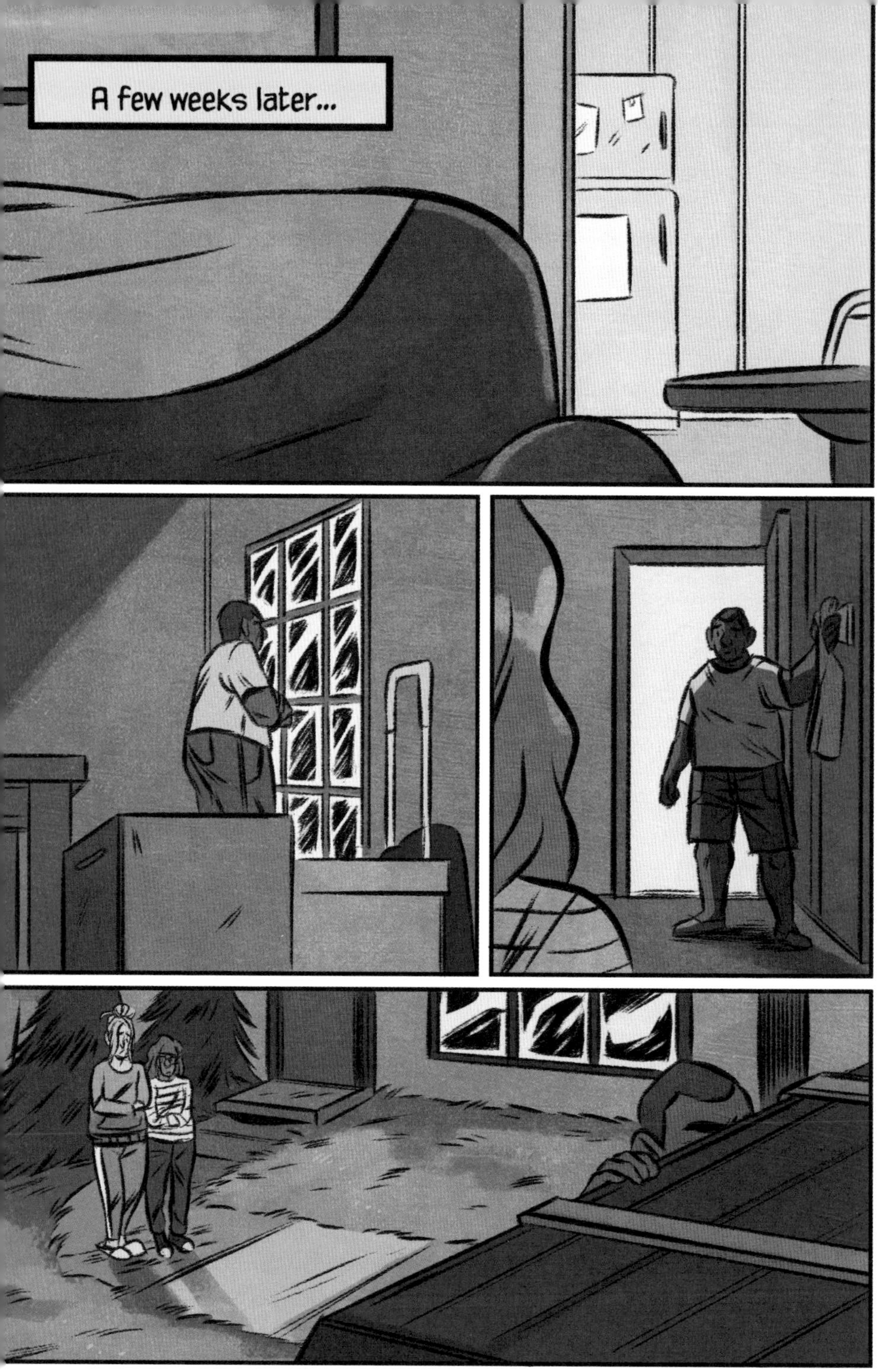
A few weeks later...

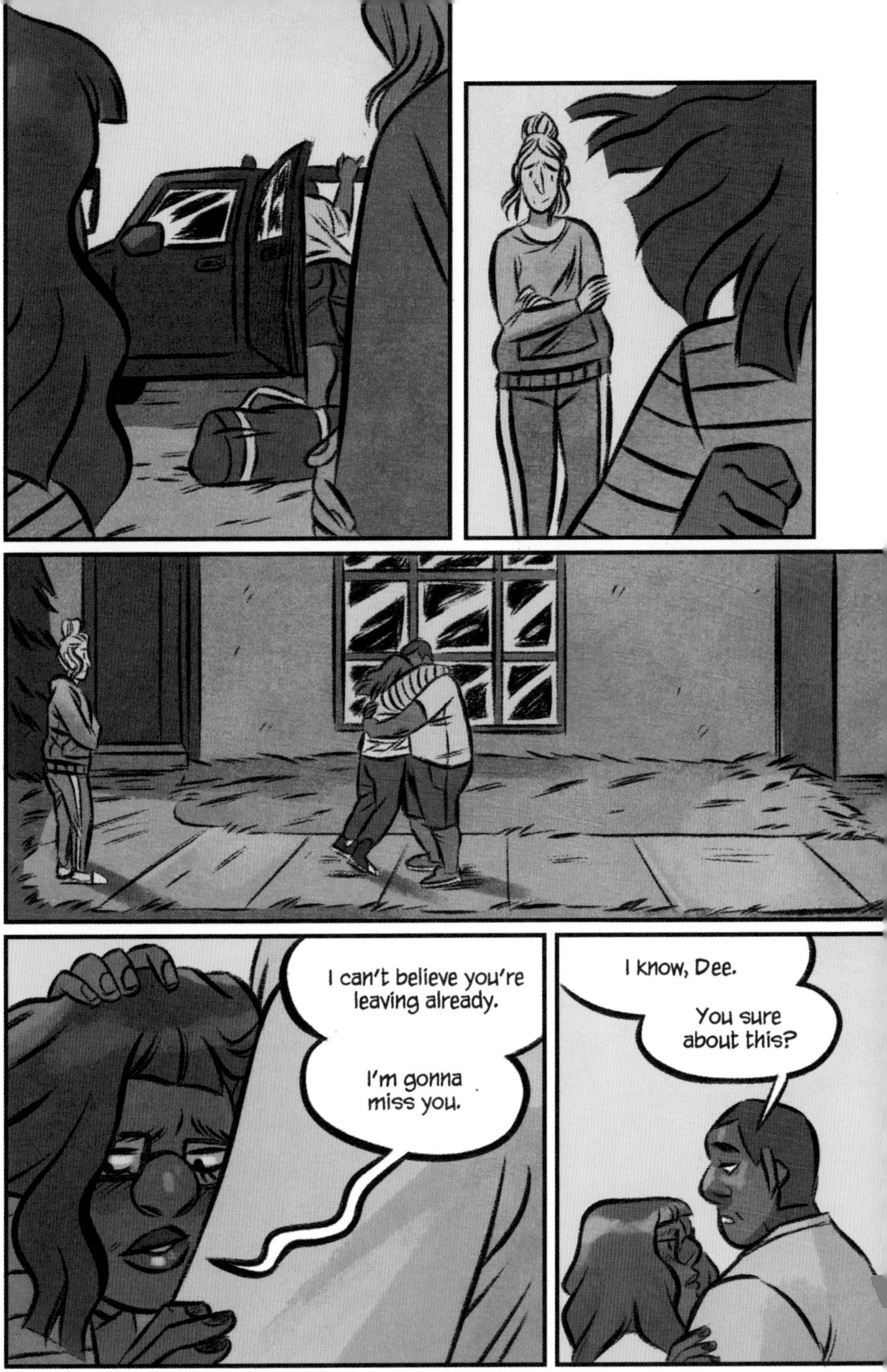
I can't believe you're leaving already.
I'm gonna miss you.
I know, Dee.
You sure about this?

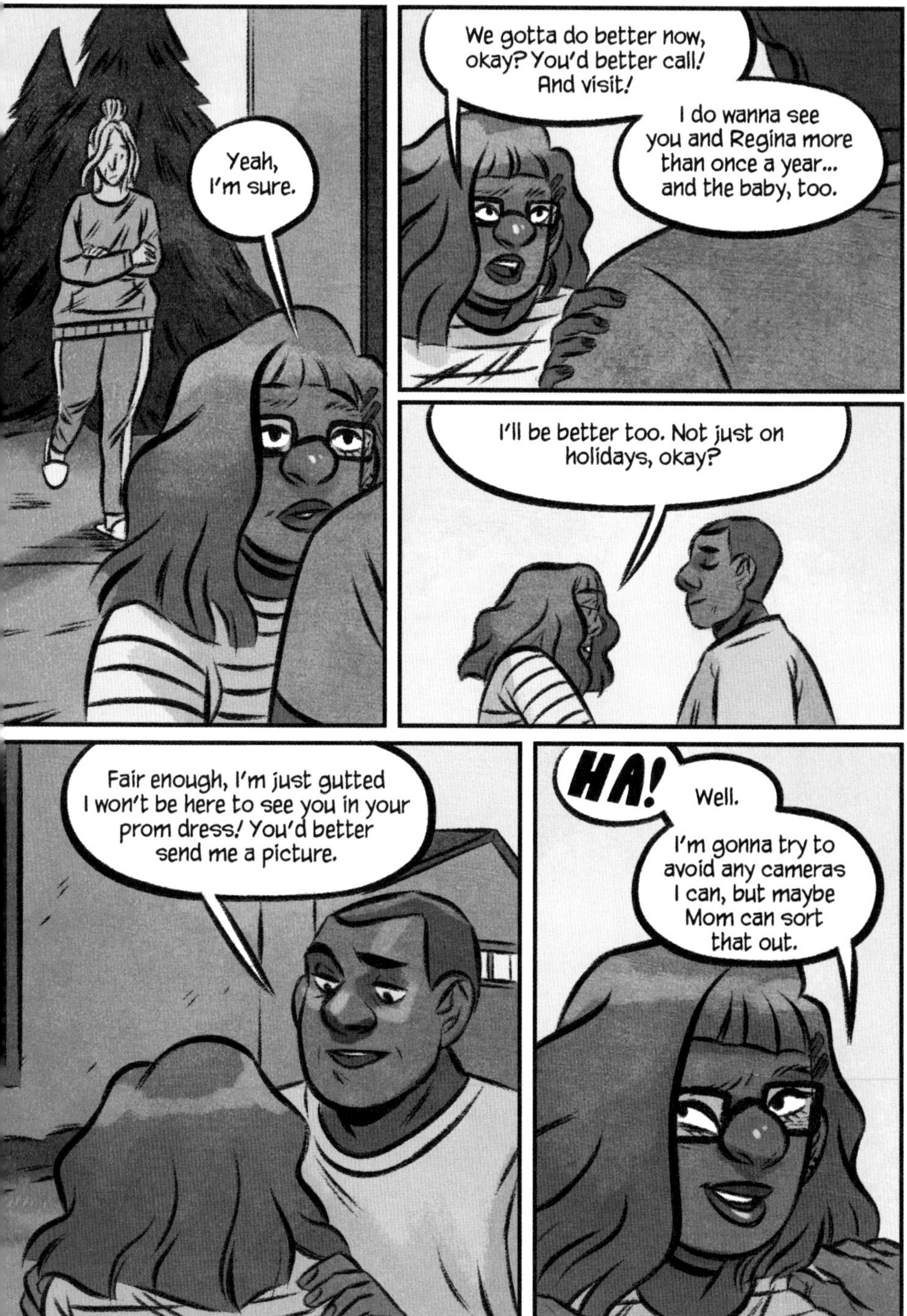
Yeah, I'm sure.
We gotta do better now, okay? You'd better call! And visit!
I do wanna see you and Regina more than once a year... and the baby, too.
I'll be better too. Not just on holidays, okay?
Fair enough, I'm just gutted I won't be here to see you in your prom dress! You'd better send me a picture.
HA!
Well.
I'm gonna try to avoid any cameras I can, but maybe Mom can sort that out.

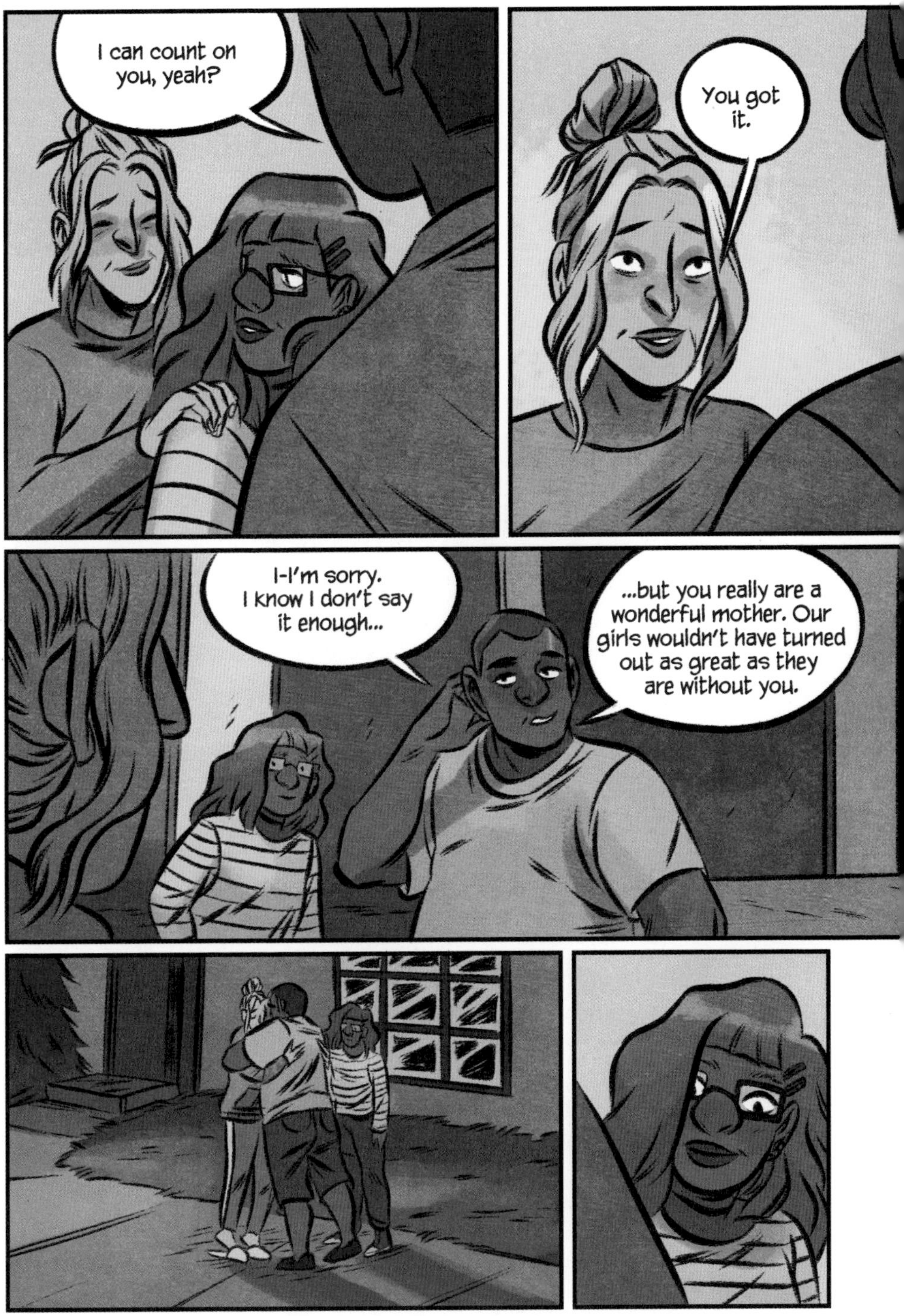
I can count on you, yeah?
You got it.
I-I'm sorry. I know I don't say it enough...
...but you really are a wonderful mother. Our girls wouldn't have turned out as great as they are without you.

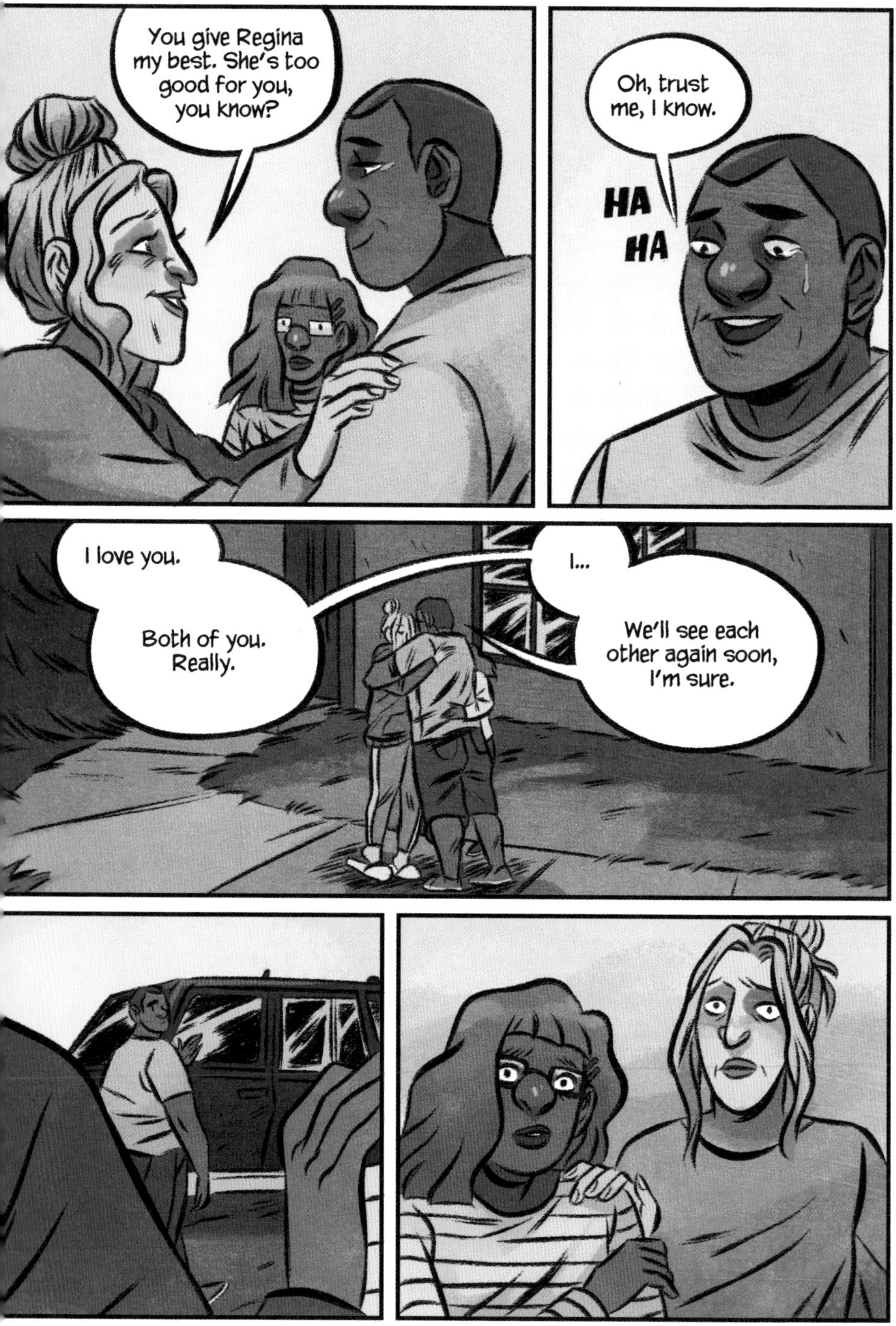
You give Regina my best. She's too good for you, you know?
Oh, trust me, I know.
HA HA
I love you.
Both of you. Really.
I...
We'll see each other again soon, I'm sure.

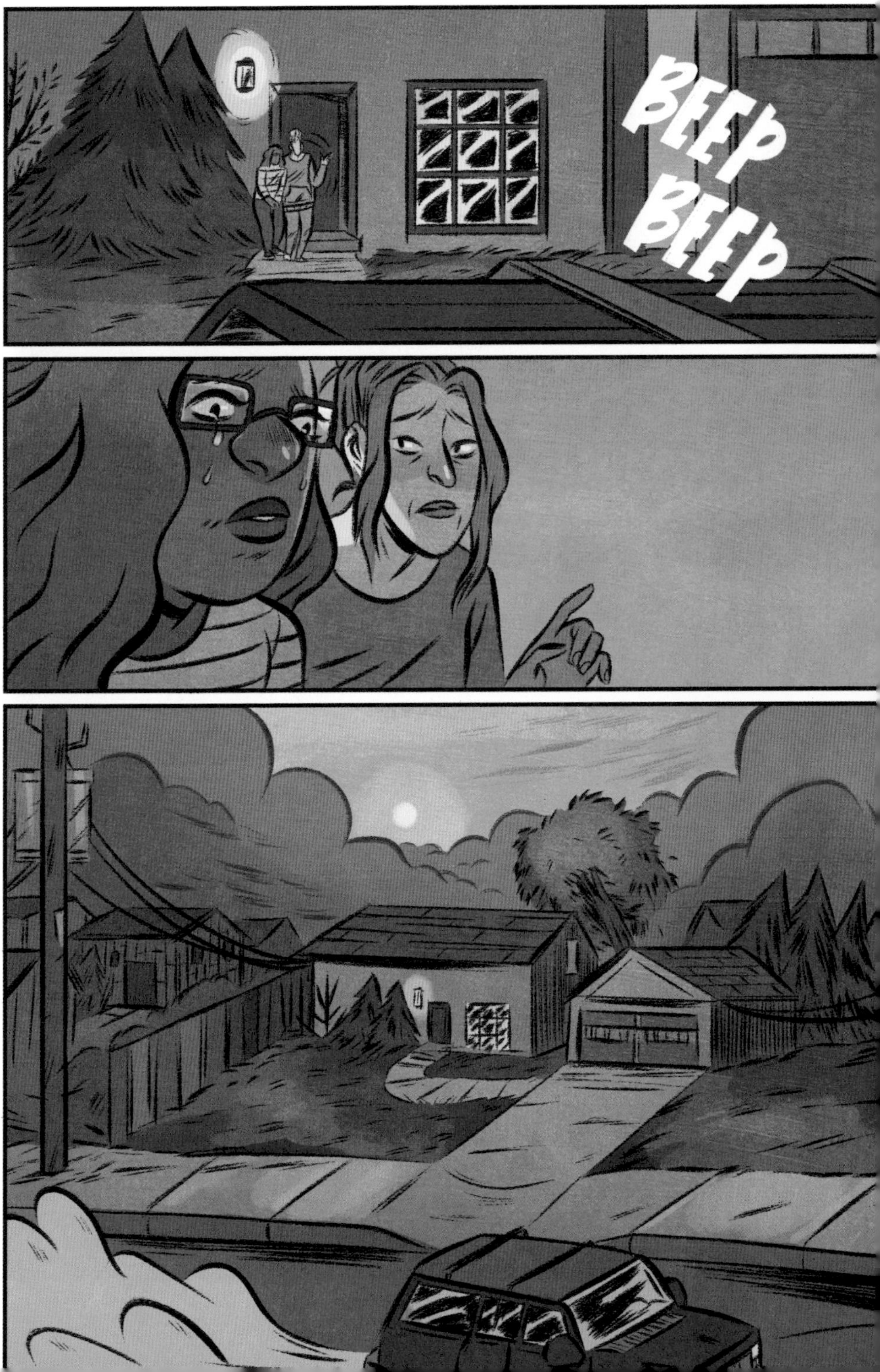
BEEP
BEEP

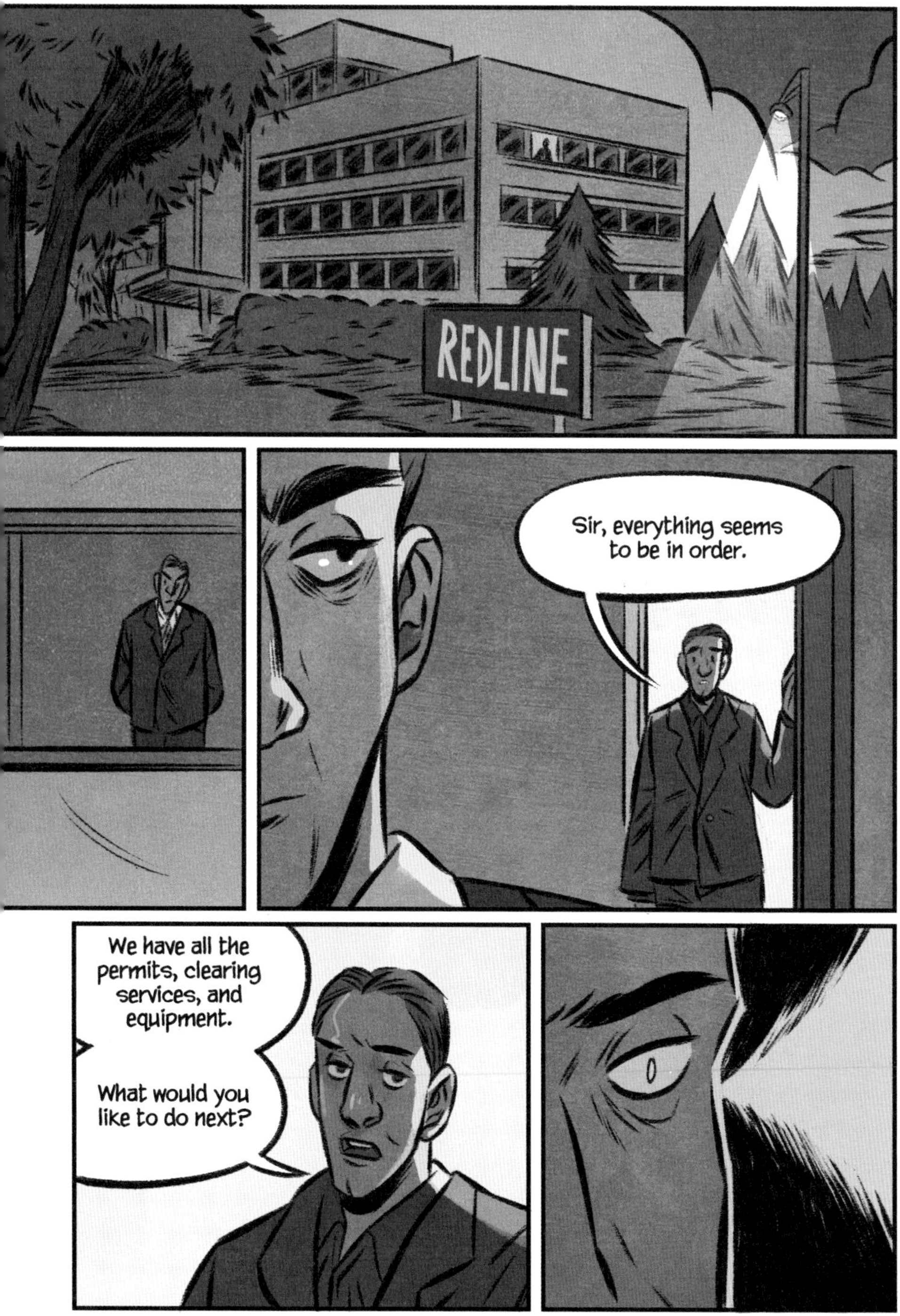
REDLINE
Sir, everything seems to be in order.
We have all the permits, clearing services, and equipment.
What would you like to do next?

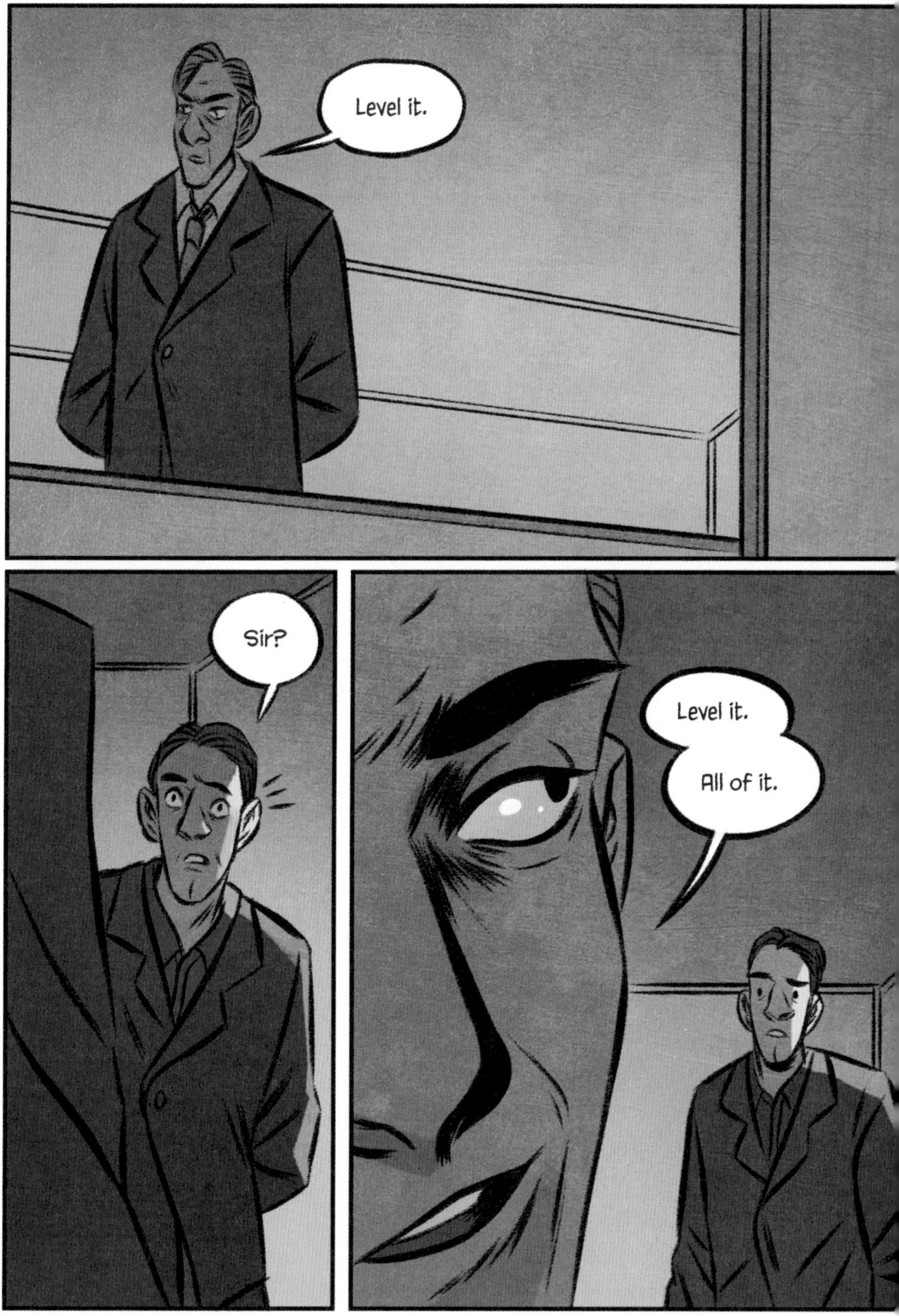

Level it.
Sir?
Level it.
All of it.

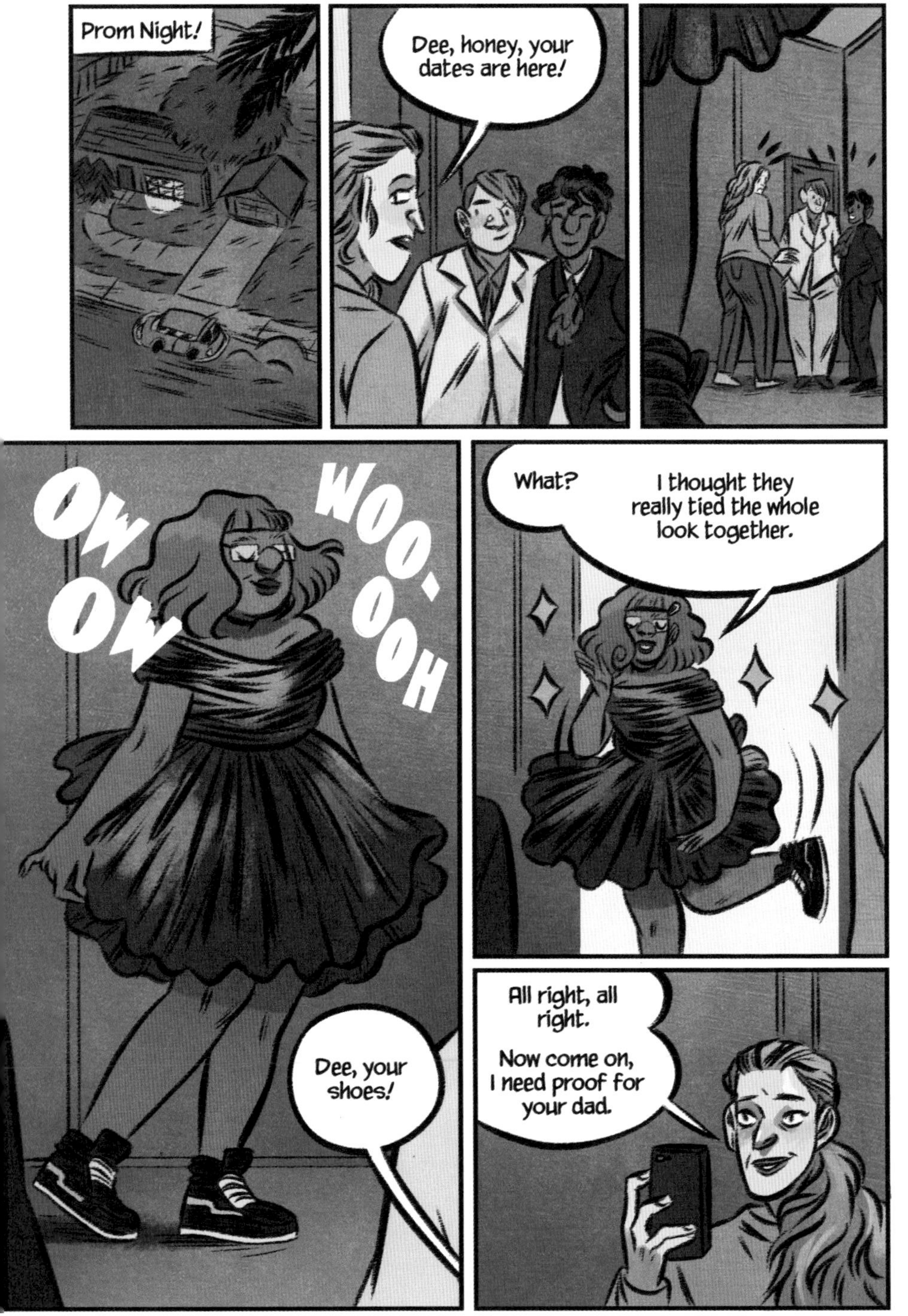
Prom Night!
Dee, honey, your dates are here!
OW OW
WOO-OOH
Dee, your shoes!
What?
I thought they really tied the whole look together.
All right, all right.
Now come on, I need proof for your dad.

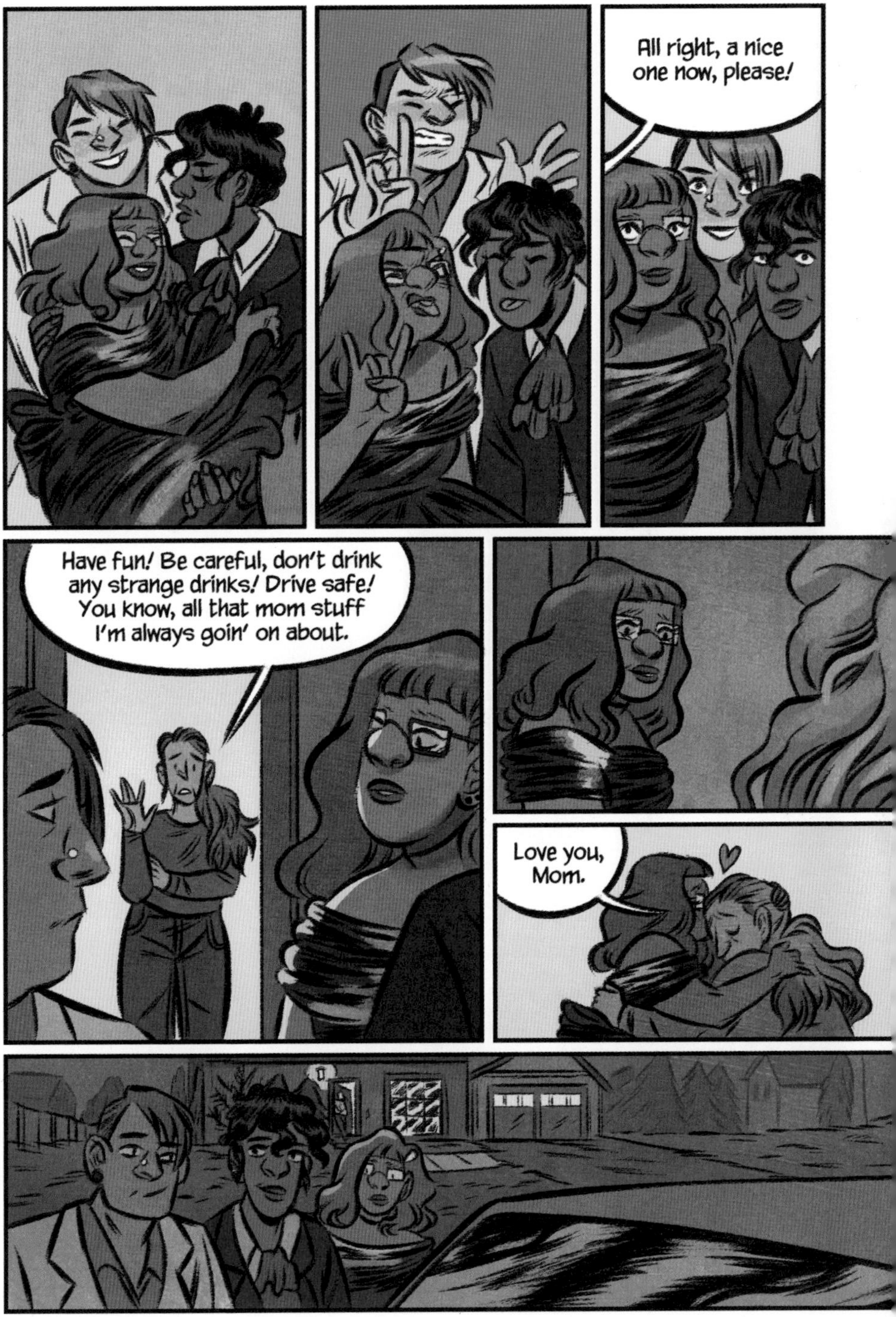
All right, a nice one now, please!
Have fun! Be careful, don't drink any strange drinks! Drive safe! You know, all that mom stuff I'm always goin' on about.
Love you, Mom.

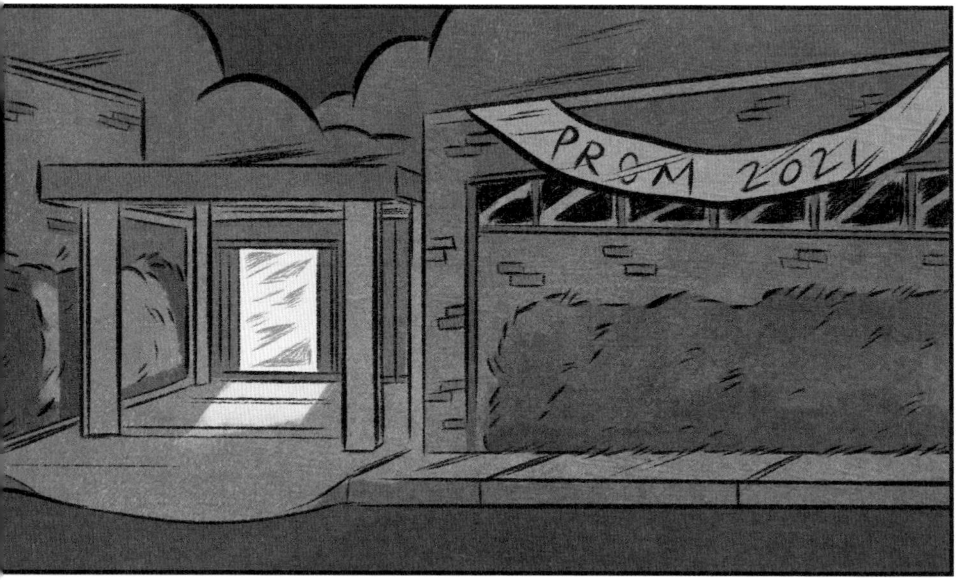
PROM 2021

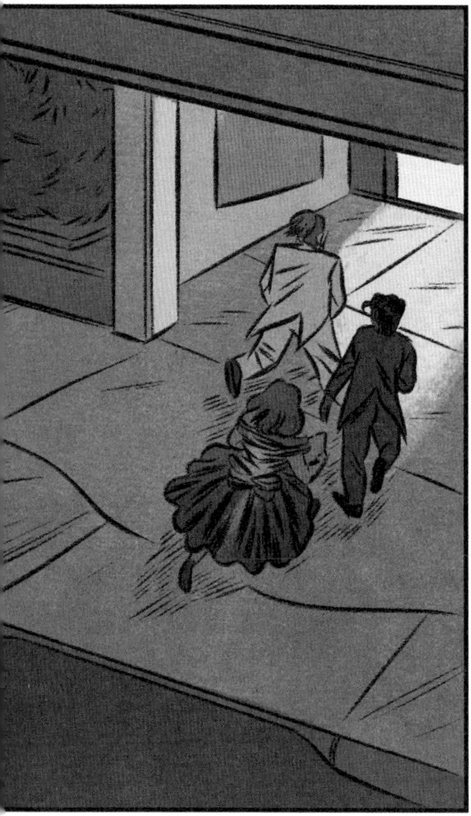

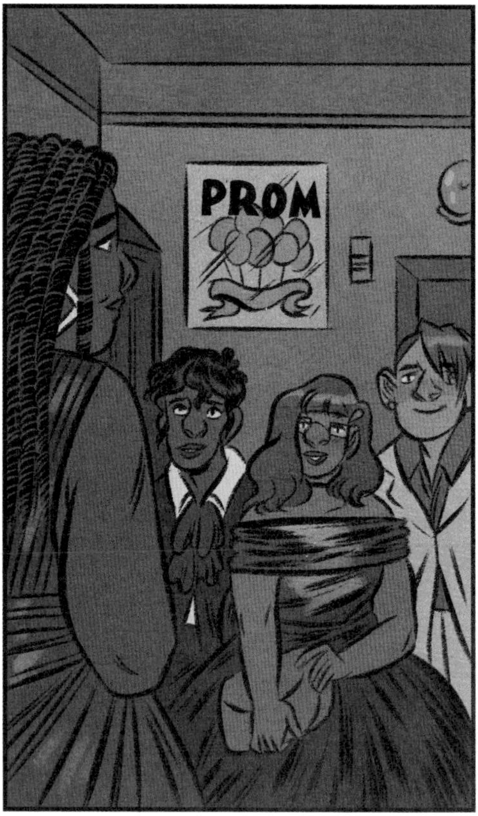
PROM

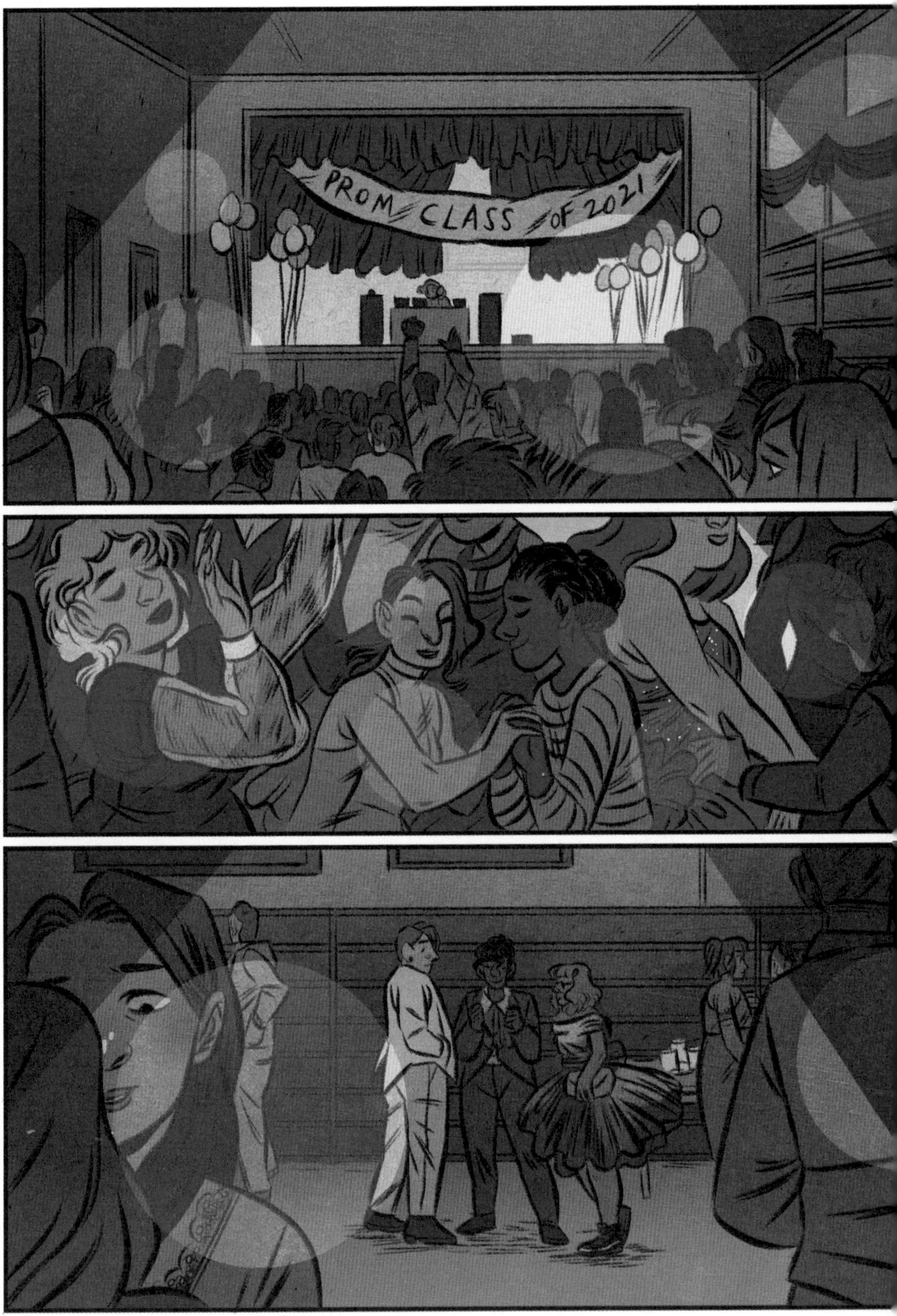
PROM CLASS OF 2021

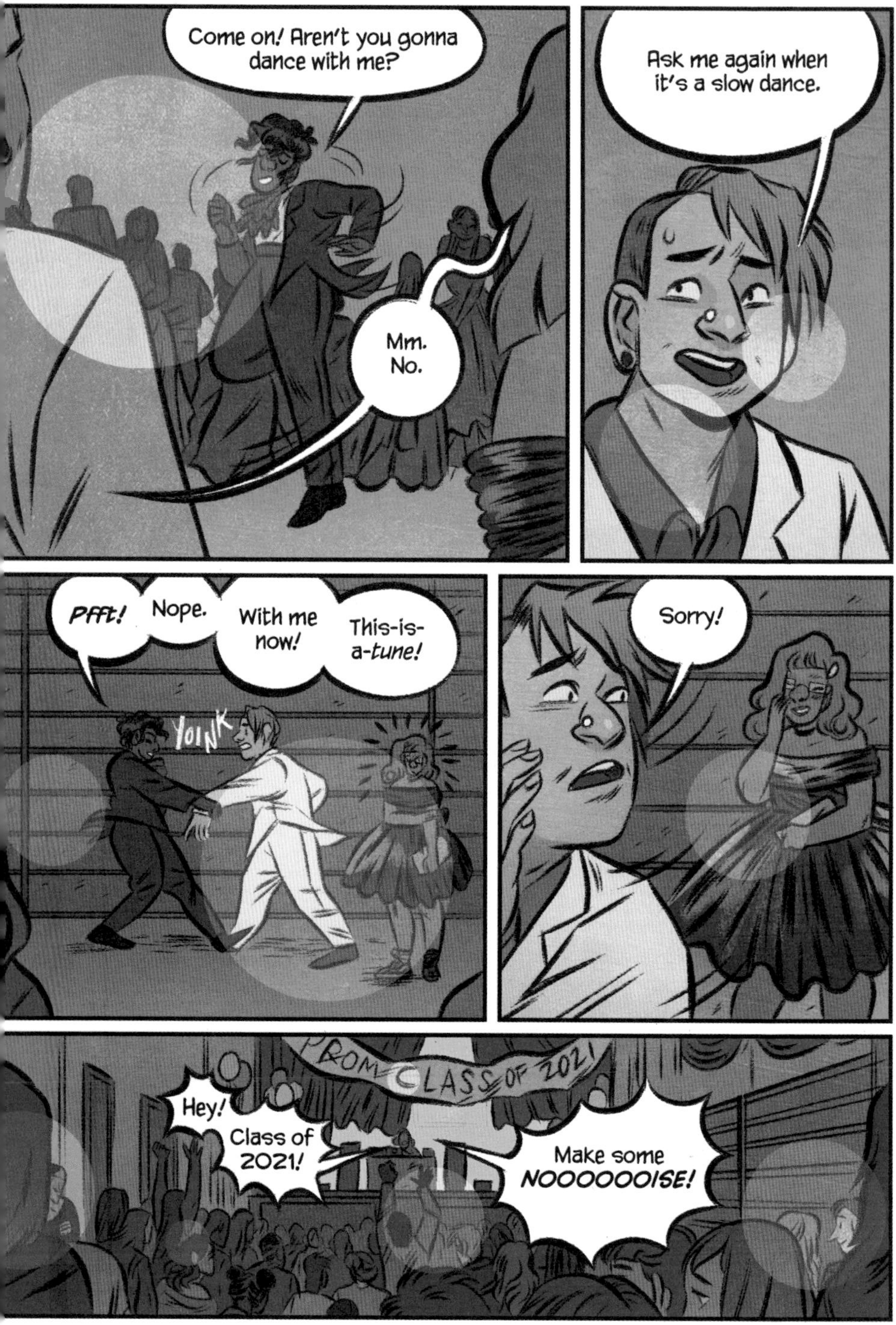
Come on! Aren't you gonna dance with me?
Mm. No.
Ask me again when it's a slow dance.
Pfft!
Nope.
With me now!
This-is-a-tune!
YOINK
Sorry!
PROM CLASS OF 2021
Hey!
Class of 2021!
Make some NOOOOOOISE!

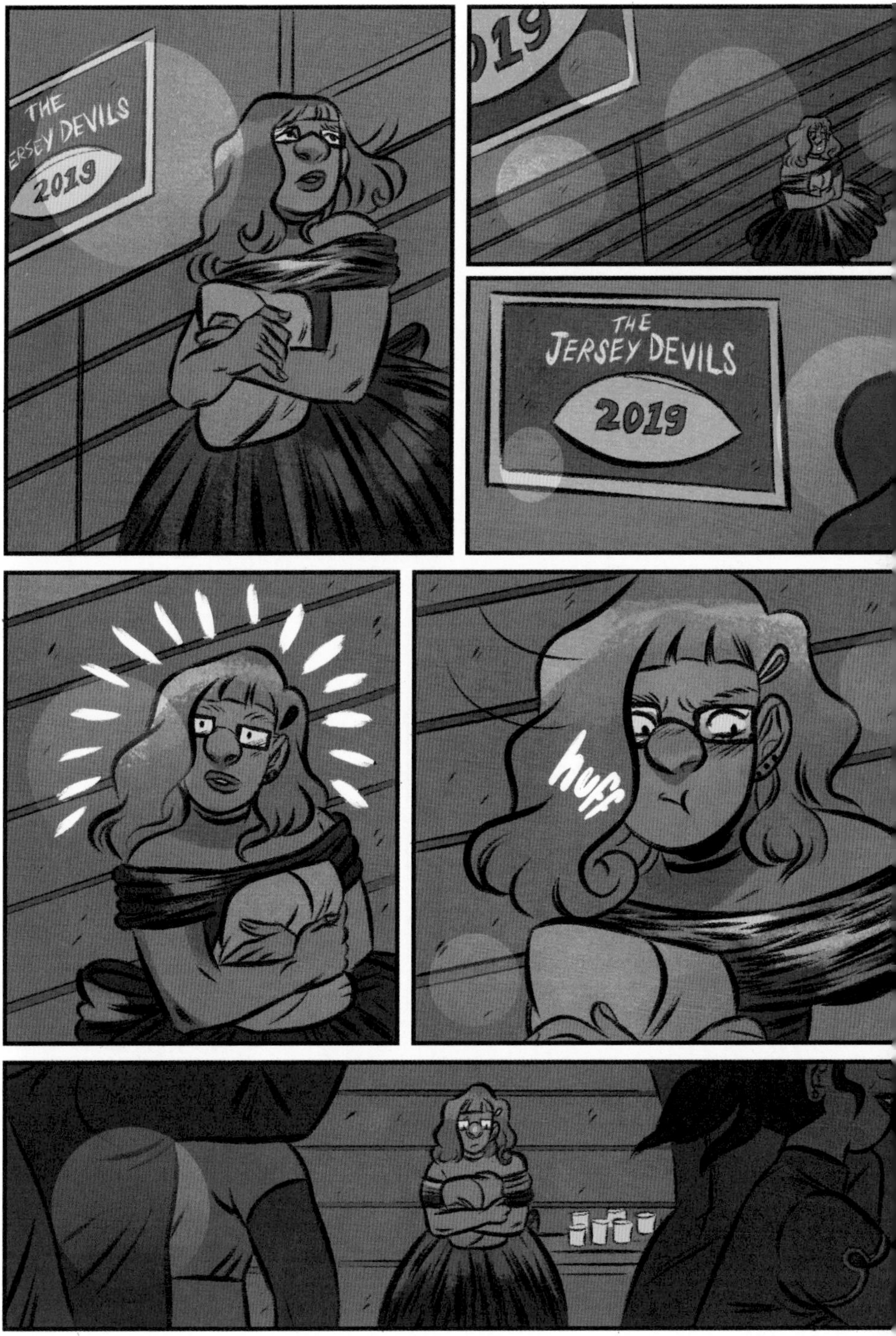
THE JERSEY DEVILS
2019
THE JERSEY DEVILS
2019
huff

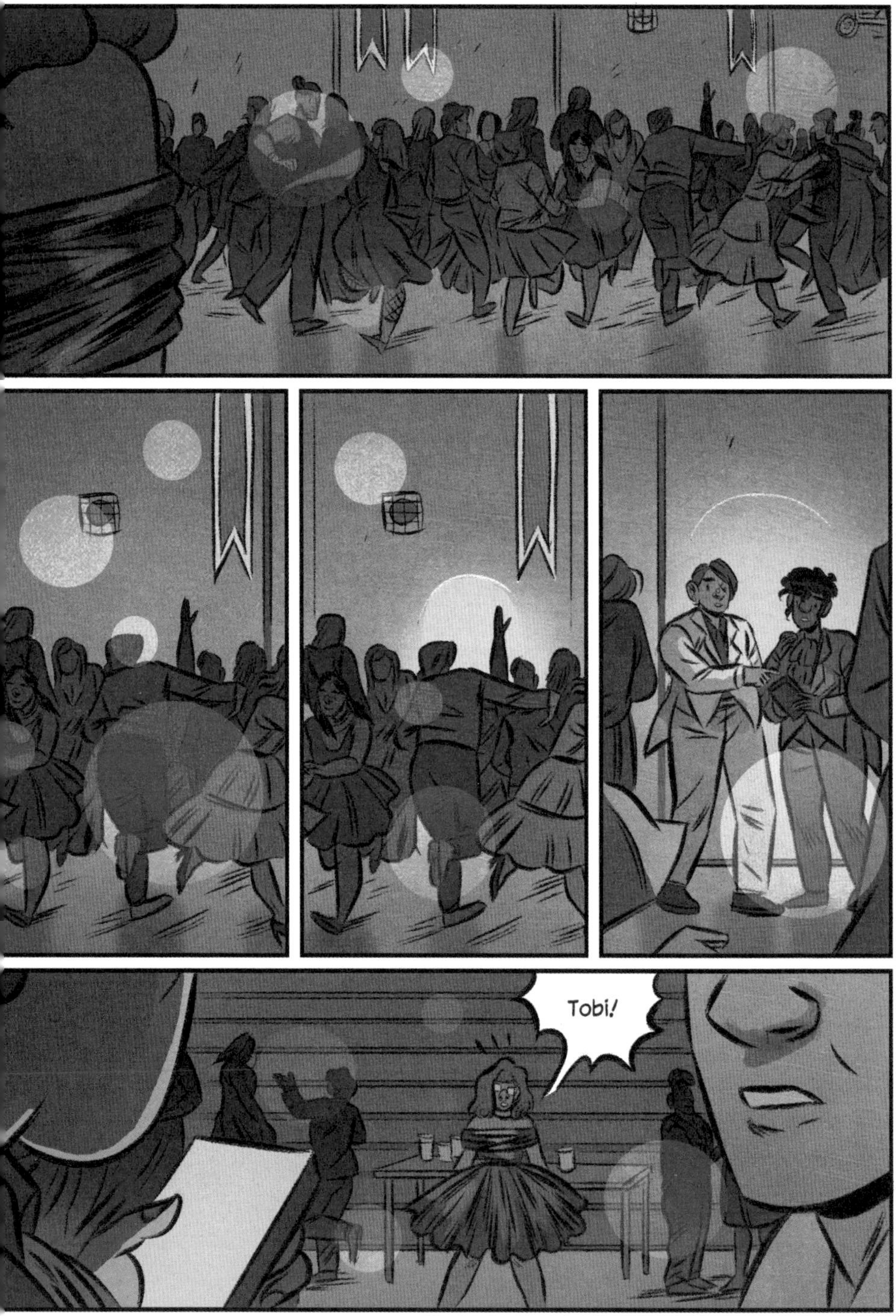
Tobi!

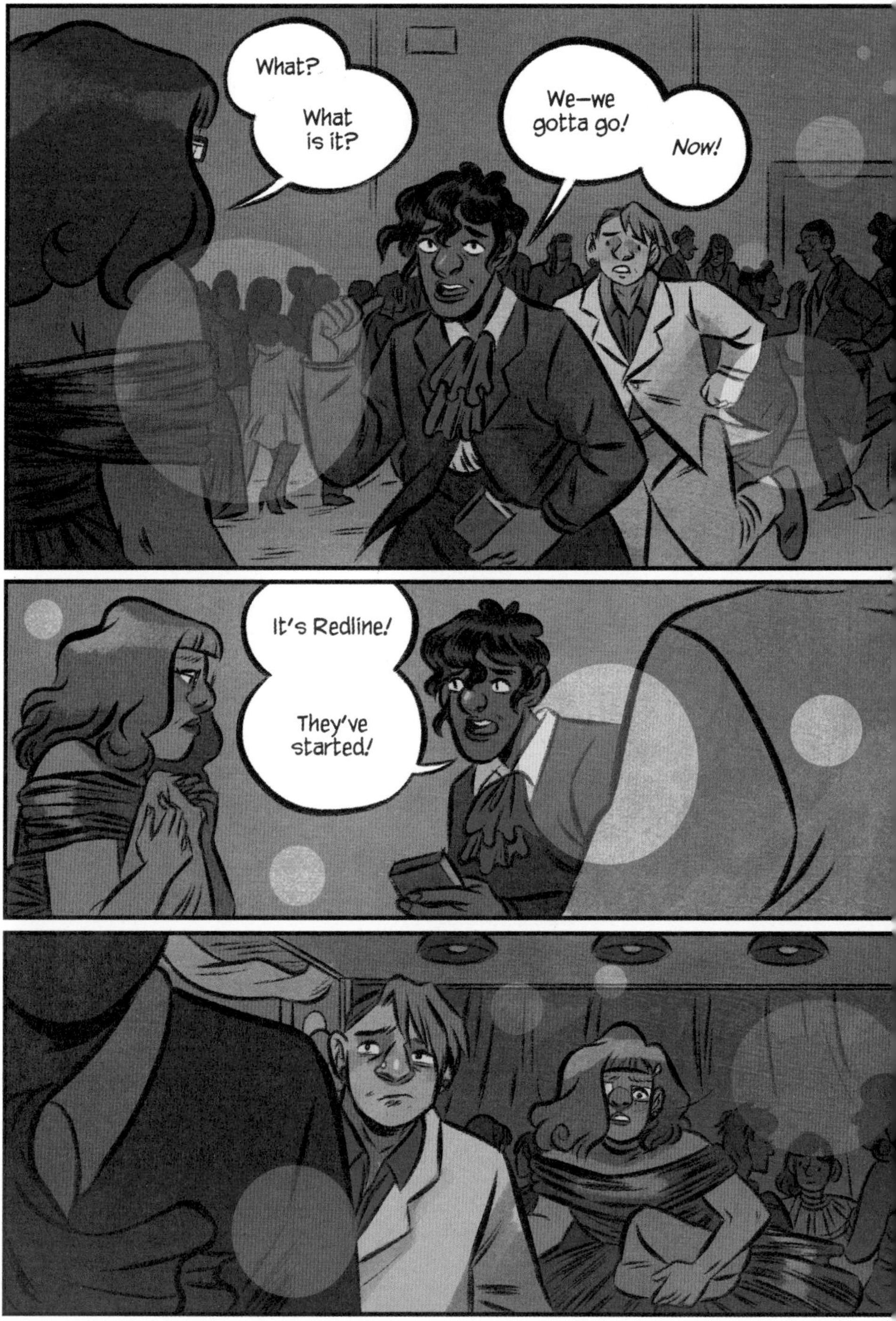
What?
What is it?
We—we gotta go!
Now!
It's Redline!
They've started!

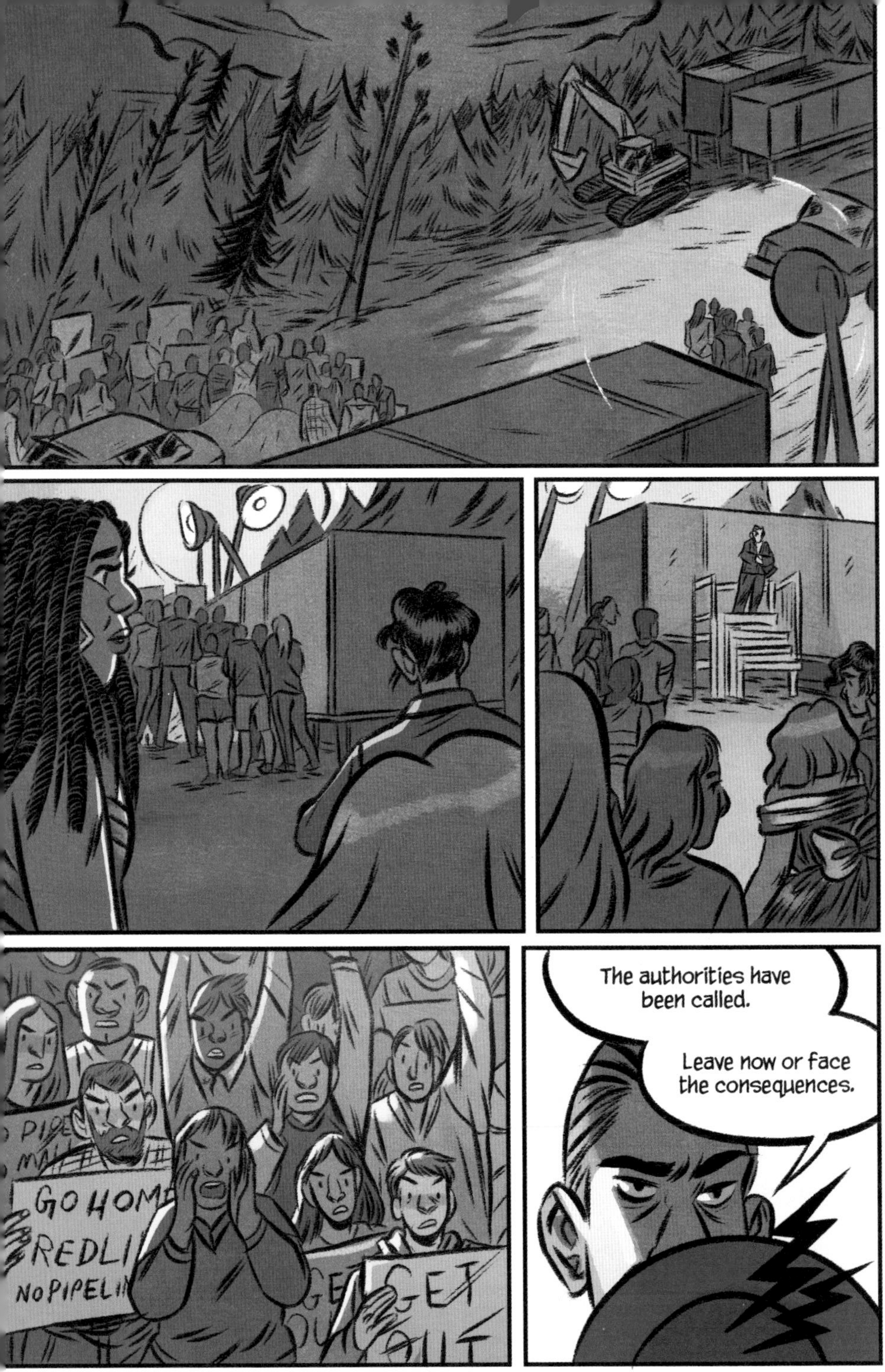
The authorities have been called.
Leave now or face the consequences.
GET

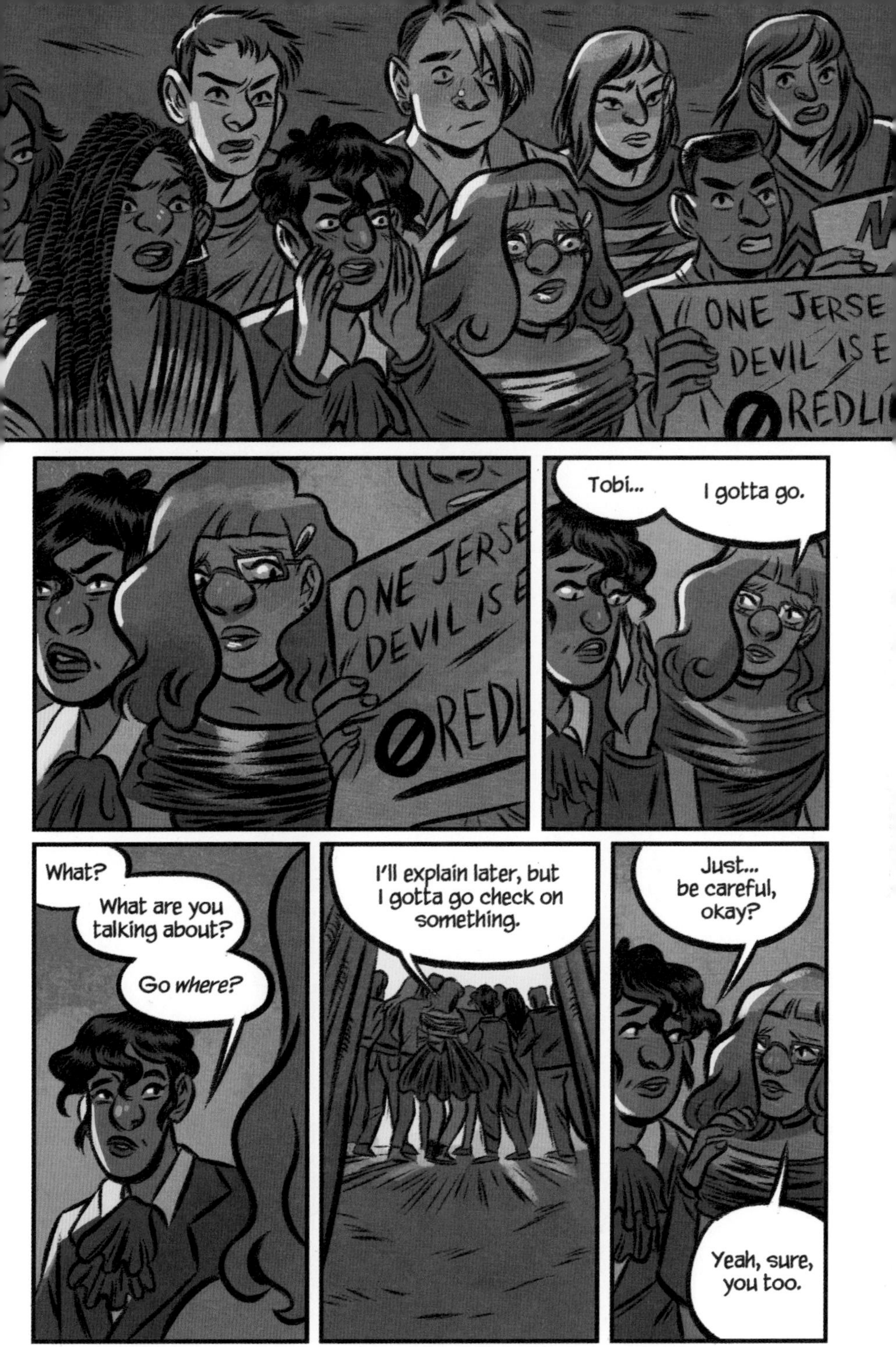
ONE JERSE
DEVIL IS E
REDLI
ONE JERSE
DEVIL IS E
REDL
Tobi...
I gotta go.
What?
What are you talking about?
Go *where?*
I'll explain later, but I gotta go check on something.
Just... be careful, okay?
Yeah, sure, you too.

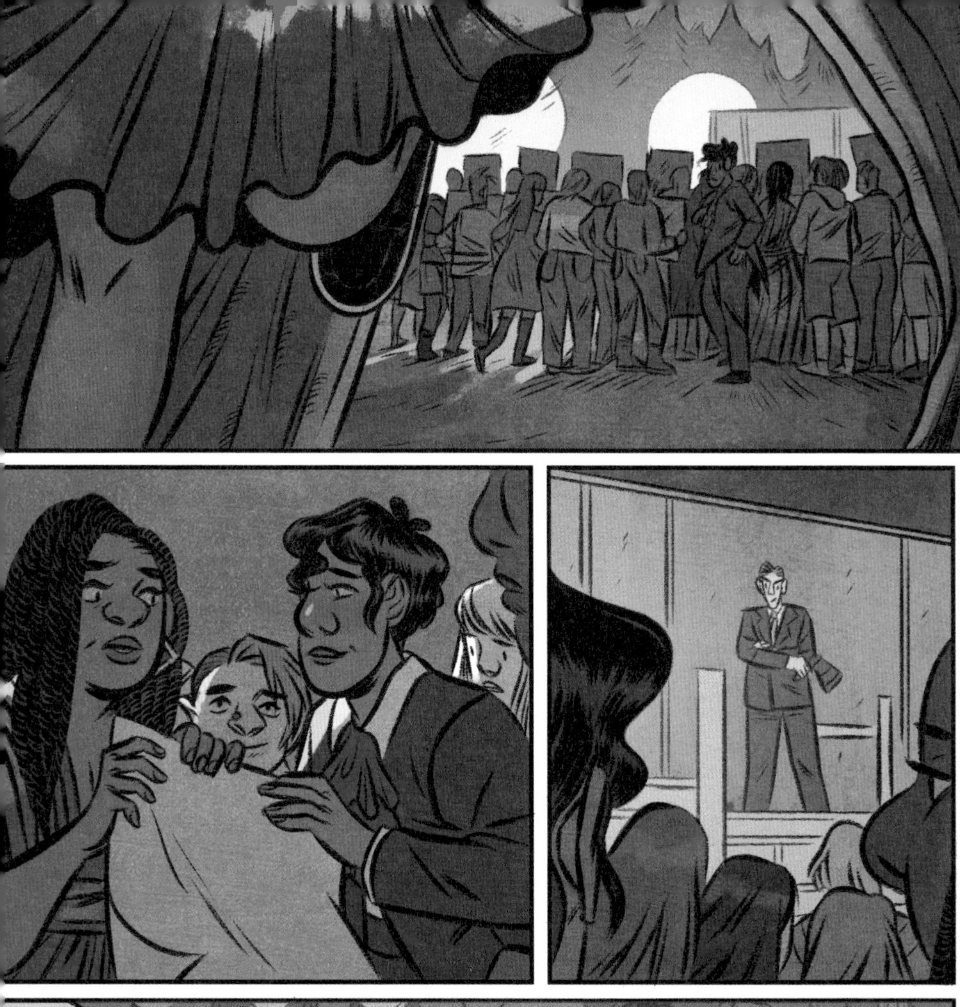
NOT OUR PINELAND STAY OUT
LEAF NOW
ELL NO!

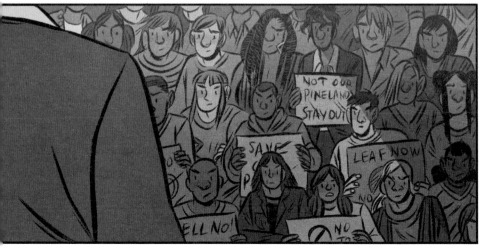

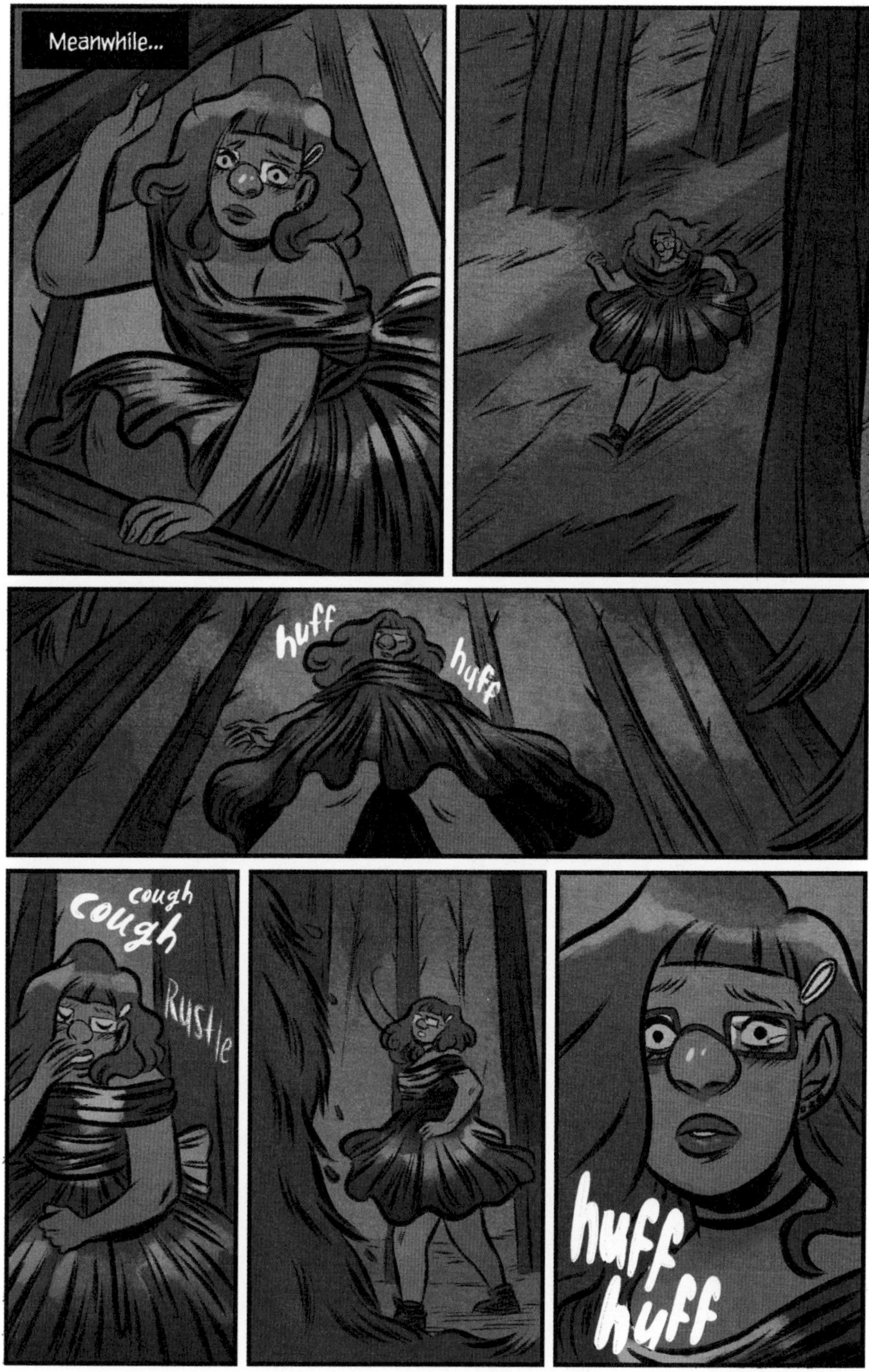
Meanwhile...
huff
huff
cough
cough
Rustle
huff
huff

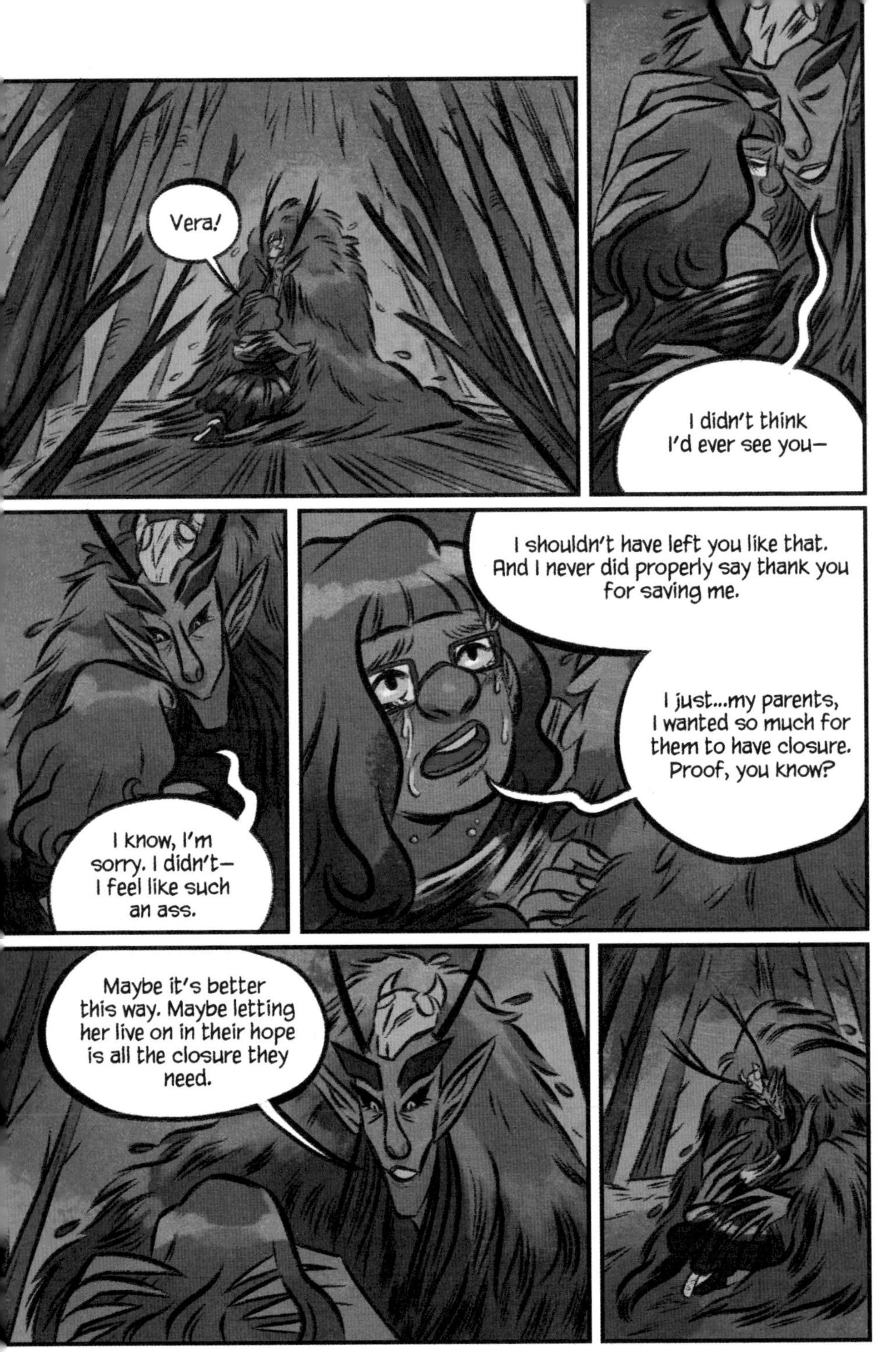
Vera!
I didn't think I'd ever see you—
I know, I'm sorry. I didn't— I feel like such an ass.
I shouldn't have left you like that. And I never did properly say thank you for saving me.
I just...my parents, I wanted so much for them to have closure. Proof, you know?
Maybe it's better this way. Maybe letting her live on in their hope is all the closure they need.

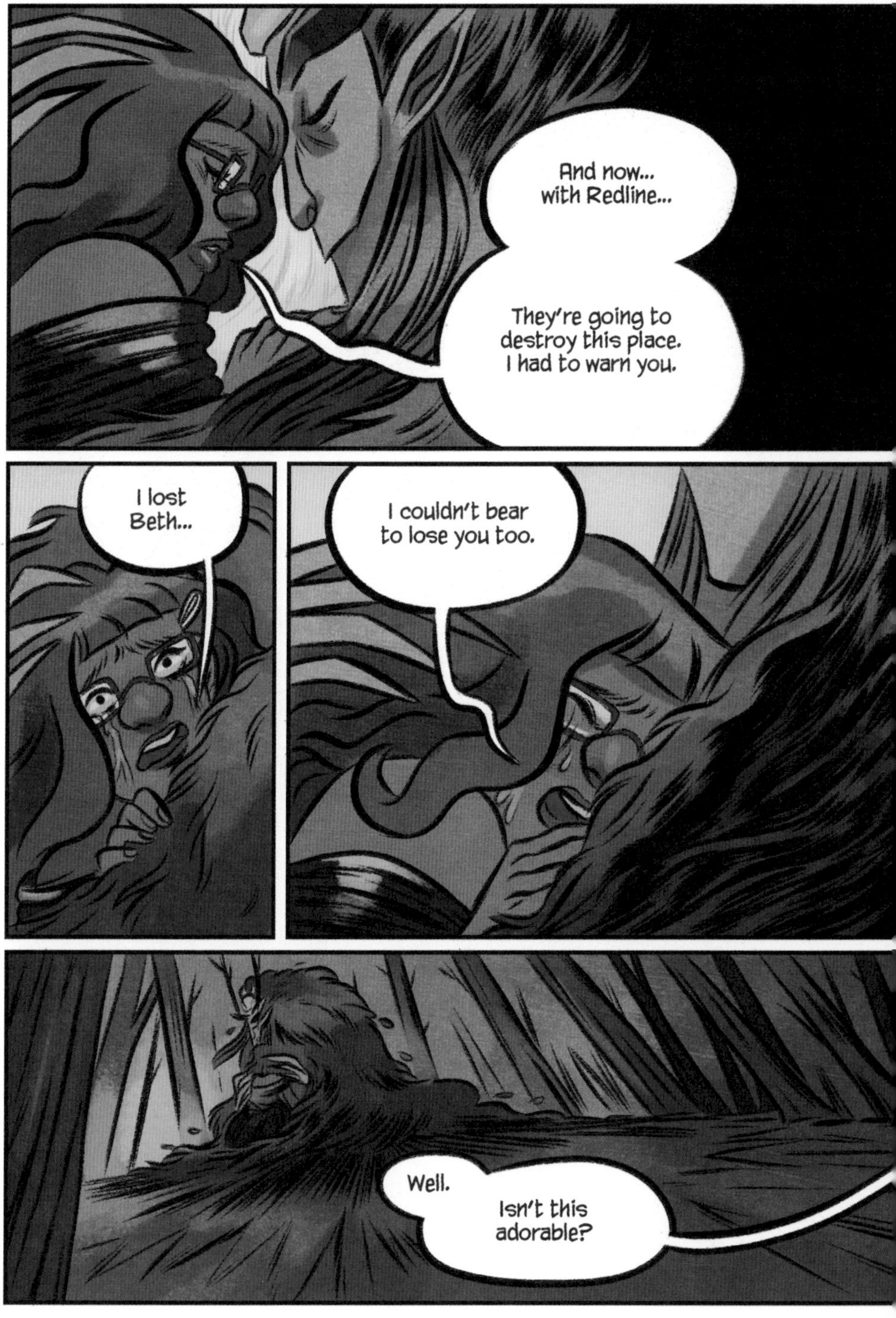
And now... with Redline...
They're going to destroy this place. I had to warn you.
I lost Beth...
I couldn't bear to lose you too.
Well.
Isn't this adorable?

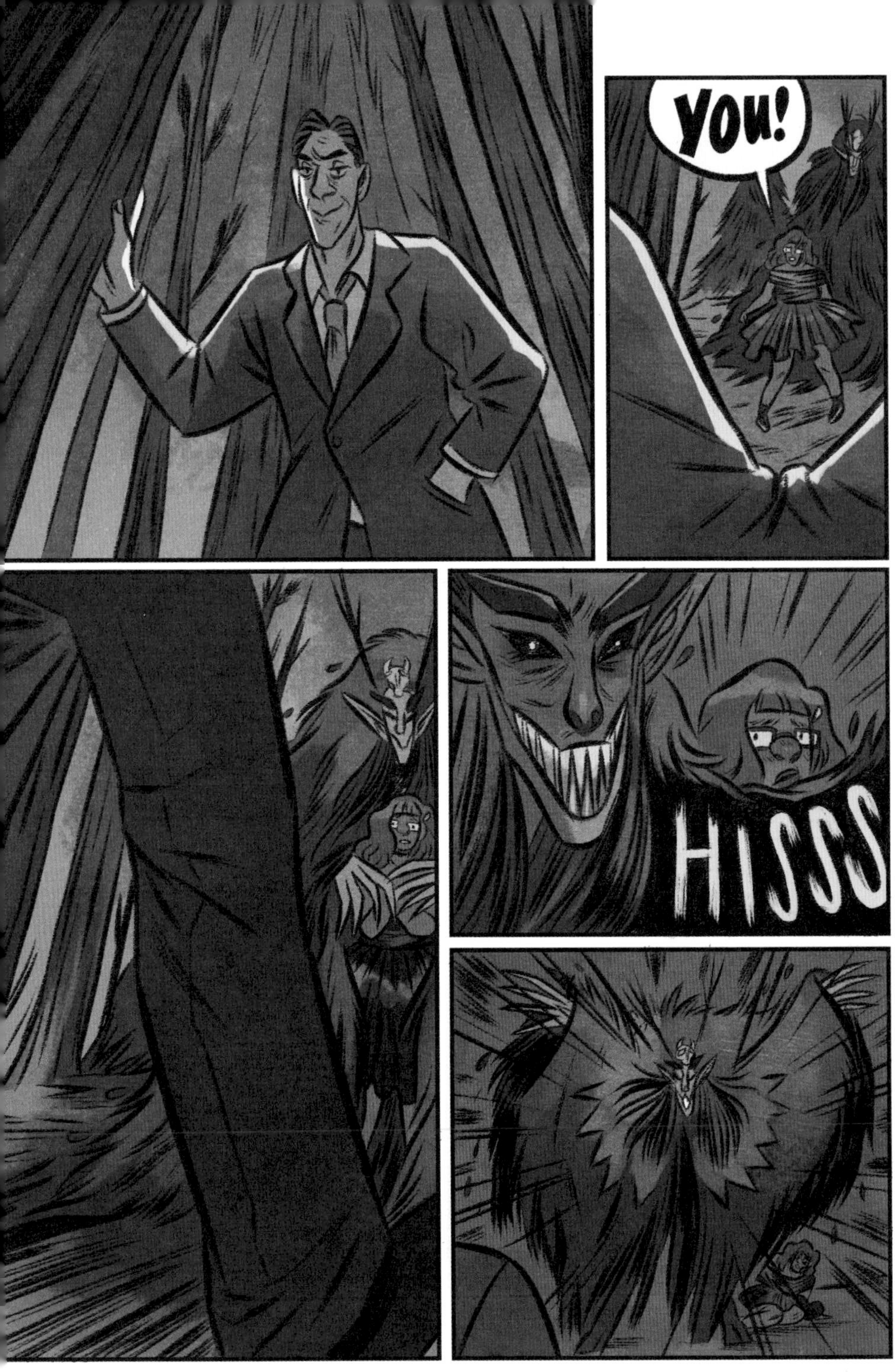
YOU!
HISSS

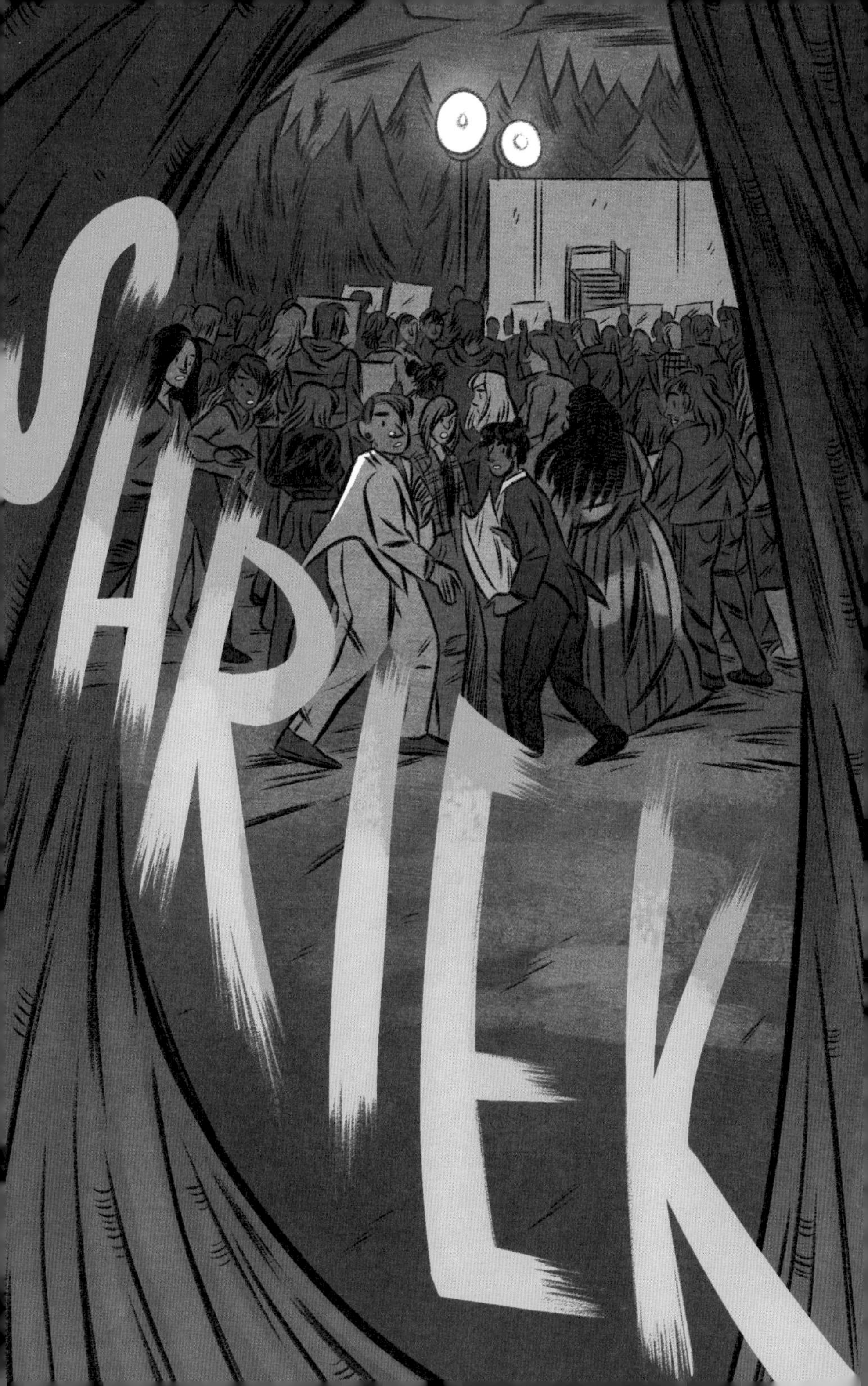
SHRIEK

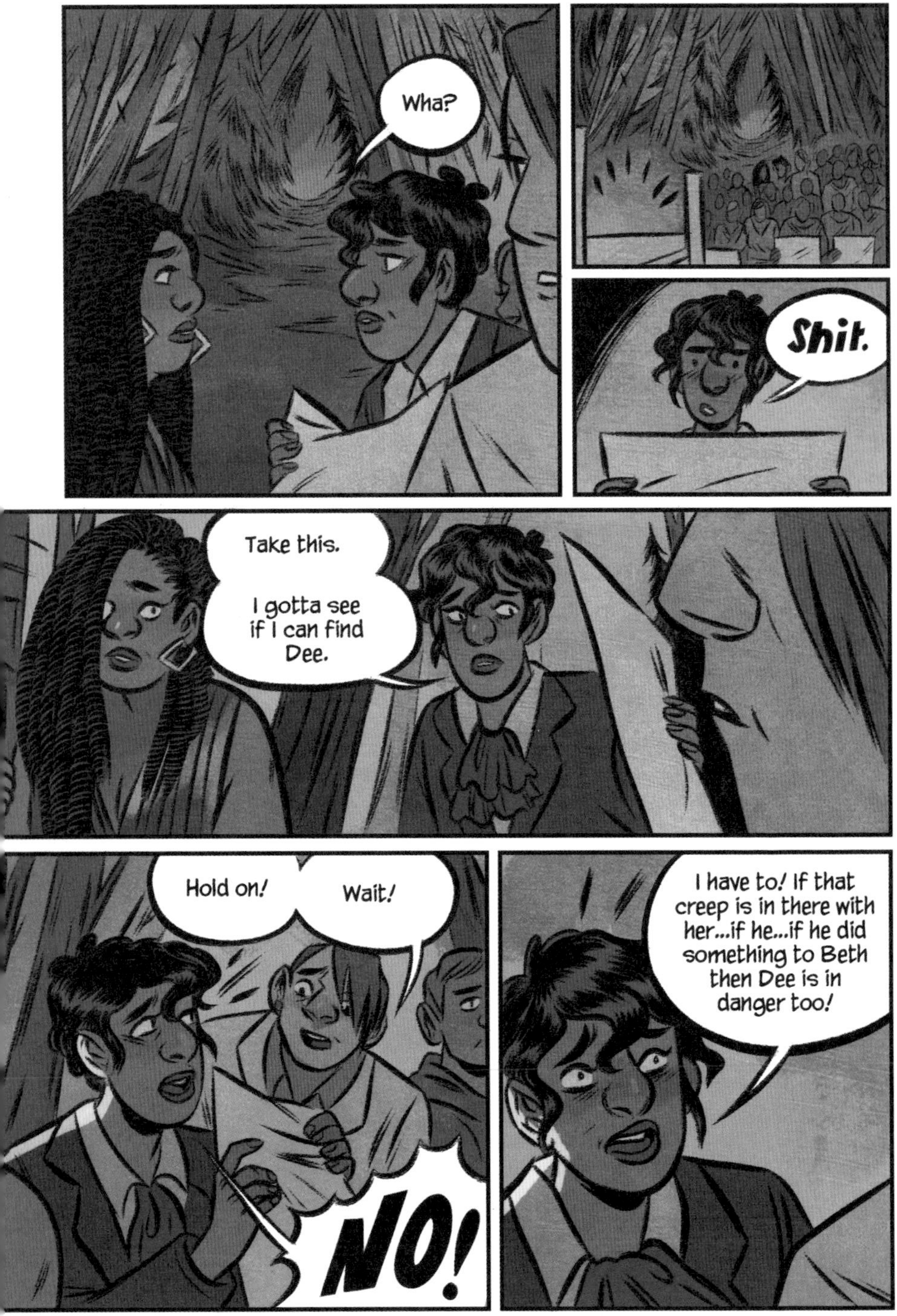
Wha?
Shit.
Take this.
I gotta see if I can find Dee.
Hold on!
Wait!
NO!
I have to! If that creep is in there with her...if he...if he did something to Beth then Dee is in danger too!

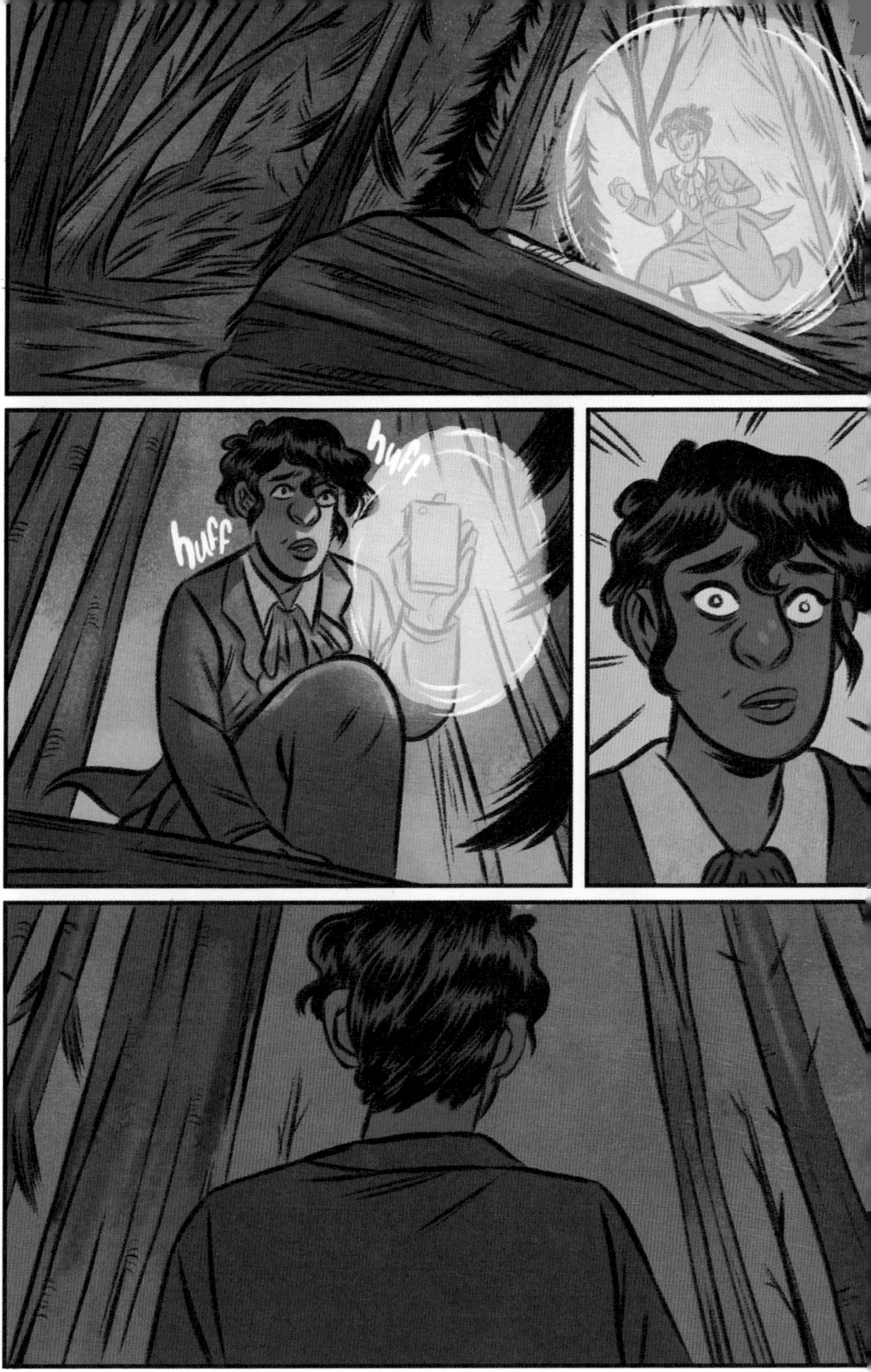
huff
huff

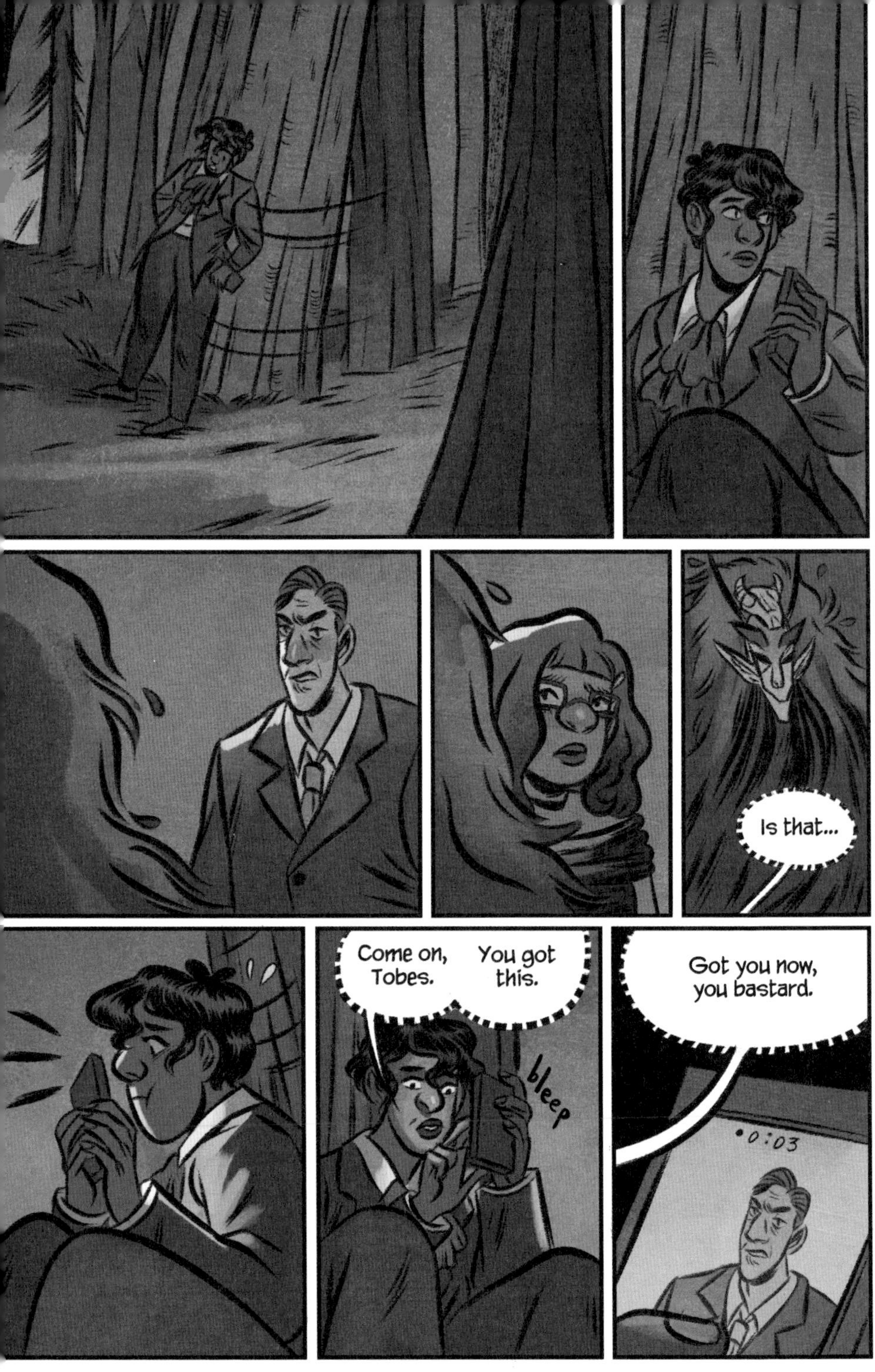
Is that...
Come on, Tobes.
You got this.
bleep
Got you now, you bastard.
0:03

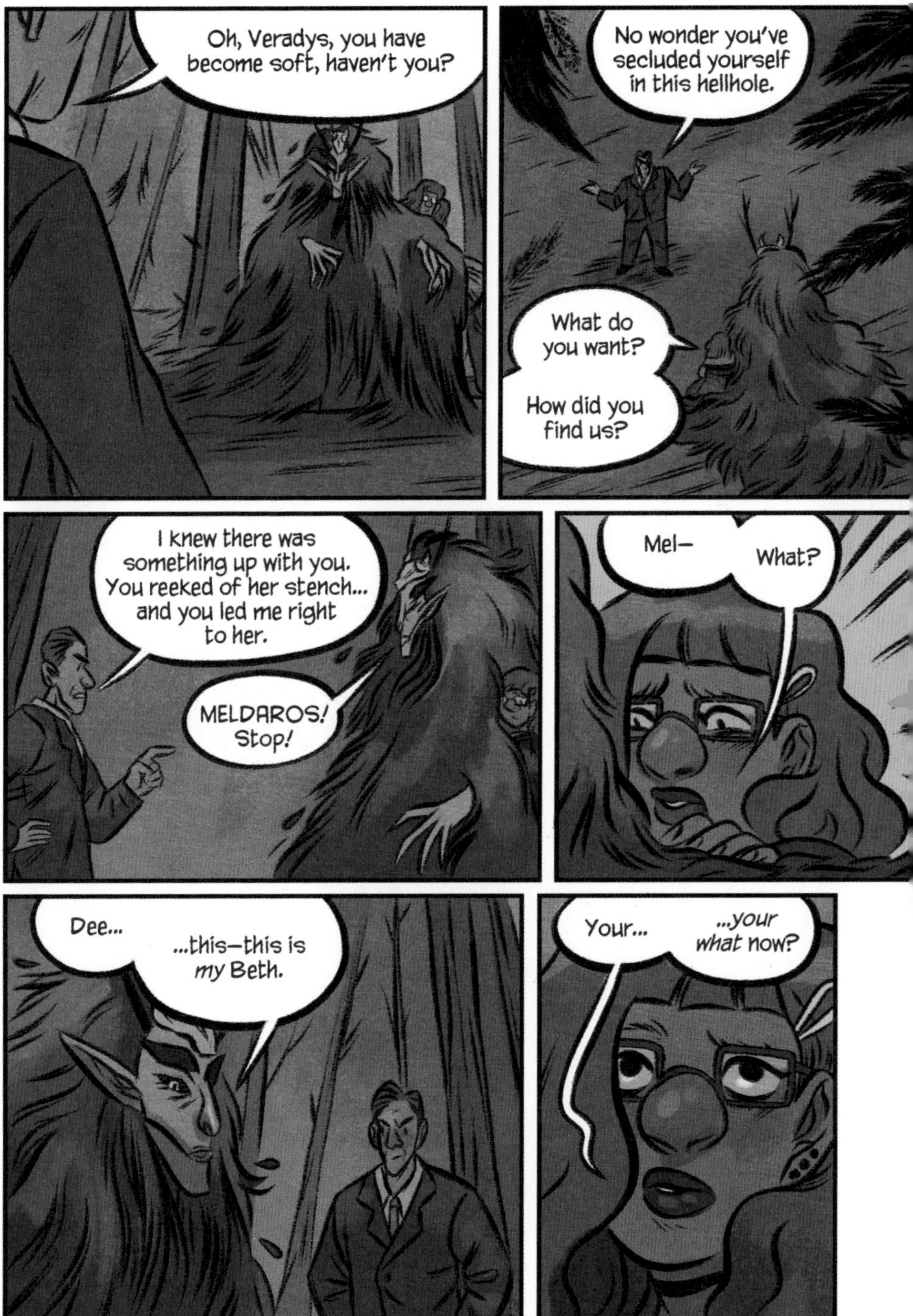
Oh, Veradys, you have become soft, haven't you?
No wonder you've secluded yourself in this hellhole.
What do you want?
How did you find us?
I knew there was something up with you. You reeked of her stench... and you led me right to her.
MELDAROS! Stop!
Mel—
What?
Dee...
...this—this is my Beth.
Your...
...your what now?

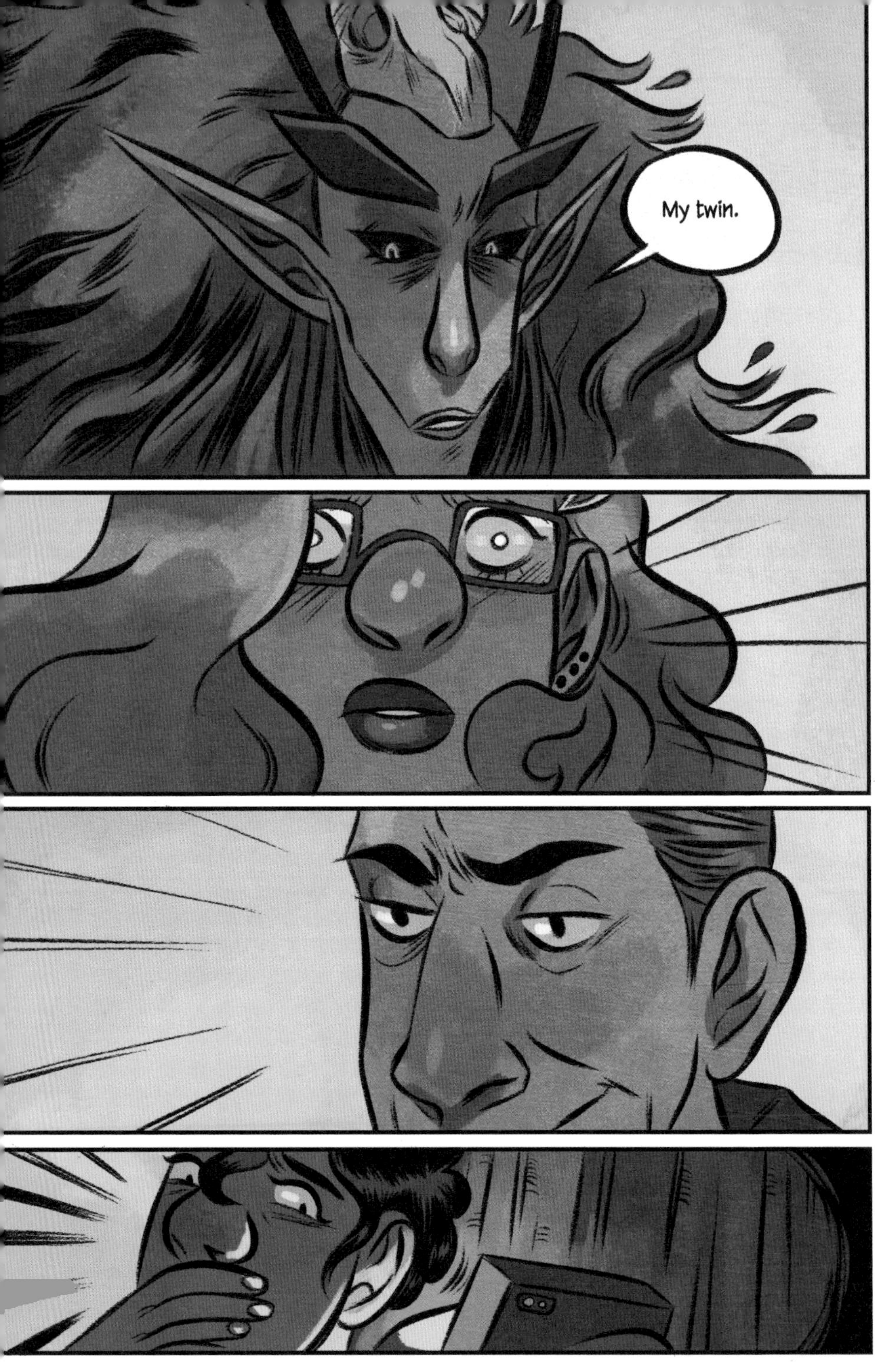
My twin.

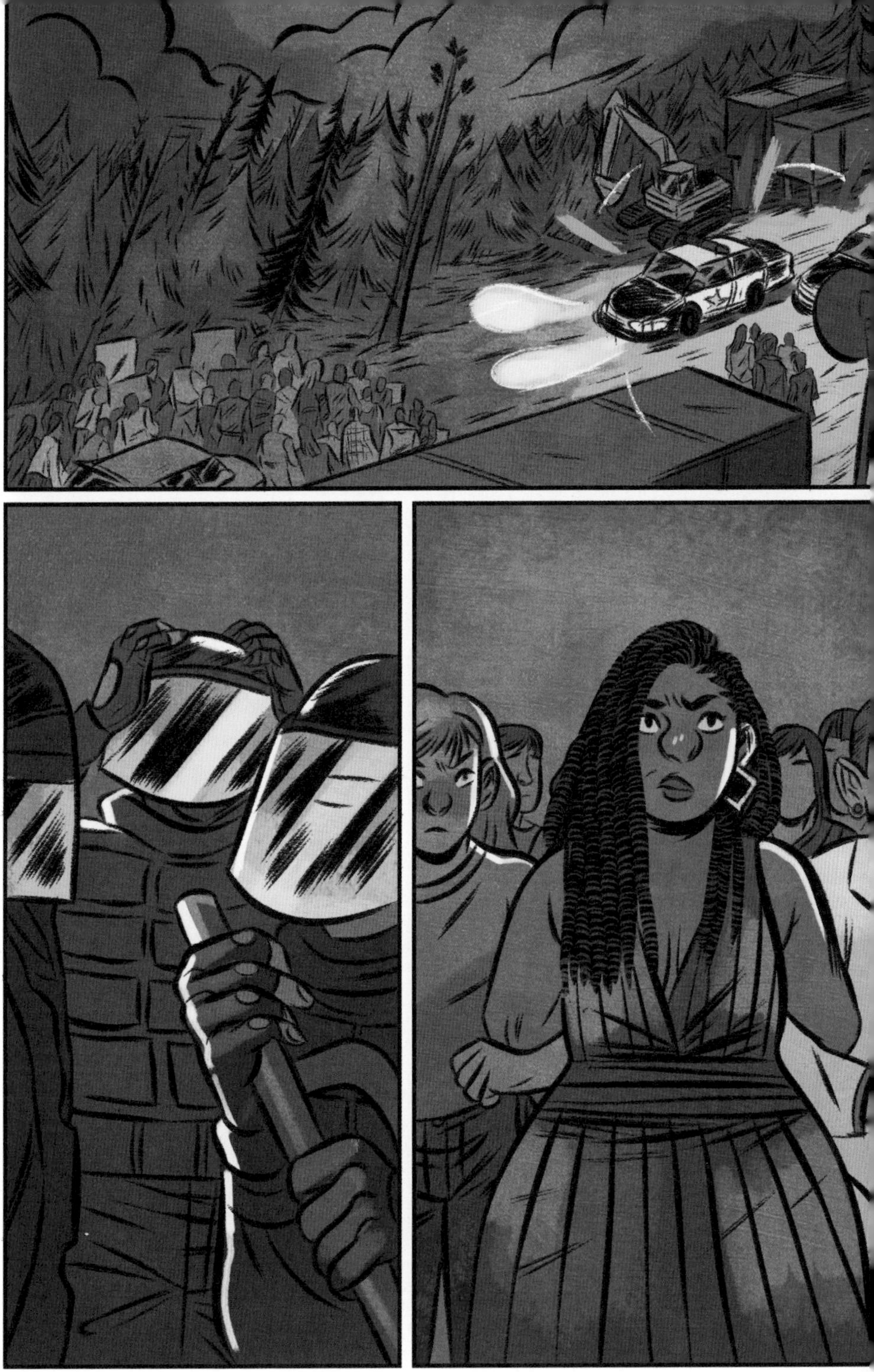

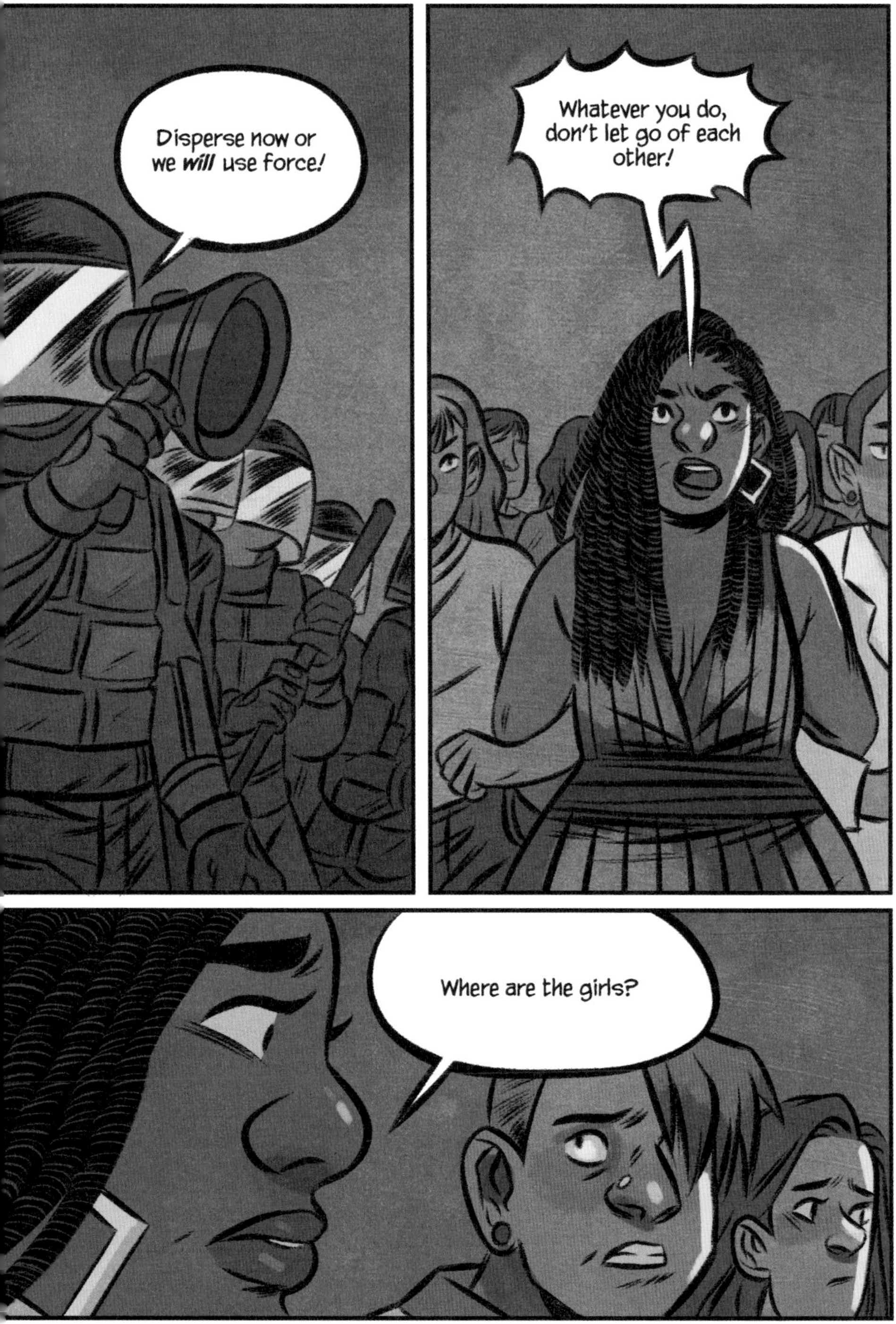
Disperse now or we *will* use force!
Whatever you do, don't let go of each other!
Where are the girls?

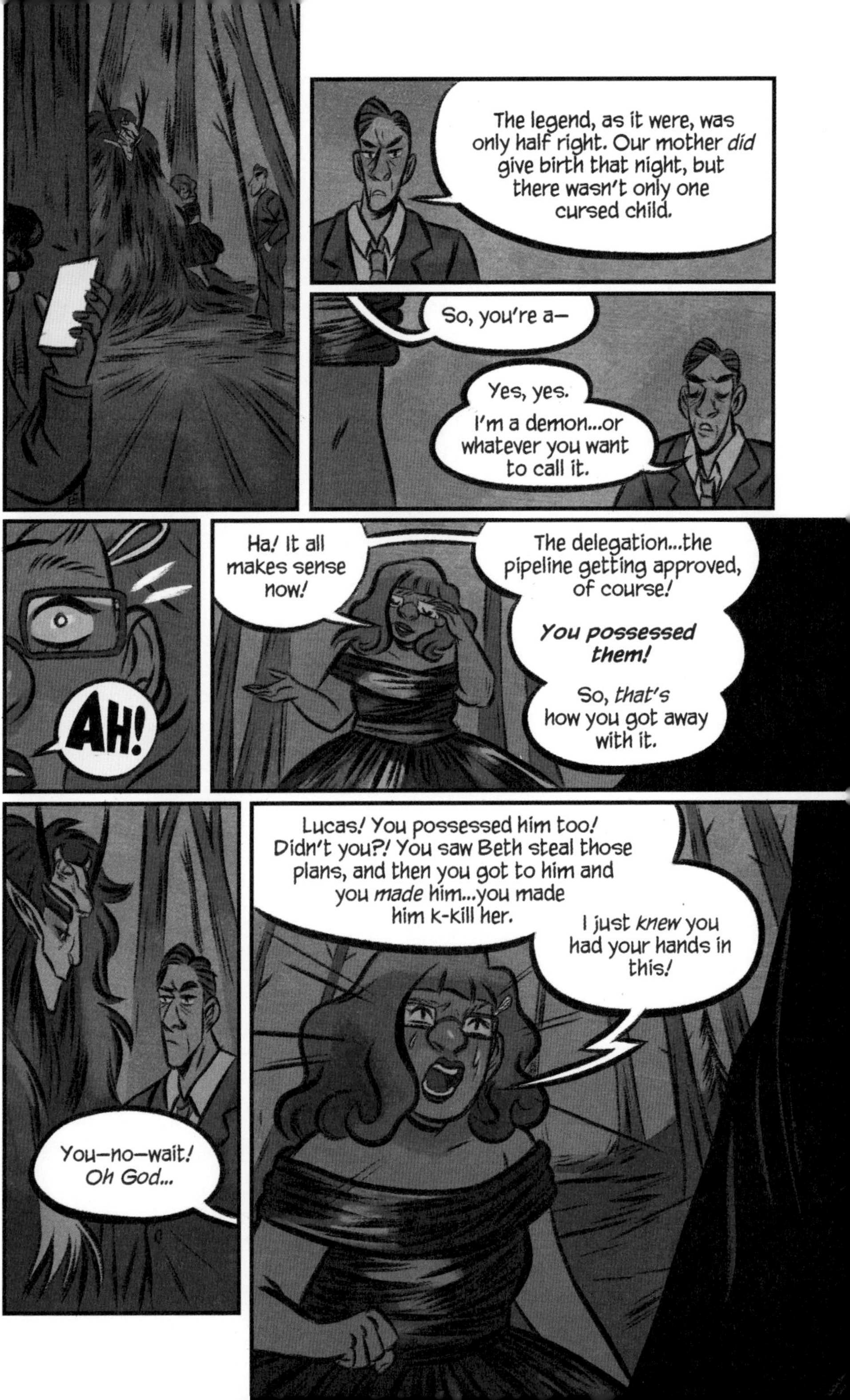

The legend, as it were, was only half right. Our mother *did* give birth that night, but there wasn't only one cursed child.
So, you're a—
Yes, yes.
I'm a demon...or whatever you want to call it.
AH!
Ha! It all makes sense now!
The delegation...the pipeline getting approved, of course!
You possessed them!
So, *that's* how you got away with it.
Lucas! You possessed him too! Didn't you?! You saw Beth steal those plans, and then you got to him and you *made* him...you made him k-kill her.
I just *knew* you had your hands in this!
You—no—wait! *Oh God...*

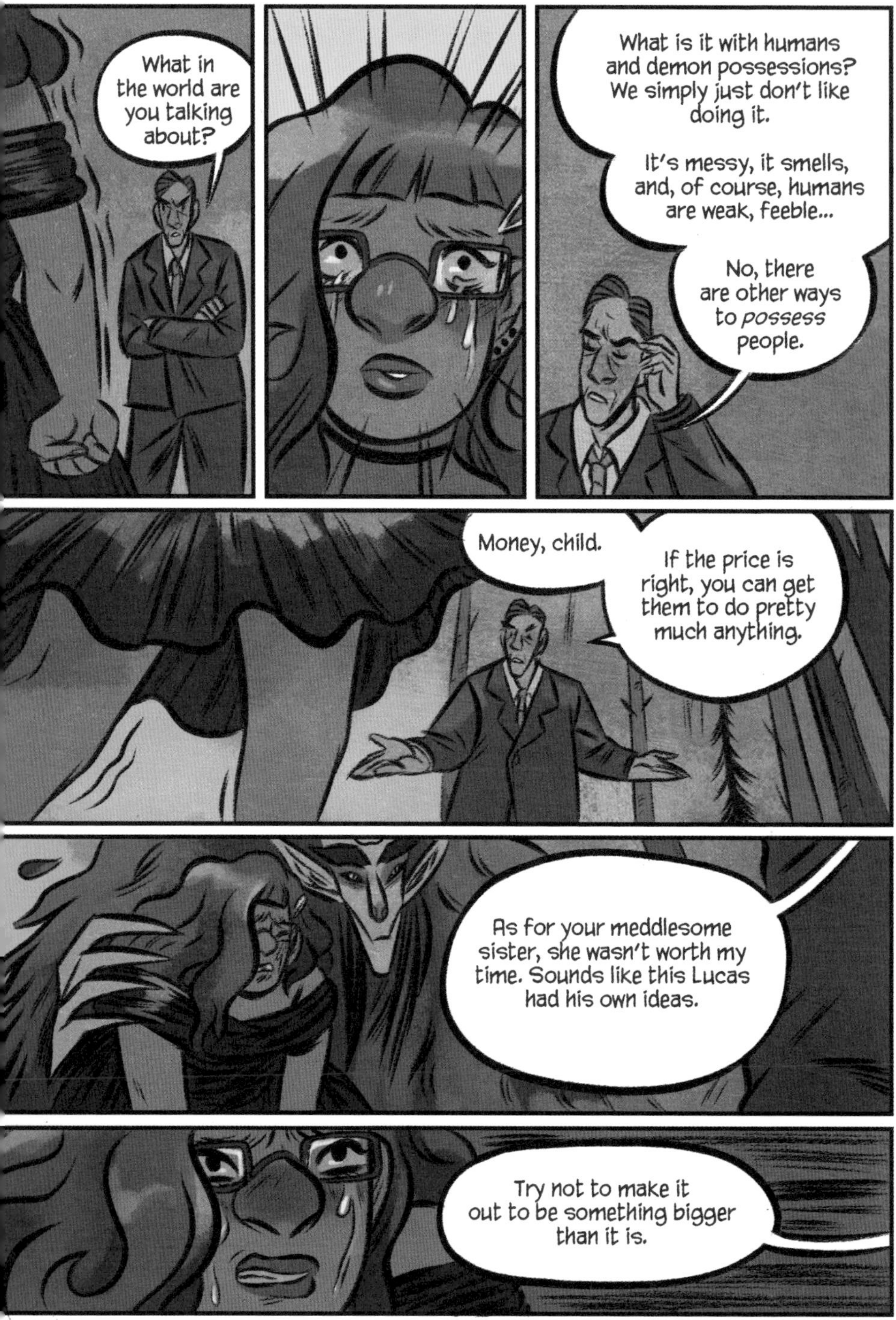
What in the world are you talking about?
What is it with humans and demon possessions? We simply just don't like doing it.
It's messy, it smells, and, of course, humans are weak, feeble...
No, there are other ways to *possess* people.
Money, child.
If the price is right, you can get them to do pretty much anything.
As for your meddlesome sister, she wasn't worth my time. Sounds like this Lucas had his own ideas.
Try not to make it out to be something bigger than it is.

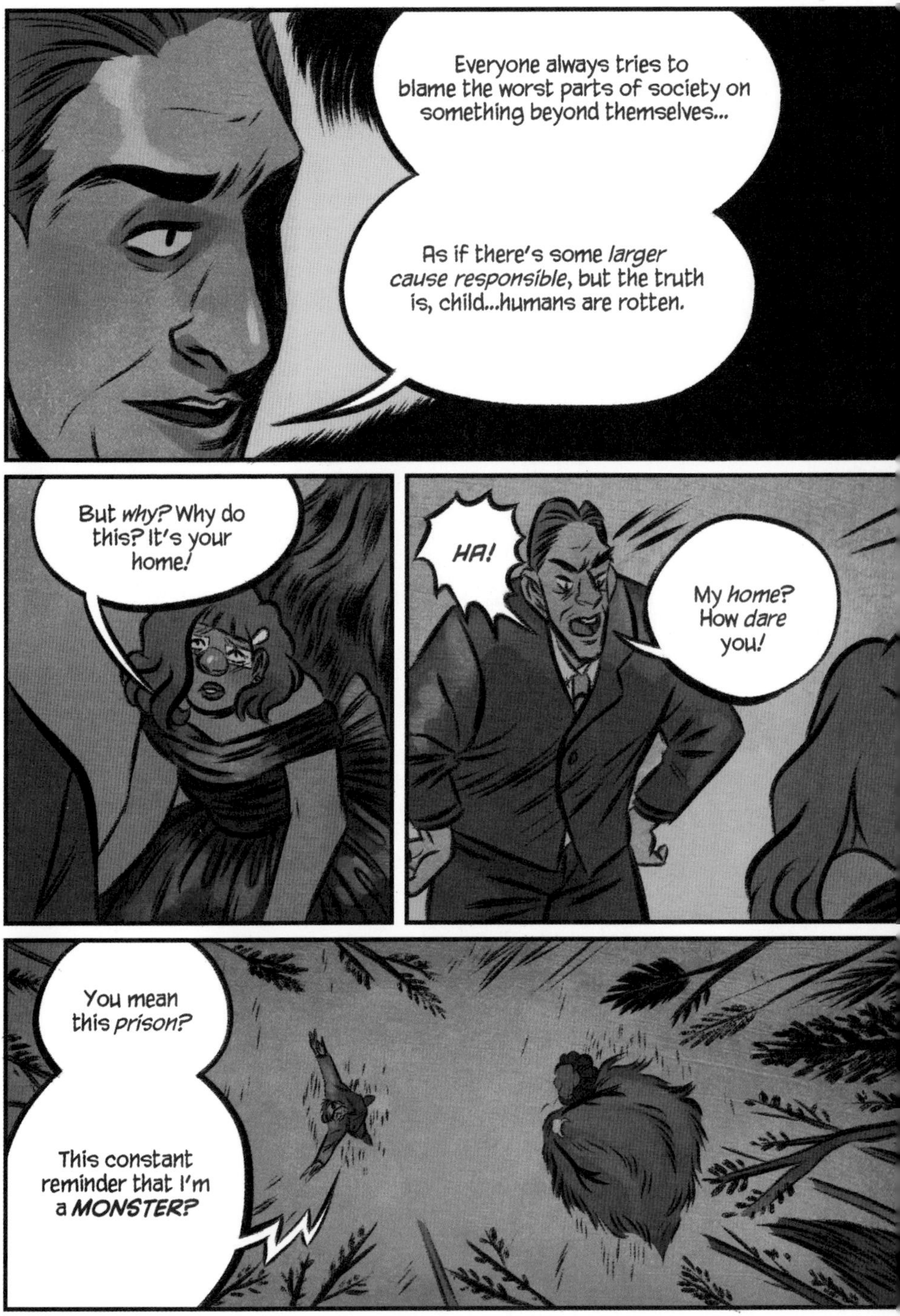
Everyone always tries to blame the worst parts of society on something beyond themselves...
As if there's some *larger cause responsible*, but the truth is, child...humans are rotten.
But *why?* Why do this? It's your home!
HA!
My *home?* How *dare* you!
You mean this *prison?*
This constant reminder that I'm a ***MONSTER?***

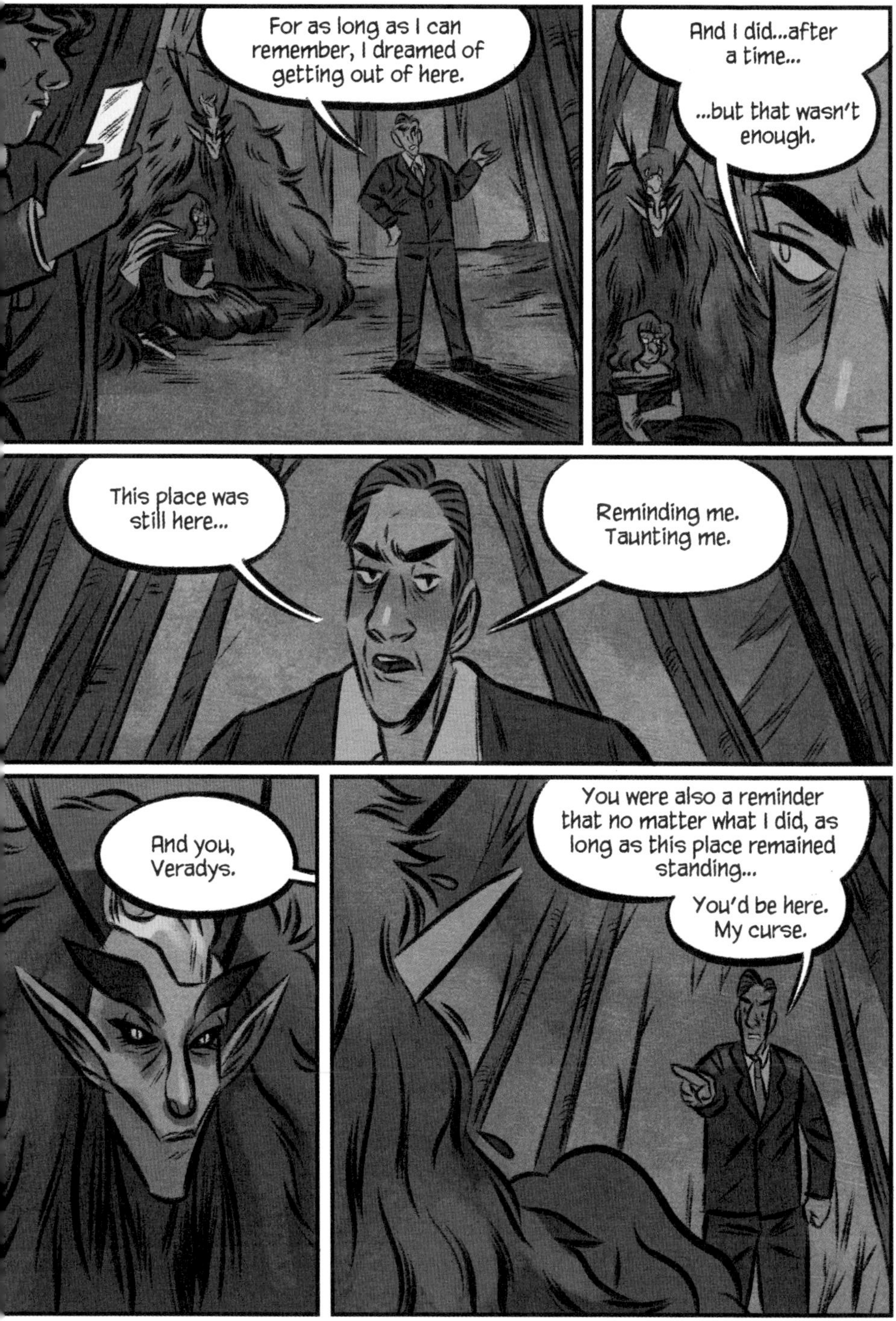
For as long as I can remember, I dreamed of getting out of here.
And I did...after a time...
...but that wasn't enough.
This place was still here...
Reminding me. Taunting me.
And you, Veradys.
You were also a reminder that no matter what I did, as long as this place remained standing...
You'd be here. My curse.

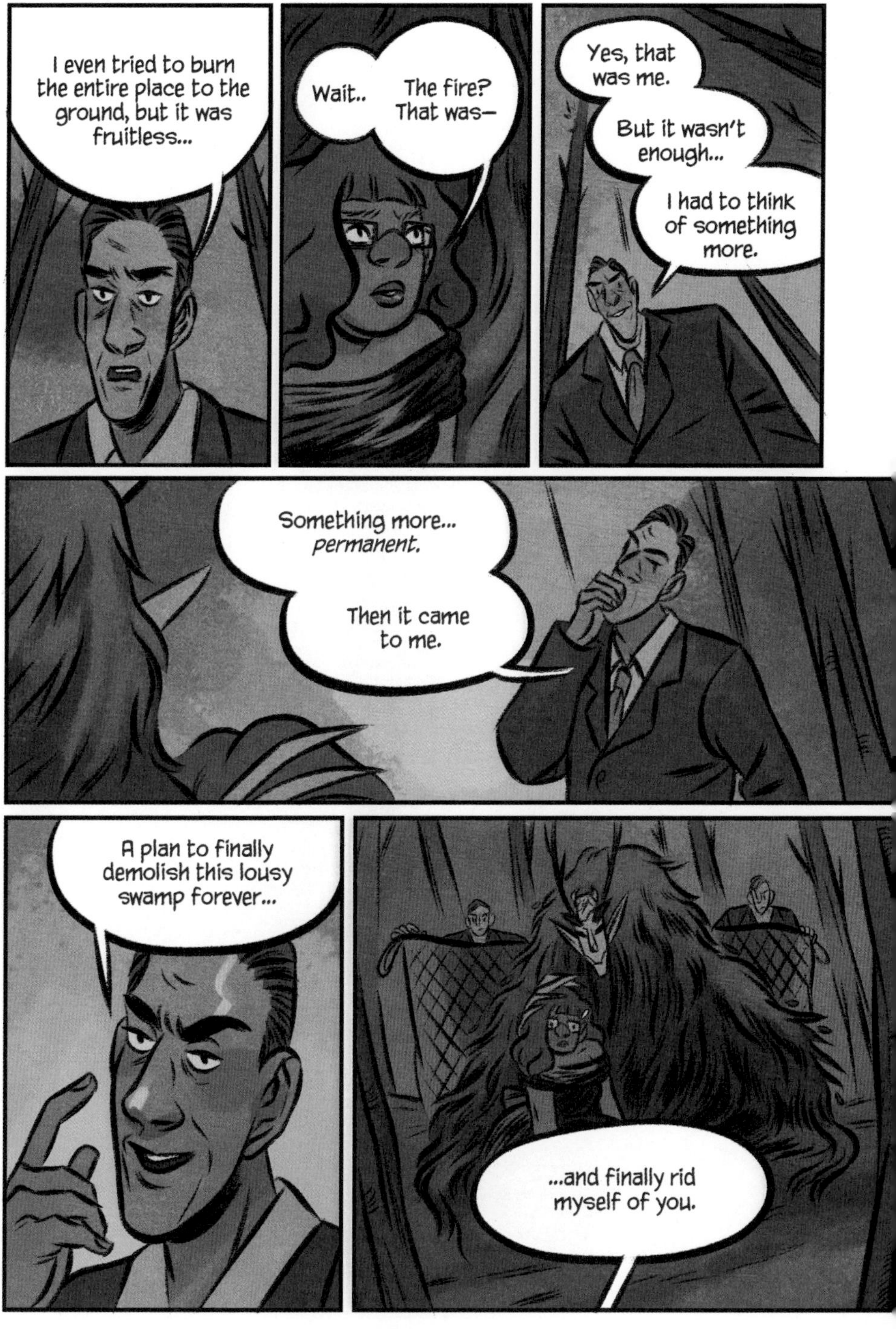
I even tried to burn the entire place to the ground, but it was fruitless...
Wait..
The fire? That was—
Yes, that was me.
But it wasn't enough...
I had to think of something more.
Something more... *permanent.*
Then it came to me.
A plan to finally demolish this lousy swamp forever...
...and finally rid myself of you.

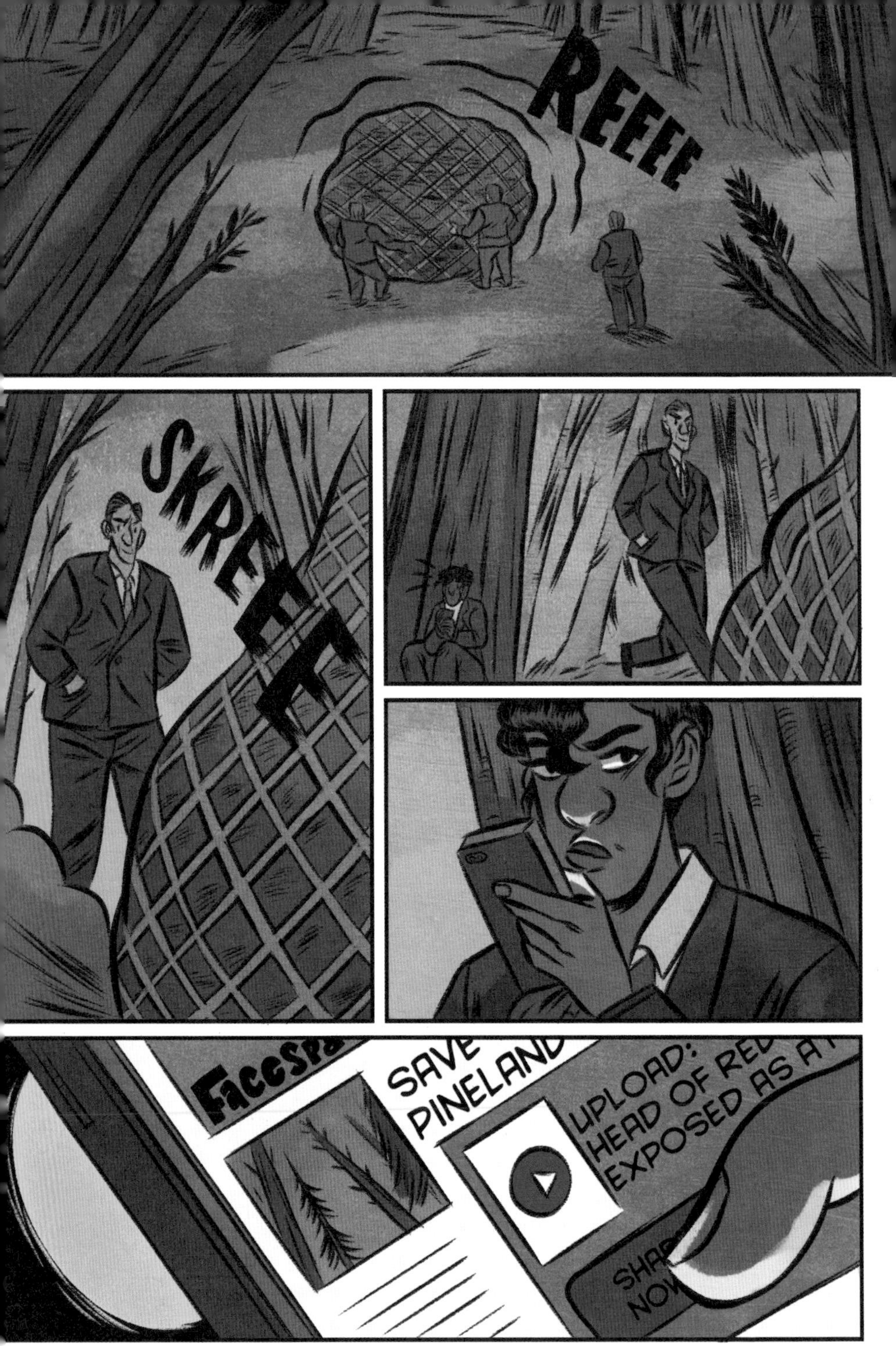
REEEE
SKREEE
SAVE
PINELAND
UPLOAD:
HEAD OF RED
EXPOSED AS A
NOW

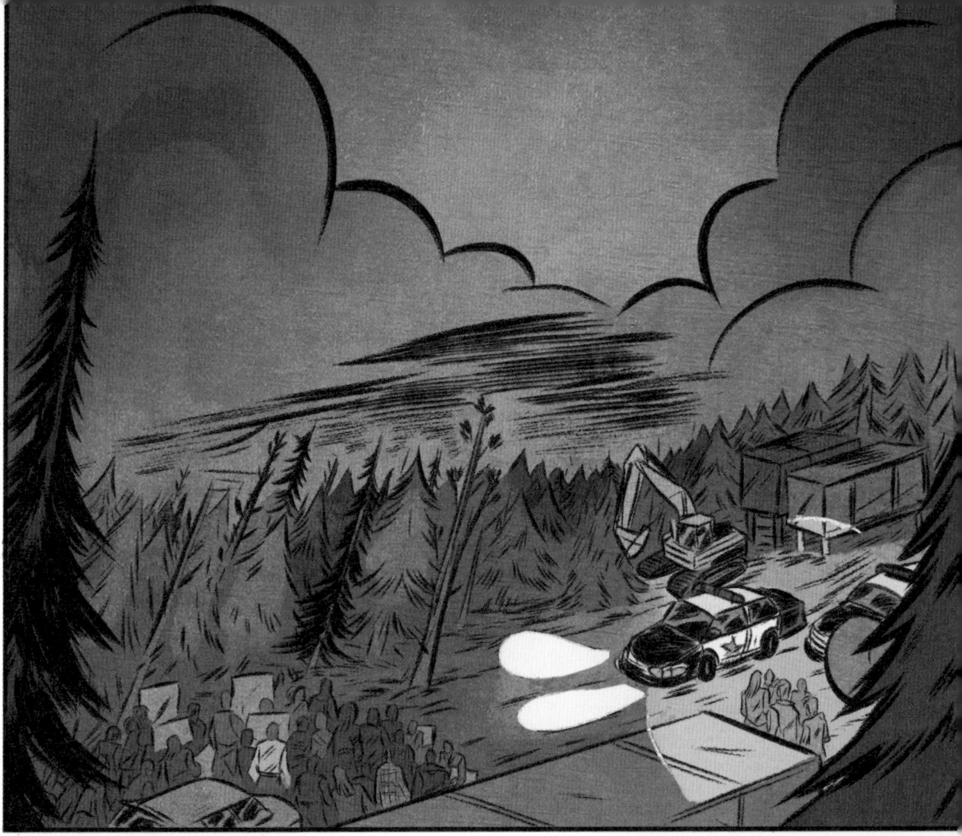

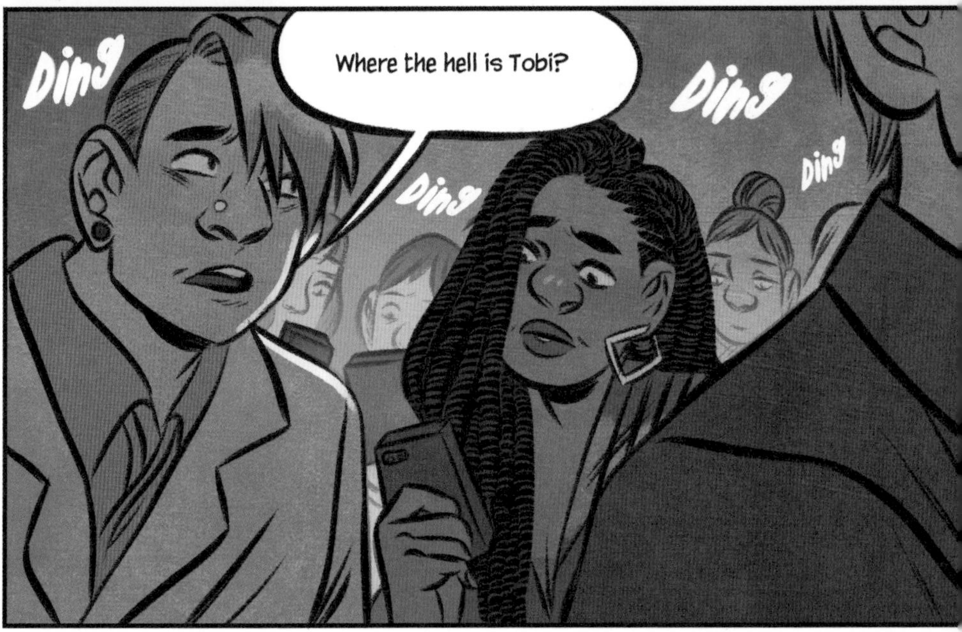
Ding
Where the hell is Tobi?
Ding
Ding
Ding

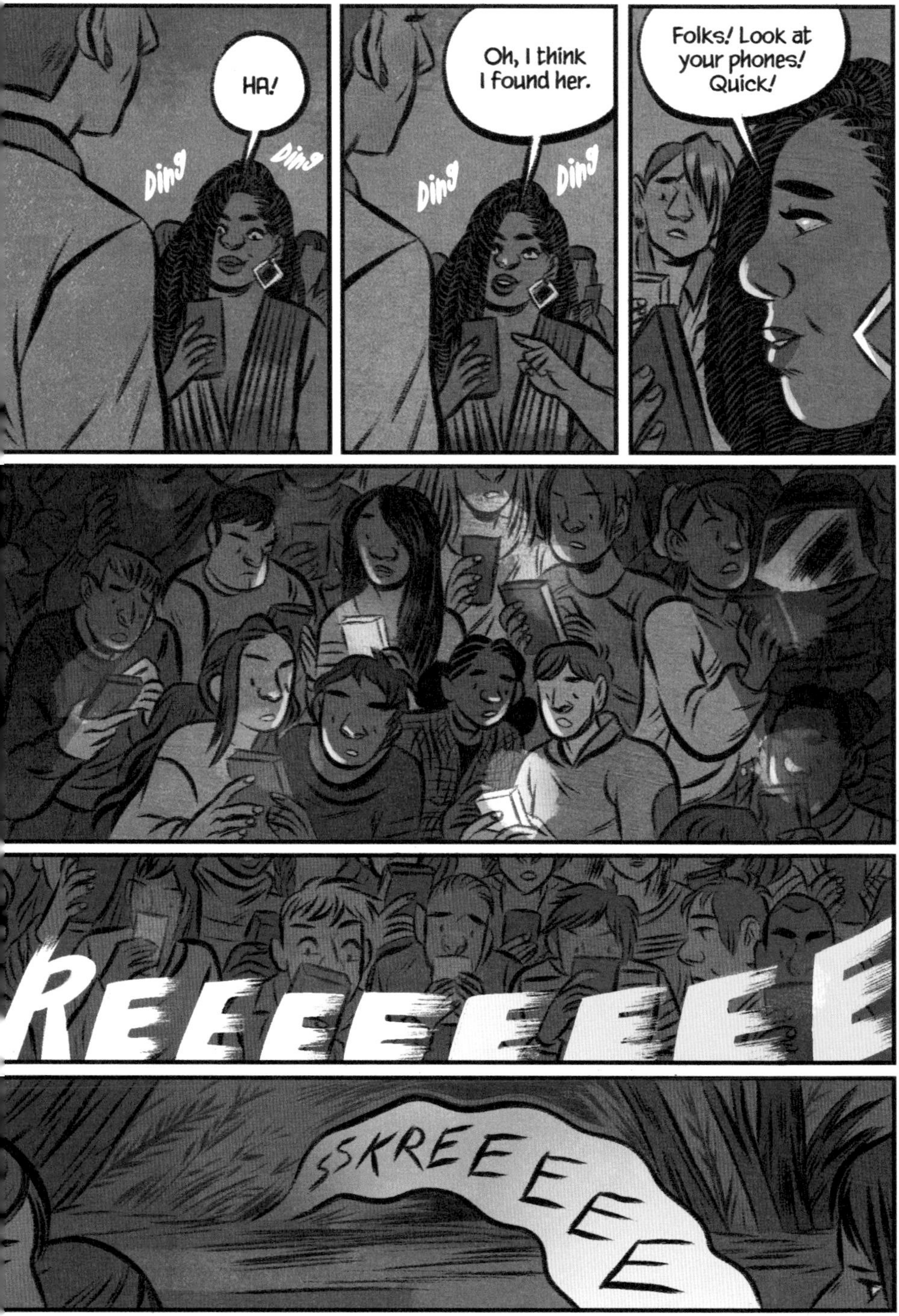
HA!
Ding
Ding
Oh, I think I found her.
Ding
Ding
Folks! Look at your phones! Quick!
REEEEEEEE
sSKREEEEEEE

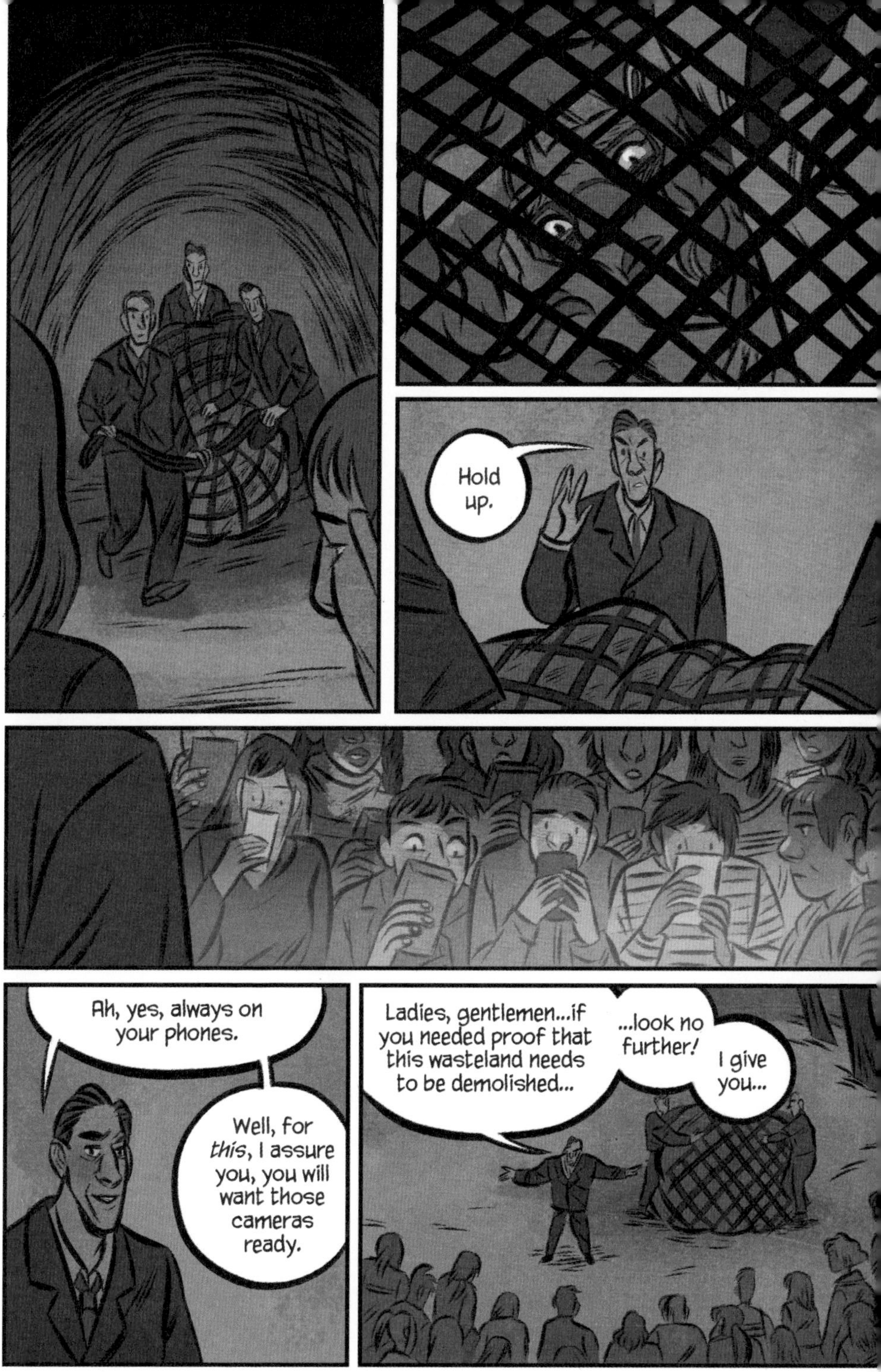
Hold up.
Ah, yes, always on your phones.
Well, for *this*, I assure you, you will want those cameras ready.
Ladies, gentlemen...if you needed proof that this wasteland needs to be demolished...
...look no further!
I give you...

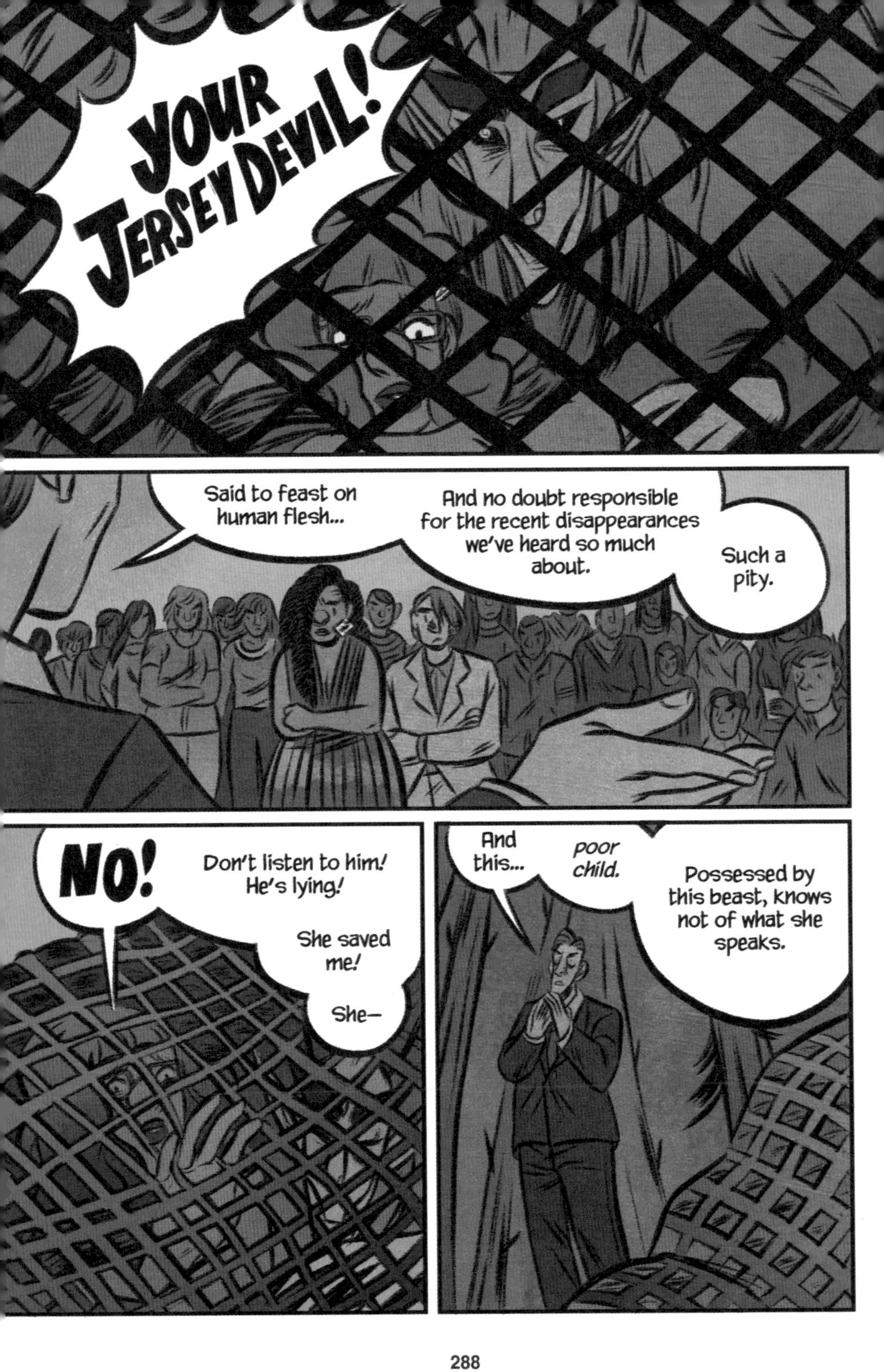
YOUR JERSEY DEVIL!
Said to feast on human flesh...
And no doubt responsible for the recent disappearances we've heard so much about.
Such a pity.
NO!
Don't listen to him! He's lying!
She saved me!
She—
And this...
poor child.
Possessed by this beast, knows not of what she speaks.

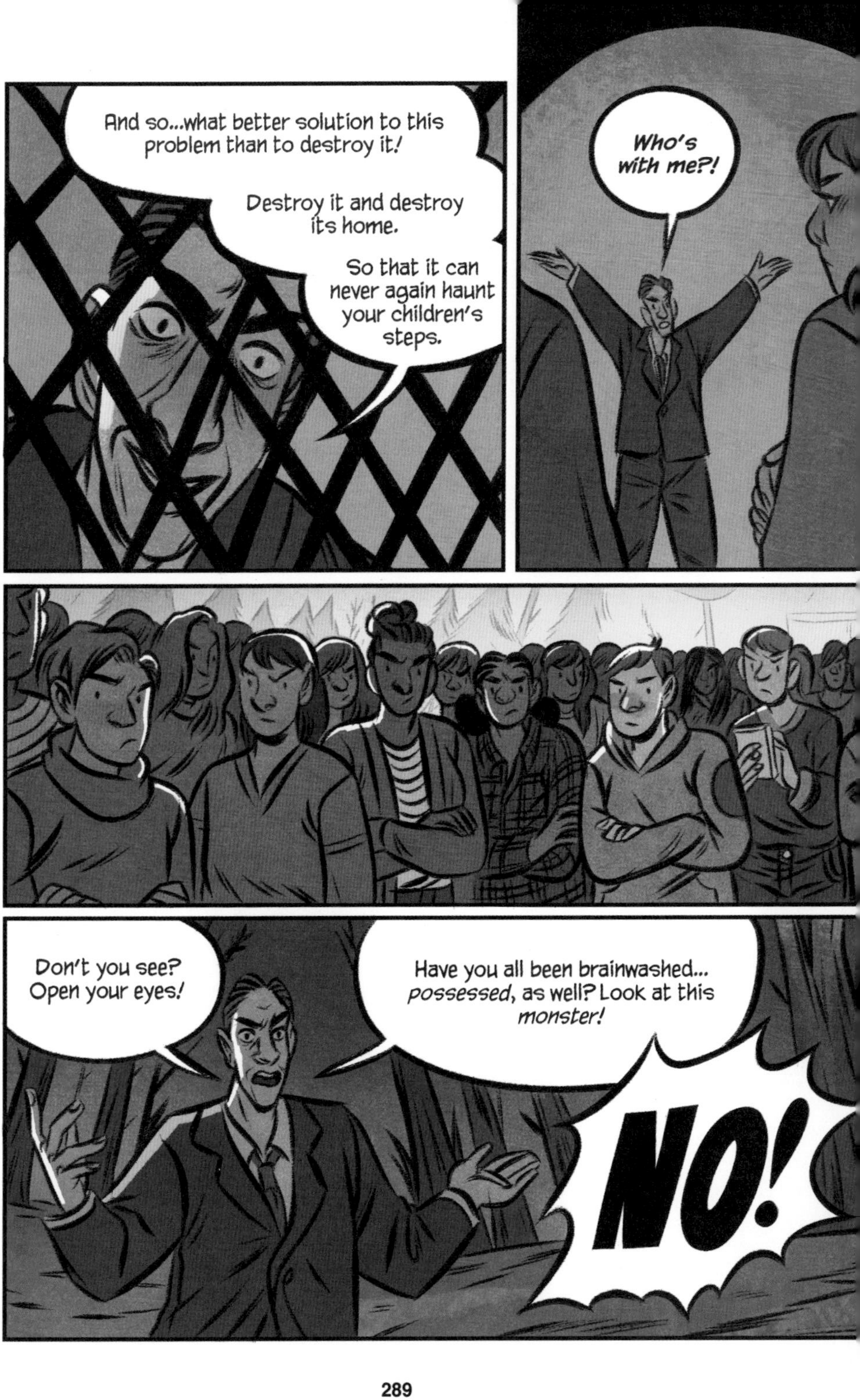
And so...what better solution to this problem than to destroy it!
Destroy it and destroy its home.
So that it can never again haunt your children's steps.
Who's with me?!
Don't you see? Open your eyes!
Have you all been brainwashed... *possessed*, as well? Look at this *monster*!
NO!

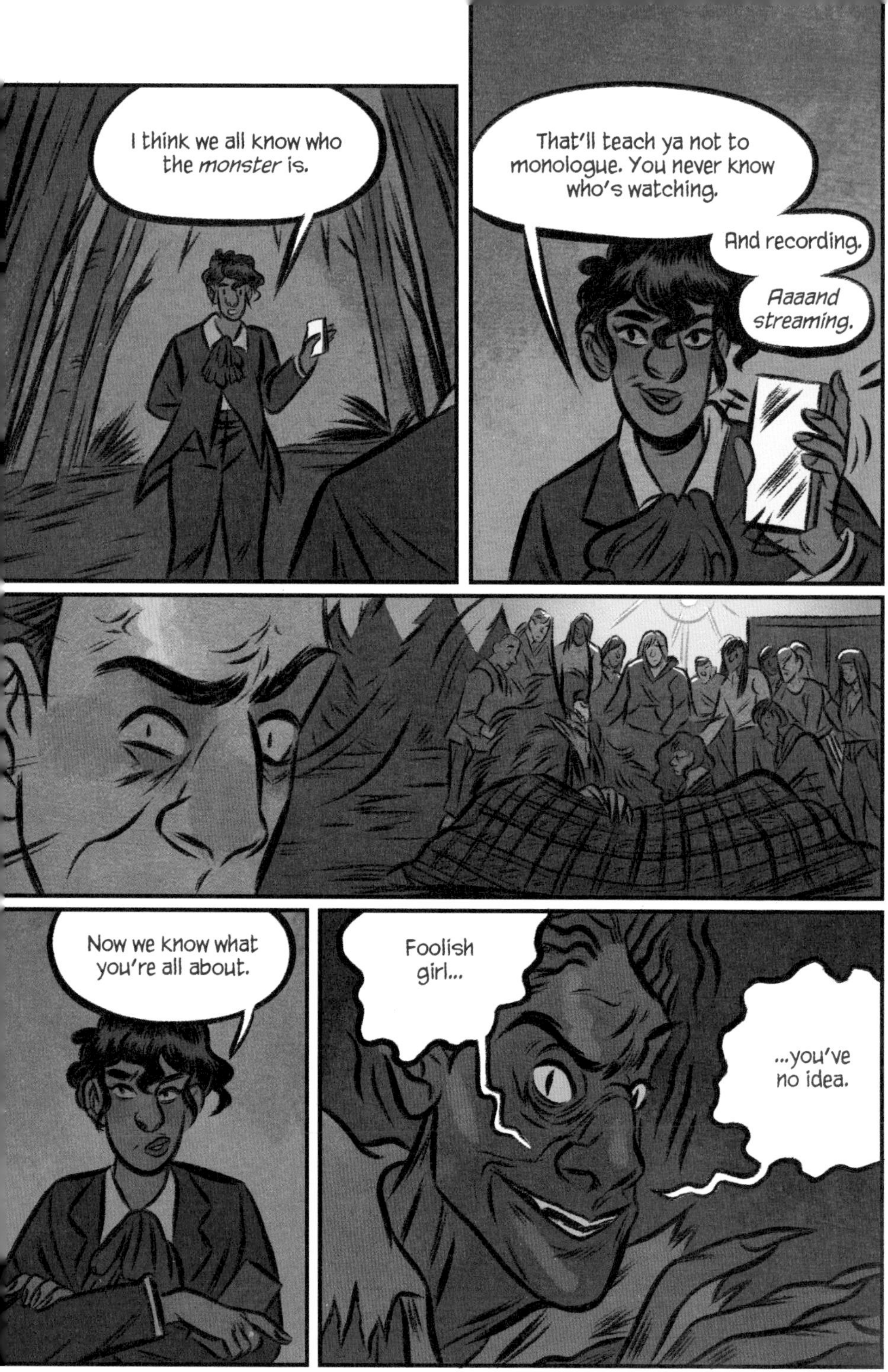
I think we all know who the *monster* is.
That'll teach ya not to monologue. You never know who's watching.
And recording.
Aaaand streaming.
Now we know what you're all about.
Foolish girl...
...you've no idea.

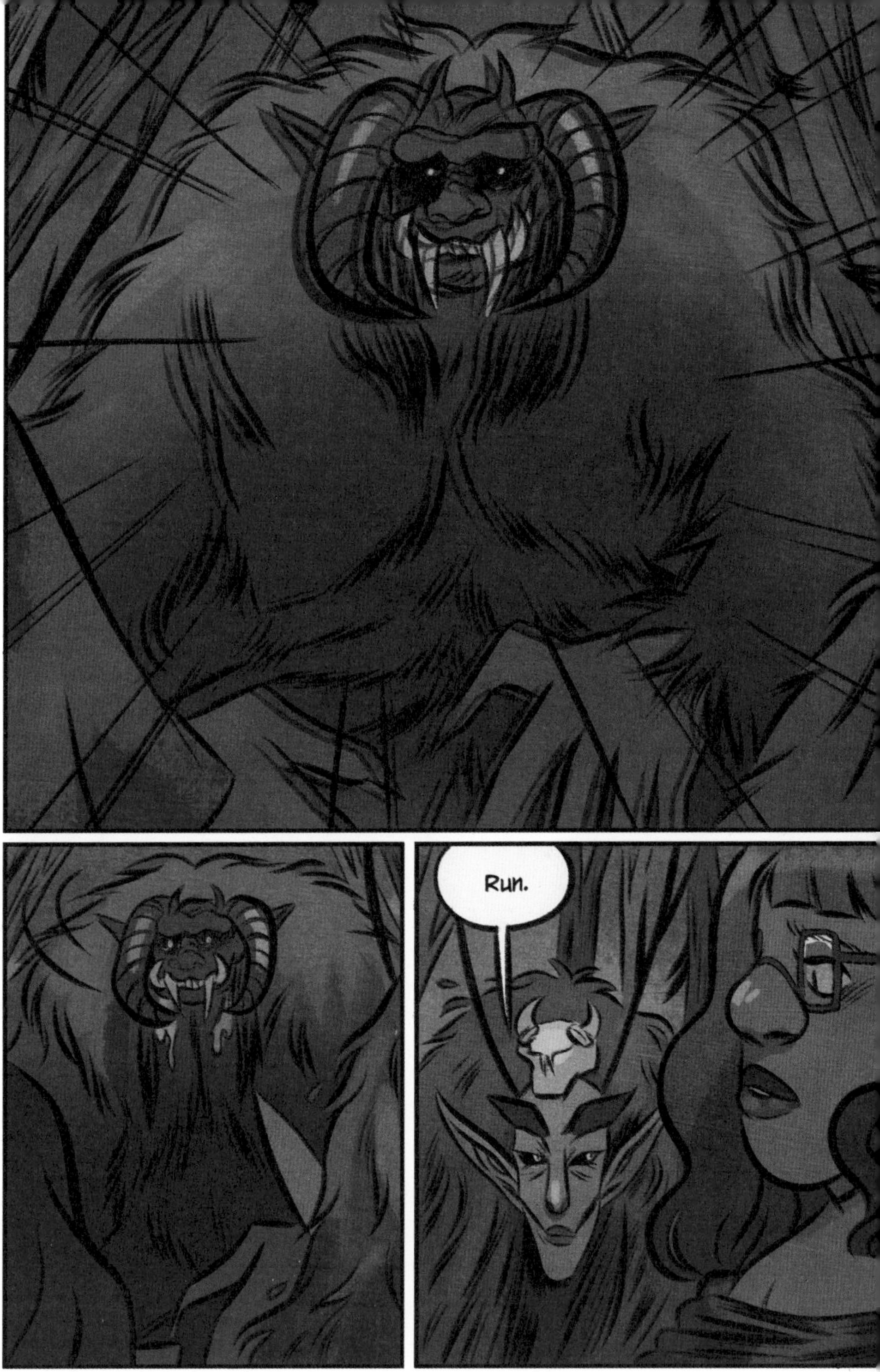
Run.

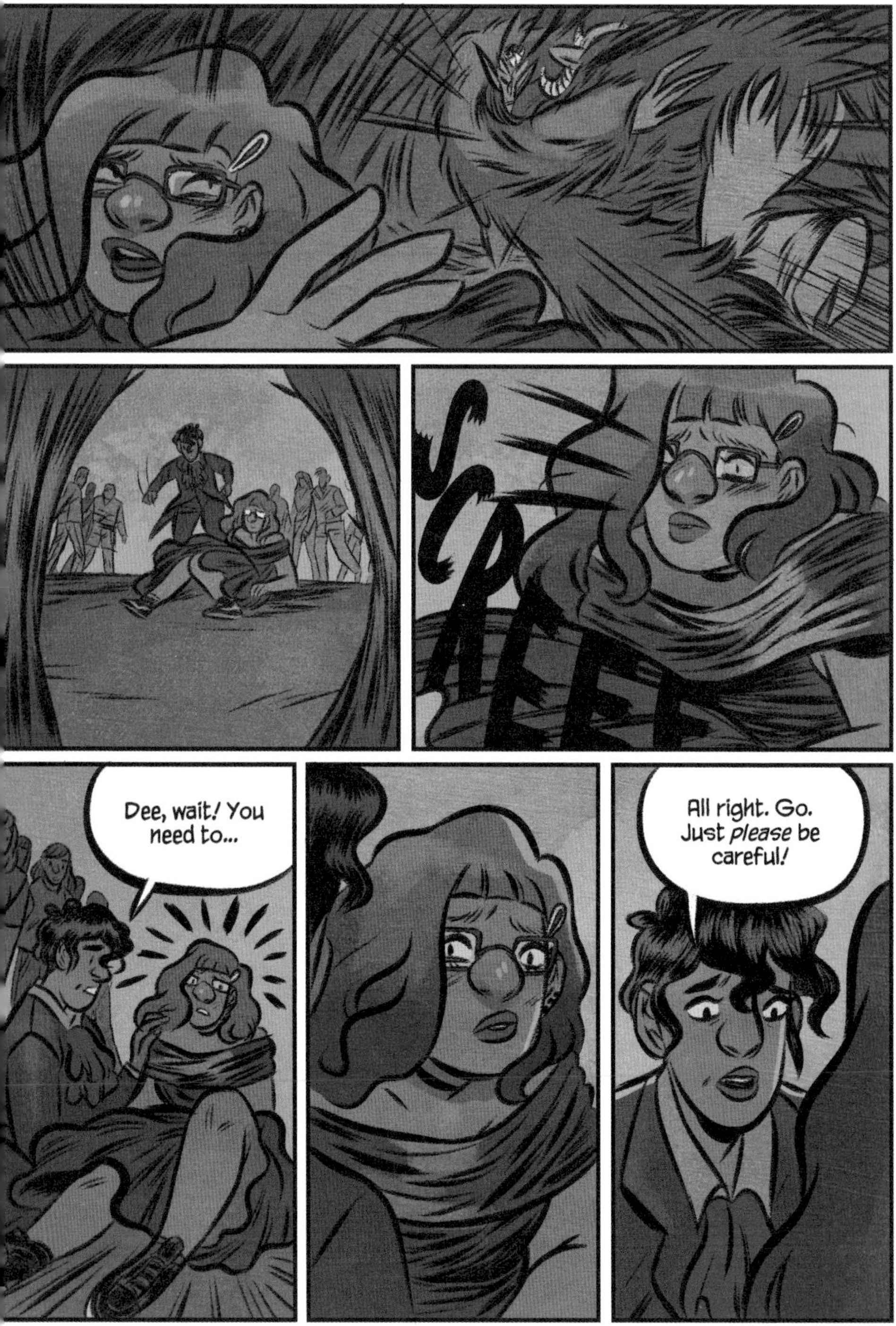

SCREEE
Dee, wait! You need to...
All right. Go. Just *please* be careful!

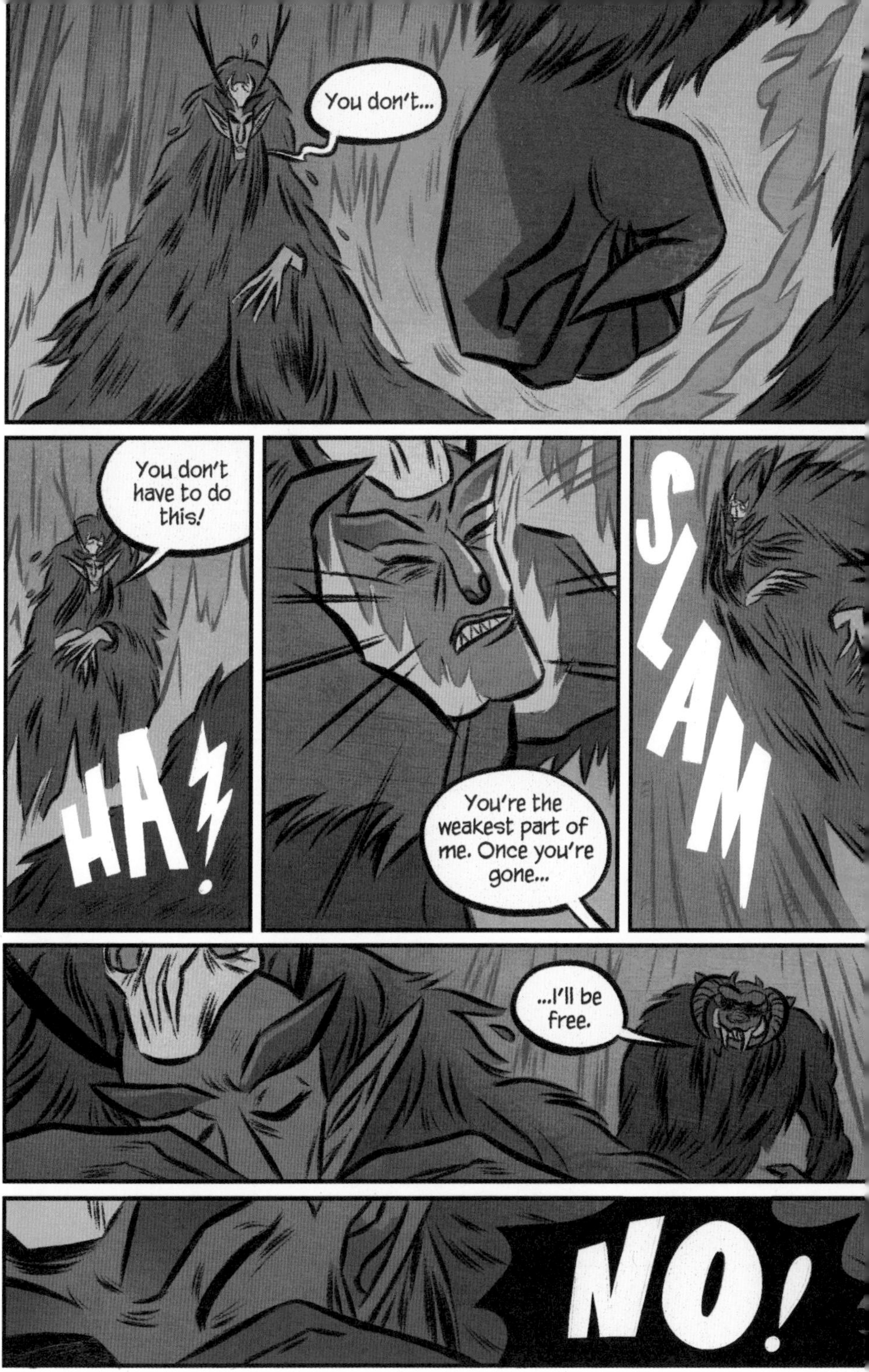
You don't...
You don't have to do this!
HA!
You're the weakest part of me. Once you're gone...
SLAM
...I'll be free.
NO!

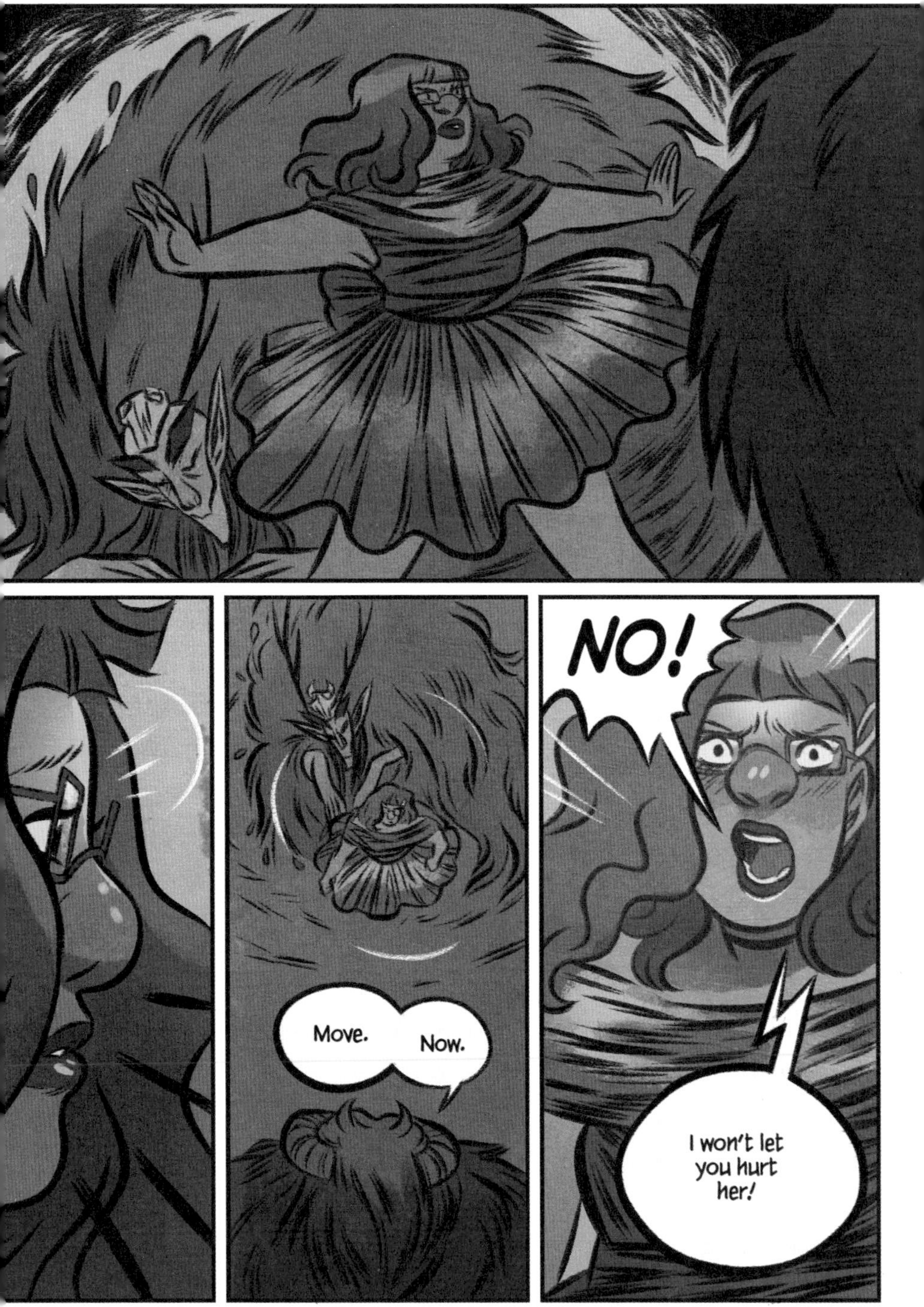
Move.
Now.
NO!
I won't let you hurt her!

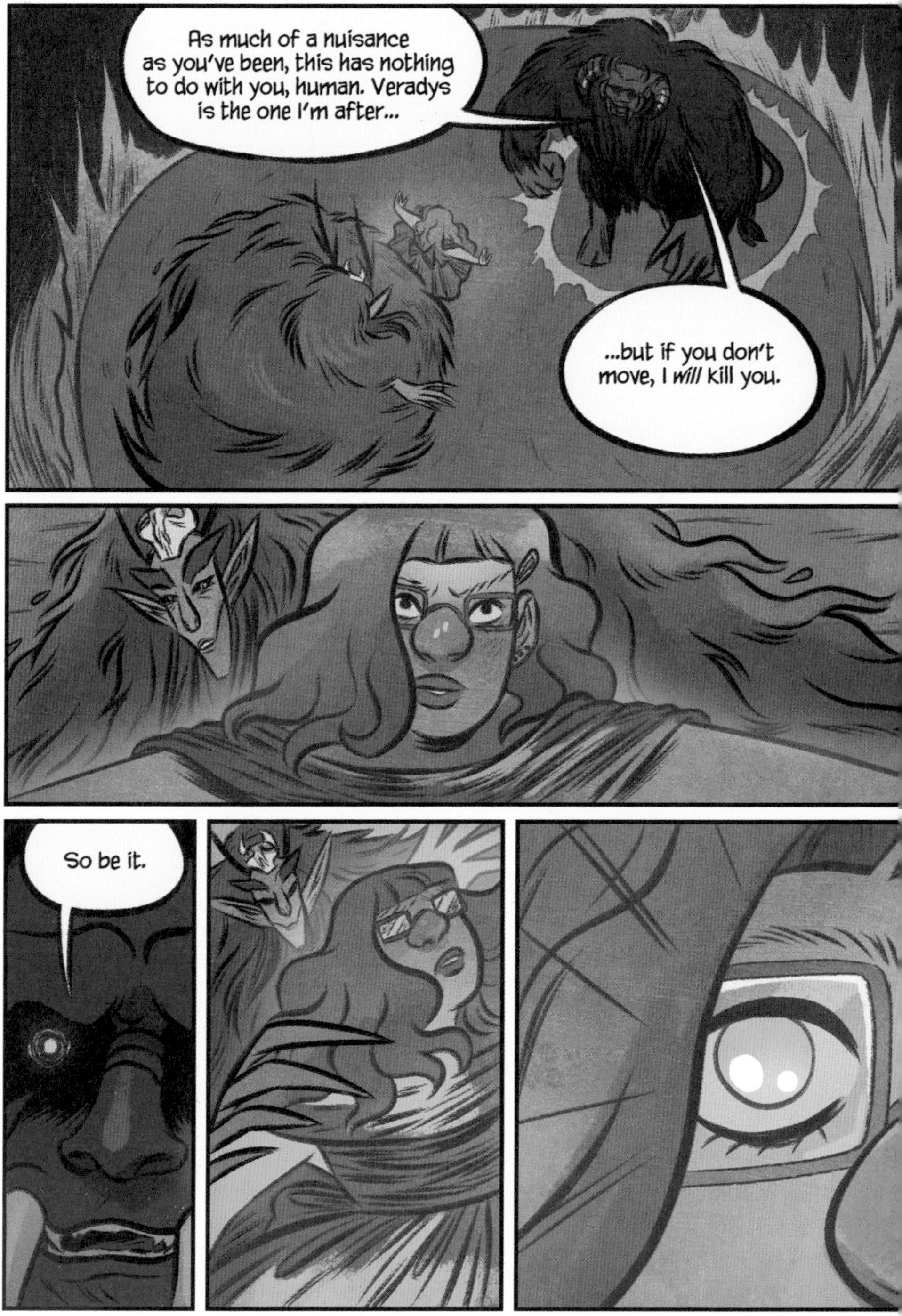
As much of a nuisance as you've been, this has nothing to do with you, human. Veradys is the one I'm after...
...but if you don't move, I *will* kill you.
So be it.

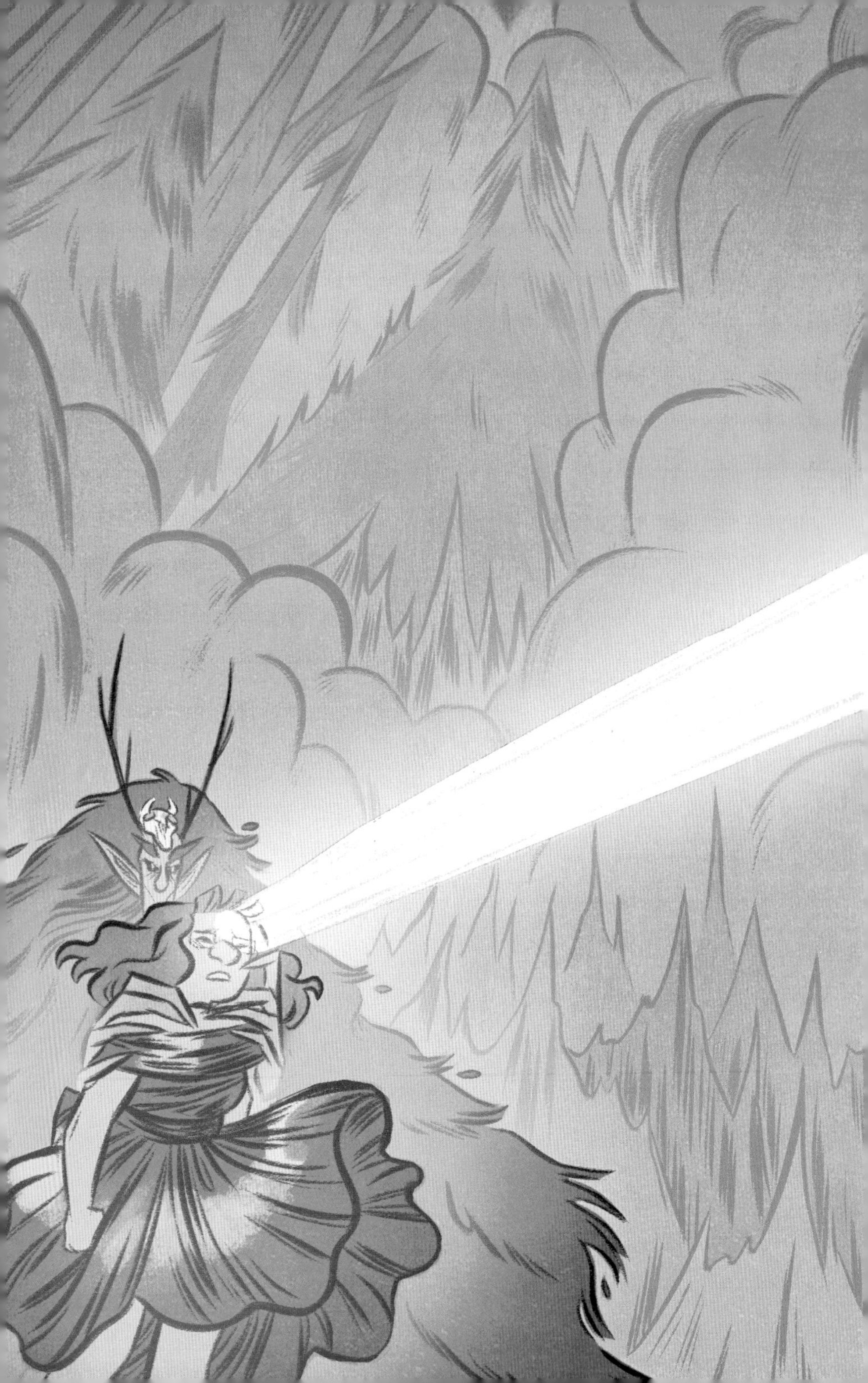

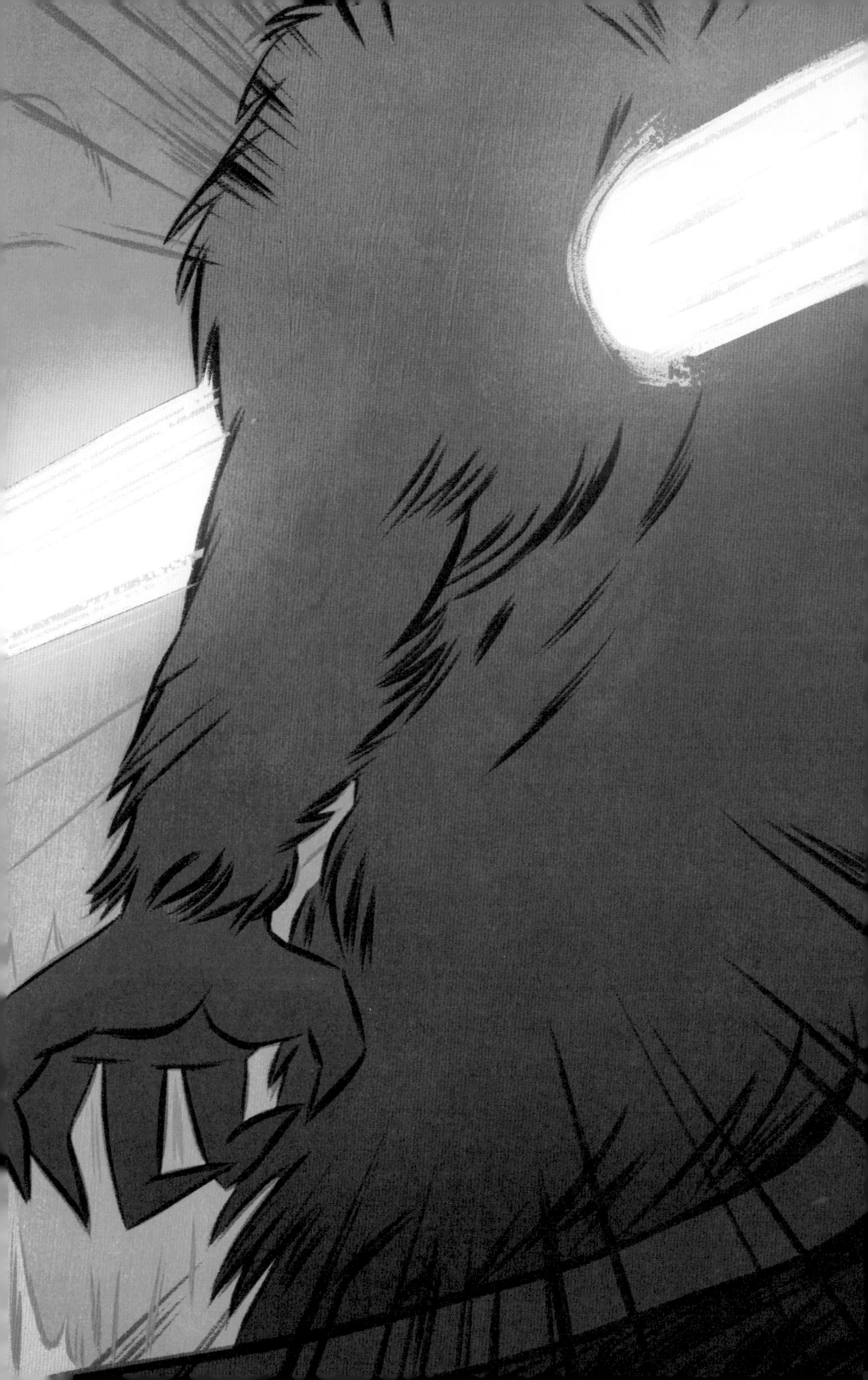

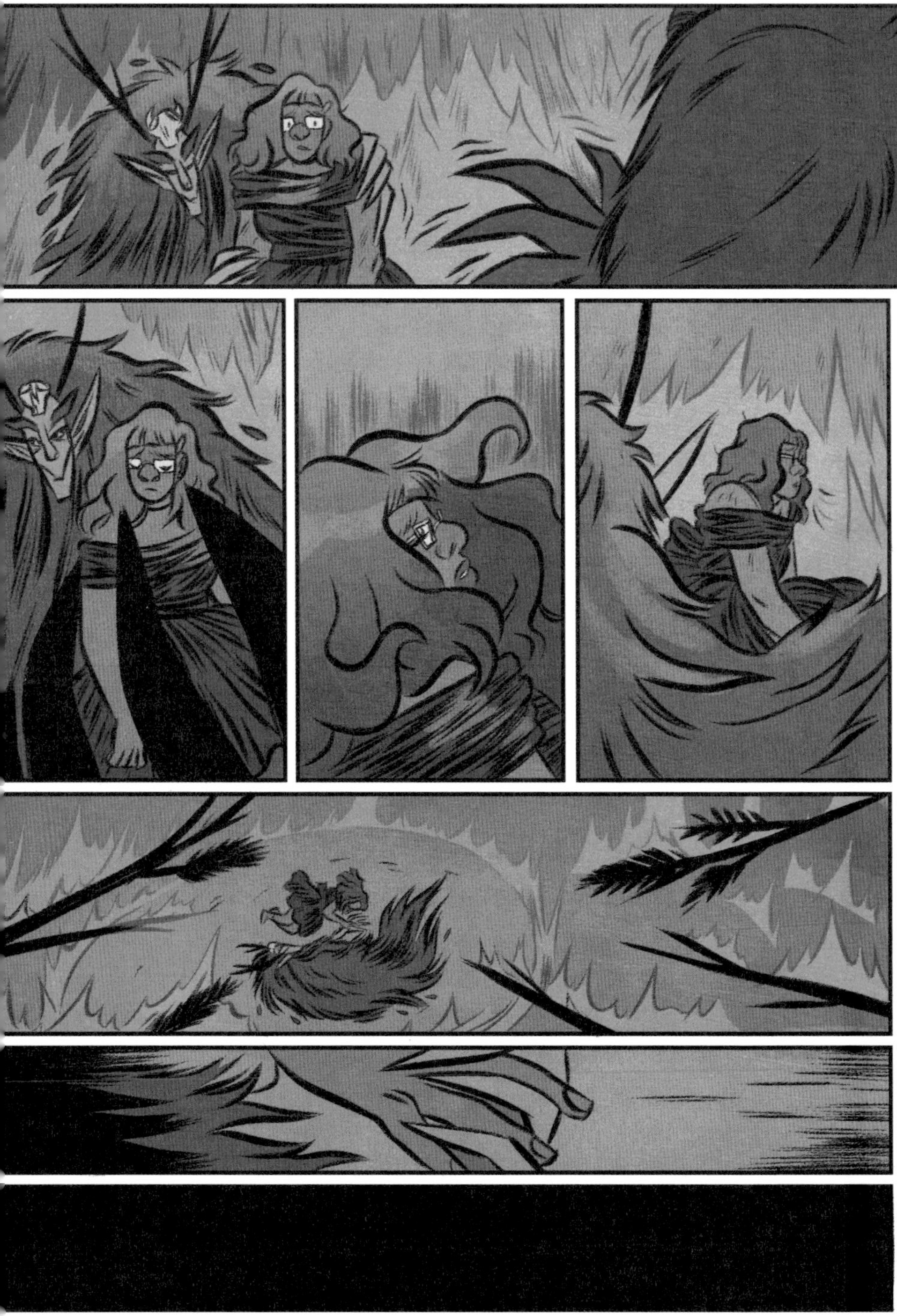

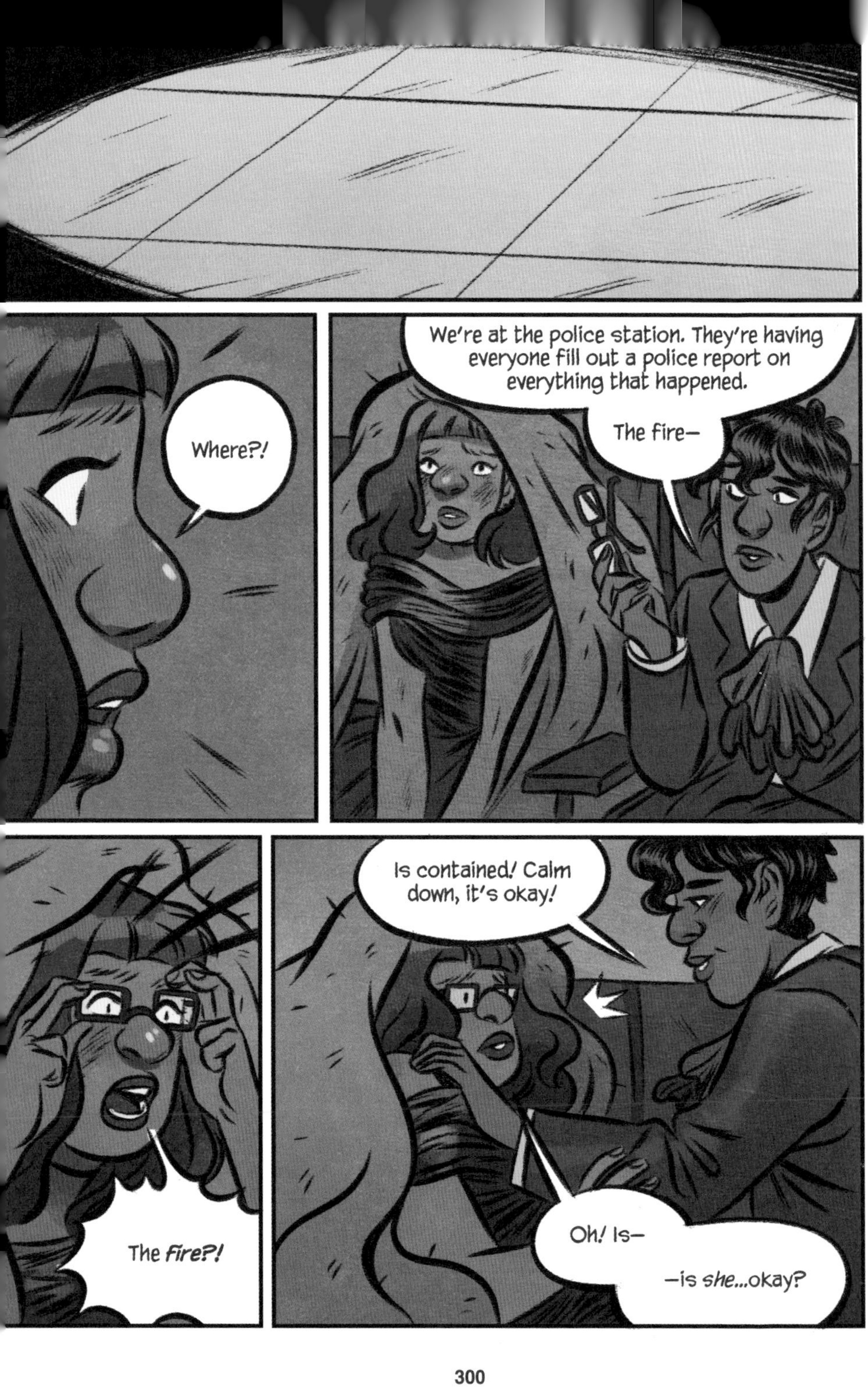
Where?!
We're at the police station. They're having everyone fill out a police report on everything that happened.
The fire—
The *fire*?!
Is contained! Calm down, it's okay!
Oh! Is—
—is *she*...okay?

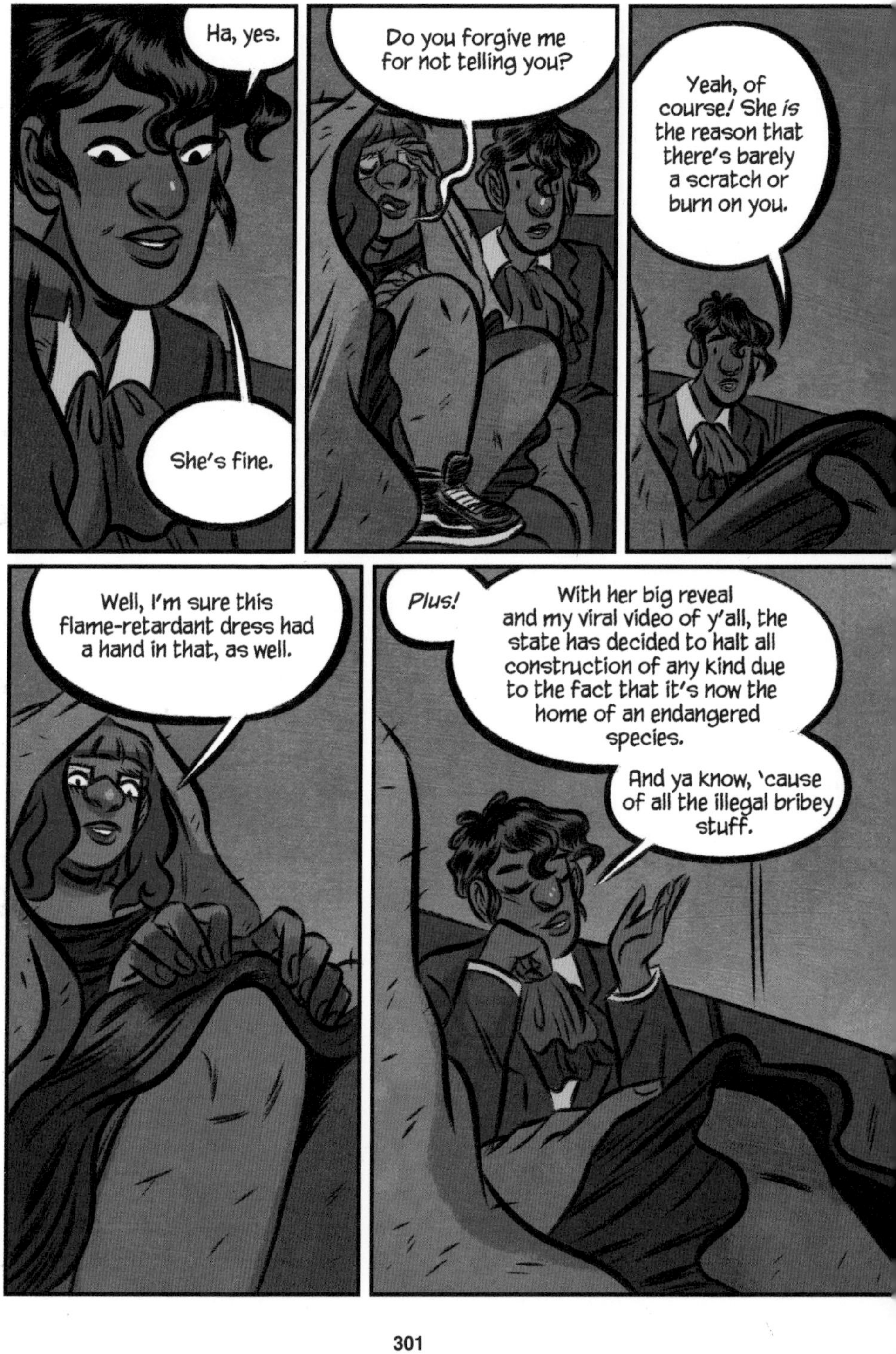
Ha, yes.
She's fine.
Do you forgive me for not telling you?
Yeah, of course! She *is* the reason that there's barely a scratch or burn on you.
Well, I'm sure this flame-retardant dress had a hand in that, as well.
Plus!
With her big reveal and my viral video of y'all, the state has decided to halt all construction of any kind due to the fact that it's now the home of an endangered species.
And ya know, 'cause of all the illegal bribey stuff.

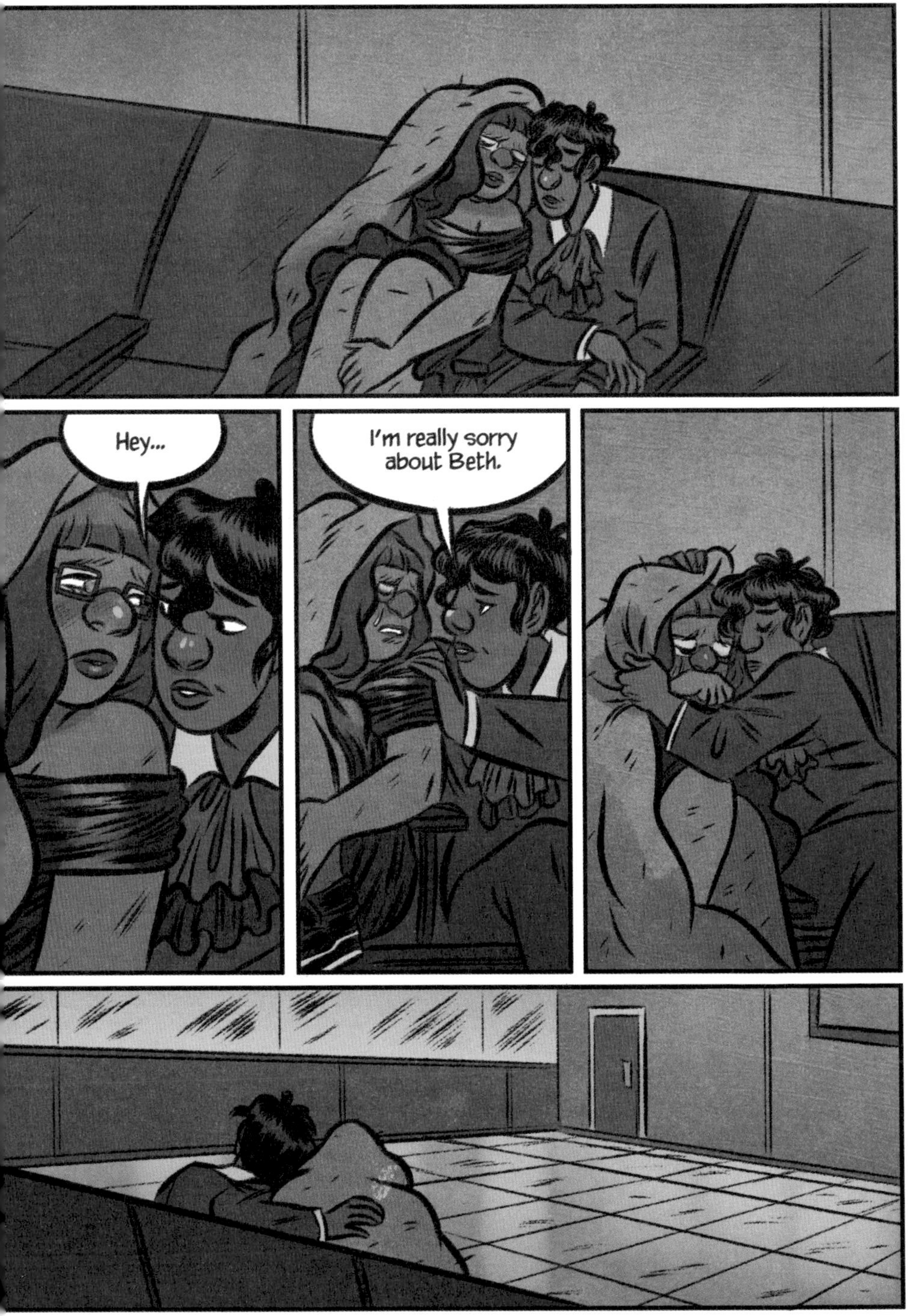
Hey...
I'm really sorry about Beth.

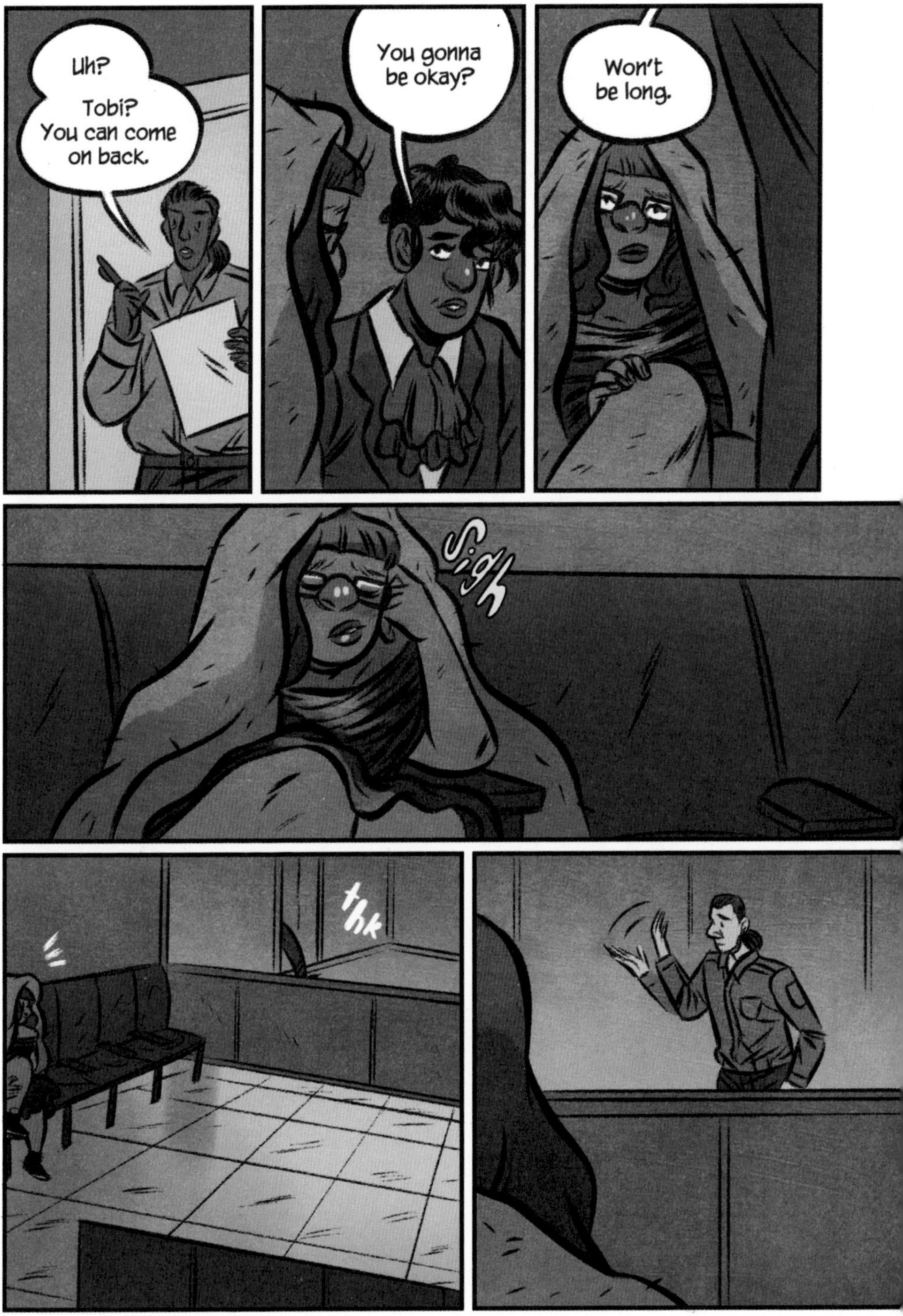
Uh?
Tobi? You can come on back.
You gonna be okay?
Won't be long.
Sigh
thk

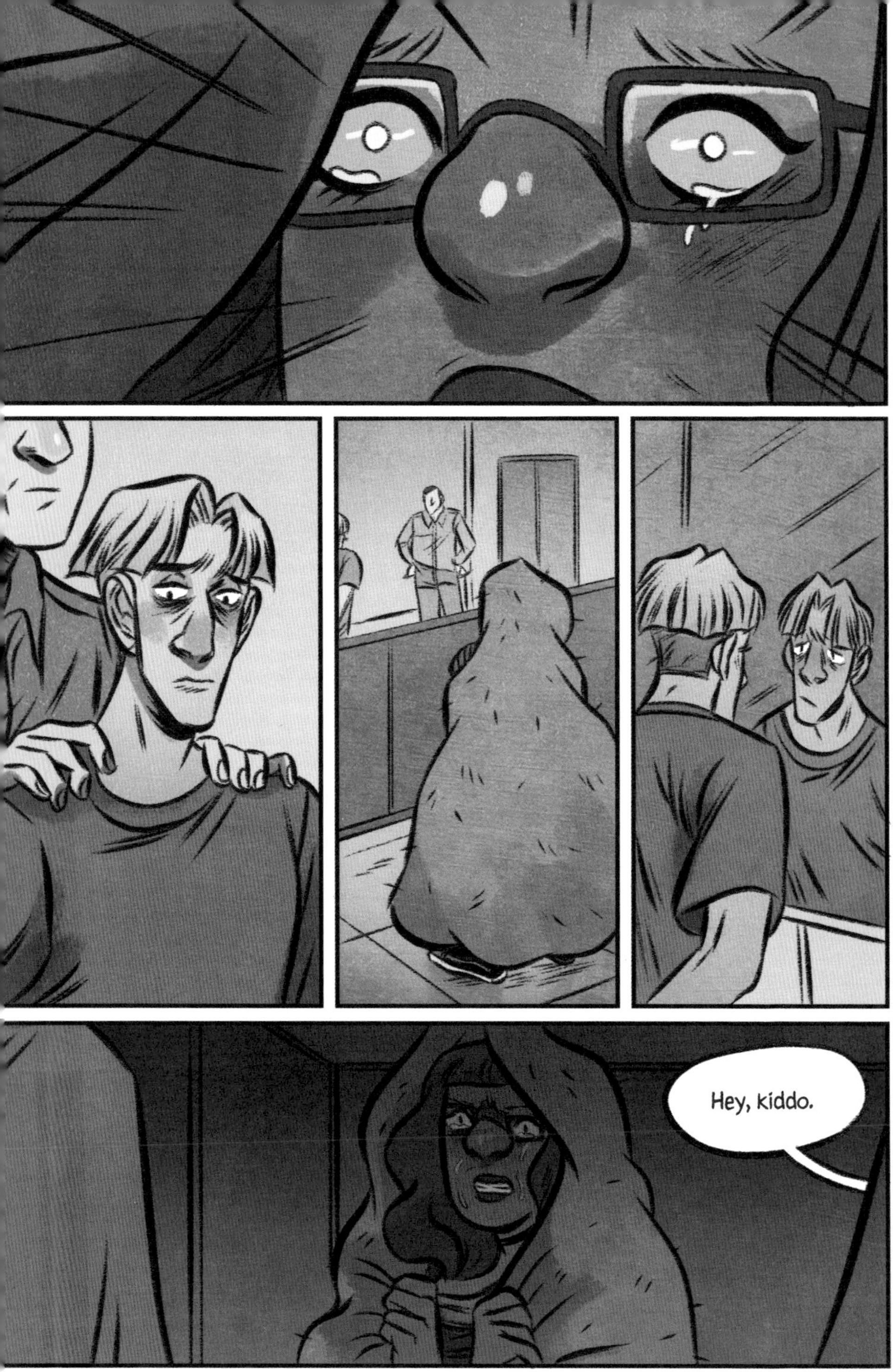
Hey, kiddo.

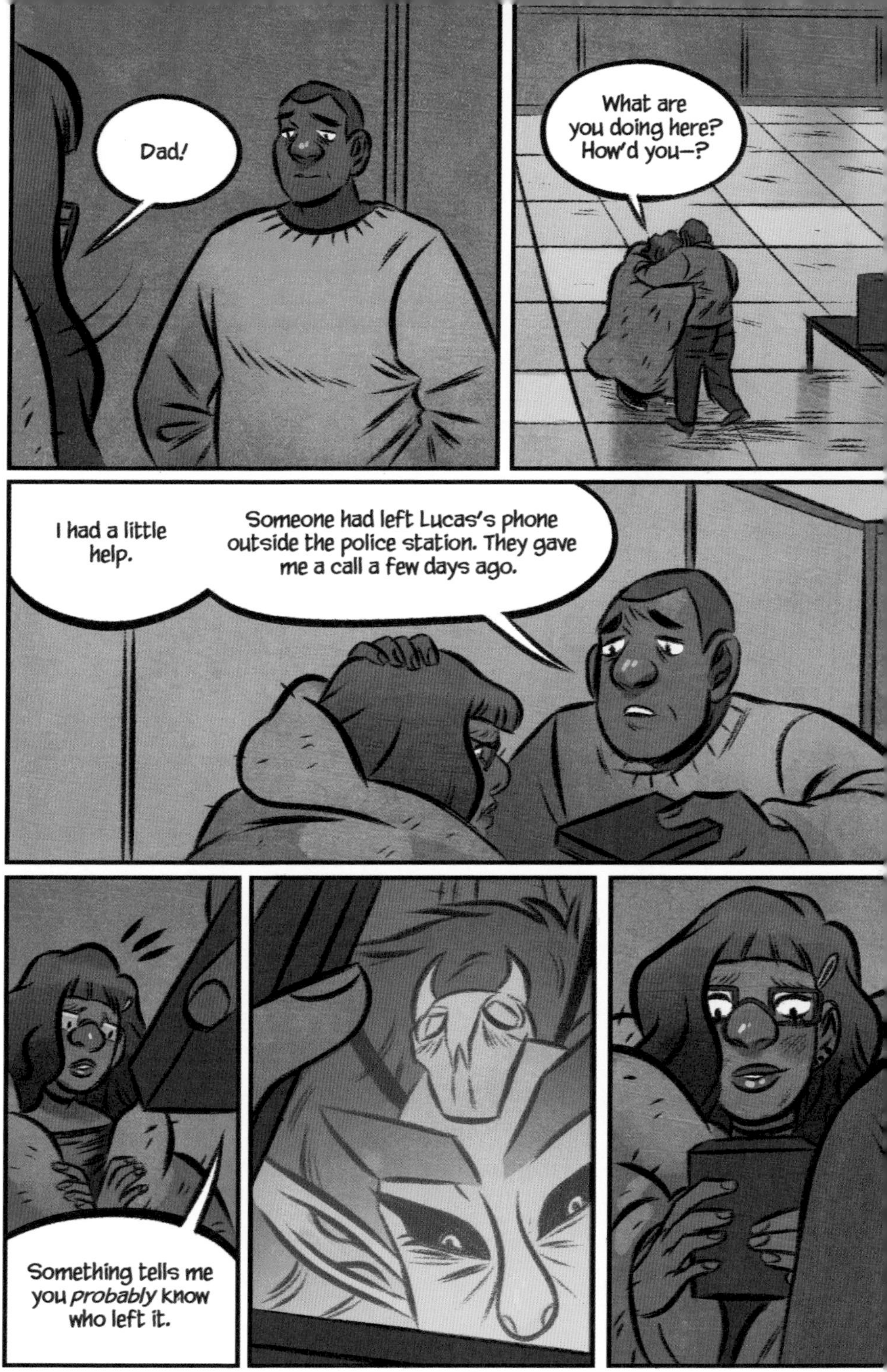
Dad!
What are you doing here? How'd you—?
I had a little help.
Someone had left Lucas's phone outside the police station. They gave me a call a few days ago.
Something tells me you *probably* know who left it.

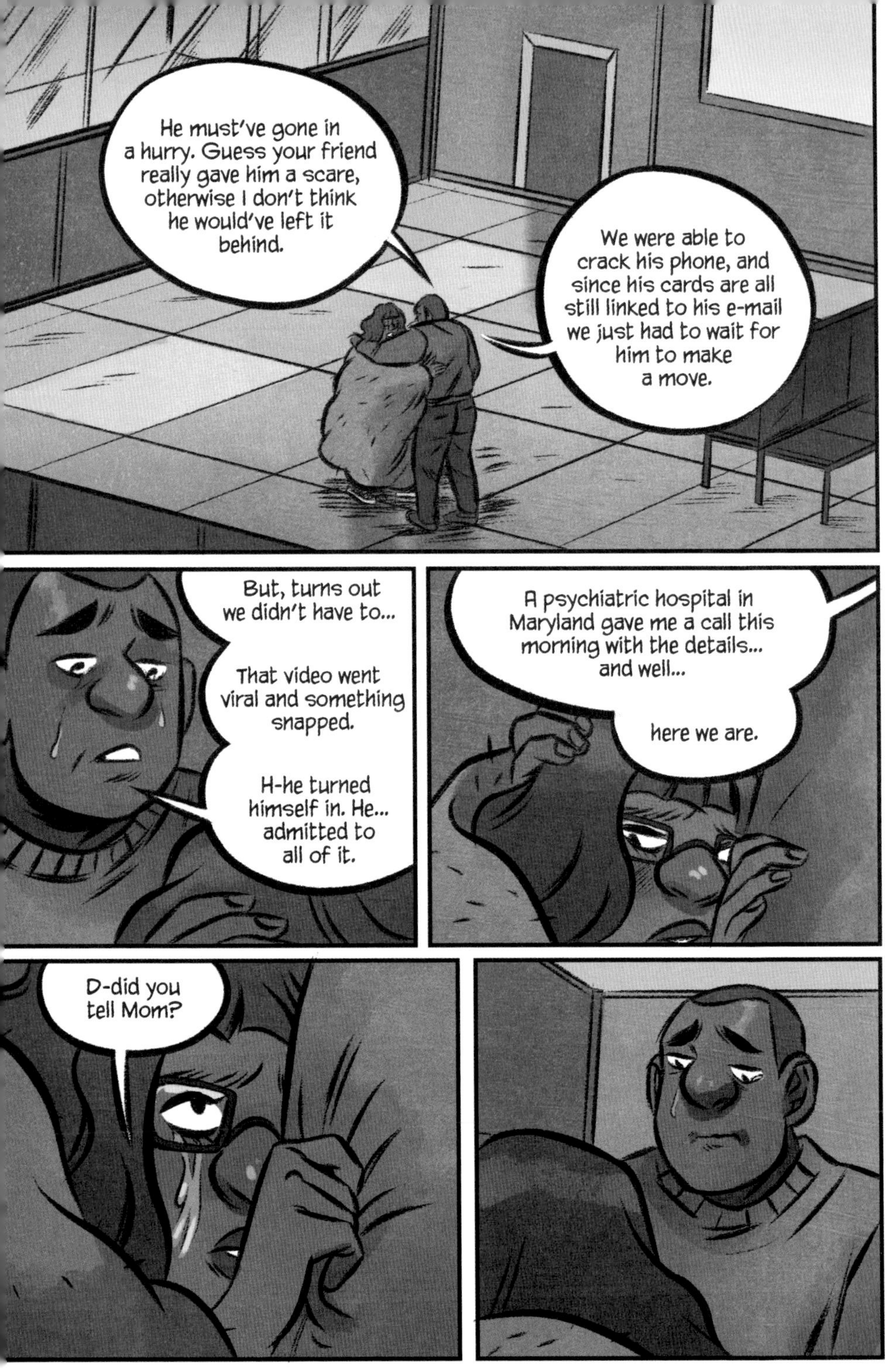
He must've gone in a hurry. Guess your friend really gave him a scare, otherwise I don't think he would've left it behind.
We were able to crack his phone, and since his cards are all still linked to his e-mail we just had to wait for him to make a move.
But, turns out we didn't have to...
That video went viral and something snapped.
H-he turned himself in. He... admitted to all of it.
A psychiatric hospital in Maryland gave me a call this morning with the details... and well...
here we are.
D-did you tell Mom?

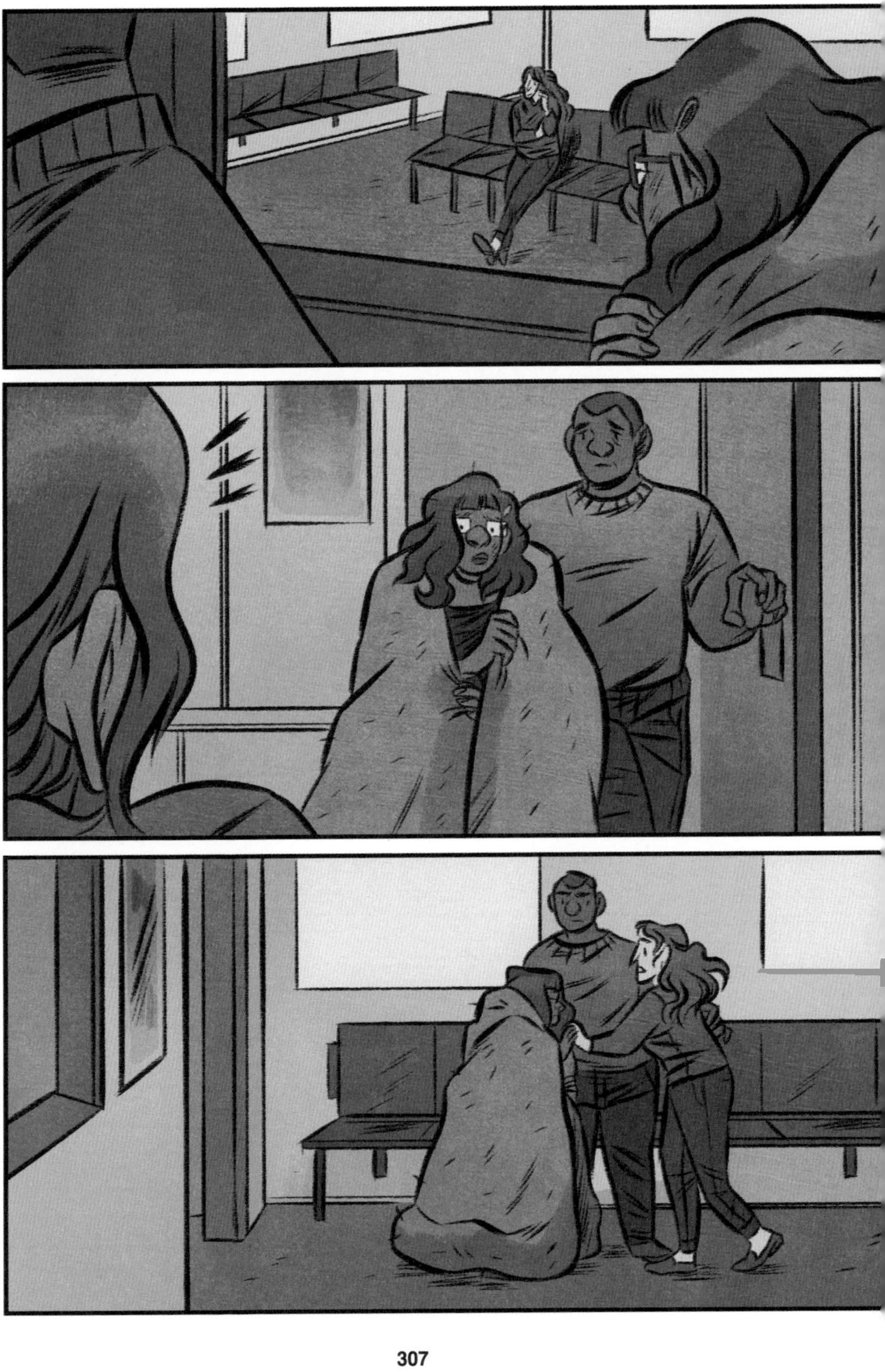

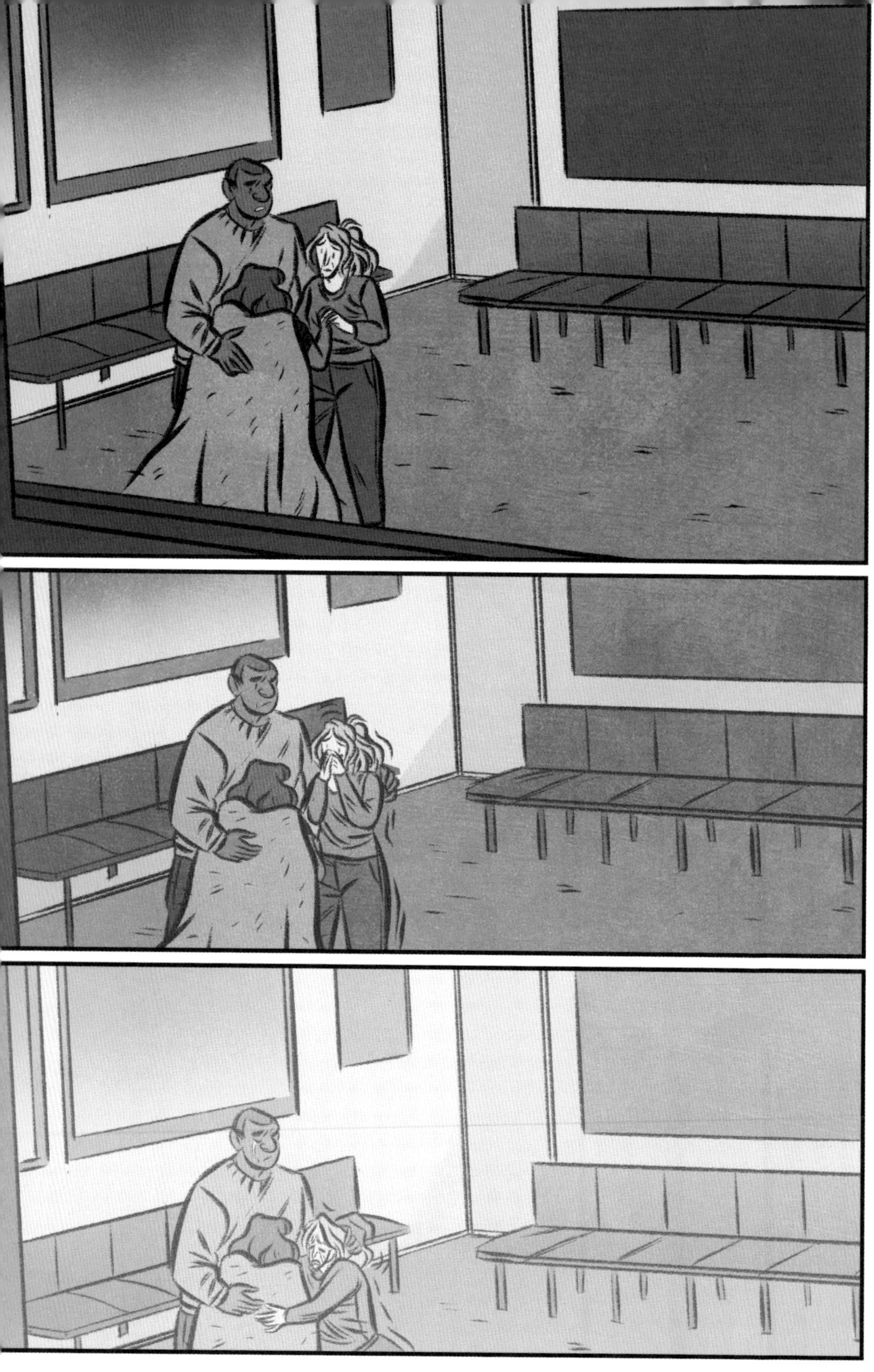

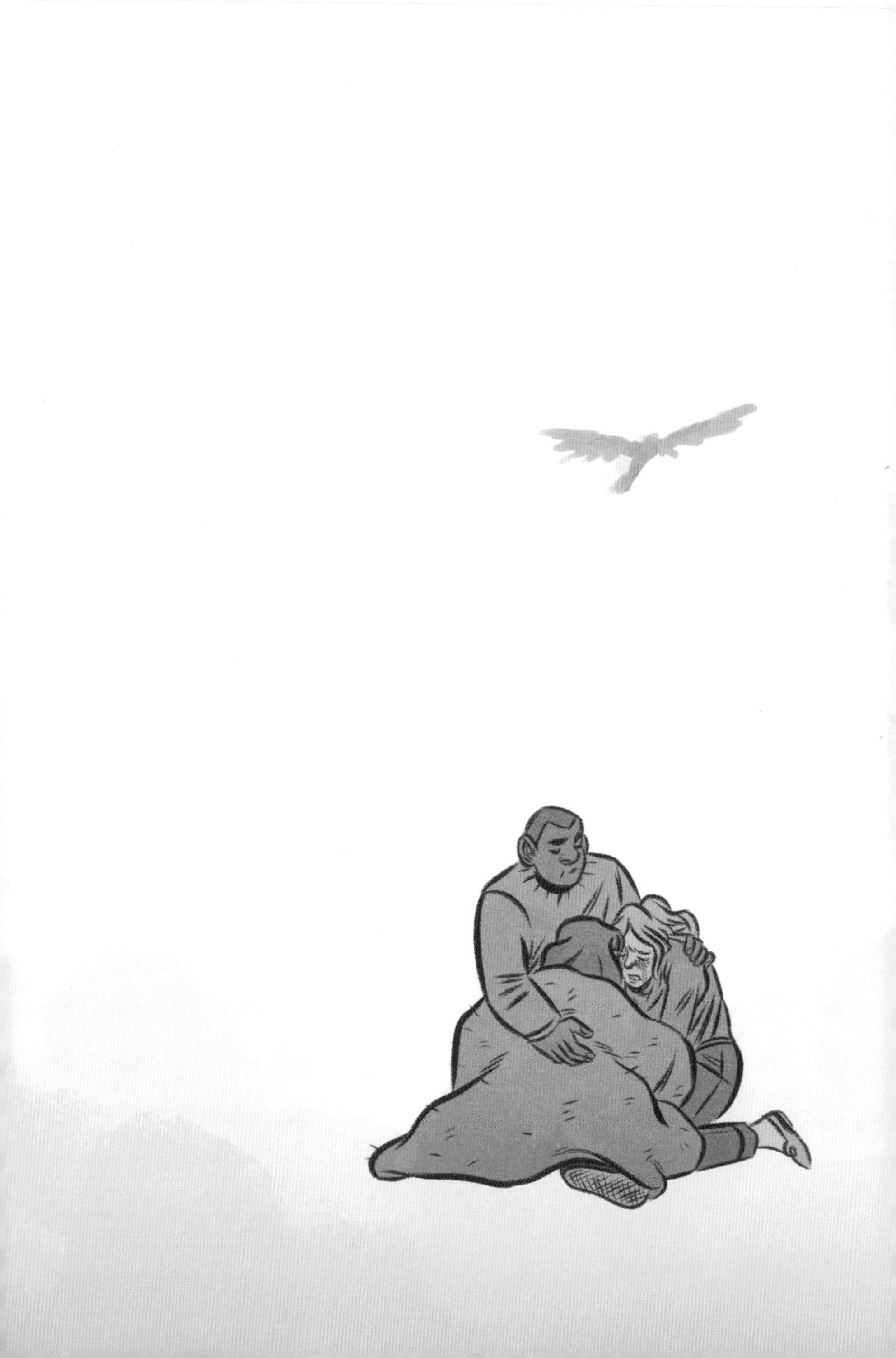

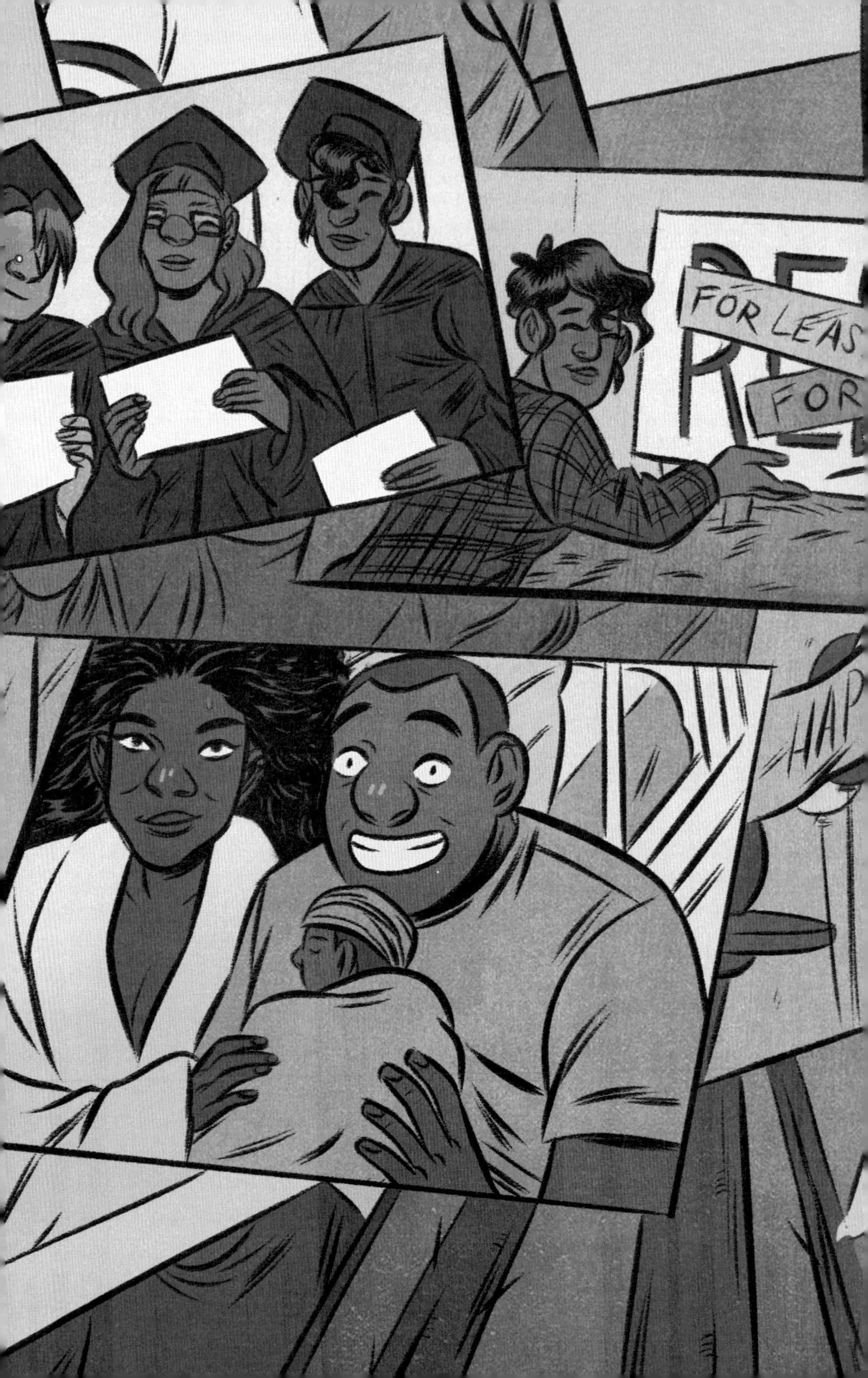
FOR LEAS
FOR

UNI
O
NJ
UNI
OF
NJ

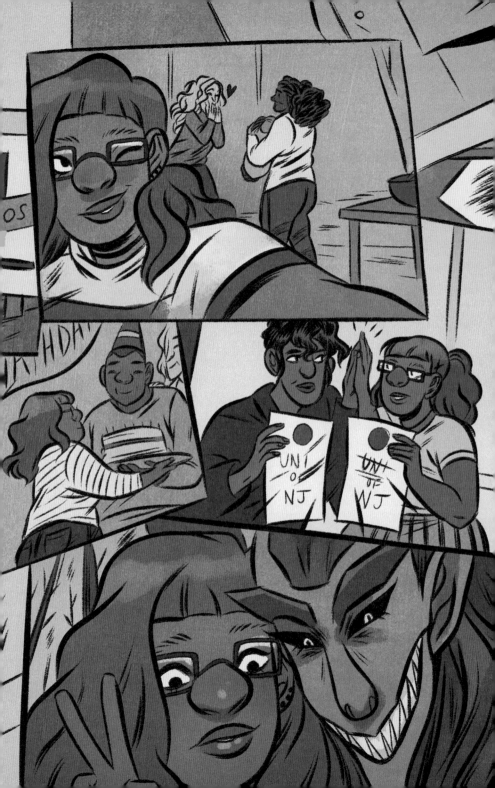

ACKNOWLEDGMENTS

There's tons of people I'm thankful for who made this book possible, especially my colorist, Triona! She put in so much work to make this book look stunning and added so much atmosphere that I never thought was possible. I can't thank her enough. This book would not be the same without her hard work!

To Whitney, my editor! She's hands-down a hero. She's come through for me in so many ways and really knew the right questions to ask to make this story as good as it could possibly be. It was an amazing experience to have her there to give me guidance and listen to my ramblings. Also many thanks to Patrick, Gina, and the rest of the Random House Graphic crew for their amazing work. This book could not have happened without them.

To Pete, my agent, who's always in my corner fighting for me and just being a wonderful friend in the process.

To John! For being there for me during all the ups and downs of this process, with coffee, hugs, and back rubs—and being the best partner anyone could ask for.

And thanks to my parents and all my family and friends for their unending support. Love you all!

BACKGROUND NOISE

Music and shows I had on in the background while I worked on this book!
- Harry Nilsson, *Aerial Ballet*
- Fugazi, *13 Songs*
- Wu-Tang Clan, *Iron Flag*
- Bad Brains, *I Against I*
- Misfits, *Famous Monsters*

M*A*S*H
Seinfeld
Peep Show
Frasier

STATS

- 689 cups of coffee!
- 235 cups of tea!
- 198 days of overtime!
- 45 times I threw my back out!
- 15 times I rewatched *Seinfeld*.

This book was drawn in 2020. Yep, *THAT* 2020. I wanna take this time to acknowledge you, yes, *YOU*—holding this book—for getting through it. You're all amazing.

MORE ABOUT THE PINELANDS

Although this is a work of fiction, I was definitely inspired by some real events that have taken place! The New Jersey Pinelands Commission had considered a proposal to install a brand-new 22-inch pipeline through 22 miles of the Pinelands and southern New Jersey. As I write this, it's been temporarily halted, but that's not to say it won't resume. As of July 2020 a key permit had been suspended after there was damage to someone's property. Hopefully by the time this book is published that pipeline will be history!

I recall reading about it and thinking: Hmm, I don't think the Jersey Devil would appreciate a pipeline running through its home. From there the idea kicked off. Whether you're a believer or not, as a Jerseyan, I have a soft spot for the Jersey Devil legend and hope this book helps keep that legend alive.

I highly recommend checking out the Pinelands Alliance, an organization devoted to preserving the natural and historic resources of the New Jersey Pinelands. Have a gander at pinelandsalliance.org for more info!

ABOUT!

Tara is a comic artist and writer. She's been making mini-comics, zines, and graphic novels for over ten years. FLY BY NIGHT is her third and longest graphic novel. She drinks far too much coffee. She lives with her boyfriend in Belfast, Northern Ireland.

You can find more of her work on taraocomics.com and on Twitter @taraocomics.

Triona is an Irish comic book colorist and has worked on titles such as CROWED, BLACK WIDOW, SPIDERMAN AND TERMINATOR. She currently lives in Dublin with her partner and her cat!

You can find more of her work on triona-t-farrell.com and on Twitter @treestumped.